CHYC

BAPT

Lucy Floy
began writi
novels (inclu Mac-
millan and Pa ed short
stories. She lives her photog-
rapher husband.

ALSO BY LUCY FLOYD

By Truth Divided (*as Teresa de Luca*)

Yesterday

Lucy Floyd

BAPTISM OF FIRE

PAN BOOKS
LONDON, SYDNEY AND AUCKLAND

First published 1992 by Macmillan London

This edition published 1994 by Pan Books Ltd
a division of Pan Macmillan Publishers Limited
Cavaye Place London SW10 9PG
and Basingstoke

Associated companies throughout the world

ISBN 0 330 31747 4

1 3 5 7 9 8 6 4 2

A CIP catalogue record for this book is available from
the British Library

Typeset by Intype, London
Printed and bound in Great Britain by
Cox & Wyman Ltd, Reading, Berkshire

CONTENTS

Map	vi
Foreword	vii
Part One	1
Part Two	271
Part Three	381
Part Four	459
Glossary	568

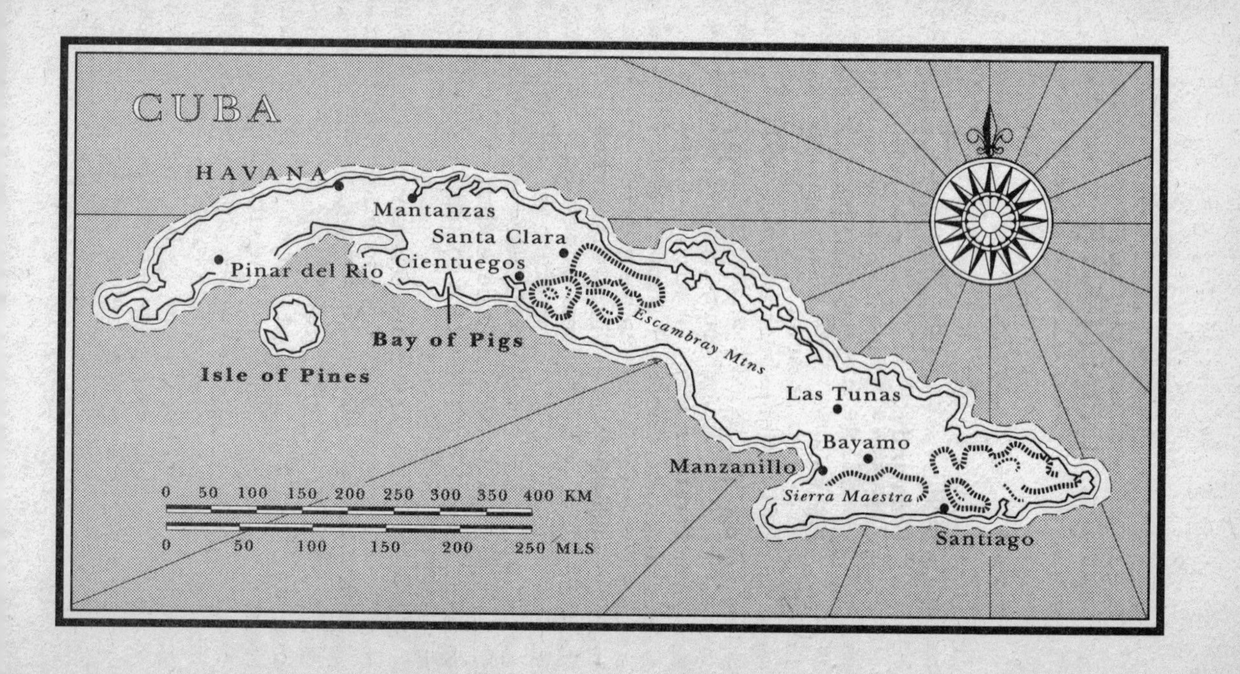
CUBA
HAVANA
Mantanzas
Santa Clara
Pinar del Rio
Cientuegos
Bay of Pigs
Isle of Pines
Escambray Mtns
Las Tunas
Bayamo
Manzanillo
Sierra Maestra
Santiago
0 50 100 150 200 250 300 350 400 KM
0 50 100 150 200 250 MLS

FOREWORD

This novel opens in 1956 and ends in 1960. For those readers unfamiliar with Cuban history, the information set out below will help put the story in context.

After centuries as a Spanish colony, Cuba fought two wars of independence, firstly in 1868–78 and secondly in 1895–98. The victory which ensued from the latter struggle was marred, from a Cuban nationalist point of view, by the last-minute intervention of the USA on the side of the rebels. This led to an interim three-year period under US military supervision before the island became a self-governing republic.

After an initial period of stability, there followed a series of corrupt and exploitative regimes, in which successive presidents ruled as virtual dictators and enriched themselves out of the national coffers; graft and gangsterism were rife. A lack of spending on welfare, health and education left a large divide between rich and poor. Cuba remained economically dependent on the US, its principal trading partner, which continued to exert considerable political influence.

Fulgencio Batista, an army sergeant, was active in overthrowing the dictator Machado in 1933, and his subsequent presidency was popular. But following a period out of office, he staged a second coup in 1952. Over the next seven years he presided over an unjust and brutal regime, which provided a breeding ground for insurrection. Revolutionary groups began a programme of urban terrorism; those arrested were tortured and sometimes murdered by Batista's secret police; this served to increase support for the rebels among the middle classes.

Fidel Castro, a young lawyer, set up a guerrilla encampment in the Sierra Maestre and became the perceived leader of the movement to oust the dictator and install a new democratic government. Ensuing rebel victories over Batista's inefficient and corrupt army were less important than the inspiration which they gave to the oppressed and underprivileged masses. Military defeats, escalating sabotage in the towns and the withdrawal of US military support for the regime finally led to its collapse.

Castro effectively came to power on 1 January 1959, promising elections which have yet to take place. A worsening relationship with the US was both the cause and the effect of a rapid shift to Communism, with the support of the USSR. This departure from Castro's pledges of democracy caused many of his former supporters to turn against him, at their peril. A witch-hunt against 'counter-revolutionaries' and the nationalisation of private companies resulted in dissenters, together with a large proportion of the bourgeoisie, fleeing the country.

The proposed invasion and 'liberation' of Cuba by US-backed mercenaries resulted in the Bay of Pigs fiasco in April 1961. This served both to consolidate Castro's position and expose covert US intervention in Cuban affairs, and led indirectly to the Cuban missile crisis of 1962.

While the novel is set against the backdrop of these historical events, I would like to stress that all the characters, and their doings, are the product of my imagination and that any resemblance to any real persons, living or dead, is entirely coincidental.

PART ONE

December 1956 – March 1957

ONE

León reached for the soft sleeping flesh beside him with the lazy lust of a husband. Being with Addy was like being married, except that she wasn't his wife, thank God. And because he was free to go today, he would still be here tomorrow.

Addy yawned in indolent compliance. Young men were a luxury, they were happy to do all the work. She found sex a bore, even with León, but it was a comforting kind of boredom. It was like playing with a child, feigning fascination with its toys, sharing its world of make-believe and magic. The pleasure was vicarious, but none the less real for that. She dreaded the day when León would finally grow up, forsake let's-pretend for a reality which would exclude her.

'Not bad,' she said drily, half an hour later, reaching for her cigarettes. 'You're improving.'

León smiled complacently and went to take a shower. Addy rang for coffee and opened the Venetian blinds, letting the brilliant December sun throw its merciless light on her dressing-table mirror. Quickly, before León returned, she removed what was left of yesterday's make-up and applied a fresh coat, reducing her galloping thirty-six years to a static twenty-nine. Even so, she still looked older than her lover. León, bless him, was a baby of twenty-five, one of those golden boys whom nothing could touch, whose life was still unsullied by shame or blame or responsibility, who could afford to waste his life because he had so much of it left. Whereas Addy had reached an age when she needed something to vindicate her past, something that would survive her fading face.

The well-appointed penthouse apartment, in the fashionable Havana suburb of Vedado, was a symbol of her progress from poverty to prosperity, from hungry hooker to thriving nightclub owner. And once her new casino, the Herradura, opened in March (with kind permission from the mobsters who would collect their share of her profits) she would be well on her way to being rich. Five more years and she could go home for good, be respectable again. Addy hadn't been respectable in twenty years. Like every other luxury in life, it came expensive.

María, the maid, tapped on the door and brought in a tray – toast, a pot of strong sweet coffee, a jug of pink, pulpy papaya juice, and a copy of the English-language *Havana Post*. There were three letters, two addressed to León and one for Addy, from Lily. She tore it open, anticipating trouble.

> 10 December 1956
>
> Dear Mom
>
> I hate you. How can you do this to me? I was so looking forward to Christmas and now I am dreading it. It will be miserable without you there. Can you imagine three weeks of hanging round St Pete's with Grandma treating me as if I was about five years old? And no, I haven't had any invitations to stay with any of my classmates. Even if I had I wouldn't accept. I hate all the girls at school and they hate me, it's even worse than the last place. Why can't I come to Havana for Christmas instead?

'Something wrong?' queried León, emerging from the bathroom, all damp hair and *joie de vivre*.

'My mother's upset I'm not visiting at Christmas,' said Addy shortly, without looking up. Having lied about her age at the outset, she had never got round to confessing to a teenage daughter. 'I told her I couldn't get away until the builders had finished.'

> . . . I understand how busy you are with the new casino, but I promise I wouldn't get in the way. And in the evenings I could work at the club, you wouldn't have to pay me. I could wait tables, check hats, anything. And then maybe, just once, you'll give me a chance to sing. You know that's all I've ever wanted to do. I can't stand the thought of coming back to this

lousy school next term. I might as well be in prison. If you make me stay here any longer I swear to God I'll run away . . .

Addy's frown deepened. Lily's grades had been the worst in her class – one of many ploys to engineer expulsion from the rich-kid boarding school in New England where she was supposed to be learning social graces, if little else. Three similar establishments had already demanded Lily's summary removal and that the fourth continued to tolerate her misbehaviour was entirely due to a sizeable donation to school funds, not to mention a judicious backhander to the stony-faced principal. Discipline was not Addy's forte – the most indulgent of parents, she preferred to delegate this unpleasant duty to others, among them her own tartar of a mother who had charge of Lily during vacations.

Addy had set the old girl up in a pleasant house in St Petersburg – a vast improvement on the dingy tenement in downtown Tampa where Addy had grown up – in which Lily was required to be polite to Ruth's card-playing cronies, to eat up all her greens, and to be in bed, having said her prayers, by ten. Addy's occasional flying visits – to leave her business unattended was to be cheated right and left – did nothing to assuage her guilt at being a bad mother, guilt which Lily exploited without mercy.

'She's spoiled to death,' Ruth had pronounced grimly. 'If you had sent her to me earlier, I might have managed to do something with her, not that I succeeded with you. As it is, she was ruined before she left Havana, and not all the finishing schools in Europe will ever make a lady out of her.'

But allowing Lily to return to her birthplace, after ten years of exile, remained out of the question. It would only be a matter of time before she discovered that Addy's, her mother's nightclub, was a whorehouse by any other name – one of many things about herself Addy didn't want her daughter to know, for all that Addy's was a cut above the usual run of Havana hooker-bars, geared to the better type of clientele. Riff-raff were not allowed past its two burly black doormen. American businessmen, army officers, senior policemen and high-ranking bureaucrats were more than willing to pay over the odds for pretty, disease-free companions and guaranteed discretion. Not that she could explain all that to an innocent sixteen-year-old. Lily was still a child, but she looked like a young woman. A beautiful young woman, as Addy herself had once been. That was the whole trouble. How could she hope to protect her in a place like Havana, the most corrupt, corrupting city on earth?

She folded the letter away; luckily León was too engrossed in his own correspondence to show any interest in hers. Addy recognised the handwriting on one of the envelopes as that of Celia, León's stepsister, of whom he was inordinately fond. So much so that Addy had begun to wonder if his attachment was more than brotherly. Whenever she teased him on the subject, he protested too much, reinforcing her cynical suspicions. Would-be rakes like León always ended up with some virginal girl-next-door.

León read Lidia's letter first, anxious to get it over with; later he would burn it. He never responded to his stepmother's outpourings, but this did not deter her from writing once or even twice a week. The contents never varied. Protestations of undying passion, embarrassingly explicit sexual reminiscences, woeful accusations of faithlessness and desertion, and fervent assurances that his ailing father was not long for this world, a prediction which León sincerely hoped was wishful thinking on her part. All the while his father was alive, Lidia would moderate her behaviour. She had too much self-interest to invite divorce and lose out on the prospect of becoming a wealthy widow. Meanwhile, the spectre of exposure hovered over León's well-being. More than he feared his father's wrath, he dreaded Celia's scorn.

Having established that she had not yet carried out her oft-repeated, if hollow threat to 'ask Enrique for my freedom', León stuffed the purple pages into the pocket of his robe before embarking eagerly on Celia's letter. As usual, she insisted on bringing him up to date with the preparations for the sugar harvest, a subject which did not interest him in the least.

The Buenaventura estate, which León was doomed to inherit one day, was situated nine hundred kilometres east of Havana in the province of Oriente. It comprised thirty-five thousand acres of cane, plus land worked by lessees and peasant farmers, all of whom were dependent on the Buenaventura *central* to buy and grind their produce. The Soler family had come a long way since León's great-grandfather, Gustavo, had arrived from Spain in 1855. A humble shopkeeper-turned-merchant, he had turned his hand to moneylending and grown fabulously rich out of the two Cuban wars of independence, when sugar prices had plummeted, enabling him to buy his debtors' land at a fraction of its true worth. Having acquired Buenaventura from an impoverished sugar baron, Gustavo had given it to his eldest son – León's grandfather – as a wedding present. The young landowner lost no time in expanding his territory by driving the local peasants off their land, foreclosing on small farmers, falsifying title deeds, bribing crooked lawyers, and disposing of anyone who tried to thwart him. Don Enrique, León's father, had carried on where his father left off, albeit with a veneer of legality, thanks to the corrupt politicians, judges and policemen who dispensed what passed for justice.

Like the old man, Celia persisted in the assumption that León would come home once he had finished sowing his wild oats. Meanwhile she was expected to fill his shoes, to act as Don Enrique's general factotum and unpaid apprentice until León saw fit to take over, even though she got little thanks for her efforts, either from her stepfather, who thought he was doing her a favour, or from her mother, who openly preferred Celia's younger brother, Eduardo. Don Enrique Soler had little time for his left-wing hothead of a stepson, just as Lidia had little time for her ageing, corpulent husband, just as Eduardo had little time for either of them. Without Celia there as a buffer, thought León, open warfare would have erupted long ago. No wonder she felt trapped. Sooner or later she would rebel, run off with the first man who offered her a chance of escape. A possibility which worried León even more than it did his father.

'How about you?' said Addy, pouring herself a second cup of coffee. 'Are you going home for Christmas?'

'I suppose I'll have to. According to Celia, the old man reckons it will be his last. She believes it, even if I don't. He never had a weak heart till I told him I wasn't going to work for him. If he does die, it'll just be to spite me.'

'Poor darling,' clucked Addy unsympathetically. 'It's tough, being heir to a fortune, isn't it?'

'It's tough all right,' said León airily. 'I don't get a cent till my stepmother dies, remember? She's not forty yet, she's good for another twenty years at least. I just hope my father lasts as long. Once he's gone, I guess I'll have to go home, whether I like it or not. Lidia hasn't a clue how to run the place, and Celia would get eaten alive, she's much too soft. Oriente's no place for a couple of women on their own.'

Addy could well believe it. From what she had learned from León, the province resembled the old American West – primitive, violent and lawless. The mountainous region to the south of the estate was running alive with bandits, and recently a young revolutionary called Fidel Castro had set up a rebel encampment in the Sierra Maestre, dedicated to the overthrow of the Batista government, of which Addy was a firm, if self-interested, supporter. You couldn't blame León for not wanting to live in such a godforsaken place, where illiterate peasants bred tribes of ragged children in palm-thatched huts, without benefit of running water or electricity, labouring in the cane fields for half the year and starving or stealing in the 'dead season' between harvests. Not that Addy felt much pity for these unfortunates. Having once been destitute herself, she was intolerant of poverty in others.

'Surely your stepmother won't want to stay in the country once your father is gone? Wouldn't she rather live in Havana?'

'Oh, undoubtedly,' muttered León. Lidia's extravagant plans for the future included a house in El Country Club, the most exclusive residential area of the capital, where she and León could be together at last, while Celia remained at home to supervise the estate in their absence.

'I suppose that will be my cue to bow out,' said Addy slyly, observing him over the rim of her coffee cup. 'I'm hardly the sort of woman you introduce to the family.'

'I don't see why not.'

'Then why haven't you told them about me?' persisted Addy. 'Because Celia would be shocked?' León coloured slightly. At heart he was a dreadful prude. 'Doesn't she wonder how you could afford to move to the better part of town?'

'Celia thinks I'm a great success as a painter,' said León, picking up the *Havana Post* and pretending to read the front page. 'But I took care to point out that it's a precarious profession and I could be out on the street tomorrow. Any time you say the word, in fact.'

It was not an idle threat. For León, hardship was a self-indulgence of sorts, a reaction to the riches he affected to shun, to the lucrative profession he refused to practise. A qualified lawyer, he could have earned a substantial living even without subsidy from his father. But he despised the legal system as corrupt and parasitic, choosing instead to amuse himself painting pointless portraits of bored, rich women. By his own admission, he had no talent, let alone a vocation; he was simply far too lazy to do what Addy would have called real work.

But it wasn't just laziness; it was a dread of responsibility, a desire for freedom. When Addy first met him, he was living on a shoestring, stubbornly surviving the stoppage of his allowance, relying on thumbnail sketches of tourists to keep body and soul together, the body being rather thinner than the one that now faced her across the breakfast table, the soul every bit as elusive.

Emerging from the Inglaterra Hotel, after a business lunch, she had sighted León with his sketch-pad, in the Parque Central, the sun glinting on his golden hair, giving him the air of a scruffy, unshaven, fallen angel. He was busily transcribing the features of a florid American tourist, who proceeded to haggle loudly over the price, while León, who had learned English at his American mother's knee, haughtily affected not to understand him. The man had turned to his wife and made some remark about goddamned Spics, whereupon León had torn the picture in two and stalked off. Intrigued, Addy had run after him and asked him to draw her instead, which he had done with virtuoso speed, presenting her with a likeness which was more flattering than accurate. When she tried to pay him over the odds, he had insisted, with devastating gallantry, that she take the picture as a gift. A gift which had proved that this self-avowed cynic was a hopeless romantic at heart – she could tell just by looking at him that he hadn't had a square meal in days.

Addy had commissioned him to paint her in oils and lost no time in inveigling him into her bed; fortunately León had been too kind-hearted, or weak-willed, to refuse her. It had been love, not lust, on her part. She hadn't felt lust in years, or love either, come to that. After some initial diffidence he had adapted remarkably well to being a kept man, but he hated her to rub it in. That she did so occasionally was to remind herself, and him, that this was an exercise in mutual exploitation, that it couldn't, and wouldn't last. It helped her confront the inevitable prospect of losing him, and if she occasionally engineered a disagreement, it was to practise for the pain of parting.

'So when do your family expect you?'

'When they see me. Next week, probably. I can't go till I've finished the picture of Captain Reinaldo's wife. It's his Christmas present to her.'

Reinaldo, a corrupt anti-vice policeman, was the nightclub's protector and León found himself obliged, at Addy's request, to be civil to him.

'Tell me,' asked Addy, casually. 'What's she like in bed?'

León had the grace to look disconcerted.

'I thought so,' purred Addy.

'We agreed . . .'

'I know what we agreed. You're free, I'm free. But for God's sake be careful. Reinaldo is a vicious bastard. I don't want you to end up in some back alley with a bullet in your guts. There are plenty of other women in Havana, much more attractive than Sofía. Why take the risk?'

León shrugged. It hadn't been a conscious decision. Like Lidia, and Addy, like all the women in his life, Sofía had made the first move. Feeble though the excuse might be, he hadn't wanted to hurt her feelings.

'Do you have a woman in Oriente as well?' continued Addy, well aware that she was annoying him. 'Besides Celia, I mean?' She enjoyed goading him out of his perpetual good humour. It was like throwing a pebble into still water, disturbing the hidden depths that passed for shallows, watching the ripples distort their light and shade.

'I wish I did,' said León, disappearing behind his newspaper. 'You've no idea how boring it is back home. The minute I arrive the old boy will be ranting and raving at me about duty and responsibility and ingratitude. With any luck he'll throw me out and tell me never to darken his door again.'

Fat chance. His father could not afford a rift, thanks to Lidia's failure to provide him with another child. Not for the first time, León regretted the loss of his elder brother, whom he hadn't seen or heard of since 1939. León had been eight at the time, Raúl fourteen. Raúl must have known that the so-called 'holiday' to the States – a vanishing act committed while Don Enrique was away from home on business – was intended to be permanent; he had always been his mother's champion and confidant. But León, the baby of the family, knew nothing of her plan to flee, taking her sons with her. He retained a confused memory of two armed men breaking into a motel room in Miami in the middle of the night and dragging him out of bed, of Mamá screaming and Raúl firing a shot at one of the intruders while the other man bundled León into a car, stopping his cries with a sweet-smelling rag. When he woke up he was on a boat, and a few days later he was back home in Cuba with his father. Raúl and Mamá had disappeared, thwarting Don Enrique's efforts to locate them; later she had sued for divorce through intermediaries, resisting huge financial incentives to send Raúl home.

León remembered his brother as tall, broad and immensely strong, as dark as León was fair. Raúl was a fine shot, an accomplished rider, a natural sportsman. Not for him the effete pleasures of books and paint-brushes that so appealed to León; even as a boy he was already touring the cane fields on horseback, taking his turn at the machete, showing himself as a future boss and born leader. León had admired and feared him; given his superior size and strength there had been no point in trying to compete, and he had learned at a tender age that it was easier to settle for the role of pampered baby, his mother's favourite, comfortably beneath his father's contempt.

Yes, if Raúl were at home, he would still be the carefree younger brother, and although he went through the motions of courting disinheritance, he knew that there was little risk, or hope, of that. Under no circumstances would his father leave the estate to Celia; blood was thicker than water, and blood ran thicker in Oriente than anywhere else on earth.The decision to make Lidia trustee of the estate for her lifetime – provided that she did not remarry – with control over its income, but not its capital, was as far as the old man dared go; meanwhile teaching Celia the business from top to bottom was his insurance policy, a way of protecting Lidia, and later, León, from the chicanery of his managers and accountants and lawyers, none of whom he trusted, with good reason. Whereas Celia was trustworthy to a fault, and assumed, in her naïveté, that León was too.

Well, so he would be in future, after a fashion. When he

got home, he would break things off with Lidia once and for all. She couldn't betray him without losing everything; he would be quite safe. Until last summer, it had been easier, and kinder, to shut her up by giving in. But that was before he had fallen in love with her daughter.

Celia sat hunched over her ledgers, brow furrowed in concentration. A year after taking up her job, she still felt like an intruder in her own office, the office that should have been León's. It was a smaller version of her stepfather's inner sanctum, with the same dark mahogany furniture, black leather swivel chair and ingrained smell of cigar – a masculine room, intended for a man. Installing her in here had been a challenge, not a compliment. Celia's lack of self-esteem was exceeded only by her pride.

Papá had asked her to come up with a list of suggestions for reducing overheads by the time he returned from Santiago de Cuba, the object being to subsidise his mounting security budget. In Celia's view, the best way to cut costs would be to spend more: a hefty increase in the annual pay-off to the union leaders would help ensure a strike-free grinding season and safeguard what promised to be a bumper harvest. Additionally, it would avert the danger of union co-operation with the rebels and reduce the risk of insider sabotage. Papá, however, would probably favour a simpler solution – abandoning Celia's expansion plans for the Buenaventura clinic. A doctor had to be on call to deal with the frequent accidents caused by viciously sharp machetes and the powerful machines at the mill; after months of subtle flattery, Celia had convinced Enrique that extending the service, to provide for wives and children, would undermine the troublemakers who accused him – quite unjustly, of course – of being a bad employer.

Mounting expenses would no doubt scupper her other pet project: establishing a free school for local children, most of whom received no education at all. The nearest state establishment had no staff, and therefore no pupils. Teaching licences, like everything else, were for sale; having bought his sinecure, the absentee incumbent of the decaying, deserted schoolhouse now drew a government salary for doing nothing.

Celia chewed the top of her pen, wondering how she could manipulate Papá into seeing things her way. Arguing with him was a waste of time; the best way to get him to agree to a suggestion was to convince him that he had thought of it himself. She looked up, lost in thought, as the afternoon breeze started up outside, provoking a hoarse, harsh cough as canestalks swayed and rubbed against each other, drowning out the whirr of the ceiling fan. Beyond the paved forecourt outside Celia's window heaved a twelve-foot-deep ocean of shimmering silver-green, ripe for the machete, full to bursting with liquid gold.

Celia loved the frantic activity of the grinding season, when ton upon ton of cane from miles around would arrive by ox-cart and private railroad to feed the voracious jaws of the Buenaventura mill. The opaque, milky juice would boil and bubble and thicken and clear and spin itself into the glistening crystals that made Cuba rich, that kept it poor. After the long lean months of unemployment, there would be work and food for everyone. Harvest time reminded her of a giant animal waking out of a long hibernation, weak and thin from its six-month fast, growing strong and fat again. It was hard to associate the crude physical vitality of the process with the sterile columns of figures that confronted her, figures that were used to thwart and discredit all her best ideas. Yawning, she picked up the telephone on its second ring.

'Celia? Are you alone?'

'León!' She took a deep breath, willing herself to sound cool. It should have been easy, it *was* easy with everyone else but him. Celia got plenty of practice at hiding her feelings. 'Yes, I'm holding the fort this week. Your father's at the Santiago office.'

'So he's better, then,' said León drily. 'Your letter made it sound as if he was about to croak.'

The line was bad, as usual. León seldom rang home, and couldn't be reached by telephone, his excuse being that he didn't have one, which Celia found hard to believe now that he had moved from his room downtown to this new apartment in Vedado. Her mother had commented sourly that he had no doubt installed some low-class mistress, and was afraid that she would answer the call. Mamá thoroughly disapproved of León's Bohemian lifestyle; Celia envied it.

'His blood pressure's still high,' she said. 'You know how easily he gets worked up. And all this rebel activity has made him worse. They fired the customs house in Santiago last week, and the flames nearly spread to the warehouse, so he's trying to negotiate a full-time army guard.'

'That'll cost him.'

'I know, it's a real racket. Santiago's got even more terrorists than Havana.' She dropped her voice. 'Eduardo has gone and joined the 26 July movement,' she hissed, referring to Fidel Castro's revolutionary network, so called in memory of a failed assault on the Santiago barracks, three years before. 'He's talked about nothing else ever since he came back from school. It's all I can do to persuade him to keep quiet in front of the parents. Papá would probably throw him out and Mamá would worry herself to death. Several students were arrested and beaten up and one boy was shot. I wish you'd talk to him.'

'It would do more harm than good. He's already written me off as a Yanqui-loving bourgeois. Never mind about Eduardo. How are you?'

'Busy as usual. We start grinding in two weeks.'

'I asked about you, not Buenaventura.'

She hesitated a moment before saying lightly, 'Missing you. Are you coming home for Christmas?' She tried, unsuccessfully, to keep the plea out of her voice.

'If you want me to. You're the only thing worth coming home for.'

As usual, it was impossible to gauge his tone, and the bad line was not the reason. It was the same story with his letters. They were full of titillating, tongue-in-cheek endearments, which could be interpreted as amorous or merely affectionate, tormenting her with their ambiguity. Celia's replies, in contrast, were robustly matter-of-fact; she had made quite enough of a fool of herself already.

Small wonder that he hadn't been home since the harvest ball, last June; most likely she had scared him off. In an ill-considered attempt to make him jealous – some hope – she had flirted quite outrageously with the son of a neighbouring *colono*, an indiscretion which had led Papá to forbid her to see the boy again. (An unnecessary prohibition. She didn't find him in the least attractive.) It was untypically crass behaviour, inspired, perhaps, by hotter than usual blood: the following day she had gone down with scarlet fever and been isolated from the rest of the household, apart from León, who had had the disease as a child. He had brought her meals on a tray, dispensed her medicine, and as she recovered, played chess and taught her poker and even painted her portrait, even though she must have looked a perfect fright. Having him all to herself had been sheer torture.

Unfortunately, she made a rapid recovery, God having ignored her prayers for a relapse, and the day of his departure, already delayed by a week, came round all too soon. He put his arms around her to say goodbye, looked at her in a way that made her hope, and then . . .

And then she had kissed him, full on the mouth, like a lover – not that she had ever had a lover – provoking an equally passionate response. Just thinking about it still made her toes curl up. Not just with pleasure but with shame. Shame that León had pulled away, left the room and left the house without another word, appalled by his lapse and hers. Not that it had been a lapse on her part. She had planned it, quite deliberately. She had been planning it, on and off, for years.

'Papá will be so pleased to see you,' said Celia brightly. 'When should we expect you?'

She had been afraid he wouldn't come. Suddenly Christmas seemed bearable again. The festive season was one long business lunch, a time for buying and selling goodwill for the following year. An invitation to the lavish Soler Christmas Eve feast was a privilege granted to some fifty hand-picked guests, which this year would include the commanding officer from the local barracks, a recent recruit to Don Enrique's unofficial payroll in return for army protection against rebel attack. Superficially, it was a glittering, happy occasion, with music and dancing and laughter, Enrique playing the benevolent host and Lidia the devoted wife. But this public display of harmony would mask an even higher than usual degree of matrimonial strife. It didn't help that Celia's father had died at Christmas, ten years before, a loss which her mother still felt keenly, much to Enrique's chagrin.

Celia was already bracing herself in readiness. It would fall to her to supervise and humour the servants while her mother tried on and discarded her entire wardrobe and complained how tired and overworked she was. Papá would carp and bluster and pick holes in everything – the table settings, the menu, the musicians, the decorations – and rather than fight with each other they would both vent their ill humour on Celia, while Eduardo kept well out of the way, with his usual Buddha-like detachment. In León's absence, it was hard, not to say impossible, to relax and see the funny side. With León there, it would be one huge private joke.

'I should be with you in a few days,' he said. 'I've decided to drive down.'

'You've bought a new car?' said Celia, well aware that he had had to sell his beloved Thunderbird to raise cash.

'Yes. A red Packard convertible.'

'Where did you get the money?'

There was a short pause.

'I've been doing this big mural for a new casino.'

'Then you must have overcharged them. You haven't been gambling, have you?'

'Only on a sure thing. See you soon.'

And with this cryptic remark, he rang off, leaving her

wondering if the low-class mistress was in fact some rich, jewel-encrusted widow. She hoped that she was old and fat, not young and beautiful . . .

Aware that she had chewed all her lipstick off, Celia got out her hand mirror and began repairing the damage with a bad grace, glaring critically at her reflection. Everyone thought Eduardo so good-looking, and everyone agreed how alike they were; it seemed unfair that the same features should afford her face character rather than beauty, earn her the epithets 'striking' or 'handsome' instead of the 'pretty' she coveted so much. Pretty women got their own way as of right, without having to work, or scheme, or wait for it. Celia got her own way by patience and stealth, if at all.

She tried to refocus her attention on the ledger in front of her, but it was no use; her concentration was shot to pieces. Locking her papers away, she decided to take advantage of the boss's absence and give herself the rest of the day off.

'I shall be working at home for the rest of the day,' she told her secretary. 'If Don Enrique calls, he can reach me at the house. Ring for the chauffeur, will you?'

The Buenaventura *batey* was the size of a large village; the office and mill buildings, dominated by a tall chimney visible for miles around, were surrounded by housing for senior staff, workers' palm-thatched huts, allotments planted with banana, plantains, yucca and maize, shops, clubhouse, cock-pit, clinic and chapel. The Soler residence, a substantial stone house, was situated at the outer edge of the compound, hidden behind tall trees, set amidst lavish tropical gardens and protected by high iron railings. Access to the long gravel driveway was restricted by the armed guards on the gate; in her more despondent moments, it seemed to Celia as if these fortifications were designed to prevent escape, rather than repel trespassers.

She reminded herself that she was lucky. In material terms, she had everything she could possibly want, plus the extra luxury of a job, albeit an unpaid one; without it she would be bored to tears. But it was not a job she could be proud of. Her seniority had been conferred, not earned, the result of nepotism, not merit. And however good at it she turned out to be, she would always be the boss's daughter, or rather stepdaughter, a mere understudy for his son, a son who would have commanded instant respect just by virtue of being male. Over-anxious to prove herself, Celia had acquired a reputation for being stern, humourless and unfeminine – deliberately so. She was damned if she would pander to machismo by pretending to be helpless, or stoop to simpering to make herself popular.

'She takes after her father,' she had overheard someone say, referring not to Don Enrique, but to Gabriel Rodríguez, his late *mayoral*, who had been shot by bandits ten years before. Celia took the remark as a compliment; he had been known as tough, but honest and fair. She had adored her father, a big, affectionate bear of a man who had called her Princess, who had left her with the painful bequest of knowing what it felt like to be loved for no reason, without having to earn it.

Her widowed mother was left poorly provided for, with no choice but to go into service at the big house, a job that had led, within a year of her bereavement, to marriage, and eventually to misery, despite a magnificent ten-bedroomed home, servants to obey her every whim, and a monthly clothes allowance that exceeded her first husband's annual income. Enrique was proud of his attractive young wife, not to say obsessively jealous. Lidia was obliged to account for every moment of her time, unable to leave the house without enduring a lengthy cross-examination as to her movements.

'Even if I wanted to take a lover,' Celia had heard her mother shout, 'no man would have me, for fear of being shot!'

This accusation had rendered her husband temporarily speechless, perhaps because it was too near the mark for comfort. Murder was too common an occurrence in Oriente to warrant excessive investigation, and men as powerful as Don Enrique could flout the law with impunity. It would certainly have taken a brave man to cuckold him, although Celia found it hard to believe that her mother would ever be unfaithful, given Lidia's carefully cultivated stance of rigid, frigid virtue, which Celia had always accepted as genuine.

The pose was not hard to maintain, given Lidia's distaste for her husband. She had briskly conveyed the facts of life – which Celia had already learned in great detail from Emilia, the housekeeper – in a manner expressly calculated to put her daughter off sex for life. Lidia dreaded her daughter falling in love and getting married, thereby depriving her of a staunch, if reluctant, ally.

'Heaven knows what I'd do without you, darling,' she would sniff. 'If I was left alone here with Enrique . . . you know what a vicious temper he has. Thank heavens I have a good, loyal, sensible daughter like you.'

Celia was neither flattered nor deceived. Good meant not pretty, loyal meant cowardly, sensible meant boring. Both her mother and her stepfather were united in their wish to keep her at home for ever. Unlike Eduardo, who had been sent away to school in Santiago, Celia had been educated by a governess, safe from the disruptive influence of her peers, and been denied the chance to take her *bachillerato*, for fear that paper qualifications might make her too independent. Marriage was likewise seen as a threat – any youth bold enough to show an interest in her was warned off in no uncertain terms. Don Enrique's greatest fear was that some upstart of a fortune-hunter would penetrate his stronghold, use Celia as a stepping stone to taking over the estate, give León the opportunity to relinquish control of Buenaventura to an outsider.

To guard against this, Enrique piled work and responsibility upon her, leaving her no time to get up to mischief. Celia's limited circle of female friends – daughters of senior employees and neighbouring *colonos* – had given up inviting her to the pool and tennis parties, movie visits and shopping expeditions that filled their unlimited leisure. As for travel to the United States –

de rigueur for any young woman of good family – that remained out of the question. The treachery of Enrique's first wife had left him with rampant paranoia on the subject; even León had been educated exclusively in Cuba, against normal practice for the sons of the rich. Like her mother, Celia lived in a gilded cage; her outward acquiescence hid a seething mass of frustration.

'You're my only comfort,' Enrique would mutter, squeezing her hand, resorting to a gruff but effective brand of emotional blackmail. 'The one person I can trust. But I suppose you'll turn your back on me one day, like all the rest of them. Even though I've treated you like my own . . .'

At such moments she felt weak with pity for him. It was hard not to return his sad, surly affection, not to respond to his naked, pathetic need for reassurance. She felt obliged to love him, if only because no one else did. If he was overbearing and demanding, at least he expected too much of her, rather than too little. And besides, with his high blood pressure, she felt obliged to put up with his black moods, to endure his peremptory demands, his bullying and tactlessness rather than answer back and provoke a rage which might result in a heart attack or a stroke.

To be *resignada* – stoical – was supposed to be a virtue, after all. Celia liked to believe that self-control was a sign of strength of character, even though Eduardo dismissed it as a symptom of weakness. To his mind, the solution was simple: she should up and leave without a word to anyone, instead of playing the martyr. If she was too feeble to risk upsetting the parents, then she had only herself to blame. That she was quite penniless – like her mother she had access to umpteen charge accounts but next to no ready cash – was, in his view, a minor detail. Eduardo despised money, and never missed an opportunity to preach revolution at her. Celia would have quite enjoyed arguing with him, except that Eduardo, like the rest of the household, always insisted on having the last word, preferably one she wouldn't understand.

Inevitably, she would soon be out of her depth and resort to a volley of home truths, berating her brother as a self-righteous, narrow-minded, supercilious little prig. But Eduardo remained unmoved, like a god deploring the blasphemies of mere mortals. 'Perhaps I am,' he would respond, equably, 'but I also happen to be right.' And then he would ruffle her hair, damn him, as if he were the elder, not she.

The only person who didn't talk down to her was León. León had always treated her as an equal, allowed her the supreme luxury of being herself. Well, not quite herself. The real, inadmissible Celia – reckless, selfish and greedy – would have gone through with the plan she had made last summer and followed him, uninvited, to Havana. The other, official Celia – cool, prim and circumspect – had thought better of it and been congratulating and cursing herself by turns ever since.

One of the two family chauffeurs, Lázaro González, was waiting for her outside, holding open the passenger door of a gleaming white Cadillac. Like many of Buenaventura's employees, he had been born and brought up on the estate where his ancestors had been slaves. Emilia, the housekeeper, was in love with him, a passion which remained unrequited despite heavy investment in magic herbs procured from the local *botánica*. Not a day passed when Emilia did not secretly sprinkle absinthe under Lázaro's bed, or wear lovage close to her heart, as yet to no avail. In his spare time, he bred fighting cocks which he trained and sold at the market in Bayamo. Thanks to Emilia, the poor doomed creatures ate like princes, as did Lázaro himself, for whom Emilia prepared traditional African specialities, his favourite dishes being *amala*, a cornmeal paste wrapped in banana leaves, and *ochinchin*, a stew of shrimp cooked with watercress and almonds. She would secretly season these delicacies with powdered orris root, an aphrodisiac which had so far failed to inflame his lust; the way to Lázaro's heart was evidently not through his stomach.

'Straight home, Lázaro, please,' said Celia. And then,

noticing his grim expression, 'Is something wrong?'

'Family troubles,' he said shortly.

Lázaro was taciturn to a degree, never using two words where one would do.

'Is somebody ill?' asked Celia.

'Not ill. Dead. My brother.' His voice was tight, cracked, his usual fierce, impassive dignity quivering with raw emotion.

'Esteban, dead?' echoed Celia, aghast.

Lázaro opened the door of the car and slammed it shut with unnecessary force before taking the driver's seat, evidently glad to have his back to her so that she could not see his face.

'I'm so sorry,' said Celia. 'Your poor mother . . . What happened?'

Lázaro didn't deign to answer, starting up the engine and putting his foot down hard on the pedal. Only when they drew up outside the house did he say savagely, 'Those white rebels killed him.'

'What?'

'He was on patrol in Santiago. A sniper shot at him from a window. In the back.'

Celia shut her eyes, appalled. Rather than be out of work for six months in every twelve, Lázaro's younger brother had recently joined the army, one of the few available jobs which lasted all year round. Like many black Cubans, he supported Batista, a mulatto president who was regarded as a friend of the Negro.

'Tell your mother we'll pay all the funeral expenses,' began Celia.

'No need. Military funeral. Army will pay.'

'Yes. Yes, of course. You must drive your mother to Santiago right away. Check into a hotel, tell them to send the bill to me. Take as much time off as you need.'

Papá would rave at her for pampering the servants, but so what? He wouldn't know anything about it until it was too late.

Lázaro nodded his thanks, opened the door for her and drove on to the garage block. Celia let herself into the house, to find Emilia weeping in the kitchen.

'That poor boy,' she sobbed, her plump shoulders heaving with distress. 'I remember the day he was born. Murderers!'

Celia put an arm round her, helpless to comment on such a pointless death, while Emilia ranted on.

'The *santero* saw it in the coconut shells. A new white leader will lead Cuba to ruin. Those rebels hate Batista because he's half black . . .'

'You're quite wrong, Emilia,' said Eduardo, appearing in the doorway. 'The rebels want equality for all Cubans, whatever their race. They want to abolish poverty and injustice. They want to—'

'Eduardo, please,' hissed Celia, seeing Emilia's eyes flash. 'Emilia, you should have a lie down. Don't worry about supper tonight, we'll help ourselves from the fridge.'

'I'm going to pay my respects to that poor boy's mother,' sniffed Emilia. She marched off, slamming the back door. Eduardo helped himself to a bottle of beer.

'I suppose you think that was a blow against tyranny,' said Celia coldly. 'Killing a young boy whose only crime was to be a soldier. Some revolution. White middle-class radicals attacking a black worker. They ought to be ashamed.'

'He was a casualty of war.'

'A war nobody can win.'

'We won against the Spanish.'

'Thanks to the Americans.'

'In spite of the Americans. They were the real enemy. They still are.'

'Rubbish. Where would we be without America to buy our sugar?'

'Where would a slave be without its master?'

Celia sighed, knowing he would use his vast political vocabulary to tie her up in knots.

'For God's sake, keep your mouth shut in front of Papá's guests over Christmas. Save your politics for your little clique of hangers-on at school.'

'No need to bite my head off,' said Eduardo mildly, removing the cap from the bottle. 'I've no quarrel with you.'

'Well, you ought to have. I don't approve of terrorism. It will only lead to reprisals and more people being rounded up on suspicion. Including you, I shouldn't wonder.'

Eduardo put his hand in his pocket and withdrew a fifty-peso note.

'Mamá gave me this for getting good grades. Will you give it to Lázaro's mother?'

'Is that what a life's worth?' challenged Celia, accepting it none the less. 'Fifty pesos?'

'It's just a gesture, that's all. I can't stand to see Batista use crude race prejudice to woo the Negroes into supporting him. Lázaro's just the kind of guy we need to join us.'

'Leave Lázaro alone, Eduardo. He's entitled to his prejudices just the same as you. And don't expect any sympathy from me if you end up in gaol. If you break the law—'

'You'd be the first to rush to my defence, dear sister. This new tough act of yours doesn't fool me, even if it has them all shaking in their shoes at the mill.' Celia tried to glare. 'What are you doing home so early?'

'I had a headache. Where's Mamá?'

'Still having her siesta. She's sulking because I wouldn't join her for lunch. She wanted me to play pet poodle in front of a couple of her pals.' As usual, Eduardo displayed a callous indifference to Lidia's devotion. ' "Eduardo got straight As again this term," ' he mimicked. ' "He takes after me, of course." '

'Can't you humour her for the short while you're home?' pleaded Celia. 'It would take the heat off me.'

'No. Try standing up to her instead. And him. Before it's too late.'

'That's easy for you to say. You don't have to live with them . . .'

The bell jangled above the door, indicating that Lidia

had awoken from her nap and was in need of the linden-flower tea she drank to calm her nerves. Celia began preparing it in Emilia's absence, while Eduardo strolled back to his room to commune with his books. Celia envied him his self-sufficiency. He was as impervious to criticism as he was to flattery, despised approval as much as Celia courted it. At the harvest ball he had been besieged by nubile admirers, none of whom had caught his fancy – but then, Eduardo could afford to be fussy. His dark, brooding good looks commanded the kind of abject admiration which is most readily accorded to those who hold it cheap.

'What are you doing home at this hour?' demanded Lidia ungraciously, as Celia deposited the tray and propped her mother up on half a dozen lace-trimmed pillows.

'Lázaro just got word that his brother was killed,' said Celia, sidestepping the question. 'The rebels fired on an army patrol in Santiago. Emilia's gone to comfort his mother.'

'All these shootings,' fretted Lidia. 'Nowhere in Cuba is safe from attack these days. I wish Enrique would send Eduardo to Miami to study.' Celia knew very well why he didn't – for fear that Lidia would join him there, desert him as his first wife had done. 'Darling, your hair is coming down again. I do wish you'd have a perm.'

Aware that her long dark hair was her best, most feminine feature, Celia obstinately refused to have it cut. Everything else about her might be neat and modest and understated, but her hair was as unruly and unmanageable as she would have liked to be.

'I was in a rush this morning. Will you put it back up for me?'

She fetched the ivory-backed brush and comb from her mother's dressing table, together with a handful of hairpins. Yawning, Lidia brushed it out and began styling it meticulously into a smooth Grace Kelly chignon.

'León telephoned the office,' said Celia carefully. Her mother had a low opinion of León – or so Celia thought. Lidia had always affected scant regard for her stepson, not just to throw her husband off the scent, but because it had suited her to foster the rift between father and son, a rift which had strengthened her own financial position.

'He's coming home for Christmas,' continued Celia. 'He's motoring down and should be here in a few days. I don't expect he'll stay long, though.'

'Why should he?' commented Lidia bitterly. 'He has somewhere else to go.'

'Yes,' agreed Celia. 'He's lucky.'

Too late, she bit her tongue. Lidia might bemoan her lot, long and loud, but the same privilege was not accorded to Celia. Her mother turned on her accusingly.

'And what's that supposed to mean? Don't you have a good home here? Don't you have everything a girl could possibly want?'

Not everything, thought Celia. But the one big lack in her life was not something she could discuss with her mother.

'I sacrificed everything for you and Eduardo,' Lidia reminded her, taking a soothing gulp of tea. 'Nobody understands how much I have to put up with. My life's over and I'm not forty yet. I'm still a young woman! A young woman shackled to a disgusting old man!'

Celia didn't comment, her sympathies hopelessly divided. Trying to be fair to both of them always made her feel two-faced.

'I know you think I'm selfish and vain and spoiled,' accused Lidia, reading her face. 'I know you think I married for money and I've got what I deserved.'

'I don't think any such thing, Mamá.'

'It's so easy for you to sit in judgement. You know nothing about life at all. Oh, do your own hair. My arms are aching.' Celia got up without a word. Lidia caught hold of her hand. 'I'm sorry I snapped, darling,' she said, switching abruptly from waspish to wistful. 'It's just that . . . you're too young to understand. Give me a big hug.'

Celia complied, well used to these mercurial changes of mood. Everything was easier to bear today, because

León was coming home. She left the room, shutting the door quietly behind her, glad to get away, to be alone with her thoughts, to hope and imagine and plan.

As soon as she had gone, Lidia buried her head in the pillows and wept as if her heart would break. Why wouldn't Enrique hurry up and die? If this dragged on much longer, she would lose León to some other woman. The thought of him getting married, belonging to somebody else, left her weak with dread. In his arms, she felt young and carefree again; without him she would wither into premature old age.

The rest of the world would call it a sin, but it was a glorious, liberating sin, a cleaner crime than the one which had cost her her self-respect, that of marrying a man she did not love. She loathed the obscene antics she had to perform to goad Enrique's flagging manhood into short-lived life, hated the travesty of love-making which defiled her first husband's memory, hated having to live a lie when she wanted to shout her secret to the world.

But she would be discreet, as always. In public she would be the disapproving stepmother, treating León with her usual coldness. If Enrique were ever to suspect the truth, both she and León would face destitution, even death. But in private, while Enrique was safely out of the house, she would be brazen, sensual, shameless . . .

León gave her hope, a hope she refused to abandon to the creeping tide of despair. Without hope, she might as well be dead.

Lily tossed her mother's letter to one side in disgust. The only good thing about it was the cheque for a hundred dollars, a so-called Christmas present which Grandma had duly confiscated and paid into Lily's savings account, which she wasn't allowed to draw on till she was twenty-one, if you please. Twenty-one! What was the point in having money if you couldn't spend it while you were young enough to enjoy it?

Mom would have bought her a car by now, if Grandma hadn't gone and talked her out of it. If she'd had a car she would have driven off into the sunset long ago. Of course, there was nothing to stop her from hitching a lift from a truck driver, pawning her jewellery, finding herself a room in a cheap motel, waiting tables until she found work as a singer. That she chose not to do so was a symptom of the cowardice that lurked beneath the bravado. She knew in her heart that she had no taste for hardship, or hard work. Spoilt though she might be, Lily retained some subliminal memory of what it was like to be poor.

She couldn't remember the vile, cockroach-infested room where she had spent the first year of her life. Her earliest recollections were of a pretty pink perfumed apartment where her mother's bedroom was always locked against her. She remembered the taste of the brandied milk she was given to drink at bedtime, remembered waking up in the middle of the night to find a man tickling her between the legs, remembered her mother screaming abuse and snatching her from his grasp, remembered her sudden, unexplained exile to Grandma's, a punishment for some unwitting crime, the prelude to ten long years of separation.

Mom was always going on about how much she loved her and how she wanted the best for her, but Lily knew better; the truth was that she couldn't be bothered with her and wanted her out of the way. She was too busy making money to care if Lily was bored and lonely. Lily's favourite fantasy centred on her long-lost father; one day he would turn up to reclaim her, and then Mom would be sorry.

Grandma often spoke bitterly about Lily's father, a small-time musician with whom Addy had eloped at the age of seventeen. For three years they had lived out of suitcases, touring seedy nightspots, moving on when the rent got overdue, finally ending up in a dance hall in Havana, where the living was cheap, but not quite cheap enough. One day he had upped and disappeared, without so much as a goodbye, leaving Addy with a baby and a pile of debts and lacking the price of a ticket home.

All this had been told to Lily as a grim cautionary tale, calculated to guard against history repeating itself. Lily knew better than to repeat it to anyone else; the official story, reserved for outsiders, was that her father had been killed in the war. Sometimes she found herself wishing it was true; as it was, she had been left with the uneasy feeling that his departure was in some way her fault. But rather than blame herself, or him, she preferred to blame her mother. When she, Lily, married, her husband wouldn't run out on her. And when she had a child, she wouldn't send it away.

'Eat your breakfast, Lily,' said her grandmother, from behind her newspaper.

'I'm not hungry.'

'You don't leave the table till you've cleared your plate. I made those pancakes specially for you.'

'I'm on a diet.'

'A diet? At your age? I never heard the like. There are starving children in Africa – don't you make faces at me, young lady!'

Lily swallowed a reluctant mouthful, knowing she couldn't win. There was no getting round Grandma the way she could get round Mom. The pancakes would appear at lunch and supper and at breakfast again tomorrow, until they were eaten.

The day stretched before her endlessly. If only she were in Havana, with Mom, what fun she could have! Havana, the Monte Carlo of the Caribbean, symbolised the glamorous adult world she yearned to join. She had nothing in common with her own generation; other kids made her feel like a freak. Other kids came from normal families, with mothers who stayed at home and fathers who went to work. She had always been a misfit, both at Grandma's and at school. She would have felt more at home in an orphanage, where everyone else was a reject, same as her.

'After you've finished you can take Baby for her walk,' said Grandma. 'And pick up some errands for me at the store.'

Lily loathed Baby, an overfed Pekinese bitch fairly

bursting with excrement, which Grandma expected her to scrape up with a little spade and wrap in newspaper. Not that Lily ever stooped to doing so. She allowed Baby to perform where she pleased, on front lawns, on the sidewalk, on the decks of empty boats by the marina, letting her run on ahead without benefit of a lead and denying all knowledge of her if anyone objected to her anti-social habits.

Having forced her pancakes down, Lily made her escape, with Baby yapping excitedly at her heels. As soon as she was well away from the house, she sat down on the nearest green bench, opened her bag and applied a liberal coating of panstick, powder, lipstick, mascara and eye shadow. On the return journey, she would reverse the procedure with cold cream and Kleenex; needless to say, Grandma disapproved of young girls covering their faces with muck. She freed her thick red hair from its pony tail and shook it out; luckily it waved naturally. The transformation complete, she released Baby who waddled on ahead while Lily followed slowly, swivelling her hips à la Lollobrigida, fluttering her eyelashes like Monroe and practising her Bardot pout – a hybrid performance aimed at the invisible admirer who followed her everywhere she went. Occasionally she would get a wolf-whistle from a window cleaner or a road-sweeper, which she would haughtily ignore, nose in air. Once a crew-cut youth in a battered Oldsmobile had stopped the car and asked her if she wanted a ride, only to be told to drop dead in a gritty gangster's-moll drawl. It was as if some unseen director had shouted, 'Action', leaving her to choose her own role, to ad lib her own script. These lonely expeditions, plastered in war-paint, with the much-despised Baby as cover, were a way of stepping outside tedious reality into a world of the imagination, a world she could invent and control.

Languidly, she followed Baby down to the marina, ever hopeful that the wretched animal would fall into the water and drown. She sat down on the grass, fished an illicit copy of *True Confessions* out of her bag, and was soon absorbed in second-hand heartbreak, deaf to the distant sounds of barking; Baby, a naturally excitable creature, yapped hysterically at the slightest thing. Lily read on, oblivious, until the squealing canine ran over her outstretched legs, closely pursued by a huge German Shepherd.

'Hold it, George,' boomed a voice, as the irate beast trapped its diminutive prey between two heavy front paws. George obeyed, still snarling at his terrified quarry, while Baby took whimpering refuge in Lily's reluctant arms. Lily looked up to see a man striding towards them.

'That your animal?' he demanded.

He was about six feet tall, with crinkly blue eyes, brown hair flecked with grey, and a leathery tan. He was wearing khaki-coloured shorts and nothing else.

'Not exactly,' said Lily, anxious to deny responsibility. 'Can you stop your dog growling? It's making me nervous.'

'George is a watchdog,' he said, ignoring her request. 'I leave him up on deck while I'm asleep. Looks like your animal was trespassing. He was only doing his job. Let's see if there's any damage.'

While George looked on balefully, he held out his arms for Baby, whom Lily relinquished without regret.

'He's given her a nip,' said the man, inspecting her hindquarters. 'I've got some iodine in the first aid box. You'd better come too, so she knows it's OK.'

He walked back the way he had come, George trotting obediently behind him and Lily bringing up the rear, still unsure which part she should play, torn between a wholesome Doris Day and a sultry Jane Russell. He jumped aboard a motor cruiser bearing the legend *Never Again*, and disappeared into the forward cabin, reappearing with a tin box.

'Sit down,' he said, indicating a battered folding chair. 'Good girl,' he continued, addressing a docile Baby, eliciting a theatrical moan of submission as he dabbed ointment onto her damaged rump.

'Thank you,' said Lily, rather piqued that the dog was

getting all the attention. And then, as Baby showed her appreciation by shamelessly evacuating her bowels on deck, Lily slipped out of character and uttered the only word appropriate to the circumstances.

'This little bitch needs to be taught manners,' said the man mildly, holding onto Baby's collar and rubbing her nose in the mess. 'You'll find what you need to clean up in the heads,' he added, sending a horrified Lily scurrying below. While she scooped up the noisome turd with tissue, crimson with mortification, the stranger clattered about in the galley.

'Coffee?' he shouted. 'Or would you prefer something stronger?'

'I really ought to be going . . .' began Lily, but he appeared not to hear her. Slapping on Baby's lead with the vigour of a hangman attaching the noose, she prepared to make a dignified farewell. A moment later, he emerged with a battered coffee pot in one hand, two tin mugs in the other, and a bottle of Bacardi wedged underneath his armpit.

'Going already?' he enquired vaguely, as if he didn't much care either way. Lily sat down again.

'I'm very sorry,' she said stiffly. 'It's not my dog. She belongs to my grandmother.'

'Who feeds her chicken breasts and chocolate chip cookies and thinks the sun shines out of her smelly little ass.'

'More or less,' said Lily, mollified, allowing him to add a slug of rum to her coffee.

'Frank,' he said, extending a big warm hand.

'Lily.'

'And how old might you be, Lily?'

'Eighteen,' said Lily, adding on a couple of years for luck.

'Are you here on vacation?'

'That's right. I work in a nightclub in Havana. I'm a . . . I'm a singer.'

'Fancy that. I do a lot of business in Havana.'

'Really? What kind of business?'

'Fishing. Smuggling. Gun running to the rebels. You know the kind of thing.'

Lily wasn't sure if he was joking or not.

'Do you know Havana well?' he continued, topping up his mug with more rum.

'Not well, no,' said Lily carefully, anxious not to have her few faint memories put to the test. 'I haven't been there very long. And I don't get much time for sightseeing. We do three shows a night, and what with rehearsals and all . . .'

'Which club is it you work at?'

'Addy's.' She was on safe ground now. Mom had sent her a photograph with the sign all lit up in neon.

'Addy's?' His expression changed, he seemed to look at her differently. 'In Obispo Street?'

'You know it?'

'Everyone knows Addy's.' He smiled knowingly. 'It's a very popular place. Prettiest hook – hostesses in Havana. I must look out for you next time I call in.'

He was obviously impressed, thought Lily, gratified.

'So, how long are you in St Pete's, Lily?'

'Just till the new year. They gave me some time off because my grandma was poorly. She brought me up, you see; I'm all she has. I'm an orphan,' she added tragically.

'Cheer up,' he said, pouring her another slug. 'So am I. But, of course, I'm an old man. Cigarette?'

Lily nodded, glad of the opportunity to demonstrate her recently acquired skill. She had misappropriated a pack from her mother's bag last summer and practised smoking them in the washrooms at school, with more persistence than pleasure. She arched her neck elegantly to accept a light, inhaled luxuriously, and blew the smoke languidly at the sky.

'How old?' she asked, curious now. It was hard to tell his age, he could have been anything between thirty-five and fifty.

'Old enough to be your father.'

'So do you have any children?' demanded Lily, emboldened by the fortified coffee.

'Not that I know of.'

'A wife, then?'

'Not any more. I'm divorced. Never again.'

'*Never Again*. That's the name of your boat.'

'That's right. So, why don't you give me a song, Lily?'

'A song?'

'You said you were a singer.' His tone was mocking, disbelieving. Probably he thought she was just a lousy cigarette girl.

'What do you want me to sing?'

'Anything you like.'

Lily hesitated, suddenly unsure of herself.

'What's the matter?'

'Nothing.' She shut her eyes to make it easier, and tried to pretend that this was an audition. Then she took a deep breath and launched into an oft-rehearsed, throbbing rendition of 'That Old Black Magic', unaware, for she knew nothing of technicalities, that she possessed perfect pitch, glorying in the natural amplification of the water all around her, giving herself up to the luxury of having an audience. After the first few bars, a heady feeling of power gave her the courage to open her eyes and fix them on his, to personalise every note, every word, to sing it just for him. When she had finished, he clapped, slowly, and this time he wasn't making fun of her.

'Who taught you to sing like that?'

'No one,' said Lily, truthfully enough. The music teachers who might otherwise have cultivated her gift had seen it as their duty to take the bumptious little madam down a peg, anxious, no doubt, to get a bit of their own back. They had reprimanded her for showing off and drowning out the feeble warblings of her classmates, thereby reducing her to sullen silence; in any case, Lily was uninspired by the dirges considered suitable for schoolgirl choirs.

'You're very talented.'

'I know.'

'Did you feel it too?'

'What?'

'That old black magic.'

He reached out for her hand and pulled her towards him and kissed her, sliding his tongue between her already parted lips. And then she *did* feel it, quite distinctly. Whether it was real or not didn't matter. She was still inside the music, on a darkened stage, under a spotlight, performing for all she was worth.

Ralph Freeman was down to his last few dollars, but you'd never have known it to look at him. His white suit and hat were still spotless, despite a day and a night in a crowded bus, sitting alongside ragged peasants and itinerant workers who stared at him with open curiosity, wondering at the rich American tourist in their midst, lacking the tact to avert their eyes from the jagged scar on his left cheek.

After a long run of bad luck, the god of gambling had given Ralph a break, enabling him to win enough to buy a new set of clothes and a one-way ticket to Havana. It had seemed a better bet than using the money to buy himself more time. Ralph was rather attached to his arms and legs, and had got to the stage where he had to choose between them. Either he settled up with Bert Orsini, and continued to walk unaided, albeit with shattered wrists and elbows, or he heeded the final warning from Carlo Panetta, which would enable him to manage his crutches. Or he got the hell out of the country and tried betting on something new.

His gambles invariably paid off. The Japanese bayonet that had sliced through his left cheek had missed his eye by a fraction of an inch – one of the many near misses which had proved him to be immortal. In fact, the war had undoubtedly been the best time of his life. He had flirted with death shamelessly, displaying a suicidal courage which had earned him two Purple Hearts and both a Bronze and Silver Star, catapulting him through the ranks to join the officers he despised.

Predictably, peacetime soldiering hadn't been the same. He hated the paperwork and tedium and bureaucracy, he hated feeling safe. But for the welcome reprieve of the posting to Korea, his career might have ended sooner, and less ignominiously. Then there had been those two tedious and ultimately disastrous years in Berlin; Ralph liked his wars hot, not cold. Making personal enemies helped raise the temperature, especially that of his commanding officer, a deskbound despot who disliked heroes on principle and Major Freeman in particular. As for risks . . . he had finally taken one too many.

He had come home to nothing and no one, his mother long since dead of an overdose of barbiturates, having fared even worse with her second husband than her first. Ralph hadn't seen her since the day he put Steve, then her lover, in the hospital; she had told him in no uncertain terms to be gone by the time he got back. By then he had been glad to leave that stinking trailer, with its stench of sex and booze and betrayal. To this day Ralph detested the smell of alcohol even more than its taste.

He could have borne it if she had been miserable. For the first couple of years, while there were still just the two of them, she had been as miserable as sin. 'You'll look after me, won't you, sweetheart?' she would murmur, snuggling up close. 'You're all I have left.' But then Steve had come along and suddenly she was happy, for the first time in her life. Not for long, as it happened, but Ralph didn't hang around to wait for the end of the story. When it came to blows, as it was bound to do, he might have known whose side she would be on. And now, fifteen years later, here he was, without money, without a job, without a roof. The army had provided all three, until it had kicked him out, just like his mother had done.

Yes, he was back where he started, in more ways than one. The last forty-eight hours had brought it all back to him – first the blast of tropical winter heat as he stepped off the plane, the fecund tropical fragrance of warm soil tainted with the smell of rotting vegetation, the whiff of tar and brine in downtown Havana, where the shriek of terns mingled with the cries of street vendors and the blare of car hooters and the wailing of beggars. Havana was a gambler's paradise, but Ralph had resisted its temptations, lured by the prospect of a much bigger game than any the casinos could provide.

And then, as the bus bore him eastwards, there had been the mournful succession of one-street, poverty-stricken villages, lined by primitive box-like dwellings, and in between them the fields of cane and corn, the stretches of uncultivated jungle, the vivid orange groves, the hedges spiked with morning glory, hosting swarms of red and yellow butterflies, the ever-present palm and bamboo and eucalyptus sprouting lushly like weeds out of the chestnut-coloured earth.

As darkness fell, Ralph had slept instantly. He could sleep anywhere, anytime, a skill he had learned as a soldier and one which had recently stood him in good stead. It seemed like a long time since he had last enjoyed the luxury of a bed. He alighted the following afternoon, stiff and yawning, at Bayamo, ten miles from his destination, carrying the one suitcase which contained all his worldly goods. There were plenty of farm vehicles and army trucks about; he might as well hitch a ride and travel for free. That way he could run to a cold drink and a shave.

Having visited the nearest café and barber's shop, he proceeded, much refreshed, to the narrow, pot-holed road leading west, towards Manzanillo, flanked on both sides by fields of cane, rippling like waves in the breeze. A few moments later he stuck his thumb out and a red Packard convertible screeched to a halt.

'Where are you headed?' said the driver, a young blond Adonis wearing sunglasses. 'I'm going as far as Buenaventura.'

'That'll do fine.'

'Hop in.'

He was dressed casually but expensively in blue jeans and an open-necked checked shirt; his fair hair was long, creeping over his collar; on his left wrist he wore a heavy gold watch. The automobile smelt enticingly new. Everything about him oozed money and privilege. Ralph hated him on sight.

'León Soler,' he said, steering with his left hand while he extended his right. 'And you?'

Ralph stared at him for a moment, absorbing the impact of the name.

'Freeman,' he said. 'Ralph Freeman.'

'You an American?'

'Is my Spanish that bad?'

'No, you'd pass for a native. But Ralph Freeman doesn't sound like a Cuban.'

'No,' agreed Ralph, without bothering to enlighten him. 'Come to that, you don't look like a Cuban.'

León Soler shrugged. 'My mother was an Anglo. I guess I take after her. Are you here for business or pleasure?'

'A bit of both. Do you live locally?'

'Not any more, thank God. I escaped to Havana when I went to law school and never came back. I'm just visiting the family for Christmas.'

'I like your car.'

'Not bad, huh? I just got it. Goes like a bird.' And then, as if he could smell Ralph's envy, 'Want to drive?'

'Are you kidding?'

'Go ahead.'

Without further ado, he stopped the car and got out. Uncertainly, Ralph moved across to the driving seat and took the wheel. As a kid, he had been addicted to joyriding; the best part had been ramming his booty into a tree, leaving its bonnet crumpled, its headlights smashed, its upholstery ripped to shreds with his penknife.

'Go on,' encouraged his benefactor. 'She won't bite.'

Ralph put his foot down hard on the gas pedal and felt the road slide away from underneath him, clenching his teeth as he watched the speedometer soar, fired by a dizzying vision of mangled steel and bleeding flesh, of infernal noise and blessed nothingness. Blindly, he roared towards the horizon, pulling out to overtake a farm cart pulled by a couple of mules, undeterred by the bend in the road which obscured the oncoming traffic.

'Slow down,' yelled his companion, alarmed. Ralph

ignored him, enjoying his fear, enjoying his own. 'Stop, damn you!'

Abruptly, Ralph jammed on the brakes, just in time to spare the lives of two startled oxen.

'Relax,' said Ralph urbanely. 'There was never any danger.'

'You don't say. This isn't an eight-lane freeway.'

'Eight-lane freeways have speed cops.' He smiled. 'I'm sorry. I didn't mean to scare you.'

'Well, I happen to scare easy. I'm not ready to die just yet.' He shook himself like a dog after a swim, and got out a pack of cigarettes and a gold lighter.

'Smoke?'

'Thanks,' said Ralph. 'Do you want to take over?' He got out of the car.

'In a minute,' said León, moving across. 'When I've got my breath back.'

He was visibly shaken and not bothering to pretend otherwise. Ralph had been terrified half out of his wits more times than he could count, but he would have died rather than admit it. Admitting it required a different kind of courage; the dividing line between coward and hero was perilously thin.

'That'll teach me to pick up a lousy hitchhiker,' continued León, looking his passenger up and down with new curiosity. 'Why didn't you take a cab?'

'No money. I had my wallet stolen in a café, back in Bayamo.'

'How much did you lose?'

'About a thousand dollars in cash.'

León whistled and started up the car again. 'You shouldn't carry that much on you round these parts. Oriente is famous for its bandits, didn't you know? We get a lot of crime during the dead season. Once grinding starts, it eases off. You ought to carry a gun.'

He opened the glove compartment and indicated a .38 revolver. Ralph reached for it, released the safety catch and pointed it at his companion.

'There's no one else around,' he said, smiling, indicating the deserted landscape. 'I could walk you into that cane field and shoot you dead. They wouldn't find you till they cut it.' How easy it would be! Too easy.

'If you're trying to scare me again,' said León, taking it as a joke, 'forget it. It's not loaded. I couldn't shoot anyone to save my life.'

Ralph pulled the trigger; there was a harmless, mocking click.

'Yes you could,' he said, replacing the weapon. 'Killing's the easiest, most natural thing in the world. If you'd been in the war, you'd know that.' Involuntarily his hand flew to his damaged cheek.

'Is that how you got the scar?' said León. Ralph nodded, disarmed by his directness. Mostly, people were too embarrassed to ask.

'I was captured by the Japs in 'forty-four and they stitched it up any old how. Still,' he added flippantly, 'you'd be surprised how women go for it. They're all suckers for Beauty and the Beast. Are you married?'

'God, no,' said León. 'You?'

Ralph shook his head. 'My parents split up when I was a kid. They were enough to put you off marriage for life.'

'I know the feeling,' said León.

'My mother died recently,' continued Ralph, inspecting the tip of his cigarette. 'So I thought it was time I made peace with my father, before it was too late. That's why I'm here. I expect he'll tell me to go to hell, but that's a chance I'll have to take.'

'Whereabouts does he live?' said León, throwing his stub out of the window. 'If it's not too far, I can take you all the way.'

'On the Buenaventura *batey*.'

León looked puzzled. 'Did you say your name was Freeman? I know most of the families on the estate. But I've never come across any Freemans.'

'My father isn't called Freeman. My mother changed our name, several times in fact. We were always on the move, never stayed any one place for long. She was afraid my father would kidnap me and take me back to Cuba . . . the way he did my little brother.'

León stopped the car, turned his head slowly, and stared.

'Show me your left hand.'

Ralph spread it out, palm upwards, revealing the truncated little finger with its missing tip, the result of an accident with a machete many years before.

'Jesus Christ,' said León. 'It's Raúl.'

TWO

SEEING THE shiny red convertible parked in the driveway, Celia had to force herself not to run.

'When did he arrive?' she asked casually, as Emilia let her in.

'They,' Emilia corrected her grimly. 'They've been here a couple of hours already.'

'They?' echoed Celia, swamped by the fear that León had brought some woman home to meet the family. 'Who's they?'

'You'll find out soon enough,' said Emilia, adding darkly, 'My blood ran cold the minute he walked through that door. He'll bring bad luck on this house, you mark my words.'

He. Celia was too relieved to be curious. Emilia mistrusted all strangers, especially those who hailed from foreign parts like Havana; as long as León's companion was male, Celia didn't much care who he was.

'Take this,' said Emilia, thrusting a muslin bag at her.

'What is it?' said Celia vaguely, tidying a stray wisp of hair and checking if her seams were straight.

'Jezebel root. To protect your virginity.' Emilia, like Lázaro, was a devotee of the *santería* cult, a blend of Christianity and African magic. Her quarters, adjoining the kitchen, were full of religious artefacts and charms to ward off real or imagined evils, among which this visitor evidently now numbered.

Celia stifled a giggle. 'Is he good-looking, then?'

'Don't mock,' said Emilia crossly. 'I shall put something in your bath tonight, to ward off danger . . .'

There was a burst of laughter from the salon; stuffing the muslin bag up her sleeve – Emilia could be very touchy – Celia headed towards the sound, curbing the childish desire to rush at León like a puppy greeting its master. That was the kind of thing little sisters did, and she wasn't his little sister any more. The buzz of conversation stopped abruptly as she opened the door of the huge reception room reserved for entertaining guests. She was unnaturally aware of the click of her high heels on the polished marble floor, and of a man's face looking at her intently, one side of it haughtily handsome, the other brutally disfigured.

'Celia, we have an unexpected visitor,' said León breezily, jumping up to greet her. Not long ago he would have picked her up bodily and swung her round and round; today he restricted himself to a brotherly kiss on each cheek. He indicated the newcomer, who bowed stiffly and met her gaze full on, daring her to look away. 'Prepare yourself for a big surprise. This is . . .'

'. . . León's brother, Raúl,' put in Lidia gushingly, leaning back in her rocking chair, flooding her new stepson with the favour of her smile, a false smile which Celia saw through instantly, her mind racing ahead. León's brother Raúl.

God. Papá would throw a fit. No wonder her mother was purring at the prospect. News of the rebel attack on the docks had produced a similar frisson of delight, betraying her unspoken hope that the shock might finish him off. And the unannounced arrival of his long-lost son would be a much greater shock than that. The son who had defied rescue, who had never once contacted him in seventeen years, who had committed the unforgivable sin of siding with his treacherous mother . . .

'I'm very pleased to meet you,' said Celia, rather woodenly, dreading the coming conflagration, fearful for her stepfather's health, a fear which nobody else seemed to share. León, with typical head-in-the sand optimism, refused to take his father's heart condition seriously, while Lidia actively desired her husband's demise and Eduardo displayed his usual sublime indifference.

'And I you,' said Raúl. He was tall and powerfully built, with an erect, military bearing; he had his father's piercing black eyes and hair and olive complexion, undiluted by the Anglo-Saxon genes so evident in his brother.

He'll bring bad luck on this house, you mark my words. Celia took an involuntary step backwards, realising too late that the stranger might misinterpret this gesture as physical revulsion, a primitive reaction, like Emilia's, to his hideous scar. She blushed, ashamed.

'Celia's terrified our father will throw you out,' put in León, making her excuses for her. 'Don't worry, *chica*. We've spent the last hour putting Raúl through his paces and reminding him how to grovel in the required manner.'

Raúl endorsed this irreverent remark with a lop-sided grimace which could have passed for amusement or derision. Lidia tut-tutted gleefully, while Eduardo smiled his usual inscrutable smile.

'Well,' said Lidia, rising. 'I must go and change for dinner. You too, Celia,' she added meaningfully, indicating that she wanted to talk to her in private. Celia met León's eye briefly and caught a flash of discomfiture behind the determined bonhomie. This might be a mountain but León would insist on treating it like a molehill; he was incapable of taking anything seriously. Including me, she thought. He's going to behave as if nothing ever happened, and expect me to do the same. A spark of well-I-won't defiance flared up and subsided, leaving behind a dull glow of frustration.

As soon as they were safely upstairs Lidia discarded her fulsome manner like a mask.

'You realise why he's turned up after all these years, don't you?' she hissed, beckoning Celia into her bedroom and shutting the door. 'To reclaim his inheritance!'

'That's rather optimistic of him, isn't it?' said Celia, taken aback, if not exactly surprised, by this abrupt change of mood. 'I expect Papá will show him the door as soon as look at him.'

'Don't you believe it. He's never stopped hoping he'd come back. Damn! Why couldn't he have waited till the old man was dead? I've always been afraid this would happen.'

'Well, I must say, you did a good job of hiding your

feelings just now,' said Celia drily. 'I thought you seemed quite taken with him.'

'There's more than one way to kill a cat,' snapped Lidia. 'I want you to be perfectly charming to him, do you hear me? I don't want him to suspect we're on to him, we have to keep one jump ahead. Don't give me that patient, pitying look of yours, young woman. May I remind you that as things stand, I will receive all the income from the estate for my lifetime. Which means that you and Eduardo will always be provided for, firstly by me, and eventually by León. If the old man changes his will in Raúl's favour, we could all be out on our ear.'

'That's a big if,' shrugged Celia. 'He's never forgiven Raúl for not coming home once he was old enough to choose. And he's bound to assume he's just after his money. He's—'

'He's getting more senile by the minute!' interrupted Lidia. 'Who knows what the old fool might do? I'm damned if I'll lose everything I've suffered for all these years. There's one sure way to make absolutely certain your father kicks him out.'

'What's that?' said Celia, chilled by the malevolent look on her mother's face. Lidia smiled at herself coquettishly in the mirror.

'Leave that to me. Just remember what I told you. Be perfectly charming to him. Don't give him any reason to act hard done by or put us in the wrong. Don't give Enrique the chance to play him off against us. Do you understand?'

Celia felt a sudden, perverse allegiance towards the intruder. Honest hostility was one thing, duplicity quite another. She might be expert at keeping her feelings to herself, but she was quite unable to pretend to feelings she didn't have.

'I shall make him welcome,' she said carefully, 'until I have reason to do otherwise.'

Her mother looked at her in the mirror, caught the sceptical expression, and turned to look at her the right way round.

'Trust me to protect our interests, Celia,' she said coldly. 'God knows, León will just stand by and let his brother steal the estate from under his nose. He's too bone idle to lift a finger to stop him. As for Eduardo, he believes money is the root of all evil. Those Jesuits have brainwashed him better than he thinks. As for you . . . don't you realise how much I care about you? Why do you always make me feel as if I'm being selfish?'

She held out her arms, looking vulnerable and forlorn. These unpredictable bursts of maternal affection always had a quality of forgiveness, fostering an obscure sense of having transgressed, an irrational need to apologise for some unwitting crime, as unavoidable and fundamental as original sin. Guiltily, Celia returned her embrace.

'Just take your cue from me, do you understand? Now go and get changed, while I do the same.'

Celia retired to her room, to find that Emilia had already run her a bath, which was tinged an unpleasant shade of green and smelt strongly of ammonia. She didn't dare ask what she had put in it; something revolting, no doubt.

'I will do this for you for the next nine days,' Emilia informed her gravely. 'Then you will be safe.'

'Safe from Raúl?'

'I knew him when he was a boy. I feared him even then.'

'Why? What did he do to you?'

'I never gave him a chance to do anything, and neither must you. When he looks at you in a certain way, you can feel the devil's power coming off him . . .' She shuddered voluptuously. 'I shall burn a candle in your name to our Lady of Mercy, Obatalá. Meanwhile, try not to look him in the eye.'

She went off, muttering to herself. Celia sniffed the water, wrinkled her nose in disgust, and got into the shower stall instead. She stood under the tepid spray for a long time, trying to think objectively. Mamá distrusted everybody on principle, perhaps with good reason; the

Solers had more enemies than friends. But Raúl was also a Soler. That was the problem, of course.

Lidia had told Celia the whole story, warning her that she must never refer to it in her stepfather's presence; Don Enrique had outlawed any mention of the subject. Even so, it was common knowledge that his first wife had fled with both children to America without leaving so much as a note. Don Enrique had despatched two hired gunmen to track her down and bring his sons back to Cuba, but Raúl had shot and wounded one of the assailants, thereby escaping capture. His mother had evaded further attempts to locate her and sued for divorce, selling her jewellery to meet the legal fees; Raúl had stood by his mother rather than return home. Don Enrique had refused to pay her a penny in child support but even the threat of penury had failed to break her, leading him to conclude that she had found herself a new protector – for how could any woman survive without a man?

Mamá certainly couldn't. However unhappy she might be, she would see her marriage through till the bitter end. To some extent, thought Celia, she revelled in her misery. Papá's jealous rages were succeeded by lavish peace offerings and profuse, pathetic apologies. Once Celia had overheard him weeping like a child and begging for forgiveness, and her mother's voice replying, cold and hard, 'Don't force me to leave you, as she did, Enrique. One day you'll push me too far . . .'

On the surface, her stepfather had all the power. But Celia had known for a long time now that her mother called all the shots. Small wonder she was worried that Raúl might provide his father with a much-needed weapon against her.

God, what a marriage, thought Celia, turning off the jets. Now she would have her mother's paranoia to cope with, as well as Enrique's. Both would confide in her, each seeking an ally against the other, ganging up together against her whenever their interests happened to coincide. If only she could get away from them!

It wasn't duty that kept her here, and it certainly

wasn't fear of poverty, whatever Eduardo thought. It was a fear of finding herself unloved and unloving, rejected, redundant, and worst of all, alone . . .

There was a tap on the door.

'Who is it?'

'Me.' León's voice. 'Are you decent?'

Celia flung on her robe and let him in, remembering her resolution to be cool, forgetting it instantly as León picked her up and swung her round and round, making her squeal with glee. For a moment everything was simple and relaxed again, just like it used to be. But only for a moment. The physical contact set off a shower of sparks which threatened to start a fire; he put her down again abruptly, as if to quench them.

'Well?' he said jauntily, putting his hands resolutely in his pockets. 'What do you think of Raúl?'

Celia sat down and began filing her nails with great concentration.

'I don't know yet,' she said. 'Why has he suddenly turned up now, after all these years?'

'Our mother just died, apparently.'

'Oh,' said Celia, chastened. 'I'm sorry.'

'There's no need. I can hardly remember her. Anyway, he says he couldn't come before out of loyalty to her. Now she's gone, he wants to make his peace with Papá.'

He flopped down on Celia's bed with his hands behind his head.

'What kind of person is he?'

León had barely mentioned his brother before, and Celia hadn't liked to ask him, knowing that the topic was taboo. She had no intention of repeating Emilia's disparaging comments, or her mother's suspicions, at least until she knew how León felt.

'He always used to be a perfect bastard,' he said equably, making it sound like a virtue. 'Did I ever tell you about that time he blindfolded me and tied me to a tree, for target practice?'

'No. You never told me anything abut him.'

'He put an orange on my head, like William Tell.'

'That was an apple.'

'Well, he used an orange. And a shotgun.'

'Weren't you scared?'

'Not as scared as I was of Raúl. He was always trying to toughen me up. He used to call me a little fairy. Anyway, I heard him count out fifty paces, one, two, three, four, and his voice getting further and further away. And then waiting for the bang, and nothing happening for ages and ages. And then, when it came, it nearly blew my head off, and then I was covered in juice and bits of fruit.'

'God. What if he'd missed?'

'He couldn't have missed. He'd crept back towards me, very quietly, and fired at point-blank range.'

'What did your mother say?'

'I didn't tell her. Even when she gave me a hiding for shitting in my pants.'

'Didn't you hate him?'

'Not exactly. I wanted him to love me. Papá was always busy, and Mamá was ill a lot of the time. Ill meaning drunk, not that I realised it at the time. Raúl took more notice of me than either of them. When he was pleased with me – which wasn't very often – I felt about ten feet tall.'

'Did you miss him?'

'I suppose I must have done. But when you're that age, you forget people quickly. You can imagine how strange it feels, seeing him again. It's like someone coming back from the dead.'

'You're pleased?'

'Of course I'm pleased,' said León, a shade over-emphatically. 'He's my brother. Lidia seemed pretty impressed with him, thank God. I was afraid she'd go on the defensive.'

He looked at her quizzically, as if expecting her to disagree; Celia chose not to disillusion him.

'So how long is he planning to stay?'

'He didn't say. He works for his stepfather in Chicago, so I suppose he can please himself.'

'What does he do?'

'He's learning the construction business. He was a major in the US army till last year but when his term was up he decided to quit. Too much pen-pushing and not enough action, he said. He got roughed up by the Japs pretty bad in the war. That's how he got the scar.'

But for the scar he would be quite good-looking, thought Celia. It gave a vicious, sinister twist to his face, which made it easy to think the worst of him.

'How do you think Papá will react?'

'God knows.'

'I'm afraid that the shock will be bad for his heart.'

'Rubbish. He piles on the agony to keep you in line. You're much too soft. He'd respect you more if you stood up to him.'

'You sound just like Eduardo,' said Celia, caught on a raw nerve. 'As I said to him, you don't have to bloody well live here.'

'Neither do you. That is . . . what I mean is—'

'What you mean,' snapped Celia, several jumps ahead of him, 'is that I don't have to live here just as long as I don't turn up on your doorstep in Havana.'

His eyes wavered away from hers and back again.

'What's that supposed to mean?'

'That I nearly did, last summer,' blurted out Celia. 'I would have done, if you hadn't made it crystal clear that I wouldn't be welcome.'

León reached out for her hand, looking at her palm instead of at her face, as if trying to read her future.

'I wanted to speak to you. About what happened last time I was home.'

She struggled to keep her mouth shut, to accept the inevitable sop, to laugh it off, even. Instead all the years of waiting and months of wondering crystallised into a split second of rage.

'What happened wasn't your responsibility. Nothing ever is, is it? You could just turn your back and walk away from it. After all, I kissed you first.'

Or more accurately, he had let her kiss him first. León

tried to remember when he had last needed, or bothered, to take the initiative. Lidia had set a precedent which other women had been repeating ever since. And like the coward he was he had imposed the same pattern on Celia, used her terrifying honesty to vindicate his own lack of it.

'I made you do it,' he said. 'I wanted you to do it. I just didn't have the guts to do it first.'

'And then you ran away.'

'And then I ran away. And now I'm back.'

'For a week or two,' she said flippantly. 'Don't worry. I won't do it again.'

She turned away from him, biting her lip. She had been so looking forward to seeing him again, allowed herself to indulge in foolish fantasies, promised herself that she would avoid a confrontation. She hadn't realised till this moment just how angry with him she was.

León hesitated, unsure just how to play it. He wanted to tell her he loved her, see her proud little face light up. And yet he couldn't, not until he had freed himself of her python of a mother. Christ, what a mess. If Celia ever found out about Lidia, he was done for. She might just forgive the deed, but not the deception. But what alternative was there to deception? How could he tell her a thing like that? 'Oh, and by the way, there's something you ought to know. Your mother seduced me when I was fifteen years old and I've been screwing her, on and off, ever since.'

'I know I behaved badly,' he said. 'I'm sorry.'

'Don't say you're sorry. You know you don't mean it. You revel in being the way you are, you think it's cute. You can talk your way into or out of anything.'

He grinned, not denying it, while she fought not to grin back.

'Look . . .' he said, playing with her fingers, bending and flexing them one by one, 'why don't we go down to Santiago tomorrow and break the news about Raúl to the old man? That way it won't be so much of a shock when he sees him. And he's less likely to shoot the ambassador if there are two of us.'

'You mean it?' she said, evidently amazed that he should volunteer for such a thankless task.

'Of course. You can drive my new car if you like.'

'All right,' she said, trying hard not to look pleased.

'Truce?'

'Truce, you swine.'

Impulsively, he pulled her down beside him on the bed, remembering all the cuddles and horseplay of the past, wondering when it had stopped being fun and started being deadly serious. It had crept up on him stealthily, taking him by surprise, or perhaps he had just been too scared to acknowledge it. He had been testing the water for the last two years, without getting more than a toe wet until Celia finally lost patience and pulled him in.

She didn't resist, but she was taut as a wire with expectation. He pressed his face into her shoulder, muffling his voice.

'I never thought that this could possibly happen,' he said, kissing her hair. The wire slackened. 'You're not my type.'

'I'm not pretty, you mean.'

'I wish you were. Then I could explain it away.' And then, making it sound like a dare, 'Kiss me. Kiss me the way you did before.'

She searched his eyes for mockery, found none, and did as he asked, with a glorious lack of subtlety, kissing him the way she had done before with almost perfect recall, as if she had relived it as often as he had.

She tasted reassuringly of inexperience and ignorance; if his own father didn't suspect him, why should she? It would be all right. It would be all right.

'Listen, Celia,' he said gently, taking her face between his hands. She was a strange mixture of painful shyness and devastating candour; the combination was startlingly erotic. 'This has got to be our secret. If the parents find out, you can imagine what they'll say. That it's incestuous, that I'm taking advantage of you, that you're just a kid. God knows, you get enough stick from them as it is.'

She smiled mischievously, enjoying the conspiracy,

seeing his self-seeking warning as a kind of promise.

'Don't worry,' she said. 'I can handle them.'

Speak for yourself, he thought guiltily, fighting a brief battle with temptation before leaving her to dress.

Frank had had a good night's fishing. His contact had met him twenty miles out of port, and now the secret orifices of the *Never Again* were filled with fresh supplies. He would get a good price from the rebels in Havana, enough to buy him another few weeks of leisure. They were well equipped with guns, the black market being run by the army itself, but the inexhaustible demand for explosives and detonators far exceeded supply. Nevertheless, he worked only when he felt like working, and always on his own terms. This was purely for profit, strictly business, untainted by any tomfool idealism or tortuous self-justification.

He neither supported nor opposed the Cuban rebels; whether they were murderers or martyrs was a moral issue that did not concern him. Saints and devils had a lot in common, and the one could transmogrify into the other with chameleon-like suddenness. Once upon a time, he had needed to think that Right was on his side, but now he knew that Right was a false friend. These days his loyalties were to himself and to hell with everyone else. And if he ever forgot his resolution, it was there, painted on the side of the boat, to remind him.

His merchandise stowed, there was no need to delay his departure any longer, just an inclination. An itch. One he couldn't resist scratching. OK, so Lily was just a kid, but she was a kid who knew the score, who sang for her supper at Addy's. And she sang the way Addy's strippers stripped – teasingly, tauntingly, leaving you wanting more.

Yesterday he had let her go, disarmed by the childlike naïveté behind the brazen façade, even though he had got a hard-on just listening to her. But if she turned up again today he would stifle his troublesome scruples, satisfy his curiosity, be disappointed. It was always a disappointment. Perhaps that was nature's way of keeping you at it, searching in vain for the elusive crock of gold. And having failed to find it, he would head back to Havana, taking care to avoid Addy's in future.

He chugged back towards shore with his illicit cargo – a calculated risk. He went out 'fishing' every day, regular as clockwork; the chances of a random search were slim. He had been clean as a whistle when he cleared customs, and if the coastguards suspected him, they had long since concluded that he was a problem for the Cuban authorities, not for them. A problem the Cuban authorities were happy not to solve, for a suitable consideration. As a regular visitor, Frank had negotiated favourable terms with the port officials in Havana, who never bothered to search him, with the collusion of the grim-faced harbour police who supervised a multiplicity of waterfront rackets.

While he was down below, fixing a liquid breakfast, he heard George barking a welcome, not a warning, indicating a visitor rather than an intruder. Frank splashed his face and chest with cold water and went up on deck, towelling himself dry.

It was Lily, strolling along the quayside, with Baby firmly attached to her lead.

'Hi there,' she said, smiling archly.

'Hi. How's the patient?'

'Limping a bit.'

'I'd better take a look. Come aboard.'

She was wearing white pants and pink cotton shirt, of which she had undone one too many buttons, giving a glimpse of lace, drawing the eye down towards her high, heavy bosom. She looked tantalisingly demure, flaunting nature and artifice with equal aplomb, her feet artlessly bare in tennis shoes, her full mouth gleaming with vampire red lipstick. He fancied he could see a glimpse of freckle peeping through the powder; she was like a bunch of wild flowers tied up with ribbon and wrapped in Cellophane.

He took her hand as she embarked and noticed the

heavy gold charm bracelet on her wrist; tasteless, vulgar, but undoubtedly real.

'It was a present,' she said, as he fingered the trinkets. 'From my . . . from one of my boyfriends.'

The euphemism was telling. He had a sudden vision of some bloated businessman buying his way into that fresh young body. A dirty old man, like himself.

'Doesn't your grandmother mind you working in Havana?' he said, lust giving way to a misplaced fatherly concern.

'Oh, she was glad to see the back of me,' said Lily, with feeling. 'As long as I send her money every month, that's all she cares about.'

His vision of a sweet, frail old lady was replaced by one of a money-grabbing harridan, eager to exploit her only asset. Lily looked at her feet and shuffled from one to the other, suddenly pathetic again.

'I can't wait to get back to Havana,' she continued. 'I wish I'd never come home. Grandma made out like she was really sick, but there isn't anything wrong with her, she just wanted to screw me for some extra money and use me as a skivvy . . .'

'In that case, leave her to stew for a bit. How about a day's fishing?'

She shook her head. 'If I'm not back in an hour she'll give me hell. She expects me to wait on her hand and foot. I only came to apologise for yesterday and to . . . to . . . because I wanted somebody to talk to, that's all.'

'I can think of a better way to pass the time,' said Frank, taking hold of her hand. He had no desire to listen to some hard luck story; he had heard them all before. He didn't want to feel sorry for her, he didn't want to be involved. 'And if you've only got an hour, then there's no time to lose.'

He bent to kiss her neck. She wriggled, either in encouragement or rebuff, it was hard to tell.

'When are you going back to Havana?' she said.

'Not until you do.'

'Do you mean that? You'll still be here tomorrow? And the next day?'

'I'll be here for as long as you are,' murmured Frank. In a few days he would be bored with her. He would give her some extra money, or buy her a nice present, and that would be that. His lips moved down towards her breasts. An hour. Time for once very quickly, and once very slowly; he found the second impossible without the first. And then she could talk as much as she liked, and he would pretend to listen. That old black magic called sex. The best antidote to thinking in the world.

He pulled her to her feet; she made a show of indecision which excited and irritated him.

'Come on, doll,' he wheedled, stifling a yawn. Having been up all night he was too damn tired to make heavy weather of it. 'Don't play hard to get. If you don't want to, just say the word, and I'll head back to Havana right now. I would have been gone already if it hadn't been for you.'

'Don't go,' she said quietly, by way of assent. She allowed him to lead her into the stuffy, airless cabin below where he peeled off all her clothes without finesse, pushed her back onto the bed, unbuttoned his fly and plunged in pretty well straight away; Lily converted a startled cry of pain into a moan of ecstasy, not wanting him to realise it was her first time. As soon as it was over – luckily it didn't take long – he rolled off her onto his back and, for no good reason that Lily could see, fell instantly asleep.

Carefully, so as not to wake him, she got up and inspected herself for damage. Her fingers came away bloodstained. She took a Kleenex out of her purse to stanch the flow, hoping that it would stop. If it didn't she would just say she had got her period. She knew instinctively that to admit her virginity would put him off. He thought she was eighteen years old, a woman of the world; she couldn't bear for him to start treating her like a kid. Specially now that she was a grown-up at last. She had quite enjoyed it, in a way. Not the act itself, which had left her cold, but the feeling of power it had given her.

She had had the chance to go the whole way before,

but till now it had given her a feeling of power to say no. There was no point in doing it just to please some boy. Every summer Grandma took a beach house on Long Island, where Lily was invited by well-meaning mothers to parties and clambakes and barbecues. She had failed to make any 'nice new friends', shunning the other girls on principle, but flirting with their brothers at every opportunity, slipping out of the house while Grandma snored to keep illicit moonlit trysts, enduring sweaty, fumbling petting sessions, learning what to do to arouse a boy while remaining unmoved herself. None of it had been remotely exciting, the way it was when you read about it in a magazine or watched it in the movies. It only became exciting if you shut your eyes and pretended you were both somebody else. And now the pretence had come true. Well, sort of. And in any case, this was just a means to an end.

The bunk was too narrow for her to lie down next to him; she sat on the floor, waiting patiently for him to wake up, unsure what was supposed to happen next, knowing only that she had to make quite sure that he would still be here tomorrow.

Raúl's ability to sleep anywhere, any time, was twinned with an ability to forgo this luxury without a trace of fatigue. Once he was sure everyone else was safely in bed, he stole downstairs by torchlight, intent on spending his first night hard at work.

The layout of the house was familiar to him from his boyhood. It had been solidly constructed, in 1825, with walls a good three feet thick – a necessary precaution against possible slave revolt, not to mention the violent hurricanes to which the region was prone. It was built around four sides of a central courtyard, where the original fountain still tinkled in the shade and orange, frangipani and pomegranate trees filled the air with their fragrance.The swimming pool at the back of the house was a recent addition, as were the air-conditioners which disfigured every window and the carefully tended garden which had replaced the untamed jungle of Raúl's youth. Lidia had planted it with more sensuality than subtlety, glorying in an excess of gaudy colour and glossy foliage. A dense forest of palm had been thinned and cleared to make way for laurel, croton, eucalyptus and avocado, mango, jasmine and papaya, giant ornamental cacti, jacaranda, poinsettia, hibiscus and bougainvillaea, roses, gladioli, morning glory and chrysanthemums, creating an effect as vivid and voluptuous as her own overblown beauty.

Raúl's former bedroom now belonged to Eduardo, as did the one next door to it, which served as the young scholar's study. The room where León had slept as a child had been converted into two bathrooms, one serving Eduardo and the other Celia, who slept three doors along from her younger brother. The corridor at right angles to this was fully occupied by the matrimonial suite, while the one on the opposite side of the house was reserved for guests, like himself. León slept on the remaining side of the square, which was broken by the wide staircase; the two rooms adjacent to his were both empty, awaiting redecoration, which appeared to be Lidia's passion in life.

She had made a point of showing Raúl round her domain after dinner, re-introducing him to the heavy framed portraits of his ancestors, pointing out all the improvements she had made, and soliciting his praise for her impeccable taste in Spanish antique furniture, Persian rugs, and American plumbing. She had obviously been given a blank cheque to indulge her harmless if expensive hobby; none the less, she had the unmistakable air of a woman who was bored and lonely and discontented, a woman who could be easily seduced.

Downstairs, there was the wide hallway, large enough for a carriage to pass through to the inner courtyard, as would have happened in former times. It was hung with saddles and bridles and housed a heavily padlocked gun cupboard. This led off into a large dining room, dominated by a massive solid mahogany table. Like the equally spacious reception room, it was lit by ornate chandeliers, their light multiply reflected by polished wood, shiny marble floors, and tall spotted mirrors in heavy gilt frames. The informal family room now contained a television set, and a modern radiogram had replaced the ancient phonograph; the gloomy stone-flagged kitchen was bright with fluorescent lights and decorative tiles, and equipped with fitted cupboards and electrical gadgets. Adjacent to this were quarters for the live-in housekeeper – the other staff slept in a separate block – and a breakfast room which looked out onto the paved patio, pool, and gardens.

One place that had escaped Lidia's refurbishments was Enrique's den, where Raúl had been frequently summoned in his youth to receive savage, if ineffectual, beatings. It was still dark and cheerless, smelling of leather and cigars and gut-wrenching fear and hatred. Raúl had never flinched at the pain inflicted on him, never once cried out loud, any more than his mother had done. The day she had finally shown Raúl her bruises was the day they had left this house for good. She was afraid, she said, that he would hurt little León too. Little León, his rival, the apple of her eye. How glad he had been when they had kidnapped him! He could have shot down that second gunman too, but he had chosen not to. He had wanted to have his mother all to himself.

Adjoining the den was the old bastard's study. The door was locked, as always, but it soon gave way to skilled persuasion, as did the drawers of the desk. Raúl spent a quiet couple of hours scanning his father's private papers by torchlight and committing salient facts to memory. There was no sign of any will, which was presumably lodged with his solicitor, but there were other documents of even greater interest, among them a thick wad of weekly reports from one J. G. Fernández, a private investigator in Bayamo, who was under contract to follow Doña Lidia's every move outside her home. For the last few years every shop she patronised, every visit to the beauty parlour, every lunch date with her friends, had been minutely recorded. Even when chaperoned by her daughter, son or stepson, the vigilance was never relaxed, and the mass of irrelevant, painstaking detail was doubtless intended to justify a dismal lack of results. Despite her coquettish manner Lidia was not, it seemed, an adulteress, although judging by the way she had been coming on to him over dinner, thought Raúl, this was probably the result of a lack of opportunity rather than inclination.

The other interesting item was a letter from his father's doctor, giving the results of some hospital tests, all of which indicated that the old man was likely to live for ever. Heart, blood pressure, kidneys and liver were all in good order, a healthy state of affairs which he evidently chose not to share with his family. Raúl was pleased to learn that he was less vulnerable to shock than he had been led to believe; it would be most tiresome if he died too soon.

He yawned, well satisfied with his research, and was just contemplating a return to bed when he heard the click of a door opening in the adjacent room. He extinguished the torch hurriedly. Damn. Why would anyone come into his father's sitting room at two o'clock in the morning?

He pressed his ear against the wall, but could hear nothing. He was beginning to wonder if he had imagined it when he heard a voice. No, two voices. A man's and a woman's.

He took a cut-glass whisky tumbler from the laden drinks trolley, held it between his ear and the wall and listened hard.

'What's the point of meeting down here?' Lidia's voice. 'What's wrong with your room? I put that brother of yours at the other end of the house.'

'I don't want you coming to my room any more. If you do you'll find the door locked.'

'What's got into you? What have I done?'

'I mean it this time, Lidia. It's got to stop. I'm involved with somebody else. It's not fair on her, or on you, to carry on with this any longer.'

'You mean you've got a mistress in Havana, I suppose.

Do you think I didn't realise that? I don't care about your other women! All I want is to see you occasionally. Then, once Enrique's dead, we can . . .'

'No. There's nothing else to say. I should have done this years ago instead of letting it drag on. Please don't make this any more difficult than it is already.'

'I won't let you do this to me. I can't bear it. I'll tell your father . . .'

'Tell him. If you want to end up with nothing, like my mother, that's up to you.'

'He'll kill you. You know how insanely jealous he is.'

'That's a chance I'll have to take.'

'How can you be so cruel?' She began weeping. 'What a fool I was to trust you! All this time you've just been using me, you've never loved me . . .'

'I never said I loved you. I was fond of you, I'm still fond of you. That's why I have to end it.'

'Don't go! Stay a little while longer. I just want you to hold me, that's all. I'm so lonely. Sometimes I feel as if I'm going insane . . .'

'I'm sorry, Lidia. I never wanted to hurt you. I'm going back to my room now and I suggest you do the same.'

'I'll kill myself!'

'No, you won't. I'm not worth it and you know it.' A long silence, punctuated by more weeping. 'Please let go of me, Lidia. It's over.'

There was a strangled curse, the sound of a door opening, and the soft thud of bare feet running away, to be followed moments later by the click of the same door shutting. Raúl lit one of his father's cigars, and sat watching it glow in the dark. Then he went back to bed and slept.

Having set off after breakfast, León and Celia arrived at the Santiago office at noon, Celia putting her foot down hard all the way. The way she drove was a dead give-away – bold, fast, exhibitionist, symptomatic of her repressed need to rebel. She made no reference to their conversation of the previous evening, but he could tell by her nervy manner that she was waiting for him to make a move. León, meanwhile, was willing himself to take it slow, to keep his head, to resist the temptation to cash in on her impatience. For once in his life, he would take control. Celia needed careful handling.

He had woken that morning in excellent spirits, and thoroughly enjoyed the drive, even though his father was waiting at the end of it. Scenery had never moved him before – he preferred painting people to places – but today the blue-misted peaks of the Sierra Maestre and its lush green foothills looked different, fresh and new, full of mystery and challenge. An early shower had cleared the air, intensifying the cool morning blue of the sky before it rose back up to meet it in a shimmering, humid haze of heat. The fields of cane and rice and citrus swayed to some silent rumba, flaunting the fertility of the rich red earth. Even the kites hovering overhead, looking for fresh carrion, seemed almost benign, part of nature's plan. The sun surely hadn't shone this brightly in years.

It was as if a huge burden had lifted from his shoulders; he only wished he had shucked it off years ago. It was the first time he had stood firm against Lidia's tears and pleas; it was always so much easier to give in. Not because he still desired her, but because he felt mean denying her the relief she craved. After all, he had been glad enough to lose his virginity to her and to let her give him a comprehensive sexual education, without once feeling the slightest pang of guilt. Whereas kissing Celia, just once, last summer, had made him feel guilty as hell.

A guilt which, like Lidia, was now in the past, buried, finished with. It would hurt Celia terribly if she knew the truth, so he was quite justified in not making a grotesque confession. And as long as they were both discreet, there was no reason why Lidia should smell a rat. Not yet, anyway. And by the time she did, their affair would be ancient history, she would have got over her rejection. There were only two tenses in León's life – not yet, and now. He never dwelt on the past, or worried about the future. Worrying about things made them happen, just as ignoring them made them go away.

The Santiago office comprised two dingy rooms partitioned off from the Soler warehouse, where a team of clerks oversaw the loading and unloading of cargo and checked its documentation. León, who hadn't shown his face there for over a year, greeted all the staff by name, displaying the phenomenal memory which had served him so well at law school, while Celia stood by, watching with cynical amusement. Their usual air of surly subservience dissolved into chatty cordiality as he asked after their wives and children, listened with feigned fascination to the story of the recent rebel attack on the harbour, and produced a twenty-peso note with the wish that they all enjoy a Christmas drink on him. He was by far the most popular of the Solers, one who would not ask to inspect the bills of loading or ask them any awkward questions, as his father, and latterly his stepsister, were wont to do. (As for young Sẽnor Eduardo, who had recently called with subversive literature urging all employees to go on strike, they regarded him with the deepest mistrust and had been quick to burn the offending pamphlets before Don Enrique got sight of them.)

On finding that his father was lunching at the local barracks and was not expected back at the office that day, León lost no time in making his excuses, anxious to get away from the dreary place and the even drearier people who worked there. He would have loved to stay longer, he said, but his sister had other plans; they would catch his father that evening at his hotel. They left to a chorus of good wishes and fervent hopes that he would call in again soon.

'What it is to have fans,' said Celia, as they drove uphill through the steep, narrow, cobbled streets into the congested city centre.

'I feel sorry for them,' said León. 'Imagine having to spend your life working in that dump.'

'You mean, imagine having to spend your entire life working, don't you? Most people don't have any choice.'

'True. But my father has. I can't understand why he doesn't sell up and retire. Spend the last few years of his life enjoying himself instead of grubbing around trying to make money he doesn't need.'

'Is that what you'd do if you inherited the lot tomorrow? Sell up and retire?'

'Probably. I rather fancy being an international playboy. Paris, New York, Monte Carlo . . . meanwhile, let's practise by having lunch at the Casa Grande. We can stick it on the old boy's account.' Don Enrique retained a suite at the best hotel in town. He was unlikely to return before four at the earliest; they would have plenty of time alone together, thought León, before he arrived.

The desk clerk smiled in obsequious recognition and confirmed that Don Enrique was out.

'My sister and I will wait for him in his suite,' said León, holding out his hand for the key. 'Please ring to let us know when he arrives.' He led Celia into the lift.

'What about lunch?'

'We'll order room service. Otherwise some god-awful bore is bound to spot us and insist on sharing our table. Come on.'

He picked up the phone and ordered lobster and champagne, waving aside her protests that she wasn't hungry. Celia vanished into the bathroom, saying that she needed a shower, and didn't emerge till the trolley arrived, looking pink and almost pretty. Surreptitiously León left the key in the door, to guard against his father's unheralded return.

One glass of wine was, as always, enough to get her mildly tiddly, which was all to the good; it would help soften her up. Even though he had not the slightest intention of seducing her, a resolution which made him feel honourable and unselfish. Celia was a long-term project, someone who would wait for him, patiently, who would be there for him when he finally got round to settling down. Celia was like a savings account, quietly accumulating interest, something you didn't touch, let alone squander, until you needed it. And he would need it, one day. But not yet. She was still absurdly young. Meanwhile, he wanted to stake his claim on her loyalty, before some other unscrupulous bastard beat him to it. Thanks to her sheltered upbringing, Celia would be a pushover for the first – or rather second – man who showed the slightest interest in her; he didn't want her wasting all that pent-up passion on anyone else but him.

'You know I'm in love with you, don't you?' he began teasingly, watching her over the rim of the glass. From long force of habit, he kept his tone light, ambiguous.

'I don't know any such thing.' She pushed her plate to one side, barely touched. 'The only person you're in love with is yourself. In a couple of weeks, you'll go back to Havana and forget all about me till the next time you come home. If you ever do.'

Persuading her of his good faith was going to be trickier than he thought. Other women believed what they wanted to believe; Celia did precisely the reverse. Better drop the bombshell on her now, jolt her out of her totally justified mistrust.

'Would it convince you I love you if I asked you to marry me?'

She cocked her head and folded her arms, determined not to take the question seriously.

'If you love me, why did you run away from me last summer?'

He hovered on the brink of a confession, looked down, and saw a yawning bottomless cavern at his feet.

'I was scared.' That was true enough. 'My feelings for you took me by surprise, I didn't know how to handle them. But I've done a lot of thinking in the past few months. I'm not in a position to support you yet, but in two or three years I hope to be independent, and then we can get married.' He would never make a living as a painter, but Addy had offered him a job as manager of the Herradura. If all else failed, he would take her up on it. At least it was better than working. 'You will wait for me, won't you, Celia?'

He refilled her glass, willing her to say yes. As she

surely would. Celia wouldn't mind waiting, he thought. Not for a few years, anyway. Her whole life was geared to compromise, to pleasing others, to giving, to accepting the bare minimum in return. Sooner or later, she would lose patience, give him an ultimatum, and then he would give in with a good grace and let her make an honest man of him. But not yet. And in the meantime he would have the best of both worlds. He would go back to Addy having got rid of Lidia and made sure of Celia. Perfect.

But she didn't answer, still too stunned, perhaps, to take it all in.

'I wish it could be sooner,' he continued earnestly, 'but at the moment, I'm still living from hand to mouth.'

'In considerable comfort, it seems.'

Her voice was cool, her eyes wary, puncturing his breezy self-assurance.

'The place I'm staying in doesn't belong to me. I'm just looking after it for a friend. I could have to move out of there any time.'

'You mean you're living with a woman.'

It was an observation, not an accusation, impossible to deny. Concealing the truth might be second nature, but lying to her face was extraordinarily difficult.

'All right.' He shrugged, as if it was a minor detail. 'I've been living with a woman. It's better than the sordid lodgings I had before. You know I don't have any money of my own.'

'I see.'

'No, you don't see. It isn't like you think.'

'How can you sit there and ask me to marry you when you're living with – not to mention off – another woman?'

'Because I don't love her. I just sleep with her. Surely you understand the difference between sex and love?'

She began scoring at the linen tablecloth with her fork.

'I wouldn't care where we lived,' she said crossly. 'You wouldn't have to support me. I could get a job. I could work in an office, or a shop. Or be a governess. Or—'

'Do you imagine my father would give his consent in

those circumstances? You're not twenty-one yet, remember. And you know how your mother disapproves of me.'

'We wouldn't have to get married.'

León looked suitably affronted.

'Are you crazy? What about the old man's weak heart? You and me living in sin would probably finish him off. We don't want that on our conscience, do we?'

'My conscience, you mean. You don't have one.'

'I do, when it comes to you. I want to marry you, not ruin your reputation. All I'm asking you to do is be patient.'

Still she didn't give an inch, fixing him with those huge disbelieving eyes of hers. Christ, this was heavy going. He had expected delight, incredulity, instant capitulation . . . gratitude even. It was the best offer she was likely to get, dammit. Switching tactics, he abandoned words as a bad job, pulled her to her feet and began kissing her, gently at first, awkwardly, inhibited by his own sincerity, worried, for the first time, that he had assumed too much, that she might be canny enough to see through him and turn him down. 'Please, Celia,' he murmured, resorting to the unpremeditated truth, 'I just can't bear to think of you with anyone else but me . . .'

That must have been what she wanted to hear. Gradually, almost reluctantly, she began to catch light. He kept piling on the kindling, so afraid that the flame would die that he didn't stop till the blaze was roaring, already out of control. He sank to his knees, pulling her down with him onto the thick carpet, sliding down the zip of her dress, revealing her small, firm, untouched breasts. No man had ever seen them before but him. No man had ever—

No, he thought feebly, as he pressed his lips against her heart, felt it hammering away at the crumbling walls of his resolve. Yes, he thought, even more feebly. He must have known when he brought her here that this was bound to happen. Proposing marriage was nothing but a sop to his scruples; proposing marriage was his way of making it all right, of justifying his own selfishness. But as long as he was careful, and didn't get her pregnant, it couldn't do any harm. On the contrary, it was the best possible way to put his mark on her, to make sure she belonged to him, that she would wait for him, that she wouldn't look twice at anyone else . . .

Celia knew she was taking a risk. Once he had got what he wanted he might lose interest. But what the hell. Three years indeed. She had no intention of waiting that long, of giving him that much time to change his mind. With luck, she would get pregnant, and then he would have to marry her sooner rather than later. That way Papá would have to give his consent. She was through with being a good girl, through with half measures and being fobbed off. And yet she was scared stiff that she wouldn't please him, that she would live to regret her recklessness. Still, better to lose him now than feed on false hopes, pinning all her dreams on something that might never happen.

'It's all right,' he soothed, sensing her tension, half hoping that she would take fright and tell him to stop. She didn't. 'Don't be scared.' Swallowing his last remaining qualm, he pulled her to her feet and led her into the bedroom. She was trembling, but she didn't resist.

'I'm sorry,' she mumbled, staring at him as he undressed, crossing her hands over her breasts, looking entrancingly pure and virginal. 'I'm just worried I won't be any good at it. Mamá never stops telling me how vile and revolting it is, and I know it isn't if you love the person, but . . .'

He covered her mouth to shut her up, fearful that images of Lidia would intrude upon the perfection of this moment. For the first time in his life, it actually mattered that it should be perfect, that nothing should happen to reinforce her doubt in him or, more importantly, in herself. This was one talent he was sure of, and like his questionable gift for art, he had wasted it, until now. But for once in his life he would paint a picture that came from the soul . . .

That she wasn't his type made it easier to start afresh. He had never held a body that was so young, so firm, so slender, so tense and taut and tight. It was like doing it for the first time. Like the Sierra Maestre, she had always been there and he had never looked at her properly until now. He avoided his customary big, bold brush-strokes, the virtuoso flamboyance that masked a lazy disregard for detail; this time he worked with painstaking care, seeking to find an essence, not to produce an effect. Slowly, surely, she began to respond, catching him up and overtaking him, while he struggled to retain his self-control, the callous detachment that made women think him a good lover. When he finally felt her sudden joyous spasm, he was grateful, not complacent, accepting it as a gift, not a tribute, humbled by the shattering intensity of his own climax, helplessly, hopelessly spoiled for ordinary sex.

She sighed and smiled and stretched contentedly, unable to hide the triumph in her eyes. Only then did it occur to him, too late, that she had outmanoeuvred him, subverted his purpose to hers. He had succumbed, unwittingly, to a will far stronger than his own, fallen headlong into the trap he had set for her. The predator had become the prey. Which was no more than he deserved.

Having seen his brother buried, with full military honours, Lázaro set off, heavy-hearted, for home. If Esteban had died in combat, it wouldn't have been so bad. But a bullet in the back was an ignoble end that cried out for retribution.

'I ought to enlist on the spot,' he told his mother gruffly. 'That way at least I'd get a chance to kill a few rebels. How can I allow his murder to go unavenged?'

She clutched pleadingly at his arm.

'Isn't it bad enough to lose one son, let alone two? What if the same thing happens to you? Why give up a good job for a soldier's miserable pay? Haven't I suffered enough? Your first duty is to the living, not the dead.'

Lázaro allowed himself to be swayed by her tears, but the rage still burned deep inside him. He had to listen to her weeping for three solid hours, all the way back to Buenaventura, where he dropped her off at the palm-thatched *bohío* he himself had built for her. It was here that she tended her plants and brewed medicinal infusions – American basil for worms, rosemary for rheumatic pain, dried guava for diarrhoea, and many other remedies whose recipes were a closely guarded secret. As the local midwife and *curandera*, renowned for her healing powers, she never had to buy food or fuel or other household necessities, which were brought to her as gifts by grateful patients in lieu of payment. If Lázaro were to leave Buenaventura, she would still have a roof over her head, she wouldn't starve. If he stayed, it wouldn't be for her sake but for the sake of the comfort and status which had corrupted him . . .

Within minutes, a stream of neighbours arrived to offer condolences; unable to bear any more tears, Lázaro drove on to his quarters above the garage. He had done well for a black man. He drove big shiny automobiles, he wore a smart uniform, he lived in a nice place and had money in his pocket. If he had been poor and unemployed, no amount of tears would have swayed him from his purpose. He was enslaved by his own prosperity.

Hearing a tap on his door, he opened it to find Emilia with a steaming tray.

'I thought you would prefer to eat in private this evening,' she said, setting his meal down on the table by the window. 'I've made all your favourites specially.'

Lázaro grunted his appreciation. He found Emilia tiresome with her constant chatter and heavy-handed sexual innuendo, but she happened to be a first-class cook, who piled his plate high with all the choicest morsels.

'Such a to-do while you were away at the funeral,' she began, as she watched him eat. 'Señor Raúl has come back from America . . .'

He listened with half an ear, shovelling food into his mouth automatically as she recounted some long-winded family saga which interested him not one jot.

'. . . and the master is due back tomorrow. I think the mistress is hoping he'll drop dead on the spot. Fat chance. If you ask me, the old man is as strong as an ox. There's nothing wrong with his appetite, that's for sure . . . or yours.'

'Thank you, Emilia,' said Lázaro tonelessly. 'That was very tasty. And now I must see to my birds.'

'There's one right here if you would only notice her.'

There were those who thought him mad to resist Emilia's advances. She had had seven husbands – not that she had married any of them – and any number of lovers, all of whom had testified to her skill between the sheets. But Lázaro knew that once he gave in to her she would never leave him alone. Every Sunday, he went to the dance at the Negro club in Bayamo, where he had the choice of any number of girls, a different one every week. There was always a spare automobile available for his private use, and the sight of one of these gleaming conveyances, with its well-upholstered back seat, was guaranteed to impress the haughtiest of females. So why settle for one whose presence he could not avoid, who would disturb his sleep and invade his privacy and exhaust him with her endless yapping?

'Forgive me, Emilia,' he said stonily. 'I have things to attend to. Good night.'

She bore this dismissal with a shrug of her well-padded shoulders and bore the empty tray away. Fortunately she had the hide of a rhinoceros; he knew from experience that this rebuff would not affect the quality of her unctuous black bean soup, her tender chicken, her meltingly crisp fried plantains, or her succulent roast pork. True, she had been a bit heavy-handed with the hot peppers lately, but Lázaro liked his food spicy.

Still dejected, he made his way to the coop where he kept his fighting cocks. Tomorrow was market day, when he would sell a couple of highly trained birds to the avid gamblers who clustered round the cock-pit in Bayamo, where the stakes were higher and competition fiercer than the one on the *batey*; having sold them, he would continue to keep them at Buenaventura, while charging the new owners handsomely for their upkeep, plus a retainer for his services. Given the high mortality rate, the demand for replacement birds was always brisk. Lázaro himself had no taste for betting, which he viewed as a mug's game.A weakness for dandified clothes was his only self-indulgence. While other young men drank and gambled and fell prey to scheming women, he had taught himself to read and write, learned a trade, bettered himself by honest labour. He had come a long way since his impoverished, fatherless childhood, wiping windscreens and washing cars at the garage in Bayamo, sleeping in its repair shop, and all for a few miserable coins a day. It had taken him twelve lean years to become a fully fledged mechanic, another five to land this plum job back at Buenaventura. When these rebels attacked the social order, they threatened his hard-won place within it. It had taken his brother's death to make him realise just how much he had to lose.

'What the hell do you think you're doing?' demanded Lázaro, his hand flying automatically to the knife he kept in his belt. A stranger was crouched in front of the row of locked cages – one of them now gaping open – with Lázaro's prize specimen in his hand. 'Put him down!'

The man turned and smiled with one half of his face. The other half creased into a hideous rictus which would have passed just as easily for a snarl.

'Forgive me. The catch was loose and I thought he might escape. A magnificent creature. Is he for sale?'

'Depends on who wants to buy him,' said Lázaro, rather thrown by the intruder's smooth manner and diction. He took charge of the bird. 'You were lucky he didn't peck your eyes out. He doesn't take kindly to being handled by strangers.'

'I have a way with animals. Do I know you from long ago? I'm Raúl Soler.'

Lázaro hesitated, rather abashed to have challenged his employer's son, wishing now that he had listened to what Emilia had said about him.

'I'm Lázaro, one of the chauffeurs.'

'I heard about your brother. My condolences.' His manner was relaxed, familiar, as if they were equals. He stroked the feathers of the bird again. 'When I was a boy I was forever sneaking down to the cock-pit in town. Is it still there?'

'It's been rebuilt. The old one got blown down in the 'forty-four hurricane.'

'Next time you go, perhaps I can tag along. When will that be?'

'Tomorrow.'

'Damn. My father's expected home tomorrow, I'd better be here when he arrives. Tell you what. Put five pesos on your best bird for me. If he wins, bet the lot on your second best bird. If that wins, carry on for me, will you, till I lose, or until all the fights are over.'

'I don't bet.'

'You'll be betting for me. You have a lucky face.' He withdrew five pesos from his pocket. 'Then afterwards we can discuss business in earnest.'

There was something about him that made Lázaro feel uneasy; probably he would turn nasty if he lost. But if he won, he could prove a good customer.

'All right. At your own risk, mind.'

'Excellent.' He slapped him on the back. 'I can tell you don't trust me. It's understandable. People tend not to at first, because of my face. It makes me look shifty, doesn't it?'

Lázaro shrugged, reluctant to endorse this inescapable truth. You shouldn't judge a man by his looks, he thought, any more than by the colour of his skin.

'I hardly recognise the old place,' went on Raúl Soler. 'The garage block used to be stables, you know.'

'They fell down in the hurricane as well.'

'There weren't so many cars in those days. I spent half my life on the back of a horse. I missed my horse more than anything else. A black stallion. No one else could ride him but me. Tell me, are you married, Lázaro?'

'No fear,' muttered Lázaro, surprised at the question.

'A man after my own heart,' approved Raúl, matily,

looking him up and down. 'Catch me giving up my freedom. Tell me, is the old bordello still there, in Bayamo? Or did that get blown down in the hurricane as well?'

'They rebuilt it, I think,' said Lázaro. 'Don't go there myself.'

'Why should you? A strapping lad like you. I bet you have a lot of girls running after you.'

Lázaro began to catch his drift. Any moment now he would ask him to procure a woman for him. With a face like that, he probably couldn't get it without paying for it.

'Not fast enough to catch me,' he said, trying to head the conversation off. He was damned if he was pimping for a white man. 'Women are nothing but trouble,' he added. 'I like my privacy.'

To his relief, Raúl Soler dropped the subject, realising, perhaps, that he had picked on the wrong man. Instead he plied him with informed questions about his birds, the one subject on which a normally laconic Lázaro could happily talk for hours. He even allowed Raúl to handle them, a privilege not granted to many. It was true, he did have a rare way with animals, picking the volatile creatures up without ruffling a feather, infusing them with a strange, hypnotic calm. Lázaro was just beginning to think that he wasn't such a bad fellow after all when young Señor Eduardo appeared, wearing his riding clothes, an unusual sight. Although his sister was an enthusiastic horsewoman, he rarely joined her on her expeditions, always preferring to bury his nose in a book.

'There you are,' he said. 'The horses are saddled up and waiting.'

'Excellent. I must show you all my old haunts . . .'

They strolled off together, ignoring him, Raúl towering above his young stepbrother, with an arm around his shoulders. Lázaro returned his attention to his birds, fingering the five pesos in his pocket. There was surely no harm in betting at someone else's risk.

Enrique Soler was well pleased with his afternoon's

work. Not only had he negotiated favourable terms for a permanent army presence outside his warehouse, but he had enjoyed an excellent and protracted lunch, reassured by the glowing terms of his latest check-up. The Soler constitution was as sound as ever, not that he believed in advertising it. His supposed heart condition was a most effective way of keeping young Celia on her toes and, besides, it gave him an excuse for his poor performance in bed – a source of great shame to him, and even greater relief to his wife.

His wife. As always, whenever he thought of Lidia, he felt a pain in his heart that was real enough. He had never had a conscience about any of his misdeeds – which were less legion than his enemies supposed, if only because his father and grandfather had done most of his dirty work for him – save the one he had committed ten years ago, almost to the day, the one which had finally delivered the incorruptible Lidia into his bed.

Had he realised then that she was frigid, or so he thought, rather than simply virtuous, Gabriel Rodríguez, her late husband, might still be alive. As it was, his ghost still stalked Enrique a decade after his violent death. He didn't fear discovery – the two men he had hired to kill him had themselves been disposed of a few weeks later, by assassins who knew nothing of their crime – but to this day he was still being punished. Lidia had proved not only cold but unaccountably barren, unable to provide him with another son to replace the one he had lost. And yet he still desired her, in the way one can only desire when one cannot have; having paid dearly for her, he would never let her go. His fear of losing her was akin to his hypochondria, with his private detective fulfilling much the same function as his doctor.

He stopped off at the jeweller's to collect the piece he had had made specially for Christmas: a heavy gold necklace set with rubies, like huge fat tears of blood. It was showy, eye-catching, designed to set off her magnificent cleavage. For Celia, there was a pair of simple pearl earrings, unostentatious but of good quality, like her. Why couldn't he have had a child like that to comfort him in his old age, instead of one who had been sired by the man he had wronged, one who looked at him with her father's eyes? At times he felt more comfortable with her brother, who had never offered nor asked affection; Celia's readiness to love and be loved was both a comfort and a constant reproach.

It was a time of year for morbid thoughts. He should have had it done at some anonymous time of year, when there were no pealing bells or whining priests to remind him of his sin. After these wretched festivities were over and the grinding season got under way, he would feel better. Celia was proving an apt and diligent pupil, one he could trust absolutely, as loyal and conscientious as her father had been before her, for all that she had a tendency to be soft, which was only to be expected in a woman. Luckily she was not flighty and frivolous like most girls her age, but on the other hand her plain looks made her easy meat, as the last harvest ball had proved. The youth concerned had been warned off in no uncertain terms. If and when Celia married, it would be to a man of his choosing.

Meanwhile any would-be suitor was a potential threat – either he would inveigle her away from Buenaventura, or he would seek to move himself in, seeking power by proxy – one reason why Enrique could never make her his heir, however badly his own son might behave.

Everyone outside the family was a potential enemy. If León were by his side, using his legal expertise for the purpose his father had intended, he would not need to check and double-check every document prepared by his crafty weasel of a solicitor. Better still, if Raúl had not been stolen from him he would be assured of a worthy successor, one who would equal him in toughness and energy . . .

He kicked this craven regret aside. He was well rid of Raúl. Any son worthy of the name would have escaped his perfidious mother, later if not sooner. Enrique chose to ignore the multiplicity of very good reasons why Raúl might have been glad to escape him. To his mind, he had been a good father, one who had striven to correct the weaknesses in Raúl's character, to make him a mirror image of himself.

He chose to forget that hatred bred hatred, to deny that his vicious treatment of his elder son had been rooted in resentment and jealousy, jealousy that Raúl had later transferred onto his younger brother, all of them rivals for the love of the same woman. That León had been spared similar brutality was thanks to his mother's disappearance; his father had had no need to compete with him. In the seven lonely years between Enrique's first and second marriages, León had been his only solace. It had never occurred to him, despite his suspicious nature, that his younger son might steal his wife, just as his elder had done.

The chauffeur dropped him off outside the hotel; Enrique dismissed him for the evening with instructions to be ready first thing next morning for the drive home.

'Your son and daughter are here, Don Enrique,' the desk clerk informed him, explaining the absence of his key. 'They are waiting for you upstairs.' He picked up the telephone and announced his arrival while Enrique strode, perplexed, towards the lift. What was Celia thinking of, leaving the office unattended? How typical of León to distract her from her duties!

Celia was standing waiting for him with the door open.

'Hello, Papá,' she said, kissing him on each cheek.'We called at the office but you'd already left.'

'What are you doing here?'

'León brought me.'

He growled a grudging greeting at his younger son, who smiled with his usual disregard for the answering glare.

'So you've deigned to visit your family for Christmas, have you?' grunted Enrique, letting Celia take his hat. 'Or are you just running short of funds?'

León and Celia exchanged looks; she was rather

flushed and her hair was falling out of its pins as usual. As if taking his cue from her, León said, very casually, 'We've got something to tell you.'

'Something that couldn't wait till I got home tomorrow? It must be bad news.'

'Oh no,' interrupted Celia earnestly. 'It's good news.'

'You'd better sit down,' said León, while Celia ran to the drinks trolley and poured a stiff measure of brandy.

'For God's sake, man!' growled Enrique, anxious now. 'Spit it out.'

León shrugged. 'All right. Raúl's come home.'

Out of habit, Enrique clutched a hand to his chest. Celia put down the brandy glass and immediately began fussing, feeling in his pocket for the pills he carried for his so-called angina. But for once his breathlessness was genuine.

'You call that good news?' he spluttered. 'No wonder it took two of you to tell me.'

'He's very nice,' began Celia, before catching the warning flash in his eyes and retreating into a barely audible sigh.

'He's not particularly nice, actually,' said León, unperturbed by his father's apoplectic expression. 'He never was, as I recall. He hasn't come to apologise or curry favour, that's for sure. If you tell him to get out, he won't hang around to listen to your insults.'

'He's in my house? Being given my hospitality?'

'Don't blame Lidia. I was the one who invited him to stay, not her. I've also warned him that you won't be pleased to see him. My mother died last week, apparently. He wanted to let me know, and to make his peace with you, before it was too late.'

Enrique sat speechless while León delivered a résumé with his usual concise aplomb; no wonder he had been assigned the role of advocate. He could have made the guiltiest man alive sound as blameless as a newborn lamb, whilst affecting complete indifference to his fate.

'. . . That's it,' he finished nonchalantly, helping himself to a cigar from the humidor. 'Quite a turn up for the book. If you like, I'll phone him now and tell him to clear off before we get home.'

'Kindly allow me to judge his *bona fides* for myself,' rapped Enrique, accepting the drink Celia had poured. 'I expect he's come to see what pickings are available. There's no need for you to be afraid of him. I've no intention of changing my will.'

'That's up to you,' said León blandly. 'It's all the same to me.'

'León—' began Celia warningly.

'Save your breath,' barked Enrique. 'We all know how your stepbrother affects to despise his inheritance. And the responsibilities that go with it. She's twice the man you are,' he added, indicating Celia. 'Luckily for you.'

'Please don't let's quarrel,' said Celia, ever the peacemaker. 'It's Christmas. Talking of which, I ought to buy something for Raúl. We can't leave him out.'

'Trust a woman to think of such trivialities,' grunted Enrique.

'Even when she's twice the man I am,' said León.

'That's enough of your insolence.'

'I'll see if I can find something in Sears,' continued Celia, picking up her purse. 'Give you two a chance to talk.'

'Don't leave me alone with him, for God's sake,' drawled León. 'I need a man around to protect me.'

Celia stifled a laugh, and much to Enrique's annoyance he found himself doing likewise behind cover of a baleful cough. Much as he berated his son for his incorrigible levity, the world was inadmissibly a happier place when he was around. Like the court jester, he was the only one who could mock the king with impunity.

'I shan't be long,' said Celia, still giggling. 'Mind you mop up all the blood by the time I get back.'

It was unlike her to be so skittish.

'What's got into her?' demanded Enrique, as soon as she had gone.

'I think she was just relieved you took it so well,' said

León, disappearing briefly behind a cloud of tobacco fumes.

'Anyone would think I was some kind of ogre.'

'Well, for some obscure reason she prefers a live ogre to a dead one.'

'Talking of which, how did your mother die?'

'Cancer, he said.'

'Did she remarry?'

'Yes. His stepfather's quite wealthy, apparently. He adopted Raúl, because he didn't have any children of his own,' he continued, repeating the story Raúl had told him. 'He's going to come into quite a pile one day.'

'Will he indeed,' muttered Enrique, annoyed.

'Tiresome, isn't it? If he'd been poor, perhaps you could have afforded to buy him.'

'Shut up and pour me another drink.'

He wasn't as surprised as he ought to have been; part of him had never stopped hoping. At first he had thought that poverty would bring him home; Raúl had grown up with the best of everything, and his mother didn't have a cent to her name. But like her, he wasn't for sale.

Enrique's late father had flown into a rage when his only son returned from business school in Miami with a low-class wife in tow, a penniless cocktail waitress already pregnant with his first grandchild. For Enrique, the knowledge that she was poor, with no family, no resources, with nothing but what he could give her, had been part of her charm. She seemed refreshingly vulgar and unspoilt, the only woman he had ever met who cared nothing for his money. Even a proposal of marriage had failed to open those long white legs of hers. She didn't love him, she said, and that was that.

In the end, Enrique had lost his head and raped her. She had spat in his face, quit her job and left her room; he had had her followed. From then on she found herself sacked as soon as hired, unable to afford a roof over her head, and still she wouldn't give in . . . until she discovered she was pregnant. Enrique had refused to pay for an abortion and offered her a husband instead.

Exhausted by the chase, she had finally admitted defeat. It had proved to be a Pyrrhic victory, a case of loser takes all.

Raúl had shared her life of sordid deprivation out of stubborn, stupid pride. A pride Enrique had been unable to knock out of him, despite any number of hidings to show him who was boss. And now that some other man had made him his heir, he had come home to gloat. A usurper had succeeded where he, Enrique, had failed, claimed the wife and son who rightfully belonged to him. What poetic justice it would be to steal his ungrateful son back again!

'So what's your news?' demanded Enrique, abruptly changing tack. 'Still pretending to be a painter, I suppose? When you said you had some good news, I wondered if you'd found yourself a wife.'

'Would that be good news?'

'It would depend on the wife. I suppose you'll end up bringing home some little tart who's got herself pregnant.'

'Someone like my mother, you mean?'

'Don't speak disrespectfully of your mother!'

'Why not? You always do.'

'Then at least learn from my mistakes. You want to find yourself a girl who's been brought up in the old-fashioned way. Not some little gold-digger, and not some stuck-up Havana heiress. And above all, not a *Norteamericana* who expects to wear the trousers. You need someone like . . . like Celia, for example.'

'Celia?'

'She'd be the perfect wife for you,' said Enrique. 'By the time I die she'll be able to run the business blindfold, which is more than can be said for you. Not that I'd give her a swollen head by telling her so. She's no beauty, admittedly, but at least that way you know she won't be running around after other men. There's a lot to be said for keeping things in the family . . . Good God, man, I do believe you're blushing.'

'I never heard of such a ridiculous suggestion in my life. Celia's only a child.'

'She's nearly nineteen. Your mother was younger than her when I married her.'

'That's hardly a recommendation. When and if I ever marry, it will be to a woman of my own choice, in my own time. The days of arranged marriages are over.'

'More's the pity. At the moment she's vulnerable to the first young buck who decides she's his key to a soft life at my expense. This way, she'd be truly my daughter at last. I'd like to have sight of a grandchild before I die.'

'I told you, it's out of the question!'

Enrique raised an eyebrow, surprised at such uncharacteristic vehemence. He had expected León to laugh the suggestion off, not treat it as a threat.

'For Christ's sake don't say anything in front of Celia,' León continued hotly. 'Or her mother. Otherwise you'll never see me at Buenaventura again. I mean it, Papá.'

Enrique shrugged philosophically. Evidently León's blood ran hotter than he thought; doubtless he would make the same mistakes as he himself had done, and allow his prick to rule his head.

'You're a fool. Marrying for love is a recipe for heartbreak. I should know, I've done it twice, and look what happened. That's the trouble with me. I've always been too soft-hearted. Especially with you. I used to beat the shit out of Raúl to make a man of him.'

'Well, you certainly succeeded. Catch me being a war hero.'

'I remember once.' reminisced Enrique, draining his third glass, 'I caught him fucking a black girl in the stables. He couldn't have been much more than twelve at the time. She was a good few years older, taught him a thing or two I dare say. Well, I sacked the dirty little bitch on the spot and gave your brother a thrashing he'd never forget. Then I took him down to the whorehouse in Bayamo, told him to use it and keep his hands off the servants in future. How old were you when you had your first woman?'

'Fifteen,' said León shortly.

'You certainly kept it quiet. But then you always were a secretive little brat.'

'Perhaps I remembered what you did to Raúl,' said León coldly. Not that he recalled this particular beating; Raúl's body had been a permanent patchwork of weals and bruises, inflicted with the buckle end of a leather belt. 'I'd run away tomorrow,' he had told León, teeth clenched, 'but the old sod would only take it out on you, and Mamá.'

'You were certainly better than he was at staying out of trouble,' conceded Enrique. 'He used to stand up to me, at least. One thing about your brother, he never had any namby-pamby airs and graces.'

'Well, he has now. He's got Lidia eating out of his hand.'

'Has he indeed?' Enrique's brow darkened.

'What I mean is,' León corrected himself hurriedly, 'he's being perfectly charming to everybody. Even Eduardo seems to like him, and you know he doesn't take to people easily.'

'Eduardo liking him is hardly a recommendation. What about you? How do you feel about him?'

León gave his all-purpose live-and-let-live shrug.

'He's my brother,' he said. 'He's your son.'

THREE

'WHERE HAVE you been all morning?' demanded Ruth, as Lily returned from walking Baby, two hours late and breathless from running. The 'once very slowly' had gone on for ever, with Lily surreptitiously glancing at her watch as she moaned and writhed. She was getting the hang of it now, and Frank seemed pleased with her. No, more than pleased, thought Lily. He was obviously crazy about her.

The very first time he had given her twenty dollars, to buy herself a little something, and since then she had never left the boat empty-handed. 'Get some new charms for that bracelet of yours,' he would say, casually, or, 'Treat yourself to some candy,' and sometimes he wouldn't say anything at all, just stuff the notes into her bag.

She wasn't in love with him, of course, but that didn't matter. He paid attention to her and was nice to her, which was much more important. Today, she had given him his Christmas present – a pair of cuff-links, even though she had never seen him wear a shirt. It was the first time she had bought a present for a man before, and cuff-links had seemed like a safe bet. She had felt very grand, buying them in the jewellery store downtown and asking for them to be giftwrapped. 'They're for my fiancé,' she had told the salesgirl, who had shown her dozens of pairs. 'That is, we're getting engaged in the new year. Can you show me what you have in diamond solitaires?' Not that she had the slightest intention of marrying Frank. Frank was just for practice.

'I've been worried sick,' continued Ruth crossly. 'I thought you must have had an accident.'

'I sat down on a bench by the pier and fell asleep,' said Lily, feigning a cavernous yawn.

'Then perhaps you should go to bed earlier. Young girls need their rest. Hurry up and wash your hands. I want some help with stuffing the turkey.'

Lily obeyed with bad grace. Tomorrow Grandma was hosting Christmas dinner for half a dozen fellow widows, who would all ask Lily how she was doing at school and what was she going to do when she grew up. Grandma would flash silent cues at her: 'Smile' or 'Be polite' or 'Don't talk with your mouth full'; the old crones would commend her on bringing up such a nice, well-behaved little girl whilst deploring the general behaviour of 'young people nowadays' and expounding the sick-making virtues of their own goody-goody grandchildren.

Sullenly, Lily followed Ruth into the kitchen and held the wretched creature down while her grandmother rammed cornmeal stuffing up its backside.

'What's that funny smell?'

Ruth sniffed the stuffing bowl, then the turkey, then Lily.

'Are you wearing scent?'

'Yes. Just some stuff Mom gave me.'

'I've never smelt it on you before. It's much too old for you. Your mother knows how I feel about that kind of thing.'

'*She* wears it.'

'She's a grown woman. Young girls should smell of soap, or perhaps a splash of cologne. Go and take a shower. And I don't want to smell it on you tomorrow, do you hear? It'll spoil people's appetite for dinner.'

'It might help hide the stink of Baby farting,' muttered Lily under her breath.

'What did you say?'

'Nothing.'

'I'm not as deaf as you think! Such language. Just for that, you can hand over the bottle right now. Go and fetch it this minute.'

'I'm not giving it to you. It's mine. It was a present.'

Frank had presented her with it that morning, an enormous bottle of Chanel No. 5, and personally applied it to all her most intimate pulse points.

'You'll do what I tell you, young lady. All the while you're under my roof . . .'

'I don't want to be under your roof!'

'I'm well aware of that,' said Ruth crisply, well used to these outbursts. In a moment the little madam would be threatening to run away again. 'I've learned not to expect any gratitude from you, but I do insist on obedience.' A policy which was proving increasingly exhausting. It would have been much easier to let her run wild, but she had made that mistake with her mother.

'If you won't hand it over,' she continued, wiping her hands, 'I'll just have to confiscate it.' She marched purposefully upstairs and into Lily's room, where she began opening drawers, searching for the offending item.

'Leave my things alone!' shouted Lily, running after her. Not that she would find anything. The perfume, along with her cosmetics and her newly acquired cache of dollar bills – infinitely more precious than the untouchable, useless ones in her savings account – was in her handbag, downstairs, in the hall.

'Then give it to me yourself.'

'No! Why should I? It belongs to me! My mother paid for it like she pays for everything! If it wasn't for her, you'd have nothing. If it wasn't for me, she wouldn't want anything to do with you!'

'And if it wasn't for her, I'd want nothing to do with you. I've had just about enough of your impudence. You've been late back every day this week, wandering around Lord knows where, falling asleep on park benches, letting poor Baby get into fights and hurt herself, answering back every time I ask you to do anything. Any more trouble from you, and you'll spend Christmas Day locked in your room.'

'Good! I'd rather spend it locked in my room! Put that down, you bitch!'

This demand was directed not at Ruth, but at Baby, who came frisking into the room dragging Lily's bag between her jaws. Lily lunged to retrieve it just as the catch flew open, spilling its contents onto the floor, including the outsize bottle of Chanel, still with its gift tag attached: *To Lily, with love from Frank.*

Desperate that Ruth shouldn't read it, Lily snatched the bottle and hid it behind her back.

'Hand it over,' said Ruth grimly.

'No!'

Baby picked up Lily's wallet and offered it to Ruth instead, enjoying the game.

'Good idea, Baby,' said Ruth grimly. 'No more pocket money until she learns to behave herself.'

She began extracting the notes, stopping short as she noticed the twenty dollar bill before counting the rest.

'Where did you get all this money?'

'Mom sent it to me.'

'Like Mom gave you the perfume?'

'That's right.'

'There's eighty dollars here.'

'So? She can afford it.'

'Don't lie to me! Have you been stealing from me, Lily?'

'No!'

Unconvinced, Ruth returned to the kitchen and began checking the petty cash she kept in the cookie tin, giving Lily the chance to remove the gift tag, which she stuffed inside her bra.

'How dare you!' she yelled, pursuing her grandmother. 'How dare you accuse me of stealing!'

Ruth continued counting. Furious now, Lily swept the tin from the worktop and sent it crashing to the floor.

'Pick that up at once,' said Ruth. 'Before I tan your hide.'

'You dare lay a finger on me and I'll – I'll—'

Ruth delivered a stinging slap to Lily's cheek.

'Go to your room and don't come out till you're ready to apologise.'

'You're the one who should apologise to me!' squealed Lily, feeling the childish tears of outrage prick behind her eyes. 'You're the thief! You're the liar! You take my mother's money for doing nothing, you never miss a chance to tell her bad things about me, you—'

Another blow, to the other cheek this time. Lily burst into tears in earnest and dropped the perfume bottle on the tiled floor, shattering it, drenching the scrubbed sanctity of Ruth's kitchen with the torrid smell of sin. Then she turned and ran out of the house and kept running, till she tripped and fell headlong, grazing both knees and an elbow. She barely noticed the pain, knowing only that she had to reach the marina before Frank went out fishing, and that this time she wasn't going back.

Half-way there she got a stitch and had to stop to get her breath back. Only then did she notice the blood running down her right arm, and both legs; only then did she realise that she was wearing no make-up and must look a perfect sight, with her face all wet from tears and her cheeks bright red from the blows Ruth had inflicted.

She moistened a finger with her blood and applied it to the corner of her mouth without benefit of a mirror. Then, for good measure, she did the same to her right eyelid. By the time she sighted the *Never Again*, she knew her latest lines off by heart.

Frank was lounging on deck, reading a book, and did not at first notice her. He had got rid of most of his library when he bought the boat, but he had kept a few old favourites, as ballast, to steady him in stormy weather. All fiction. You could rely on decent fiction to tell the truth, which was more than could be said for facts. Facts were for lying with. Hearing George bark a cheerful greeting, he looked up and saw an almost unrecognisable Lily running towards him. She looked about fourteen years old.

'What happened?' he said, as she leaped aboard and threw herself into his arms, sobbing. Lily shook her head, unable to reply. Frank sat her down on deck, fetched iodine and cotton wool, and began cleaning her up, as he had once done with the injured Baby.

'I can't go back there,' sniffed Lily, wincing at the sting

of the ointment. 'Next time she might kill me.'

'The old lady?' said Frank. Lily had already told him about her grandmother's vicious temper and her fondness for hard liquor, but he had assumed she was exaggerating.

'When I got back I found her going through my drawers, looking for money. When I asked her what she was doing, she threw a hairbrush at me. Then she ripped my bag out of my hands and took my wallet. When I tried to snatch it back she began punching me and kicking me. I s-said I was leaving and I wasn't coming back, and then – and then – she got hold of my passport and air ticket and ripped them up and said I wouldn't be going anywhere. Then she threw me out of the house . . .'

'It's OK,' murmured Frank. 'Give her a while to cool off, then I'll take you home.'

'No! If she sees you she'll go berserk! Oh, she'll be fine and polite to your face, but after you're gone she'll start lamming into me again. I think she's insane. I've tried to get her to see a doctor, but she won't. I came home because I was worried about her, but . . .' She clung to him, weeping. 'I know you'll think I'm wicked and selfish, but I just can't take it any more! Will you give me a ride to Havana? I've got no other way of getting back!'

Frank held her close and ran his hands through her hair.

'Think it over for a while,' he said. 'It's Christmas Day tomorrow. Once she sobers up she'll be sorry.'

'Oh, she's always sorry afterwards. I'm her meal ticket, she doesn't want to lose me. I'll send her money every month, just like I always do, but I'm not going back there ever again!' She wiped her eyes on a corner of her shirt, pulling it free from her waistband to expose a tantalising expanse of bare white midriff.

'Please help me, Frank. At least this way we can have a few whole days together . . .'

She kissed him with a dreadful desperation, as if to muzzle a refusal, pressing her breasts into his chest, coiling her arms tight around his neck. Frank tried not to feel sorry for her, and failed. Taking her to Havana was no problem in itself, nor was her lack of documentation, thanks to his harbour contacts. No, the problem would be resisting the temptation to visit Addy's, to keep seeing her, just to make sure she was all right. The problem was the insidious, creeping affection that had nothing to do with the luscious softness of her body or the pert prettiness of her face, or her mechanical competence in bed. Those things had just been an excuse, and he had needed an excuse. She evoked a quixotic need to protect and spoil her, if only to relieve the crushing burden of his own misanthropy, if only because she was a victim, like himself.

'What about all your stuff?'

'Let her sell it. Once I'm back at work I can buy more.'

'Do you want to pick up a few things downtown?'

'No. I might run into her. Can we leave right away?' She began scratching her nose on his stubble. 'Well, perhaps not right away . . .'

'You stay down below,' said Frank. 'I'll go buy some supplies for the trip. Give me a list of things you need and I'll get them for you.'

Her handwriting and spelling were better than he had expected; her list shorter and more precise, quoting the exact makes and shades of cosmetics she required. Frank added some fancy underwear, to cheer them both up, and a girlish pink gingham dress to wear on top of it – pink was her favourite colour – and another bottle of perfume, to replace the one she had lost, despising himself all the while as an old fool. But what the hell. It was Christmas, after all.

Raúl rather enjoyed the festivities; the artificial seasonal benevolence worked in his favour. He found himself guest of honour at the Soler Christmas Eve feast – which took place by candlelight, the rebels having sabotaged the power lines – not to mention an object of eager speculation amongst curious, indiscreet and inebriated guests, to whom he spoke with bilious cordiality and listened with abstemious contempt. He was doubly glad he had invented the rich-stepfather story, for all that it wouldn't bear checking out; his pride could not have borne the assumption that he had come home cap-in-hand. One lie led, inevitably, to another, increasing the chances of being caught out, but this danger dignified the enterprise, adding a welcome element of risk. An honest, poor-me approach would doubtless yield quicker, easier results; the old man would relish the chance to pity and patronise and punish him with fatuous generosity, generosity which would cost him nothing. Raúl intended to cost him everything he had.

It was hard to credit that this ageing, feeble man was the brute who had beaten him senseless as a boy and subjected his mother to violence, rape and sexual degradation. Raúl had been barely six years old when he had heard her crying out in the middle of the night, rushed to her aid, and witnessed the hideous scene that had haunted him ever since. It was that night, he was sure, that his brother had been conceived . . .

Raúl had paid dearly for his intervention, bearing the brunt of his father's guilt, guilt which the old hypocrite had evidently sought to expunge by treating his second wife and younger son with kid gloves – fearful, no doubt, of losing them as well. A self-serving reformation which served merely to intensify Raúl's loathing and stiffen his resolve.

The presence of outsiders inspired in Enrique an embarrassing degree of patriarchal pomposity, hence all the maudlin speeches about not being long for this world and letting bygones be bygones, none of which took Raúl in for a moment. Clearly his father thought that he could use him to bring León into line. León, meanwhile, seemed pleased rather than perturbed at this reconciliation, putting up a show of easy-going, fraternal goodwill, confident, no doubt, that he was in no real danger. Raúl kept him at arm's length; the last thing he wanted was to find himself charmed, like everybody else, into liking him. He had been a charmer even as a kid.

He had grown up into a sharp-witted fellow, despite the languid pose of couldn't-care-less sang-froid. He might well have proved something of a threat if he hadn't had his mind on other things, to wit his troublesome liaison with his bitch of a stepmother, and his burgeoning affair with her charming *ingénue* of a daughter, which Raúl would never have suspected, given the latter's shy, prim demeanour, had Eduardo not observed them in a furtive embrace and blurted out his disgust. This snippet provided a welcome reprieve from talk of revolution, a subject in which Raúl was careful to show an intense, seductive interest.

'León's just amusing himself, of course,' Eduardo said bitterly, during one of their rides round the estate. 'Poor Celia. Talk about taking sweets from a baby. I expect she's getting desperate for a man.'

'Surely not. I would have thought there were any number of young men eager to marry an heiress.'

'She's not an heiress, and everyone knows it. And even if she was, nobody would ever get past your father. Or my mother come to that.'

'Perhaps León will succeed where others have failed.'

'I hope not, for her sake.'

'Why do you say that? Don't you like him?'

'Of course I like him. Everybody does That's his whole trouble. He thinks he can get away with anything. He's completely amoral and he's got no principles. How do you suppose he got that flashy car and the apartment in Vedado? You can bet your life he's got a rich mistress. And that he doesn't give a damn about her, any more than he does about Celia. It sickens me the way women fawn over him.'

'I've heard that they fawn over you as well.'

'Who told you that?' He coloured charmingly.

'Your mother. She was telling me what a big hit you were at the last harvest ball.'

Eduardo shifted his shoulders uncomfortably.

'I'm not interested in women.'

'Come now.'

'That is, I don't think of them just as sex objects, the way León does. When I marry, it will be to a woman I can respect. Not that I've met one yet. Apart from Celia, that is. She's quite intelligent. At least I used to think so.'

'Perhaps you should have a brotherly word in her ear.'

Eduardo shook his head. 'It would only make things worse. She's stubborn as a mule. Especially when she knows she's in the wrong.'

'Then perhaps you should talk to León.'

'Much good that would do. He'd just laugh it off. I told you, he always does exactly as he pleases and to hell with everyone else.'

'Your mother, then?'

'What do you take me for? A grubby little sneak? If they want to slobber over each other, that's up to them.' He gave an involuntary shudder, betraying the very real distaste that had loosened his tongue on the subject. 'I shouldn't even have told you. For heaven's sake keep it quiet. I don't want to start another god-awful family row.'

'My lips are sealed,' said Raúl, adding casually, 'Tell me, have you ever had a woman?'

'Of course,' said Eduardo, too quickly. 'Three of us went to this place in Santiago.' Another giveaway shift of the shoulders. 'You know what it's like at school. They're all obsessed with sex. Everyone passing dirty pictures round the dorm and so on.'

'And so on?'

'Oh, for heaven's sake. You were a pupil there too.'

'Only for a couple of years, thank God. But I think I know the kind of thing you mean. One of the senior boys was always trying to touch me up. In the end I had to fight him off. Luckily I was big for my age.'

Eduardo changed the subject hurriedly, confirming Raúl's suspicions. He was much too desirable not to have been approached, and much too proud to have succumbed. With every day that passed, he was struck more and more by how alike Eduardo and Celia were, not just physically but temperamentally. Both of them put a great deal of energy into hiding their feelings, with Eduardo taking refuge in political cant and emotional self-sufficiency, Celia in the role of peacemaker and modest, dutiful daughter. It was easy to imagine Eduardo shunning admirers of both sexes; it was equally hard to imagine his demure elder sister locked in a passionate embrace with anyone, even a seasoned womaniser like León; in his presence she was, if anything, more subdued than usual, a fact that became significant once you knew she had something to hide. Presumably León had sworn her to secrecy, for fear that Lidia, with all the fury of a woman scorned, would sabotage his little adventure. He was a degenerate, two-faced bastard. Raúl had to give him credit for that.

Raúl was in little doubt that Lidia had lined him up as her next victim, a role which might be worth playing, albeit discreetly. Unfortunately, she did not attract him in the least. But he couldn't afford to make an enemy of her by spurning her advances. When she brushed her hand against his over dinner, and wound her right leg purposefully round his left, under cover of the table, he fully expected her to come to his room, once her husband was snoring, and invite him to carry on where his Don Juan of a brother had left off. And when she made a great point of telling Enrique that Raúl had kindly offered to drive her to the hairdresser in Bayamo next day, he felt obliged to pretend that he had, wondering whether she had plans to stop off on the way and invite him to ravish her in the nearest cane field. Perhaps she didn't realise that she was being watched. Thank God he did. He would have to be very, very careful.

His father grunted something about Raúl having better things to do and what did they employ chauffeurs for, whereupon Raúl said that he had business in town in any case, it would be no trouble. The chance to be alone together might yield some useful information; a disgruntled, oversexed wife could prove a powerful weapon against her husband.

That night he braced himself for a nocturnal visit – at

least the house itself appeared to be safe from surveillance – resolving to play things by ear. Mercifully, however, his rest that night was undisturbed, and having slept well he rose early, to find Celia sitting alone at the table on the patio. Enrique and Lidia always took their breakfast in bed, whilst León invariably rose late, out of sloth, as did Eduardo, out of industry, it being his habit to pore over his books well into the small hours.

'Good morning,' he said, sitting down opposite her as a surly Emilia dispensed coffee, juice and hot toast. She was dressed in a businesslike grey costume and white blouse, with her hair scraped back into a less than tidy chignon. 'I take it you're going back to work this morning?'

'Yes. Grinding starts in a few days, there's a lot to do.'

'I'd be very interested to come with you. I gather you more or less run the place.'

'Hardly. But Papá's out and about a lot. So technically, I'm second in command.'

'Technically?'

'I'm female. I wouldn't be accepted at all except that nepotism's so normal. I don't know if it's the same in the United States, but in Cuba no one takes women seriously, especially in business.'

'All the more reason for you to prove them wrong. I know my father thinks the world of you. He told me so himself. I have to take your mother into town today, but perhaps tomorrow . . .'

She began fiddling with her napkin.

'There's something I ought to tell you.' She took a deep breath. 'I don't think you should go to Bayamo with Mamá. I think you should make some excuse.'

'But . . . why?'

'Because Papá is terribly jealous. He might get the wrong idea.'

'About me and your mother?' said Raúl, raising a suitably incredulous eyebrow.

'I don't mean . . . oh, I know how absurd it must sound. I asked León to talk to you instead, but he said I was being silly. The thing is . . . my mother is out to make trouble for you. She thinks you're here to cheat León out of the estate. Well, it wouldn't be cheating exactly, you are the eldest son, but . . .'

'It's all right,' said Raúl drily. 'I can quite see her point of view.'

'I know I'm being disloyal to her, telling you this. But I can't stand by and let Papá be upset. He's got a weak heart, you know. He'd get terribly angry if he thought that you . . . that you and Mamá . . . what I'm trying to say is . . . Mamá would like Papá to throw you out.' She hung her head. 'I don't think you should be alone with her if you can help it. It would be her word against yours, you see.'

She blushed hotly. She looked even more like her brother when she blushed. The same high forehead, the same long dark lashes, the same determined chin and full, generous mouth . . .

'You can imagine how awful I feel, telling you this. It's just that Papá gets himself worked up so easily. And even if he didn't have a weak heart . . . I have enough trouble keeping the peace round here as it is!'

For the first time he caught sight of the impatience and exasperation that simmered beneath her surface calm.

'I'm sorry my presence here has caused you such a problem.'

'I'm the one who should apologise,' she said. 'This is very embarrassing. You probably think I've got an over-active imagination.'

Not quite active enough, thought Raúl. No wonder León had ducked out of warning him off, which showed that he was less of a hypocrite than he seemed. Celia broaching the subject must have brought him out into a cold sweat.

'Naturally, I wouldn't suspect you of actually *doing* anything,' she went on, disconcerted by his silence. 'Or my mother either, of course.'

'Naturally,' he said gently, amused, touched, grateful. He had nearly fallen into Lidia's little trap, his thinking blurred by too much knowledge. What a devious, dangerous bitch she was. 'I appreciate how difficult it must have been for you to warn me.'

'I didn't do it for your benefit,' she said. 'I did it for Papá.'

She fell silent as Emilia appeared with more coffee.

'Emilia,' said Raúl pleasantly, ignoring the evil eye the housekeeper gave him at every opportunity. 'When Doña Lidia comes down, would you mind telling her that something has cropped up and I won't be able to take her to the hairdresser's today? Please convey my profuse apologies.'

Emilia responded with a surly nod and withdrew.

'I think she and Lidia feel the same way about me,' he sighed self-mockingly. 'You don't trust me either, do you?'

'Not entirely, no.'

'I don't blame you. Well, as I'd better be out of the way before your mother comes down, can I hide out in your office for a while? And then perhaps later you can show me round. Things must have changed a lot since I was a boy.'

'It would be better if you left it till tomorrow. Papá's going to be out all day today.'

'So much the better,' said Raúl gallantly.

She wasn't used to being noticed, that much was clear, which would make her wary of flattery but susceptible to genuine interest. And he was genuinely interested. He hadn't been before, not once he had established that she had no claim on the estate, but now that she had proved herself an ally, albeit an unwilling one, he realised that she could be useful to him in circumventing the hidden landmines that made Soler territory so dangerous. She was too honest to mislead him deliberately, if too canny to tell him everything.

'Well, if you're sure you wouldn't be bored . . .'

'León may find it boring,' said Raúl, 'but I always used to take an interest in the estate. In those days, I expected to take over one day. But now I owe it to my stepfather to follow in his footsteps. So your mother has really no need to worry. Like you, I have a strong sense of duty.'

She relaxed slightly. 'Don't you miss the army?'

'No. It's not the same in peacetime.'

'You prefer war?'

'Peacetime's like the dead season. Except that you keep on marching up and down waving your machete, even when there isn't any cane.'

Unexpectedly, she laughed, relieved, perhaps, to have got her little ordeal over with. She looked quite different when she laughed, and the sound had an almost earthy quality which took him by surprise. She got up. 'If you wait for me in the car, I'll join you in a moment.'

She went back indoors. Raúl strolled round to the front of the house where a white Cadillac was waiting, and got into the front seat next to Lázaro, who handed him an envelope without speaking. Inside was a hundred pesos.

'Well done,' commented Raúl, returning ten of them. 'Next time I must come with you.'

This was a godsend. Supposedly he had wired home for more money, to replace what had been 'stolen'; this way he would be spared the embarrassment of asking his brother for another loan, and with any luck his winning streak would continue.

'Our secret,' he added, looking Lázaro up and down with interest. Small wonder that Emilia lusted after his strong young body, encouraged, no doubt, as Raúl was himself, by the fact that he was still unattached. Casual enquiries had revealed that the chauffeur kept himself to himself and sought his pleasures outside the estate. With good reason, perhaps. Or was that just wishful thinking? There was only one way to find out.

'Good luck only lasts if you keep it quiet,' he continued, smiling. 'Agreed?'

Lázaro pocketed the money without speaking, silence indicating consent, and a moment later Celia reappeared, slightly flushed; judging by the total disappearance of her lipstick, she had just been kissed very thoroughly.

As a boy, Raúl had taken a delight in misappropriating

León's toys. Their mother was forever drooling over her baby and telling Raúl not to bully his little brother, but his little brother had learned very quickly that to cry, or to tell tales, would lead to severe reprisals. Frustratingly, however, León had not been possessive about his things. He had a natural inclination to share, to offer up sweets and playthings before they were taken away, mistaking spite for need. Raúl wondered if he displayed the same generosity of spirit when it came to women.

He remembered vividly the day León was born, the sound of his mother screaming in agony in the bedroom, and then the silly, doting look on her face when she held that ugly, wrinkled bundle in her arms. She had never been the same after that. All her love had been transferred to his brother. Even after León was kidnapped, and Raúl became an only child again, she had pined for her lost baby, and then Steve had come along and the pattern had been repeated all over again. He had to listen to her screaming in ecstasy while a rival ripped her apart, had to witness that stupid, sated look of joy. Celia looked a bit like that now. He experienced a destructive urge to wipe that secret smile off her face and replace it with one which owed its origins entirely to him, or failing that, cleansing tears.

'What would you like to see first?' she asked, as they arrived at the compound. 'The mill's not operating at the moment, of course. All the machinery is being cleaned and serviced ready for next week. Would you like to start off there?'

The process of converting raw cane into sugar was well known to Raúl: his father had begun teaching him the business as a child. But in deference to Celia, he pretended to have forgotten all he knew, asked her to explain the functions of the huge rollers that crushed the cane, the vats that boiled and clarified the syrup, the centrifuge that spun it and trapped the glistening crystals, leaving a residue of raw molasses, and the additional machines, new since his day, which packed the dry granules ready for export. He took a ride on the private railroad that transported the crop to the mill from the farthest reaches of the estate and the dependent *colonias* beyond. Celia's commentary was fluent, well informed, and leavened with brisk, anecdotal humour. In the presence of her family, she tended to say little, rather than be drowned out by Don Enrique's sounding brass or Lidia's tinkling cymbal, even though – or perhaps because – both Eduardo and León interrupted them both constantly, the one displaying a studied arrogance, the other irreverent good humour. The presence of guests drove her further into her shell, but you could tell that she was listening and watching, never missing a thing. Except what she was too blind to see.

Not surprisingly she flourished, like a plant used to struggling in the shade, in the unaccustomed sunshine of close attention. Their conversation over breakfast had produced an instant, unsought, but inescapable, intimacy, found a chink in her natural reserve that she hadn't had time to repair.

'So what do you really think about the rebels?' he asked, as they returned to the railhead. Beyond the silver-green fields towered the mist-swathed peaks of the Sierra Maestre, reminding him of how much he had loved this place, how much he had missed his native land with its womb-like warmth and its rampant lushness, and its natural tendency to excess, so similar to his own. The air was perfectly still, reducing the early-morning rustle of the cane to a dry, papery whisper, producing the semi-silence that invites indiscretion, like the sound of waves lapping on the shore, or the muted hum of voices in a restaurant.

'You've heard Papá's views and you must have heard Eduardo's,' shrugged Celia. 'Between them they say all there is to say.'

'But surely you have an opinion of your own?'

'Not a cut and dried one like they do, no.' It sounded like an equivocal response, but she said it with a certain passion.

'Then that makes it all the more interesting. Tell me.'

'It's not so much an opinion as a gut reaction. I keep thinking of what happened last time, that's all. My mother's grandfather, Camilo Acosta, was a peasant farmer, a third-generation Cuban. He ran supply lines to the rebels in the second war of independence against Spain. One day an army unit arrested him at his house and disembowelled him in front of his wife and children. Meanwhile, my other great-grandfather, Angel Rodríguez, a Spanish immigrant worker, was a firm supporter of the government. His employer refused to pay the rebels for permission to grind, so they attacked his fields and butchered the workers who'd defied the ban rather than let their families starve. One of them was my grandfather. The rebels chopped off his arms and legs and left him to bleed to death. So you see, both sides were as bad as each other.'

'I take your point.'

'I dread the same kind of thing happening all over again. But if it does,' she added with spirit, 'I won't care which side my menfolk are on, as long as they stay alive and don't get hurt. That's a typical woman's view, I suppose. What do you think?'

'Soldiers are trained to obey orders, not to think. And, of course, I'm completely out of touch with Cuban affairs.'

'Even if they get rid of Batista,' she said, 'someone else just as bad will take over. It's inevitable. Every president we've ever had, including him, has promised sweeping reforms, but nothing ever changes. The system's still as corrupt as it was under the Spanish.'

'Then why not get rid of the system, once and for all?'

'At what price? Burning cane fields and destroying property will just antagonise American investors and destroy the economy. Well, that's what the rebels want, of course. I'm sure you've heard Eduardo's treatise on how the US is the real enemy.'

'He did stress that I shouldn't take it personally. Kept reminding me that I was really a Cuban. Not that I've ever forgotten it.'

He had never stopped feeling like an exile adrift in an alien land. From being a scion of one of the richest families in Oriente, sure of his place in society, he had been suddenly and savagely demoted to the rank of fatherless Hispanic, a problem child from a poor home. He had learned first-hand that without money and status you were nothing, nobody, that he who had thought himself a prince was merely his father's chattel, without rights or fortune of his own.

After Raúl's fight with Steve, in which the latter had sustained a broken jaw, his mother had had the nerve to suggest that he go back to Buenaventura. At the time he would rather have starved. It would have smacked of selling himself, of begging his father's pardon, of admitting his mother's betrayal. Even now, he refused to sink that low. He was a gambler, not a beggar.

'My stepfather was very good to me,' he went on. 'He brought me up like his own. But I never lost sight of whose son I really was.'

'I know what you mean,' she said warmly, with a flash of fellow feeling. 'It was much the same for me. You must be relieved that Papá is making you welcome.'

'I expect he's doing it for his own reasons. He never used to have a forgiving nature, and I can't believe he's mellowed that much.'

'Perhaps not,' said Celia guardedly. 'But at least you've made a start.'

'So I have,' agreed Raúl, smiling. A start on his long-delayed revenge. Which was beginning to look as if it might be sweeter than he had dared to imagine.

Ruth telephoned Addy on Christmas Day to tell her, briskly and factually, that Lily had run away, assuring her that she was bound to turn up, it was just a silly tantrum. The foolish child had left without clothes or money, she couldn't possibly have gone far. The police had circulated a description, and her photo had been flashed on television. There was no need for panic.

For three long days Addy sat tight, waiting for news,

nurturing the hope and dread that Lily might somehow turn up in Havana, or at least telephone to demand the fare. But this possibility waned with every hour that passed; unable to bear the suspense any longer, she decided to fly home. The likelihood was that she hadn't gone far, and Addy wanted to be on the spot when she was found.

If only she'd gone home for Christmas as usual, none of this would have happened. She had got her priorities wrong yet again. Even now, sitting on the plane to Miami, she found her mind slipping into the familiar furrow, worrying about the builders falling behind schedule, and the burden of the repayments on the loan, and how important it was that they open sooner rather than later, and how every day's delay was a day's less profit. I must be a monster, she thought, thinking about money when my only daughter is missing, perhaps dead, and all because I wasn't there to protect her. Perhaps it was just a defence mechanism, a refusal to think the unthinkable. And besides, what was the new casino for, if not for Lily? It was the gold mine that would enable her to sell Addy's and put her past behind her, set her darling daughter up for life. That way Lily would never find out her shameful secret, Lily would never want for anything, and all because she, Addy, had put her daughter first . . . or had she?

She took a connecting flight to Tampa, arriving in St Petersburg to find her mother red-eyed and grey-faced; she seemed to have aged ten years since the summer. A lingering, sickly smell of perfume hung about the house, perfume that had been, according to Ruth, the cause of all the trouble.

'But I didn't give her any of my perfume,' protested Addy, sniffing the air. 'It's not one I use, in any case. And I certainly never sent her eighty dollars in cash . . .'

'Well, somebody did,' accused Ruth. 'I can't watch her every minute of the day. For all I know, she's been shop-lifting and taking the stuff to a pawnbroker's, like you used to do.'

'Mother, please. That was a long time ago.'

'There's no way you can bring a girl up decent without a man. I learned that after your father died. It would never surprise me if Lily hadn't run off with some boy.'

'What boy?'

'How should I know? I've been through all this before, remember. You managed to elope with that no-good bum without me even knowing he existed.'

'Could it be someone she met at the beach house last summer?'

'You said you wanted her to have some fun. You said you wanted her to meet some nice boys from good families. Don't blame me if she got up to mischief with one of them . . .'

Addy tried to keep calm, wondering too late why she had thought that Lily would knuckle under to Ruth when she herself had defied her. Even now, she found it easier to identify with her daughter than her mother, not that that made things any easier. Of all the things she dreaded, it was Lily falling for the wrong man, a bad man, a man who would break her heart and make it impossible for her to believe in love ever again.

'I called you after a week,' she said, casting her mind back. 'If she's run off with a boy, she'll do the same. I don't care, as long as she's all right.' She stifled a sob under cover of blowing her nose.

'She only did it to bring you running,' said Ruth bitterly. 'You realise that, don't you? And now that she's set a precedent, the same thing will happen again, and again, and again. I'm getting old, Addy. I love the child dearly, but I can't cope with her like I used to.'

'It won't be for much longer. Another couple of years and I plan to sell up, come home for good.'

'Don't bother. By then it will be too late.'

'If you're trying to make me feel guilty—'

Their bickering was interrupted by the sound of the telephone. Ruth got to it first.

'Yes,' she said faintly, her face ashen. 'Yes. Right away.'

'What is it?' demanded Addy. 'Have they found her?'

'There's a body . . . been washed up . . . on the shore,' began Ruth. Her speech was slurred, her features contorted, her breathing laboured, as if she were drunk. 'A young girl. They want us . . . to go down to the m-morgue . . . to iden – iden—'

It happened in slow motion. Addy saw her mother's mouth move soundlessly, like a fish, saw her hand lose its grip on the receiver, saw her slump shapelessly into her chair. She kept trying to talk, but the sounds made no sense, her eyes flashing helplessly, her left arm and leg struggling to pull herself upright while her other side lay limp and lifeless, like a puppet without strings.

As the bout neared its violent, uncertain end, a raucous babble of excitement filled the cock-pit in Bayamo, which was crammed to bursting with men of all classes and colours. Raúl stood in the front tier, quietly watching, his fists clenching in silent fury as his fancy was wounded yet again. He had staked all his afternoon's winnings on this fight, despite, or rather because of the unfavourable odds; as an untried bird, it had yet to prove itself, but Lázaro had assured him that it would win, while advising him not to risk his money until it had shown its mettle.

If it won, Raúl stood to collect three thousand pesos, which should be more than enough to strike a deal with Fernández, his father's private detective. If it lost, he would be penniless again. He held his breath as the two combatants circled each other, their feathers flashing blue and russet and gold, and swore in exasperation as his bird keeled over, apparently unconscious. Lázaro, as its trainer, stepped forward and picked up the injured creature, blowing gently down its beak to clear the blood clot that was choking it. A puff of alum in its eyes and a mouthful of *aguardiente* over its head and the cock returned bravely to the fray, biting, clawing, nipping and dodging, until finally its craven bully of an opponent ran away, eliciting cheers and boos from the crowd. A few seconds later, the victorious bird fell down dead from exhaustion, but by then the battle was already won. A flurry of settling up ensued; relieved, Raúl collected what he was owed and pressed a hundred pesos upon Lázaro.

'That's too much.'

'I'll be the judge of that. I don't want you training birds for anyone else in future, and you'll get your share of any winnings.' He slapped him on the back. 'I have private business to attend to. I shall need the car for an hour or so. Then I'll pick you up here and you can drive me home.'

Lázaro fished in his pockets for the keys, his attention already fixed on the next fight. Raúl left quickly before he was tempted to double his money. The stakes he would be playing for from now on were much, much higher than that.

'We'd better start dinner, Emilia,' said Celia, looking into the kitchen. 'Señor Raúl must have been delayed. Please keep some back for him.'

Emilia, who was busy doctoring the portion of stew she had set aside for Lázaro, grunted her acknowledgement without looking up. As she put down the phial, Celia picked it up, intrigued, pulling out the cork and sniffing the cloudy liquid. It smelt nearly as bad as the stuff Emilia insisted on putting in her bath, unaware that Celia was taking showers instead. As for the jezebel root, she had tossed the muslin bag out of León's car on the way to Santiago. It was enough to make you believe in magic. She wrinkled her nose. 'I think you'd better add some extra spices.'

The potion allegedly contained the ground-up heart of a humming-bird and the juice of a green Cantharis fly; a shard of Lázaro's tobacco had been ritually burned and the ash added to the brew. The resulting concoction had cost Emilia a whole week's wages.

'Patience,' muttered Emilia to herself. 'That's the secret. Patience.'

Patience, thought Celia. She had been patient for so long, and now that it had finally paid off she was already getting greedy. And careless. What did it matter if Mamá and Papá found out? Why was León so sure they would disapprove?

At first the sense of subterfuge had added to the excitement. León's untypical caution, his fear of discovery, his excessive concern for her reputation had provoked Celia towards deliberate recklessness. Telling him it was safe when it wasn't, for example, so he wouldn't use one of those horrible things that would stop her having a baby. And he had been too weak to argue. She had exploited that weakness ruthlessly, finally proved what she had always known – that she could wind him round her little finger, whether he realised it or not. The knowledge was intoxicating. She didn't care about Buenaventura, didn't care about being poor, didn't care about the prospect of a blazing family row. All she cared about was marrying León, as soon as possible.

Patience. It had all been a sham. She had never been patient, or tolerant, or long-suffering, never been soft-hearted and unassuming, never been shy and modest. She had spent most of her life pretending, compromising, doing things she didn't want to do, seeking approval, compensating for her lack of beauty, her lack of confidence, her lack of alternatives. But now she didn't lack for anything, and having experienced a taste of power, she was determined never to be powerless again.

She sauntered back into the dining room and took her place at the table. Her mother was still in a filthy mood, perhaps because Raúl had been avoiding her. León was listening good-naturedly to Papá droning on about the estimated size of the harvest, while Eduardo was lost in a world of his own as usual, counting the days, no doubt, till he went back to school. They all underestimated her, every one of them, even León. But soon all that would change . . .

They were half-way through desert before Raúl made his belated appearance.

'My apologies,' he said, throwing open the door and lurching into the dining room. 'I was unavoidably . . . detained.'

His urbane manner contrasted sharply with his dishevelled appearance, as if he were unaware that his clothes were filthy, his face scratched and streaked with dirt and his left sleeve torn and soaked through with blood. There was a long moment of startled silence, followed by general commotion. León jumped up to take his brother's weight and help him to a chair. Lidia called out to Emilia to fetch a glass of brandy, Eduardo ran to get his first aid kit and Enrique barked at Celia to call the doctor. She ran to use the telephone in the hall to find Emilia wringing her hands.

'Where's Lázaro?' she demanded of Celia. 'I just asked *him* but he looked straight through me. Has there been an accident? I've been out to look at the car, but there's no damage—'

'We don't know what happened yet.' Celia put through a call to the family doctor and asked him to come immediately. Emilia fetched the brandy, knocking back a steadying swig herself before she took the glass to the patient, Celia following.

'. . . Bandits. Rebels. Whatever you want to call them,' Raúl was saying. Emilia let out a cry of alarm.

'What happened to Lázaro?' asked Celia, taking the glass from her before she dropped it.

'A good question,' said Raúl, waving the drink away with a gesture of distaste. 'If he'd been with me at least it would have been two against two.'

'But where was he?' asked Celia, puzzled. Usually Lázaro was so reliable. 'Wasn't he supposed to drive you home?'

'Evidently he had better things to do. I had some business to attend to at the telegraph office, so I gave him an hour to amuse himself in town. That's the last I saw of him. In the end I got fed up waiting for him and decided to drive myself.' Eduardo began cutting through his torn sleeve, exposing a deep gash. 'About half-way home I was forced to stop by a farm cart parked across the middle of the road. Two men wearing masks jumped out from behind it. One of them threatened me with a knife and told me to hand over my money.'

'I warned you,' began León. 'That's the second time you've been robbed . . .'

'I wasn't,' snapped Raúl. 'I didn't learn unarmed combat for nothing.' He produced his wallet from his inside pocket. 'But next time I'll take your advice and carry a gun.'

'I shall dismiss Lázaro as soon as he returns,' blustered Enrique, 'and replace him with an armed bodyguard. Any fool can drive a car . . .'

'You were lucky they didn't slice through an artery,' said Eduardo, inspecting the wound. 'As it is you'll need stitches.'

'So will they. I managed to get hold of the knife. That's when they took fright and ran away.'

'That's my boy,' muttered Enrique approvingly. 'Just as well it happened to him and not you,' he added, turning to León. 'Now perhaps you'll put some bullets in that bloody useless gun of yours.'

'I'd have given them my money,' said León. 'It's not worth dying for, or killing for come to that. They were probably just a couple of starving peasants with umpteen kids to feed. The rebels don't bother to steal wallets, holding up banks is more their line.'

'Rebels, bandits, there's no difference,' snapped Lidia. 'Don't make excuses for the scum.'

'León's right,' said Eduardo, cleaning the wound with professional deftness. Ever since childhood he had played doctor, mummifying his guinea-pig of a sister; since then he had acquired a whole library of textbooks, determined to master as much theory as possible before he started medical school next year. 'If people could be sure of a living wage all year round, there wouldn't be any need for crime. Is that bandage too tight? It's just till the doctor arrives.'

'I hate doctors. Look at the mess they made of my face. Why don't you stitch it up now and be done with it?'

'You need a local anaesthetic. We've got some, in the clinic, but I'm not licensed to administer it. And a tetanus shot.'

'I don't need an anaesthetic. And I had a tetanus booster last year. I'd rather trust myself to you than another ham-fisted butcher.'

'But—'

'Do as he asks,' interrupted Enrique. 'He'll soon change his tune once the needle goes in.'

'Papá . . .' began Celia, fearful that Raúl was delirious.

'What's the matter with you?' demanded Raúl of Eduardo. 'Are you squeamish, or what?'

'Of course I'm not squeamish.'

'Quite the reverse,' put in León drily, lighting a cigarette. 'He's dissected every other species he can lay his hands on. You'll be his first human.'

'Then get on with it, before I bleed to death.'

Catching the mocking gleam in Raúl's eye, Eduardo's expression hardened. Without another word, he began preparing a suture.

'I can't watch this,' said León, making as if to leave the room while Lidia looked on, riveted.

'Stay here,' said Eduardo. 'I need you to hold his arm steady. It'll jump otherwise.'

'I'll do it,' volunteered Enrique.

'You're not strong enough. It has to be kept absolutely still.'

'What's the matter?' jeered Raúl, seeing his brother's reluctance. 'Afraid you're going to faint? Celia, you'd better be there to catch him.'

León shrugged and pinioned the bleeding arm on the dining table, gripping it tightly at both wrist and elbow. Celia averted her eyes from the damaged limb, looking instead at the watching faces, seeing this bizarre tableau through their eyes. León visibly flinched every time steel pierced flesh, Eduardo's concentration was impassive, absolute, Papá had the intent, hypercritical look he used to scrutinise a balance sheet, Mamá stared with ghoulish fascination, and Raúl – Raúl didn't move a muscle, only the unnaturally tight set of his mouth betraying the gritted teeth within. Emilia stared as if hypnotised, white-faced, trembling all over, her eyes full of fear. Thinking that she was about to cry out and disturb the steadiness of Eduardo's hands, Celia took her arm and led her quickly, quietly out of the room.

'Are you all right?'

Emilia shook her head.

'I just seen a devil. Only a devil can give power like that.'

'Don't be ridiculous,' said Celia sharply. 'The man's a war hero, he's been through worse pain than that, I daresay.'

'He's got the devil in him,' repeated Emilia. 'I always felt it, but now I know for sure.'

'You're just worried about Lázaro, that's all. Have another shot of brandy and lie down. He'll be back tomorrow, you'll see.'

Emilia shook her head. 'Something's happened to him. I can feel it.'

'You and your feelings,' chivvied Celia, more gently. 'Come on, I'll put you to bed.'

Emilia had her own quarters adjacent to the kitchen, a small, fussy room which was festooned with holy pictures, artefacts, candles, and other accoutrements of the *santería* cult. An altar to the goddess Oshún, patroness of love and marriage, overlooked the large double bed which took up most of the floor space. Until conceiving her passion for Lázaro, Emilia had shared it with a succession of lovers, but in order for the charms to work, she had taken a temporary vow of chastity. In Celia's view, it was sheer frustration that was making Emilia so nervy. It must be difficult, being used to having a lover and then having to do without. The same thing would not happen to her.

Hearing the doctor's car draw up outside, she went to open the door, wondering what he would make of Eduardo's needlework. But by the time she showed him in, the injured arm was neatly bandaged and its owner refused point blank to have it re-examined.

'I'm rather tired,' said Raúl. 'If you'll excuse me, I think I'll take a bath and go to bed. Can you lend me an arm, Eduardo? I feel rather giddy.'

Eduardo picked up his medical kit and led his patient away, leaving behind a strange, awkward silence.

'Can I offer you something to drink, Doctor Lucero?' twittered Lidia. 'I've been meaning to talk to you about my back . . .'

'I'd better go see if Eduardo needs any help,' said León, exchanging an imperceptible glance with Celia before retreating upstairs; a few moments later, having consumed an obligatory cup of coffee, Celia yawned a good night, and ran up to her room, to find León waiting for her.

'How long have we got?'

'An hour at least. You know what Mamá's like once she starts rattling on about her aches and pains. And Doctor Lucero never leaves till he's had at least three cocktails.'

An hour. They began undressing themselves, to save time, feverish with haste. León almost resented her for reducing him to this pitiful state. He had never felt so damned scared before, not even when the untimely return of Captain Reinaldo had necessitated a precipitous escape through his wife's bedroom window. That hardly counted as danger compared to this. I'm in love with you, he had told her glibly, not expecting this terrifying assault upon his well-being, this hollow dread of losing her twinned with the paradoxical, perverse need to escape her. He had envisaged something cosy, comforting, above all controllable, thought to provide himself with an emotional nest-egg, not intending to draw on it so much and so soon. It was a not-yet situation that had turned into a now, a process that couldn't be reversed. She had taken that smug, self-seeking love of his and peeled away its layers, exposed the naked, neglected need within. He felt trapped, powerless, haunted not so much by the prospect of Lidia's venom as that of the old man's approval. If he got wind of this, he would lose no time in rushing them to the altar, post-haste. Celia would get her own way in that as well . . .

'Like this?' she murmured, as if for all the world she were the pupil and he the teacher; after ten years of gleeful promiscuity and self-congratulation on his supposed sexual prowess, he felt ignorant, inadequate, a fraud, unable to function unless he drew upon her superior strength, her secret knowledge. A part of him had always been detached, observing his own performance, manipulating his partner into thinking him generous, tender, sensitive, when in fact he was merely preening his own ego, a midget masquerading as a giant.

She let out a spontaneous cry, and he smothered the sound in a guilty kiss, feeling like some monstrous mother stopping the breath of a newborn infant.

'Ssh. Eduardo's just two doors along and—'

'Don't fuss,' she teased. 'I checked his room when I came upstairs. He wasn't there. I expect he's still with Raúl, lecturing the poor man about the revolution.'

But her little brother, had she but known it, had other things on his mind.

Lázaro squeezed his way between the towering stalks of cane, not stopping until he knew he was safe from pursuit. Still shaking, he examined himself for injuries, but the blood on his clothes was all his attacker's.

Exhausted, he sank to the ground, as fear receded and fury took its place. He cursed himself for letting down his customary guard, for responding to Raúl's open, friendly manner, for appearing to encourage him. It was as if he had fallen under a spell, unable to recognise the danger signals until it was too late.

If he had heeded Emilia's warnings, he might have thought twice before taking that suggested short cut, before stopping the car, well off the beaten track, to enjoy the proffered cigarette and discuss his beloved birds, lulled by the money in his pocket and the promise of more to come. Not once had it occurred to him, in his stupidity, what the purpose of the detour might be. He had marked Raúl Soler down for a taller, broader, uglier version of his philandering brother, a soldier who had seen active service, a fine horseman, the embodiment of *machismo*, a man's man. He was a man's man all right.

As realisation dawned, he had tried to play it stupid, to

pretend he did not understand the lewd talk of handsome cocks, the purpose of the crisp banknotes pressed into his palm. But when action took the place of words, invading his body with caresses more degrading than a slave-owner's whip, he had panicked and reached for his knife, overcome by a potent, primitive mixture of disgust and fear.

'What are you afraid of?' Raúl had said softly, ignoring the twitching blade. 'Do you imagine I would stoop to forcing you? If you didn't want it, then why did you smile and simper at me, why did you lead me on? Surely you're not so stupid that you didn't understand me? Or are you just playing hard to get?'

Affronted by this slur on his manhood, Lázaro had reviled him for a dirty *maricón*, defending his besmirched honour with the huge obscene vocabulary devoted to that much-despised species. It was another mistake. Belatedly regretting his volley of abuse, he had seen those pleading, mocking eyes erupt into flashing fury, known what it was to be a virgin threatened with rape . . .

'So you think you're more of a man than I am, do you?' Raúl Soler had hissed with ominous quietness. 'Then let's see you prove it.'

Big and strong though Lázaro might be, his adversary was bigger, stronger, easily wrenching the knife from his grasp and pinning him, face down, helpless, on the ground.

He had very nearly paid for his insults with the ultimate degradation. But at the very last minute, when Soler had him weeping with terror and begging for mercy like a girl, he had unaccountably relaxed his hold, enabling a disbelieving Lázaro to free himself, retrieve his weapon, and drive the blade into his enemy's unresisting arm. Scrambling to his feet, he had left it embedded in his bleeding flesh and run like hell.

'Some man you are!' Soler had yelled after him in triumph, compounding his sense of shame. 'I wouldn't soil myself on a pathetic coward like you. Go on, beat it, before I kill you! And I will do, too, if I see you again!'

If only he had plunged the knife into his heart! But he would have paid dearly for such short-lived satisfaction. He would have been the automatic suspect, they would have hunted him down like a dog and tried him for murder. Useless to plead self-defence, for who would believe his word against the son of Don Enrique Soler, who owned every judge and could buy any jury in the province?

As it was, a mere flesh wound was a poor revenge, rendered meaningless by his enemy's passive acceptance of it. Lázaro felt defiled, defeated, diminished, not just by the sexual assault, but by the bitter knowledge that Soler could easily have overpowered him, that he had chosen instead to make him grovel before showing his contempt by letting him go. Worst of all, he had all but accused him of being a *maricón*, like himself, the lowest of the low.

It was cold comfort to know that he would not name him as his assailant, for fear of exposure. None the less, Lázaro dared not return to Buenaventura, where his very life would be at risk. Raúl's threats and taunts still rang in his ears. *Coward!*

The omens were clear. He must shirk his duty no longer. He must turn his back on the soft, easy life that had led him to ignore the call of his murdered brother. Only then would Changó, god of thunder, be disposed to grant the favour he would ask of him. The death of Raúl Soler.

Eduardo's anti-social habit of spending whole days studying alone in his room was too normal to provoke comment, and his sudden desire to go back to school early met with little resistance, other than from his doting mother. In Lázaro's continuing mysterious absence, León drove his young stepbrother to the railway station, too preoccupied with thoughts of Celia to notice his pallor or the circles under his eyes.

'Goodbye, then,' he said, as the porter loaded the luggage. 'See you in the Easter vacation, I hope. Don't get yourself into trouble in the meantime, will you?'

'Trouble?' Eduardo looked at him vaguely, his mind far away.

'Celia's worried you're going to do something stupid and end up in gaol. I wouldn't rely on the old man to bail you out if I were you. You know how he feels about the rebels.'

'I can look after myself.' Eduardo reached into his pocket and produced a Colt .38 revolver. 'Anyone who tries to arrest me will have to kill me first.'

'That's a bit melodramatic, isn't it?'

'So is what they do to people in prison.'

'Listen to me, Eduardo. If you shoot a policeman, not even my father will be able to save you. And think how distressed your mother and sister will be. You can do more good by finishing your studies and becoming a doctor than by joining a bunch of half-baked revolutionaries and getting yourself shot.'

'Oh, for God's sake. I don't need a sermon, OK? Specially from someone who doesn't give a damn about anyone but himself.'

It was unlike Eduardo to be so aggressive. For all their differences, he and León had always got on well together, exchanging routine insults without malice on either side.

'What's biting you?' said León. 'Something on your mind?'

'Nothing. I just couldn't stand to stay in that house a minute longer.'

'I know the feeling. A pity you've done nothing but stay in the house all week. You know what you need?' he added, grinning. 'A girl.'

Eduardo scowled. 'That's your solution to everything, isn't it? God, you make me sick!'

'Come off that high horse of yours, for God's sake,' said León mildly. 'A bit of fun would do you the world of good.'

'Fun? Is that what you're having with Celia?'

'Celia?'

'I saw you pawing her the other day. Can't you even keep your hands off your own sister?'

'She's not my sister,' said León coldly. Damn. He might

have known this would happen, Celia was getting more careless by the minute, almost as if she wanted them to be discovered. Thank God it was only Eduardo, he thought. At least he would keep it to himself. 'Haven't you anything better to do than play peeping Tom?'

'Women. That's all you think about. You disgust me.'

'Now, wait a minute . . .'

'Have you slept with her?'

'That's none of your business.'

'You have, haven't you? I ought to lay you out.'

'That's enough! What the hell do you know about it anyway, you po-faced, snotty little virgin . . .'

'I know the difference between love and lust, which is more than can be said for y-you!'

'Eduardo . . .' León caught hold of his sleeve. 'You're crying!'

Eduardo sniffed noisily and wrenched his arm free, wiping his eyes with his cuff.

'Leave me alone!'

'Look, you've no need to worry about Celia. I promise you faithfully I won't do anything to hurt her—'

'I couldn't give a shit about Celia and I couldn't give a shit about you either! You can fuck each other's brains out for all I care!'

'But you just said . . .'

'Piss off, will you?' He hauled himself aboard the train and sat down on the opposite side of the compartment, leaving León standing on the platform, speechless. He could quite understand Eduardo's anger, but not his anguish . . .

I know the difference between love and lust . . . So that was it. He was eating his heart out over some girl and was too repressed to do anything about it. Hence the holier-than-thou tirade. His indifference to women had always struck León as a pose, an arrogant front for a profound shyness of the opposite sex, a reaction to the constant harassment of match-making mothers and their husband-hunting daughters. León sympathised, having had much the same experience himself, but there were plenty of safe, uncomplicated outlets for adolescent libido – the estate employed any number of young females, and such girls were not normally averse to granting their favours in return for some modest token of appreciation. But Eduardo was hamstrung by his high-flown ascetic principles and outdated notions of chivalry. It was typical of him to run away from temptation; he had the haggard look of a lad who had spent half the night masturbating and woken up more frustrated than before. What he needed was an older woman to take him in hand . . .

His mind flew unwillingly to Lidia. She seemed to have taken the hint, thank God, though that could be simply the result of his father being at home; the old man was a very light sleeper, and their encounters had always been confined to his absences from the house. León had hardly thought about her lately; Celia was proving a much bigger headache than her mother had ever been. The harmless, wholesome tonic had proved to be a potent drug, and an addictive one at that. The prospect of returning to Havana filled him with gloom, and yet he couldn't wait to get away, to feel safe and free again.

He arrived home just as Celia returned from the office for the midday meal; she snatched an illicit kiss in the hall, giggling at his discomfiture.

'Papá's going to be late,' she told her mother breezily. 'He's got someone with him. I do hope he won't be long. I'm ravenous.' She gave León a saucy look behind Lidia's back.

'I wish Eduardo had your appetite,' sniffed Lidia. 'He's hardly touched his food in days.'

'You know what he's like when he's studying. He has his mind on higher things.'

'And I do hate him using the train,' went on Lidia. 'There's talk of the rebels blowing up the tracks.'

'It's just as dangerous going by road,' said Celia. 'Look what happened to Raúl the other day.'

'Where is Raúl, by the way?' enquired León.

'Out riding,' said Lidia, rather sourly. 'He took a packed lunch.'

'Any sign of Lázaro yet?'

'Not a word. Emilia's still behaving like a wet dish-rag.'

'I'm beginning to think Emilia's right,' said Celia, helping herself to a piece of bread. 'That something's happened to him. I mean, why would he just disappear, walk out on a good job like that?'

Strange how indifferent she had become to other people's troubles. She ought to feel concerned for Lázaro, sorry for Emilia and his mother, but her normal sensitivity was blunted by joy. Nothing mattered any more except being in love, nothing was capable of deflating her high spirits. Already León had promised faithfully to come home again next month; if he didn't, she had warned him, she would visit him.

'Oh, good,' she said, pulling out her chair. 'There's Papá now.'

Pleasantly preoccupied, she did not immediately notice her stepfather's thunderous expression as he marched into the room; her first inkling that something was wrong was a slight blanching of Lidia's complexion, which reacted to the nuances of her husband's moods with the immediacy of a weathervane.

'Take that away,' he barked as Emilia entered with the soup tureen. 'Shut the door and stay in the kitchen and don't come back till I ring for you.' He turned on Celia. 'What are you smirking at?'

'I wasn't smirking,' mumbled Celia, suddenly feeling eight years old again.

'Leave the room. I wish to speak to León in private.'

Celia stood up, as did Lidia.

'Not you,' hissed Enrique, to his wife. 'This concerns you too. Go, Celia.'

Celia knew straight away what was coming next. *If the parents find out there will be hell to pay . . .* Somehow or other their delicious secret had been discovered, and León was about to be warned off, because she was 'still a child', because his intentions were assumed to be dishonourable, because she was his so-called sister . . . She felt a thrill of trepidation.

'No,' she heard herself saying. 'Anything you have to say to León can be said in front of me.'

'I'll be the judge of that. Now get out.'

Celia didn't move. Enrique grabbed her roughly by the arm.

'Let go of her,' snapped León. 'Celia,' he added, gently. 'Do as Papá says. I can handle this.'

'I'm staying!' said Celia, drunk with her own daring, emboldened by the astonished look in her stepfather's eyes. She had long ago ceased to answer back, unable to bear the consequences – the retaliatory chest pains, the accusations of ingratitude, the icy atmosphere that would prevail until she ate humble pie and apologised. But today she felt full of courage and strength and, above all, impatience, impatience to have all this out in the open and damn the consequences. If Papá threw León out, so much the better, she would have the perfect excuse to follow him . . .

'That's enough of your impudence, young woman!' bellowed Enrique. 'Who do you think you are, laying down the law to me? May I remind you—'

'That I'm not your daughter, that you took me in, that but for you I would have nothing? There's no need. You've never let me forget that I'm not your flesh and blood, so you can hardly object to León and me getting married!'

The ensuing perfect silence shimmered like the blanket of still hot air over the cane fields outside. Lidia's jaw dropped open, León shut his eyes, and Enrique let go of Celia's arm as if drained of strength. Suddenly all her defiance collapsed into the old, crippling concern.

'Please don't be angry, Papá,' she said. 'We would have told you before, but León thought you and Mamá wouldn't understand . . .'

Lidia shot León a look of undiluted loathing.

'How could you?' she hissed. 'How long has this been going on?'

'I asked Celia to marry me shortly before Christmas,' said León, rather woodenly. 'She accepted. We agreed to wait a couple of years. I realise that she's very young and that I'm not in a position to support her yet. I—'

'Animal!' yelled Enrique, his face purple with rage. 'Is there no limit to your baseness? You lied to me! You told me you weren't interested in her!'

Celia looked from one to the other, confused. Had Papá already challenged León? If so, why hadn't he told her?

'You seduced her behind my back,' continued Enrique, showering the tablecloth with spittle, 'when all the while you – you—'

'He didn't "seduce" me,' interrupted Celia, walking round the table and taking León's arm. 'I've been in love with him ever since I can remember. If you want to blame anyone, blame me.'

Enrique thrust himself between them and prised them apart. 'Take your filthy hands off her!' he shouted. 'This is where they really belong!' He pressed León's palms against Lidia's ample bosom, nearly knocking her over.

'Don't be shy,' he jeered, as Lidia recoiled in horror, overturning a chair. 'Why shouldn't a son share his father's taste in women?'

'I don't know what you mean,' whimpered Lidia hoarsely. Celia looked on stupidly, refusing to understand.

'Whore! Don't lie to me! I know all about your grubby little affair! I have enough evidence to divorce you and cut you off without a cent.'

'It's not true!' shrieked Lidia, turning to León. 'Tell him it's not true!'

León didn't answer. He turned and looked Celia full in the face, making her blood run cold.

'Tell me it's not true,' she said.

'Of course it's true!' roared Enrique. He withdrew an envelope from his pocket and held it aloft. 'I know you've been meeting each other in secret. I have all the evidence here, in black and white!'

'But that's not possible!' whimpered Lidia. 'We always . . . that is, we never . . .' Her voice tailed off guiltily.

'Is it true?' repeated Celia, never taking her eyes off León. 'Tell me!'

'It was true,' said León quietly, speaking to her as if there was no one else in the room. 'But it's over. It was over before I asked you to marry me.'

'Get out of my house!' roared Enrique. 'Before I kill you! And don't ever show your face here again!'

'León,' pleaded Lidia, panicking. 'Take me with you . . . Don't leave me here with him . . .'

'Don't be ridiculous,' said León icily. And then, 'Celia? Are you coming to Havana with me or not?'

Lidia began sobbing hysterically. Enrique sat down, looking suddenly very small and crumpled. Celia didn't reply, trying to find the anger that would release the writhing demons inside her.

'Please, Celia. I need to talk to you before I go.'

'There's nothing to say.'

León got hold of her arm and pulled her out into the hallway. He gripped both her shoulders tightly, hurting her. 'Listen to me. I don't know what his "evidence" is, but I swear to you it was all over between me and your mother last summer.'

'Last summer? So when did it begin?'

'Does it matter? From the first time I kissed you, I've never . . . never . . .'

'I don't believe you. Why should I believe you? No wonder you told Papá there was nothing between us. No wonder you didn't want Mamá to find out! You were afraid she'd tell on you!'

'You mustn't blame your mother. It wasn't her fault, it was mine. She was lonely and frustrated, and I . . . I felt sorry for her.'

'Like you felt sorry for me?'

'You know that's not true.'

'I don't know anything any more. I thought I knew all your faults, I thought I could cope with them, I didn't mind you being weak and lazy because I thought you were honest. And all the time you were lying to me! I *loved* you, you bastard!'

And the worst of it was, she still did. It was that which appalled her even more than his monstrous behaviour. She didn't want the truth. She wanted excuses, and more lies, she wanted to blame her mother, she wanted anything that would enable her to hold on to her happiness.

'I know I've behaved like a perfect shit, I know I should have told you. But I was scared of losing you. Come with me now. I'll get a job, we'll manage. Celia . . .'

'Let go of me.' She wrenched herself free, not trusting herself not to weaken. 'It's too late. I—'

A bloodcurdling shriek sent both of them rushing back to the dining room, to find Lidia prostrate on the floor, and Enrique standing rigid, with his back to her, staring into space.

'Celia,' moaned Lidia. 'Don't leave me. Don't leave me alone with him . . . I'm frightened. He h-hit me.'

'It's all right, Emilia,' said Celia, as the startled housekeeper appeared at the doorway. An icy calm took hold of her. No one must ever know. This would only be bearable if nobody ever found out. 'Leave this to me. Go back to the kitchen.'

Emilia, inured to matrimonial rows, shrugged and closed the door.

'It's all right, Mamá. I'm here.' Celia knelt down beside her mother and took her hand.

'It wasn't my fault,' she sobbed. 'I knew it was wrong but he wouldn't leave me alone . . .'

'Celia—' began León.

'You heard what Papá said,' she hissed, not daring to look at him. 'Get out. I never want to see you again. Don't say another word. Just go.'

He went. He went without pausing to pack, slamming out of the house and into the forecourt where his car was parked, cursing viciously under his breath. Thank God he was out of that madhouse. At least now he was a free man . . .

No he wasn't. He was more trapped than ever, he

would never be free again, he would be in hell until he got her back. One way or another, however long it took, he would get her back.

FOUR

IT WAS Frank's second experience of a honeymoon. The first, conventionally enough, had taken place after his wedding, a last-minute affair followed by a trip to Europe, not that the honeymoon had been in Europe. Frank had travelled there alone after a mere three days with his bride, the best three days of his short-lived marriage, and that wasn't saying much.

The second had been this last week with Lily. It had the same quality of postscript and prologue, of regrets in the making, of live-for-the-moment urgency. She made him feel young again, which proved, as if it needed proving, that he was getting old.

Knowing that she wasn't expected back at Addy's until the new year, Frank had suggested a leisurely cruise, stopping off at the Keys on the way, fishing, swimming, giving the poor kid the first real vacation of her life. He enjoyed making a fuss of her, enjoyed having something soft and warm to hold on to at night, justified this hazardous self-indulgence by reminding himself that it was only temporary. There was all the difference in the world between a honeymoon and a marriage, and the first was undoubtedly better without the second.

He had married Maggie in 1942; she had divorced him in 1945. In all that time they must have spent less than six weeks together. It had been one of those whirlwind wartime romances followed by a just-in-case wedding. If anything had happened to him, Maggie would have been provided for, along with any children, not that there had been any children, which perhaps was just as well. He must have seemed quite a catch in those days. A brilliant young academic, a linguist and historian, a man of passion and principles, engaged in hazardous hush-hush work that gave him an air of mystery and romance. As it happened, his liaison work with the Free French, from an office desk in London, England, had turned out to be a great deal less dangerous than the term 'intelligence' suggested, and the secret-agent skills he had learned at the training centre in Washington – silent killing, field-craft and marksmanship – had never been put to the test. The risks he had taken had been much more subtle than those which threatened life and limb, and he hadn't come a cropper till the war was technically over. War itself had been a kind of honeymoon, a prelude to the sour disenchantment of so-called peace.

He had loved Maggie more in retrospect than in reality; missing her had proved more pleasurably poignant than being with her. The same would doubtless apply to Lily. The sooner she became a memory, the sweeter that memory would be. In less than an hour he would put in to Havana and that would be that. He felt bad about leaving her, of course. Like Maggie, she seemed frail and dependent, awakened his protective instincts. Like Maggie, she would be better off without him. She was vulnerable, yes, but she was also tough, and with luck she would find herself some rich old fart who would be stupid enough to marry her. Girls like that either did exceptionally well for themselves, or ended up in the gutter, and he wanted to believe that Lily fell in the first category, not the second.

'Havana,' he said, pointing. She put a hand up to her eyes and squinted towards the harbour, her face betraying more eagerness than was good for his ego. On the port side loomed the massive ramparts of the Morro Castle, on the starboard the fort of La Punta, bulwarks against the buccaneers and invaders of old. The Spanish had always been possessive about this jewel of an island, repeatedly rejecting US offers to purchase it. But by helping to liberate Cuba from its masters, in 1898, America had shrewdly got it for free. It had been an unofficial colony ever since.

'You stay down below,' said Frank, 'while I deal with

the port officials. Addy's is just a short walk from the jetty, I'll see you to the door.'

'No,' said Lily quickly, desperate to keep Frank away from her mother. 'I share an apartment with a girlfriend, in Vedado. I'll get a cab.'

'Fine. I'll come with you.'

'I'd rather go alone. I hate goodbyes,' she added, as an afterthought, squeezing his hand.

'I'll drop by at the club one evening, next time I'm in port.' A promise Frank had no intention of keeping. He rooted in his pockets for the last of his money and gave it to her.

'For the cab,' he said. 'If you need more . . .'

'I won't need any more. Thanks a million, Frank. You've been good to me.' She put an arm around his waist and kissed his cheek. 'I'll miss you.'

'I'll miss you.'

It was disconcertingly true. He would miss seeing her face light up when he suggested some mundane treat like a shrimp dinner or a bicycle ride round Key West or skinny-dipping by moonlight. He would miss the sweet sound of her voice on the night air, and the mess she made of the cabin, and the unfamiliar sense of being needed, even if needed was just a euphemism for used. He would miss all that much more than having sex with her, needing her, using her . . . Christ, what a load of sentimental crap.

Lily went down below and changed out of her shorts into the pink gingham dress Frank had bought her. Mom must be absolutely frantic by now, she thought. She would be too relieved to see her in one piece to be angry. Although eager to reach her destination as soon as possible, Lily had seen the advantages of spinning the voyage out. The longer she stayed missing, the harder it would be for Mom to send her home and, besides, it had been fun. She hadn't had to go to bed early, or eat breakfast, or go to church, or walk the dog. Instead she had drunk beer and wine and rum, slept late, spent as long as she liked getting dressed and doing her hair and fixing her make-up. She had done whatever she liked. She had visited waterside bars and restaurants, sung for an appreciative audience of one, tasted the oft-imagined bliss of being a grown-up. She would never go back to being a child again.

Mom wouldn't send her home, not now she knew that the threat to 'run away' was for real, that she was capable of fending for herself. She wasn't, of course. She couldn't have done it without Frank, Frank who had turned up in his boat like a pirate and carried her off. She felt a bit sorry for him, knowing that he was crazy about her and all, but he would get over it. She began singing to herself, full of anticipation. *When I fall in love . . .* It would happen, for sure, in Havana. He would be young and handsome and preferably rich, but if he was poor it didn't really matter, she could always ask Mom for money. He would be a musician, or a professional card-player, or a poet. Something unconventional and exciting, not some boring adult version of the 'nice boys' she had met last summer. In Havana all her dreams would come true.

She just hoped Frank didn't turn up at Addy's one night and ask her mother about a redhead called Lily. She didn't want him to find out that she wasn't an orphan, or a singer, or eighteen years old. Or Mom to hear the dreadful whoppers she had told about Grandma. Being much the same age, they would probably gang up against her. On the other hand, once Mom gave her a job, the whoppers wouldn't matter any more.

She packed her belongings – all emergency purchases made by Frank prior to their departure – into the box the dress had come in. Tomorrow Mom would take her out and buy her a whole new wardrobe. And then soon she would be fitted for the slinky spangled dress she would wear to make her début. Mom wouldn't say, 'Wash all that muck off your face' or bawl her out for wearing perfume. She wouldn't dare.

Havana harbour opened its narrow jaws and sucked in the *Never Again* like a snake swallowing its prey. The city hung above them like a giant canvas daubed with whites and blues and yellows, as if to match the sun and sky, its hot red roofs blurring in the haze, its steeples rising proudly like so many swords held aloft. It all looked instantly familiar, it felt like coming home. Somewhere in the distance Lily fancied she could hear drums and guitar and maracas, belting out the raucous street serenades that had once lulled her into sleep. Above her, gulls and cormorants and terns clamoured as if in greeting, and pelicans, roosting on the pilings, grinned a benign welcome.

After they had tied up at the jetty, Lily stayed out of sight while Frank began talking to a man in rapid Spanish, a language which Lily had picked up as a child from her ever-changing minders, and the only subject she had ever shown an interest in at school, in readiness for this day. She couldn't catch what he was saying, but there didn't seem to be any problem because a few moments later Frank called down to her to come out now and helped her ashore.

Lily inhaled the hot, pungent smell of the harbour, a mixture of fish and creosote and diesel. The dockside was swarming with life – policemen, port officials, vendors trundling pushcarts and sailors – but the crowd seemed to render her invisible, because no one asked to look inside her cardboard box or inspect any papers.

'See you around, then,' said Frank, as they reached the taxi rank.

'Yes,' said Lily. Suddenly she felt frightened. He had taken care of her, and now he was going away.

'Sure you don't want me to see you home?'

'No need. Goodbye, then.'

It was so much easier to fake emotion than to show it. For the last week she had pretended passion, without any trouble at all, and now that she was actually *feeling* something, she found herself unable to express it. She had intended to shed a few tears, because the script required it, but her eyes stayed stubbornly dry, defying her talents as a performer, betraying the genuine distress within.

She kissed him quickly on each cheek. Taking his lead from her, he kept his embrace light, casual.

'I meant to buy you a little something but I was running short of cash.'

He wasn't crazy about her at all, she thought, with a dismal flash of insight. He was just like Mom at heart. She had liked him giving her things, but presents were always a substitute for something better. 'You know how much I love you, sweetheart,' Mom would say, just before she deserted her yet again, and there would always be some extravagant gift to ease the moment of parting. On reflection, she was glad that Frank had not bought her anything. She might not be in love with him, but she wanted to cling to the delusion that he cared about her, that he wasn't just buying her off.

'That's OK. So long.'

The cab driver took her box and put it in the trunk; Lily got inside, anxious now to be away, and murmured her mother's address in a low voice, so that Frank wouldn't hear it. He raised a valedictory hand as the car took off at breakneck speed.

As a child, Lily had lived in the old part of the city. Her memories were of dark, narrow, noisy streets, overlooked by rusty wrought-iron balconies, shaded by striped awnings and thronged with ambling, unhurried humanity of every hue. But instead of plunging into the familiar crowded thoroughfares leading off from the harbour, the cab shot off along the Malecon, the wide boulevard which ran the length of the sea wall, towards the spacious serenity of the suburbs, where new hotels and apartment blocks looked down on rows of pastel-painted Spanish-colonial houses with columns and arches and stone balustrades. A few minutes later the driver turned left into a broad avenue lined with spreading banyan trees and drew up in front of a four-storey building screened by royal palms and flowering shrubs. A uniformed commissionaire stood guard outside its gleaming plate-glass doors; Lily paid off the cab and approached him regally, clutching her rather battered cardboard box. He tipped his hat and asked which apartment she wanted.

'Number seventeen,' she said, pleased with herself that she had understood him. 'Señora Herbert.'

'The Señora isn't at home. Is she expecting you?'

'Yes. I'm her daughter.'

'Her daughter?' He seemed surprised.

'That's right,' affirmed Lily haughtily. 'I have come from the United States to visit her.'

The doorman inclined his head in a stiff bow and held the door wide, giving access to a cool, air-conditioned lobby full of mirrors and potted plants.

'Then please go up. Her . . . her maid will let you in.' He pressed the elevator button for her, still looking at her oddly. Lily was rather annoyed that Mom wasn't sitting at home, anxiously waiting for her. She was probably at that precious new casino of hers, supervising the builders, not concerned about her at all. Still, it would give her time to freshen up before she got back. She couldn't wait to take a leisurely bubble bath and help herself to some fresh clothes from her mother's wardrobe. It would be nice to sleep in a proper bed tonight.

She got out at the top floor, still slightly giddy from being on dry land again, and pressed boldly on the doorbell which was answered instantly by a small, squat, swarthy woman wearing a black dress and a white apron and cap.

'Señora Herbert is expecting me,' announced Lily. 'I'm her daughter. I have come from America to visit her.'

The woman looked at her stupidly; Lily said it again, extra slowly and clearly. Half-way through her reprise, a man appeared in the hallway, looking at her curiously over the maid's shoulder.

Lily tailed off in mid-sentence. It was him. He was already here, waiting for her. The most handsome man she had ever seen in her life. A bit like James Dean, with dark golden hair and blue eyes you could die for . . .

'I've come to see my mother,' faltered Lily, staring at him, lapsing into English. 'Mrs Herbert.'

He stared right back, making her blush. 'You're . . .

you're Addy's *daughter*?' he said, replying in the same language. Lily nodded, still transfixed, taking his open-mouthed expression for admiration. He must have felt it too, she thought dreamily.

'I'm sorry,' he said, recovering himself. 'I never realised that she had one. You'd better come in.'

She followed him into the living room, which was all in pale blue, with floors as white and shiny as a frozen lake. The furniture was modern, expensive-looking, like the kind of thing you saw in magazines, not old-fashioned stuff like Grandma had, and there were vases of flowers everywhere, filling the air with their scent. Lily inhaled luxuriously. Grandma's apartment smelt of polish and embrocation and flatulent, overfed dog. A sense of well-being restored some of her composure. She arranged herself prettily on a blue shot-silk divan.

'Addy has gone to St Petersburg, to visit her mother,' said the man, rather awkwardly, still looking at her strangely. He can't take his eyes off me, thought Lily, thrilled. 'Did you say she was expecting you?'

'Er . . . not exactly,' said Lily, smoothing her skirt. 'She couldn't come home for Christmas this year, so I thought I'd spend the New Year with her instead. It was meant to be a surprise.' It would sound childish to say she had run away. Grandma must have sent for Mom, thought Lily, repressing a chortle of glee. The pair of them must be crazy with worry by now. Serve them both right.

'I see. Then perhaps we'd better call her, to let her know you're here.' He said something to the maid, who consulted a leather-bound pad by the telephone, dialled the operator, and recited Grandma's number in Spanish.

Belatedly, Lily wondered what this man was doing in Mom's apartment while she was away. As if reading her thoughts he said, extending a hand, 'I'm León Soler. A business associate of your mother's.'

'Lily Herbert,' said Lily, smiling the smile that had worked so well with Frank. He didn't return it and his grip was disappointingly brief. She wondered what he meant by 'business associate'. It suggested a fat man in a suit smoking a cigar. 'What part of the States are you from, Mr Soler?'

'I'm not,' he said. 'I'm from Oriente. I've just got back from spending Christmas there. In fact,' he added, rather hurriedly, 'I didn't realise your mother was going to be away. I called round on the off-chance, just before you arrived.'

'Are you in the entertainment business too?' enquired Lily hopefully.

'I'm an artist. I'm painting a mural for your mother's new casino, the Herradura.'

Lily caught her breath. He was tall and handsome and he was an artist too! This was definitely fate.

'No answer, Señor,' said the maid, displaying the receiver as if to show that it was empty.

'Try again in ten minutes,' he said. 'Fetch some coffee.' And then, turning to Lily, 'How old are you?' The question rather broke the spell.

'Eighteen. I mean . . . sixteen.' Pointless to lie, he would find out the truth from Mom.

'Why didn't you tell your mother you were coming?'

'It was a sudden impulse. Some friends of mine brought me on their yacht. We had such a delightful voyage. Do you know Key West? You'd simply adore it. There's an artists' colony there . . .'

The maid reappeared with a tray and handed her a minute cup. There was no milk or sugar and Lily didn't like to ask for any. She took a sip of strong thick coffee, relieved to find that it was already sweetened.

'Who normally takes care of you?' persisted León Soler, ignoring this attempt at small talk. Why was he suddenly talking to her like a kid? thought Lily crossly. If only she really was eighteen!

'I'm at boarding school,' she admitted, reluctantly.

'Do your teachers know you're here?'

'No. I spend the vacations with my grandmother, in St Pete's.'

'Does she know you're here?'

'No,' said Lily with a toss of the head, going on the

defensive. 'She wouldn't have let me come. She says Havana is no place for children. Well, I'm not a child any more.'

To demonstrate, she uncrossed her legs and crossed them again, wriggling the upper part of her body as she did so, thrusting her bosom forward. Such small gestures were enough to bring a gleam to Frank's eye, it was as easy as flicking a switch. But León Soler didn't seem impressed. The stare which she had taken at first for admiration had hardened into a steely, critical gaze which made her squirm.

'No wonder your mother rushed off like that. She must be out of her mind with worry.'

'There was no need for her to worry,' said Lily, airily. 'I can take care of myself.'

'So it seems. Is that all the luggage you've brought with you?'

'I thought I could buy more clothes when I got here. I didn't have much time to pack.'

He lit a cigarette from the silver box on the coffee table without offering her one, or asking her permission. Rather piqued, Lily helped herself.

'Can you give me a light?' she purred, getting up and leaning over him, flooding him with her perfume. She took hold of his hand and lit her cigarette from the glowing end of his, glad to have perfected this little trick over the last week. It was an artist's hand, with long tapering fingers. Frank's hands were hard and leathery from handling ropes, rough against her skin. This one was soft, but firm as well, beautiful, like the rest of him. She had touched him now, and he hadn't disappeared. He was real.

'Does your mother know you smoke?' he demanded, spoiling the moment.

'Why shouldn't I? She does.'

'María!' he called, raising his voice. 'Try that number again.'

The maid scurried to do his bidding, with no more success than the last time. León Soler fished a notebook out of his pocket and wrote down the number. Then he beckoned María into the hallway, shutting the door behind him; Lily could hear them talking in low voices. She seized this opportunity to get out her compact and touch up her lipstick. God, her hair was a mess. A few minutes later, León reappeared.

'You must be tired after your voyage,' he said. 'I'd better leave you to get some rest. María will show you to your room. Your mother will be very relieved to find out where you are. Nice to have met you. Goodbye.'

Lily held our her hand; he shook it briskly, the way he might have shaken hands with a man.

'I'll tell her you called,' she said pertly. 'I expect we'll meet again soon.'

'Perhaps.' He saw himself out, leaving Lily alone with María, who ushered her into a spacious bedroom done up in various shades of yellow. There was a pale lemon counterpane on the bed and a corn-coloured silk lampshade overhead, covered in the same fabric as the curtains. The rugs either side of the bed were of a burnt ochre and the wallpaper was a riot of yellow flowers. Lily had always hated yellow. Her mother knew that. That she had chosen it for the guest room was proof that she had never intended to invite her here.

María indicated the closet and the chest of drawers and the switch for the air conditioning, and showed her where the bathroom was, jabbering all the while.

'I don't like this room,' said Lily petulantly, in Spanish. 'Is there a different one?'

María made a gesture of apology and shook her head. Undeterred Lily went to open the door next to hers. It was locked.

'It's locked,' said María, unnecessarily, shrugging to indicate that she did not have the key. Lily tried another room, but that too was locked. The next one, however, opened straight away.

'My room,' said María. It was small, with a single bed, no bigger than a boxroom. 'I will show you round the apartment,' she added, helpfully, leading Lily first into the fitted kitchen, which wasn't remotely interesting, then into the dining room adjoining it, dominated by a long white lacquered table adorned by a bowl of vivid orchids. A portrait of her mother as a young woman hung on the wall, and Lily looked round for a photograph of herself, but there wasn't one, even though she had sent her one quite recently, a studio pose taken on her sixteenth birthday. Presumably Mom kept it by her bedside, or on her dressing table. She must have locked her door to stop the maid stealing her jewellery while she was away.

'I will run you a bath,' said María, speaking extra slowly for her benefit, endorsing her words with unnecessary sign language, fuelling Lily's irritation. She was rather fat, with a wart and bad teeth. Lily wondered why her mother chose to employ such an ugly woman. She returned to the yellow bedroom and undressed, annoyed not to have access to her mother's clothes. There was nothing in the cardboard box except some underwear and the shorts and blouse she had been wearing when she took flight. Presumably Mom had her own bathroom, because the one next door to Lily's room had nothing in the cabinet over the mirror except a few spare bars of soap and tubes of toothpaste, and there was no bubble bath. Mom always used bubble bath.

Lily watched the tub fill with plain clear water. There wasn't even any shampoo. At school you weren't allowed bubble bath, so she used shampoo instead; it worked nearly as well. If she washed her hair with ordinary soap, it would be like straw.

'María,' she called, draping herself in a towel. 'Do you have any shampoo?' She indicated her hair, stiff and dull from the salt air. No wonder León Soler hadn't looked twice at her. He was an artist, and artists noticed things like dirty hair. She had done her best to keep it nice on the boat, but Frank would keep mussing it up.

María disappeared briefly and returned with a large bottle of shampoo, the same kind Mom always used. Had she made María a present of it, or had María got a key to her room? And if she had the key, why hadn't she let Lily into it?

'And some bubble bath, *por favor,*' added Lily, mimicking a pouring motion beneath the tap. She nodded helpfully and scuttled off. Lily peeped outside briefly in time to see her unlock the door of her mother's room, and promptly followed her inside. María, emerging from the *en suite* bathroom, seemed panic-stricken to see her. Perhaps she wasn't supposed to have the key, perhaps she had had it copied, with some criminal intent.

That did not concern Lily now. Glad to have outwitted her, she flung open the door of Addy's closet.

It was a large, walk-in affair, lined with sequinned full-length evening gowns, low-cut cocktail dresses, silk blouses, skirts, jackets and furs, with rows of shoes neatly arranged on racks, dozens and dozens of pairs, all with high spindly heels, some in silver or gold. Excited, Lily selected a black strapless dress with a beaded bodice, held it up against herself, and turned in search of the nearest full-length mirror.

It was then that she saw the rail of men's clothes. Suits, jackets, pants, a white tuxedo, a special hanger for ties, and a stack of folded shirts on a shelf above. So that was why her mother had never invited her. She was living with some man!

'Señorita . . .' began María helplessly, wringing her hands. Ignoring her, Lily strode into the bathroom. Sure enough, there was a razor and a stick of shaving soap by the basin. She shuddered, remembering the succession of 'uncles' who had blighted her childhood. She had hated all of them, because as soon as they arrived she would be sent out for a walk with her nursemaid, or banished to her room, clutching a candy bar, and then, as now, her mother's door had been locked against her.

That was why she had sent her to Grandma. She had got in the way. She imagined some ugly, whiskery old man – they had all seemed terribly old – using that razor, opening the closet door, getting into that bed . . .

María was prattling on about her bath getting cold, but

Lily was still staring at the bed, a four-poster with a lace canopy above it. There was a photograph on the bedside table in a silver frame. Not the one of her on her sixteenth birthday, oh no. It was a picture of her mother, arm in arm with a man, the man. And he wasn't ugly or whiskery or old.

Lily fled and shut herself into the bathroom, slamming both doors behind her. Suddenly everything made sense. Her mother didn't want her to know about León, she wanted to keep him all to herself. 'I didn't realise Addy had a daughter,' he had said. That was why there were no photographs of her anywhere. It was as if she didn't exist, as if she'd never been born.

Her fury was spiked with bitter triumph at having caught her mother out. This was why she had come home at vacations, instead of letting Lily visit her. She was afraid that León would fall in love with her, because she was younger and more beautiful. Lily knew that Mom was scared of getting old, like Grandma. She would spend hours at her dressing table, applying her make-up, and went to bed at night plastered in cold cream, to prevent wrinkles.

Lily lay back in the hot water, letting her hair fan out, remembering all the lies Mom had told her. That she couldn't wait to leave Havana, that she was so lonely and miserable without her girl. She hadn't believed her, of course, but there was all the difference in the world between not believing her and finding out the truth. The truth was that the spare room was done out in yellow, and that her mother lived with a young, handsome man. The truth was that Mom didn't want her any more than Grandma wanted her, or the schools wanted her. Probably Frank didn't really want her either. Frank wanted sex, Grandma and the schools wanted money, Mom wanted León all to herself. And she, Lily, had nothing, nobody.

She tried to cry and couldn't. She was too upset, and besides there wasn't any point in crying when there was no one to see the tears. She poured half a bottle of shampoo over her head, spinning flecks of foam all over the bathroom, immersing her head beneath the water, wondering what it felt like to breathe it in. That would teach Mom a lesson, if she drowned herself, if she died. But you couldn't die if you'd never really existed. From now on she would exist with a vengeance, she would make her presence known.

She got out of the bath and dried herself carefully, wiping away the steam on the mirror so that she could see herself, but the image was fogged, ghost-like, mocking her resolution. You only exist through somebody else, even God wouldn't exist unless people believed in him. Or the devil, come to that. If you couldn't get people to love you, making them angry with you was the next best thing.

María had locked her mother's door again, but this time she didn't dare not open it on demand. Lily helped herself to the black beaded dress and a wired strapless half-cup bra, which pushed her breasts upwards, brimming over the low neckline. She found some black nylons and squashed her feet into too-small sling-backed shoes. She picked out a pair of long, dangling diamanté earrings with a matching pendant and helped herself liberally to face powder, rouge, lipstick and scent. Her wet hair rather spoiled the effect, so she hid it under a black silk turban before swanning into the hall, resplendent in all her finery.

María gaped when she saw her.

'I'm hungry,' said Lily, imperiously. 'Bring me something to eat and a bottle of wine.'

She sat herself down at the head of the long table in the dining room, imagining León at the other end and half a dozen glittering guests between them, all thinking what a beautiful couple they made. How jealous Mom would be! She would try everything to come between them, but nothing would work, because they were made for each other. By stealing him, she would steal her mother's power, by stealing him, she would *become* her mother, the mother she admired and envied, the mother whose love she had sought in vain. Poor Mom. Lily would be kind to her. She would send her home to live with Grandma, and from time to time she would visit and give her nice presents, but she wouldn't invite her to Havana, because she would be too busy. And she would never send away her daughter, León's daughter, never part with that ultimate proof of her own existence.

María covered the table with a starched cloth, and laid it with silver cutlery and cut glass. She poured iced water from a matching jug, and red wine from a crystal decanter. Lily had never tasted wine till last week and was determined to get to like it – Grandma disapproved of both alcohol and tobacco, making their bitter flavour seem sweet. María brought her a bowl of soup and a basket of bread. The soup had beans and rice in it, and shreds of chicken, and other unidentifiable bits and pieces, and although it was good, Lily left half of it, just for the pleasure of not having to clear her plate. A dish of cold cuts followed, pork and sausage and ham, which she rejected, demanding an omelette instead. It was the best omelette she had ever tasted, unctuous and creamy, not hard and leathery like Grandma made, but seeing the anxious look on María's face, she pushed the plate to one side after a couple of mouthfuls. There was fresh fruit for desert – mangoes, pomegranates and figs – but they were all too messy to eat, so Lily ignored them and poured herself another glass of wine, enjoying the warm glow it gave her inside. Some of the things Frank had asked her to do would have been impossible but for the wine she had drunk beforehand – and sometimes afterwards as well, surreptitiously while he snored, to take away the taste of his thing and the stuff that squirted out of it.

Every now and again, she heard the ping of the telephone being lifted in the next room and María earnestly repeating Grandma's number. She imagined Mom and Grandma trying to blame each other for what had happened. She had often heard them quarrelling in the night, when they thought she was asleep. 'You spoil the child!'

Grandma would complain. 'What use is it me trying to raise her right if you come here and upset everything!' And Mom shouting back, '*I'm* her mother, not you! I love her more than you ever did me! *You* love her more than you ever did me!' She had enjoyed them fighting over her, enjoyed playing them off against each other. She hoped they were shouting at each other now, blaming each other, and so they should.

She had just poured her third glass of wine when the phone started to ring, and a few moments later María appeared and said that the Señora was on the line. Lily took her time, wiping the corners of her mouth on the linen napkin, brushing the crumbs off the black dress, checking that no stray tufts of hair had escaped from the turban.

'Lily?' Her mother's voice was strained, tearful.

'Hi, Mom,' said Lily casually.

'Thank God. Thank God.' She broke into stormy sobs, the same sobs she used when it was time to go back to Havana. 'Are you all right, sweetheart?'

Lily fell to ferocious inspection of her bitten-down fingernails. Hearing her Mom cry always made her want to cry as well, but the wanting to blocked the tears somewhere deep down, producing a gnawing pain at the pit of her stomach.

'I'm fine.'

'León – Señor Soler just telephoned me. He said you'd been on a yacht.'

'That's right. Some friends offered me a ride.'

'What friends?'

'No one you know. I'm not going back to Grandma, I'm not going back to school. If you don't want me here, there are plenty of other places I can go. The yacht's still there in the harbour, my friends are heading for Mexico, they want me to go with them. If you don't want me, say so, and I'll leave right now, and you won't see me ever again.'

There was a short silence.

'Don't be like that, darling. You're welcome, you're

more than welcome. I can't wait to show you Havana and take you shopping and buy you lots of nice clothes. María will look after you. She'll buy you anything you need and get you all your meals and do all your laundry . . .'

'When are you coming home?'

'Lily . . . your Grandma's in the hospital, I've been there with her all day. She's very sick. They think . . . they think she might die.'

'What's wrong with her?'

'She had a stroke, sweetheart.' The pain in Lily's gut burrowed deeper, making her bite her lip. 'But you mustn't blame yourself. It wasn't your fault. She's getting old.'

Lily didn't answer. She would rather Mom had said that it *was* her fault, so that she could deny it.

'It was mine,' continued her mother. 'I should have known, I should have . . . Listen, darling.' She blew her nose. 'I have to stay here for a while, I can't leave Grandma right now. But I've asked Señor Soler to look after you till I get back. He'll take you out and make sure you have a nice time. Honey, whatever you do, don't go out on your own. Havana is full of bad people, and very dangerous at night. Don't go anywhere without María or Señor Soler. Promise me.'

So 'Señor Soler' was going to 'look after her', was he? Which just proved that Mom didn't see her as competition, that she still thought of her as a child . . .

'I promise.'

'I love you, sweetheart. I love you so much. You won't run away again, will you? You won't go to Mexico, to punish me?'

'No,' mumbled Lily, swallowing the lump of mucus at the back of her throat, groping for her anger like a lifeline. She would punish her by staying.

'Papá?' Silence and then a hideous strangled sob. Celia took a deep breath. 'I rang the Santiago office, but they said you hadn't been in. And the hotel said you weren't taking any calls. I had to tell them there was an emergency.'

'I don't want to talk to anyone. Including you. What time is it?'

'Eight o'clock. I hope I didn't wake you. I'm phoning from the extension in the den. I wanted to catch you before I went to work. Grinding starts today, remember.' She tried to keep the reproach out of her voice.

Silence, punctuated by heavy, squeaky breathing.

'Are you ill? Have you seen the doctor?'

'What can a doctor do for me? I'm ready to die, the sooner the better.'

'Papá, I'd come down there to see you, but Mamá's not well either. I can't leave her.'

'What . . . what have you told Raúl?'

'That León went back to Havana early. That you were called to Santiago on business and that Mama's got a migraine.'

He began crying like a baby. 'I should have killed him,' he seethed. 'He . . . he didn't touch you, did he?'

Celia gulped. 'Not in the way you mean,' she lied.

'You're still a virgin?'

'Of course.'

'Thank God for that. How's . . . how's your mother?'

Lidia was holed up in her room like a wounded animal in a burrow, refusing food and threatening suicide.

'Terribly upset. I'm very worried about her. You mustn't blame her, Papá. It was all León's fault—'

'You think I would turn her out, wear my horns in public? My first wife made me a laughing stock, I can't go through all that again. Not in front of Raúl.'

Celia offered up a silent prayer of relief. As long as none of this came out, all might yet be well. Papá would never speak to León again, but León was already a black sheep, people would not be surprised if he ceased to visit.

'Besides,' sniffed Enrique, 'if your mother left, she'd take you with her. You'd turn your back on me as soon as she said the word.'

'Papá—'

He hung up abruptly. 'Damn you,' hissed Celia, under her breath. Her patience was stretched to breaking point. Controlling herself, she replaced the receiver, collected a breakfast tray from Emilia, and went back upstairs into her mother's room. Lidia was awake, staring sightlessly at the ceiling. Celia pulled back the mosquito netting and poured her a cup of coffee.

'I've just got through to Papá,' she said brightly, sitting on the side of the bed and taking her mother's hand. 'Everything's going to be all right. There's not going to be a divorce, there's not going to be any scandal. No one will ever find out.'

'Emilia . . .'

'Emilia doesn't suspect a thing, she's well used to you two quarrelling. And neither does Raúl. In a few days, Papá will come home and we can put all this behind us.' Thank God Eduardo wasn't here. It would kill Mamá if he ever found out. Celia had hoped that she would perk up at the news of this reprieve. But Lidia just looked at her blankly and repeated the now familiar refrain.

'He pestered me and pestered me. And once I gave in, he threatened to tell Enrique if I refused him . . . you do believe me, don't you?'

Celia wasn't sure that she did. She could still see Lidia clutching to León's arm and saying, 'Don't leave me. Please take me with you.' It wasn't just fear or shame that was eating her up like this – it was a sense of loss, the same sense of loss that was burrowing away at Celia's guts like a maggot. Lidia had loved him too. Probably she still did.

'Men are all the same,' continued Lidia. 'All they're interested in is sex. They'll lie and flatter and promise you anything, just to get you into bed . . . We're both victims, can't you see that? You don't hate me, do you? Do you?'

If only she could. It would make things so much easier.

'Of course I don't hate you.'

'Then let me have my sleeping pills,' she pleaded, like a child begging for ice-cream.

'But you've only just woken up!'

'Please, Celia. I can't bear the thought of lying here in torment all day.'

'Then get up. Go into town, do some shopping . . .'

'No. I don't feel well enough. If you won't give me one, I'll send Emilia round to the doctor's to fetch some more and I'll take the lot!'

Following a similar, earlier threat, Celia had confiscated her mother's supply. But it seemed cruel to deny her the relief she craved. She went to her room, unlocked her bureau drawer, and returned with a solitary tablet. Lidia sat up in bed and gulped it down with her coffee.

'I wish I was dead,' she groaned, lying down again. 'I wish I'd never been born.'

'Don't talk like that,' said Celia, quelling a surge of irritation. Here she was, dispensing sympathy to both Mamá and Papá, and not once had it occurred to either of them that she too might be suffering, that she too was in need of comfort and support. Suppose she had taken to her bed, gone to pieces as they had done? Who would be left to cover up, to lie and smile and pretend?

She sat with her mother till the pill took effect, and went down to join Raúl for breakfast.

'I hope your mother's feeling better this morning?' he said, rising to greet her.

'Not really. These migraines of hers are very severe. They often last a week or more.'

'If I were a sensitive soul, I would think that people were trying to avoid me. First my father rushes off to Santiago, then León goes back to Havana without a word . . .'

How brilliantly his plan had worked! It had been quite pathetically easy to bribe that grubby private eye into giving false – but essentially true – information. Whether his father divorced Lidia or not, he would surely not leave her in charge of the purse strings once he was dead. Nor would he allow León to inherit. Everything was going according to plan. And yet his triumph was marred, unexpectedly, by the sight of Celia bravely concealing her pain. She must, in her naïveté, have truly loved his brother.

'I told you, that's typical of him,' said Celia. 'He does everything on the spur of the moment. And he never stays long. He gets terribly bored here, the same as Eduardo. Everyone pleases themselves in this house.'

'Everyone except you.'

'Nonsense. I assure you, I'm every bit as selfish as everybody else. I'm just better at hiding it, that's all.'

'If I'm outstaying my welcome, I wish you'd tell me.'

'Of course you're not.' If only he would stop asking questions, she thought. Every nerve in her body, every cell in her brain, screamed with agony, and she had to sit here, pouring coffee and making small talk and being the perfect hostess.

Raúl reached across the table and took hold of her hand.

'Something's wrong, I can tell. Why aren't you eating anything?'

'I had something upstairs earlier with Mamá. Nothing's wrong. I always feel a bit flat after Christmas. With León and Eduardo gone, the place always seems very quiet. And with Mamá being ill, and Papá away, I'm afraid you must find it rather dull.'

'Not while you're still here. Can I join you again today? I always used to look forward to the first day of grinding.'

'So did I. I mean, so do I. Naturally, it's more worrying this year, with all the rebel activity and so on.'

'Specially with your brother in the thick of it.'

'He told you?'

'In confidence, yes. I warned him not to do anything stupid. With this latest spate of bombings, the police will be out for blood. Have you seen the paper yet?' He handed it to her. 'Several students were rounded up last night.'

Celia felt a stab of alarm. Was that why Eduardo had gone back to school early? To keep some rendezvous with his revolutionary friends?

'Don't say anything to Papá. If he knew about Eduardo it would be the last straw.' She bit her lip. 'That is, he'd be bound to take it personally.'

'Naturally. No doubt the rebels would like to see his fields in flames. Which makes it all the more inconsiderate of him to leave you alone here for days on end. He takes you completely for granted. It would serve him right if you upped and left.'

'I'm used to being taken for granted. And anyway, where would I go?'

'Anywhere you like.'

'I've no money and no qualifications. And besides, I like it here. I enjoy my job, lots of girls would envy me.'

She spoke irritably, angrily even, torn between the need to hide and the urge to flee. What little self-esteem she still possessed was vested in her work, her social status, her identity as the boss's daughter, the things she had once held cheap. She would have sacrificed all those privileges for León, but she would not give them up for nothing. She was trapped by pride, by a sense of duty, but most of all by fear, preferring to cling to the shipwreck than strike out for an unseen shore.

'You've no money?' he echoed, surprised. 'I never realised the old man was a miser.'

'On the contrary, he's very generous. If I want something, I only have to ask for it.'

'Except freedom and independence. Eduardo told me you wanted to go to college and he wouldn't let you.'

'It wasn't quite like that. He asked me to join the business, and I said yes.'

'Because he made you feel guilty and ungrateful?'

'Because it was a chance to earn my keep.'

'Why should you? Nobody else does. I'm surprised at León. He should have taken your side against Papá instead of letting you shoulder his responsibilities. If you like, I'll talk to the old boy myself. After all, I've got nothing to lose.'

'It's very nice of you to offer. But I'm really quite content.'

She didn't want kind words and sympathy and offers of moral support, not from him. It could only be a matter of time before Papá rewrote his will in Raúl's favour. Her mother's predictions had come true, she reflected, without Raúl having to lift a finger; Lidia and León had handed Buenaventura to him on a plate, whether he wanted it or not.

She rose from the table and took the jacket of her plaid costume off the back of her chair. Raúl stood up and helped her on with it. She shivered as his hands brushed against her shoulders, remembering what Emilia had said about him bringing bad luck. Ridiculous, of course. León and her mother had been having their affair long before Raúl came on the scene. This had never been a happy home. The Soler marriage had been a time bomb, waiting to explode. León had always been selfish and irresponsible. And she, Celia, had always been a stooge.

Raúl offered her his damaged arm and they walked out towards the waiting car; he had scorned to wear a sling. Yesterday he had asked her to renew the bandage for him; she had looked at the row of neat stitches puckering the flesh and envied him his ability to bear pain, wished that her own wound could be sewn up with twine and left to heal itself. The important thing was to keep busy, to occupy her mind with other things. Today she would visit the mill to see the first of the cane disappear between the giant rollers. She would look on intently while the sugar master tested the juice and pronounced on the likely yield, she would watch while the syrup was boiled and skimmed, nod approval when the first batch of dry white sugar emerged from the centrifuge, ready to be packed and transported. And all the time her mind would be whirling, boiling, hissing, as if trying to burst out of the confines of her skull.

Later León would phone her at the office, as usual, and she would cut him off, not wanting to hear his excuses and explanations, dreading the words she had once longed to hear. 'Come to Havana now, right away.

I'm waiting for you . . .' All this was quite bad enough without temptation too.

She stumbled as she got out of the car, dizzy from lack of sleep. Perhaps tonight she would take one of her mother's pills, rather than lie awake reliving those moments of tainted joy. Had he done *that* with her mother, and *that* and *that*? She supposed he must have done. Presumably everybody did the same things with everybody, there was nothing special or new or exclusive about any of it. And her mother would have cried out, as she had cried out, and León would have covered her mouth with his to silence her and reminded her to be quiet, in case anybody heard, in case she, Celia, heard. God, how she hated him. So why couldn't she stop loving him?

They arrived at the mill just as the first train-load of cut cane was being unloaded. The chief engineer greeted Celia with his usual air of patronising respect, slighted, perhaps, that Don Enrique should be absent on the first day of grinding. The trucks were uncoupled and pulled by winch and hawser onto the hydraulic lift, which tilted, tipping the thick stalks onto the waiting conveyor belt. Celia followed their progress as they passed under a set of revolving blades, emerging as a mass of giant splinters, ready for the ruthless, greedy rollers which would drain them of every last vestige of juice, reducing them to firewood, fuel for the giant boilers which would transform sap to syrup and syrup to crystals.

Like the cane she had been torn apart and crushed and squeezed dry. She felt limp, exhausted, deafened by the din of the machines, faint with the heat from the furnaces and the sickly smell of raw sugar. She wanted to go somewhere cool and quiet where she could be alone, but she smiled and spoke and answered Raúl's questions, explaining the new machinery which had recently been installed, fighting the pounding pain in her head and the waves of nausea rising from her empty stomach.

The juice was being pumped into the boilers now,

ready for clarification. A precise quantity of lime was added to coagulate the impurities, creating a thick sludge to be drained off to fertilise next year's crop.

'These clarifying pans are new since your day,' she said, as the clear amber liquid flowed into the first of the evaporators. 'You can watch the whole process through these glass panels. The vacuum pans and the centrifuges are due for replacement next year. Papá has ordered the latest American machinery.'

'That must come expensive.'

'It will pay for itself in five years. One has to plan well ahead.'

Five years. In five years she would look back on all this and find that it didn't hurt any more. In five years León would have married some rich Havana beauty whom he would deceive without compunction, as he had deceived her without compunction, and her mother, and his mistress, and no doubt countless others. In five years, or three, or one, or less, Papá would probably be dead, and Raúl the master of Buenaventura. What would become of Mamá then? What would become of Eduardo? What would become of—

'Celia!'

Raúl's voice seemed to come from a long way off. She was lying on the stone floor, with no memory of how she had got there. He was dabbing her forehead with a damp handkerchief and people were standing all around her, gaping. Her head ached more than ever.

'Don't get up,' said Raúl. 'I'll carry you to the car. You're ill.'

'I'm all right,' insisted Celia, scrambling to her feet, appalled to have made such a spectacle of herself. Someone approached with a glass of iced *guarapo*, freshly pressed cane juice from the stall outside which served refreshments to the workers. She took a sip of the cold, grassy-flavoured liquid. 'It's just the heat in here,' she said, smiling her thanks. 'I think I'll go and sit down for a bit. Excuse me.'

She began walking unsteadily out of the mill and

towards the office building. Raúl took her arm.

'Don't be so stubborn,' he said. 'You shouldn't be at work today. You must go home, to bed. You're ill.'

'Nonsense. I just need a couple of aspirin. Please go back and take my place. It's traditional for a member of the family to be there, everyone expects it.'

'I don't count as a member of the family,' he said, following her into the office. 'I only came today to keep an eye on you. I knew you weren't well.'

'I'm perfectly well,' snapped Celia, dreading kindness and concern. Kindness and concern would reduce her to a gibbering wreck. She poured herself some water from the carafe on her desk and tipped two Alka-Seltzers into it. They fizzed loudly, making the liquid spit, showering tiny droplets onto the polished wood. Raúl sat down opposite her, looking at her intently.

'Please don't stare at me like that,' said Celia, avoiding his eye, keeping her gaze fixed on the two white discs as they trembled and heaved. 'It makes me uncomfortable.'

'Forgive me,' he said. 'I was just thinking how like Eduardo you are.'

'I know,' she acknowledged wearily. 'Everyone comments on it.'

'I didn't mean just your looks. I was thinking of your personalities.'

'Our personalities are completely different. Eduardo's an intellectual, an idealist. I'm very down-to-earth and practical.'

What a trivial conversation this was, she thought, but at least it was safe. Eduardo was neutral territory, the only member of the household who wasn't implicated in this fiasco, the only one with nothing to hide.

'You've chosen different suits of armour, that's all. You're both very self-assured, and very shy.'

'That sounds like a contradiction in terms.'

'Not in the least. The two things often go together.'

'It sounds as if you've been analysing us.'

'I expect you've been analysing me as well. Tell me, Celia, honestly, what do you really think of me?'

He had extraordinarily penetrating eyes. Inky black,

glittering, unfathomable. She felt light-headed, loose-tongued, liable to say something stupid.

'I'm a bit scared of you.'

'People usually are. I look pretty sinister, I know.'

'It's not that. It's just that ever since you came . . . Why have you really come?'

He smiled with one side of his face. The other side looked more like a frown.

'You still don't trust me, do you? But then, why should you? Naturally you all think that I have designs on the estate. Naturally you all feel protective towards León.'

'I'm sorry we've made you feel so unwelcome.'

'On the contrary. You've been too welcoming. I arrived in expectation of a hostile reception. And instead you've all gone out of your way to be nice to me. My father does it to spite my brother, your mother does it to compromise me, Eduardo does it to convert me to the revolutionary cause, León does it because he'd like nothing better than to offload his responsibilities onto me and go back to being the carefree younger son.'

The merciless accuracy of this statement revived her like a bucket of cold water.

'You seem to have got us all worked out.'

'All except you. You're full of contradictions. Drink your Alka-Seltzer, it's stopped fizzing.'

She swallowed it too fast, making herself choke. He got up and thumped her on the back, picking up her telephone as it rang, beating her to it.

'Well, hello, brother,' he said blandly. Celia sat very still. She didn't want to speak to León, she couldn't speak to León, especially not in front of Raúl. 'Nice of you to rush off like that without bothering to say goodbye . . . Oh, yes. A likely story.' He chuckled. 'Tell the truth. Was some woman pining for you? Why didn't you bring her home to meet the family? Is she someone Papá wouldn't approve of?'

Celia felt herself flush a deep brick red. She drained the gritty dregs of the glass in a vain attempt to hide her face behind it.

'Yes, she's here,' continued Raúl. 'She's not at all well,

in fact. She passed out at the mill this morning and is refusing to go home and rest. Perhaps you can talk some sense into her, I can't.'

He passed her the receiver.

'Celia? For God's sake, don't cut me off.'

She couldn't very well in front of Raúl and he knew it.

'León! No, I'm fine. It was just the heat.'

'Listen. I want you to come to Havana. Today, tomorrow, as soon as you can get away. We'll stay in a hotel till I can find us an apartment, I've already got a job lined up.'

'Yes, Papá is in Santiago at the moment. And Mamá has got one of her heads. She's been in bed for three days now.'

'What do you want me to say? Your mother was lonely and unhappy, I gave her what she wanted. I never knew I was going to fall in love with you.'

'Yes, Raúl's arm is healing nicely. Eduardo did a marvellous job.'

'What more can I say? This is what you wanted all along. You wanted to tell the parents straight away, you didn't want to wait. You've got your own way, dammit!'

'Yes, I'll give your love to everyone. Take care now. Bye.'

She hung up, her face still locked in an artificial, twitching smile.

'I think you were right,' she said. 'I think I'll go home and lie down.'

León slammed down the phone in the lobby of the club and strode out into the morning sunshine, bleary-eyed. He had passed a restless night in one of the rooms upstairs, and the lurid sound effects either side had kept him awake till dawn, not that he would have slept in any case. Phoning her was proving to be a waste of time; he would have to put it all in a letter. An unashamed piece of can't-live-without-you supplication, calculated to exploit that incorrigibly soft heart of hers, to beat Lidia and Enrique at their own game. Her mother was clearly piling on the agony for all she was worth, desperate to keep Celia at home to protect her from Enrique who, not to be outdone, was no doubt clutching his chest and threatening to die any minute, fearful of losing his only ally. She had always been pig in the middle in that house, never more so than now. With luck they would be driving her crazy and straight back into his arms.

He might have known Lidia would do something stupid. She must have taken his rejection to heart, confided in one of her idiot female friends, someone jealous and spiteful enough to send an anonymous note to her husband. Well, perhaps it was for the best. As soon as Addy got back, he would come clean with her, collect all his stuff, and move out. He wanted to have all his cupboards clear of skeletons by the time Celia cooled off and agreed to join him. Addy had always said he was free to go whenever he wanted, always nagged him, albeit mockingly, to settle down with a nice girl. And now, God help him, that was that he was going to do, given half a chance.

Meanwhile, the last thing he felt like doing was babysitting for Addy's brat, but what with this dying mother of hers, he couldn't very well refuse to help out. Addy was obsessed that she was going to run away again, some garbled story about her threatening to go to Mexico and how all this was a judgement on her for being a bad mother. The world was suddenly full of hysterical women. 'And whatever happens,' she had pleaded, 'don't let her find out about the club. Take her to see it one morning, when it's closed, to satisfy her curiosity. But for God's sake keep her away during business hours.'

In happier circumstances he would have seen the funny side. The floor show at Addy's, although tasteful by Havana standards – no women with donkeys, or anything like that – was explicitly designed to encourage patrons to retire upstairs with one of the scantily clad 'hostesses' who circulated from table to table, trawling for prey. Hardly the sort of place you wanted to show off to your sixteen-year-old daughter, even a would-be *femme fatale* like Lily who managed to behave, despite Addy's precautions, just like the kind of little tart who worked there. Still, at least he had had the foresight to lock the master bedroom, and his studio. A source of great relief to Addy, who thought Lily was 'too young to understand'. Or rather, old enough to understand only too well.

He arrived to find María full of woe.

'The young lady saw me go into the señora's room, I am sorry, Señor, I could not keep her out. She is asleep in the señora's bed, she did not like the yellow.'

León let out an oath and flopped down onto the couch.

'She saw the photograph of you with the señora,' went on María haplessly. 'She told me to take it away . . .'

'It's OK, María,' said León wearily, rubbing his eyes. 'That's the least of my troubles right now. Go and wake her, it's high time she got up.'

A few moments later, Lily appeared, wearing one of her mother's négligés, a diaphanous feather-trimmed concoction of pale pink chiffon. Her large, erect nipples were clearly visible underneath, as was the luxuriant mound of copper-coloured hair between her legs.

'*Buenos días*,' she said, mincing towards him on high-heeled mules with a grotesque degree of coquetry.

'Go and put some clothes on immediately,' barked León, in English. 'You look ridiculous.'

She flushed angrily. 'Do you prefer to see it on my mother?'

'Frankly, yes. Now go and make yourself decent.'

She opened her mouth to retaliate, thought better of it, and ran back to the bedroom, slamming the door behind her.

'Excuse me, Señor,' began María again, wringing her hands.

'What is it now?' León picked up the morning paper, wishing to God he was somewhere else.

'Captain Reinaldo called last night, to see the señora.'

'Oh, really? Come to collect his rake-off, had he?'

'The señorita had changed for dinner. Into one of her mother's dresses. The black dress, with the beads, and no straps.'

León hadn't a clue which dress she meant, but he got the general idea.

'The señorita asked Captain Reinaldo to stay for coffee. She told me to go to bed. Captain Reinaldo did not leave till very late.'

'What?'

'Twice, I made an excuse to go in. The young lady was very annoyed with me and told me to go away. I tried to phone you at the club, from the extension in the señora's bedroom, but they said you were out. Please, Señor, it is difficult for me. I am a servant here. I do not want to upset the señorita. I do not want to lose my place. She does not like my cooking, she does not like her room. I cannot tell her what to do. Please do not leave me alone with her, Señor, I do not want the blame if Captain Reinaldo comes again. Captain Reinaldo is very important, I cannot tell him to leave. But the señora said on the telephone that I was to take care of the young lady, and . . .'

'Don't upset yourself, María. You did what you could. I'll deal with it.'

Relieved, María waddled off, leaving León to mull over this latest unwelcome development. Reinaldo, like most of his kind, was a model of public respectability. He was never seen at the club, calling at Addy's apartment to collect his monthly bribe in cash. When he wanted a girl, Addy would send one over gratis to a love-nest he kept in Miramar, having paid the poor bitch a hefty bonus to service his pet perversions. Addy would go absolutely berserk at the thought of her precious daughter bursting out of some strapless dress, being ogled by the likes of Reinaldo without benefit of a chaperon.

Lily spent a good hour on her toilette, finally making her entrance in one of her mother's less revealing dresses, a floral cotton shirtwaister with a very full skirt and umpteen stiff petticoats swaying underneath like a crinoline. She was wearing far too much make-up but

León couldn't face another drama and pretended not to notice. María appeared unbidden with coffee and toast on a tray, looking like a dog expecting to be kicked.

'I'm not hungry,' sniffed Lily, still sulking.

'Then you'll just have to sit there till you get an appetite.'

'You sound just like my grandmother.'

'Who's had a stroke because of you.'

'It wasn't my fault.'

'No. I'll bet nothing ever is. What's all this nonsense about Mexico?'

'My friend has a boat moored in Havana harbour. I can leave here any time I give the word.'

'A male friend, I assume?'

'Naturally.'

'Last night you said friends, plural.'

'Last night you said you were my mother's business associate.'

'Well, now you know I'm not you can move back into your own room. I shall be staying here till your mother gets back. So if Captain Reinaldo calls again, you won't have to entertain him all on your own.'

'At least he was polite to me.'

'I don't doubt it. Now eat your breakfast and shut up. Your mother wants me to buy you some clothes. Mariá has a niece about your age, she'll come with us and choose something suitable.'

'I don't like María. She gives me the creeps.'

'If you'd said that in Spanish I'd wallop you,' said León, as María smiled nervously at the sound of her name. 'You'll be polite to her in future.'

'I think you're a jerk.'

'And I think you're a spoilt bitch. Say one more word and you'll stay in the apartment all day, tied to a chair. I mean it.'

He left the room, afraid he would lose his temper with her. His nerves were raw enough today as it was. He called to María for the key to his studio, it didn't matter if she saw it now. He located the unfinished water colour he had done of Celia last summer and propped it up on the easel. Superficially it was a good likeness, but it depicted only the body, not the soul. Like all his pictures, it was the work of a hack, it had come too easy to be any good. You had to suffer to produce real art, and he had never been prepared to suffer. He had given himself up to it like the act of love, or rather sex, untroubled as to whether it was sincere or meaningful, content that it was gratifying. He was a phoney, a flatterer of rich, bored women, women who hired him because he was young and good-looking, who paid him to do more than paint. It had seemed less dishonest than practising what was laughingly called the law, less subservient than working for his father, less parasitic than simply living off Addy. But it was just a soft option, an excuse to waste time, to procrastinate, to escape. And now reality had caught up with him at last; it was almost a relief.

'Who's she?' demanded a voice behind him. León sighed. There was no getting away from her.

'No one you know.'

'Did you paint that picture of my mother as well?'

'Yes.'

'It doesn't look anything like her.'

'It wasn't meant to.'

'Will you paint me?'

'Certainly not. You're quite vain enough as it is.'

'Are you and Mom getting married?'

'No.'

'Why not?'

'That's really none of your business.'

'Yes, it is. I'm her daughter. You'd be my stepfather.'

'Well, I'm not going to be your stepfather, so you can relax.'

'You don't like me, do you?'

'Not much.'

'Nobody does,' she said plaintively, switching to poor-me mode.

'What about your friend with the boat?'

'He's in love with me. That's different. All the girls at

school hate me. So do the teachers. So does my grandmother. She only puts up with me because Mom made it worth her while. Mom can't be bothered with me either.'

'Stop feeling so sorry for yourself.' He stacked the painting back against the wall. 'If you've finished your breakfast, we'll go out and get you some clothes.'

'Will you take me to the club tonight?'

'No. There's no admission to people under eighteen.'

'Why not?'

'Because that's the law,' said León improvising rapidly. 'But I'll show you round this morning, before it opens, if you like. And now for God's sake stop bleating. You're getting on my nerves.'

'If you carry on being nasty to me, I'll tell Mom.'

'Tell her whatever you like. I couldn't care less.'

'Screw you!' she shouted, stamping her foot. 'I'm going to leave right now! I'm going to get my friend to take me to Mexico!'

León stifled an unseemly urge to take her over his knee and give her a good hiding.

'I wish you hadn't said that, Lily. Because now I'm going to have to lock you up till your mother gets back.' He seized hold of her arm and frog-marched her into the hated yellow room. She began screaming blue murder, some of it very blue indeed. He locked the door and left her hammering on it, shrieking obscenities at the top of her voice. María appeared, looking more tragic than ever.

'It's all right,' he said. 'Ignore her.'

He pocketed the key and went out, like a harassed parent fleeing a fractious baby. He walked round the block twice, to clear his head, to give her time to simmer down, wondering if he had overdone it. She was pathetic, really. She was like a toddler with tits. It could only be a matter of time before she got herself into trouble and broke poor Addy's heart.

An ice-cream van stopped on the corner, attracting an ant-like procession of domestics carrying chilled dishes. Languidly, he joined the queue and bought three large tubs, one vanilla, one guava, and one chocolate chip, to give her a choice. Then he crossed the road again, unaware that a dry-eyed, smirking Lily was watching him from her window.

The sleeping pill wore off at three a.m. Celia tossed and turned in a vain attempt to get back to sleep; in the end she put on the light and re-read León's letter, cursing herself for the way it brought the tears to her eyes, made her heart beat faster, filled her full of a sense of having wronged him.

> I make no excuses for myself, except to admit that I'm weak, that I need your strength. I can't promise to change overnight, to stop being selfish and lazy and irresponsible, but if anyone can shame me out of it, it's you. Meanwhile I give you my most solemn pledge that I will never give you cause to doubt me again, that in future I will always be as honest with you as you have been with me . . .

But she hadn't been honest with him. She too had lied and cheated and manipulated. At this very moment she might be pregnant, thanks to her deliberate attempt to nail him by fair means or foul. She found herself hoping she was . . .

> I won't phone you again, Celia; I don't want you to despise me for having no pride. This letter says all there is to say, and now it's up to you to forgive me or condemn me. When you've reached your verdict you can call me; I'm staying on in the apartment in Vedado while the owner is away in America. (I know what you're thinking, but I would hardly give you the number unless that was true.) If I don't hear from you, I'll know that you never really loved me and I'll never trouble you again.

He meant it. He hadn't rung since posting the letter, three days ago. And already she was beginning to panic that he never would, already she was weakening. She buried her head in her pillow and let out a muffled volley of abuse, giving vent to all her bottled-up feelings. She wanted to pummel at him with her fists, to see him bleed and cry out in pain; she wanted to reform and redeem and, in time, to reward him. But more than that, she wanted to quell her own feeling of helplessness, to regain control, to salvage something out of this hideous mess. She wanted to speak to him, right now this minute, and give him a piece of her mind . . . well, that was as good an excuse as any.

She got out of bed, tiptoed downstairs to her father's den, and put through a call to Havana, heart racing. She felt rebellious, sinful, excited. She felt alive again. But when she heard the operator say, 'You're through,' her courage suddenly failed her, robbing her of speech.

'Hello?' León's voice. Celia hesitated. Why was she doing this? Was this an act of courage or merely desperation? 'Hello?'

'It's me, Celia.' She kept her voice hard, cold.

'You got my letter?' His was warm, anxious.

'Yes. You've got a nerve, trying to soft-soap me. I'm only phoning you to tell you to go to hell.'

'I'm there already. What about you? Are things very bad at home?'

'Absolutely bloody.'

'He's going to divorce her?'

'No. It's all being hushed up. Mostly so he doesn't lose face in front of Raúl. God, I'm so angry with you . . .'

'Good. I deserve it. When you come to Havana, you can beat me black and blue, call me every name under the sun. You've got to get away from them, Celia, before they wreck your life.'

'I couldn't leave even if I wanted to,' she hissed, struggling not to cry. What a relief it was to talk about it! 'Someone's got to run the place while your father's in Santiago. He's been sulking for nearly a week now. And how can I leave my mother in the state she's in? She's been in bed since it happened, threatening to kill herself . . .'

'She tried that one on me, time and time again, every time I tried to finish it. It's pure bluff, can't you see that? Lidia's a survivor. Don't let her make you into a victim.'

'I hate you!'

'Then catch the first flight tomorrow and show me just how much.'

'I'm not coming to Havana, damn you.'

'You know what? I'm glad this has happened. I don't care if Raúl gets the estate, it sets us both free. In a few weeks, your mother will be making up to him like mad and my father will be all over him. They won't need you any more. They never needed you. You're the one who needed them . . .'

She hung up, trembling all over, re-energised, revived. He was right, of course. Mamá was laying it on with a trowel, using her as a shield. As for Papá . . . 'You're all I have left now,' he had whimpered, and it patently wasn't true. He had Raúl. And given a choice between her and Raúl, Raúl would win hands down, because he was a man, because he was a Soler, no matter what he had done in the past. 'Promise me you'll never see León or speak to him again! Promise me!' And she had promised. How could she not promise? And yet she despised herself for it.

'You've got to get away from them before they wreck your life.' And they would, infecting her with their bitterness, draining her dry. She couldn't bear it. Better to be bad and happy than good and miserable, better to live with guilt than die racked with regrets . . .

She looked up as she heard a sudden, accusatory noise directly above her, like a piece of furniture being knocked over. It was coming, right on cue, from her mother's room, as if to say, 'What about me? I need you too!' Trust her to intrude at this particular moment. Perhaps she had got up in the night, groggy with her pills, and fallen over. Wearily, resentfully, Celia walked slowly back up the stairs and past her own room, turning right at the end of the corridor. Sure enough, there was a thin yellow band of light under Lidia's door. Celia tapped gently and went in.

She wasn't aware that she was screaming until Raúl came running in answer to her cries. She tried to look away and couldn't, tried to shut her eyes and couldn't, till he pressed her face into his chest, lifted her into his arms, and carried her, still screaming, from the room. But it didn't do any good. She could still see it, she would always see it, in merciless detail. The overturned chair, the two bare feet dangling in mid-air and the white face, full of silent reproach, looking down at her from on high.

FIVE

EDUARDO SPUN the chamber of his revolver, unsure if he would be able to bring himself to use it, except in self-defence or self-destruction. A paradox, that. To neglect the former would achieve the latter. Martyrdom was heroic, suicide an act of cowardice, even though it took guts to kill yourself. That was another paradox. Life was suddenly full of them. Why should the memory of pleasure fill him with such profound pain? How could anything so beautiful be ugly? But he only had to look at Raúl's face to know that beauty and ugliness could sit side by side in mutual mockery.

'It's natural that you should feel frightened,' Raúl had said, 'and that you should try to deny it. I felt the same way myself, often I still do. In my case, it took me years to find out the truth about myself, longer still to accept it. If I had known early on, like you, I could have spared myself a great deal of torment.'

Raúl had opened the door to an enchanted garden of delight, shown him a vision of peace and plenty, and yet he had fled from it, returned to the field of battle, denied himself the blessed relief of surrender in a show of false hostility. He could still hear Raúl's voice, low and gentle, tempting him from the other side of the bedroom door he had locked against him.

'Why are you treating me like this, Eduardo? Have you any idea of how much you make me suffer?'

'I don't want to make you suffer. That's why I'm going back to school tomorrow, to make it easier for both of us.'

'Where you will listen to a bunch of frustrated priests preach hypocrisy and repression. Do they still fill your heads full of sin and damnation? Didn't they tell you that women are the quickest route to both? Especially for the likes of you and me . . .'

He still felt as if he had betrayed Raúl's trust, insulted his dignity, his frankness. Like him, Raúl knew the anguish of being different, of fighting his own nature, of seeking relief in conflict. Raúl had needed the war, he said, in the same way that Eduardo needed the revolution. And now he needed the revolution more than ever.

At least politics, unlike life, presented clear, definable notions of right and wrong. Eduardo's only doubt was about his capacity to kill; as a would-be doctor, he was dedicated to the preservation of life, not its destruction. In one of his recurring dreams he shot a policeman in the chest, and then operated to remove the bullet. The policeman always died, leaving him consumed with guilt – not so much for having killed him as for failing to save his life.

Hearing footsteps in the corridor outside his study, he replaced the gun in the foot of a riding boot and dipped his pen in the inkwell, adopting a look of intense concentration. There was a perfunctory knock on the door, and the abbot entered.

'You have a visitor,' he said, as Raúl appeared, hat in hand, head bowed, by his side. Eduardo blushed and stood up clumsily, sending a book crashing to the floor.

'I am sorry, my boy,' continued the priest. 'You must prepare yourself for some sad news.' He turned to Raúl. 'I will leave you alone together. Please take as long as you like. I will see that you are not disturbed.' He left the room, shutting the door behind him.

'Is it the old man?' said Eduardo, less concerned at his stepfather's long-predicted demise than at the prospect of being alone with Raúl, even for a few minutes, a few minutes that he wanted, despite all his resolutions, to last as long as possible. Raúl didn't answer. 'I expect Mamá is shedding crocodile tears,' he went on, seeking refuge in flippancy, 'all the way to the bank. Poor old Celia. She was fond of the old bastard, God alone knows why. I suppose I'm expected to drop everything and come rushing home for the funeral?'

'Eduardo . . .' Raúl walked up to him quickly and placed both hands on his shoulders.

'Don't do that,' said Eduardo, removing them. 'Not here. For God's sake.'

'It isn't my father,' said Raúl. 'It's your mother.'

'What?'

Raúl pushed him into a sitting position and pulled up a chair beside him, taking hold of both his hands. 'I wish I didn't have to be the one to tell you this. Your mother has committed suicide. She hanged herself with the cord of her dressing gown last night.'

Eduardo stared at him blankly.

'But . . . I don't understand. Why would she do such a thing? Why—'

'She'd been drinking. Doctor Lucero said she'd been suffering from depression. Something to do with the change of life.'

'No,' said Eduardo loudly, as if to wake himself up from a bad dream. 'I don't believe it.'

'I've prevailed on him to issue a death certificate giving the cause of death as a heart attack, to avoid unpleasant gossip. But I told Celia you had a right to know the whole story. Not even Lucero knows that, thank God. I didn't know it myself till a few hours ago, when my father broke down and told me everything. We must all pull together now, Eduardo, as a family. Whatever happens, none of this must ever get out. The family honour depends on it.'

'What are you talking about?'

Raúl's grip on his hands tightened, as if trying to infuse him with some of his own strength.

'You thought what we did together was dirty, didn't you? You said you wished you could be like León, because he was normal. Well, there's something neither you nor I would ever do, pariahs though we may be. But he did it. All the while he was trying to seduce your sister, he was having an affair with her mother, his father's wife, right under her husband's nose.' His voice thickened. 'The old man found out, banned León from the house and threatened to divorce your mother. The fear of public disgrace drove her to end her own life.'

'Oh, God.' He wished he could feel something, but it was all unreal. The only thing that was real was Raúl's face, which was contorted in stoic, silent grief, as if reliving the bloody moment when the bayonet had torn it apart.

'I'm sorry,' said Raúl, moved by the sight of his young friend's pain. 'I meant to break it to you more gently. Your sister found the body. I had to cut it down. I'll never forget that moment as long as I live. It was worse than all the things I saw on the battlefield. And then having to tell my father, and now you . . .' He put his arms around him, and this time Eduardo did not resist him.

Raúl's distress was genuine. Just seeing Eduardo again had produced that sharp, unfamiliar pain beneath his ribs, and even as he held him close, and closer, and finally as close as two people can be, he knew that it would never be quite close enough. It was different from all the other times. Painfully, exquisitely different. It was free of shame and anger, it was pure and clean and true, it was full of the poignant, piquant fear of loss. It was love.

'What does it say?' demanded Lily, as León tore open the cable. 'When will Mom be home?' He didn't answer. 'Is Grandma dead? Tell me!' She tried to read it over his shoulder, whereupon León got up and marched out of the room. Thwarted, Lily followed him.

'Go away,' he barked. 'It's nothing to do with your mother.'

'Then who's it from?'

'For Christ's sake, María, get this brat out of my hair, will you?'

He slammed the door of Addy's room and reached for the telephone by the bed, crumpling the cable into a tight ball.

LIDIA FOUND DEAD LAST NIGHT. CELIA AND I LEAVING IMMEDIATELY FOR SANTIAGO TO BREAK NEWS TO FATHER. PHONE ME HOTEL CASA GRANDE TONIGHT. RAÚL.

He imagined Raúl and Celia driving to Santiago, just as he and Celia had driven to Santiago. Raúl would break the news while Celia hovered anxiously, and then his father would fumble for his pills, the three of them re-enacting that little tableau of three weeks ago. Was it really only three weeks ago? He spread the cable out again while he waited for the call to come through. Found dead. Could it possibly mean . . .? No, surely not.

'Raúl? It's me. Is Celia there?'

'She's with your father. The doctor's here at the moment.'

'I have to talk to her . . . Raúl?'

There was the sound of an altercation in the background and then Eduardo's voice came on the line, almost unrecognisable, choked with rage.

'You filthy bastard, you stinking murderer. If you ever lay a finger on my sister ever again, if you ever come near her, I'll kill you.'

'Eduardo, I'm so sorry about your mother, I—'

'Sorry? You've got the nerve to say you're *sorry*? She'd still be alive if it wasn't for you! She hanged herself because of you!'

'What?'

More commotion as the receiver was wrested from him, and Raúl saying, 'Control yourself. Leave this to me,' and then the sound of a door slamming.

'I didn't want to put it in the cable,' resumed Raúl, matter-of-factly. 'The official cause of death is a heart attack.'

'But—'

'I can't talk now. Give me your number and I'll call you back.'

She had meant it then. She had threatened time and again to kill herself, used that threat to blackmail first him, and then Celia. 'She's bluffing,' León had told her only yesterday. 'Don't let her manipulate you the way she did me. She's a survivor . . .'

'Give me your number,' repeated Raúl. León found he couldn't remember it and had to read it off the dial, clearing his throat several times. All the muscles in his larynx seemed to have gone into spasm, robbing him of his usual fluency.

'I'll get back to you,' said Raúl brusquely, and hung up.

León sat staring at the receiver, shaken by the hatred in Eduardo's voice, remembering the time he had warned him off Celia, not knowing about Lidia, wept with rage, rage he had shrugged off as sexual frustration. He hadn't taken him seriously, any more than he had taken Lidia seriously, any more than he had taken Celia seriously when she had said she would never forgive him. He had taken refuge in the cynical optimism of a spoiled child reared on empty threats and undeserved rewards. He lit a cigarette with shaking hands. Lidia had been tiresome, manipulative, a thorn in his flesh, but he had never wished her dead. Eduardo's fury would be nothing compared to Celia's, Celia who would no doubt blame herself even more than she did him.

It was twenty interminable minutes before Raúl finally called him back. León leaped to pick up the phone as soon as it rang.

'Well, little brother,' said Raúl drily. 'You've really excelled yourself this time. No excuses, please, Papá has told me the whole sordid story.'

'How's Celia?'

'How do you think? She doesn't wish to talk to you. And she doesn't want you at the funeral, she's afraid the sight of you would finish the old man off. So perhaps you'd better come straight away, before he gets round to changing his will.'

'For God's sake, Raúl. It's no joking matter.'

'You're telling me. Eduardo's taken it very badly. Worse than Celia, even though she was the one who found her mother's body, swinging from the light fitment.'

'Oh, God. Oh, God.'

'She blames herself, for taking Lidia's sleeping pills away. She thinks pills would have been a more pleasant way to die. She keeps asking me if she would have suffered. I told her she would have died instantly.'

'Would she?'

'Not necessarily. Damn you, León. I intended to go home in a couple of days. And now I find myself saddled with a family drama.'

'Keep an eye on Celia for me, will you? I'm afraid . . . I'm afraid she'll do something stupid.'

'Isn't one woman killing herself over you enough? Tell me, were you really intending to marry the poor child? Or were you just trying to get her into bed?'

'I love her,' said León helplessly. 'Please tell her I love her.'

'If you love her, you'll leave her alone for a bit. She's got quite enough to cope with at the moment.'

'Yes. Yes, I guess she has.'

'Look, I'll wire my stepfather and tell him I have to stay a bit longer, till things calm down. I can't see my father going in to work for a bit, he seems to be on the verge of a breakdown. At least I've got some idea what goes on at the *central*, so I might as well make myself useful and give Celia a break. In the meantime, don't go blabbing your remorse to any of your lady friends. You can imagine what the newspapers would pay for a juicy piece of scandal like this. Lucero drove a hard bargain, I can tell you.'

'I won't tell anyone. Raúl . . . thanks.'

'Don't call the house, don't go upsetting Celia. If you must phone, phone me at the office.'

'Right.'

It seemed natural to take orders from his elder brother again; in fact, it was a relief. Raúl was the only one of them not emotionally involved, thought León; Raúl would cope impassively, calmly, his thinking unclouded by rage or grief or guilt. Thank God he was there.

'I'll keep you informed,' said Raúl. 'Meanwhile, remember what I said. I must go.' He hung up.

'León!' bawled Lily, from the other side of the door. 'What are you doing in there? We'll be late for the movies!'

León put his head in his hands, sorely tempted to

throttle her. But he didn't want to be alone right now with only his thoughts for company. Lily was trivial, silly, irritating, someone he could take it out on without compunction. He opened the door and glared at her with all the loathing he felt towards himself.

'Anything to shut you up,' he said.

'A death spell is not for any petty grievance,' said the *mayombero* gravely. 'What is your enemy's crime?'

'He raped me,' mumbled Lázaro, less than truthfully. So what if he had let him go? He had done so out of contempt, not mercy. A contempt which had struck at the heart of his masculine pride, leaving him defiled, diminished. It was rape by any other name. 'The man is white, and rich, and powerful. This is the only justice I can hope for.' The witch doctor communed silently with the spirits, considering this request, while the supplicant waited anxiously, head respectfully bowed. 'Did you bring me a strand of this man's hair?' he asked at length. 'Or a nail clipping?'

Lázaro proffered the shirt he had been wearing at the time of the attack, impregnated with the very essence of his enemy.

'This is his blood.'

'If your claim is just, your request will be granted. If not, be warned, the spell will turn against you.'

Lázaro watched intently, breath bated, as the priest took a live black chicken and plunged a gleaming blade deep into its breast. While the wretched creature squawked in agony, he anointed the raw, exposed flesh with rum, sulphur, pepper, garlic and graveyard dust and wound the bloodstained shirt around it, calling down curses on the head of Raúl Soler and invoking the god Changó to hear Lázaro's plea for retribution. This done he buried the bird alive at the foot of a palm tree, with its head poking through the soil to prolong its death throes; as its flesh rotted, so would the evil-doer's punishment commence.

'You must be patient,' the priest counselled sagely, dismissing him. 'Evil-doers have evil spirits to protect them.'

Lázaro nodded, mumbling his thanks and leaving behind a generous donation towards the *mayombero*'s living expenses. A soldier's pay was poor, but his sergeant had been quick to pick up on his knowledge of fighting cocks and entrust him with the care of half a dozen birds. Lázaro's share of their winnings had enabled him to pay for the sacrificial chicken and the brand new knife used to slaughter it.

His mission complete, he hurried back to the bar adjoining the cock-pit where a group of NCOs were busy celebrating a successful evening's gambling; they would assume he had been with a whore. As a rookie, Lázaro was officially confined to base, but this rule had been flouted to enable him to tend his charges during combat. Discipline was lax in any event; privileges were for sale and charges dropped in return for a suitable bribe. Most recruits had joined up for the sake of a square meal, rather than any desire to serve their country.

Lázaro's sergeant waved him over to his table and called for more beer.

'We'll miss you when you get your posting,' he burped. 'Beats me why a guy like you joined the army. You could make a good living training birds.'

'The rebels killed my brother,' said Lázaro stonily. 'I aim to even up the score.'

'You mean you want to fight?'

'Of course.'

'Then more fool you. You're not likely to get the chance, mind, unless you're sent to some godforsaken garrison in the Sierra.'

'There's plenty of rebels in the towns,' pointed out Lázaro.

'True enough,' conceded his mentor, wiping his mouth with his sleeve. 'If you're lucky, you might get the chance to beat up a few rich-kid students. Or watch them being tortured, eh?'

'Maybe,' said Lázaro, hiding his distaste. He found

his new comrades an uncouth bunch and was already disillusioned with army life, which little resembled the glowing picture he had chosen to give his mother. He had sent her a short note explaining his disappearance: he had fallen in with a couple of soldiers in Bayamo, who had talked him into enlisting. He hadn't returned home first for fear she would talk him out of it, as she had done once before. After eight weeks' induction, at a boot camp near Santiago, he hoped to get his first taste of active service.

She had been quick to reply dictating her letter to a literate neighbour.

Dear Son

Such a relief to hear from you at last. Sad as I am to lose you, it's right that you should try to avenge your brother. I wanted you by my side for selfish reasons.

I pray for you constantly, as does Emilia. The poor woman wept for joy when she heard you were safe. She visits most days and brings me food and news from the big house, which is all in uproar.

Doña Lidia died of a heart attack, not long after you left. There was a terrible fight, Emilia says, with the master stomping off to Santiago and leaving the poor woman in hysterics, which no doubt brought it on. I feel sorry for young Celia. Señor León is keeping his head down as usual, leaving her to cope all on her own, not even coming back from Havana for the funeral. Meanwhile her brother Raúl is running the business and acting like he owns the place while poor Celia stays at home with her father, who is in a pitiful state, sitting in his chair all day, staring into space, the guilt has no doubt turned his brain. The boy, Eduardo, has gone back to school, he's another one who's less than useless. Emilia always said that Raúl Soler would bring bad luck on the family. Looks like she was right.

You are in trouble for leaving without giving notice. Señor Raúl had to drive himself home from Bayamo and got attacked by a couple of bandits, who sliced his arm through to the bone, so you had better not show your face here till he has gone back to America. If he goes. Don Enrique is a broken man, it would never surprise me if he retired and left the running of the business to him . . .

Whether Raúl Soler stayed or left, he would not escape his fate; magic could travel over land and sea. Lying on his bunk that night Lázaro could still hear the black chicken's anguished cries, soothing as a lullaby, dragging his enemy's spirit slowly downwards into the dark, unforgiving earth.

Raúl was well pleased with his progress to date. The house of cards had been ready to topple, he had barely had to breathe to blow it down. But his sweetest victory so far – the seduction of Eduardo – was one he could never flaunt. Their weekly meetings at the Casa Grande left him buoyant, burdened, filled with doomed, devastating hope.

Celia, bless her heart, was grateful to him for filling her shoes at the office, a place in which Raúl contrived to spend as little time as possible. He had never had any patience for pettifogging detail, for paperwork, for long-winded meetings. A few hours out in the fields wielding a machete, a half-day operating the centrifuge, an early-morning stint driving the cane-train, all served to make it clear that he was not content to communicate through flunkeys, that there wasn't a job he couldn't tackle himself if need be. Celia might be more thorough, more methodical, more knowledgeable, but Raúl knew from his army days that such virtues cut little ice with the rank and file. Leadership was a theatrical, physical thing, requiring flamboyance, arrogance and the ability to show off, qualities which were admired in men and deplored in women, qualities which had been trained out of Celia since childhood. She had been given the job but forbidden the tools she needed to do it well. She was expected to be a son without ceasing to be a daughter, she had been saddled with the worst of both worlds. What had started off as an attempt to usurp her had softened, insidiously, self-indulgently, into a mission of rescue.

He had spent the afternoon at the packing shed, stripped to the waist, tirelessly tossing heavy sacks of sugar and barrels of molasses with scant regard for his damaged arm, now unbandaged and exposed to public view, giving credence to Emilia's ghoulish account of Eduardo's *ad hoc* surgery. Having proved his physical strength equal to the burliest of his workmates, he showered, dressed, and returned to the admin. block to find a visitor waiting for him.

It was Fernández, the odious private detective from Bayamo, a short, fat, bald individual with small pig-like eyes, wearing an old cheap suit, an expensive silk cravat and a servile, insolent expression. His visit came as no surprise. Raúl had half expected him to double-cross him, a possibility that had spiced their squalid transaction with a welcome element of risk. Not just welcome, essential. Once he stopped taking chances he would cease to be a hero, become one of life's miserable conscripts, concerned only with the sordid business of survival.

'I came to offer my condolences at the death of your stepmother, Doña Lidia,' he began, bowing his head obsequiously. 'A tragedy.'

'What are you doing here?' demanded Raúl, unmoved by this preamble. 'I warned you never to contact me.'

'My work incurs heavy expenses, Señor. I am finding it difficult to make ends meet. You assured me, as part of our bargain, that you would have other jobs for me in future.'

This promise had been superfluous. The sight of three thousand pesos in ready cash – Don Enrique was notoriously slow to settle his debts with tradesmen – would have induced this money-grubbing upstart to sell his entire family. His false report to his employer, relating half a dozen illicit rendezvous between León and Lidia, had revealed a natural talent for invention. Raúl felt no remorse at the deception he had instigated, if deception was the right word; they were both of them, after all, as guilty as sin. He had not bargained on Lidia's suicide, but in Raúl's view she was no loss. Celia, poor kid, would be better off without her.

'If I have any further use for you I will contact you,' he said coldly. 'Good day.'

'And in the meantime, the cupboard is bare. I thought, if you couldn't see your way to giving me any more work, I could call in at the house and pay my respects to Don Enrique. A valued client. A very valued client.'

'Who would have you shot if he knew you had misled him.'

'Oh, I wouldn't dream of damaging my professional reputation. I pride myself on being a very reliable informant. When Don Enrique telephoned me, just before Christmas, and asked me to check up on your credentials, I spared no pains to come up with a full dossier on your background. I have many valuable contacts in the USA. I learned the business in Miami, you know.'

Raúl didn't speak.

'Your father wanted to know exactly how much your stepfather in Chicago was worth and how much you stood to inherit. He also asked me to check out your army record. Need I say more? I'm sure he'd be shocked to know that you were cashiered, and even more shocked to know the reason why. To think that a son of his . . .' He shook his head sadly. 'Regrettably, we Cubans are a narrow-minded, old-fashioned breed. Woefully intolerant of sexual . . . ambiguity.'

'Are you trying to blackmail me?'

'That's an ugly word, Señor. I prefer to think of it as a business arrangement. And in case you've any bright ideas about killing me, there's an envelope in a very safe place, to be opened in the event of my death.'

Raúl lunged at his tormentor and lifted him by the throat, pinning him up against the wall, making him fight for breath.

'Listen to me, you fat pig. Let them open your envelope after you are dead. But bear in mind you won't die quickly. You will die the most horrible death you can imagine. Or perhaps you can't imagine it. If you were a soldier, instead of a stinking parasite, you'd know all about pain and how to inflict it. Go and tell my father whatever you like. Tell him straight away, because you won't get another penny out of me, not now, not ever.

And then run as fast as your fat legs will carry you, enjoy what's left of your life while you can. I know exactly how I'm going to kill you, it will make hell seem like a blessed release.'

In one lightning movement he transferred his grip from neck to testicles, producing an animal howl of pain.

'There's one thing you should have noted when you checked up on me. Unlike you, I'm not afraid to die. I had a row of medals to prove it, until they took them away. And because I'm not afraid to die, I'm not afraid to kill. You disgusting piece of dog-shit. Get out of my sight.' He released his victim and spat juicily in his face.

'A m-misunderstanding,' croaked the good detective, groping for a grubby handkerchief, mopping the sweat and spittle from his florid features. 'I m-merely wished to seek your instructions as to what exactly I should t-tell your father.'

'I will furnish you with all the necessary information, which you will relate to him verbatim. And if you ever try to threaten me again, I'll twist your balls off, one by one, and make you eat them. Now beat it.'

He watched him through the window as he scuttled towards his car and drove off as if pursued. A disappointing adversary. Contempt was a poor substitute for fear. He hadn't felt real fear since he had come to Cuba, not even when Lázaro had pulled that knife. Fear, a constant companion in wartime, was something he still missed sorely. Fear, like love, made you feel alive. Fear and love were twin emotions, so similar as to be almost indistinguishable. Perhaps that was why he was half in love with death. Death was the ultimate threat, the ultimate temptation, the ultimate release.

He returned his attention to the papers on Celia's desk – correspondence about the new plant which had been ordered from America, representations from a neighbouring *colonia* concerning their quota for the coming year, a report from the Santiago office regarding the new security arrangements. Terrorist activity continued unabated, and the premises of pro-Batista businessmen, together with government buildings, were prime targets. Raúl found the new arrangements at Buenaventura – a permanent contingent from the local barracks, whose commanding officer's palm had been well greased – totally unsatisfactory. The Cuban army was a disgrace, without any experience of combat, its soldiers poorly trained and concerned only with money-making rackets. If he, Raúl, were a rebel leader, he would need less than a dozen hand-picked men to hold the whole place to ransom. An attack at night would find the guard napping: one contingent would storm the house and take Don Enrique hostage, while their comrades took control of the mill, the admin. buildings, and the staff accommodation. Few of his father's employees would be prepared to die defending his property. With the right strategy and enough nerve it would be a walkover.

Which wasn't to say that he supported the revolution, although it suited him to give Eduardo that impression – not only for the sake of cementing their relationship but because any dispute would have been painful. It did no harm to agree with him, and besides there was no arguing with an idealist. But the more Raúl listened to him, the more sceptical he became.

As Celia had said herself, the history of Cuba was littered with fallen despots, all of whom had presented themselves as great democrats and reformers. And any despot, Batista included, reminded Raúl of his father, the epitome of tyranny, injustice and hypocrisy. But why should this Castro be any different? Already a personality cult was building up around the man, which boded ill if he ever came to power. Why should a dictator of the left be any better than one of the right?

But be that as it may, he welcomed anything that threatened the peace, and if it came to a war there was only one place he wanted to be: in danger.

'Celia?'

'Yes. Papá, I'm here.'

'Where's Raúl?'

'At work. He should be home soon.'

'Have I been asleep? What have you been doing while I've been asleep?'

'I've been sitting here beside you, like I promised. Look,' she continued brightly, 'Emilia's made you some broth.'

She picked up the bowl and began feeding him like a baby. The smell of it made her feel nauseous. After a few mouthfuls, he waved the spoon away.

'Try,' coaxed Celia wearily. 'You must keep your strength up.'

'For what purpose? The sooner I follow your mother's example the better. Why should I wait for nature to take its course?'

'Don't talk like that, Papá. What would I do without you?'

'I must speak to my lawyer,' he went on. 'I could die tomorrow. You and your brother will be provided for.'

'Don't worry about that now.'

'I suppose you think I'm going to leave everything to Raúl.'

'I hadn't thought about it.'

'He must be laughing up his sleeve at this fiasco.'

'I'm sure he's not. He's been a tower of strength. I don't know how we would have coped without him.'

This eulogy lacked conviction, for all that it was well deserved. He had been too good to be true, embarrassed, perhaps, to be the likely beneficiary of so much misfortune. Lidia's words had rung in her ears more than once in the past few weeks. *He's come here to curry favour with the old man. He's come here to reclaim his inheritance.*

She wanted to believe that it was true. She didn't want to believe that Raúl was as kind and considerate as he seemed. She wanted to believe that all men were cheats and liars, as León was; she resented any assault on the fortress of her bitterness and cynicism. Even so, she was glad he was here to share her burden, whatever purpose lay behind it. León had always made her feel strong; Raúl encouraged her to be weak. And now she felt weaker than ever, too weak to inflict yet another savage blow on

Papá, too weak to bring more shame and disgrace upon the family . . .

'You've got to understand, Celia, that if I were to leave Buenaventura to you, I would be making you vulnerable to the worst kind of man. It doesn't mean I don't love you, quite the reverse.'

'I know you love me, Papá.'

'And besides, why should I enrich some young buck who's only interested in your money, who doesn't bear my name?'

'Please stop, Papá. I'm not interested in money. If I stay here, it's because I care about you, no other reason.'

'Why couldn't you have been mine, Celia? Why couldn't you have been a boy?'

'It would certainly have saved a lot of trouble. Now please finish your soup . . .'

There was a tap at the door.

'Señor Raúl is here to see you,' announced Emilia sourly.

'Leave us alone, Celia. I have things to say to him in private.'

Celia rose and left the room, glad of this reprieve. But for the old man's self-obsession he would surely have guessed that something was wrong, noticed her inability to look him in the eye.

'How is he today?' asked Raúl, in the corridor.

'Much the same.'

'More importantly, how are you?'

'I'm fine.'

She wasn't fine, thought Raúl, concerned. She looked pale and haggard, exhausted by the strain of another harrowing day at his father's side. He watched her slim figure disappear down the stairs. Her movements were quick, almost impatient, betraying a vast well of trapped energy, energy that she rationed and suppressed, as if afraid of it. He was torn between a desire to propel his last remaining rival into his brother's arms and a wish to deprive him of the one thing he valued, the only thing he wasn't prepared to share.

León telephoned the office every day without fail,

seeking news of Celia, reiterating his good intentions, prevailing on his brother to intercede for him. Which Raúl had duly done, relishing the role of devil's advocate. To have spoken ill of León would have roused Celia to defend him; to make excuses for him hardened her heart. To Raúl's mind León's promises weren't worth shit. He was too bone idle to work for a living. Once he got Celia back he would forget all his resolutions, she would end up scrubbing floors to support him while he amused himself with other women. Well, so what? Why should he, Raúl, care what happened to Celia? Once she was out of the way he would be indispensable, the field would be clear for him to recover all his losses. And yet he did care; to let her go would be a kind of loss, an admission of defeat.

'Well?' demanded his father, with a liveliness which would have astonished Celia. 'What's been going on in my absence?'

It was the first time he had shown any interest in the month since Lidia's death. Raúl delivered a precise, if laconic bulletin while the old man fired questions at him, as if trying to catch him out.

'You seem much better today,' commented Raúl.

'Sorry to disappoint you. As it happens, I've no intention of dying till I've put my affairs in order. I suppose you're expecting me to change my will in your favour.'

'Well, you would suppose that, wouldn't you? Don't expect me to try to convince you otherwise.'

'The only person who deserves to inherit is Celia. She's been a good daughter to me. But leaving it to her would be tantamount to leaving it to your scoundrel of a brother. It would never surprise me if he talked her into marrying him after I was dead.'

Raúl affected a bored lack of interest.

'You took your time about coming home, I must say. But you're still my son. And you take after me, no doubt about that. I could see myself in you, even when you were a boy.' Raúl stared straight ahead of him, hands clenched behind his back. He hated to think that he was like his father, hated the old bastard for having the nerve to congratulate himself on the resemblance. 'Tough, ruthless, single-minded, and with the same fundamental weakness. You were too damned fond of your mother, just as I was, God rot her.'

Raúl stared straight ahead of him, registering no emotion.

'León takes after her. Her hair, her eyes, her confounded stubbornness. He was never for sale, any more than she was. He couldn't give a fuck if I left you the lot tomorrow, damn him to hell, he sees this place as a millstone. You've got good timing, Raúl, I'll say that for you. You'd like to be my heir, wouldn't you? It would give you a second string to your bow. As it is, that rich stepfather of yours owns you body and soul.'

'Well, it's better than being owned by you.'

'You always were a bloody-minded bastard,' growled Enrique, approvingly. 'When you wanted something, as a child, you could never bear to ask for it. You either helped yourself, or went without.'

'Well, I haven't changed. And as far as Buenaventura is concerned, I'm happy to go without. The terms of your will don't interest me in the least. There's only one reason why I'm still here. I'm not here for you, or for your money. I'm here for the sake of that poor kid downstairs.' He was surprised at the passion in his voice, for once he spoke from the heart, compelled by a strange, sweet sense of responsibility. 'You lie there wallowing in your guilt without thought for how she might be feeling. She's lost her mother, she's been betrayed by the man she loved, and she's worried sick about losing you as well. If I can take some of the weight from her shoulders, then that's what I propose to do, whether or not you think I've got hidden motives. I couldn't care less for your good opinion, or your bad opinion, come to that.'

His father smiled like the sly old fox he was. Raúl knew before he spoke that he had devised some sting-in-the-tail device to tempt and thwart him.

'To get back to what I was saying. I propose to change my will. Buenaventura will go to my first grandchild born within wedlock. I'm not interested in any bastards either of you may have sired, I expect there are at least a dozen. The proviso is that my heir be born and raised in Cuba until his or her majority. In the meantime, the child's father will have full control over the income from the estate.'

Raúl lit a cigarette.

'Lucky fellow. This new will of yours sounds tailor-made for León. I'm sure he'll be delighted to marry Celia and impregnate her as soon as possible.'

'Which is why I don't propose to tell either of them. And you won't either, if you've got any sense. In any case, Celia can't marry without my permission till she's twenty-one.'

'If you're not telling them, why are you telling me?'

'Because I want you to give me a grandchild, before I die! A boy, preferably, but even a girl would be better than nothing. At least she would have my blood in her veins.'

Raúl's lip curled in contempt. Like some ancient tree, his father was desperate to bloom once more before he withered into nothingness.

'That's the one thing Celia lacks,' his father continued. 'My blood. You like her, don't you?' There was a new tone in his voice, wheedling, anxious. 'She's no beauty, granted, but she's strong and healthy, loyal and sensible. And still a virgin, thank God. She swore to me she never let your brother touch her. If he hadn't dirtied his hands on my wife, I would have given the pair of them my blessing . . .'

'Are you seriously suggesting that I marry her instead?'

'She'd be a better wife than you deserve. How old are you now? Thirty-one? Thirty-two? It's high time you settled down.'

Marriage. He had never considered it before, even for money. The sort of female who aroused him sexually was tolerable only in small doses; the thought of being tied to such a creature, day in day out, didn't bear thinking about. He was attracted to women, and to men, who provoked his need to abuse, who provided a release for his demons; lust and disgust were inextricably linked. At least, so he had thought, until he had met Eduardo, Eduardo who had proved that love was not an antidote to desire.

He could never marry Eduardo, never have him except in secret, but he could marry his sister, who resembled him so closely in everything except for sex. If he had to beget a child by anyone, it might as well be by a woman who carried Eduardo's genes . . .

'Of course,' continued his father slyly, 'she'll take a lot of persuasion. You're hardly an Adonis, like your brother. But if you're half the man I think you are, you won't take no for an answer.'

Raúl felt the tingle of challenge. At least this would be easy. It would doubtless take time and guile, but if he succeeded it would be a major triumph, one in the eye for his golden boy of a brother. He had to admire León, however grudgingly, for breaking through the thick wall of Celia's reserve; he wondered what lay behind it, wondered if she was as passionate as Eduardo, succumbed to a sudden dizzying vision of having them both at once.

'Well?' rapped Enrique, impatient at his lack of response. 'Isn't she good enough for you?'

'Too good,' said Raúl, with perfect sincerity.

'Does that mean you'll consider my suggestion?'

'You'll just have to wait and see, won't you? Though how I'm supposed to court her I don't know, given that you won't let her out of your sight.'

'Tell her I'm feeling much better,' said Enrique. 'Tell her to take the evening off. Spend as much time with her as you like . . .'

'I'll take you up on that much,' said Raúl, 'if only to give her a break from nurse-maiding you.'

'Then get on with it!' rapped Enrique. He reached for

the telephone. 'Leave me now. I need to speak to my solicitor, in private.'

Raúl met Celia at the foot of the staircase, already on her way back up.

'The old man doesn't need you again tonight,' he said. 'We can have dinner together for once.' He offered her his arm. 'Come and sit down. You look tired.'

'But—'

'I gave him a piece of my mind. Told him it was time he pulled himself together. He's feeling thoroughly ashamed of himself. Don't ruin my good work.'

'Well . . . thanks a lot. To tell you the truth, he's been driving me insane. How were things at the office today?'

He saw the unspoken question in her eyes and took his time about answering it, bringing her up to date with the minutiae of his day before saying casually, 'My brother rang. Said all the usual things. Seems pretty confident you'll join him once Papá's recovered.'

'I trust you put him right about that?'

'Far be it from me to put my oar in. Perhaps you should speak to him yourself. It's a thankless task, being a go-between. You of all people should know that.'

'I don't want to speak to him.' She looked away. 'I can't.'

'Then why don't you speak to me? It can't be good for you, bottling things up like this. Why is it that you still don't trust me, Celia? What do I have to do to prove my good faith?'

'I trusted León and look where that got me.' She bowed her head, struggling with herself, and then the words all came rushing out at once. 'The night my mother killed herself, I was talking to him on the phone, trying to find an excuse to join him in Havana. Even after what he'd done. Can you believe that? I remember thinking, if I don't get away from here now, soon, I'm going to be stuck here for ever. Papá kept telling me I was all he had left, and Mamá kept threatening suicide . . . I'm sorry. You don't want to hear all this.'

'No, no. Go on. It's better that you talk about it.'

'León said she would never do it, that it was just a bluff. Just like he said Papá wasn't really ill, that he was just putting it on. And all the while I was listening to him, wanting to believe him, she was tying that cord around her neck and climbing up onto that chair and—'

'Don't torture yourself,' murmured Raúl, reaching for her hand. 'It wasn't your fault.'

It seemed the most natural thing in the world to put his arms around her and hold her close, comforting her like a frightened child; it required no premeditation. It was luxury to hate them all for her sake, rather than his own.

'León would have used you too,' he said. 'You would have gone straight from the frying pan into the fire. If your mother's death saved you from that, then she didn't die in vain.'

'I shouldn't have needed saving. I've always thought of myself as a strong person, because I'm good at putting up with things, but that's just a sign of weakness, isn't it? I stay here out of weakness, and if I were to leave now, that would be out of weakness too. I'm pathetic.'

'No, you're not. You're brave and determined and proud, and I admire you for it. One day, all this will just be a bad memory. You will fall in love again. You may not believe it now, but I promise you that it will happen. But don't give that love away lightly. Save it for a man who cares for you, who'll look after you and above all, who'll be faithful to you. Not one who takes and gives nothing in return.'

She shook her head.

'I don't want anything to do with love ever again.' She buried her face behind her handkerchief. 'Will you excuse me? I don't feel very well.' She stood up too quickly and sat down again giddily. She was very pale.

'You look terrible,' said Raúl, alarmed. 'Let me call Doctor Lucero.'

'No!'

'Why not?'

'Because I'm not ill.'

'You soon will be, if you're not careful. You mustn't

neglect yourself, Celia. Think how much your father depends on you. He told me today that having you here was all that keeps him going. You owe it to him to stay well.'

'Oh, God,' she said in a low voice. 'I don't know what to do.' And then, urgently, impulsively, 'Can I really trust you?'

'With your life.'

'If I tell you something in confidence, you promise on your honour that you won't betray me?'

'You have my word as an officer and a gentleman.'

'The thing is . . . I need your help.'

'Anything you ask.'

'I want you to find me a doctor.'

'But you just said—'

'Not that kind of doctor.' She swallowed hard. 'I think I'm pregnant.'

'What?'

'Papá mustn't find out. I lied to him, I told him we never . . . I had to lie. He would have blamed it on León and it was my fault. I . . . I tricked him. So that we'd have to get married.' She turned away, so he couldn't see her face. 'It'll cost money. A lot, I should think. I've got some jewellery of Mamá's. Can you sell it for me? There's no one else I can ask. Then next time you go to Santiago perhaps you could find me a doctor who would . . . who would . . .'

'Am I hearing you right? You're asking me to help you murder your child?'

She flinched at his deliberate choice of words.

'Well, what choice have I got? Can you imagine what this would do to Papá, on top of everything else? I don't know which would be worse, me giving birth to a bastard, or asking for permission to marry León. And in any case, I don't want to marry León, I don't want León's child. I don't want anything that's going to remind me of him!'

For one foolish, quixotic moment, he regretted what his father had told him, wished that his motives were pure.

'No,' he said. 'I won't let you do it. You said you hadn't got any choice. But you have. You can marry me.'

'What?'

'Unless marrying me is even more repulsive to you than butchering your unborn infant.'

She stared at him.

'You're not serious,' she said.

'Please don't think I'm being noble or selfless. For once I do have an ulterior motive. One that any other woman would have guessed at long ago. Or perhaps I'm even better at hiding my feelings than I thought.'

'I don't understand—'

'Yes, you do. I know you don't love me, but that hasn't stopped me loving you, or enduring agonies on your behalf. Especially now.'

'But—'

'I was too proud to declare myself and risk a rebuff, knowing you still cared for my brother. I'm good at suffering in silence. Haven't I already proved that?' He held up his arm, reminding her. 'Or did you really think I felt no pain? It was nothing, believe me, compared to the pain of loving you.'

She stood up, bewildered.

'Please stop,' she said. 'Please don't talk like that.'

'I'm sorry if I've embarrassed you. I'm afraid I lack my brother's gift for words. I also lack his conceit, his complacency, and his complete lack of conscience. Not to mention his good looks. If you find me physically repugnant, I am even prepared to forgo my conjugal rights. What more can I say?'

She sat down again.

'You're willing to do all this for me?'

'I would be a fool to let my chance slip by. What other hope would I have of getting you to marry me? I don't flatter myself you would do so under any other circumstances.'

'But Papá . . .'

'Leave my father to me. If we marry quickly, we can pass off the child as mine.'

'But won't he think it odd?'

'His greatest fear is that you will run away to Havana and desert him, he told me so himself. This way he can be sure of having you by his side. Naturally I wouldn't expect you to leave him while he lives. Let him think you are marrying me to spite León. That should ensure that he gives his consent.'

She shook her head, confused.

'No. It's very kind of you, but . . .'

'Kindness has nothing to do with it. I cannot compel you to marry me. But neither can you compel me to stand by and allow you to risk your life, to do something you know is wrong, something you'll always regret. Trust me, Celia. I swear to you that I will love your child as my own.'

Abruptly, she burst into tears, and he felt his heart turn over. She was so small, so helpless, so afraid, so alone. Just as his mother had been, all those years ago . . .

The memory of that betrayal was like a timely warning. Once again he was in danger of falling prey to sentiment and delusion. But then, danger was what made life worth living.

'I'm fed up with being fobbed off all the time,' complained Eduardo's classmate, César Mendoza, a fellow revolutionary. 'The same little clique have things all their own way. You and I never get a look in.'

The two boys were on their way to a meeting of their cell. For once, they had not had to break bounds to attend, it being a Saturday afternoon when senior boys were allowed to go into town.

'Stop belly-aching,' said Eduardo wearily. 'We'll get our chance sooner or later. The important thing is to show you can take orders. Arguing with Pérez will get you nowhere.'

'He's had a down on me right from the start. Just because I used to be in the Communist Youth . . .'

César had left the party as a protest against the recent Soviet invasion of Hungary. But his former membership still counted against him; there was no love lost between the 26 July movement and the Communists, who regarded each other as rivals rather than allies.

Eduardo let him rant on, thinking ahead to his next meeting with Raúl. The abbot had raised no objection to his dining with his stepbrother once a week, little suspecting the purpose of these encounters. As Raúl kept saying, no one would ever know. It didn't mean he was effeminate, and it couldn't do any harm. The ancient Greeks had thought nothing of it, it was perfectly natural.

Raúl, of course, had no reason to doubt his masculinity. Raúl had already demonstrated his strength and courage. He wasn't beset by the fears which plagued Eduardo, who had yet to prove himself a man. Eduardo, like many self-styled rebels, was at heart deeply conventional; Raúl followed his own rules. Which made it all the more gratifying that he deferred to Eduardo in all matters political, admitting his total ignorance on the subject. His sympathy for the cause had done much to seal their relationship.

The meeting was taking place in an empty house whose owners, the parents of one of the group, were away in the USA. In response to a coded knock, the door opened and the two boys went inside, donning their black and red armbands as they did so. Pérez, the leader of the cell, arrived last, flanked by two senior henchmen. He was a veteran of the attack on the harbour and customs house, when three hundred members of the movement had effectively controlled the city for two days, until a crack corps arrived from Havana by air lift to crush the rebellion. Even that had been bungled, and most of the revolutionaries had escaped. Their daring assault had attracted a flood of new recruits, among them César and Eduardo.

Until now both boys had had to content themselves with routine jobs – distributing pamphlets, raising black and red flags, petty acts of vandalism against government property and fly-posting sessions in the dead of night. All dangerous enough activities, if they had been caught red-handed, but not quite dangerous enough for their self-esteem. Eduardo knew better than to complain; César was openly disgruntled.

'*Patria o Muerte!*' Pérez reminded them, getting down to the business of the day. Automatically they repeated this catchphrase, like acolytes responding to a priest. 'The recent rebel strike on the barracks at La Plata disproves all Batista's lies about Fidel and his followers being dead. By the time they establish a base camp, we need to have our supply lines all set up and ready to go.'

Once that happened, he explained, it would only be a matter of time till the revolutionary army, swelled by eager peasants, workers and students, cut a swathe through the province in the grand tradition of the war of independence and advanced, growing in numbers by the hour, towards Havana, while Batista's troops, underpaid and demoralised, defected to the revolutionary cause.

'My orders are to organise a raid on a gun shop,' he continued. 'It's a six-man job. A driver, two look-outs, and three operatives, led by myself. Volunteers?'

Everyone present raised a hand. Eduardo had little hope of being chosen. The best he could hope for was to be a look-out, it was the kind of thing they tried out on a beginner . . .

'Rodríguez, you can be look-out.'

'Right,' said Eduardo, barely able to believe his luck.

'I take it you can arm yourself?'

'I've got a revolver.'

Pérez continued to reel off the names of the chosen. César's brow darkened. 'You five stay behind after the meeting to be briefed. Now, as far as the rest of you are concerned, these are your assignments for the week.'

César had to be content with cutting the telephone lines of one of the pro-Batista newspapers and other acts of minor sabotage – pouring sugar into the petrol tanks of army vehicles, and so on.

'That's the third time you've passed me over,' he accused Pérez sullenly. 'I'm fed up coming to meeting after meeting and never getting any responsibility. I told you before, I'm a crack shot.'

'I'm delighted you went dove-hunting with your papá as a lad,' said Pérez coldly. 'As for your marksmanship, the last thing we need is some trigger-happy kid who'll get himself captured and blow the whistle on the rest of us under torture.'

'I'd rather die!' César was getting very red in the face. Eduardo swallowed a sigh.

'So you can withstand torture, can you?' sneered Pérez. 'Well, let's just put that to the test.' In two quick strides he advanced on César, spun him round and pinned both arms behind his back.

'Tell me the names of three people in this room.'

'No.'

Pérez wrenched one arm into a vicious lock. César squealed in pain.

'I can't hear you,' said Pérez, increasing his leverage on the unfortunate limb, eliciting another involuntary howl. 'Speak a bit louder. What's my name?'

'Let him go,' said Eduardo quietly. 'It won't prove anything. Except that everyone breaks under torture.'

Not everyone. He cast his mind back to Raúl, who had never flinched as that needle had dragged its way through his bleeding flesh. Eduardo had found the experience almost unbearably arousing, he could see now that it had been an act of seduction, creating a physical bond between them, serving as foreplay to everything that had followed.

'Would you like me to do it to you instead?' enquired Pérez, without relaxing his grip. César was very white, he looked about to faint.

'I might stand you breaking my arms. But we all know they do worse than that. If you want to test me properly, you'd better give me *mazeppa*,' he added, referring to the ultimate, much-dreaded torture, perpetrated by the Spanish against the Cuban rebels of old and still practised, unofficially, by the SIM, Batista's secret police. The victim was tied by his wrists to the bumper of a car – it used to be two galloping horses – and dragged at high speed over a rough road. Sometimes his hands were torn off altogether; he invariably lost the use of his arms for good. 'But first, volunteer for it yourself.'

Pérez laughed and let his victim go.

'You've made my point for me,' he said. 'The important thing is not to get caught, because few of us will be able to bear the kind of pain those bastards enjoy inflicting.'

Dismissing the rest of the group, Pérez kept the chosen few behind, spread out a plan on the floor, and began outlining details of the proposed raid. His second-in-command, another veteran by the name of Barrio, had stolen a van the previous evening, which was currently housed in a lock-up outside the city. The three chief operatives would meet up at an agreed assembly point at 18.50 precisely, just before closing time, and enter the gun shop, where the two look-outs would already be stationed front and rear, at 18.55. At the same moment Barrio would park the van outside the back of the shop, to ensure a swift getaway. The area was a no-waiting zone, but as the raid would only take three minutes, this was deemed to be an acceptable risk. In the event of Barrio being troubled by the police, the rear look-out, Eduardo, was to create a diversion. The shop had an alarm button, but its location had been discovered via a cousin of Pérez, whose grandmother worked for the proprietor as a skivvy. The owner and his assistant would be inveigled well away from the alarm before the actual hold-up took place; they would then be gagged and tied up, together with any customers, to delay contact with the police.

The raid complete, the stolen rifles would be transported by van to a secret location known only to Pérez and Barrio, who would drop off their comrades en route.

'No problems with playing hookey, Rodríguez?' he added, turning to Eduardo.

'I'll get César Mendoza to cover for me.'

'As long as you don't tell him too much. If he can't learn to take orders, we'll have to kick him out, and I don't want to do that. He might turn coat, out of spite, and betray us. "You never give me any responsibility!" ' he snivelled, reproducing César's whine exactly. 'It would never surprise me,' he added witheringly, 'if he wasn't a lousy queer.'

Eduardo felt a hot spurt of anger, wondering if Pérez would write off Raúl as a lousy queer, Raúl who was twice the man of any of them. In the new, just, society he yearned for everyone would be equal. Except *maricóns*, of course.

'Lily!' called León, hammering on the bedroom door. 'If you're coming with me, hurry up.'

'You go on ahead,' called Lily peevishly, burying her head in the pillow. 'I'm too tired.'

'Get up this minute, you lazy cow. Your mother will be disappointed.'

'No, she won't. I'm sure she'd rather have you all to herself.'

'Oh, have it your own way.'

Lily lay staring at the ceiling until she heard the door slam, picturing the fond embrace at the airport. She had hoped to seduce him well before Mom got back, imagined León breaking the news to her, 'Lily and I are in love . . .' But nothing worked. The more she acted like an adult, the more he treated her like a child. It was worse than being at Grandma's.

At least Grandma had let her go out on her own; here she wasn't allowed to set foot outside the door without a chaperon. She should never have made that threat about going to Mexico. León insisted on taking it seriously, just for spite. And he had been so bad-tempered lately, biting her head off at the slightest thing. The worse he treated her, the worse she behaved; even his anger was better than indifference.

Even the club had been a big disappointment. Not that Lily had seen the cabaret, but having been taken there by León one morning, on a carefully supervised visit, she didn't much want to any more. It wasn't much more than a glorified bar, and a pretty sleazy one at that, a far cry indeed from the glittering nightspot of her imagination. All her hopes were now pinned on the Herradura, which looked a much better place to launch her career, but it was still just a shell, she couldn't imagine it ever being finished. At this rate she would never get a chance to sing. Perversely she felt as if she had been lured to Havana on false pretences.

She got up and flopped into a chair in the living room, still in her nightgown. María began rattling together a tray in the kitchen, singing to herself, glad, no doubt, that her mistress was coming home at last. Grandma, having hovered on the edge of death for weeks, was now out of danger and safely installed in a convalescent home; Lily should have been glad that she would take many months to recover completely, that there was no question now of her continuing as her guardian, that there had been no talk of sending her back to school. But she couldn't bear the thought of playing gooseberry. She wished now that she had kept in touch with Frank; at least he thought of her as a woman.

She reached for a cigarette, but the box on the table was empty, thanks to León, who chain-smoked from morning till night.

'María! Go out and buy me some cigarettes.'

'But the señor said you were not to smoke . . .'

'Did you hear me? Go out and buy two packs of Chesterfields this minute, or I'll tell my mother that you left me alone with Captain Reinaldo!'

Cringing, María did as she was told. As soon as she had gone the phone rang.

'Hello?' said Lily languidly.

There was a short pause.

'Do I have the right number?' said a woman's voice, in Spanish. 'I'd like to speak to León Soler.'

'Who is this?' demanded Lily, in her most peremptory tone.

'Can you tell him it's Celia?'

Celia. He had been working on a painting of someone called Celia all week. To Lily's mind she wasn't in the least pretty, but when she had commented, cattily enough, on her lack of allure, León had jumped down her throat.

'Of course she's not pretty, you little idiot,' he had barked. 'She's beautiful. Which is something you'll never be.'

She had wondered at the time if her mother knew about this Celia, and whether Celia knew about her mother. She had been cheeky enough to ask him, but he had told her to shut up and mind her own goddamned business.

'Hello?' said the voice anxiously. 'Are you still there?'

'Just a minute.' Lily held the receiver a few inches away from her face and murmured huskily, 'Are you awake, *mi amor*? It's a woman called Celia asking for you . . .' She embellished this with a squeal and a giggle. 'Shall I tell her to ring back later?'

There was a click as the caller hung up. Lily smiled to herself. So much for the beautiful Celia. At least Mom was the devil she knew.

'I want you to cover for me this afternoon,' said Eduardo to César. 'I'm supposed to be supervising study hour for some junior boys. I want you to do it for me instead.'

'Why?'

'Why do you think? I'm not expected back for supper. I got permission to dine out this evening, with my step-brother. I have done, several times, since my mother died, so they didn't query it.'

'Right. Good luck, then.'

A few minutes later César tracked down a classmate who owed him a favour.

'I'm taking study hour,' he said, 'and I want to slip into town. Will you cover for me?'

César knew that he would never be given a chance to prove himself, unless he seized it for himself. What a triumph it would be if, as self-appointed third look-out, he managed to save the life of one of his *compañeros*! That would teach them to pass him over in future.

As the bell rang for study period, Eduardo exchanged glances with César and walked quickly out of the science lab into the corridor where a crowd of boys was milling about, moving from one classroom to another, giving César cover to follow him. He had already strapped his revolver round his calf.

He held back, watching, as Eduardo returned briefly to his study and slipped out of the fire exit at the end of the passage. The school premises were bounded by spiked iron railings; to climb over them without injury was a rite of passage among the senior boys. César hoisted himself over them in Eduardo's wake and tailed him for some twenty minutes, following him down the steep hill which led into the town centre, where he took up his position to the rear of a gun shop. Its frontage was well known to César, who had often inspected the merchandise through the plate-glass window.

Opposite the back entrance to the shop there was an alleyway at right angles to the road, sandwiched between two buildings. César disappeared into it quickly, crouching behind a brimming dustbin, displacing a scavenging cat which yowled in protest as he kicked it out of the way.

Unaware that he was being watched, Eduardo stood flicking idly through a newspaper, his dark glasses hiding the movement of his eyes as he looked this way and that for any sign of approaching trouble. César saw him glance down at his watch and stiffen, anticipating, perhaps, the moment of attack. They would enter, no doubt, from the front and exit via the back way – a theory which was confirmed when a van, driven by Pérez's sidekick, Barrio, drew up outside the back door, blocking César's view of what happened next.

Seeing the vehicle stop, Eduardo acknowledged a signal from Barrio. Three minutes, that was all that was needed. Three minutes. In three minutes it would all be over.

He despised himself for being afraid. It wasn't so much the fear of being caught as the fear that he might fail in his mission, neglect to spot some danger or issue the necessary warning in time. Two and a half minutes. In two and a half minutes it would all be over . . .

It was then that he spotted a solitary policeman at the far end of the street, advancing purposefully on the illegally parked vehicle. As agreed, Eduardo gave three warning knocks on the door and prepared to create a diversion; he was to inveigle the policeman into the alleyway opposite and then hit him over the head with the butt of his revolver; it was vital not to make any noise. He waited behind the van until the policeman was almost level with it, and then ran into view, panting.

'Officer,' he began, 'come quickly—'

César did not hear or see this exchange, his view blocked by the vehicle. The first he knew of it was when he saw Eduardo come rushing into the alleyway, with a policeman apparently hot on his tail. Almost instantly, he heard the shots ring out, one, two, three, four times, unaware, until he saw the smoking barrel, that they had come from his own gun.

'What are you doing here?' yelled Eduardo, bending over the policeman's body. 'You bloody fool! You've killed him!'

'I did it to save you. I thought—'

'It was a decoy, damn you!' There was the sound of a siren. 'Shit! You'd better run for it. Go on, get the hell out of here!'

Still clutching his gun, César took off down the alleyway, more afraid of the wrath of his peers than pursuit by the police. Eduardo ran back into the street, where Pérez and co., alerted by the gunshots, were piling into the van.

'What happened?' demanded Pérez, but at that moment a police car came screaming down the street. 'Get in!' he yelled.

Barrio put his foot down hard and the vehicle lurched forward, thwarting Eduardo's attempt to jump aboard. Suddenly the air was full of shots, Pérez and his comrades returning the police fire, while Eduardo instinctively threw himself flat to avoid being hit, too late to avoid the bullet which tore viciously into his side. But the police did not bother to stop to arrest him, intent on pursuit of the van, reassured, perhaps, by the blood gushing from his wound, that he would not get far.

Suddenly the street was deserted. Eduardo dragged himself to his feet and staggered into the alleyway. If they caught him, they would rush him to hospital in order to save his life; then they would torture him to find out the names of his comrades. He must find somewhere to hide, where he could bleed quietly to death, before they found him.

'This way!' Two strong arms caught him as he stumbled, dragged him through a dark doorway and pulled him, backwards, up a flight of stone steps, making him cry out in agony. 'Quiet! Be quiet!'

And then, thank God, he must have died.

SIX

Buenaventura, 21 February 1957

Dear Brother,

As I told you on the telephone yesterday, I shall be away from home on private business for the next week or so. This note will serve to bridge the gap until we speak again.

I am sorry that Celia returned your letter unopened, but be assured that I conveyed your deep concern for her missing brother. As of today's date, there is still no news of him, and our father's lawyer confirms that there is little defence that can be offered if he ever comes to trial. His fellow revolutionaries were all captured and lost no time in naming him as the missing member of the group; we can only hope that he is lying low somewhere, being sheltered by rebel sympathisers.

Raúl paused and re-read what he had written, to satisfy himself that no trace of his real emotions had seeped through. Celia had shed his tears for him, her distress made crueller by the knowledge that Enrique cared little for Eduardo, and felt that he had got what he deserved.

'I warned him time and again not to dabble in politics!' he had roared. 'Was there ever a man with a more ungrateful family? How much more disgrace am I supposed to bear? What is the next shock in store for me?'

A question which had helped to make up Celia's mind; by her own reckoning she was already two months' gone.

It goes without saying that Eduardo's disappearance has been a terrible blow for Celia, especially coming, as it does, on top of all her other troubles. In these last weeks, she has turned to me more and more for advice and support, having lost three of the people closest to her – her mother, her brother, and you. I hardly thought myself capable of filling such an enormous breach in her affections, but she assures me that I have; it will no doubt surprise you to know that later today, with our father's blessing, Celia will become my wife.

He imagined León's face as he read the letter – the open jaw, the wide, disbelieving eyes, the ploughing of the first furrow on that smooth, untroubled forehead. He had always enjoyed wiping that infuriating sunny smile off his chubby infant face, envied him his inborn ability to be happy. An ability that would survive this blow, no doubt. He would soon find someone else.

'You're a fast worker and no mistake,' his father had cackled. 'How on earth did you manage it?'

'She jumped at my offer. The poor girl is desperate to get married and have children. Thanks to your policy of warning off potential suitors, she imagines she is ugly and doomed to a life of spinsterhood. No wonder my brother found her such a willing victim.'

'Well, naturally I will give my consent, but I don't see the need for all this rush. It will provoke malicious gossip.'

'Then put the wedding off by all means. Quite honestly, I'm worried that she's rushing into this. You don't imagine she cares for me, do you? She just wants to pay León back. Given time to think, she might change her mind . . .'

A risk Enrique had not been prepared to take. Celia's own account of herself was hardly that of a woman in love.

'I need someone to look after me,' she had said, eyes downcast. 'With Eduardo gone, what will become of me if anything happens to you, Papá?' It had stuck in her throat, he could tell, to profess such abject dependence but, like it or not, she would never be independent now.

'You'll treat her with respect, do you hear me?' his father had hectored. 'She's not some loose-living American girl, she's been brought up the old-fashioned way. God help you if you make her unhappy . . .'

I can hardly expect you to rejoice at this news, which is why I chose to conceal it from you until the last minute. Frankly,

I wouldn't have put it past you, even after all that has happened, to turn up and cause a scene in the hope of preventing our union. Naturally I wished to protect Celia from any public indiscretions on your part. No one knows that you took advantage of her – not even our father – and I intend to guard her reputation with my life. She told me everything, protesting that she was not fit to be my wife, imagining that I would blame her for your lack of self-control. I only wish I could undo all the pain you have caused her.

Having said all that, I am still your brother, and I hope that my marrying Celia will not make us enemies. You must agree that you lost her through your own stupidity and self-indulgence and you can hardly blame me for sharing your regard for her. Rest assured that she will be well looked after by a man who loves her as much as, or rather more than, you would have done. I have no doubt that with your looks and charm you will not lack for female consolation.

Your brother Raúl.

Leaving this letter on the post tray in the hall, Raúl returned to his room to spend his last hour as a bachelor. Despite the glib tone of his letter he felt troubled, anxious. Why couldn't Celia be a bitch, like other women? Then the prospect of his wedding night might be less daunting. Reason might tell him that she was neither pure nor innocent – she carried the proof of that in her belly – but she seemed it, none the less, filling him with paralysing respect.

He veered jaggedly between a foolish, fanciful wish to make her happy and a bitter knowledge that he was bound to make her suffer. He dreaded losing control, dreaded treating her as he treated other women, endlessly reliving and embellishing the scene he had witnessed as a child. He pictured her shock and fear and revulsion, pictured her confiding, one day, in her child, the way his mother had drunkenly confided in him, filling his young mind with disturbing images, images which had appalled and aroused him . . .

The safest thing would be not to touch her, at least till the child was safely born. In any case, it wasn't her body he wanted; he wanted the invisible, inaccessible part of her which still belonged to León, which lay beyond his reach. He wanted with her what he had had with Eduardo. With Eduardo there had been no need to visualise violence, or vengeance, no need to draw on that bottomless well of disgust. It had been like the touch of a dove on his shoulder, filling him with the sense of peace he had always despised in life, the peace he had thought to find only through death . . .

It was to be a quiet ceremony, with no celebrations afterwards, in deference to Celia's bereavement and concern for her missing brother. The honeymoon would be in Santiago, ostensibly because Celia wanted to be within reach of home, in case the old man had a relapse, but in reality because she felt too ill to contemplate a longer journey.

'Book the honeymoon suite at the Casa Grande,' Enrique told Raúl expansively. 'Champagne, flowers, no expense spared. Charge it all to my account. I propose to double your salary as soon as you get back, so you can tell that stepfather of yours you won't be needing his help in future. I'm damned if I'll let a son of mine live off another man's charity . . .' Old fool.

Quiet ceremony or not, a huge crowd of women and children were waiting outside the tiny Buenaventura chapel, ready to shower the bridal pair with rice and flowers. The responses were almost drowned out by the sound of Emilia sobbing away like the mother of the bride. Celia looked wan in white, and even thinner than usual, but she made her vows in a firm, clear voice and put up a convincing show of being happy, smiling and waving to the cheering throng as she emerged on Raúl's arm.

'Aren't you worried I'll take her away to America?' goaded Raúl, waiting downstairs with his father while Celia changed out of her wedding dress. 'Perhaps I married her to double-cross you. Perhaps I married her to set her free.'

If the rich stepfather had existed, that was precisely what he would have done; it frustrated him that this gesture was beyond him.

'You're forgetting that she doesn't love you. As you said yourself, she's marrying you to spite your brother. Besides, she'd never leave me for you.' Enrique endorsed this confident prediction with a self-satisfied smile, well pleased, no doubt, to have found a groom who did not stir her passions, who would not be any threat. You selfish old sod, Raúl seethed to himself, weren't your own two loveless marriages enough for you?

'Are you sure you'll be all right without us?' asked an anxious Celia, finding Enrique slumped in a rocking chair, wheezing away as if ready to breathe his last. 'If you're feeling poorly, we can always go away some other time.'

'Home is no place to spend your wedding night. A newly married couple need time alone together. And let's hope you won't be alone for very long.'

The poor girl blushed crimson at this innuendo, looking every inch the virgin bride. Then she made her goodbyes, while Emilia started weeping anew and intoning all kinds of mumbo-jumbo, much to Raúl's irritation. Anyone would think she was marrying the devil himself.

The new chauffeur was waiting outside to drive the happy couple to Santiago, together with an armed bodyguard. Celia hung out of the window waving, blinking back the tears.

'What's the matter?' said Raúl, sliding shut the glass partition so that the servants couldn't hear. 'Aren't you glad of the chance to get away for a bit? For the next week I want you to rest and relax. The last couple of months have taken their toll.' He put an arm round her. 'You look tired. Why don't you try to sleep, during the drive? Stretch your legs and use my lap as a pillow.'

She did so, falling asleep almost instantly, betraying the exhaustion left by a long succession of sleepless nights. He had been half expecting her to change her mind; even now his victory rang hollow. He hadn't had to woo her, merely to exploit her condition, the condition she owed to his brother, the condition she had feared to reveal to his father, the father who had engineered the match. That she was now his wife seemed inevitable, it reflected no credit on him. She had married him for the very same reason his mother had married his father, except that her child wasn't his.

It shouldn't have mattered. At least León, ignorant of the terms of his father's new will, would not be rushing to the altar in some sordid race for legitimate progeny. But it did matter. How much sweeter his triumph would be if she were doing this for love!

He looked down at Celia's sleeping face, his eyes caressing Eduardo's high Castilian cheekbones, Eduardo's long straight aristocratic nose, Eduardo's firm, full mouth and stubborn chin, and, yielding to a sudden impulse, he bent his head and kissed her on the lips. He had not kissed her before, except in the most perfunctory fashion, not attempted physical intimacy of any kind, sensing her reluctance, dreading the dutiful, frigid compliance with which she would respond. She woke instantly and put her hands behind his head, returning his kiss with unexpected ardour. No, not ardour. Gratitude.

'Thank you, Raúl,' she said shyly. 'Thank you for all you've done for me.'

'Don't thank me,' he said coolly, withdrawing from her embrace. 'It's my privilege to be able to help you.'

'I hope you don't think I'm using you. That is, I . . . I like you. I didn't at first, but then I'm not a very good judge of character.'

'Perhaps not. But I am.'

She sat up, troubled.

'You know so little about me,' she said, awkwardly. 'You think I'm everything I appear to be.'

'Not quite. I know that to survive in that madhouse it becomes necessary to hide one's feelings, and that hiding one's feelings gets to be a habit. I had much the same experience myself, when I lived here as a child.'

'Tell me.'

Raúl hesitated. He had never confided in anyone, never unloaded the pathetic sob-story of his miserable childhood. Nor would he do so now. He wanted her respect, not her pity.

'Like you, I craved approval. But like you, I was very proud. The two things are very difficult to reconcile, as you must surely have discovered. In the end, something has to give. I rebelled, as you tried to do. I didn't want you to have to pay the price I paid for freedom. The old man never forgives, never forgets.' And neither do I, he thought.

'He seems to have forgiven you.'

'I doubt it. It just suits his purpose to pretend he has. He's only consented to this marriage to keep you away from my brother. Like he's only making me his heir to punish León. You still love him, don't you?'

'No.'

'Celia, I had hoped that you would be as honest with me as I have been with you.'

'I was infatuated with him,' she said bitterly. 'I was flattered that he wanted me. I suppose I must have seemed a pushover. I've always been very ignorant about men apart from the things Emilia told me.'

'What things?'

The ghost of a giggle lit up her face. It was a long time since he had seen her smile.

'Oh, you know. About her lovers and so on. She marks them out of ten, a point for this and a point for that.'

He caught a fleeting glimpse of that secret side of her. Something earthy, almost coarse, something that disturbed and excited and repelled him. It was an image of her with León – not a passive, if passionate, ingénue, blinded by love, but a typical all-devouring female, greedy, knowing, critical . . .

'So how many points out of ten do you give my brother?'

She recoiled, taken aback by the sudden venom in his voice.

'I'm sorry,' she mumbled. 'I didn't mean to sound crude. It was just a joke.'

'These Negresses get up to all kinds of tricks, so I'm told. You must have found her talks very instructive.'

'Please, Raúl. You're embarrassing me. I don't know what made me mention it.'

'I apologise for embarrassing you,' he said stiffly. How easy it would be to cow and humiliate and destroy her! 'Let's speak of something else.'

She bowed her head, and then, after a pause, said. 'No.' She tilted her head defiantly. 'Please don't make me afraid to speak frankly. I've had enough of that from Papá. With him I had to play the little girl all the time. My mother was just as bad, she was always a dreadful prude, the same as Eduardo. Or rather, I thought she was a prude. I don't want to live a lie, like she did. If I'm to be your wife—'

'I told you,' said Raúl, 'I don't propose to exact my conjugal rights, especially with your being in such a delicate condition. It would be quite crass of me to expect you to sleep with a husband of convenience. If you ever find it in your heart to love me back, that will be soon enough for me.'

'That's very considerate and generous of you,' she said firmly. 'But I don't propose to take you up on it. It wouldn't be natural. When I took my vows, I meant to keep them. I intend to be a good wife to you, if you'll let me.'

'Thank you, but I don't want any favours. Self-control is my one talent, remember? Now try to get some rest.'

She stared at him for a moment, and he recognised the expression in her eyes. She had the pained, puzzled look of an unjustly reprimanded child, schooled to think itself always in the wrong, eager for a kind word, a pat on the head, forever making amends for some unwitting misdemeanour, hemmed in by resentment and frustration and guilt. And then his anxiety was submerged by a huge wave of tenderness, because he understood exactly how she felt.

'What's the matter?' asked Addy, as León tossed her suitcase into the back seat. He seemed tense, irritable, quite unlike his usual carefree, nonchalant self. 'Is it Lily?'

'Lily? No, she's fine. Apart from driving me to distraction.'

'I'm sorry if she's been playing up. I know I took advantage of you, but . . . there's something else, isn't there?'

'Addy . . . we have to end it. I'm moving out.'

Addy sighed with regret and relief. 'That's really sweet of you, darling. I didn't want to have to say it first. But with Lily there—'

León started up the engine and switched it off again.

'It's not that. When I was home at Christmas, I asked Celia to marry me.'

'Celia?' Already? she thought. He didn't seem very happy about it. Perhaps he had got her pregnant. 'Well . . . congratulations. I always suspected you were more than just fond of her. So when's the wedding?'

'Good question,' he muttered, as if to himself. Then, rather fast, as if to pre-empt further questioning, 'There was a row with the parents, neither of them approved. Then Celia's mother died suddenly, and my father had some kind of breakdown. So everything had to be shelved.'

'Your stepmother died? But . . . why didn't you go home for the funeral? You should have told me, I wouldn't have expected you to—'

'It was nothing to do with looking after Lily. My father went off the deep end and banned me from the house, to keep me away from Celia. He refuses to give his consent to the marriage.'

'But why?'

'Why do you think? Because I refuse to work for him. Because I haven't got a steady job, or anywhere to live.'

'Say no more. I told you, I need a manager for the Herradura. And I can easily loan you some cash.'

'I don't want your money,' he said testily. 'You've got enough debts already. But I'll take you up on the offer of a job. Just pay me the going rate, OK? You've patronised me enough.'

Addy flinched at the unaccustomed sharpness in his voice.

'I offered you the job because you won't cheat me, not to do you a favour. You know what a den of thieves Havana is. God knows who's had their hand in the till while I've been away.' A headache began burrowing a three-day niche behind her right eye. She dreaded what she would find when she got back to the club. León had been so good, keeping tabs on the builders and minding Lily, she hadn't liked to ask him to do a nightshift as well . . .

He started up the car again. 'I've found a cheap room downtown, to be going on with. No point in paying out for somewhere decent until I know when Celia's going to join me. I want to save as much as I can between now and then.'

This was a new, disconcertingly adult León; the good-tempered overgrown adolescent had aged with alarming speed. She ought to have taken a maternal pride in his new-found sense of responsibility, but she found his uncharacteristic gloom disheartening, infectious.

Lily gave her a cool welcome, dampening her spirits further. Understandably, she resented her staying away so long. Lily had no idea, of course, how dreadful these past weeks had been, with Ruth sustaining a second stroke and developing pneumonia while the medical bills clocked up daily at a terrifying rate. More than once Addy had found herself wishing that her mother would do the decent thing and die.

'Cheer up, darling,' she pleaded. 'I know you're upset about Grandma, but I wouldn't have left her if there was any danger. She has a lovely room in the convalescent home, and everything she wants. She's learning to walk again, and her speech is improving every day. When she goes home, one of her friends is going to move in with her, so she won't be on her own. She wouldn't want you to fret over her.'

But Lily wasn't fretting over Grandma. Lily was simply acting up, displaying a sullen ill humour which proved impervious to bribes or blandishments. Appalled at the sober, serviceable clothes León and Maria had bought her, Addy went to the other extreme and let her have her pick of all the latest fashions, entranced, as always, to see herself young and beautiful again, spoiling her with the artless pleasure of a child dressing a doll, wanting only to see her smile. But nothing worked.

'Why won't you let me sing at the new casino?' grumbled Lily.

'I told you, darling. You're too young.'

'I look much older than my age. Everybody says so. Captain Reinaldo thought I was at least eighteen. Why was León so angry when I asked him to stay to coffee?'

'León was only angry because you sent María away. In Cuba, it's not normal for young girls to entertain without a chaperone.'

'What about when I was alone here with León, when María was out?'

'León was your chaperon, darling. I asked him to look after you. That's different.'

'I've seen lots of girls, while we were out shopping, hanging around with their boyfriends. They didn't have chaperones.'

'They're low-class girls, sweetheart.' And then, seizing her chance, 'Talking of boyfriends, you haven't told me about yours yet. The one with the boat.'

'What's the point? You wouldn't like him.'

'Why wouldn't I like him?'

'Just because.'

'Did you . . . you didn't do anything, did you, Lily?'

'Do what?' A wide-eyed insolent stare.

'On the boat. He didn't make a pass at you, did he?'

'Of course he did.'

'And what happened?'

'Why do you want to know?'

'Because I'm your mother. Tell me, darling. I won't get mad at you, I promise. Did you . . . you didn't sleep with him, did you?'

'If I tell you, will you tell me about León?'

'What about León?' As if she didn't know.

'Are you in love with him? Why didn't you tell me he lived with you? Is he the reason you never asked me to come? Has he moved out because of me?'

'The reason I never asked you to come is because I knew I'd never be able to part with you again, and I wanted you to finish your education. And León intended to move out long before you came. It was never a permanent thing. I didn't tell you about him because . . . because I thought you would disapprove.'

'Well, so I do! I think it's disgusting! He's much too young for you!'

Such conversations invariably culminated in Lily flouncing off to her room in disgust, thus evading counter-interrogation. In any case, Addy didn't have the heart for it. Perhaps she didn't want to know what had happened on the boat, didn't want to find out that Lily took after her, that all Ruth's grim predictions were coming true.

No point in forcing her to attend school; she would only misbehave and start people talking. Instead Addy bought a piano and hired a singing teacher. Señora Valera, a retired Spanish prima donna, informed Lily sternly that she would not take her on as a pupil unless she showed signs of talent. This challenge worked like a charm; for two hours every morning Lily submitted to the most ferocious discipline, trilling her scales to order into a tape recorder, and harmonising with herself with breathtaking virtuosity. In the afternoons Addy took Lily with her to the Herradura, where she distracted the workmen, grumbled that she was bored, and was cheeky to a hostile León at every opportunity. In the evenings she would take her out to dinner or an early movie, delaying her departure for the club until Lily was in bed. Not that she went to sleep. Impervious to María's pleas, she sat up playing records so late and so loud that the neighbours threatened to sue.

'She won't listen to me,' complained María, when Addy took her to task. 'When the Señor was staying here, she did as she was told.'

'Well, he isn't staying here any more!' interjected Lily.

'More's the pity,' muttered Addy, exasperated.

'I suppose you go to his place these days,' accused Lily.

'I assure you I don't,' said Addy, truthfully enough, thinking of León's unsavoury one-roomed apartment, chosen for cheapness rather than comfort.

'You're lying!' accused Lily. 'I'm telling you right now, if you marry him, I'm moving out!'

Addy dismissed María hurriedly.

'Of course I'm not going to marry him! Look, don't tell him I told you, because it's not definite yet, but he's practically engaged. To a girl called Celia, from his home town. So you see, you've no call to worry.'

She had thought that this information would reassure her, but it had quite the opposite effect.

'Well, I wish he'd go back there and marry her! The sooner the better. I hate him!' And with that she ran off to her room with much slamming of doors.

So that was it, thought Addy, with belated enlightenment. It had taken her rather longer than it should have done to diagnose Lily's symptoms, symptoms which she had misread in the light of her own guilt. She had thought that Lily didn't want to share her, that she viewed León as a threat. But the truth was that Lily didn't want to share León. Her little girl was in love.

She should have seen it coming. Or perhaps, subconsciously, she had done, right from the moment she had asked León to take care of her. A pity he was already attached. A lifetime's experience of men had left Addy with no illusions, but León, although no angel, was not a typical man. He was fundamentally kind and decent. He was also selfish, unreliable, promiscuous and lazy, but those failings had been thrust upon him by other people, herself included.

Seeing him in his new mood of industry and independence, she had caught a glimpse of his untapped reserves of strength and tenacity, qualities that had never had a chance to develop. She cast her mind back to their first meeting, when he had been poor and hungry and proud; he had wanted so badly to prove himself, but neither she nor his weak-willed bully of a father would let him. She had taken him in, corrupted his purpose; his father had balked at cutting him out of his will. Even now, she was undermining him, for all that it suited her purpose, by setting him up in a job that was well beneath his abilities. It was León's fate in life, and his tragedy, to have things made easy for him. That would-be hedonist had a thwarted need to struggle, a struggle which had always been denied him.

Until now. Addy had to hand it to this Celia, she had the poor guy in one hell of a state. She would have liked to meet her, work out the secret of her charm. She had an image, from the photographs she had seen, of a shy, shadowy sort of girl, the downcast eyes betraying a lack of confidence, the fixed smile hinting at hidden sadness. A dark horse, evidently. Addy couldn't help being jealous, not so much for her own sake, but for Lily's. Still, Lily would get over it. She would no doubt fall in love again. And again, and again.

That was precisely what worried her. She couldn't keep her on a leash for ever. She would have liked to introduce her to some hand-picked young men, scions of the American business community in Havana, with whom she had connections. But their fathers knew only too well what Addy was and what she had been; the sins of the mother would be visited cruelly on the daughter. She imagined Lily falling for some nice, well-bred boy, being rejected by his outraged family, finding out just why she wasn't good enough for their son. It didn't bear thinking about.

Once they got back home, it would be different. They would move to a neighbourhood where nobody knew anything about them, where Addy would be just another rich widow with a beautiful daughter. Once the loan was reduced to manageable levels, releasing her collateral, she would sell Addy's, leave León to manage the casino, and set about finding Lily a suitable husband. She was the kind of girl who needed to be married young, to a strong man who would correct and protect her, who would provide a safe outlet for her sexuality. Meanwhile she was vulnerable to creeps like the unknown sailor who had brought her to Havana and who might call again, at any time, to lure her God knew where.

She was pondering these problems in bed one morning when María tapped on the door to say that Señor León was here. It was unusual for León to call so early in the day; like Addy he was a late riser. She kept him waiting while she fixed her face before joining him in the living room. He hadn't shaved and his hair was dishevelled, as if he had dressed in a hurry.

'What's the matter?' she said, alarmed at his haggard appearance. 'Have you had bad news of some kind?'

He held out a letter. 'Read it.'

Addy was a slow reader, especially in Spanish. She could sense his impatience, as she fetched her glasses and scanned each line with her finger, silently mouthing the words. He didn't wait for her to finish it before exploding into a vitriolic commentary.

'What a bloody fool I was! All this time he's been working on her behind my back, bad-mouthing me, turning her against me. Even when we were kids, he took my things, even when he didn't want them. I thought, so what if he wants Buenaventura, let him have it, but I never thought he would want Celia!'

'Why not?' said Addy quietly. 'Why wouldn't he want her?'

'He only wants her because she's mine. Celia's quiet and shy, she's not even pretty. He's only marrying her to spite me. And she doesn't love him either! She's doing this to get back at me for . . . forget it.'

'For what? Did you and Celia quarrel, before you left? There must be more to this than you've told me.' Addy got up and put her hands on his shoulders, searching his face. 'What did you do to upset her? Was it because she found out about me?'

At that moment Lily strolled into the room, yawning.

'Oh,' she said sulkily, feigning surprise. '*He's* here.'

'Go back to bed for a moment, honey, I'll get María to

bring you a tray. León and I have business to discuss.'

'Business? Don't make me laugh.'

'Why do you put up with it?' demanded León, rising to the bait. 'Show your mother some respect, damn you!'

Lily tossed her head and stomped out of the room, muttering obscenities under her breath, words she could only have learned from the stranger with the boat.

'Well?' demanded Addy. 'Was it because of me?'

'No, no, it was nothing to do with you. It was . . . something else.'

'Is it that terrible?'

He tried to give his characteristic shrug but it came out as a shudder. 'You would think so, yes.'

'Nothing shocks me,' said Addy confidently. She could guess the kind of thing that had happened. Perhaps he had been caught *in flagrante* with some nubile servant girl, even got her in the family way. Addy set no store by sexual fidelity, she understood men too well for that, but young Celia probably thought differently. She imagined the stormy scene which had led to León's premature departure. Loud voices raving at each other in Spanish, Celia in floods of tears, violent threats from the servant girl's father or brother, the overture to yet another blood feud, much ado about nothing. Cubans were never happy unless they were at each other's throats. León, who chose to ignore his own Anglo blood, had often accused her, fondly, of being a typical cold-fish Yanqui, which was perhaps why he found her company so restful. Strong emotions frightened him, especially in himself.

'Leave it alone, Addy. It doesn't make any difference now. I rang my brother, as soon as I got the letter, I thought it might just be some gross practical joke, like he used to play on me when we were kids. My father's secretary answered the phone. Giggled and said that Señor Raúl was on his honeymoon.' He lit a cigarette with an unsteady hand. 'He'll make her miserable, I know he will. How could she do this to me, to herself? I never realised she hated me that much. Suddenly everyone seems to hate me.'

It was odd to hear him echo Lily's favourite nobody-loves-me lament, León, who had always accepted love as his due.

'I don't,' she said. 'I'm still your friend.' She held her arms wide and let him cling to her for comfort, quivering with suppressed emotion.

'Good luck to her,' he muttered, breaking free abruptly. 'I would have made her a lousy husband anyway. This way at least I'm still a free man.'

Yes, thought Addy, thinking of Lily sulking in her room. It was an ill wind all right.

'I guess you won't want that job any more, right?' she said sadly. 'God knows how I'll cope without you. Specially with Lily being so difficult. You've seen how she answers back to me.'

'She needs taking in hand,' said León grimly. 'She's got all the makings of a juvenile delinquent. If I were you, I'd send her to a convent.'

'And risk her running away again? I can't. Oh, León, I know you've got your own worries at the moment, but . . .' She began sobbing piteously. León stubbed out his newly lighted cigarette and offered her his handkerchief.

'Don't cry,' he said helplessly. He had never learned how to cope with tears.

'How about moving back in?'

'What? What about Lily?'

'I meant as a lodger, not a lover. It was such a comfort, knowing you were here in the evenings, to keep an eye on her for me. She knows how feeble María is, and . . . wouldn't you consider free bed and board, in exchange for—'

'Absolutely not,' said León, interrupting her. 'My babysitting days are over.' And then, relenting at her woeful expression, 'It's you Lily wants to be with. I'll cover for you at Addy's, so you can stay home nights. Poor kid. She's spoilt rotten, just like me, that's why she drives me crazy.'

Well, thought Addy, that was a start. It was better than indifference.

'Thanks, sweetheart,' she sniffed, adding hopefully, 'Cheer up. You'll fall in love again.'

'Not if I can help it,' he said.

Eduardo had a fevered recollection of self-diagnosis, of searching through the torn fragments of medical text-books that littered his once-tidy brain. He knew that he had lost a lot of blood, that his wound was throbbing and festering, that there was a risk of septicaemia. But gradually he lost track of when and why and how the injury had occurred as fever wiped his memory clean, robbing him of all sense of time and place, trapping him in a shifting nightmare world somewhere between heaven and hell.

One moment he would be in the enchanted garden with Raúl, happy and at peace. And then the mirage would dissolve, Raúl would vanish like a ghost, and the flowers would shrivel and decay before his eyes, leaving behind the rank odour of putrefaction, making him choke for breath. The garden became a waste ground, and he knew he was doomed to rot into its sterile soil, unloved and unmourned and alone . . .

He wasn't alone. He was lying on a lumpy mattress, and there was a woman bending over him, a pale-skinned mulatta with slanting, oriental eyes.

'Who are you?' he said, blinking. His own voice sounded unfamiliar, hoarse and cracked. She didn't answer. He tried to sit up and fell back, gasping, as his torn flesh protested. His chest was bare, but for a wide bandage just above his waist. He prodded at it, wincing. 'Where am I?'

For reply, the girl ran from the room, leaving Eduardo none the wiser. In a corner was an altar to the Virgin of Charity. An odour of the farmyard seeped through the narrow slit which served for a window; outside he could hear the clucking of hens.

A moment later she reappeared, together with an older woman and a young man.

'So you're awake,' said the latter, crouching down

beside him. 'We were afraid you weren't going to make it. You were burning up. The bullet went straight through you. But you bled like a pig, and it grazed one of your ribs.'

Eduardo looked at him stupidly. Was he supposed to know this man?

'Jorge Diego,' he said, reading his thoughts. 'This is my mother, and my sister, Mirella.'

They all looked vaguely familiar now, like people he had met in his dreams.

'Eduardo Rodríguez.'

'We know who you are. You're famous, my friend. You killed a policeman. Don't you remember?'

A faint recollection floated just beyond reach. Shots, a smoking gun, blood, and then someone dragging him through a doorway . . .

'Where am I?'

'Not far from Punta Brava. About thirty kilometres south of your stepfather's spread.'

'In the Sierra? How did I get here?' He rubbed his eyes. 'I remember . . . I remember being in a cellar. It was dark.'

'They couldn't keep you there, it was too dangerous. A friend of my sister's brought you in a farm truck, hidden under a pile of sacking. By that time your wound was septic and you were delirious. My mother here prepared a poultice to get rid of the poison. How do you feel now?'

'Thirsty.'

The girl jumped up and proffered a baby's bottle full of milk.

'That's what's been keeping you alive,' grinned the man. 'Mirella here's been feeding you like a big baby. Or don't you remember that either?'

'I thought I was dreaming.' He had dreamed he was an infant, back in his mother's arms, smothered, trapped, impotent, helpless. But he had sucked and swallowed none the less, driven by some primitive survival instinct, knowing that nourishment would make him grow, that size and strength would bring him freedom. 'Thank you.'

The girl wrested the teat from the bottle of milk and

gave it to him to drink like beer. It was warm and goaty.

'You're in the movement?'

The man exchanged glances with his sister.

'It's Mirella you have to thank for this, not me. I don't much approve of you people, if you want to know the truth. On the other hand, I've good reason to hate the police. Pity you only killed one of them.'

'But I didn't. It was César who . . .' suddenly it all came flooding back. César appearing in that alleyway and the sound of the gun going off, César's gun . . . 'It wasn't me.'

'Well, in that case you've been well and truly framed. Show him the newspaper, Mirella.'

There was a picture of him on the front page, blurred and grainy, which must have been enlarged from the school photograph taken the previous summer. Underneath there was an account of the raid on the gun shop. Five terrorists were now in custody awaiting trial. César's name was not included, he must have got away; the others would not have known he was there. There was a reference to the missing killer's wealthy stepfather, proprietor of the Buenaventura Sugar Company. A search of his study at the Jesuit College in Santiago had revealed subversive pamphlets, but as yet no other pupils had been implicated. There was a reward of five thousand pesos for information leading to his arrest.

'Mirella, go and fetch the boy some soup,' said the older woman gruffly. 'He must be hungry.'

The girl disappeared through the low doorway. Jorge stood up. 'Sorry about the lack of home comforts,' he said. 'But at least we've still got a roof over our heads. Plenty of others have been driven off their land, to stop them helping the rebels.'

'It won't work,' muttered Eduardo. 'It will just turn them against the army.'

'Or against the rebels. Can you blame us? We peasants are uneducated, ignorant people, remember. Not like you and your friends.'

He followed his sister out of the room, leaving Eduardo to absorb this rebuke in silence. The mother rearranged the pillows and helped him into a sitting position.

'I can't thank you enough,' began Eduardo, embarrassed to be beholden to people who had so little, who could have sold him for five thousand pesos.

'If it was up to me, you wouldn't be here,' she said gruffly. 'I blame you young troublemakers for what happened to my daughter.' She straightened up. 'She was working in service, in Santiago. Fell in love with the master's son. He was mixed up in politics, like you. I knew no good would come of it, told her to find a boy of her own class. But she wouldn't listen. He took her off to Havana with him, got her involved with these 26 July people. They planted a bomb in the railway station and somebody betrayed them, so he had to go into hiding. The police came looking for him and took Mirella instead. She told them nothing, because she knew nothing, but that didn't stop them beating her, and raping her and worse. She lost the baby she was carrying and she's never uttered a single word from that day to this.'

She gave Eduardo a meaningful look; this little speech was clearly intended to warn him off her.

'One of his other comrades betrayed him,' she went on, 'so her loyalty was in vain. He was shot trying to resist arrest, so they said. Jorge fetched Mirella back home, he thought she would be safer here. But she cares nothing for safety, she's still mixed up with the rebels in Santiago. It's thanks to her they dumped you on us. They know very well we can't refuse her anything.'

'I'll leave tomorrow,' began Eduardo. 'I don't want to put you in danger.'

'And where will you go? Will your family shelter you?'

'My sister would. But not my stepfather. He might not turn me in, but he'd certainly throw me out.'

'Mirella won't let you leave until you're better,' said the woman, resigned. 'Then no doubt you'll want to join the rebels.'

'Er . . . yes.' Was he up to being a guerrilla fighter? And yet, where else could he go?

'Mirella knows these mountains like the back of her hand, if anyone can find them for you she can. Here she is with your soup. Then you must sleep.'

Yes, he must sleep. The effort of talking, and thinking, had quite exhausted him, he barely had the energy to swallow.

The older woman left them alone, and the girl handed him the spoon and held the bowl for him, eyes downcast. Knowing that she wasn't going to speak was a relief, it meant he didn't have to either. He forced himself to stay awake long enough to drink every drop and smiled his thanks. She took the bowl back, handed him an empty bottle, and left him to deal with it in private. He wondered what had happened while he was in his delirium. Had he wet himself like a baby? Had he screamed and wept in pain, like a coward? He was glad Raúl had not been there to hear him. Raúl . . .

Raúl would be worried about him, and Celia too. He must send them a note, saying that he was safe. Perhaps he could arrange a rendezvous, to get hold of a rifle . . .

Soon he slept. When he awoke, much refreshed, he managed to drag himself out of bed and stagger into the next room where a pot was bubbling over a crude makeshift stove – a rough wooden box, filled with soil and topped with bricks. It was a typical, poor Oriente farmhouse, a home-made dwelling of palm thatching with a tin roof and a packed earth floor, treated with water and ashes to make it as hard and smooth as concrete.

Eduardo stooped to look through the open door. There were chickens scratching in the yard, which was shaded by breadfruit, papaya and plantain trees. A recent shower had left the warm earth damp, intensifying the rich tropical smell of simultaneous growth and decay. Beyond the clearing the ground rose skyward, leading high into the Sierra Maestre, its dense green carpet of vegetation draped by a gauzy veil of mist. Eduardo took a big gulp of humid air, as if to reassure himself that he was still alive.

At that moment Mirella appeared, carrying two buckets of water from the well, and shooed him back into bed.

'Do you have a pen and paper?' he said. The request sounded fatuous. 'I must get word to my family.'

She nodded and fetched a lined exercise book and a pencil, but he found it hard to grip it tightly enough to mark the page, and then he broke the point and lay back again, hating himself for being so feeble. Mirella took a penknife from her pocket, sharpened it, and wrote, in a large, childish hand, 'I will write for you.' He was surprised that she was literate, and it must have shown because she scribbled, as if in explanation, 'I never went to school. But my *novio* used to teach me.'

'Thank you,' said Eduardo, humbled. He cleared his throat. ' "Dear Celia" – that's my sister.' She nodded gravely. ' "I can't tell you where I am, but I am alive and well. I was shot, but it was only a scratch, and when I am fully recovered I shall be heading for the rebel camp. You are not to worry about me, I am among friends. I know that this has happened at a bad time for you and I hope that Raúl is still there and able to give you some support. Tell him you have heard from me; you can trust him. Eduardo." '

He would have liked to write to Raúl, and say much more. But no doubt the police were waiting for him to contact his family and would be intercepting any mail. Raúl would understand the reason for his silence. He wondered if he would ever see him again.

Mirella handed him the sheet of paper for signature. Her letters were neatly formed, but her spelling was poor. She pointed apologetically to a word she was not sure of, and rather than insult her by pretending, he spelt it out to her. She nodded gratefully, fetched a rubber and changed it. Then she pointed to another word, repeating the process, her expression intent, determined.

'Your *novio* taught you well,' said Eduardo, touched, and then, eager to redeem some of his debt, 'I will carry on teaching you, if you like, while I am here.'

He found himself speaking slowly to her, as if she were an idiot, and reminded himself that she wasn't stupid, she wasn't even deaf. She was just dumb, as if to prevent herself from ever speaking of the things they had done to her, as if she had surrendered the power of speech to ensure she would never break under torture.

She smiled to indicate her thanks. Three different races, distilled through several generations, had given her almond-shaped eyes, straight black glossy hair, skin the colour of fudge. She was Spanish and African and Chinese, she was more completely Cuban than he would ever be. There was a quiet nobility about her that came from knowledge and endurance. She would not flirt or giggle, she would not embarrass him, as other girls did. She had Celia's virtues without Celia's vices. She was that most elusive of creatures: a woman he was not afraid of, a woman worthy of respect.

Frank hung around outside Addy's for a good half-hour, inventing good reasons to break his resolution and go in. A visit to the pool hall and two nearby bars had merely served to make him more twitchy, like an iron filing responding to some unseen magnet. It was nearly two months now, and he was still missing her like hell. By seeing her again he would put a stop to that, prick the foolish bubble of illusion. The winsome waif who haunted his memory would be exposed as a seasoned hustler, more than capable of looking after herself.

He walked into the purple plush lobby, with its dimpled banquettes and simpering hat-check girl, paid the admission fee – designed to keep the rabble out – and passed through a double door, guarded by two burly black bouncers, into the club beyond. There was a long curved bar at one end, a dais at the other, and small round tables crammed around a patch of dance floor. The minimal lighting was fogged by a haze of cigar smoke, as if to obscure the identity of the patrons. Hostesses in low-cut dresses with skirts slit to the waist flitted from table to table like tinsel butterflies, while others settled on their prey, drank over-priced champagne, danced crotch to crotch, led the way through a curtained alcove to the rooms above. Coloured spotlights created a sudden garish sunrise, indicating the start of the floor show; half a dozen dusky girls wearing pink ostrich feathers began moulting sensuously in time to the rumba, while the band, sated by the sight of too much flesh, hid their yawns behind their hands and counted the hours till dawn.

Frank sat at the bar and bought a glass full of ice and a bottle of Jack Daniel's. Within seconds a girl was perched at his side, a blonde Negress in a gold lamé dress.

'Long time no see,' she drawled in English, ordering a frozen daiquiri at his expense.

'Yeah,' confirmed Frank.

'Where you been?'

'Around.'

'So how's the smuggling racket?'

He couldn't for the life of him remember what he had said to the girl, he could barely remember screwing her. Perhaps he hadn't quite managed it. Probably he had been too drunk. More than likely he had given her the life story. You could say anything to a whore, it was like telling a priest. Oddly enough, he hadn't told Lily anything.

'Not bad. Where's Lily tonight?'

'Lily?'

'The singer.'

'You mean Patrice?'

'Could be.' She might be calling herself anything. Had she told him her surname? Not that it would make any difference, in a place like this. 'A white girl. Red hair. Green eyes. About five-five.'

'Patrice is a brunette. Then there's Donna, but she's black. Don't know no Lily.'

'She might not be a singer, then.' Girls like that always called themselves singers, or dancers, or actresses, or models.

The blonde shrugged. 'Look around. You want a white girl tonight?' She half slid off the stool, preparing to leave her drink untouched and move on to more profitable pastures.

'Don't know if I want a girl at all,' said Frank, truthfully enough. Christ, he was getting older than he thought. 'Where's Addy?'

'You can't have Addy,' grinned the girl, shaking a finger at him. 'Nobody gets to have Addy. Anyway, she ain't here. Señor León's in charge.' She indicated a fair-haired man in a white tuxedo sitting alone at a side table. 'But he won't know this Lily, it's his first night as manager. Addy just sacked the old one for ripping her off.'

'Perhaps I'll stay a while and see if she shows up. Tell the other girls not to waste time on me, will you?'

She nodded and left him, using some kind of silent, secret code to pass on his message; for the next hour he was left alone to work his way steadily through the bottle, eyeing the swishing curtain as the hostesses entered and exited, and the changing spot-lit cabaret, featuring first the strippers, then Patrice, the dark-haired *chanteuse*, with a neckline that reached down to her navel, and then a female conjuror, who toured the tables producing coloured scarves out of unbuttoned flies. Frank yawned. He would finish the bottle and go; it must be Lily's night off, thank God. Or perhaps she had quit and gone to work someplace else.

He wasn't the only one who was off his oats; two men at a neighbouring table got up abruptly, deserting a pair of pouting hostesses, and proceeded to make their way, unsmiling, out of the room. Frank knew one of them by sight, but he couldn't quite place him. His memory was getting worse and worse these days, his brain pickled by booze. As the two men passed him, the one he recognised caught his eye, frowned, hesitated briefly, and hissed in Spanish, 'For God's sake get out of here, quick!'

He ran to catch his companion up and disappeared, leaving Frank scratching his head, puzzled. Was he one of the customs officials on his night out? If so, why should he advise him to leave? Was the place about to be raided by the authorities? Perhaps Addy had committed the ultimate crime of being late with her protection money . . .

Christ. He had never seen him in a suit before, that was why he hadn't recognised him. It was one of his customers, a guy he knew only as Pedro, a member of the Directorio Revolucionario, one of the numerous rebel splinter groups. Only then did Frank notice that he had left his briefcase, lying under the table. *For God's sake get out of here, quick!* He jumped off his stool, knocking over his glass, and lurched unsteadily towards the man in the white suit.

'You're got to evacuate the building,' he slurred. 'Someone's planted a bomb.' He hiccuped and blinked to clear his vision.

The man got up. 'Can I help you outside, perhaps?' he said, with frigid courtesy. 'Call you a cab?'

'I tell you there's a bomb!' repeated Frank, pointing at the recently vacated table, where a couple of newly arrived punters were giving their order to a cocktail waitress. 'The Directorio have left a briefcase under that table. You got army people here, right, and police? That makes this place a target!'

The band had started up again and he was shouting to make himself heard above the music and the babble of voices. Heads turned to see the cause of the commotion, and the two enormous black guys appeared from nowhere, like guard dogs awaiting the order to pounce.

'Listen, will you?' exploded Frank. 'I know I'm drunk, but I'm not that drunk. At least look before you throw me out! You want all these people to get killed?'

The man looked at him properly for the first time, as if returning from some far-off world of his own. From the bored, irritable expression on his face he did not enjoy his work.

'OK,' he said. 'I'll look. And then you'll leave quietly, agreed?'

He strode towards the table in question, excused himself blandly, and looked underneath it.

'Can we check this in for you sir?' he enquired of a

portly, red-faced man, holding the briefcase aloft.

'Do what you like with it. It doesn't belong to either of us.' The man continued with his order. Addy's deputy bowed stiffly and began making his way towards the exit, slowly, too slowly. *For God's sake get out of here, quick!*

Frank snatched the case from him and ran hell for leather into the street, hotly pursued by the two bodyguards who assumed him to be absconding with stolen property. Obispo was crowded with pleasure-seekers; he dodged this way and that, heading for the water's edge, five interminable blocks away, propelled by a drunkard's strength and a hideous vision of death, death they had bought from him . . .

His pursuers were almost upon him when he hurled the briefcase high into the air and over the quayside. It soared, barely visible against the night sky, and exploded into a deafening roar as it drowned its fleeting brilliance in the black waters of the harbour.

'I told you,' muttered Frank, keeling over. 'I fucking well told you.' Waving aside the helping hands, he struggled to his feet unaided and saw the manager running towards him.

'I saw it,' he panted. 'I heard it.'

He wasn't the only one. There was a sound of an approaching siren.

'I've got to get back to my boat,' said Frank thickly. 'I don't want the police asking questions . . .' No use. His legs wouldn't carry him any further. 'That way,' he croaked, pointing towards the nearby jetty. 'Just get me on board my boat and forget you saw me, will you?'

The manager shouted an order at one of the bouncers, who lifted Frank bodily and carried him, following his directions, to his berth. The ever-vigilant George, thinking that his master was in trouble, leaped into action and closed his jaws round the man's leg, causing him to drop Frank ungently on deck. Frank groaned, countermanded the attack, hauled himself onto his knees and ejected most of the bottle of Jack Daniel's over the side.

'You two can go now,' said the boss-man, while George

continued to growl unhappily. 'You don't know anything about the explosion, OK? You chased a thief and lost him.' He shoved some money at them. 'Are you all right?' He turned to Frank. 'I owe you an apology. Not to mention my life.' He held out his hand. 'León Soler. Do you have a name?'

'I've had quite a few in my time,' said Frank, returning his grip. 'But you can call me Frank.'

'You could have been killed. Addy – the owner – will want to reward you.'

'Reward me? For selling those bastards the stuff in the first place? Let's just call it quits, shall we?'

'You're a rebel sympathiser? Then why—?'

'I'm not the sympathetic type. It was a business arrangement. The two guys at that table recognised me, warned me to get the hell out. Typically Cuban, that. They should have left me to fry. They were due to collect more stuff from me tomorrow, as it happens. Help me chuck it over the side, will you?'

He went below, knelt down, removed a panel from the floor of the cabin and disappeared into the space beneath. A moment later a disembodied arm appeared, bearing an oil can with a false bottom, followed by several more.

'Get rid of them,' shouted Frank. 'Hurry up, before I change my mind.'

León took them up on deck, two at a time, observed by a still mistrustful George, and lowered them soundlessly into the water. A moment later Frank reappeared, streaked with dirt.

'I must be crazy,' he grunted, pouring himself a medicinal measure of rum.

'Do you want me to stick around for a while? Or arrange a bodyguard? Or put you up in a hotel? They're going to come looking for you.'

'Which is why I'm going to cast off right now before they show up. You better go.'

'At least let us pay you for it instead. How much do you want? Give me an address I can send it to . . .'

'Forget it.'

'If you change your mind, the offer still stands. It might be safer if you contact Addy privately at home.' He scribbled briefly on the back of a book of matches and handed it over.

'Just tell her from me that she's in danger. They'll try again. To their mind, places like Addy's represent everything that's wrong with Cuba.'

León Soler raised a cynical eyebrow. 'Of course. Once we've kicked Batista out, and the Americans, there will be no more prostitution, no more graft, no more human nature, right?'

'To their mind, I said. I'm just in it for the money.'

'And they're just in it for the power. Or the glory. Which makes your hands cleaner than theirs. At least you don't kid yourself about your motives. Or didn't until tonight, I should say.'

Frank couldn't quite make this Soler guy out. His speech and manner suggested education, breeding, intelligence, qualities rare in the glorified pimps who presided in places like Addy's. Evidently Soler couldn't make him out either. And right now Frank couldn't have enlightened him.

'Let's just say I had a skinful,' he growled. 'You'd better go. The sooner I get out of here the better.'

'Good night, then. And thanks again.'

Frank watched him disembark and poured himself another drink, not wanting to be sober when Pedro and co. arrived. He was damned if he was going to run away from them, hide from them, forgo his right to come and go as he pleased. But neither was he going to fight them. To stand his ground, unarmed, was the best way to play it; defiance was the best defence. The rebel code respected courage, even the insane, misplaced courage of a man prepared to risk his life for the sake of some little *puta* who numbered soldiers and policemen among her clientele.

But it wasn't so much courage, thought Frank, as a kind of capitulation. In the past, rebel bombings had left him unmoved – easy enough when you didn't give a shit about anyone, least of all yourself – until the thoughts of Lily dead or injured had broken through the armour of his misanthropy, exposing the sentimental slob within. And anyway, what could they do to him? They couldn't put him on the stand, sling him into gaol, destroy his career, ruin his good name. They could only kill him.

In any case, he was already dead, spiritually at least. Six years of cold warfare as a spy – sorry, diplomat – in Eastern Europe had left him weary, disenchanted, so much so that he had resigned from the Agency, intending to go back to teaching, only to find worse troubles awaiting him at home in the shape of Senator Joseph McCarthy. Frank's flirtation with socialism in the thirties – particularly his pro-Republican stance in the Spanish Civil War – was now deemed an un-American activity, one which could only be expunged, it seemed, by naming and giving evidence against fellow heretics.

Frank had been called before the House Committee, refused to testify, taken the Fifth Amendment and gone to gaol for contempt, emerging to find himself unemployed and unemployable, denounced by those very same people he had sought to protect. Among them a close friend and one-time colleague, who had returned the compliment by selling his old buddy down the river. Not that it was fair to blame him, or any of the others, come to that, frightened family men with wives and kids to think of. Compared to them, Frank had had little to lose, apart from his reputation, his job, and the few illusions he had left.

And now he felt the same what-the-hell urge to look them in the eye and say nothing, to condemn himself by his own silence, to confess, without speaking, to the moral fatigue that made every cause seem false, worthless. If nothing was worth dying for, then it wasn't worth living for either. He poured himself another drink and waited.

Alarmed at her violent bouts of nausea, Raúl insisted that

Celia see an obstetrician in Santiago, who gave her a thorough check-up and assured her that there was nothing to worry about. The sickness was quite normal, it would soon pass.

Celia relayed this news to Raúl, hoping that it would quell his anxieties. 'He said there was no reason why we shouldn't . . .' She tailed off awkwardly. What she really wanted to say was, 'Please, please, let's get it over with. The longer we put it off the more difficult it will be.' Perhaps he didn't actually *want* to. She had never felt less attractive in her life.

'Even so,' said Raúl. 'We don't want to take any chances, do we? Better to be safe than sorry.'

'It's very nice of you, to be so considerate, but—'

Why couldn't she just be grateful to him for leaving her alone? thought Raúl irritably. It was as if she couldn't wait to compare him with his brother and find him wanting. She would lie, of course, pretend to enjoy it, anxious not to offend him. And knowing that, it would be all he could do not to turn on her, provoke the fear that would compensate for her lack of love. She wasn't Eduardo, she could never be Eduardo, and already he couldn't forgive her for it. It took every ounce of self-control he possessed not to punish her for her unwitting crime.

Celia fell silent. It seemed indelicate to persist, hypocritical even. God knows, she didn't feel much like it either. But she couldn't help being piqued that he wasn't tempted. Was it unselfishness or just indifference?

He began diverting her attention, as one might distract a sulky child, regaling her with some amusing anecdote, forcing her to laugh, as if knowing that laughter was her weak spot. But unlike León, he seldom laughed himself, it was never a shared experience, and even as she succumbed to his peculiar, sinister charm, she began to feel self-conscious, absurd, aware that he was observing, analysing, recording, while giving nothing of himself away. Once or twice when she had allowed herself some gesture of affection – a tentative kiss or a squeeze of the hand – he had patted her head, as if in reproof, making her feel like an over-demonstrative dog.

Every day that passed compounded her sense of failure. Having slept alone on the couch, Raúl would rise early, before she awoke, leaving her to breakfast alone. Then the chauffeur would be summoned, Celia having declared that she felt perfectly well, and an expedition planned, to the beach or the mountains. Picnics would be packed, tables reserved, routes discussed. But the motion of the car invariably made her retch, necessitating a sudden stop by the roadside, followed, more often than not, by a premature return, at Raúl's insistence, which the knowing desk clerk no doubt ascribed to newly-wed lust.

In the evenings, when she felt at her best, they would dance after dinner in the hotel restaurant. He was a very good dancer, correct and stylish, but he never abandoned himself to the music, never let himself go. Everything he did was disciplined, deliberate, there was nothing spontaneous about him. Even that impassioned proposal of his had sounded like a speech in a play. His only unpremeditated act had been the sudden kiss in the car, which she found herself reliving, wondering what she had done right then, what she was doing wrong now. It was strange. He was such a physical person. A fine horseman, a strong swimmer, a keep-fit fanatic. Once she had observed him, unseen, through the crack in the door, doing his morning work-out in the adjoining room: first a hundred punishing sit-ups without any visible sign of effort other than a glistening sheen of sweat, followed by press-up after press-up after press-up, as if he were making love, inexhaustibly, to the floor . . .

It was hard to believe that this was the man who, according to Emilia, had spent his boyhood in precocious pursuit of servant girls. Once Celia had dared to tease him about it, only to elicit a solemn admission that he had been very wild as a youth and that he hoped she would not demand to know the sordid details of his past. Celia found his reticence titillating. He knew the worst of her, why shouldn't she know the worst of him?

It was something of a relief, no doubt for both of them, when their disappointing week together came to an end.

'Poor Celia,' said Raúl on the drive home. 'You must have found me very dull company. I'm afraid army life is not conducive to social graces. I don't feel at home in fancy hotels full of flunkeys, unlike my lounge-lizard of a brother . . . Forgive me. I mustn't remind you of happier times.'

'Stop it. If you had a boring week, it was my fault for being sick all the time.'

'Your fault. Of course. Everything always is, isn't it?' There was a goading, sarcastic edge to his voice. 'Even the condition you find yourself in. "It was my fault, I tricked him." Why couldn't you have told me that he tricked you?'

'I don't understand . . .'

'Why couldn't you have painted him as the vile seducer, yourself as the innocent victim? Why did you make excuses for him?'

'I wasn't making excuses for him. I was telling you the truth!'

'You know, there is nothing more irresistible to a man than a woman who is willing to bear the burden of his sins. Would you do that for me, Celia?'

'Do what exactly? What sins are you talking about?'

Another infuriating pat of the hand. 'Forget it. I was wrong to bring the subject up.'

'But I want to talk about it!'

For reply, he slid the glass panel and spoke briefly to the chauffeur, leaving it open to preclude further private conversation. His sins. Whatever they were they couldn't be worse than León's. She welcomed them, she welcomed anything that would bring him down to her level, make him human, fallible, weak . . .

Don Enrique had survived without them remarkably well, having risen from his sick-bed to resume charge of the office, where Celia's presence, formerly so essential, was now deemed not only expendable but undesirable.

'Your working days are over, my girl!' he decreed, on the morning of her first day home, Celia having overcome her nausea to put in her normal appearance at breakfast. 'A married woman's place is in the home. Especially now your mother is gone. That Emilia is a law unto herself, she needs taking in hand.'

'But . . . but what will I do all day?'

'Do? What do other women do?'

Celia thought back to her mother's arid existence, an eternal round of shopping, fittings, hairdos and social calls to other bored, under-occupied wives, with whom she would commiserate on the shortcomings of the husbands and domestic staff who reduced them to pampered uselessness.

'I'm not other women.' She shot a look of appeal at Raúl, but he smiled blandly and said, 'Indeed you're not. You're mistress of Buenaventura now. Which should be more than enough to keep you busy.'

'Raúl's more than capable of taking over your former duties,' went on Enrique. 'He knew more about the business at fourteen years old than you would have learned in a lifetime. I always felt bad about expecting you to do a man's job. At the time, there was no one else I could trust. But now that Raúl is back . . .'

'Now that Raúl is back, I don't matter any more, is that it? Not that I ever did.'

There was the familiar frozen silence that greeted any attempt to answer back.

'Who would have thought it?' said Enrique witheringly. 'Jealous of her own husband. Raúl, you speak to her. She's your responsibility now, thank God. Perhaps you will succeed where I have failed.'

He stalked off, leaving his coffee untouched, and a moment later she heard the car drive off. He wouldn't speak to her again, for days if necessary, until she humbly begged his pardon. Mamá had adored such disputes, revelled in any rift between them. Not that Mamá had ever stood up for her. Or Eduardo, come to that. Eduardo would merely raise his eyes to heaven. As for León . . . such petty quarrels never seemed to happen when León was at home. And now they were all gone.

León, Mamá, Eduardo. Now there was only Raúl and Papá.

'What was that little outburst in aid of?' said Raúl mildly. 'I would have thought you would be glad to be your own mistress at last. You never enjoyed your work, you only pretended to, to keep him happy.'

'It was better than doing nothing.'

'You'll have plenty to do once the baby comes.'

'That's not the point. Papá doesn't even know I'm having a baby.'

'There won't be one unless you look after yourself. Why don't you go and lie down?'

He spoke patiently, wearily, making her feel foolish. All her frustration came bubbling to the surface with volcanic force.

'Stop treating me like an invalid!' she exploded. 'You make me feel as if I don't exist! This is what you wanted all along, isn't it? To take my place, León's place. You married me to give yourself an excuse to stay, to take over Buenaventura. You don't love me any more than León did, any more than Papá does!'

She had no idea where the words were coming from. Not from her thoughts, that was for sure. She hadn't allowed herself to think like that, wanting to believe he really cared for her, to avoid further damage to her battered self-esteem. He looked at her coldly.

'I'm sorry you feel that way,' he said. 'I will, of course, return to Chicago immediately if that is what you wish. Our marriage is as yet unconsummated, you can apply for an annulment. Then you can join the man you really love, as perhaps you should have done in the first place.'

He got up and walked quickly out of the room, just as his father had done, leaving her to repent at leisure. What had possessed her to attack him like that? 'He's heir to a fortune as it is,' Papá had grumbled, lamenting the necessity of making Raúl his heir. He could have stayed on as long as he liked, without marrying her, without taking responsibility for his brother's child. He had treated her with courtesy and respect, and she had repaid him with abuse.

It was her own dependence on him that was choking her. He seemed determined to put her firmly in his debt, to occupy the high moral ground, just as Papá had always done. So that when and if he chose to ask something of her, it would prove impossible to refuse, whether she wanted to do it or not. What a burden gratitude was!

Emilia came in, to discuss the menus for the day, as she had once done with her mother, and to present her with the latest tradesmen's accounts. The day-maids had arrived and were already sweeping and polishing furiously; the gardener wanted instructions about the plants Mamá had ordered from the nursery. Some new bedroom furniture was due to be delivered that afternoon. There was nothing wrong with the old bedroom furniture, but spending money had been Mamá's only solace . . . apart from León.

Was this to her life from now on? The tedium of it stretched out endlessly before her. She was a married woman now, with a rich husband, she had lost what little identity she had. León would have given her a free hand, to work at anything she pleased. León would not have cared a fig for convention, or wifely obedience, or other people's good opinion. With León . . . she would have got her own way. Subtly yet surely she had always dominated him, but she would never dominate Raúl. León had made her feel like a woman, Raúl made her feel like a child.

'What's the matter with you?' demanded Emilia, with her usual lack of deference. 'You look terrible.'

'Well, you warned me not to marry the devil, didn't you?' Celia bit her lip. She mustn't confide in Emilia. She mustn't confide in anyone.

'And you wouldn't listen. Did he hurt you?'

'Hurt me? Don't be ridiculous. He's the kindest, gentlest man imaginable.'

'Then why have you got those circles under your eyes?'

'Because I've just been on honeymoon,' snapped Celia, rallying. 'Why else?'

'Devils make good lovers,' said Emilia darkly. 'But bad husbands.'

'I'll be the judge of that. And kindly don't speak to me in that familiar manner in future.'

Emilia pursed her lips.

'I got hold of some nice red snapper for tonight. And then there's fried chicken, and then *coco quemada*.'

Fish. Just the smell of it would send her rushing from the table.

'Señor Raúl doesn't care for fish. Make something with eggs instead. And a chocolate cake.' The thought of a chocolate cake was irresistible. 'It's his favourite. And when the new furniture arrives, have them put it in one of the spare rooms till I decide what to do with it. Don Enrique won't be back for lunch today, he has a meeting in Manzanillo. Señor Raúl and I will eat upstairs, cold cuts and fruit will do. We won't want to be disturbed.'

'Upstairs?' Emilia gave her a knowing look.

'Upstairs. I have letters to write and then I shall take a nap, I'm rather tired. Please don't bother me with anything unless you have to. That's all.'

A little black girl was in the bedroom, cleaning already spotless windows. Celia sent her away. She knew now what she had to do. She had married Raúl for all the wrong reasons, but she was still his wife, or rather she wasn't his wife, yet. What was it he had said? 'Once you feel able to return my love, that will be soon enough for me.' Well, she would just have to pretend. She had spent most of her life pretending, after all. Anything was better than carrying on like this. It wouldn't be like it was with León, but she didn't want it to be. If it proved to be a duty rather than a pleasure, so much the better, it would serve to redress the uneven balance of give and take.

Suddenly she didn't feel sick any more. Perhaps it had been psychological, a form of retreat, an excuse. The doctor said it couldn't do any harm, as long as they practised 'restraint'. It was hard to imagine a man more restrained than Raúl, however 'wild' he had been in the past. But he was still a man, for all that. If she didn't fulfil his needs, some other woman would, her marriage would become a farce, as her mother's had been. If she could make him happy, what did it matter whether she enjoyed it or not? It was the least she could do.

She got undressed and put on the slippery silk nightdress she had purchased as part of a hastily chosen trousseau; a store in Santiago had brought half their stock to Buenaventura for her approval. It was cut very low, revealing the tops of her breasts. There had seemed no point in wearing it to sleep alone. She sat down at the dressing table and released her hair from its pins; normally she tied it back in bed, to stop it getting in her eyes, but now she let it hang in loose profusion. Patiently, she began applying extra make-up, embellishing her usual dab of powder and lipstick with rouge and mascara and eyeshadow. She had watched her mother often enough, but had always been too impatient to copy her technique, too self-conscious to invite the close scrutiny that any change in her appearance would provoke – and besides, Papá would have been sure to disapprove. And yet he had liked to see Mamá all made up like a model in a magazine, on the grounds that she was a married woman, and a married woman should look her best for her husband.

Well, she was a married woman now. Perhaps Raúl had just been trying to spare her feelings by saying that he loved her. More than likely he didn't find her attractive at all. And she wanted him to find her attractive. She wanted him to want her. Once that barrier was broken, everything else would follow, they would be relaxed and easy in each other's company, this dreadful sense of strain would go. Better still, it would help banish León from her thoughts, from her dreams. Damn him. She could still hear that giggly American voice purring, 'León, *mi amor*, there's someone called Celia for you . . .'

No use. She could still see that heart-melting, treacherous smile, still feel the touch of his hands and lips, still remember what it was like to have him inside her. And part of him was still inside her, growing every day, she would never be able to forget him. She could never have gone through with that abortion. She had confided in Raúl on false pretences, in the hope that he would talk her out of it. She had wanted to hear him say, 'There's only one solution. You must tell León, and I will intercede for you with my father. He'll have to let you get married now. Leave everything to me.' She had got more than she bargained for. And now, God help her, she would see it through . . .

Raúl arrived home at noon to find the dining room table a bare expanse of gleaming mahogany, reflecting the fiery glow of a bowl of red roses.

'The mistress asked for lunch to be served in your suite,' Emilia informed him. 'When I took it up she was fast sleep.' She made it sound like an accusation.

Raúl went upstairs, still smarting over Celia's attack on him, an attack which seemed, to him, quite uncalled for. He knew what was really biting her. Why didn't he just screw the silly bitch and be done with it, give her something to complain about? Once or twice he had come near to taking her while she slept, roughly, cruelly, viciously. He had wanted to fuck his brother's bastard out of her, make her pure and clean again, obliterate all traces of his rival, crush her like fruit and slake his thirst on her warm, weeping juice. And yet he knew he would despise himself for it, create a vicious, endless circle of violence . . .

He entered quietly. She was still asleep. Her mouth was slightly open, revealing the pinkness within, and one of her smooth, slender legs was outside the cover. There was lipstick and powder and a smudge of eye-black on the pillow; her pallor was hidden behind a mask of paint, paint he had not noticed at breakfast this morning. Lying there, oblivious to his presence, she had reverted to her secret self, exposed the sensuality which sometimes showed through her demure façade, which infected her girlish laughter.

On their honeymoon, in Santiago, there had been a fiesta, the narrow cobbled streets thronged with dancers and musicians, the air vibrating with drums; as they watched the sweating bodies gyrate and shudder, her feet had begun to tap, her hips to sway, her shoulders to heave, her whole body had been twitching to the insistent, primitive African rhythms, as if she too would have liked to splay her legs and shake her breasts, to join in their collective sexual frenzy. Later that night, he had asked her to dance with him, in more civilised surroundings, on the polished square of floor in the hotel restaurant. He had led her through a waltz and a foxtrot and a cha-cha-cha, but her movements had been stiff, precise, self-conscious, like his own. That flash of angry desire had not been re-ignited, the brazen hussy had fled, to be replaced by the violated virgin he feared to touch.

She opened one eye and smiled and reached out a thin, bare honey-coloured arm. She had painted her nails a bright pink, to match her mouth.

'I'm sorry about this morning,' she said. 'It was unforgivable of me to say all those stupid, wicked things. It must be something to do with being pregnant, I'm not usually so ill-humoured.'

She got out of bed. She was wearing a nightdress he hadn't seen before, which clung to her breasts and her belly and her hips, which caught the light as she moved.

'Don't get up on my account,' he said. 'I'll bring the tray to you in bed.'

'All right.' She sat down on top of the covers and patted the space next to her. 'Sit on the bed beside me, so we can talk.'

'I prefer to sit at the table here.' He began piling two plates with slices of pork and chicken.

'You're still angry with me. I don't blame you. I haven't been much of a wife to you, have I?' She got up and drew up a chair next to him. She smelt of lemon blossom.

'I'm not angry. I've already forgotten it. There's no need to discuss it any more. Would you like some rice?'

'I'm not hungry. Raúl, look at me. Please look at me.'

He turned and looked at the red mouth, the sticky lashes, the mass of heavy tumbled hair.

'I'm looking at you.'

'Do you find me ugly?'

'How could anyone with looks like mine presume to find anybody else ugly?'

She put her hand up to his cheek and traced the line of his scar with her finger. There was no pity in her face, no patronage, just curiosity and that strange, shy candour; her touch was infinitely titillating. Then she lifted his hand to her own face, forcing his fingers to explore it, to move on to her neck, and her shoulder and then, of their own free will, to her breasts. She did it all innocently, wantonly, inflaming him, inhibiting him, filling him with tenderness and fury.

She moved across and sat on his lap and kissed him, as he had once kissed her. He had never risked it again. Since then their embraces had been brief, desultory, on her part as well as his, but now she slid her tongue between his lips, filling his mouth with the taste of hers, while she fumbled with the buttons of his shirt, clumsily, nervously.

'Celia—'

'Please, Raúl. You said you loved me. I want to love you back.' She was plaintive and vulnerable again, but insistent, demanding. She slipped the straps of her nightdress, letting her small, high breasts spill out of it, pressing them into his chest. Raúl felt the blood begin to pound in his head. He had never wanted a woman so much in his life. And yet he held back, torn between the fear of hurting her and the inadmissible, irresistible desire to do just that.

'Cover yourself up,' he said harshly, pushing her away.

'What?' Her eyes were huge, uncomprehending.

'I said, cover yourself up! I don't expect a wife of mine to behave like a common whore.'

'I'm not your wife,' she said, standing there half-naked, too stunned by his icy tone to obey him. 'You won't let me be your wife. I thought—'

'Is that how you behaved with my brother?'

'Raúl, *please . . .*'

'Perhaps I judged him too harshly. What man could

resist such an overture? You're very seductive, aren't you, underneath that innocent pose of yours? Like mother, like daughter.'

He had thought that the insult would cow her, but she went on the attack, slapping him hard across his mutilated cheek. He imprisoned her wrist and twisted it, making her cry out, but then she ducked her head and bit his hand savagely. Incensed, excited, he slapped her back, sending her reeling, waiting for the first sign of fear. But she was much too angry to be scared of him.

'You bastard!' she spat. 'Don't you dare speak ill of my mother!'

'How did he give it to her, do you think?' He seized her by the shoulders, pressing his fingers deep into her flesh, but she didn't flinch, her eyes blazing into his. 'The same way he gave it to you? How did he give it to you, Celia? Like this?'

There was no going back now. It had been bound to happen like this – brutally, angrily, without finesse. Every so often this ritual would be re-enacted, punctuating the sterile prose of their marriage with flashes of obscene poetry. He had been a fool to expect anything else.

He dragged her onto the floor and ground himself into her savagely, as if to deny her power and demonstrate his own. But she didn't struggle, making this show of force redundant, ridiculous. It was as if he had tried to break down a door, only to have it fly open, sending him hurtling into thin air, robbing him of balance.

She didn't even shut her eyes. She watched him all the way through it, with defiance, with dignity, with a terrible, terrifying insight. And when it was over and he tried to roll off her, already bitterly ashamed, she put her arms round him and held him fast and said, 'It's all right. I know why you're angry. I understand.'

Her arms were strong, her embrace uncompromising. She didn't understand, of course, she didn't know the half of it. But the half she did know was more than enough, she must never find out the rest . . .

'I want to love you back,' she said again, and this time

he almost believed her. Believed her enough to let her see his first tears in twenty years.

SEVEN

AFTER THE near-miss bombing, Addy took immediate but discreet steps to improve security. The two bouncers were well paid to keep their mouths shut; if people got the idea that her premises were a target they would stay away, just when she needed all the money she could get. Lily was likewise told nothing of the attack; Addy didn't want her to worry.

León proved to be a tower of strength, running the club by night, and monitoring progress at the Herradura – due to open at the end of March – by day. For once in his indolent life, he seemed anxious to keep busy, whereas Addy, usually so industrious, was glad of the chance to stay home and play Mom. Renewed familiarity bred a measure of trust and brought down Lily's guard. The laconic, moody teenager gradually became a prattling child again, albeit with a woman's preoccupations.

'If anything happened to you, who would look after me? Would I have to go back to Grandma?'

'Grandma's not well enough to take care of anyone, darling. But nothing's going to happen to me. By the time I die you'll be married with a home of your own.'

'How will I ever get married if I don't get to meet any men?'

'There's plenty of time for that. You're only sixteen. In a couple of years, we'll be going home and you'll be spoiled for choice.'

But Lily had already made her choice; that much became clearer by the day. Addy decided not to mention Celia's marriage; a little jealousy would do no harm at all. Meanwhile, things were progressing nicely. Lily evidently enjoyed being bullied, enjoyed it far more than being spoiled. And León had a soft spot for her too, however hard he tried to hide it.

'She can sing all right,' he had acknowledged grudgingly. Sometimes he would buy her sheet music, or a gramophone record, which he would toss at her with a curt, 'Here. Perhaps this will stop you whining for a bit.' And Lily would glower and affect indifference, ignoring the gift until León was out of the way, when she would play the record or practise the song over and over again. He picked the classic cabaret numbers which suited her style; Lily haughtily despised rock 'n' roll, embracing the tastes of the older generation she longed to join. She was still at the age when youth seemed a burden.

She continued to plead for a singing spot at the Herradura, but that was one issue on which Addy remained adamant. Having started her own career as a dancer, she knew that one thing led to another; she didn't want Lily running off with some greaseball piano player or ending up as a married man's plaything.

'I told you, you're too young,' repeated Addy, a week before opening night. León had called in with a sheaf of cheques for her to sign; her brow was furrowed in anxious concentration. 'Perhaps when you're older.'

'Stop mollycoddling her,' interjected León. 'She might as well use the only talent she appears to have.'

Lily flung him a grateful-suspicious look, but he didn't meet her eye.

'Kindly don't interfere,' said Addy, annoyed. He knew very well what her feelings were on the subject. 'I'm her mother, and I know what's best for her.'

'I'm not so sure. It would do her the world of good to have to earn her own living.' It was the first time he had ever contradicted Addy in front of Lily, breaking an established ground rule. Addy's eyes flashed.

'I might say the same for you,' she snapped.

'I rather thought I had done, recently.'

'Recently being the operative word.'

'Well, if you're not satisfied with the hours I've been putting in lately, go ahead and fire me. I hate the lousy job anyway.' He gathered the cheques together. 'Time I got back. I'd hate you to think I was slacking.' He left the room and a moment later the front door slammed. Lily turned on her mother.

'Why did you have to talk to him like that?'

'Because he had no right to question my decision,' said Addy calmly. 'Don't worry, he'll get over it. He just needs time to cool off.' León had a short fuse these days; the bland, imperturbable charmer had fled for ever. 'Lily!' she called out at her as she stormed out. 'Where are you going? Come back here this minute!'

The door slammed again, even louder this time. Sighing, Addy went to the window and looked down into the street. León was just about to get into his car when Lily arrived on the scene, panting. There was a short exchange, with León apparently telling her to go back inside, whereupon Lily installed herself in the passenger seat, arms folded, stubbornly refusing to budge. Eventually León threw up his hands in a typically Latin gesture, got in beside her, and roared off. Addy smiled.

'Your mother will have my guts for this,' said León, drawing up outside the Herradura. 'That'll teach her to leave it to me to hire the cabaret. You realise you can't be top of the bill. I had to buy a big name to bring people in.'

He wondered why he was doing this. Perhaps it was because Lily, unlike himself, had a genuine gift, a saving grace. Addy would let her waste it on church choirs and amateur operatics, drain her talent of all its vigour, refine it into something polite and respectable, make her dance the minuet to the rhythm of the rumba.

The elegant contralto Lily could produce for the redoubtable Señora Valera left him unmoved; her voice was at its best when it came down to earth, wrapped itself round cheap music, elevated it into a kind of poetry. It was the only thing she did that wasn't choked with pretence, that made her seem like a real person instead of a posturing brat. When she sang, she became, briefly, tantalisingly, a woman, someone who understood love and pain, even though she couldn't possibly know the first thing about either.

The Herradura was located in the fashionable suburb of El Country Club, home of Havana's wealthiest citizens, a prime site for the high-class nightspots and bars which had mushroomed in the economic boom of recent years. Addy had conceived a hushed, discreet, intimate sort of place, less public and brash than the casinos in the big Vedado hotels, one designed to appeal to discerning residents rather than mug tourists, to build up a regular clientele rather than attract passing trade. Such a small-scale enterprise was seen as no threat to the large, Mafia-controlled establishments; Addy's underworld connections had given it their blessing, just as long as she paid her dues on the nail. The gala opening night, by invitation only, was to feature complimentary gambling chips, free drinks and a lavish buffet.

Lily teetered after him into the lobby, her high heels buckling on the thick red carpet. 'I've been meaning to ask you,' she said boldly, pointing to his mural. 'What's it supposed to mean?'

León had grown to hate it. It featured oblong dice, circular playing cards and square roulette wheels, presided over by a wall-eyed Lady Luck; Addy, oblivious to its cynicism, had been impressed by its Picasso-esque pretensions. At the time, it had seemed clever, mocking, but now it seemed like a bad joke, one which had turned against him.

'That you should never trust to luck.'

'Surely you don't want the customers to think that?'

'People who gamble don't think. Come on, let's see what you can do.'

The lobby led through an arcade of fruit machines into a large gaming area for roulette and blackjack, flanked by several smaller rooms for private poker games. Beyond it was a spacious cocktail-lounge-cum-restaurant, at one end of which was a dais for the cabaret, equipped with microphones and spotlights, as yet disconnected. Workmen were still busy putting the final touches to the décor, which was intended to be sophisticated and elegant. The sparkle of the chandeliers was reflected endlessly in mirrors, glass and chrome, but the effect was, to León's mind, still reminiscent of cheap, showy jewellery. The whole place reeked of Addy's frustrated snobbery, her longing for what she called 'class'; it had none of the honest vulgarity which had made her fortune. The sex peddled here was the untouchable kind – pert hands-off waitresses, sultry singers who were paid only to sing, voluptuous female croupiers who were strictly forbidden to date the punters. The idea was to offer light relief, not an alternative, to the serious, respectable business of gambling.

'Go on, then,' said León. 'Get up there and show me what you can do.'

Even without an accompaniment, her voice was bang on key. Even without a microphone, it reached every corner of the room. The workmen stopped what they were doing, stood up and took notice, while she belted out 'Ten Cents A Dance' followed by 'Love Me Or Leave Me'. Strange how someone so shallow and immature could invest each word, each note, with a lifetime of experience. All the bitterness was there, all the disappointment and broken dreams of a woman twice her age. Listening to her was almost painful; when she finished there was a burst of spontaneous applause from her listeners, which she acknowledged graciously, as her due, before tripping down off her pedestal and becoming herself again.

'Well? Do I get the job? Will you talk to Mom?'

'I can talk, but I can't make her listen. She doesn't have a very high opinion of me, as you'll have gathered.'

Addy's taunt had stung, for all that it was well deserved. Work was merely the drug that kept despair at bay, that crammed his mind with things he didn't care about. His brushes and paints would have given shape to too many disturbing images, and he had quite enough suffering to cope with already without exploring the uncharted realms of self-expression. In the past, art had been fun, fantasy, falsehood, now it threatened to bring him face to face with the truth.

'Yes, she does,' said Lily. 'She always sticks up for you

when I . . . that is, I'm sure she didn't mean what she said. But she still shouldn't have said it.'

Lily rather relished apologising for Mom; normally it was the other way round.

'Why shouldn't she say it? It was fair comment. I'm a spoilt rich kid, same as you. I never worked for a living until a few weeks ago. And I'm only doing so now for selfish reasons.'

'You mean you're saving up to get married,' said Lily, tossing her head to hide her chagrin.

'What gave you that idea?'

'Mom said you were engaged to a girl from your home town,' shrugged Lily, affecting indifference. 'Does that mean she'll be coming to Havana?'

León didn't deign to answer. Lily pulled a face.

'In other words . . .' She sighed and dropped her voice an octave. ' . . . "Mind your own god-damned business." '

She caught the curl of the lip, the tone of voice, and the sudden jerk of the head with savage accuracy, provoking a reluctant smile.

'Not bad. Who else can you do?'

Lily promptly shrunk several inches and adopted María's abject sing-song and fidgety, cowering stance. ' "Please, Señor, the señorita has been smoking again. I told her to stop and she stubbed out her cigarette in my" ' – heartrending sobs – ' "in my *arroz con pollo*." ' And then, in a flash, she had grown to the statuesque proportions of Señora Valera. ' "You must breathe from here, child!" ' tapping her midriff, and then, inspecting some imaginary music, ' "What is this? Who is Cole Porter? I have never hearrd of him!" ' She giggled, pleased with herself, treating him to an artless naughty-kid grin, quite unlike her usual sly, malicious smirk.

'So when's the wedding?' she continued, pushing her luck.

León gave her a playful cuff around the ear.

'There isn't going to be one. Didn't your mother tell you that too?'

'No. What happened?' She had all the persistence of a child demanding a bedtime story.

'She jilted me. She married somebody else.'

'You don't say?' sympathised Lily, hiding her delight. 'Why would she do a thing like that?'

'Because she's not as much of a fool as I hoped. Or perhaps she's more of a fool than I thought. Talking of which, I don't want any foolish behaviour from you. Havana is full of sharks waiting to gobble up pretty, gullible young girls. All kinds of guys will send flowers backstage and ask you to have dinner with them. Dinner meaning sex. That's what your mother is trying to protect you from. If you want to prove how grown up you are, you'll smile sweetly and tell them to get lost. If I catch you fooling around with any of the customers, I'll fire you on the spot. The same applies if you start playing up or indulging in any kind of artistic temperament. I expect you to be professional. Is that understood?'

'Yes, boss,' said Lily meekly, all smug docility now that she had got her own way.

'It's a four-piece band, piano, trumpet, sax and bongo, I'll arrange a rehearsal for tomorrow. The pianist is very good-looking, he has a wife and two children. So watch it.'

'What about a dress? I've got to have a new dress.'

'You can talk to your mother about that. Assuming I can persuade her to give her permission. Just stay well out of it and leave me to do all the talking, OK? And if it doesn't work, you abide by her decision and don't come snivelling to me. I just hope I'm not making a rod for my own back.'

On arrival back at the house, Lily fled straight to her room as instructed, barely able to contain her glee. He wasn't getting married, after all. He liked her singing, he had given her a job, she would see him every night at the Herradura, he had forbidden her to go out with other men. This restriction pleased her. He obviously wanted her for himself, and didn't want Mom to know. That was why he was always so rude to her, to throw Mom off the scent. All this time he had probably been crazy about her. In romantic novels the hero and heroine always hated each other at first, and then, in the middle of a violent quarrel, they fell into each other's arms.

She could hear raised voices; much as she relished the

thought of Mom and León fighting over her, she didn't want it to end up with León walking out for real, or her mother firing him. Gingerly, she tiptoed out into the corridor and listened outside the door.

'You can't keep her locked up for ever,' León was saying. 'It will only make her even more rebellious.'

'If I agree to this, it will be on condition that you accept full responsibility for her.'

'I'll watch the little madam like a hawk, don't worry. I don't trust her any more than you do.'

'It's other men I don't trust. Frankly, I'd rather it happened with you than anyone else.'

'What?'

'Don't be coy. You must have noticed that the poor child is madly in love with you.'

Lily clapped her hand to her mouth. God, was it that obvious?

'Don't be ridiculous. If she is, it's because I'm the only man available.'

'And that's the way it's going to stay. All I ask is that you don't break her heart.'

'It's bound to get broken sooner or later. But not, I assure you, by me. Look, I must go. I've got an appointment.'

'An appointment? With Sofía, I suppose?'

'Why not? No chance of breaking her heart, at least. Or mine, come to that. Now take the kid out and buy her a new dress.'

Lily crept back to her room, her bubble of elation burst. 'I'd rather it happened with you than anyone else.' Her mother *approved*, dammit. This was just an extension of the child-minding role she had given him at the beginning. And meanwhile, he was seeing Captain Reinaldo's wife!

Trust Mom to go and spoil everything. It was just another present, another way of keeping her quiet. 'Look, darling, would you like that nice man in the window?'

The annoying thing was, she would.

'Raúl? It's me. Can you talk? Are you alone?'

Eduardo's voice was cool, impersonal. Raúl's heart went into spasm.

'Good morning, Señor. Hold the line just one moment.' He turned to his secretary. 'That will be all for now. Please see that I'm not disturbed, will you? I have an important contract to discuss.'

He waited impatiently till she had left the room before hissing, 'Where are you? Your letter didn't tell us anything.'

'I was afraid it might be intercepted. Are the police watching the place?'

'Not officially. But I expect they've recruited plenty of informers. How are you?'

'This isn't a social call. Are you still willing to help us?'

Raúl cast his mind back to those long, wearisome political discussions, when he had painstakingly laid the foundations of their relationship.

'More than ever. One of your comrades – the one called Pérez – died in prison, did you know?'

'I heard,' said Eduardo thickly.

'God only knows what they did to him, the boy's parents are kicking up a hell of a stink. More and more people are turning against Batista—'

'Half a dozen of us are leaving for the rebel camp. We need rifles and ammunition. Urgently.'

'You can count on me.'

'Then take the road to Punta Brava tonight and wait for me where it crosses the stream, near the place you showed me once, where your horse threw you as a child. I'll be there between ten and midnight. Be careful that you're not followed. How's my sister? Or should I say, your wife?'

So he had heard. Hence the icy, reproachful tone.

'She's fine. Eduardo, listen to me. I had a good reason for marrying her. I—'

'Don't tell her I called you. I don't want her involved in any of this. The less she knows the better.'

He hung up. Raúl shut his eyes, too excited to be perturbed by Eduardo's rancour. Once he explained, the hostility would shift onto León. All that mattered was that they would be alone, in a secret place, after dark. Perhaps for the last time . . .

He battled briefly with an urge to abandon his plans and follow Eduardo to the mountains. But it wouldn't work. Two men could never be together in an army. There were better ways. If he were to offer to supply the rebels on a regular basis, such clandestine meetings could become a regular thing; he could refuse to deal with anyone else but Eduardo.

He sprang into action immediately. Helping himself from the gun cupboard, under the eye of the round-the-clock army guard, would be to arouse unnecessary suspicion. Better to pick up some new supplies, which would mean absenting himself for the rest of the afternoon. He tapped on the door of his father's office. The old man was slumped in his leather swivel chair, staring into space; by his glazed look, he had been drinking steadily since lunch.

It had not taken Raúl long to undermine his crumbling authority; underneath all the bluster he was a broken man, haunted by images of his dead wife, racked by guilt, prone to sudden irrational rages. His memory was erratic, making it a simple matter to convince him that he had approved Raúl's plans or given him certain instructions, or to get his signature on a cheque. He would always pretend to be *au fait* rather than admit his ignorance, sinking ever deeper into a mire of confusion.

Seeing him in such a pitiable state, Raúl might have found it in his heart to forgive him, if he had deigned to ask for that forgiveness, to admit his crimes against him. Instead he persisted in behaving as if he was the one who had been wronged, and been magnanimous enough to let bygones be bygones. And yet, even now, the old man couldn't bear to restore the status quo, couldn't bear to make his elder son his outright heir. Damn him, thought Raúl. Why should I feel sorry for him? Why should I weaken now?

'I'm just leaving now for the Gómez *colonia*,' he said casually.

'What? Why?'

'He anticipates a surplus, remember? We discussed it. You asked me to strike a deal with him. I'll drive a hard bargain, don't worry.'

'Er . . . right. You do that. When will you be back?'

'Oh, I might do a few spot checks in the area. See if anyone's trying any fiddles behind our backs. Rojas tells me he was offered a bribe to accept short weight from Figueroa. I gave him a bonus, of course. I thought I'd make it clear that anyone else who tries it will find themselves without a contract for next year.'

Anything which fed the old man's paranoia was guaranteed to meet with his approval.

'Good man. Well, what are you waiting for? Get on with it!'

Raúl drove himself into Bayamo, where he bought half a dozen Winchester .22 rifles and a hundred rounds of ammunition; all sales of firearms were closely monitored by the authorities, so he took the precaution of calling in on the local police chief to alert him of his purchase.

'I'm not satisfied with those so-called soldiers,' he confided, knowing that there was no love lost between the army and the police. 'I intend to recruit and train a few hand-picked men of my own, as back-up.'

This was a plausible enough story. The recent increase in revolutionary activity had caused all plantations to invest heavily in security. Rebel forces were reported to be growing daily; disgruntled peasants were allegedly flocking to join them, eager to strike back at the big landowners who had oppressed them for so long. An American journalist had been invited to Fidel Castro's camp in the Sierra; the ensuing spread in the *New York Times* had made him into an international hero. Meanwhile, in Havana, revolutionaries had had the temerity to storm Batista's palace, albeit unsuccessfully; it all went to show that nowhere was safe, that you couldn't be too careful.

'Very wise,' approved the policeman. 'But finding good men isn't easy. There's no one you can trust these days. Take your stepbrother, for example . . .'

'Talking of which,' said Raúl, dropping his voice to a confidential murmur. 'He telephoned today. From Cienfuegos.'

'Cienfuegos?'

'To let my wife know that he was safe. He wouldn't give his address, of course, but you can probably close your files. I don't think he'll show his face in Oriente again. Er . . . don't mention to my wife that I told you. If your colleagues in Cienfuegos were to catch up with him, I wouldn't like her to think I had tipped them off. For your benevolent fund,' he added, extracting some notes from his pocket. 'Well, good day.'

Leaving the rifles in the boot of the car. Raúl arrived back at the house in time for dinner. Celia smiled serenely at him across the table, behaving normally as always, giving his father no reason to suspect their violent quarrel of the night before, provoked, as always, by Raúl and won, as always, by Celia.

He had broken his rule not to confide in her, found himself telling her things he had never told a living soul. The misery of his early life at Buenaventura, the way his brother had always been the favourite, the brutality he had suffered at his father's hands, his resentment of his mother's remarriage, the bitterness of exile. He had sought her sympathy, got it, wallowed in it, and then turned against her for giving it, ashamed to have confessed to so much weakness.

The taunts he flung at her were always the same. That his brother had made a fool of her, that she had behaved like a slut, that he wasn't taken in by her lies and pretence, that he knew very well she thought of León every time he made love to her. That she was plain and dull, and no bloody good in bed. Anything to make her cry, anything to make her seem even more feeble than himself.

But she didn't cry easily. And she didn't sulk either. She hit back, revealing the hot temper she had spent her life suppressing. He could tell that it was almost a relief for her to vent it on someone who appreciated it, deserved it, welcomed it. To watch it erupt and explode before his eyes was almost unbearably erotic. Already a quarrel had become an essential prelude to lovemaking. And after passion, came penitence, and pardon, and a measure of temporary peace.

Immediately after the meal Celia excused herself and went up to bed.

'Well?' roared his father. 'Can't you take a hint? Go up there and join her, man!'

'I think she's rather tired.'

'I should hope so too. Any signs yet? Has she bled this month?'

Raúl scowled, appalled at his crudity.

'No,' he said.

'Then she might be pregnant already?' said his father, counting the weeks back to their wedding.

'It's possible.'

'Excellent. Still, it's too early to be sure. Get up there and do your duty.' He shuffled off to his den, shedding cigar ash everywhere, creating an eddy of stale air. Since Lidia's death, he had taken to neglecting both his dress and personal hygiene. What a disgusting apology of a man he was. No wonder his poor bitch of a wife had fallen headlong into her handsome stepson's arms . . .

As had Celia, who 'understood'. She thought he took after his bully of a father, she identified with his mother, her mother, both of whom had preferred León. And now she was condemned to follow in their footsteps, for all that she wouldn't accept it. She needed to believe it was possible to love to order, that she would succeed where they had failed. Her self-respect depended on it. The harder it proved to be, the more determined she would become. How much would it take before she gave in and admitted defeat?

She was pretending to be asleep. He sat down on the bed and drew back the covers, displaying the marks his fingers had left on her shoulders. She bruised so easily, dammit. He hadn't intended to hurt her. She had hit back, as always, with spirit, kicking and biting and gouging her nails into his flesh, drawing blood, satisfying some unspoken need of her own. And afterwards she had licked clean the wounds she had inflicted, held him in her arms until he slept, rendered him abject, helpless, the victim, not the victor. Every time he abused his strength, he increased her power.

'Celia?' He bent down and took her hand. 'Are you awake?'

'I am now.'

She looked at him uncertainly, unsure, as always, what to expect, trying to gauge his mood.

'My father heard a rumour there were cane-burners in the area,' he told her. 'I'm going to take a drive around tonight and see if I spot anything suspicious.'

She sat up. 'Don't. It might be dangerous.'

'Nonsense. I'm only doing it to put his mind at rest. You know how worked up he gets. I'll sleep next door, so as not to wake you.'

Was it relief on her face, or disappointment? He took her face between his hands and kissed her forehead. 'Good night, my angel. Don't dream about him, will you? I'm jealous even of your dreams.'

He walked round to the garage block and transferred the rifles from the trunk of his sedan into the Jeep used for cross-country journeys. The dirt track to Punta Brava was undulating and narrow, full of gulleys that flooded with every storm, making it impassable to ordinary vehicles. Giving the guards on the gate the same story about cane-burners, he drove off into the night, his spirits lifting as he rose higher and higher into the mountains, passing tiny villages and isolated homesteads. The risk of meeting an army patrol was slight. Manpower was concentrated on fortifying garrisons and protecting vulnerable property, rather than inviting the possibility of ambush in the middle of nowhere.

He stopped by the stream and got out of the car, leaving his headlamps on. A moment later, two figures and a mule appeared from behind the trees. Shit, thought Raúl, he's not alone.

'Eduardo,' he said, running forward and grasping his hand.

'This is Mirella,' said Eduardo coolly. 'She's a courier.'

He had the beginnings of a beard, and, like the girl, he

was dressed in rough peasant clothes. Raúl stared at him, seething with frustration, like a child looking through a cake shop window, able to see but not touch.

'I assumed you would be alone. I need to talk to you in private.'

'Where are the rifles you promised?'

'If you want them, send her away.'

Eduardo hesitated.

'Mirella,' he said. 'Kindly leave us alone. I'll call for you when we've finished.' She nodded and disappeared into the darkness. 'Don't try anything,' continued Eduardo, keeping his voice low. 'One yell from me and she'll come running.' And then, his rage seeping through his frigid manner, 'Why did you do it? Is your father leaving the estate to her, or what?'

'On the contrary, he's leaving it to me.'

'Then why? You said—'

'León made your sister pregnant. I married her to protect her reputation and give the child a name. My father has no idea, of course. The child is due in September. Prematurely, of course.'

Eduardo swore violently.

'I knew it,' he hissed. 'I knew the bastard was screwing her, I could see it in her eyes . . .'

'It doesn't make any difference to us,' continued Raúl. 'Surely you understand that?'

Eduardo looked at him in amazement.

'Thank you for doing the decent thing by her,' he said stiffly. 'I appreciate it. But there can be nothing between us in future. Not now that you're married to my sister.'

It wasn't even healthy pique any more; it was his ridiculous, debilitating sense of honour.

'The marriage is in name only,' said Raúl. 'Thanks to León, Celia finds any thought of sex repellent. She told me I was free to seek other liaisons, as long as I left her alone. Nothing we do together can hurt your sister. Do you want me to force myself on her out of sheer frustration? I though you would respect me for what I did, not turn against me.'

Eduardo searched his eyes; Raúl's returning gaze did

not waver for an instant. Trust, however misplaced, created its own truth.

'It's pointless to discuss it.' said Eduardo. 'By tomorrow I'll be gone, we may never see each other again.'

'Listen, I can be useful to you. I can supply you with food, arms, drugs, ammunition. Everything you need. But only if you collect the goods, and only if you come alone.'

'Are you trying to bribe me?'

'If I must. I can't live without you, Eduardo. If I can't see you any other way, I'll just have to join you in the mountains.'

'No!' He dropped his voice. 'Please, Raúl, don't do that to me. We'd get caught. You know we would. It would be suicide.'

'Then do as I ask. Tell your *compañeros* that you've talked me into supplying them, but that I refuse to deal with anyone else but you.'

Eduardo shut his eyes, fear and temptation fighting open battle all over his face.

'They won't wear it. I'm a new recruit. I can't dictate terms to them.'

'Then I will. Don't force me to pursue you, Eduardo. Don't expect me to give you up, not now . . .'

He reached out to touch him, felt his answering tremor. Eduardo took a step backwards.

'I'll get word to you. Let's have those rifles. Mirella!'

The girl emerged from the trees, barely visible in her dark clothing. Raúl handed over the weapons and ammunition, which they loaded onto the mule, concealed among bundles of palm-thatch. Then they slid away from him like a disappearing dream, leaving him heavy with hope.

Frank had not had to wait long for his visitors. He had muzzled and tethered George in readiness, fearing that they might shoot the dog if it tried to defend him.

'I know one of the girls who works at Addy's,' he told them coolly, while Pedro and his mate, trigger fingers twitching, made great play of deciding whether to shoot him. 'That's why I did it. And that's why I've dumped my cargo over the side. From now on you can get your stuff from somebody else.'

'Such noble scruples,' Pedro had sneered. 'Have you any idea how many lives are lost every day thanks to this stinking government? Quite apart from the people they arrest and torture and kill? There are the children who die for lack of food and medical care, the peasants who are hounded off their land, the innocent people who are sentenced to death because verdicts can be bought and sold, the—'

'Cut the crap. Just go ahead and kill me and prove how brave you are.'

'It will be a pleasure, Yanqui,' began the other man, poking the barrel of the gun in his chest, but Pedro stayed his hand.

'We can do without American help,' he snarled. 'We made that mistake in the war of independence, the war you pretended to win for us so that you could rule Cuba by proxy. You sold us the stuff because you wanted our money, no other reason. Like all your kind you worship the dollar. You're not worth the bullet it would cost to kill you. Go to hell.'

And with that they had spat on the ground and marched off, leaving him dizzy with relief. They would learn in time, as he had learned, that wars were never won, only lost.

The next day he decided to deal in more innocuous, if less profitable cargo. There was always a ready market for dope. Senior policemen masterminded its distribution via cops on the beat, who would pick up unemployed youths off the street and offer them a cut to sell the stuff in Havana's teeming slums, this crime to be committed under full police protection. So what? thought Frank. At least it didn't kill anyone.

He made enquiries of the harbour officials, using the appropriate circumlocutions; next day he received a note asking him to call at an address in Miramar to discuss new import regulations. Frank duly presented himself and agreed terms with one Captain Hector Reinaldo, a balding, dapper little guy with a waxed moustache, narrow deep-set eyes and unnaturally small hands and feet. He made Pedro and co. seem like a bunch of pussy-cats. Double-cross him and you were dead.

Perhaps he should give it a miss, clean up his act, try to do something legal for a change. It was a bit pathetic to be playing the pirate at the age of forty-three . . . Forty-three. Much too old to start living by the rules. Breaking them was the only point of honour he had left.

'How do I look?' demanded Lily, inspecting herself in the mirror.

'Absolutely gorgeous,' said Addy, blinking back the tears. She looked so grown-up tonight, so beautiful in her silver-spangled dress, with her vivid hair piled up on top of her head. It was like looking back twenty years into the past. There was a spray of lilies on the dressing table, with a card which said simply, 'Make your mother proud of you, for once. León.' A much larger, flashier bouquet had arrived from Captain Reinaldo, which Addy had been quick to intercept.

'Did you see how many flowers arrived for Rhonda Carroll?' grumbled Lily, referring to the American cabaret star who had been imported from Miami at vast expense. 'Nearly as many as arrived for you.'

'Would you trade yours for hers?' smiled Addy, plucking one of the lilies and putting it in its namesake's hair. 'Or mine, come to that?'

'The ones León sent you were nicer,' said Lily churlishly. 'I expect he was trying to keep up with all your other admirers.'

'They're not admirers. Mostly they're people I do business with.'

'Well, it looks like a hospital out there. I wouldn't be surprised if I started sneezing half-way through my first number.'

'Don't be nervous, darling,' said Addy. 'I just know you're going to be a big success.'

'I'm not nervous. I'm a better singer than *her*. Even León says so.'

There was a knock at the door and León came in, looking immaculate in a white tuxedo.

'Addy, Captain Reinaldo has honoured us with his presence. He's sitting at your table waiting to kiss your hand. Unfortunately, his wife couldn't come tonight.'

'What a shame,' said Lily innocently. Addy exchanged glances with León.

'When Lily joins us, after her act,' she said, touching his arm, 'I want you to head him off, pronto.' She embraced her daughter fiercely. 'I'll be rooting for you, darling. See you later.' She went off to greet her guest.

'Why do you have to head him off?' demanded Lily of León, as if she didn't know. 'I think Captain Reinaldo is very nice and polite.'

'A nice polite old lech,' said León. 'Take that flower out of your hair, it looks ridiculous.' He removed it and looked at her critically. 'You're putting on weight.'

'Don't you start,' muttered Lily, who was proud of her burgeoning bosom, if rather sensitive about her thickening waistline. Her mother had made the same comment. She had kept asking her when her period was due, and so Lily had pretended to come on, languishing on the couch with a hot-water bottle just to shut her up. Her cycle had always been erratic; sometimes she went for months without anything happening, provoking stern questions from the matron at school, who recorded such things on a chart. Mom was nearly as bad. But Lily stubbornly refused to worry; the week with Frank on the boat was like a dream, immune from consequences. More likely the change of air had upset her system, not to mention María's cooking.

'Spotlights show up every bulge,' continued León pitilessly. 'You'd better cut down on the ice-cream and candy in future. Apart from that you look OK.'

'León . . .'–a heart-melting tremble of the lip–'I'm scared.' She was, too. Too scared to allow her real fear to bubble to the surface. Putting it on was safer.

'I should hope so. Don't worry. Once you hear the music, you'll be fine.'

'But s-suppose they don't like me?'

'Then I'll have to fire you.'

'Trust you to be horrible to me just before I go on! G-go away!' She began mewing into a handkerchief.

'You'll ruin your make-up.'

Lily had already considered this, but none the less she sent two glistening teardrops cascading down her powered cheek. It would only take a minute to repair the damage.

'Stop blubbering, there's a good kid.' Relenting, he gave her a brief, placatory hug. She clung to him, wanting to make the moment last. It didn't. León unwound her arms without ceremony.

'I stuck my neck out for you, remember? Don't you dare let me down.'

He left her to finish preening herself, wondering, not for the first time, if he had done the right thing in talking Addy into this. Not that he had done any such thing; Addy had well and truly set him up. 'You're responsible for her, remember,' she had said. Responsible for a kid who had a crush on him. 'I'd rather it was you than anyone else.' So that he could protect her against men even less scrupulous than himself. It was like some crazy inside-out version of the Celia/Lidia nightmare, and in some ways no less threatening. Women. There was no getting away from them.

He returned to the bar-cum-cabaret area, where Addy was holding court to a hand-picked first night clientele – rake-off merchants like Reinaldo, Mafia loan sharks who had provided her capital, suppliers who hoped for regular orders, and a cross-section of Havana's business and social community plus their bored, pleasure-seeking wives, eager for new ways to spend their excess time and money.

'Thank you for the beautiful bouquet you sent,' Addy was warbling at Reinaldo.

'I see I was not the only one to want to pay tribute to a

very successful lady,' said Reinaldo smoothly, indicating the profusion of floral displays. The biggest one was from the girls who worked at Addy's, who had clubbed together to buy a huge horseshoe woven out of jacaranda, bougainvillaea and mariposa, studded with rare *Flor San Pedro* orchids.

'I hope you'll spread the good word for me, Captain,' cooed Addy. 'Any friends of yours will be assured of an extra special welcome.'

'I gather that your charming daughter is singing tonight. Not that I believe she's really your daughter. You look much too young. No wonder you kept her a secret. I've no doubt that she will prove to be a big attraction. I confess myself quite enchanted with her.'

León saw Addy's mouth tighten imperceptibly and knew what she was thinking. Reinaldo was quite capable of asking for payment in kind, and of making life extremely difficult for her if thwarted.

'You're not the only one,' put in León, appalled by a sick-making image of those tiny manicured hands examining Lily's charms in detail. 'I'm afraid the young lady has already acquired an admirer. One who works on the premises and keeps a very close eye on her.' He gave Reinaldo a steely smile and offered him a cigar. 'One who enjoys her mother's full approval.'

'A very generous mother,' said Reinaldo, eyes narrowing, looking from León to Addy and back again.

'And a very protective one,' said Addy sweetly, squeezing León's hand gratefully under cover of the table. 'He's someone I know I can trust absolutely. A mother can't be too careful these days.'

'And being from Oriente, he's one of those possessive types,' continued León, lighting Reinaldo's cigar and then his own. 'You know how passionate these provincials are about defending their womenfolk's honour.' He exhaled a dense plume of smoke, relishing the irony of his new role. Only yesterday he had been consoling Reinaldo's neglected wife; today he was playing the jealous lover.

Reinaldo shrugged. 'Women are fickle, alas. Especially

young, beautiful women. We men are but helpless victims, vying for their favours . . .' His eyes lit up as the first act was announced.

'And now, returning to her birthplace for her singing début, a warm welcome please for Miss . . . Lily . . . Herbert!'

A rustle of polite, disinterested applause, a barely perceptible reduction in the babble of conversation. León had warned her not to expect silence, or attention, or appreciation, stressed that she was just a supporting act, there to provide decorative background noise, but none the less he had to resist the urge to stand up on the table and shout, 'Shut up, damn you, and listen!'

Lily fixed her eyes on her mother's table, unable to see León in the gloom, but knowing he was there. She always sang for one special person, even when there was nobody to hear her, and tonight she would sing just for him. She launched straight into a rasping, gritty rendition of 'Luck Be A Lady Tonight', drowning out the hum of conversation, which, unable to make itself heard above her powerful vocal cords, lapsed into an unaccustomed hush, ready for a husky, infinitely suggestive 'Bésame Mucho'.

God, she was sexy when she sang, thought León. It wasn't even deliberate, otherwise she would surely contrive to be so in real life. In real life she had the exaggerated, embarrassing sex-appeal of a whore. He wondered if she was capable of genuine emotion. Or perhaps she had already learned the dangers of feeling anything, except under cover of a song.

'Bravo!' he called out, rising to his feet to applaud her, inspiring others to do likewise. Reinaldo clapped with polite restraint, licking his lips as Lily made a deep bow. Addy blew her nose; could that really be her little girl up there? She called to one of the waitresses for a bottle of champagne; on cue León bore Reinaldo off to the roulette table.

Lily appeared a few minutes later, glowing and breathless.

'You were wonderful, darling,' said Addy, embracing her. 'Let me introduce you to Señor and Señora Valdez.

Señor Valdez is at the Department of the Interior, he's a personal friend of the President. He has a daughter about your age, studying in Miami . . .'

All those hours spent being polite to Grandma's cronies stood Lily in good stead. She smiled and listened politely while Señora Valdez, already flushed from too many free cocktails, toasted Lily's health and began the inevitable eulogy to the absent daughter; meanwhile her husband was giving some boring account of the recent attack on Batista's palace.

'A fiasco,' he droned. 'We were in fact fully prepared for the assault. As always, the rebels were betrayed by one of their own. They have no unity, no programme, they are the spiritual descendants of the gangsters of the nineteen-thirties . . .'

'. . . of course, my daughter would like to settle permanently in the United States,' Señora Valdez went on. 'Her elder brother married an American girl, he has his own business over there. They have two adorable little children . . .' She began rummaging in her purse for the photographs. Lily's fixed, false smile became momentarily spontaneous as she saw León approaching from the other side of the room.

He never reached her. He disappeared behind a blinding flash, the lightning to the most tremendous clap of thunder. Suddenly the room was full of dense swirling dust and the sound of screaming.

'Lily!' yelled her mother, gripping her arm. 'Hold onto me! Out into the street, quick!'

Another explosion, even louder than the first.

'León!' screamed Lily, ignoring her mother's plea, wrenching her arm free, heading towards the place where she had last seen him. 'León!'

She was knocked headlong by the weight of bodies stampeding to get out. She banged her head hard on the corner of a table, felt someone's foot in the small of her back, and then a final deafening blast robbed her abruptly of all her senses.

León was not so fortunate. He saw everything, heard

everything, endured the horror of finding Addy's inert body pinned down under a fallen beam with its left leg blown off at the knee. He picked her up and carried her to safety before returning inside, soaked with her blood, to search for Lily, fighting his way through the rubble, ignoring the other casualties till he found her, unconscious but not visibly injured.

Reinaldo, to do him credit, got them both to hospital double quick, commandeering the first ambulance to arrive. It hurtled through the darkened streets, siren shrieking, while Reinaldo followed in his own vehicle with León as passenger.

'Your security arrangements left a lot to be desired,' he said tightly, inspecting his right sleeve, which had been torn at the shoulder in the fight to get out of the building.

'I don't understand it,' muttered León to himself. He had been careful to take every precaution, mindful of the American's warning that the rebels would try again. Every workman had had his tool kit inspected, every item checked into the cloakroom had been opened by its owner, every crate of bottles and box of foodstuffs had been examined, every bag had been searched . . .

'The flowers,' he said suddenly. 'It must have been the flowers.' Huge displays in baskets, with explosives lurking beneath the blooms. How could he have been so stupid?

'Scum,' hissed Reinaldo. 'We'll catch the bastards who did it, never fear.' And even if they didn't, León found himself thinking, others would be convicted in their place, or die in police custody, to save the tiresome inconvenience of a trial. He shut his eyes and started to pray, for the first time since childhood.

Addy and Lily were whisked into the emergency room on arrival; León and Reinaldo sat in the corridor outside, waiting interminably for news.

'What sort of insurance did she have?' enquired Reinaldo, offering León his umpteenth cigarette. 'It's virtually impossible to get cover against terrorist attack these days. Unless you're willing to pay the earth.'

'I don't know,' muttered León irritably. Trust Reinaldo to think about money at a time like this. 'And I don't care, as long as they both get out of here alive . . .'

After what seemed like hours a doctor emerged and approached them quickly, evidently in a hurry to begin work on his next case.

'Relatives of Lily Herbert?' León jumped up. The doctor drew him aside, and said quietly, 'Would you be the fiancé, by any chance?'

León cast a sideways glance at Reinaldo, who was affecting not to listen.

'Yes. Yes, I am. Is she all right?'

'She's still unconscious, due to concussion, but luckily there's no damage to the baby.'

'The baby?' echoed León faintly.

'Naturally we'll be keeping her under close observation. She'll need complete bed rest for the next few days. You can see her as soon as she comes round.'

'And her mother?'

'She's still in theatre. You'll be kept informed.'

He hurried off. Reinaldo coughed.

'I couldn't help overhearing . . .' he began.

'I'd appreciate your discretion,' said León stiffly.

'Naturally.'

'I think I'd rather wait alone now, if you don't mind. Thank you for your help.'

Reinaldo stood up. 'As you wish. I will telephone for news later tonight. Please convey my best wishes to both mother and daughter. If I can be of any assistance, I am at your disposal. Don't hesitate to call me, at home or at the office.'

'Thank you.'

León shook his small, smooth hand and watched him walk away. His discretion wasn't worth shit of course. The first person he would tell would be his wife, who would promptly tell half of Havana. Not that it mattered. Nothing mattered, as long as they were all right.

Did Lily even know she was pregnant, or had she done what he would have done, in her place – buried her head in the sand and waited for the problem to go away? How the hell was he going to break the news to Addy? Addy who had lost a leg, lost her casino, possibly lost her entire fortune. And what about Lily? If Addy died, how was he going to tell Lily?

He froze as a surgeon in a green gown came out of a swing door and advanced towards him relentlessly, like an angel of death.

'She's gone, isn't she?' He felt numb, blocked.

'I'm very sorry. The internal injuries were beyond surgery. I understand that her daughter has regained consciousness. She's very confused and keeps asking for her mother. We don't advise telling her yet, for obvious reasons. Please bear that in mind when you go in to see her.'

'Yes. Yes, of course.'

He must have sat there for several minutes, in a daze, without moving, unaware till the tears splashed on his hands that he was crying. Addy would have been surprised and touched to see him weep for her. He had never let her know how much he cared for her, never admitted it to himself till now. Strong, gutsy, independent, she had made few demands on him in life. But now that she was dead, he could not ignore the last request she would surely have made. She would have asked him to take care of Lily. Not just Lily, but her child, Addy's grandchild . . .

Oh, God. Reinaldo already believed that the baby was his, and so would everyone else. He would have to track down the real father, drag him to the altar, or failing that, marry her himself. Otherwise Addy's ghost, like Lidia's, would haunt him for ever.

Lidia. It was as if she was trying to punish him from beyond the grave. If so, he could hardly blame her. As long as she didn't do the same to Celia. As long as she left Celia alone.

PART TWO

June – September 1957

EIGHT

'GET A load of that mulatta,' said Lázaro's fellow private, an exceedingly inept trainee mechanic who tried his patience sorely. 'Stop the truck and let's take a closer look.'

Lázaro hesitated, torn between curiosity and a chivalrous wish to leave the poor girl in peace. Curiosity won.

'The two white guys with her might be carrying weapons,' he conceded gruffly. 'We'd better check them out.' He pulled up, and called out to the party to halt.

'What have you got in that basket?' he demanded of the girl, keeping his voice low, courteous.

She put it down on the ground without speaking, tacitly inviting him to look inside. It was a moment before he could tear his eyes away from her. She was beautiful, with clear skin the colour of caramel and hair as shiny as tar, her full skirt billowing around her slender waist, her bare legs tapering into fragile ankles.

'Where are you going to, darling?' put in Lázaro's companion jeeringly. 'How about riding with us?' She didn't answer.

'We're on our way back to our village,' put in one of the men. 'We've been to the market in Santiago, to sell eggs and vegetables.' He indicated her empty basket and the sacks thrown over their shoulders.

'I asked her, not you.'

'She can't speak,' said the second man. 'She's been dumb ever since she was attacked by bandits last year. We're her cousins. Her father won't let her go out alone.'

Lázaro gestured them towards the truck and frisked them both while his comrade kept his weapon pointed at them, if not his eyes. His eyes were still fixed, lasciviously, on the girl.

'When you've finished,' he called, 'take over the gun and I'll do the same to her. Check if those tits of hers are for real.'

The mulatta stood very still, her face registering no emotion, eyes downcast. Only the set of her shoulders changed, imperceptibly, registering silent terror.

'You'll keep your hands to yourself,' snarled Lázaro. And then, to the girl, 'It's all right. Don't be frightened. No one's going to hurt you.' He jerked his head at the two men. 'That's it. Clear off back to your village.'

The girl shuddered in visible relief. No wonder the father wouldn't let her out alone, thought Lázaro. It was not uncommon for peasants to be attacked on their way to or from market, either for the food they carried or for the proceeds of the sale. Many bandits now called themselves 'rebels' to sanctify their crimes, not that Lázaro saw much difference; both breeds were bent on robbery and murder. But a girl like that wasn't safe anywhere . . .

'Don't be a fool, man,' chivvied his comrade. 'Put her in the back of the truck and we'll take it in turns.'

'You heard what I said.' He got back into the driving seat and started the engine. 'Are you coming back to the barracks with me or would you prefer to walk?'

'But—'

'I said, leave her alone!'

Scowling, his companion rejoined him.

'What the fuck's the matter with you?'

'We came out to test a new back axle, not to rape some peasant girl. And all the while you're my trainee, I give the orders, not you.'

For the past two months, Lázaro had been assigned to the motor pool at the Santiago barracks, maintaining and repairing military vehicles and acting as driver to senior officers. Technical skills such as his were rare among recruits; Lázaro knew he was in line for promotion to corporal and a permanent cushy billet as an instructor. The prospect of killing any rebels seemed as distant as ever.

'Rape? Don't make me laugh. She was screaming for it. You're soft, that's your trouble. These scumbag peasants all support the rebels, they'd sell their souls to anyone who promised them a patch of land. And their women are all whores. They say Castro has a regular harem up there in the hills.'

'And you're soft in the head. Don't you know that half the peasants are informers in the pay of the police? For all you know, that girl was one of them and you could have ended up on a charge. So watch it. I'm damned if I'll lose my chance of getting a stripe, thanks to a cretin like you.'

Seeing the dangerous glint in his eye, Lázaro's comrade wisely chose to let the insult pass.

'All right, all right. She was only some little slag. Not worth fighting over . . .'

Not for the first time, Lázaro blessed his powerful build and naturally truculent expression. It wouldn't do for his fellow soldiers to know that he had never once struck a man except in self-defence. Though he would have done, if that animal had dared lay a finger on the girl. Thank God he had been there to protect her.

He wished he had thought to ask her name, and the whereabouts of her village. Perhaps he could find an excuse to come this way again next market day, on the off-chance that she might come back. After weeks of making do with whores he longed for a different kind of girl, one who was pure and delicate, who would soothe his troubled spirit and restore his masculine pride.

Revenge wouldn't be enough, he knew that now. Revenge was like an all-consuming fire that purged and cleansed, revenge would leave him drained, empty, weightless. But then what? For the first time in his life, he longed for love.

Three months in the mountains had been a test of stamina, but not, so far, of courage. Eduardo had been prepared for hunger, hardship, exhaustion, and, above all, fear. What he had not bargained for was being bored.

The rebel camp was situated in the upper reaches of

Pico Turquino, some fifty kilometres south-west of Buenaventura. It comprised several semi-permanent structures, made of the palm which covered the area like some giant weed; long hours were devoted to heavy building work, erecting the workshops which would make the rebels as self-sufficient as possible. Plans were in hand to set up a shoemaker's, a gun repairer's, a bomb factory, a hospital, a butcher's and even a cigar factory.

The rest of the time was spent in mind-numbing route marches, laden like beasts of burden, subsisting on iron rations and sleeping rough on hammocks made of sacking. Not surprisingly, many recruits succumbed to the effects of heat, fatigue, insect bites and fever; desertions were frequent, as were summary dismissals of men deemed unfit for service due to moral, ideological or physical shortcomings.

New arrivals were mercilessly grilled to weed out informers and spies. Although the camp's location was undoubtedly known to Batista's agents, its elevated position made it immune to ambush and all but inaccessible to conventional forces. The jungle terrain was an effective camouflage, hampering air reconnaissance, as was the blue mist which hung over the area like a veil. So far there had been no engagements with government troops, let alone the special task force charged with eliminating all guerrillas.

Advisedly so; the rebel army was much smaller than was commonly supposed; hence its cautious attitude towards combat. Certainly there was less action up here than in the towns, where bombings and sabotage continued unabated despite savage police reprisals. To Eduardo's disappointment, he had no access to his heroes, Fidel Castro and Che Guevara, apart from compulsory attendance at their political lectures. The sheer tedium of camp life would have been intolerable but for the respite of his meetings with Raúl.

Buenaventura was a rich and inexhaustible source of much-needed supplies, thus enabling Raúl, if not Eduardo, to name his own conditions for collection. At first

Mirella had been sent in Eduardo's stead, accompanied by a local peasant who acted as a full-time courier. They had returned empty-handed, but for a note from Raúl, addressed to Eduardo, but read first – as it was intended to be – by his superiors.

> I was most reluctant to deal with strangers whom I neither know nor trust. It is well known that your forces are riddled with spies. With all due respect to your *compañeros*, I must in future refuse to meet with anyone other than yourself, whose loyalty to the cause I know to be as fierce as my own, and who I know will not betray me to the authorities. If these terms are unacceptable, I propose to offer myself for active service. In my absence, there will be no one else whom I can trust to continue to supply you, other than your sister whom I refuse to put at risk in view of her delicate condition.

'We need supplies more than we need an extra man,' Eduardo's lieutenant had barked. 'You'd better meet with him yourself next time. Arrange a regular rendezvous and squeeze him for as much you can get.'

It was, inadmissibly, a relief, to be forced to fall in with Raúl's plan. He had needed an excuse for his own weakness, and Raúl, realising this, had provided him with one, as if to relieve him of responsibility. Given that his marriage to Celia was in name only – a claim which Eduardo preferred not to challenge – it was all too easy to convince himself that neither of them was guilty of betraying her.

Their meeting place was about four hours' walk from the camp. Raúl would drive into the mountains as far as the road would take him, there to transfer sacks of beans, flour and rice, ammunition, tools and drugs onto Eduardo's waiting mule. He would combine such expeditions with routine overnight absences from Buenaventura, to avoid arousing suspicion; their encounters were always under cover of darkness, giving them a few precious hours together before Eduardo could commence his return journey at daybreak – a few hours when he could be truly himself, however briefly, sure of his prearranged escape, able to walk away, until the next time. It made it seem as if he was in control, as if he was still free. And in any case, there might not be a next time. The prospect of premature, sudden death in battle intensified every moment they spent together.

Unlike him, Raúl knew the terrors of battle first-hand. Hearing about his wartime experiences, Eduardo could only envy him his courage and rage at the way the US Army had treated him. He felt honoured that Raúl should have seen fit to tell him the real reason for his discharge, a dark secret he had never confided in anyone else and one which brought them closer together, as did their joint commitment to the revolution.

'I'm very ignorant about politics,' Raúl had said, allowing him to take the lead. But despite his admitted lack of textbook knowledge, Raúl believed unreservedly, as Eduardo did, in the principles of democracy and free elections, purged of the corruption that had brought Batista, and others, to power; Eduardo had been quick to build on this, eager to convert him to the cause.

Raúl had been shocked to learn that all workers at Buenaventura were required to surrender their voting cards, a common practice amongst employers, thus disenfranchising themselves and ensuring the return of a candidate chosen by his father. He deplored the evils, as expounded by Eduardo, of the ruthless monoculture which provided work for only half the year for the sake of guaranteed profits. He expressed admiration for Celia's plans – so far blocked by Don Enrique – to introduce new schemes which would enable the workers to share Buenaventura's profits. Eduardo had in fact pooh-poohed his sister's suggestions as 'petty reform', but they sounded bold and adventurous coming from Raúl, Raúl who epitomised strength and daring, Raúl who carried a machine-gun under the seat of the car to disable any patrol foolish enough to stop and search him.

Not that it had happened yet. Troops were spread thin, especially now that so many of them were hired out to provide paid protection for businesses and plantations, lining their commanding officers' pockets and leaving vast tracts of land as virtual 'free territory'. In any case, most soldiers were incompetent, ill-motivated and unwilling to put themselves in danger. Attacks on army personnel were frequent, with rebel supporters issuing guns to children as young as eight. Recently a little girl had shot a lone soldier fatally in the stomach, even as he bent to pat her on the head, before making off with his rifle. It was all part of the war of attrition which would prepare the way for the eventual rebel push towards Havana.

Meanwhile, by mutual agreement, Celia remained ignorant of Raúl's involvement in the struggle. In the event of his being apprehended, it would be best if she genuinely knew nothing. And besides, as Raúl was quick to point out, her support could not be guaranteed. Much to her distress, several of Buenaventura's fields had been set ablaze, though this loss would make little odds in a year which had yielded a bumper harvest. The culprits would never be identified. It was an easy matter to attach a paraffin-soaked sponge to a rat and put a match to it, leaving the frenzied creature to cut a jagged, blazing swathe through the cane. But so far such attacks had proved few, perhaps because workers, unable to grasp the importance of depriving the government of sugar revenue, had a vested interest in protecting the crop which gave them their livelihood.

Mirella, who knew every inch of the Sierra, was a frequent visitor to the camp, meeting and guiding groups of volunteers from the surrounding area. She always made a point of seeking out Eduardo, even waiting a day or two till he returned from an exercise, whereupon they would disappear into the trees together for a few hours of privacy. Naturally, everyone assumed that they were lovers. It occurred to Eduardo that perhaps Mirella wanted them to think this, in order to protect herself from unwelcome attentions, and so he fostered this illusion, perhaps for his own benefit as well as hers, while taking care not to do or say anything that might destroy her gratifying trust in him.

The pattern of their meetings never varied; Eduardo would speak – sometimes reciting a chunk of poetry, sometimes reading an extract from a book or newspaper – while Mirella wrote down everything he said, after which he would read it through and check and correct her spelling. Then, in response to her silent, persuasive prompting, he would talk about his ambition to be a doctor, the importance of eliminating the diseases of poverty and ignorance, and the need to make medical care readily available to all.

Uneducated she might be, but there was no doubt in Eduardo's mind that she was highly intelligent, sensitive and refined. Their bond was mutual respect and a common cause; they were comrades, with nothing to fear from one another, if more than enough to fear on each other's behalf.

This morning he had awoken with the surge of elation that heralded his weekly rendezvous with Raúl. Just as he was setting off with his mule, he caught sight of Mirella, accompanied by a panting pair of new volunteers, haggard and wheezing, as he had once been, from the punishing climb. Her face lit up as she spotted him, but unusually, for her, she looked weary; her face was filmed with sweat and a red flush was visible beneath her smooth brown skin.

She stood silent by Eduardo's side while the self-elected spokesman of the group recounted their brush with an army patrol just outside Santiago; the soldiers had searched both men, unaware that Mirella carried their weapons suspended from a belt, hidden beneath the stiff petticoats of her dirndl skirt.

'Two thick-as-shit niggers, luckily for us,' he went on expansively. 'One of them was obviously smitten with Mirella, stopped his buddy hauling her off to be strip-searched . . .'

Mirella froze him with a look, reproving either his racism or the lewd tone of his voice; at that moment the platoon lieutenant arrived and hauled the newcomers off for vetting. Mirella indicated that she wished to unburden herself and disappeared briefly into the undergrowth, returning with a couple of army-issue revolvers.

'I'm just leaving,' Eduardo told her, apologetically, 'to collect supplies.'

She smiled and indicated that she would accompany him part of the way; her village was well to the east of his meeting place with Raúl, where he would arrive at sundown and camp till dawn. He noticed the shadows under her eyes, the furrow of fatigue across her brow.

'Are you sick?' She shook her head. 'You look tired. Stay here and rest. I'll be back by tomorrow morning.' She gestured another negative and took hold of the mule's bridle.

'Enjoy yourselves,' someone yelled after them. 'If you don't come back, Rodríguez, we'll know she's finally shagged you out!'

Mirella bowed her head, embarrassed.

'Apologise to the lady,' said Eduardo tightly. The man concerned was a big, burly peasant with forearms as thick as hams. 'And mind your language in future. Do you suppose she's deaf as well as dumb?'

There was a rumble of sheepish support, indicating to the aggressor that Eduardo spoke for them all. Several of those present had been guided to the camp by Mirella and all of them lusted after her without any hope of success.

'No offence, Mirella,' grunted the man, without looking at her. 'It was only a lousy joke.'

She ignored the apology, staring straight ahead of her, dignified, untouchable, and Eduardo couldn't help feeling proud that his comrades thought she was his woman, if disgusted at the crude interpretation they put upon their relationship. As he led her away she grasped hold of his hand, the first time she had ever touched him. It felt small and fragile, filling him with pity and protectiveness; if he hadn't met Raúl, would he have thought, perhaps, that this was love?

Her silence invited secrets; knowing that she wouldn't repeat anything he said, Eduardo fell to talking about his childhood, his family, his feelings, himself – something he had never done with anyone else but Raúl. He told her about his hazy memories of his father and the shattering effect his death had had on the whole family. Celia, the most boisterous and extrovert of sisters, had transformed overnight into surrogate head of the family, consoling their prostrate mother, taking care of her younger sibling, suppressing her own tears, inspiring him to do the same. Their childhood had ended at that moment, never to be fully resumed.

'I never liked my stepfather much,' he said. 'But Celia can't bring herself not to like anyone, she's always making excuses for people. It disgusted me that my mother sold herself, even though I did all right out of it. My own father could never have afforded to give me a fancy education . . .'

He wanted her to know that he had once been poor, albeit nowhere near as poor as she. It was a monologue, but it didn't seem like one. Her rapt attention was a response in itself.

'Celia was a sitting duck for my stepbrother, León. Or perhaps I should say duckling. Ugly duckling. She's not ugly, actually, but my mother brainwashed her into thinking she was. So what chance did she stand with a womaniser like him?'

It was tempting to tell her the whole story, but loyalty to his sister and mother forbade it. León had taken up with another woman, he said, breaking Celia's heart – true enough, in its way – and she had married Raúl on the rebound.

'I used to have a lot of time for León,' he said. 'I respected the way he refused to crawl to his father. I admired his intellect – he was a brilliant scholar, even though he was so damned lazy. But now I despise him. I don't believe he's capable of loving anyone . . .'

No more than he had been, until recently. He tailed off, feeling like a hypocrite. Which was worse, having an affair with your father's wife, or your sister's husband? Was he just using León as a scapegoat for his own guilt?

León who, despite all their differences, had always been kind to him, León who was tolerant and broad-minded, who believed in live-and-let-live if nothing else. Would León judge him as harshly as he had judged León?

'Love requires courage,' he muttered, thinking aloud. 'Raúl says cowardice is a natural state, that courage is acquired, not given. You don't find it till you're tested, till you overcome fear . . . Mirella?' He shot out an arm to catch her as she stumbled. 'Are you all right?'

Normally so sure-footed and indefatigable, she sank to the ground, apparently exhausted.

'What's the matter?' he said, alarmed, tugging the mule to a halt.

She clasped her hands over her belly, shutting her eyes against the pain. Eduardo felt her forehead to find it was burning hot.

'Why didn't you say?' he began, angry with himself for rambling on and not noticing her distress. 'Show me where it hurts.'

Mirella rolled over onto her side and was violently sick, the vomit a tell-tale shade of yellowish green. Eduardo wiped her face with his handkerchief. Gently, he prised her hands away and began prodding her abdomen, eliciting a stifled moan.

'When did it start? This morning?'

She nodded and began struggling to her feet. He pushed her down firmly onto her back and continued his examination, asking her yes-or-no questions, his heart sinking rapidly. It looked like a textbook case of appendicitis.

'Listen, Mirella. We have to get you to a hospital. You may need an operation.'

Her eyes opened wide in terror. Like most working people, she associated surgery with death. Public hospitals were overcrowded, underfunded and understaffed, a last resort; the best doctors and the best equipment were reserved for the private clinics which catered for the moneyed classes. No doubt that was why she had ignored her symptoms, hoping they would go away.

His mind flew over the various possibilities; Che Guevara was a qualified surgeon, but they would never get back to the camp before nightfall, especially as Mirella would have to ride on the mule, slowing down their pace. Taking her home to her family wouldn't help; their farm was miles from anywhere, let alone a hospital. The only solution was to complete his journey, taking her with him, and get Raúl to drive her into Bayamo.

Gently he helped her up and set her astride the mule, explaining his plan to her gently, trying to calm her fears. They continued their journey, slowly but steadily, weaving their way through the palms and scrub, while Eduardo kept a close watch on his patient, hoping that his diagnosis was wrong. He hated to think of her under the knife, at the mercy of some other man's skill, beyond his protection. He shut his mind to the fatal consequences of peritonitis, of a bungled anaesthetic, of some unforeseen complication, cursing both his excess of knowledge, and the insufficiency of it. Every so often he squeezed her hand to give her courage. She had saved his life; now it was his turn to help save hers.

It began to rain.

Celia kept her headlights off, so that Raúl wouldn't know she was behind him. She knew perfectly well that he was being unfaithful to her, that these eternal 'business trips' and 'security checks' were cover for clandestine meetings with some woman.

Like León, he lied sweetly, seductively, took her for a fool. Well, she wasn't, not any more. All her life she had made the best of things, refused to feel sorry for herself, counted her blessings. And paid the price of her cowardice. The time had come to fight back, to pretend, at least, to be brave.

Tonight he was supposed to be dining out in Bayamo, as the guest of a traveller in farm machinery; so why was he driving in the opposite direction, towards Manzanillo? Celia gritted her teeth, resisting the craven temptation to turn round and go home rather than face up to the bitter truth: that already he was tired of her, dependent on someone else to slake that inexhaustible desire of his, to meet his limitless needs. But she kept going; the truth, however unpalatable, was better than not knowing.

To her surprise, he left the main road and turned south, into the mountains, the road getting rougher and narrower by the minute, the rain pelting down, too fast for the wipers to keep up with them, making it hard to see. Where the hell was he going? There was nothing up there but ramshackle farmhouses. Surely he wasn't seeing some peasant girl?

He disappeared briefly into a gully in the road, re-emerging on the other side. A few moments later Celia followed. There was a spatter of stones, a swish of water and a whir of wheels as the car stuck fast in the mud. She tried reversing to no avail, the engine roaring uselessly, mockingly, as she watched Raúl's tail lights disappear into the distance.

She groped for a torch and flashed it to the right and left, but there was no sign of habitation, no chance of getting help. She would be stuck here till Raúl found her on his return; the road led nowhere and he couldn't get back home without retracing his route. Catching him out was one thing; having to admit that she had tried and failed was quite another.

She began laughing, or crying, she wasn't sure which. How absurd and pathetic she was. She must be in love with him, to behave like this. Love. What a miserable business it was. Even when she was happy, it hurt like hell; their most intense, rewarding, intimate moments were haunted by a terrible, shared sadness, a sense of something missing, something missed.

Every time she thought she was making headway, getting close to him at last, he would turn on her, subject her to that cruel tongue of his, force her to hurt him back, almost as if he wanted to turn her into a shrew. And however sweet their reconciliations, they were overshadowed by the spectre of conflicts to come.

She ought to tell him, 'I've had enough. I want nothing

more to do with you. Leave me alone and take as many mistresses as you like. Take your complexes out on them instead of me.' She had married an angry, bitter man, all iron control on the outside and raging chaos within. She had married a frightened little boy who believed himself unlovable. However much she gave him, it would never be enough.

Why, when she wanted only to forget León, would Raúl insist on using him as a weapon against her, against himself? Why couldn't he leave that ill-starred love to die a natural death, instead of feeding it with his jealousy, inviting disloyal comparisons, infecting her with his own rabid insecurity? The old Celia would never have gone looking for a fight like this. She would have turned a blind eye, possibly played the martyr, told herself she didn't care. It was as if he were taking her apart, piece by piece, and rebuilding her, with all her faults magnified and all her strengths stretched to breaking point . . .

Seeing headlights bearing down on her she switched on her own so that she wouldn't be hit by the oncoming vehicle; it was going much too fast. Fearing that the dip in the road made her invisible, she pressed hard on the horn.

It stopped, thank God. Celia's initial relief was quickly swamped by alarm. It was Raúl's Jeep. She felt her throat go dry in anticipation of the most stupendous row.

'What are you doing here?' he demanded, throwing open the passenger door and getting in, showering her with droplets of rain.

'What do you think?' said Celia sullenly, thrown by his premature return. Whoever she was, he had given her very short shrift. 'How was your dinner in Bayamo?'

'I can explain . . .' he began.

'Don't insult me with lies and excuses!' hissed Celia, determined not to lose the initiative. 'You can move into one of the guest rooms tonight, do you hear me?'

'Celia—'

'I've suspected for weeks that you were up to something. Who is she?'

The baldness of the question seemed to rob him of speech. Then he said, 'So that's it. You think there's another woman.' He looked away, not even bothering to deny it. 'You're jealous.'

The word carried a ring of incredulity, which she took for sarcasm.

'Oh, I get it! You're trying to pay me out. Because *you're* eaten up with jealousy, you want me to suffer too! Damn you! I should have known better than to fall in love with a two-timing bastard like you!'

This backhanded declaration of love seemed to stun him. She had never said the words outright before, partly because she hadn't been sure until now, partly because she knew he wouldn't believe her, that he would take the words as a sop. Now that they were said she felt absurd, defenceless. Against all her resolutions, she burst into tears.

Raúl tried to put an arm around her. She swatted it away like a wasp.

'I swear to you, Celia,' he said quietly, humbly, 'that you are the only woman in my life.'

How badly she wanted to believe him! He pulled her close and this time she didn't pull away.

'Then why . . .?'

He kissed the top of her head.

'Shut up,' he said softly, 'and listen.'

Eduardo peered anxiously through the windscreen, cursing the other driver for holding them up. Mirella moaned in her sleep. Luckily Raúl had brought medical supplies, which had enabled Eduardo to give her a sedative, but it was vital that they continue their journey quickly, before her appendix ruptured.

He was just about to get out of the car and hurry things up when Raúl tapped on the window and shouted, 'I want you to drive and keep on driving till you've pushed the car out of the mud. Don't worry about doing any damage, we haven't got time to mess about.'

He returned to the stranded vehicle. Eduardo locked

the Jeep into a low gear and advanced relentlessly, forcing it backwards and upwards, until its wheels engaged, whereupon Raúl reversed it into a level space by the side of the road. Eduardo drew up alongside, blinking in disbelief as his sister jumped in beside him and pinioned him in a fierce embrace.

'Celia! What the hell are you doing here?'

Raúl got into the driving seat without speaking, squeezing Eduardo into the space between them.

'I was following Raúl,' she said sheepishly, exchanging glances with her husband. 'I was such a stupid, jealous idiot, imagining all kinds of nonsense . . . And all the time he's been seeing you! I'm so *furious* with you both for not telling me before!'

Raúl drove on impassively, displaying an impenetrable sang-froid, while Celia plied her brother with questions. Woodenly, Eduardo answered them. So much for their platonic marriage, he thought bitterly, so much for Celia giving Raúl permission to conduct extra-marital liaisons. She wasn't an idiot, and she was right to be jealous. He could barely bring himself to look her in the eye.

'Why did you hold out on me like that? Surely you didn't think I'd give you away? Taking me along would have been good cover. I could have said I was visiting a sick peasant . . . didn't you realise that I'd want to help?'

'Because you support the cause, or because I'm your brother?'

'If you joined Batista's army tomorrow, you'd still be my brother. I'd send you parcels, you'd come home on leave. Politics be damned.' She mollified this feminine heresy with another enthusiastic hug, quite winding him. 'I'm really hurt that you kept me in the dark.'

'We thought it was safest if you didn't know anything,' mumbled Eduardo. 'Raúl didn't want you implicated. Specially with you being pregnant. Er . . . congratulations.'

She coloured slightly.

'Papá is over the moon, it's really bucked him up. He can't wait for November.' She turned round and looked at Mirella, who was still in a restless doze. 'What's her name?'

'Mirella. She's a courier. Her people took me in when I was injured.'

'Are you sure it's appendicitis?'

'She has all the signs. Either you or Raúl will have to do the talking for her . . .' Briefly, he explained her history, while Celia's eyes grew wide with horror.

'I'll stay with them while they examine her,' she said immediately, 'and wait till she comes round. I'll have them all jumping to attention, never fear. Then she must convalesce at Buenaventura. I'll dream up some story or other to tell Papá.'

'Thanks,' said Eduardo, relieved. Left to herself, Mirella would be shinning up and down the mountains before she was properly well. 'Her people are too poor to look after her properly, and too proud to accept help. If you give her a job of some sort, it won't look like charity. And at least it will keep her out of danger for a bit. God knows she's suffered enough.'

'What about you?' demanded Celia. 'Haven't you done your bit, getting shot up and accused of a murder you didn't commit?'

'It was just a scratch. And I would have killed that policeman if I'd had to. My innocence was circumstantial.'

Celia pulled his shirt free and inspected the scar left by the bullet wound.

'You call that a scratch?' she said. 'You could have been killed! You could still be killed!'

'Not much chance of that,' said Eduardo. 'I haven't fired a shot in anger yet. The most exciting thing we've done so far is to capture an army corporal, and we didn't even kill him, even though he was a well-known butcher. We re-educated him and then let him go, would you believe. The policy is that we shouldn't kill or torture prisoners the way Batista's men do.'

'You sound as if you think you should.'

'Hardly. I don't even know if I'm capable of killing

anyone, yet. We uncovered a spy in the camp, just a few days after I joined. Court-martialled him on the spot. I forced myself to watch the firing squad, it was the first time I'd seen a man die. I thought it would make it easier to shoot someone, when the time came. But so far I haven't had the opportunity.'

'Let's hope you never do.'

'Don't say that. We're going to have to kill a lot of people before Cuba is free.'

'Free? We got our freedom once before and look where that got us. Listen. We can get you to the States. Raúl will be able to arrange it.' Raúl didn't comment on this suggestion, driving on impassively. 'You can go to medical school there. Surely a live doctor is a lot more use than a dead soldier?'

'I wouldn't go to America on principle.'

'Why not? Lots of people there support the rebels.'

'Like the two journalists who came to the camp last week? All they wanted was a cheap, sensational story to sell their newspapers.'

'But Cubans in America can lobby the state department, influence government opinion. Especially intelligent, educated Cubans like you. We could arrange false papers for you, we could—'

'No. I'm not running away. Don't argue with me, Celia, my mind's made up. Why should I leave people like Mirella to fight my battles for me?'

Celia sighed and shrugged, well used to losing arguments with her brother.

'She's so beautiful,' she said. 'Even when she's ill, even in those old clothes. Are you and she . . . involved, by any chance?'

Suddenly Eduardo wished to hell they were.

'We've become very close these past few months. Look after her for me, won't you?'

'Don't worry,' said Celia. 'We'll take great care of her, won't we, darling?'

She reached across and touched the back of her husband's neck in a fleeting, familiar gesture, before letting her arm come to rest on Eduardo's shoulder. For the first time in his life, he felt close to her. Like him, she belonged to Raúl.

After dosing his corroded digestive tract with useless patent remedies, Frank had finally plucked up courage to visit a doctor, who referred him grimly to a specialist in Miami. He had not intended to keep the appointment, but a night of white-hot pain had scared the shit out of him, and it came as no surprise to find out that he had an ulcer the size of a silver dollar and a swollen liver that was well on its way to packing up. If he didn't go on the wagon, the quack had said, he'd better start shopping for a headstone and a coffin-sized plot of land.

Frank duly chucked a crate of bottles over the side and treated himself to a few weeks off, fishing, swimming, reading, renewing the brightwork on the boat, reminding himself of his vocation to be a bum, a man who could survive without friends, without possessions, without love, without a sense of purpose, without a future, or a past. A past which popped up, like a shark's fin, during a routine visit to Montego Bay.

He was re-reading *Huckleberry Finn* on deck, with George snoring by his feet, when he heard a voice boom,

'Frank? It's Frank Maguire, isn't it?'

He blinked to see Harry Jordan, a colleague from his Agency days, hailing him from the foredeck of a gin palace tied up alongside. He had begun to lose his hair, but otherwise looked exactly the same – invisible. Harry Jordan was medium height, medium build, medium colouring, with the sort of nondescript face people forgot instantly, an easy man to underestimate, a natural-born spy.

Frank briefly considered denying his identity, or feigning amnesia. Harry hadn't wanted to know him when it mattered, after all. His closest friend, a guy he had known since college, a left-wing idealist in his youth as Frank himself had been, had subsequently proved himself a patriot by shopping all his old pinko associates, including the one he was beaming at now.

'Harry,' acknowledged Frank coolly. 'What are you doing here?'

'Fishing. A bit late in the season, but I have to grab time off when I can. And you?'

'Resting.'

'I thought you were dead.'

'You must have known I wasn't. There isn't anything you people don't know.'

Harry smiled, not denying it. Frank knew for a fact that tabs were kept on all 'retired' personnel.

'Come aboard and have a drink.'

'I'm TT.'

'Drying out, you mean? I know the feeling.'

Harry disembarked and jumped aboard the *Never Again*, subjecting Frank to a bonecrushing handshake.

'Good to see you looking so well,' he lied. Frank knew he looked terrible. All he had drunk all day was half a bottle of bismuth. 'I'm sorry about what happened, Frank. I didn't have any choice . . .'

'Forget it.'

'If there's anything I can do to make it up to you—'

'Look, you don't owe me any favours, OK? You didn't say anything about me that wasn't true, I daresay. I always was my own worst enemy. How are you doing these days?'

'Pretty well, as a matter of fact. You know me, Frank. A survivor. How about you?'

'I get by.'

'The *Never Again*,' mused Harry. 'Have you kept to your motto?'

'I'm through with having principles, if that's what you mean.' And then, as if to prove the point, 'I was hawking explosives to the rebels for a bit. Now I'm pushing dope instead, it's easier. But then you knew that already.'

Harry made tut-tut noises, smiling.

'Don't flatter yourself, Frank. We can't keep a tail on every Commie in the Caribbean.'

The unjust epithet still stung.

'You know me better than that,' he growled.

'Indeed I do. No self-respecting Commie would stoop to helping the rebels. Not that most people appreciate the difference between the two. Let's hope to God they never join forces. What do you think?'

'I don't have an opinion on politics any more.'

Harry pulled out a folding chair and made himself at home.

'Take Castro, for example. He'd never make the grade as a party member, he's too much of a maverick. Personally, I think we should support him, as the lesser of two evils, not that many of the guys upstairs agree with me. You know how it is.'

'I know how it is,' agreed Frank.

'What they do agree on is that our friend Batista is becoming a major embarrassment. Corruption, bribery, torture, they're just not the American way. You know, Frank, you could be very useful to us right now. You speak the language, you're pally with the rebels—'

'Not any more. Look, I don't know any names, I haven't got any information, and if I had I'm not poor enough to want to sell it to you.'

'Hell, Frank, I'm offering you a job, not trying to bribe you.'

'Because you've got a guilty conscience?'

'Because it's the least I can do now I'm in a position to do it. And because you were one of the best in the business.'

'You must be desperate.'

'For good people, yes. Informers are a dime a dozen. Come on, Frank. For old times' sake. Let's talk about it over dinner.'

'Thanks. But I'm going fishing tonight. And then I'm heading back to Havana.'

'Perhaps we'll run into each other there. If we do, I'll thank you not to know me. Listen . . . if you could use a loan—'

'I told you, I get by.'

'Lucky you. You know, I envy you sometimes, Frank. No ties, no responsibilities, no worries. I've got three sons to put through college and a daughter who's going to cost me more than all the boys put together. Remember that next time you judge me.'

'I never judged you, Harry.'

'You can contact me via this number if you ever change your mind.' He produced a bogus business card from his inside pocket. 'Think it over. "Never again" sounds like an excuse to me, not a reason. When you don't believe in anything, you end up despising everyone. Including yourself. So long, then.'

Frank watched him jump onto the pier and hop aboard the neighbouring boat, whence a dusky female appeared from the forward cabin, looking sultry and rumpled, with a highball in each hand. He found it hard to believe that Harry just happened to be here, equally hard to believe that his job offer was more than a sop. He had trusted him, once. It seemed a lifetime ago.

Thinking about the past was bad enough, without seeing his present through Harry's eyes, Harry, sleek and smug and successful, eager to make things up to him and do a burned-out buddy a good turn. That night, for lack of any other anaesthetic, Frank got well and truly stoned, for the first time. It proved to be a revelation. Whereas alcohol fuelled his pessimism, marijuana proved to be the stuff of hope. It was in this unfamiliar mood of fume-induced euphoria that he discovered, quite by accident, the book of matches bearing Addy's private address and telephone number and decided to resume his quest for Lily. Booze had told him loud and clear that she was just another hard-nosed little whore, more than capable of looking after herself. Dope said she was a damsel in distress, waiting to be saved.

Innumerable smokes later Frank arrived, light-headed, in Havana and lost no time in dialling the number, only to find the line disconnected. Probably the rebels had sabotaged the exchange. Undaunted, he took a taxi ride to the address in Vedado, which turned out to be a ritzy apartment block, where he was intercepted by a surly doorman.

'Señora Herbert doesn't live here any more,' he said, in the weary manner of one who had repeated this many times. 'If you're another debt collector, you're wasting your time.'

'Debt collector? You mean she's gone bust?'

'She lost everything when the rebels bombed her club. The bailiffs were round before the poor woman's body was cold. There's nothing left.'

Frank stared at him, horrified. So Pedro and co. had got their own back after all . . .

'They bombed Addy's?'

'No. The Herradura. A new gambling joint out in El Country Club. Four dead, forty-odd injured. Must be three, four months ago.'

Suppose Lily had gone to work at this Herradura place? Four dead and forty injured . . .

'What about . . .' he groped for the name '. . . León somebody or other? Do you know where I can get in touch with him?' He might know whether Lily was among the casualties.

'Señor Soler? You won't get any change out of him. I told you, there's no money.'

'I'm not after money. I'm a friend.' He produced five dollars to prove it. 'If he's in trouble, I want to help him. Did he leave a forwarding address?'

The doorman peered at the note, unimpressed. Frank produced another, impatient now.

'Mail's been redirected to 257 Tejadillo. That's all I know.'

That figured. Tejadillo was in the dock area, near the red-light district, where he had no doubt found alternative work. Frank got back into the cab and continued his journey, alighting in a dark, cobbled road typical of the old town, its iron balconies draped with laundry like bunting, its garish awnings almost meeting across the middle of the narrow thoroughfare. Number 257 was a wide, heavy doorway leading into a courtyard, infested with ragged, shrieking children and surrounded by run-down apartments. An old mulatta woman was mopping one of the stone stairwells, an evil-smelling pipe between her lips.

'Soler?' enquired Frank.

She jabbed a finger without ceasing her labours.

'Top floor, three along. He's out. But his woman's there.'

Frank walked up the wet slippery staircase and along the communal balcony which connected four sides of the square. There was a smell of fermenting garbage and stale cooking oil, a cacophony of crying babies. Behind splintering shutters a woman was screaming blue murder while a man roared in counterpoint.

He stopped outside Soler's door and knocked loud enough to make himself heard over the din of the radio, which was blasting out 'Love Letters In The Sand' at full volume. There was no answer. He knocked again, and a female voice called out, accusingly, 'Who's there?'

'A friend of León's.'

'He's at work.'

'Whereabouts can I find him?'

'What?' She switched the radio off and opened the door a fraction, on the chain. 'He drives a cab. He could be anywhere.' She had a strong American accent and the voice was instantly familiar. Frank squeezed his face between the edge of the door and the jamb and saw a mass of red hair framing a freckled face free of make-up, a face so naked he hardly recognised it.

'Lily!'

'Frank!' She flung open the door and fell into his arms, laughing and sobbing at once. 'Oh, Frank! Am I glad to see you!'

'How the fuck did you end up in a place like this? Jesus, Lily, what a dump. If I'd known . . .'

It was then that he felt the bulge under her robe. He drew back and looked down at her distended belly, unable to hide his horror.

'You're pregnant,' he said woodenly.

She nodded, hiding her face behind a curtain of lank, greasy hair and adding meekly, 'It's all right. I'm married.'

'What?' He had quite forgotten, in the shock of seeing her, that he had come here looking for León Soler. Christ. She had gone and married a lousy pimp . . .

'What was I supposed to do? I had to marry someone.' She showed him in to a small, dingy room crammed with good-quality furniture. There was a double bed, a chest of drawers, two chairs, a dressing table, and a wardrobe, leaving barely enough room to move. A basin filled with dirty gold-rimmed china plates sat atop a small mahogany coffee table; there was the unmistakable odour of unemptied chamber pot.

'It's your baby, Frank,' she said plaintively. 'But I didn't know how to find you. I thought I was never going to see you again.' She put her arms around his neck. 'Oh, why couldn't you have shown up before? I'm so miserable, living in this crummy room. But it's all we can afford . . .' And then, rather anxiously, 'How did you find me?'

'I kept looking for you at the club but nobody knew you. In the end I went round to Addy's house in Vedado and they told me about the bombing and gave me this as a forwarding address. I was afraid you'd been working at the casino, that you'd been killed.'

'I nearly was. I was singing there that night. I ended up in hospital and nearly lost the baby. Oh, Frank, it was horrible!'

Frank felt nauseous. At least this time he hadn't supplied the explosives, but morally he might as well have done. He held her tight, thanking God. It was his child she was carrying . . . so she said.

'Come away with me now,' he said impulsively, before he had time to think better of it. 'I'll find us a decent apartment, look after you and the baby . . .'

'Oh, Frank, you were always so good to me! I hate to ask, but would you have any cash on you? The thing is, I haven't paid the rent, and the electricity man is due this afternoon. I spent all the housekeeping on the lottery, anything for the chance to get out of this lousy place. León will kill me if he finds out. I had to borrow ten pesos from the woman downstairs to get my groceries, and she's starting to get nasty . . .'

'Never mind about all that. Hurry up and pack your things. The sooner I get you out of here the better.'

She drew back. 'I can't leave. I told you, I'm married.'

'So? You don't love this guy, do you?'

The question seemed to throw her for a moment.

'That's not the point,' she said evasively. 'He's my husband.' And then, speaking very fast, 'He doesn't know anything about you, you see. I told him it was his child, I had to. I'll let you see the baby, I'll meet you in secret, but please, please, please, don't give me away.' She looked quite panic-stricken.

Frank knew then that she was conning him. Perhaps she had conned this Soler guy as well. More than likely she couldn't be sure who the father was. Even so . . .

'I can't leave you to rot in this god-awful place. Can't he do better for you than this?'

'There were debts,' she mumbled. 'When my – when Addy died. León lost all the money he had put into her new casino. The insurance people wouldn't pay out after it was bombed, and he doesn't get on with his family so he can't ask them for any help and Grandma's had a stroke so I couldn't go home and . . . oh, God, everything turned out such a mess!' She wiped her eyes. 'Fifty pesos would make all the difference,' she sniffed, getting back to the point. 'I'll never waste it on the lottery again, I promise. León keeps me short, he puts money in the bank for medical bills and such, so that I can't spend it, he doesn't understand how hard it is to manage. He's always nagging me to clean the place up, but I feel so tired all the time. I keep saying, it wouldn't cost much to get a black girl in.' She gestured helplessly round the room. 'I get so lonely. León works all hours, he's hardly ever here. But you mustn't come here again. If the neighbours told him about you, he'd go loco. You know what Cuban men are like . . .'

She might be poor, and pregnant, but she hadn't changed. She was still the same grasping, manipulative, fly little Lily that he knew and loved. He didn't have to carry her off, didn't have to stop being a bum. He could have her on the side, without responsibility, enjoy a tarnished version of the cosy fantasy that would never have stood up to the bright white light of day. His child – if it was his child – would never call him father, but perhaps that was no bad thing. In his blacker moments he would always have doubted its provenance; this way it didn't matter either way.

His mood was already on the downward curve from mawkishness back to misanthropy. It was a compromise, but so much the better. All the while he kept coming up with the cash, she would pretend to care for him, which was a hell of a lot safer than the real thing. No doubt she had him down for a mug, one she could bleed white . . .

Well, why not? Harry Jordan's parting shot had hit a raw nerve. 'Never again' was an excuse, not a reason. An excuse not to stick his neck out, a refuge from his own weakness, a denial of his own strength. Yes. It was high time he made a fool of himself again.

'Please make yourself at home,' said Celia, showing Mirella into a pretty, white-walled bedroom, well aware that it would not feel like home. Home was a palm-thatched shack without running water or electricity or privacy. Home was plantains at every meal and home-made furniture and unrelenting drudgery. She remembered vividly how grand Buenaventura had seemed to her, once. How much more intimidating this house must be for Mirella.

'I hope you'll find the bed comfortable,' she continued, smoothing the crisp, sprigged counterpane. 'The doctors want you to get plenty of rest. They warned that the drugs would make you very tired.'

A thorough medical check-up had revealed a kidney infection, mild diabetes and serious anaemia; a regime involving rest and a special diet had been prescribed for the next three months. By that time the baby would be here; Celia had offered her the job of nanny, to please Eduardo, who was anxious to keep her out of danger.

It had taken time to win the girl's confidence, to change the hollow-eyed mistrust into a welcoming smile. Her avid interest in Celia's pregnancy was heartbreaking, her questions penned in a large round childish hand. Did she want a boy or a girl? What was she going to call it? She had been five months' gone when they had kicked her own baby out of her and thrown her, bleeding, into the gutter.

'I would have told them where my *novio* was,' she had written once. 'If I had known.'

'Is that why you won't speak? You can speak, you know, if you try . . .'

But she preferred not to. Silence and suffering had become twin vices, the one linked inextricably with the other. She had climbed those mountains with a chronic backache caused by her bleeding kidneys, pain that would have crippled anyone else, she had borne her grumbling appendix without complaint, conquered her dizzy spells through sheer determination. That she had finally agreed to take care of her much-abused body was entirely due to Eduardo. She would get better for his sake, not her own.

'It's nearly time for dinner,' continued Celia. 'You'll be taking your meals with Emilia, she's a bit gruff but very kind. She has a sweetheart in the army, by the way, so be careful what you say to her . . .' She broke off, smiling at her gaffe. 'The other servants don't live in the house, they have their own quarters nearby. Come with me.'

Celia had bought her new clothes suitable to her position in the household. Even without a scrap of make-up she looked lovely, thought Celia wistfully, with her luxurious black hair braided on top of her head; small wonder Eduardo had fallen in love with her. She led the way downstairs and ushered her protégée into the kitchen.

'Now remember what I said,' she told Emilia. 'Mirella's been ill recently, so she's to have plenty of meat and eggs and green vegetables to build up her blood. And she isn't to do any housework.'

Emilia glared, making her disapproval plain. Clearly she thought Celia quite mad to have employed a mute, sickly girl to do nothing but act as a companion. As for looking after the new baby, how would the poor little mite ever learn to talk if its nanny was dumb? It was just another example of her young mistress's pregnant whims.

'So what is she going to do all day? The other servants won't like it.'

'She's going to keep me company. At least she won't nag me all the time like you do.' Or chatter on inanely like women of her own class. Or bully her like Papá or torment her like Raúl, sometimes so loving, sometimes so scathing, always unpredictable.

She should have been reassured to learn that her jealous fears were unfounded. But she still felt as if she had a rival – not a woman, but something less tangible, more insidious. Perhaps it was the lure of combat. Raúl never said so, but she knew in her heart that he envied Eduardo, that he nurtured a nostalgia for war, that he was at heart a man of action, who found his role at Buenaventura increasingly irksome. Sometimes he would return home with a pile of papers under his arm and hand them to her, saying, 'Look through these for me, will you? You know I've got no head for figures.' The proposals he put before the old man were invariably Celia's, proposals which would surely have been rejected had she suggested them herself. Which explained why Raúl never ascribed them to her, but it was galling, none the less, to be left out of their discussions, as if her married state had robbed her of the power to think.

Celia joined the men in the dining room; Mirella watched with interest while Emilia dished up the meal, marvelling at the quantities of food required to feed three people. She began making herself useful, washing the soup plates while Emilia served the tortillas and admiring the modern American kitchen. She cast her mind back to her late *novio*'s family home in Santiago, where she had worked as a maid. She had thought that those people were wealthy, but their home was humble indeed compared to this. If she had grown up in such a place, she would surely oppose the rebels, not support them, as Eduardo did. Eduardo did things for complicated, clever reasons, well beyond her comprehension; he used long words, thinking that she understood. Silvio had known full well the limitations of her mind, he had been interested only in her body. But Eduardo assumed she was intelligent. Speech would have revealed her coarse vowels, her ignorance, her limited stock of words; muteness covered a multitude of sins.

'A girl comes in to do all that in the morning,' snapped Emilia. 'I don't want you claiming that I put you to work against Doña Celia's orders. I've known the mistress since she was a little girl, so you may as well know I don't stand for airs and graces from anyone, not even from her, and least of all from you.'

Mirella took this warning in good part, understanding the other woman's resentment. She felt uncomfortable about her role in the household and most certainly wouldn't have agreed to convalesce here had not Eduardo sent a note to the hospital pleading with her to be sensible. He had written of her duty to get strong, in order to participate fully in the revolution. But what had really swayed her had been the sentiments expressed between the lines, as unspoken as her own emotions. For the last year she had been prepared, no, determined to die, as her lover and her child had done; now she wanted to live again.

It was easy to like Celia, if only because she resembled her brother so strikingly. And the fact that she was pregnant made her less daunting than a woman of her class might otherwise have been. More than Mirella envied her wealth, her beautiful house, her fine clothes, she envied her that baby. After the rape and beating, she had shrunk at the thought of letting any man touch her, ever again, resigned herself to childlessness, until she had met Eduardo. He was so gentle, so respectful. He made her feel clean again. And she knew he would make the most wonderful father.

Ever since her ordeal she had carried a gun with her at all times, a small automatic her brother had bought her after her return from Havana. So far, she had never had to use it, although she had come pretty near it that day those two soldiers had stopped her on the road. But if the time ever came, she would not hesitate to shoot; she would kill herself, if necessary, rather than endure such horror again. Celia, understanding her fear, had kept the weapon safe while she was in hospital and had given it back to her this morning, raising no objection to her wearing it strapped to her thigh. The house was full of guns, after all.

The bell in the kitchen jangled loudly, summoning Emilia into the dining room. 'That'll be his lordship,' she muttered. 'Celia never rings like that.'

She got up and waddled off, leaving the door open. A moment later Mirella heard a commotion, and hurried after her to see what was wrong.

Celia was lying on the floor, with her husband loosening the collar of her blouse and her father-in-law crashing round the room like a caged elephant.

'Help my son look after your mistress,' he snapped at Mirella. 'I must telephone for the doctor. She fainted and fell, the foolish girl may have damaged the child . . .' He shuffled out into the hall, muttering to himself.

'What happened?' demanded Emilia of Raúl, too worried to be polite, her manner openly accusatory.

'There was a news bulletin on the radio,' he said curtly. 'The rebels attacked the barracks at Uvero. At least a dozen of them are reported dead with several more injured. Celia fears that her brother may be among them.'

Alarmed, Mirella crouched down on the floor and took Celia's hand. She wanted to say, 'Don't worry. Eduardo will be all right. It might not even have been his unit that mounted the attack. And even if it was, the radio always exaggerates rebel casualities . . .' She wanted to say it to convince herself, if not Celia, and for the first time in months she made a conscious effort to speak, but the words wouldn't come, perhaps because they might not be true.

Celia moaned and opened her eyes.

'It's all right, my pet,' soothed Emilia. 'Mirella, fetch some brandy from the cabinet over there.'

Mirella did as she was bidden and noticed that Raúl had left the room, by the french windows. She could see him on the terrace, with his back to the house, head bent, shoulders slumped, face covered by his hands.

NINE

'WHERE TO?' barked León, not bothering to look at his umpteenth fare of the day. As usual, his mind was not on his work. Money – a topic he had always despised – was now a constant preoccupation. The forced sale of all Addy's assets had raised barely enough to cover her debts, let alone provide for her unborn grandchild. Medical bills were his biggest headache, especially if there proved to be unforeseen complications; consigning Lily to the gruesome inadequacies of a public ward didn't bear thinking about.

Responding to a clipped voice, he began the drive on automatic pilot, fighting his way through the clogged arteries of downtown Havana towards the broad leafy avenues of Miramar, lined with palms and flowering shrubs. León found the suburbs sterile and snobbish, preferring the teeming heart of the old city, but the fact remained that Tejadillo was no place to bring up a kid. Summary eviction from the apartment in Vedado had left him no choice but to take Lily back to his room, but once the baby was born, he would have to find a decent apartment in a better area. Meanwhile, it made sense to stay put and save every spare cent.

Saving every spare cent was easier said than done. Sudden penury had made not the slightest impact on Lily's inborn extravagance. Instead of buying food and ice and toothpaste, she would spend a week's housekeeping on a stuffed toy for the baby or, on one occasion, a silk cravat for León, bought on impulse during one of her window-shopping sprees. In an attempt to recoup her expenditure, she would invest her last few pesos in a lottery ticket, thus incurring further losses. She was no more capable of budgeting than the unfortunate child she was carrying. León now bought the groceries and paid the rent himself, leaving Lily with the kind of pocket money appropriate to a little girl, a little girl who bawled and sulked and called him an old skinflint. But her recent decision to give English lessons, 'to buy things for the baby', seemed like a step in the right direction, even though the things she bought were pretty rather than practical, just like Lily herself.

He glanced in the driving mirror and met his passenger's eye. A smiling, malicious, derisive eye.

'You'd make a much better lawyer than you do a cab driver,' commented Captain Reinaldo. 'You've committed at least three traffic violations in as many minutes.'

León turned left without indicating. 'I told you when Addy died that I wasn't interested in practising what you call the law.'

'Such a waste of an expensive education. I gather your professor had high hopes of you.'

'He had high hopes of selling my father a phoney diploma, you mean.'

'And so you, in your bloody-minded way, had to come top of your year and deprive the poor fellow of his dues. But why do the same to yourself? You know, they're sorely in need of capable people in the public prosecutor's office. Specially after what happened with that old fool Urrutia.'

Manuel Urrutia, a prominent Santiago judge, had caused a sensation by dismissing the case against a number of captured rebels.

'If there were a few more independent judges like him,' said León tersely, 'I might be tempted to change my mind. As things are, I prefer my present occupation.'

'Tut, tut,' mocked Reinaldo. 'Do I detect rebel sympathies? Of course, rebel sympathies are all the rage at the moment. The smart set have quite taken Castro to their hearts.'

'You think I support the bastards who murdered Addy? Until the law rises above politics, I want no part of it.'

'Integrity is a luxury you can't afford, my friend. Lack of money destroys a marriage quicker than anything else.'

'My marriage is my business.' He stopped the cab. Reinaldo proffered the fare plus an outsize tip.

'Take it, man,' he growled, as León hesitated. 'Spend it on that poor little wife of yours. When the time comes for her confinement, I can arrange excellent care for her through the department's benevolent fund. It's the least I can do, out of respect for her late mother.'

'Thank you, but I can't accept your charity. Or accrue a debt I've no hope of paying back.'

'I had a feeling you would say that,' sighed Reinaldo. 'But remember good doctors come expensive. When you finally tire of slumming it – as you will – don't be too proud to let me know, if only for your child's sake.'

His child. Would he have acted differently if it *was* his child, if Celia was its mother? Would he have expected Celia to live in that vile little room, to endure the hardships he had forced on Lily? Wasn't he revelling in guilt and self-flagellation and sheer perversity? Wasn't he punishing Lily for not being Celia, Celia for whom he would have betrayed any principle rather than let her live in squalor? Except that it wouldn't have been squalid, with Celia. Not just because she would have made the place clean and decent, but because passion would have dignified their poverty, passion he would never feel for Lily, nor she for him, except in the fanciful make-believe of her mind.

She needed to believe that this was love, to pretend that he would have married her anyway, to convince herself that it was fate, rather than circumstance, which had brought them together. It seemed cruel to deny her that comforting illusion, to make things as difficult for her as they were for him, to reject her pathetic attempts to please him. And yet he was cruel sometimes, no, often, unable to curb his exasperation, a situation which Lily had quickly learned to exploit to her advantage.

She would rage and weep, make him feel like a

monster, and then inveigle him into making things up in bed, the one place she was guaranteed his undivided attention. Despite her overt enthusiasm for sex, León was pretty sure that she was faking it, playing her role to the hilt like the incorrigible actress she was, so wrapped up in her own performance that it carried a reality all its own. Sex was a trade-off for affection, a plea for approval, a chance to show off. But who was he to complain if she was less than sincere?

He got home that evening to find her sprawled over the dirty bedclothes, gorging herself on a box of coconut candy. As usual, there was no food prepared and the place was a pigsty.

'Hi, honey,' she purred, rolling onto her back and stretching like a cat. 'I wasn't expecting you back so early.' She manoeuvred herself off the bed. 'Dinner should be ready. I gave Concha downstairs two pesos to cook a bit extra every night this week. Be an angel and fetch it, would you? My back's killing me.'

She put her arms round his neck and gave him a squelchy welcome-home kiss.

'What have you been doing all day, you lazy cow?'

'Giving lessons to Señora Mendez. I bought these for the baby.' She displayed a pair of pink bootees. 'Aren't they cute? I got you some cigars, to put you in a good mood. Why don't you stay home tonight?'

'I can't afford to. We need the extra money for the baby.' He tried to keep the resentment out of his voice and failed; luckily, if annoyingly, Lily didn't seem to hear it.

'I wish it would hurry up and be born,' she said, yawning. 'I hate being fat.'

'Once it's born, you have to feed it and change it and look after it. Once it's born you won't be able to lounge around all day eating candy.'

'Once it's born I'll find work as a singer and earn enough to pay for a nurse. And move out of this crummy room.'

'It wouldn't be so crummy if you cleaned it up once in a while.'

'They said at the clinic that I was to take it easy,' said Lily, aggrieved. 'I get these terrible backaches.'

'Then cut out the shopping trips and save your energy for the housework. And don't waste your money buying me cigars in future. I don't even like that brand.' He tossed them to one side.

'You ungrateful bastard! I won't ever buy you anything again!'

'Good. Now go downstairs and fetch my dinner.'

'Fetch it yourself. If you wanted a skivvy you should have married a Cuban girl!'

'And if you wanted to be the boss you should have married a Yanqui. Preferably the one who got you pregnant.'

'That's right! Throw it in my face! You never miss a chance, do you? I should have had an abortion!'

'You insisted that you wanted to keep the baby.'

'That was before I knew how awful it would be, being married to you!'

She picked up an ashtray and threw it at him. León ducked, and it bounced off the thin lath-and-plaster wall, leaving a dent and producing a puff of distemper. She followed on with a shoe, a cigarette lighter, and the baby-care book León had bought her, the last of which struck home, hitting him on the nose.

'Bitch,' muttered León, catching the spurt of blood in the handkerchief he used to wipe his windscreen. Predictably, Lily began boo-hooing her apologies.

'I'm sorry,' she burbled. 'I never meant to hurt you. Why must you be so c-cruel to me?' She put her arms around him and began kissing it better. 'Come to bed,' she said.

Five days after the attack on the barracks at Uvero, a different courier showed up for the rendezvous with Raúl, bringing with him a note from Eduardo.

> I am confined to the camp hospital with a badly fractured ankle sustained during the attack, the result of an accident with my rifle whilst trying to drag a wounded comrade to safety. My injury obviously prevents me making the journey

> to collect supplies in future; even after the bones have knitted, it seems likely that I will be left with a limp, which would make the climb impractical. If deemed unfit for active service, I propose to stay on as a medical auxiliary. I trust that you will continue to supply us, bearing in mind that this has been the first engagement of a major campaign.

Raúl's relief that Eduardo was alive, if not well, was quickly superseded by dismay at this abrupt end to their meetings. And yet he knew he ought to welcome this chance to free himself from the chains of his obsession. Ever since Celia's jealous outburst, he had found it harder and harder to lead a double life. He had not been prepared for the impact of her declaration of love, or for the effect it would have on his peace of mind. For the first time in years, he found himself burdened with a conscience.

Eduardo had tried time and again to finish the affair, but both of them had been too weak to go through with it. No doubt he welcomed his injury, as a means of escaping his seducer, a thought which made Raúl feel as if he had pulled the trigger himself.

'I want you to take me to him,' he demanded of the courier. 'His sister won't rest till I can report that I have seen him for myself.'

'That's not possible this time. Civilians are not permitted access to the camp except in special circumstances. But I'll pass on your request.'

'It's not a request, it's a demand. Next time, be prepared to take me back with you, blindfolded if need be. Otherwise, there will be no more supplies, and I'll ask the girl, Mirella, to guide me to the camp with or without your permission.'

For two pins he would have added that he thought Castro and Guevara and co. a bunch of prize bunglers, who had sacrificed the lives of eight trained men for the sake of a histrionic gesture, that their alleged 'victory' demonstrated the ineptitude of the garrison at Uvero, rather than the military skill of the guerrillas. But he held his tongue, knowing that such an outburst would sever the connection for good.

'He's all right,' he reassured a wakeful Celia on his return; Mirella had kept vigil with her, waiting for news. The two women hugged each other, fuelling his irritation. 'But the fracture sounds quite serious,' he added, showing Celia the letter. 'I've told them I want to visit him. I intend to put pressure on him to leave the camp and see a specialist.'

'Would that be wise?' she said. 'He's still wanted for murder, remember.'

'The rebels have safe houses, and access to sympathetic doctors. If we foot the bill, no doubt something can be arranged.'

Mirella scribbled her willingness to accompany him. Raúl looked at her with contempt. The foolish girl was obviously besotted; how could Eduardo tolerate such banal, dog-like devotion?

'That's out of the question,' he said coldly. 'Eduardo would be most displeased if I allowed you to make the climb in your present state of health. I haven't paid out a small fortune in medical bills just so that you can invite a relapse. Leave us now. I wish to talk to my wife in private.'

'There's no need to be so sharp with her,' said Celia mildly, after she had gone. 'She was only trying to be helpful.'

'I don't trust her. I don't like the way she creeps about the house.'

'She doesn't mean any harm. She's frightened of you, that's all. She's frightened of all men, except for Eduardo. She might have better luck persuading him than you would. He's in love with her, after all.'

'I find that hard to believe. The girl's a half-wit.'

'She's uneducated. That's not the same thing. And even if it was, who needs brains with looks like that?'

He heard the unspoken plea and chose to ignore it. This was the second time he had lost Eduardo; in his present mood he would vent all his frustration on Celia. Frustration she would subvert with the callous skill of a lion tamer, forcing his caged energy through hoops of her own devising. As he got into bed she reached out for him. Raúl turned his back.

'What's the matter?'

'It's late. Go to sleep. You need your rest.'

'What's wrong? Why are you angry with me?'

'You ought to be glad to be left alone. If you had any regard for your child you would refrain from tempting me, knowing what a brute I can be.'

Now the plea was in his voice, not hers; he cursed himself for making it. He felt her skinny little arms wind themselves round him like steel hawsers, felt her brazen little hands search out his most sensitive spots, provoking him, subduing him, using her own vulnerability as a weapon against him. Why couldn't she be frigid and make this marriage easier for both of them? Then he wouldn't need to feel so damn guilty about deceiving her.

'We don't have to make love,' she murmured. 'I just want to feel close, that's all.'

Trust her to exploit his craven, childish need for comfort. She cradled his head in the crook of her arm, asking nothing of him, relieving him of the need to be a man, allowing his anger to trickle uselessly away, forcing him to lay down his arms and surrender on her terms.

She had all the warmth her brother lacked. Eduardo had passion, yes, but not warmth. Deep down Eduardo feared him, even as Raúl feared himself. He had never feared anyone, except himself, until Celia. Every time she risked his anger, she depleted it, brought him one stage nearer capitulation. She would never be content until she had sucked all the life-giving poison out of him, distilled it into milk and water, rendered him a harmless pet, a willing slave.

The process was relentless, irreversible, threatening. Inexorably, irresistibly, he was falling in love with his wife.

A week later, Raúl's request to visit the camp was granted.

'Leave the car here,' said his guide, as the dirt road narrowed to a footpath. 'We go the rest of the way on foot.'

Another man appeared from nowhere with a couple of mules and began unloading sacks of rice and coffee with guns and ammunition buried in their depths. Raúl slung one of them over his shoulder, never faltering once during the arduous climb, his pace constrained only by that of his companions. He felt no fatigue, propelled by the thought of seeing Eduardo again.

Some hours later, they reached the camp – not the primitive bivouac Raúl had been expecting, but a series of well-constructed buildings built of palm. Not only was its hospital well equipped with drugs, dressings and surgical equipment but it featured a bakery, a schoolhouse where recruits were drilled in literacy and ideology, an armoury, and a leather factory. There seemed to be plenty of food available; the supply line to Buenaventura was clearly one of several established in the last six months.

He found Eduardo seated on a stool in the dispensary, with his foot encased in plaster.

'Why did you insist on coming here?' he demanded, not looking at him. 'I got word to you that I was safe.'

'I came to persuade you to apply for a discharge. Celia's orders.'

'How is she?'

'Considerably better than you.'

'And . . . and Mirella?'

'As much in love with you as ever.'

He handed over two envelopes, one addressed in Celia's bold italics and the other in Mirella's childish scrawl.

'I suppose you've had a good read?'

'Check the sealing wax. I assume it's a love letter, otherwise why would she have bothered?'

Eduardo stuffed both missives in his pocket.

'I happen to care for her, believe it or not.' His voice sank to a whisper. 'Just like you claim to care for my sister. I told you last time we met we have to end it. You may not have any respect for Celia, but I do.'

'I have the greatest respect for her. Was it my fault that she turned to me for love and affection? What was I supposed to do? Spurn her, humiliate her, make her feel unattractive and undesirable? Would you really have me treat her so heartlessly? How can you begrudge her a share of what I feel for you?'

'Keep your voice down!'

'Then let's walk. Find somewhere private, where we won't be overheard.'

'Where you can jump me, you mean. You just can't take no for an answer, can you? I might have known you'd show up here. I would have thought you'd have more pride than to run after me like this . . .'

'Listen, Eduardo. The courier told me that the surgeon advised you to seek specialist treatment. That otherwise you may end up a cripple.'

'I can't leave the camp. I'm a wanted criminal, remember? If I show my face in a civilian hospital, someone might recognise me and turn me in for the reward.'

'I can take you to Havana, book you into a private clinic under a false name.'

'No. I've already persuaded them to let me stay on, as a medical aide.'

'Nursing is women's work. An army is no place for a hanger-on with a game leg.'

'I can help run the literacy classes as well,' protested Eduardo hotly. 'Che says every man must learn to read. There are lots of things I can do—'

'You seem to have it all worked out,' said Raúl. And then, taking a chance, 'What really happened to you, Eduardo?'

'I told you what happened. I was dragging a wounded comrade to safety and my rifle went off by accident.'

'An accident? Are you quite sure?'

'What are you implying?'

'Unlike your rookie superiors, I've had fifteen years' experience in the field. I'm not as easily fooled as they appear to be.'

All the colour drained from Eduardo's face, confirming Raúl's suspicions. His heart went out to him. It had always worried him that he would panic under fire; he was completely lacking in the killer instinct which was the life-blood of so-called courage.

'How dare you! How dare you accuse me of . . . it wasn't like you think!'

'Let's get out of here,' said Raúl, taking him by the arm, 'and you can tell me all about it. I'm not going to condemn you. I'm just glad you're alive, that's all.'

Scowling, Eduardo reached for his crutches and thrust himself towards the outer perimeter of the camp.

'What do you want me to say?' he hissed, as soon as they were out of earshot. 'All right, so it wasn't an accident. I'm a coward. A snivelling, miserable, lying coward. Satisfied?'

'I didn't say you were a coward. What you did took a different kind of courage.' Eduardo had what it took to commit suicide, he thought, not without envy. 'Tell me,' he said gently. 'Tell me the whole story.'

Eduardo leaned back against a tree, eyes tightly shut, his voice choked with shame.

'The plan was to attack the barracks from all sides and keep firing at it until the order for the advance. But I knew that when we did advance, there would be no cover, that some of us were bound to get picked off. I was . . . scared.'

'Rightly so. Go on.'

'When the order came, we all ran forward, and the guy next to me was hit in the chest. I stopped and rolled him over and I could see straight away that he was dead, but I thought, if I drag him back, out of the line of fire, it will give me an excuse to retreat. But he was so damn heavy and the bullets kept coming so I just lay down flat, beside him, too terrified to move. By the time I realised what I'd done, it was too late. I knew if they found me like that I'd end up in front of a firing squad. So I shot myself instead.'

Raúl winced with pain at the thought of it.

'Did you have to do yourself quite so much damage?'

'They might not have believed me otherwise. And besides, I deserved it. At least this way I'll never have to fight again. So now you know. You can't possibly despise me more than I despise myself.'

'I don't despise you. I would never have the guts to do what you did.'

'Guts? Are you kidding? I was so determined to prove myself a man. And now I've proved the exact opposite. Not that it needed proving.'

'Meaning what exactly?'

Eduardo made an obscene gesture. 'That I'm a fairy,' he lisped viciously.

'Stop wallowing in your own self-pity. Not everyone's cut out to be a soldier.'

'Well, I'm not a soldier any more. But I can help save the lives of men who are. And that's what I'm going to do.'

'After you've had that ankle seen to, there's nothing to stop you coming back.'

'You won't let me come back. Once I'm out of here you'll never let me go. And I'll be too damn feeble to do anything about it. You think you can set me up in some love-nest, where you can carry on cheating on my sister. Well, I'm not giving you the chance. You're no better than bloody León! Just because I'm less than a man doesn't mean you can make a mistress out of me!'

'Eduardo, you're feeling guilty about losing your nerve, and that's understandable. But that guilt has nothing to do with what there is between us—'

'Was between us. Was, was, was. My days as your bit on the side are over. Find yourself some other nancy-boy!'

He swung round and hauled himself back towards the camp. Raúl tried to catch hold of his arm but Eduardo lashed out at him with a crutch.

'Leave me alone, damn you! If you ever lay a finger on me again, I'll tell Celia! I'll tell everyone!'

Raúl didn't pursue him; this was no place for a lovers' quarrel. And besides, truth to tell, he was relieved, for all that he was disappointed. He would never have had the will power to make the final break himself, but now he found himself ready to cede to *force majeure* . . . or fear.

'I'll tell Celia!' The threat was probably hollow, but it had struck home none the less. Once upon a time the risk of exposure had added a certain spice to his adventures, but recently he had begun to have recurring nightmares in which Celia discovered his vice and shrank from him in loathing and disgust. He would wake up bathed in sweat, thinking that he had lost her, drenched by the knowledge that he would rather die than face her scorn.

He was escorted back down the mountain to the dusty track where he had left the Jeep; the descent, unlike the climb, left him weary, breathless, labouring under the burden of bitter thoughts. He must have driven a couple of miles before his normally acute sixth sense, blunted by too much introspection, picked up a scent of danger. A split second later he heard a voice say, in English, 'Pull over,' and felt the cold kiss of a gun against the back of his neck.

He looked in the mirror. The man was unfamiliar and unremarkable – slightly balding, with a bland, expressionless face, the kind of face it was hard to remember afterwards. He must be some Mafia hit man, an emissary of Bert Orsini or Carlo Panetta, sent to collect his unpaid gambling debts.

'Get out of the car. Keep your hands where I can see them.'

'How much do you want? I can give you the money by tonight.'

'I said, get out of the car.'

The rebel guide had disarmed Raúl as a precondition of his visit. There was a gun under the seat and another in the glove compartment, but if the guy was worth his hire he would be too quick for him. Raúl alighted and allowed the enforcer to frisk him.

'Move,' he said, pointing towards the trees.

'I told you, I can get the money. I just haven't got it on me right now. Give me twenty-four hours.'

'I didn't come here for money.'

God, thought Raúl, what a stupid way to die.

'If they sent you here to kill me, get on with it,' he said, preparing to lunge at his attacker and go down fighting.

'Relax. I didn't come to kill you either. The gun's just for self-defence, don't force me to use it. Now keep walking till I tell you to stop.' He marched him into trees till they came to a clearing, well hidden from the road. 'That's far enough. Nice and private. Sit down, Major Freeman, and make yourself at home.'

'What is it you want?' demanded Raúl, jolted by the use of his former name and rank. 'Who the hell are you?'

The man pocketed his weapon and withdrew a pack of Pall Malls.

'You can call me Harry,' he said.

Another month to go. Another month until she could be herself again. Lily was fed up with being pregnant. And even more fed up with being poor.

At first she hadn't minded. Being pregnant proved that she was really grown up, and being poor seemed kind of Bohemian and romantic. But the novelty had soon worn off, specially once León started driving that cab and leaving her all by herself. Frank had turned up at just the right moment. It was nice to be spoiled again and have a bit of money to spend. Even though it came as a hell of a shock to find that he had once met León, that León would therefore recognise him if he ever saw him again. To make sure he never did, Lily always met him down in the harbour, aboard the *Never Again*, where there was no chance of getting caught. Far from being the typical jealous Cuban husband Lily had described to Frank, León would probably jump at the chance to offload her, and Frank would be only too happy to take her off his hands.

Lily knew in her heart that León hadn't really wanted to marry her. Given half a chance he would have tracked down the baby's father and forced him to do his duty by her. Lily had therefore been very careful not to give anything away. A guy she knew only as George had offered her a ride to Havana; she couldn't remember the name of his yacht. She hadn't realised what he was after until they were far out to sea, leaving her with no escape. She had been too frightened to refuse him and now no man would ever want her again . . .

'Men will want you all right,' León had sighed, while she sobbed strategically in his arms. 'That's the whole problem. God, Lily, what am I going to do with you?'

She soon found out. León's way of doing it was nothing like Frank's. Frank was crude and clumsy and sweaty, but León was detached, confident, self-controlled, to the point of seeming almost cold-blooded. Frank was grateful for every little thing she did. León was never grateful. He didn't care a bit if she said no – a bring-him-to-heel tactic which she had quickly abandoned, well aware that there were plenty of other women who would say yes. To guard against this she made a point of exhausting him to the point when he would roll over and groan, 'For Christ's sake, Lily, give me a break. I've got to get some sleep.' In bed, at least, she felt she had something to offer him.

Luckily he had swallowed that fib about her giving English lessons, a cover-story Lily had invented to explain where the extra money was coming from. Lily saw no harm in accepting it; it was only right that Frank should help support his child. She kept meaning to save the cash he gave her, but sooner or later it always burned a hole in her purse. She was incapable of going inside Fin de Siglo or El Época without buying herself some itsy-bitsy item to cheer herself up, and because that seemed selfish, she would buy something for the baby as well, and she would have bought stuff for León too except that he would only get mad at her for being extravagant and perhaps start realising that she was spending more than the few pesos she claimed to earn. So most of her purchases ended up hidden at the bottom of the chest of drawers, one of the items of furniture León had rescued from the bailiffs. León had sold most of her mother's jewellery, but nearly all the proceeds had gone towards Grandma's medical bills; León said that if they didn't pay them, the old girl would be forced to sell her home. The rest was tucked away in the bank, safely out of Lily's reach. León was a real old Scrooge.

'You look a bit puffy round the face,' he commented, as he dressed one hot, humid August morning. Lily yawned. With Frank away on another fund-raising 'fishing trip' she was looking forward to a well-earned rest. Just recently she had begun to feel tired and heavy, so tired that she could barely find the energy to go shopping. And yesterday's headache was still banging away, worse than ever. 'What did they say at the clinic?'

'That I was doing too much,' said Lily, improvising. She had been to the clinic once, five months ago, and never gone back. The minute they heard her address they had asked her to pay in advance, then a snooty nurse had asked a lot of personal questions about her bowels and her bladder and had she ever had VD, then some ugly old doctor had poked and prodded with stubby fingers and hurt her arm taking her blood pressure and made her take off her panties and put her legs in the air while he stuck some horrible cold instrument inside her. It had all been thoroughly unpleasant, not to mention a complete waste of money, and Lily had resolved not to go back until the baby was ready to be born.

Every second Wednesday, León would pick her up and take her to the clinic himself; Lily would hang around the lobby until he had driven off before making her getaway in the opposite direction. She had told him that they had insisted on cash payment up front – that much, at least, was true – so he would give her the money just before he dropped her off, enabling her to visit the ice-cream parlour, go to a matinée, and spend the rest on whatever took her fancy.

It wasn't that she was selfish. She had offered to sell the watch Mom had given her for her sixteenth birthday, so that León didn't have to work so hard, but he wouldn't hear of it. Lily had shoved the watch in a drawer and never worn it again. Just the sight of it made her moody and maudlin, renewing the vicious sense of loss which struck her down at her most unguarded moments. She could be stuffing herself with peanuts, or lapping up the scandal in a movie magazine, or singing along to the radio when some memory of her mother would smite her like a hammer blow, causing spontaneous, threatening tears to spurt suddenly from nowhere, filling her with grief and terror. Usually it happened when she was alone, but once or twice León had been there, and he had been so sweet, so comforting, so kind, that she had felt even worse, wriggled free of his embrace, told him to get lost, and the worst of it was, he didn't argue, he seemed to understand that she wanted him to stay near her, but ignore her, to leave her alone but not lonely. At moments like that she loved him to pieces, loved him too much to show it . . .

Sometimes, when he was very late home, she would be gripped with fear that he had had an accident; when the radio gave out news of a bomb going off – an almost daily occurrence in Havana – she would worry that his cab had been driving through the area at the time, that he, like Mom, had been blown to smithereens by the rebels. Most people in the block were ardent supporters of the rebels, and León had warned her repeatedly to keep her views to herself and not get into any political arguments with the neighbours.

Not that she would have dared. The neighbours were a rough crowd, but luckily they proved friendly enough, on account of her being pregnant. Or perhaps sympathetic would be a better word. The woman on the ground floor had four children under five, all of them crammed into two rooms, and Concha, three doors along, had recently given birth to twins who suffered horribly from eczema. Yolanda downstairs, newly abandoned by her latest lover, had a tribe of urchins, all with different fathers, who had never been to school and worked shining shoes or washing cars or delivering groceries for a few coins a day. Lily had no intention of ending up like any of these harassed mothers. Her daughter would wear little pink frilly dresses with a matching bow in her hair, and white socks and patent leather pumps. She would not cry or dribble or get dirty. She would win bonny baby contests and learn ballet and tell Lily she was the best mommy in the world. People would stop Lily in the street and say, 'What a beautiful little girl! She looks just like you!' They would go shopping together.

Yesterday she had put down a deposit on an enormous plum-coloured baby carriage with a white tasselled hood and white wheels and shiny chrome fittings. When they had asked for the delivery address Lily had told them she was in the process of moving to a new house in Miramar and would contact them in due course. The saleslady had been duly obsequious and persuaded her to equip the carriage with a pretty little pink quilt and a row of brightly coloured balls to keep the little darling amused when her nurse took her out for a walk. On her way out of the baby department, Lily had passed through children's wear and fallen in love with a dinky little cream lacy party dress designed to fit a three-year-old, but it seemed worth snapping it up now because it wouldn't be there in three years' time and she might never find anything quite like it again. On the next rail there were some cute little petticoats on special, reduced by 20 per cent, so it made sense to buy a couple of those as well. But while the assistant was wrapping them up, Lily began to feel quite dizzy and had to ask them to hail her a cab to take her home. Today she would take it easy for once instead of rushing round the shops. And in any case, she was broke, until she saw Frank again next week.

After León had gone she hauled herself out of bed and gave herself a spongebath, in an attempt to cool off. Half-way through, she began to feel dizzy again, and flopped back on the bed, naked, without bothering to dry herself. Oh, for air conditioning! That stupid little fan was worse than useless and the heat today was overpowering, no wonder she felt so lousy. She vaguely remembered learning at school that heat made things expand, and her body was no exception to the rule. Her ankles – not that her ankles were visible any more – had swollen up like balloons, as had her fingers, making her wedding ring pinch into her finger like an elastic band. The headache had grown to fill her entire skull and was slowly invading the rest of her body; she felt as if she weighed a ton. God, what a drag it all was. And to think she had another month of this to go!

Eventually she must have slept, but she had no recollection of sleeping. One minute she was lying there, succumbing to one of those awful black longings for her mother, and the next León was bending over her, shaking her awake.

'Lily! What's the matter with you? Lily!'

She sat up in bed and found she could hardly breathe. Her limbs were too heavy to move, as if they were full of water.

'I don't feel well,' she managed to say. Was it really evening already? 'I was so tired . . .' The words sounded thick and slurred in her mouth.

León helped her into her nightdress, manipulating her arms through the sleeves; they were floppy, unresponsive like a rag doll's. Then he disappeared briefly, returning with Concha's current co-habitee, a burly stevedore, who grabbed hold of her feet while León lifted her by the shoulders.

'What are you doing?'

'Taking you to the clinic.'

'I'm all right,' insisted Lily. 'I just need to rest.'

'Don't argue. You look terrible. I'm going to insist they check you over.'

Ignoring her protests, the two men installed her in the back of the cab. Oh, God, thought Lily, panicking. Now León would find out that she hadn't kept her appointments and he would ask what she had done with the money. She imagined him bawling her out in front of that horrible, stuck-up nurse on reception, who would no doubt wag a finger at her and call her a naughty girl. Better get it over with, now, in private.

'León, I've got to tell you something. I never kept the appointments.'

'What?'

'I spent the money on things for the baby instead. A perambulator and stuff. I mean, I've felt fine up to now and—' A sudden searing pain in her temple robbed her of further excuses. For a moment she couldn't see, blinking frantically to clear the black spots from her vision. León looked at her sharply in the mirror.

'Just keep still and don't bother to talk,' he said quietly, not angry at all. 'You're going to be just fine.'

Only then did it occur to her that she wasn't going to be just fine. Otherwise why would León be so nice to her? She wanted him to rant and rave at her and call her a silly bitch; that way she would know everything was all right. But he didn't. He smiled at her nervously in the mirror and kept saying things like 'Nearly there' and 'Relax, sweetheart' so that by the time he drew up outside the clinic she was well and truly terrified.

They seemed reluctant to look at her, saying she wasn't their patient, until León got very angry and refused to leave until they produced a doctor. Lily sat very still, trying to wish away the pain in her head, the throbbing, septic feeling in her arms and legs. Eventually a man in a white coat appeared, not the one she had seen before, and summoned her into a cubicle where he fired questions at her and conducted a hurried examination. Then he left her alone. She could hear him talking to León in the corridor outside, and León's voice getting angrier and angrier. Alarmed, Lily crawled off the couch and made towards the raised voices.

'If she dies, I swear to God I'll sue you,' León was yelling.

'I regret, we are not a charitable concern. I would suggest you take her to a public hospital.'

'Public hospital be damned. Let me use your telephone, now! Lily, what are you doing here? Find a chair for my wife, damn you!'

A nurse ushered Lily into a waiting room, where she sank into a soft chair which claimed her like quicksand, robbing her of the power to move. Her mouth was parched and she could hear strange buzzing noises in her head, as if a swarm of flies had settled on her brain. After what seemed like forever, León appeared.

'It's OK,' he said, taking hold of her hands. 'Everything's taken care of. Listen, honey, you need a Caesarean. Your blood pressure's very high, it could kill the baby and you as well. This way they'll put you to sleep, you won't have any pain and when you wake up it will all be over.'

Lily nodded numbly. She had heard about Caesareans. Rich women had them to avoid being stretched and torn. She was relieved. Her neighbours had regaled her with ghoulish tales of their own agonising labours; this way there was nothing to fear.

'The trouble is, this place won't do it unless I pay them beforehand and I haven't got enough cash on me and the banks are shut. But I've fixed up for another hospital to send an ambulance for you, so there's no need to worry . . .'

It arrived a few moments later, siren blaring, and took her to a brand new building near her mother's old apartment, where everyone was very polite and treated her like a lady. It was bliss when the needle went into her arm robbing her of consciousness, such bliss that she rather resented waking up only a few seconds later with a terrible searing pain in her gut.

León was sitting by her bed, smiling that awful hearty smile that didn't suit him at all. Then a nurse walked in with a squalling bundle in her arms, and held it out to her, grinning all over her face, mocking her.

It couldn't possibly be her baby. It wasn't pretty and it wasn't smiling. It was bright red, shrivelled, ugly, *angry*. Worst of all, it was a boy.

Harry Jordan had been subtle, flattering, devious, but Raúl knew what it all boiled down to. Either he co-operated, or his wife would discover – quite by chance, of course – the real reason he had left the army. The bastards must have known that one day he might be useful to them, which explained why they had hushed things up at the time.

'You got a raw deal,' Harry had said smoothly. 'This is your chance to put all that behind you, Ralph. We badly need first-hand intelligence from inside the rebel camp. From someone who'll achieve quick promotion, from a native-born Cuban they'll accept as being one of their own. From someone with quick wits, experience and guts, someone who deserves a second chance. It'll be risky, but then you like risks, don't you? Your record proves it.'

'Like you said, I'm a native-born Cuban. I'm not a lousy traitor. If you think I'm going to help the US prop up that shit Batista, you've got the wrong man.'

'We want to see Batista out as much as you do, believe me. But we don't want the Communists getting in. And neither do you. One thing we know about you, Ralph, is that you're not a goddamned red. If Fidel's the democrat he claims to be, then good luck to him. But if he's not, then he's got to be stopped. No one's asking you to betray your country. Just to help protect it, that's all. Your loyalties are to Cuba, not to Castro.'

Eduardo would still call it treachery, no doubt, thought Raúl with some disquiet. But unlike Eduardo, Raúl was ever more suspicious of the real aims of the revolution, and of Fidel Castro himself. To his mind, the man was a politician, not a soldier, and like all politicians he wanted power.

'You've been in Korea, you've been in Berlin,' continued Harry. 'You don't need me to tell you what Communism means. This is a job for a patriot, Ralph. For someone who wants to make sure that freedom means freedom.'

Even without the threat of exposure, Raúl would have jumped at this chance to prove himself. Spying was the most dangerous game of all, one that would test his nerve as never before. The prospect was irresistible.

'In that case remember one thing,' he had said, fixing Harry with a steely glare. 'You're not using me. I'm using you, OK? I'm doing this for my country, not yours.'

His only regret would be in leaving Celia to his father's tender mercies. Making her miserable – or happy, for that matter – was a right he reserved exclusively for himself. Would she be sorry to see him go, or secretly glad to be rid of him? However much she reassured him of her love, he still couldn't quite believe in it, even though perhaps it wasn't that surprising. Her most irritating habit was to love people who didn't deserve her, people like his father, like his brother, like himself.

He was due to begin his mission shortly after the baby was born. Best not to tell her till the last minute, no point in upsetting her prematurely. He would miss her. Another danger sign, proof of her ever-growing power. He had almost forgotten why he had married her, almost lost sight of the reason he had come back home. Almost but not quite. Never a day passed but that his father didn't remind him of it, with his frequent drunken diatribes against his mother, his endless distorted reminiscences. He seemed to live more and more in a paranoid past, forever droning on about what a good husband and father he had been and how badly he had been treated and how big of him it had been to welcome his errant son back into the fold. Raúl might have taken pity on him, wretched ruin of a man that he was, if he had displayed one shred of remorse, or self-knowledge, or humility – the three creeping, cancerous conditions which Raúl most feared in himself.

Celia's son was healthy, perfect, beautiful. Too beautiful.

'He looks just like his father!' the midwife had crowed, and the trouble was, he did, despite that merciful crown of dark hair. Already she could see León in those crumpled features, and as the baby grew and developed she would find herself searching out similarities, not an earlobe or a toe would be safe from inspection and comparison, fuelling the painful memories she had striven so hard to suppress.

She smiled as Raúl appeared in the doorway. He looked drawn, haggard.

'I heard you crying out,' he said tightly.

'It's over now. I'm fine. The baby's fine . . .'

'He looks like you,' said Raúl, with relief, glancing into the crib. And then, with a strangled sob, he knelt down by the bed, put his head on her lap and wept with relief that she was all right. But even as Celia put her hands on his head and bent to kiss it, Don Enrique lurched in without knocking and interrupted them. Raúl swore under his breath.

'A boy,' he burped, rubbing his hands, inspecting the sleeping infant. 'I knew you wouldn't let me down. Not a bad weight for a seven-month baby, either.'

Celia exchanged glances with Raúl, waiting for some accusation, but luckily Enrique was too pleased with this particular gift horse to look it in the mouth. And even if he did, he would no doubt jump to the same conclusion as Emilia.

'So that's why you had to get married so sudden,' she had commented drily. 'Not that I didn't have my doubts. I warned you what he was like but you wouldn't listen . . .'

'You were lucky you didn't go full term,' continued Enrique, hiccupping. 'Solers breed big babies. Raúl nearly split his mother in two. After he was born, she couldn't bear for me to touch her . . .'

'She couldn't bear for you to touch her, period,' muttered Raúl, *sotto voce*.

'What was that?' said his father vaguely, not hearing him. 'Have you decided on a name yet?'

'We're going to call him Gabriel, after my father,' said Celia, steeling herself for a fit of the sulks.

'Good,' said Enrique unexpectedly. 'I was going to suggest it myself. Your father was a good man, Celia. A good man. Did you know, I've had a mass said for his soul every week since he died?'

'No,' said Celia, not believing him.

'Every week, without fail. If he didn't get to heaven, it wasn't my fault. Now that his blood and mine are one, perhaps he'll stop punishing me for marrying your mother. I shall raise my glass to him tonight. The colonel has invited us to dine at the barracks, don't expect us back till late . . . Raúl, we must wet the baby's head before we go. I put a bottle of Dom Pérignon on ice.' He ambled off.

'Old sod,' seethed Raúl. 'He didn't even ask how you were.'

'I told you, I'm all right. Just tired.'

'I've never been so frightened in all my life. I was afraid you were going to die. I hated to think of you in pain. I hated my brother, and the baby, for causing it.'

'Raúl . . .'

'Don't worry. I'm not going to take it out on the child. I'm going to make him love me, like I made you love me. You do love me, don't you, Celia? In spite of everything?'

'As long as you love me, in spite of everything. Sometimes I'm not sure you do.'

He sighed and took her hand and played with the fingers, running his thumb up and down each one, sending a tingle up her arm. Then he pulled back the bedclothes and undid her nightdress and put his mouth to her swollen breast, pulling hard at the nipple, as if trying to recapture some vision of vanished bliss. And Celia wished that it was that easy, that she could simply put him to her breast like an infant and take away his hunger and distress, that she could fill that terrible empty space inside him.

'I do love you, Raúl,' she murmured, and it was true, she did. Not in the way that she had loved León, but it was love none the less. Loving León had been effortless, natural, involuntary, a product of her own weakness; loving Raúl was hard work, testing her strength and stamina to the limits. León was like freewheeling down a hill; Raúl was a slow, arduous climb, full of rocks and hidden pitfalls. But if she ever made it to the top, she told herself, the view would surely make it all worthwhile.

'That's a gem of a wife you've got there, my boy,' slurred Enrique, emptying the last of the bottle of champagne. 'You've certainly been luckier than I was. Mind you, now she's got a baby, she won't have any time for you. Your mother was just the same. Women always put their children first. Mind you have another one straight away, or she'll spoil it half to death and turn it into a little queer.'

Raúl clenched his teeth.

'The important thing with a boy,' went on Enrique, 'is to bring him up tough, like I did with you. Don't make the mistake I made with León. Spare the rod and spoil the child.'

'I don't need any advice from you as to how to bring up my son. And I'll thank you not to interfere.'

'Gabriel is my heir, remember? Which gives me the right to interfere, as you call it, as much as I please. Celia's far too soft to be given a free hand. As for you . . . I remember what you were like with your brother. Forever jumping to the little blighter's defence.'

It was true. Raúl might have bullied the hell out of León, in private, but he had protected him fiercely against his father. His resentment towards the former was as nothing compared with his hatred of the latter. The thought of him laying a finger on Gabriel filled him with renewed fury.

'This baby has given me a new lease of life,' continued Enrique smugly. 'I don't intend to oblige you by dying for a good few years yet. I shall leave the running of the estate to you and spend most of my time with my grandson. Then, when he's old enough, I shall start teaching him the business, the way I did you . . .'

'Come on,' said Raúl abruptly, looking at his watch, hauling his father to his feet. 'It's nearly eight o'clock. We'll be late.'

Enrique yawned malodorously. 'Very well, then. You'd better ring for the chauffeur.'

'No need. I'll drive. My car's outside.'

Enrique tottered into the hall, where Emilia dispensed his hat and stick. Raúl took his weight as he staggered drunkenly towards the Chevrolet sedan, which was parked, unlocked, in the driveway at some distance from the house. He installed him in the passenger seat and sat down beside him briefly before saying, 'Damn. I've left the key in my other jacket. I won't be a moment.'

He walked back briskly towards the house, glancing at his watch again just as he heard a massive explosion behind him. The blast threw him forwards, momentarily stunning him, and blew out the ground-floor windows. With his usual immaculate timing, he had missed death by seconds.

'Don't you like it?' demanded Lily, pirouetting in the centre of the spacious drawing room, making her skirts spin. 'Three bedrooms, two reception, two bath, kitchen, balcony, telephone, refrigerator, air conditioning. All fully furnished and we can move in right away.' She stopped twirling abruptly, reading León's folded arms and baleful expression. 'What's wrong with it?'

'We can't afford it.'

'Yes, we can.' She waltzed him towards an easy chair, sat down on his lap, and took a deep wait-for-it breath. 'It belongs to the police department,' – León let out an oath – 'and Captain Reinaldo's arranged for us to have a special deal.'

'Forget it. I don't want any more favours from Reinaldo.'

'Oh, don't be so pig-headed,' said Lily, getting up. 'If it hadn't been for him getting me into that fancy hospital, I might have died, and the baby too. You ought to be grateful to him.'

'I don't want to be grateful. I told him I was prepared to pay, all I asked for was credit. I don't like someone else paying my bills.'

'You never minded Mom paying your bills.'

'That was completely different!' rapped León, caught on a raw nerve. 'I told you, I don't want to be in Reinaldo's pocket. You accept a favour from someone like him, and one day he demands a favour in return.'

'Don't start all that again. Look . . .' She grabbed his hand and pulled him into the hallway. 'This room here will be perfect for the nursery. And the one next door can be for the nanny . . .'

'And who's going to pay for the nanny? Captain Reinaldo?'

'I'll pay for the nanny. I shall find work as a singer.'

'You'll do no such thing. If you think I'm going to let a wife of mine sing in some sleazy nightspot . . . your mother would never forgive me.'

'But you were the one who suggested it! You were the one who wanted me to sing!'

'That was before we were married.'

'Hypocrite!'

'Listen to me, Lily. Singing at your mother's place, with me there to keep an eye on you, was one thing. Working for some Mafioso of a nightclub owner is quite another. And besides—'

His argument was drowned out by a loud wail from Leonardo.

'Oh, God,' groaned Lily. 'It's bleating again.' She peered into the carrycot – the baby carriage was still awaiting a delivery address – and wrinkled her nose in disgust. 'Yuk. It's shat itself.'

'Then I suggest you change its diaper.'

'I can't. Just the thought of it makes me nauseous.'

She flung open a window while León attempted to deal with it himself, spearing the poor infant with the safety pin and producing heart-rending howls of anguish. God, neither of them knew the first thing about babies, how on earth were they going to cope?

Leonardo – Lily had insisted on the name – had only just been discharged from the maternity home where he had spent the first month of his life, ostensibly on account of his low birth weight, but mostly because Lily had refused point blank to take him home to any of the places León had found within their price range. That she had agreed to collect the baby today was evidently a ploy to force León's hand, part of the little plot she and Reinaldo had hatched between them. Much as León resented their benefactor's interference, he was increasingly anxious to reunite Lily with her baby before the tenuous bond between them was severed altogether. During her two weeks in hospital, she had shown no affection towards the child, playing the post-operative invalid for all she was worth and fretting resentfully about the size of her scar.

After her return home, it had been all León could do to persuade her to visit. His heart had gone out to the poor kid, mewing pathetically in its crib, bottle-fed by uniformed nurses, like some orphan in an institution. Would she have been any different with a girl? Searching for clean underwear to take to Lily in hospital, he had come across a treasure trove of pink baby clothes, pink frilly dresses, and half a dozen elaborate dolls, one of which warbled a plaintive 'Mamá', dolls which represented what Lily thought a baby ought to be: clean, quiet, pretty, and above all, female. He put an apoplectic Leonardo over his shoulder, trying in vain to soothe his distress.

'All right,' he said wearily. 'We'll give it a trial. But only for the baby's sake. And if I catch you entertaining Reinaldo behind my back, I swear to God we'll move out the very next day.'

'Oh, León! I feel so much better already! I'm sure this dreadful pain in my gut has been made worse by all the worry. I knew you'd understand!'

She began showering him with exuberant kisses, unsettling Leonardo, who redoubled his cries in protest.

'Here,' said León, handing her the baby. 'I'll go fetch the crib and some overnight things. You stay here and give him his feed.'

Lily sat down in a mahogany rocking chair and shoved the teat in the child's mouth without finesse.

'You're not supporting his head properly,' fussed León. 'He'll choke.'

'Can I ring up the agency and get them to send a nurse round right away? We can easily afford it. Think of all the money we saved on the medical bills . . .'

'For God's sake,' said León, exasperated, as he showed

her how to hold the child correctly. It was just common sense, she was doing it deliberately, homing in on his fear that she would drop it. 'Do what you like.' She smiled and gave the baby a big kiss.

'Poor Leonardo. He's got such a useless mommy. But he still loves her, don't you, honeybunch?'

Unimpressed by this maternal overture, Leonardo responded by sicking up some too-hastily swallowed milk all over Lily's silk blouse. Lily insisted on taking it off straight away and dabbing the stain with a wet handkerchief; while León fed the ravenous baby in her place she went to the telephone and arranged for some prospective nannies to be sent round to the apartment immediately.

With some misgivings at leaving Lily alone with her own child, León finally got in the cab and drove back from the tree-lined avenues of Miramar towards the dark alleyways of downtown Havana. Once again, he thought despondently, he had landed on his feet – or rather Lily had, but it boiled down to the same thing. Like him, she had a knack for attracting patronage, and it was pure hypocrisy to judge her for it.

'Pride is all very well, my friend,' Reinaldo had told him smugly, 'except when you force your wife and child to suffer for it. This flirtation with poverty is a gross act of self-indulgence. An educated man like yourself driving a cab, and living among the lower orders – what are you trying to prove?'

He might as well have said, 'Let's do a deal, my friend. You turn a blind eye while I pay my respects to your luscious little wife, and you can have a sinecure in the public prosecutor's office. Now what could be fairer than that?'

Lily denied that Reinaldo had given her money, or presents, but the other items León had uncovered told their own story – bottles of French perfume, silk lingerie, and items of jewellery which he had never seen her wear.

'I shoplifted them,' she had told him sullenly. 'There were so many things I wanted and you never gave me any money, so I helped myself. It was easy. I just told the salesgirl I felt faint and needed a glass of water, and by the time she got back I'd put it in my bag. Nobody ever suspects you when you're pregnant.'

He hadn't believed her, there had been a terrible row, and she had succeeded, as usual, in putting him in the wrong.

'I couldn't bear for anyone to touch me but you,' she had whimpered. 'How can you think such dreadful things of me? Just because I made one stupid mistake, out of ignorance . . .'

As he got out of the cab, one of the urchins who lived in the block thrust a copy of the evening paper in his hand. León tossed the boy a coin and cast his eye down the front page as he climbed upstairs. The headlines declared a record sugar harvest and foretold increased foreign investment for the following year. An army commander in Holguín had been assassinated by members of the 26 July movement. Twenty-two terrorists had been arrested in Oriente. Nothing interesting.

He began stuffing the contents of the drawers and wardrobe into a couple of suitcases. It was only when he saw page five of the newspaper, exposed as he used its outer leaves to wrap some shoes, that he spotted the photograph of his father.

> Don Enrique Soler, proprietor of Buenaventura, one of the largest sugar producers in Oriente province, was killed last night, the victim of a terrorist bomb . . . An explosive device was planted in a car belonging to his son Raúl, who narrowly escaped the blast . . . The two men were on their way to dine in nearby Bayamo, to celebrate the birth of Don Enrique's grandson . . . This is the third outrage of this type in the last month . . .

León knelt back on his heels and read it again, shocked not so much by the death, as by the birth, his mind flying back nine months and reaching one inescapable conclusion.

All these months and he hadn't known, hadn't even

suspected. He had never replied to Raúl's letter informing him of the wedding, preferring to lose touch completely in the hope of putting Celia out of his mind. Not that it had worked. And now it never would.

So that was why she had married Raúl. More correctly, that was why Raúl had married her; she was too honest not to have told him the truth. Not content with stealing his girl, Raúl had stolen his son as well . . .

Trust him to 'narrowly escape the blast', flaunting that charmed life of his yet again. If only the bomb had killed him instead of the old man! Such grief as León felt for his father was tempered by a sense of inevitability. He had spent his life making enemies and now he had paid the price. God. Suppose it had been Celia? If Raúl cared anything for her, he would take her back to America, to safety. And then she would be lost to him for ever . . .

She was already lost. She was married, he was married. What had happened was irrevocable, there was no hope of a second chance. Perhaps she was happy with his brother, and he hoped for her sake that she was, that she didn't feel as miserable and trapped as he did. Not that she would admit it, but he would be able to tell, just by looking at her. He had to see her again, one last time. He had to know for sure if it was his child, and to let her know he knew.

No point in telling them he was coming; if they had wanted him there, they would have sent a cable. The only way to handle this was to turn up, unannounced. He was entitled to be at his father's funeral; they couldn't turn him away, black sheep though he was, without inviting public censure. If she was happy, perhaps she would forgive him. That was about the best he could hope for.

He got home to find Leonardo being bathed in a basin by a cheerful gap-toothed black girl.

'She's got excellent references,' beamed Lily. 'She used to work for an American family who've gone back home. She's very cheap, and she can start right away . . .'

'Hire her.'

'What?'

'I said hire her. I've got to go home. I've booked a flight to Bayamo first thing tomorrow morning.' He handed her the newspaper. 'My father's dead.'

'Oh, León!' She put her arms around him. 'First my mother and now your father! Those dirty lousy stinking rebels! How terrible to read it in the paper! Why didn't anyone let you know?'

'I'm not on speaking terms with the rest of the family. But I have to be at the funeral.'

'Do you think he's left you any money?'

'For God's sake, Lily. Of course not. I told you, he more or less disowned me, that's why I couldn't ask him for help when your mother died.'

'Can't I come too?'

'No. The baby's too young to fly.'

'The baby can stay here, with Gracia.'

'I said no.'

'You're ashamed of me.'

'I'm not ashamed of you. Try to understand. This is difficult enough as it is. I don't expect much of a welcome. I don't want to involve you in a family row. I'll phone you to let you know when I'll be back.'

Her crestfallen look made him feel guilty; God only knew what she would get up to while he was gone. But this was important. Why should he put another man's child before his own, a woman he was merely married to before the one he loved?

His teeming thoughts kept him awake all night. The old man had presumably changed his will, left everything to Raúl. León had never wanted Buenaventura, but now the loss of it stuck in his throat, not because he cared anything for the estate itself, but because it represented a much greater loss, or perhaps theft would be a better word. He would have given Raúl his inheritance, but that wasn't enough, because Raúl wasn't interested in what was freely given. Raúl had always had an uncanny knack for finding some hidden, prized belonging and taking that as well. A host of forgotten grievances rose from their collective grave, making him feel like a helpless kid again, filling him with a long-denied desire to pay his brother back.

He left Lily still sleeping, undisturbed by Leonardo's waking wail. The flight touched down at Cienfuegos, arriving in Bayamo shortly before noon, where León hired a cab to drive him to Buenaventura. The gates were manned by armed guards, men he did not recognise; a telephone call was made to the house to seek permission to admit him before they finally waved him through.

All the flags were at half-mast, all the windows draped in black. Emilia was standing by the door, waiting for him. She ran forward to greet him, eyes red from weeping.

'It was terrible,' she said. 'Bits of the master all over the drive. They could barely find enough of him to bury. Your brother is in Bayamo, at the solicitor's. Celia's in bed . . . poor darling, the shock has stopped her milk.'

'Can I see her?'

'Why did you never come before? Why didn't you come when Doña Lidia died? You bad, bad boy . . . don't go upstairs. She's sleeping. The doctor gave her a sedative. Wait while I check if she's well enough to see you.'

She ushered León into the salon, just as a mulatta nursemaid came down the stairs, carrying a baby in her arms.

'Can I look?' said León, well aware that he might not get another chance. The girl halted in her tracks and looked at him dubiously.

'It's all right, Mirella, this is Gabriel's uncle.' Emilia lowered her voice. 'Let's pray he takes after his mother, not his father. Seven-month baby, my eye.'

The baby was his all right. At the last moment, he had begun to have doubts, prepared himself for some sickly premature infant like Leonardo. This one was plump and placid-looking, with Celia's dark hair, dark hair that would pass for Raúl's . . . He held out his arms, but the girl ignored the gesture, walking past him into the kitchen, returning with a bottle of formula, and following

Emilia back upstairs, as if resenting his interest. The whole tableau seemed to illustrate the hopelessness of his position; he could make no claim, enforce no rights, without causing a scandal. Dispirited, he went into the salon to wait. The only possible way forward was a reconciliation; he would have to swallow his pride. The alternative was an angry confrontation, in which he would surely be the loser. He jumped up as he heard footsteps on the stair and Emilia's voice saying, 'You shouldn't be up. The doctor said—'

'Celia!' He ran out into the hallway to greet her. In front of Emilia, at least, she would have to put up some show of normality. Taking advantage of this, he put his arms round her. She was stiff, unresponsive.

'Lay an extra place for dinner, will you?' she said to Emilia. 'And get a room ready. I assume you'll want to stay overnight?' she added coolly. 'The funeral is tomorrow.'

She led León back into the salon and sat down in her mother's old rocking chair, gesturing him to take the seat furthest away from her. She looked different, older. Paler too, though perhaps that was the effect of the black dress she was wearing. She was formidable, dignified, self-assured; all the schoolgirl gawkiness had gone.

'The paper said he died instantly.' He sounded stilted, polite, like a visitor.

'Yes. The police have taken away all the evidence. I expect they'll round somebody up sooner or later, they always do.' No tears, but her bloodshot eyes told their own story. He wanted to hold her close and comfort her; he didn't dare.

'Why didn't you let me know?'

'You had no respect for him in life, why should you have any in death?' Her voice was ice-cold.

'I've seen the child. No wonder you didn't want me to come.'

'I don't know what you mean.'

'For God's sake, Celia. I'm not a fool.'

'No. You were the clever one. I was the fool.'

'You should have told me. I had a right to know.'

She shot him a look of pure venom.

'You have no rights. Over me or the child. Once the funeral is over, I want you to leave and never bother us again. Is that understood?'

'No. No, it's not. Haven't you punished me enough, by marrying Raúl, by giving him my son? Don't you know that I've never stopped loving you for a single minute? Can you imagine what it cost me to come here and face you, face him?' He checked the counter-accusation that sprang to his lips, remembering his resolution. 'I didn't come here to make any demands on you. I came to ask your forgiveness humbly and to make peace with my brother.'

She looked away. For one sweet moment, he thought she was about to weaken. Then she met his eyes full on.

'Liar. You came here to cause trouble between us. You came here hoping to find me unhappily married and still pining for you. Well, I'm not. Raúl's a good man and I love him. More importantly, he loves me.'

'If that's true, I'm glad for you. Do you suppose I want to see you miserable?'

'You never loved me. You used me, just like you used my mother. I hate you. I'll never forgive you as long as I live.'

If she had been as happy as she claimed, there would have been no room for hatred. Her anger shone out of her like some dreadful light, filling him with inadmissible hope. Of course he didn't want her to be happy. Her misery was his only consolation. Rightly or wrongly, he was angry with her too. Angry with her for wrecking the carefree equilibrium of his life, for burdening him with guilt, for condemning him to a lifetime of regret. Love wasn't the cosy, comforting thing he had thought he wanted. Love was the stuff of greed and jealousy and conflict. Love was pain.

'There's Raúl's car outside,' she said, standing up. 'I'm going back upstairs. I don't want to be in the same room with you when he comes in. I don't want you to look at me over dinner, I don't want you even to speak to me. If you do, I won't hear you, I won't answer.'

Her voice was calm. But the raw emotion in her eyes was like a challenge, an invitation, a promise. He wanted her back. God, how he wanted her back . . .

She left the room. León heard the front door open and Emilia announcing that Señor León was here. A moment later Raúl strode into the room, all smiles. Bereavement sat well on him.

'León!'

'Don't pretend you're pleased to see me. You might have sent me a cable.'

'It must have slipped my mind. Have you seen Celia?'

'Very briefly. She's busy with the baby. Or, should I say, my baby.'

'Oh, I wouldn't say that if I were you. Not unless you want to ruin her reputation. Still, you ought to be glad for the little fellow. I've just got back from the solicitor's. Young Gabriel has just become a very rich little boy.'

'What?'

'My father's will leaves Buenaventura to his first grandchild, with the child's father as trustee and beneficiary until he attains his majority. Legally, of course, Gabriel is my son. In fact, I registered his birth this morning. Cigar?' He helped himself from the humidor. 'Don't worry, little brother. You can rely on me to do an excellent job on your behalf.'

León stared at him, vividly recalling that satanic smile from long ago. It was the smile that accompanied the execution of some diabolical practical joke, a smile that was full of malice, a smile that said, 'You may be the favourite, but I'm the clever one. Squeal on me if you dare.'

'You knew,' said León. Suddenly it all made sense. 'He told you what he was going to do. That's why you married her, isn't it?' He remembered his father offering Celia to him in marriage; the old sod had gone and done the same thing to Raúl, sold her to him like a lump of meat. Raúl lit his cigar, unperturbed by the accusation.

'You didn't marry her for love. You married her for control of Buenaventura.' Raúl inhaled luxuriously and blew a dense plume of smoke towards the ceiling. 'Worse, you made her think you were doing a favour. You made her feel *grateful* to you.'

'You're the one who should be grateful. Thanks to me, you have no responsibilities, no ties, no worries. Not every man would agree to bring up his brother's bastard as his own. As for Celia, she's a charming girl. Passionate too. I must say, you taught her well.'

The cigar soared like a rocket as León landed a blow to his jaw, sending him reeling backwards, overturning the laden drinks trolley. There was a satisfying tinkle of shattered glass. Raúl's hand flew inside his jacket and produced a gun.

'Get out,' he hissed, pointing it at him. 'I only threaten you with this to prevent myself from breaking your neck with my bare hands. She's mine now. So is the child. So is Buenaventura. Your days of taking what belongs to me are over. Now I've done the same to you, perhaps you have some idea what it feels like.'

'Shoot me,' said León. 'Kill me. Then find out which one of us she really loves.'

Raúl tossed him the gun. 'No. You kill me. Go on. All you have to do is pull that trigger. But you won't, of course. You haven't got the balls. You don't love her enough.'

'Was it you who told my father about Lidia and me? How did you know? Did she tell you? Were you screwing her as well?' He pointed the gun at his chest and cocked it. 'Tell me the truth, damn you.'

'Stop it!'

León dropped the weapon as the door flew open and Celia ran between him and Raúl.

'How dare you accuse my husband like that! How dare you threaten him! Get out! Get out of here and don't come back!'

'Calm yourself, my love,' said Raúl smoothly. 'My brother became over-excited when he heard the terms of our father's will. All his capital goes to his first legitimate grandchild. A position which has just been filled by Gabriel. The income passes to me, his father, until he is twenty-one.'

Celia stared at him and León knew straight away what she was thinking.

'Ask him why he really married you,' he said viciously. 'Ask him if he knew all along.'

'Ask, by all means,' said Raúl, putting a proprietorial arm around her and kissing the top of her head. 'I knew nothing about it till I visited the lawyer this afternoon. As a matter of fact, Papá expressly told me that he was leaving everything to me. Personally, I'm delighted that Gabriel will be the beneficiary. And so should you be, brother, in the circumstances. But I can't allow you to upset my wife any longer. Please do as she asks and leave this house.'

León fought a brief battle with his conscience and lost. Raúl's complacency was just too much for him. His father had left everything to his first legitimate grandchild, hadn't he? Well, so be it. So be it.

'You've no right to ask me to leave,' he said. 'In fact, you're only here with my permission. As trustee of the estate, I'm the one with the right to throw you out.'

'León,' said Celia, alarmed. 'Don't do this. How can you dishonour me by claiming Gabriel as your son? And in any case you can't prove it!'

'And even if you could,' said Raúl smoothly, 'Celia isn't your wife. The will specifies that the heir must be born within wedlock.' He pulled Celia closer. 'Don't worry, my sweet. Leave this to me.'

León reined in his anger with a supreme effort, forced himself to say the words calmly, quietly, clearly, slowly, cruelly, wanting to savour every last morsel of his triumph.

'Gabriel has an elder cousin. The son of my marriage, born last month in Havana, the legal heir to Buenaventura. I shall be filing the necessary documentation with my father's solicitor without delay. Meanwhile, you may remain here with my permission. I would not dream of turning my own brother, let alone my own son, out onto the street.'

For a moment nobody spoke, causing him to wonder if he had said the words, or merely imagined them.

'You're married?' said Celia faintly. 'With a child?'

'Why not?' said León, relishing the moment. 'You are.'

The anguish in her eyes made it all worth while. But the look on Raúl's face was even better. There was fury, yes, astonishment, yes, hatred, yes, but there was something even stronger and sweeter and more precious. For the first time ever, his elder brother looked at him with respect.

TEN

'SO WHEN are you expecting your husband back?' murmured Frank, passing the reefer to Lily.

'Dunno,' she shrugged, still piqued by León's refusal to take her with him. 'He called me from a hotel in Bayamo, said he'd be a few more days.'

'Then let me see the baby,' pleaded Frank. 'You can tell the neighbours I'm a relative from the States.'

'Why do you want to see it? All babies look the same.'

Frank didn't like to say, 'To convince myself it's really mine,' not that that was really the reason. He was only too ready to be convinced, overcome by a morbid middle-aged need to feel he had cheated death, acquired some stake in a shrinking future.

'Because he's my son. While your husband's away, what harm can it do?' Lily pouted, undecided; Frank reached for his wallet, counted out a wad of dollar bills, and put them in her purse.

'Oh, all right,' sighed Lily. 'If it matters that much to you.'

'Then let's go right now,' said Frank, pulling her to her feet before she could change her mind.

Rather unhappily, Lily complied. She hadn't wanted Frank to see the new apartment, or the uniformed nurse-maid, she had wanted him to think she was still destitute, relying on neighbours to mind the child while she sneaked out to keep their illicit trysts aboard the *Never Again*.

'We've moved,' she said casually, correcting the address he gave the driver.

'Up in the world, by the sound of it,' remarked Frank, surprised.

'Thanks to you,' said Lily, nuzzling up to him. 'We

could never have afforded the rental otherwise. I had to tell León I'd got some more pupils. But we're still living from hand to mouth. I just couldn't bear to bring up our child in that other place . . .'

Frank knew she was lying; he hadn't given her nearly enough to finance such an improvement in her fortunes. Perhaps she was milking some other guy as well. No doubt on the very same pretext.

'Tell me the truth, Lily. I'm not stupid.' Though he undoubtedly was.

'I'm telling you the truth!' Her head was beginning to ache, that stuff gave you a hangover worse than booze.

'Like you tell the truth to your husband?'

'I told you, I don't want to hurt him! He was there when I was in trouble, which is more than can be said for you! If you make things hard for me, I'll have to stop seeing you altogether. And if León ever finds out . . .' She began sniffing piteously.

'Heck, Lily, I don't want to bust up your marriage.' Was it tact or cowardice that made him keep up this charade? Either way it meant kidding himself. But then, kidding himself had always been his forte. 'I'm sorry. Forget I spoke.'

The cab drew up outside a modern apartment block, where Lily swept regally past the doorman, saying loudly to Frank in Spanish, 'If you can give me an estimate for the work by tomorrow, I'll discuss it with my husband as soon as he returns.'

'*Si, Señora,*' muttered Frank humbly, following her into the elevator, fighting a desire to laugh. You had to hand it to Lily, she was one tough cookie. A maid in a white apron opened the door to a small square hallway, which was almost fully occupied by an enormous baby carriage.

'This gentleman is a painter and decorator,' said Lily briskly. 'I'll just show him what work needs doing in the nursery.'

'Leonardo is asleep, Señora. He'll be waking up for his feed any minute.'

'Never mind about that. Go out and fetch me two packs of Chesterfields, will you?' She took some of Frank's money out of her bag. 'And some coconut candy. Oh, and I need some aspirin, so you can go to the drugstore while you're out.'

'If he wakes before I return,' said the girl, 'his formula is all ready in the kitchen.'

She went off to do as she was bidden, while Lily showed Frank into the baby's room. The infant was asleep in a pink canopied crib, overlooked by two rows of immaculately dressed dolls, sitting stiffly like sentinels on opposite shelves. Absently, Lily picked one of them up, and began rocking it to and fro, confident that it would not cry, throw up, or dirty its diaper. Frank put a finger into the cot and touched a tiny clenched fist. He felt an absurd lump in his throat.

'Hiya, Leonardo,' he said softly. The choice of name had hurt, at first, but now that it had a face to it, it didn't seem so bad. The child wriggled in its sleep, as if in response. Frank bent down and picked him up, luxuriating in the warmth and weight and smell of him.

Lily dropped the doll on the floor. 'For God's sake, don't wake it,' she said, irritably. 'At least not until Gracia gets back. Once it starts crying, it won't stop.'

'It?' echoed Frank, looking down at Leonardo, who continued to dream on. Before the birth, she had always referred to the baby as 'she'. He looked round the room, noting the predominance of pink and the army of brand-new dolls. 'Too bad you didn't get the girl you wanted. Perhaps you'll be luckier next time.'

'There isn't going to be a next time,' she said vehemently. 'I never want to go through all that again. I nearly died, remember?' She picked up the discarded doll and began straightening its dress. 'I want you out of here as soon as the maid gets back,' she added. 'And you mustn't come here again. People will talk.'

'I don't have to come here. There's no harm in you taking the baby for a walk in the park, is there? Like tomorrow?'

'I guess,' muttered Lily. She had looked forward to parading round with her huge perambulator, graciously accepting homage from passers-by, but both times she had tried it, the baby had woken and cried itself into a frenzy, and she had had to come home again. 'Oh, shit,' she groaned, covering her ears as Leonardo opened his eyes. 'Wait for it.'

But for once his waking whimper was short-lived. He stared curiously at the big blue eyes staring down at him and appeared to mimic the expression on the stranger's lips, producing a chortle of glee.

'Hey, Lily, did you see that? He smiled at me!'

'That usually means he's about to crap.'

'So?' He began dandling the baby up and down. 'Attaboy! Can you crap, all by yourself? My, but you're a clever kid!'

Lily raised her eyes to heaven. The worst thing about a baby was that it hogged all the attention. She was almost gratified when Leonardo's contented gurgle erupted into his customary howl.

'What did I tell you?' she said, as Frank continued to pull silly faces.

'Whassa matter, little guy? You hungry?'

'He's always hungry. Gracia will give him his bottle when she gets back. I think it's time you were leaving.'

'In a minute.' Frank carried the baby into the kitchen; the motion seemed to soothe him. Spying the ready-warmed bottle of feed, he put the teat in his mouth, producing instant silence, apart from the sound of frantic sucking.

'There you are. Nothing to it.' He walked into the living room uninvited and made himself comfortable on the couch, fascinated. Lily began filing her nails, thoroughly bored with this, jumping up as she heard the maid return. 'I'll see you in the park tomorrow,' she said, taking the baby from him. 'Around four o'clock, OK?'

She began ushering him out, just as Gracia opened the door, admitting a visitor as she did so.

'Good day,' smiled the newcomer, bowing. He

extended a beribboned bouquet. 'A small housewarming gift from my wife.'

He was small and bald with a waxed moustache. Frank did a double-take. It was the crooked cop who ran the drug racket.

'Why, thank you, Captain Reinaldo,' warbled Lily. 'What a thoughtful gesture.'

'Such a beautiful child,' continued Reinaldo, taking a perfunctory peek. 'Just like his charming mother. I do hope I haven't called at an inconvenient time.'

'Not at all,' said Lily graciously, handing the baby to Gracia, and filling her arms with the flowers instead. 'Can I offer you a drink? I've had a tradesman in to give me a quote for some decorations, he's just leaving.' She turned to Frank. 'I'll look forward to receiving that estimate,' she said regally. 'I'll let you know my decision when my husband returns.'

'Thank you, Señora.' Frank fielded a steely you-don't-know-me look from Reinaldo. What the hell was he doing here?

Captain Reinaldo, meanwhile, knew precisely what Maguire was doing here. He had always suspected that young Lily was truly her mother's daughter, and the surveillance under which he kept all his suppliers had finally put an end to speculation. Nevertheless, he would have thought her more selective than to number a boat bum like Maguire among her clientele, let alone allow him into her home. Until now, she had been reasonably discreet with her visits to the *Never Again*, proof that her poor fool of an overworked husband knew nothing of the liaison. At last he had the little bitch exactly where he wanted her.

'I was very sorry to read the sad news about your father-in-law.'

'Yes, León's in Oriente at the moment, for the funeral. He wanted me to go with him, but I thought the journey would be too much for the baby, and naturally I couldn't bear to leave him behind. We're so delighted with the apartment,' she added, showing him into the salon, and serving him from the newly stocked cocktail cabinet. She handed him a bourbon on the rocks and sat down next to him on the chintz-covered settee. 'I can't begin to thank you enough for all you've done.'

'I think you can.' Reindaldo smiled, reached across for her hand, and kissed it, his mouth moving slowly up her bare arm. Lily withdrew it, simpering.

'Really, Captain, you mustn't flirt with me. I'm a married woman.'

'A married woman whose husband is unable to provide for her adequately. Or for her child.'

Lily acknowledged this remark with a long-suffering sigh.

'I do wish you could persuade León to take that job at the public prosecutor's office. I've tried, but he won't listen to me. I begged him to make things up with his father, and now it's too late. He cut him off without a penny, you know.' She sighed tragically. 'We're finding it a terrible struggle to manage. I'm so anxious about Leonardo's education. And what if he's sick? We can't even afford a health plan. It's such a worry, being a mother.'

'It would be my pleasure to help you, you know that, Lily. May I call you Lily? Your mother and I were such good friends . . .'

Not for the first time, Lily wondered if Reinaldo had been her mother's lover. That would account for why León was always so touchy about him. Lily enjoyed Reinaldo's elaborate flattery, which made a welcome change from León's constant criticism and Frank's rather crude line in compliments, but she didn't like anything about him physically, not his shiny bald head nor his carefully manicured moustache nor his twisted, twitching mouth, and she didn't like the slight but sinister cast in his left eye. But it would have been stupid to refuse the apartment; after all, he had always behaved with perfect politeness, never giving any credence to León's claim that he was a dirty old man. But now, as his soft damp hand reached out again and began entwining its fingers with hers, she began to have a few qualms.

Emitting a naughty-naughty giggle, designed to spare his feelings, she slapped his hand and tried to pull free, but his grip was like a vice.

'You can repay me, Lily,' he said softly. 'And in return, I will give you anything you want. I am a very powerful man. I can help you, help your husband. All you have to do is be kind to me.'

'Please let go of me, Captain. The nurse may walk in any moment.'

'Don't worry about the nurse. She's been well paid to keep her mouth shut.'

'But—'

'You wouldn't like to lose this apartment, would you, Lily? And you'd hate your husband to find out about Mr Maguire, wouldn't you?'

'Mr Maguire? I told you, he's just—'

'There's no need to make excuses. Why shouldn't you amuse yourself as you please? Your visits to the harbour will be our little secret. As this will be. Now, shall we go somewhere more comfortable? Gracia is just about to take the little one for a walk and she won't come back until she sees me leave.'

Even as he spoke, Lily heard the front door slam shut.

'Captain Reinaldo, I—'

'Come now,' he rapped. 'Don't be coy. I have been very patient. I respected your pregnancy, I waited for you to recover from the birth. Now the time has come to keep your side of the bargain.'

Lily understood bargains. But it was generally she who struck them. She had always regarded herself as a saleswoman of sorts; now she felt like goods on a shelf, powerless to choose their own buyer. How had Reinaldo found out about Frank? She had been so careful! Oh, God. If she refused him, he would tell León. And then León would go to Frank and say, 'She's all yours, pal. Be my guest. I never wanted her anyway.' And Frank, of course, would be only too delighted to have her and the baby all to himself . . .

Even if León didn't dump her, they would have to

move out of this apartment, and go back to that awful room. León would forbid her to see Frank again, rob her of all the little extras that made life bearable. And besides, she didn't want to lose Frank. Frank loved her a hell of a lot more than León. This way, she could keep both of them, and the apartment too. It was only sex, after all, the one thing she knew she was good at . . .

Gulping, she allowed him to lead her out into the hallway and into the main bedroom; of course, he already knew where it was, having picked out the apartment himself.

'Take your clothes off,' he said, shutting the door. His lips were twitching faster than usual, like a rabbit's, and his voice had acquired a sharp, staccato rasp, quite unlike his normal oily tones.

Nervously, Lily began unbuttoning her blouse. 'I've just had a baby,' she reminded him, clutching at straws. 'I'm still—'

'Don't worry. I won't touch you there.' He made 'there' sound like somewhere very nasty. 'I said, take your clothes off, Lily.' His voice was soft again, his eyes ranging up and down her like a searchlight, making her feel shy. And she had never been shy before, not even the first time, she had always been proud of her body, enjoyed showing it off, relished the effect it had on Frank, and to a lesser extent, on León. The pregnancy had left it unmarked, apart from the scar left by the Caesarean. It annoyed her, even in front of a creep like Reinaldo, that she wasn't physically perfect any more.

'Aren't you going to undress?' she said pertly, wanting only to get this over with quickly. And then, in a desperate attempt to take charge, 'Here, let me help you.'

He flung her hand away. 'Whore,' he hissed, producing a switchblade from his pocket. He flicked it open and advanced, blade gleaming. Lily gasped, too terrified to move.

'Don't scream. Not yet, anyway. I won't hurt you, as long as you don't scream.'

'It's OK,' croaked Lily, struggling to keep calm. She

forced a smile. 'I'll do whatever you want, there's no need for that.'

'You're afraid of me,' said Reinaldo, baring a row of crooked teeth. 'Aren't you?'

'Of course I'm not.' It's just a game, she thought desperately. Perhaps he needed a bit of help, like Frank sometimes did, on account of being so old. Her best bet was to go along with it, act normal, otherwise he might get mad and hurt her. He held the point of the blade under her chin.

'Are you scared yet?'

Lily blinked as the steel moved to the corner of her eye, realising just in time that he wanted her to be scared, that the erection poking out from his open flies depended on it. Gee, but he was small. She would never have thought they came as small as that.

'Yes,' she said quickly, changing tactics. 'Yes, I'm scared.'

'That's good. Now lie face down on the bed.'

Lily did as she was told. Reinaldo straddled her from behind and gagged her with his cravat.

'It's all right,' he said softly. 'You can scream all you like from now on. In fact, I shall be very disappointed if you don't, because you're going to be very, very frightened.'

Lily blanked her mind out, and imagined she was a movie star playing a scene in a film. The script said she was supposed to be scared, so she would act scared . . .

'No,' she tried to say, dragged unwillingly from the refuge of her imagination. She made an effort to roll over onto her back, but he immobilised her with his full weight. 'Not that. Not there.' But the gag robbed her of all her consonants, making her sound like a braying donkey.

'Some women like it this way,' said Reinaldo, pressing the knife against her throat, 'but I'm so glad you don't. And then afterwards, you can taste for yourself just how dirty you are inside.'

He smiled as her muscles went into spasm in a vain

attempt to exclude him; it was better than raping a virgin. And her muffled scream of protest made it even better, the kindling to his flame.

For once, Lily wasn't faking. She had never been so damned scared in all her life.

'We can't possibly stay at Buenaventura,' repeated Celia. 'What if he brings his wife and child to live here? The sooner we leave the better.'

His wife and child. The words stuck in her throat. He hadn't lost much time. The child must already have been conceived when he came home at Christmas. Had he promised to marry that woman too? Had he asked her to wait two or three years? Had she trapped him even as she, Celia, had hoped to trap him? Why did it hurt so much? Why did it hurt more than everything else put together? It only hurt because she let it, seizing upon this new grievance, seeing it as an antidote to the poison of regret.

'Raúl? Can't we go to your stepfather, in Chicago? I know you said he was angry about you staying here in Cuba, but surely now . . .'

'I have no stepfather,' he said quietly. 'I have no fortune, no family, no expectations. I have nothing. I lied. I lied about everything. You married a pauper.'

Celia sat down on the bed. It was less of a shock than it should have been. She could hear her mother's voice saying, 'I don't trust him. I don't believe a word that man says . . .'

'My father gloried in having power over people,' he continued in the same, flat toneless voice. 'I would rather have died than come to him as a beggar. If I hadn't lost my livelihood, I would have kept my solemn vow never to see or speak to him again. But I had nowhere else to go. I didn't leave the army by choice, Celia. I had an affair, unwittingly, with a Russian agent in Berlin. It was hushed up to avoid a diplomatic incident, I was forced to resign my commission. I gambled, got into debt, came here to escape my creditors, to reclaim what was mine by right.'

There, thought Raúl. Now she knew the truth, except for the sex of the agent. If only he had had the guts to tell her that too, to tell her about Eduardo, to watch her shrink from him in revulsion. It seemed almost preferable to lose her outright, now, in one fell swoop, than endure the torment of losing her by degrees to his handsome, charming, unscrupulous brother, the brother who had the right to come here any time he pleased and who would surely not hesitate to take advantage of his absence.

Celia didn't speak for a moment. Then she said dully, 'So León was right. You didn't marry me for love. You knew about the will, didn't you? Didn't you?'

The desolation in her voice tore him apart. He had never hated himself so much as at that moment.

'Yes. What I didn't bargain for was falling in love with you.'

She searched his face, looking for more lies. Raúl grasped both her hands and met her gaze full on.

'Listen, Celia. I refuse to stay on here as my brother's lackey. But I can't expect you and Gabriel to live in poverty. As long as you stay here, you won't lack for anything, León has a moral duty to support his son. And one day, I swear, I'll come back for you.'

'I don't understand. Where are you going? Are you leaving me? If you're leaving me, at least have the guts to say so!'

She began flailing at him with her fists, seeking the familiar release of conflict. Raúl trapped them behind his back, imprisoning her in a fierce embrace, kissing her savagely, hungrily, as if for the last time, forcing an equally desperate response.

'You still love me, don't you?' he murmured. 'Even though I lied to you. But then, you have a special weakness for liars.'

'Stop it! Stop tormenting me! Wherever you're going, I'm coming too. I don't care about being poor, I'll work, we'll manage. Don't force me to live on León's charity, I can't bear it!'

He seized her by the shoulders, his eyes alight with the

passion she had learned to fear, passion that was none the less precious, like an uncut gem, promising hidden riches.

'You can't come with me, Celia.'

'But—'

'Hear me out. Have you any idea how much pain it has cost me to pretend to share my father's politics, to toady to the police chief and that bumbling fool of a colonel, to see the workers break their backs for a pittance while we live in luxury?'

He would rather have told her the real purpose of his mission, but she might not have understood, and besides, the need for strict security forbade it. He had dreaded breaking the news of his departure; now the least he could do was to make his reasons sound convincing. Otherwise she might think he was running out on her.

'I had planned to make so many changes here, once my father was dead. And now the only way I can make those changes is to fight for them. There is only one place in Cuba where a man is judged by his courage and strength, rather than the size of his wallet.'

Celia stared at him in horror. First Eduardo, now Raúl. They would both end up dead . . .

'You're going to join the rebels? After they killed your father? After they tried to kill you?'

'The rebels cannot be held accountable for every action of terrorism committed in their name. Such atrocities will never cease until we put an end to injustice and poverty. Would you condone the crimes my father has committed over the years? The land he has stolen, the people he has oppressed and exploited? Can you blame those who thought that I came out of the same mould, who assumed me to be his heir, who no doubt would prefer, in their ignorance, to see Buenaventura run by someone as weak and spineless as my brother?'

'You're condoning murder?'

'It was an act of war. I'm a soldier. One who must fight for what he believes in, whatever the personal cost.'

'What about the cost to me, to Gabriel? Can you imagine what my life will be as the wife of a rebel?'

'No one will know. Everyone must be told I have returned to Chicago, and that I will be sending for you. My father's death will serve to divert suspicion. Why would a rich Yanqui ally himself with his father's killers? Trust me, Celia. When Cuba is free, we can build a new and decent life together. If you are prepared to wait for me. If you really love me. If you can resist the renewed assault my brother will make on your affections.'

So it was a test, thought Celia. The cruellest, most heartless test he could devise for her. To leave her alone and defenceless against someone almost as ruthless as himself.

'I'm glad this has happened,' he said. 'Glad I've got this chance to redeem myself, to prove my love for you and yours for me. I was never cut out for a soft life, like my brother. I was born to strive and struggle and suffer.'

He knelt down at her feet, pressing his head against her belly.

'And no one has ever made me suffer like you. Why do I wallow in it so? I don't deserve your love, Celia. It's like a scourge, a penance. No one else has ever loved me, why should you?'

And yet she did, even now, understanding his terrible doubt in himself, knowing from bitter experience what it was to feel second best, rejected, disappointed, dependent. And he knew that she knew. He manipulated her need to love and be loved, used her as the mirror that reflected his own troubled spirit.

If she pleaded for him to stay he would only despise her for it. And if he gave in, he would despise himself. War was his natural habitat. Raúl needed enemies – better for him to fight Batista than turn his aggression inward on himself.

'You won't betray me, will you?' he whispered, plaintive and vulnerable again. 'You won't betray me as she did?'

Celia made a silent, solemn vow never to make Gabriel

love her as much as Raúl had loved his accursed mother.

'I won't betray you,' she said.

Frank hung around outside the block, stubbornly waiting for Lily's visitor to leave. It had taken him all of thirty seconds to put two and two together, to work out that this Reinaldo guy must have been getting freebies at Addy's, and that Lily had kept on her erstwhile client to help make ends meet. And when the maid had taken the baby for a walk, minutes after his arrival, it served to confirm his suspicions.

Bitch. Now was the time to cut his losses. It wasn't as if he wanted her for sex, the cheapest commodity in the world. He wanted her for something else, something she couldn't give him, something the baby had given him instantly, automatically . . .

Something he didn't want to lose. It had been a mistake to see the child, to hold it, to feel responsible for it, to fancy he saw himself in its unformed features. If he walked away now, he would be free to see her again, act like nothing had happened. And instead he was waiting, watching, stewing, building up to a showdown that would probably finish everything and make him look like a jealous old fart.

'You don't have to do this any more,' he would say. 'Why don't you leave that lousy pimp of a husband before he turns you into a raddled old whore?' Only nine months ago, there had been a kind of innocence about her. If he'd acted then, it might not have been too late. Perhaps it still wasn't. So much for not having a conscience any more. Harry would bust a gut laughing if he could see him now . . .

He ground out his cigarette with his heel as Reinaldo emerged from the building and walked towards his car. He was hunched, as if in pain, taking the slow, deliberate steps of a man who has had too much to drink, and yet he couldn't be drunk, he had been quite sober half an hour before . . .

The nanny, who had been wheeling the baby carriage

round and round the block, promptly accosted him; Reinaldo shoved some money at her and drove off, whereupon the girl pushed the pram back into the lobby, a routine that served to dispel any lingering doubts Frank might have had. He marched past the doorman, who acknowledged him with a nod, rode up in the elevator and rang the bell. The maid answered.

'The señora is resting.'

'She's expecting me.' He walked straight in and rapped on the bedroom door. 'I have the estimate you asked for,' he bellowed. 'I need to talk to you right away.'

The door opened instantly and Lily appeared in her robe. She pulled him inside and threw her arms around him convulsively, shaking from head to foot.

'When I heard the door I thought it was him. You've got to help me, Frank. I've got to get out of here, before he comes back.'

'Did he hurt you?' She nodded. 'Tell me what happened!'

'I c-can't. It was horrible. He bribed the maid to leave me alone with him. I'm afraid to stay here. He's got a knife. Oh, Frank! Thank God you're here!'

Thank God he was here. And to think he had so nearly walked away . . .

'You'd better pack a few things. I'll call for a cab and see to Leonardo.'

'Leonardo?' She nodded vaguely, as if she had forgotten him. Frank rang for a taxi and barged in on the nursemaid.

'Pack all the baby's things together,' he said. 'The señora is going on holiday. You can take some time off, till she gets in touch, OK? Hurry up!'

Startled, she began assembling baby paraphernalia, with Frank's assistance, to the sound of Lily crashing about in the bedroom, intent, it seemed, on packing everything she possessed. A good sign, in Frank's view, proving she had no intention of coming back. Despite her frantic haste, she made him go up and down several times, until every last item was stowed in the trunk of the cab, packed or not, including the pathetic family of dolls. At last they set off, Frank with the carrycot on his lap, Lily clutching a teddy bear. Every so often, she shuddered, as if remembering what had happened, but he didn't ask for any more details, not wanting to know. Soon all that would be behind her for good.

They arrived at the jetty just as the brief tropical twilight plunged them abruptly from day into darkness. Frank tipped the driver to help transport all the luggage onto the *Never Again*. Once they were back home, he would sell the boat and settle down. It would fetch enough to set them up in a small apartment, and then he would get a job, any job. . .

'Will you telephone León for me?' she asked, sitting on the edge of the bunk with Leonardo lying in his carrycot beside her. Confused by all the commotion, he was grizzling piteously. 'He's staying at the Hotel Alvara, in Bayamo.'

'Sure I will. Once we're safely away from Cuba.'

'I don't want to leave Cuba,' she said. 'Not without León.'

'What?'

'Reinaldo threatened to tell León about you. He must have been watching us. So you've got to tell León that you're my uncle, from the States, and you've been giving me money, but I didn't want him to know in case he was too proud to take it. He'll believe you. I mean, if you really *were* my lover, you wouldn't have the gall to talk to him, would you?'

'Wait a minute—'

'I don't want to lose him, Frank! I love him! He's my husband!'

This was too much. 'Your pimp, you mean.'

'My *what?*' She stared at him. 'How dare you! If he's a pimp, what does that make me?'

'Cut it out, Lily. I know what you are, I've always known what you are. Let's stop pretending, shall we? Why do you think I've let you take me for a sucker? Because I care about you, that's why. How many girls like you end up with a knife in their guts? How many of them end up dead in the gutter?'

'Girls like me?' She jumped up, eyes flashing. 'You're as bad as Reinaldo! I'm not a whore, I'm not, I'm not, and neither was my mother! He said horrible, horrible things about her, he said he'd done it to her, the same thing he did to me, he said she *liked* it . . .'

'Your mother?'

She went very red. 'Addy was my mother,' she said in a small voice. 'I came to Havana to be with her. I wanted to be a singer. I ran away from Grandma's because I didn't want to go back to school.'

'School?' Christ almighty. 'Lily . . . how old did you say you were?'

She sniffed. 'I'll be seventeen in a couple of months. I said I was older so you wouldn't treat me like a kid. You were the first, I swear it! I wanted you to like me! It was the only way I could get you to take me to H-Havana, so I could be with Mom. I thought you gave me all those presents because you c-cared about me, not because you thought I was a . . . a . . . You rat! If I'd known it was that easy to get pregnant, I wouldn't have done it. I wish to God I hadn't. I hated it if you must know. I hated every minute of it!'

She broke down into stormy, face-twisting sobs, quite unlike her usual stage-managed tears. Frank put an arm round her helplessly, his mind going into reverse, re-evaluating everything she had ever told him, every cynical conclusion he had jumped to, every piece of counter-evidence he had wilfully ignored. *When you don't believe in anything, you end up despising everyone*. It took a pretty determined misanthropist to mistake a virgin for a whore.

'If it wasn't for you I wouldn't be in this god-awful mess! And now León won't love me any more! Oh, God! I wish I was dead!'

'It's OK. Lily, please don't cry, it's OK. I'm sorry. You're right, it was all my fault. I'm sorry.'

He held her close while her tears subsided. But not too

close. He felt enough of a child molester already.

'Will you go and phone León right away?' she pleaded. 'Before Reinaldo speaks to him first? Tell him I'm your niece, like I said? Please, Frank. He'll believe you! After all, you are old enough to be my . . .' She faltered and left the sentence unfinished, in a belated attempt at tact.

It should have been the final moment of truth, and in a way, it was. She put her arms round his neck, and for the first time he got from her what he got from the baby, got what he really wanted. He had never been much good as a lover. He had to learn to be a father now.

León lost no time in calling in on his father's solicitor, where he lodged a formal claim on the estate in the name of his legitimate son. Pending Leonardo's majority, León would enjoy absolute control over the management of Buenaventura, the voting stock in several Cuban- and American-owned companies, and the income from both the property itself and a large portfolio of investments, the provisos being that he could not dispose of any capital and that the child must be raised and educated in Cuba. If Leonardo died or left the country before his twenty-first birthday, the estate would pass to the next eldest surviving grandchild, subject to the same provisions. Celia would retain the absolute right to live at Buenaventura for her lifetime at the expense of the legatee. The old man had predictably failed to leave her the one thing she would have valued: her independence.

And now León had deprived her son, his son, of his inheritance, enriched a child fathered by a stranger, perpetrated a gross act of legal embezzlement. But it was too late for scruples now. In any case, his first duty was to Lily and Leonardo. He wasn't going to sacrifice them at the altar of self-indulgent guilt or give in to fear of reprisals. It would have been just as dishonourable to have kept quiet, let Raúl have his way, reverted to the play-safe behaviour of his childhood. For once, he had invited retaliation, and he would undoubtedly get it.

Perhaps he should have pulled that trigger while he

had the chance. The challenge had been typical of Raúl. He recalled an episode from his childhood, when his brother had given him his treasured Swiss army knife, one of his rare, unpredictable acts of generosity. León had stammered his thanks, overwhelmed by the enormity of the gift, while Raúl crouched down beside him, grinning from ear to ear. 'Now cut me!' he had whispered, baring his arm. 'Good and deep. Try to make me cry out! Do it or I'll thump you!'

Unable to bring himself to execute this fiendish request, León had chosen the thumping instead. Holding Raúl's arm steady, while Eduardo stitched up the gash in it, he had caught a mocking look in his eye, a look that said, 'Remember?'

Well, he had struck back now, without the crude aid of steel or lead, he had fulfilled the dare at last. From now on he would match his brother in guile and ruthlessness. He was through with being soft, and weak, and nice. Or perhaps he never had been nice. Perhaps unhappiness was the catalyst which had fired his true self into life, perhaps he and Raúl had more in common than he thought. Even now, he felt an inkling of sympathy for him, understood, imperfectly, how bitterness and loss could warp the soul, as they were even now warping – or tempering – his own.

'It will take several weeks to complete all the formalities,' the solicitor advised him obsequiously, well aware that his client had a first-class diploma and would double check everything he did. 'Meanwhile, you may draw an advance on income, if you wish, pending verification of the information you have given me and processing of the will.'

'I'll send you copies of the birth and marriage certificates. You'll find everything in order. Naturally my brother still has a home, and a job, if he wants it. I've no interest in the day-to-day management of the estate and don't propose to take up residence. Perhaps you will convey this to him formally on my behalf.'

Might as well rub salt in the wound, as Raúl would

have done in his place. Would he return to America now, taking Celia and the child with him? Or would he stay on and plot behind his back? With the law on León's side he would have to find some other way to hit back. One thing was for sure. Whatever he did would not be what it seemed.

After calling in at the bank with a letter of authority, and withdrawing a sizeable sum in cash, León checked into a hotel and telephoned Lily, to let her know he had arrived, holding back the news of Leonardo's inheritance until he got home; he was in no mood for whoops of glee. As soon as he got back to Havana he would move her out of that apartment, cancel out his unwanted debt to Reinaldo. The income from the estate was well in excess of a quarter of a million a year. Enough for an easy, indolent life of leisure. He wouldn't have to drive a cab any more, wouldn't have to do anything at all. He could play at being a painter again, indulge Lily's every whim, give that poor kid of hers a decent start in life. Raúl could always fall back on his rich stepfather for money, it wasn't as if Celia and Gabriel would have to go without. Inadmissibly, he would have liked to see them penniless, so that he could distribute largesse, make them dependent on him, have them in his power . . . Christ. He was getting as bad as his father.

He arrived at the funeral next morning to find Celia and his brother already outside the church, receiving condolences. Much to his embarrassment, León soon found himself similarly surrounded, being forced to listen to false eulogies from those seeking to ingratiate themselves with the new master of Buenaventura. Raúl, meanwhile, was the picture of bland composure. Inside he must surely be seething, but outwardly he appeared to be giving in gracefully. Too gracefully.

'Now that the estate is in my brother's capable hands,' León overheard him saying, 'I shall be returning to Chicago immediately. Celia and the baby will remain here while I make preparations for them to join me . . .'

What was he playing at? Was he planning to ditch

her? That seemed like too much to hope for. Celia's face, invisible behind her black veil, gave nothing away. She remained silent throughout the mass, but as the coffin was carried from the church and laid to rest in the family vault, next to that of her mother, she broke down and wept, with her husband's comforting arm around her shoulder. As soon as the funeral was over, he led her to a waiting car, which drove off slowly, heading the convoy back to the house. Then he turned to León and said, quietly, as they watched the mourners depart, 'I saw the way you were looking at her. The minute my back's turned you'll be sniffing round her like a tom cat. You probably think I'm a fool for leaving her alone.'

'I think you've got no use for her any more. Have you had the decency to tell her, or are you keeping her on a string?'

'You'd love to believe that, wouldn't you? The truth is, my stepfather objected to our marriage, especially my decision to remain here in Cuba. He felt I'd betrayed my mother and turned my back on him. I can't be sure of a welcome, or a home, or a job. Otherwise, I can assure you, I wouldn't permit her to invoke her rights of occupation, even temporarily. Meanwhile, of course, you will do your utmost to turn her against me.'

'Like you turned her against me, you mean?'

'You misjudge me, brother. And her. The more you try to malign me, the fiercer her loyalty will be. You're ignoring one important thing. Celia loves me. And I'm going to make her prove it.'

The words sounded complacent, but the voice betrayed a glimmer of tell-tale doubt. Instinctively, if unwisely, León pounced on it.

'And what if I manage to prove that she loves me more?'

Raúl smiled with one half of his face.

'I'll kill you,' he said pleasantly. 'I'll kill you both.'

Lily was getting anxious. Frank had been gone for what seemed like hours, and the baby wouldn't stop crying.

She rolled herself a reefer, to try and calm herself down, but as usual it made her feel slightly sick, and puffing the smoke in Leonardo's face didn't have the required effect of shutting him up.

'Be quiet!' she pleaded, bouncing him up and down on the bunk, redoubling his cries. 'You're giving me a headache!' She picked his discarded dummy off the floor and shoved it back in his mouth, but he ejected it again, showering her with spittle. In despair, Lily began crying along. She had been stupid. She shouldn't have lost her head like that, shouldn't have made Reinaldo mad. But no one had ever forced her before, no one had ever insulted and abused and humiliated her. And when he finally removed the gag and forced his stinking thing inside her mouth and started saying filthy things about her mother, she had suddenly remembered that God had given her teeth . . .

It had been a moment of pure, primitive triumph. The howl of anguish had caused him to topple to one side like a felled tree, dropping his knife, releasing her from his weight, and enabling her to make a dash for the bathroom and lock herself in.

'You come near me, you motherfucker, and I'll cut it off!' she had screamed, smashing Leon's shaving mirror against the tiles to give herself a weapon. A few breathless moments later, she had heard the door slam, but afraid that he might have tricked her, she stayed put until reassured by the sound of Gracia returning with Leonardo. By that time her courage had collapsed into horror at what she had done. Reinaldo would never let her get away with this.

Hurry up, Frank. I can't stand another moment alone with this baby . . . She jumped up expectantly as she heard George barking up on deck.

'Frank?'

The barking became a growl. Lily jumped as several shots rang out, silencing the poor creature for ever.

'Frank!'

It wasn't Frank. It was three armed policemen.

*

'Serves you right,' said Sofía Reinaldo, inspecting her husband's penis. 'I see you got it in all the way. In your case, of course, that's not very far.'

'Shut up,' growled Reinaldo, wincing, his arm still sore from the tetanus shot. His doctor had been only marginally more sympathetic than his wife. The thought of Lily languishing in gaol, on a trumped-up drugs charge, was the only thing that helped to soothe the pain.

'Let her go,' wheedled Sofía. 'She's only a child.'

'She's a tramp, like her mother. I paid her enough in advance, damn her eyes. Her medical bills, the apartment, a nanny for the price of a cleaning woman . . . what did she expect?'

More to the point, what had León expected? Sofía nurtured fond memories of her favourite lover, and still retained hopes of luring him back into her bed. She had seen him only once since his marriage, a meeting engineered by her when he had stubbornly declined her offer of financial help. Seeing the misery in his eyes, she had filled him full of liquor, loosened his tongue, wrung the whole story out of him. The poor darling had got his come-uppance at last, thanks to this heartless creature in Oriente, and as for this child bride of his . . . She hadn't known whether to laugh or cry.

She gave this absurd marriage a year at most; you only had to look at the girl to know what she was. Not that she would ever make the grade if she carried on like this. But she felt sorry for her, admired her guts. She had struck a much deserved blow for all her kind. With luck, the damage she had inflicted would prove to be permanent.

'Think what you are doing, Hector,' Sofía chivvied him. 'Do you want the girl to expose you in court?'

'It will be made very clear to her,' said Reinaldo, 'that keeping her trap shut and pleading guilty is her only hope of clemency. I'll teach the little *puta* to make a fool out of me!'

'She'll tell her husband.'

'Tell him what? That she invited me into her bedroom?

The maid will confirm that she did just that, before telling her to go out and leave us in peace. She will also confirm that one of her other lovers, the Yanqui dope dealer, had only just left the apartment.'

'And what if the American turns state's evidence against you?'

'He'd be a dead man, and he knows it. Besides, who would believe his word against mine?'

'You're a shit, Hector.'

'Just like your two brothers, who both owe their jobs to me. Just like our son, who will one day follow in my footsteps. A son who believes his mother to be the Virgin Mary. Keep your nose out of my affairs, Sofía, as I keep mine out of yours.'

He stepped gingerly into his trousers and left the house, with his wife's laughter ringing in his ears. As soon as he was gone, she dried her eyes and picked up the telephone.

Buenaventura, 25 September 1957

Dear León

Raúl will have made you aware of his problems with his stepfather. For the sake of the child it seems prudent for me to exercise my right to live here until he has made some alternative provision for us.

The solicitor informs us that you do not propose to take up residence yourself. In Raúl's absence, you will have to employ a manager. I am the person best qualified for that job. Accordingly, until Raúl sends for me, I am willing to take over the running of Buenaventura, at the same salary Raúl received from his father. If you have any respect for me at all, you will allow me this opportunity to pay my way, rather than reduce me to the status of poor relation and parasite . . .

Hearing a whimper from the baby, Mirella scooped him out of the crib, glad to have beaten Celia to it. She settled down happily into a rocking chair and offered him his bottle; already she felt as if Gabriel belonged to her. In the last few months she had played the expectant mother, knitting and crocheting and sewing exquisite tiny garments, in readiness for his arrival. Even though Celia could well afford to buy a ready-made layette, it gave Mirella pleasure to make these things herself, as she had once done for her own baby. And now Gabriel would fill the breach until she could have one of her own, with Eduardo.

He hadn't asked her to marry him yet, but Mirella knew that he cared for her. He wrote to her every week, via the courier, expressing concern for her health and making her promise to stay at Buenaventura, in safety, until the war was won. Once the revolution triumphed, there would be a general amnesty for all those wanted by the police. And then Eduardo would be able to come out of hiding and would surely claim her as his bride . . . Life was suddenly full of hopes and dreams again.

The doctors had reassured her that she was still able to conceive, and with every day that passed she felt stronger – the gnawing pain in her back had gone, her urine was no longer tinged with blood, and the combined effects of medicine, rest and good food had put paid to the giddy spells which had threatened, more than once, to make her lose her footing and tumble headlong down the mountain.

She had grown used to the comforts of her new life at Buenaventura. She liked her soft bed and her pretty room, her well-being marred only by Raúl's ill-concealed dislike of her. No doubt he disapproved of his brother-in-law, an educated white boy, falling in love with a poor, ignorant mulatta. Mirella was glad that Raúl had gone off to the camp, if fearful that he would try to turn Eduardo against her while he was there. She cast this uncomfortable thought aside, smiling down happily at Gabriel, her face the picture of madonna-like adoration. She only had to look at him to forget all the bad things in life.

Celia, watching her, stifled a pang of jealousy and tried to concentrate on her letter. Don Enrique's death, the arrival of León, the violent confrontation between the two brothers, the funeral, and Raúl's subsequent departure for the camp, had made heavy demands on her time and emotions, denying her the luxury of recovering from the birth and enjoying her baby. But it seemed churlish to resent Mirella for doing such an excellent job. With so much else on her mind, it was a relief to know that Gabriel was not being neglected, that every moment of his life was bathed in love and affection. And if León agreed to let her run the estate she would have to rely on Mirella more than ever.

This way there would be no handouts, this way she could keep her pride. This way she could safeguard the supply line, keep in touch with Raúl and Eduardo. Papá would no doubt turn in his grave, but her loyalties were to the living, not the dead. How could she turn her back on her husband and her brother?

> If acceptable to you, this arrangement will be on the understanding that you give me a free hand and that you do not visit or telephone. I will furnish you with a weekly report and monthly accounts, and keep you informed of any decision I choose to make. I would appreciate an early reply.
> Your sister-in-law
> Celia Rodríguez de Soler.

She had just rung the bell for Emilia, to despatch this note via the chauffeur to León's hotel, when she heard the telephone ring for the twentieth time that day. Suddenly she was at the top of everyone's guest list, besieged by fulsome invitations from those gossips avid for all the details of the latest family drama. Who was this girl León had married in secret in Havana? Would they be coming to live at Buenaventura? How unfair that Raúl should lose out after all the hard work he had put into the estate, small wonder he had upped and left for the States, and when did Celia and the baby plan to join him?

She ignored the extension ringing at her elbow; Emilia had been told to say she was unavailable. But in a few days, she would have to face the world again. Assuming León agreed to her terms, she would get her girlhood wish with a vengeance, she would earn her own living at last.

'Give him to me, Mirella,' said Celia, putting the sealed

envelope to one side and holding out her arms. How tiny he was, how defenceless. What a simple, safe, uncomplicated love this was, sane and wholesome and pure and right. Just to sit still, holding him, was like lying in the sun after braving a stormy sea, the strength she needed to dive back in was surely to be found here, on this peaceful shore . . .

There was a knock on the door and Emilia came in.

'There's a woman on the line, from Havana, asking to speak to Señor León. That's the second time she's called. I put her onto his hotel in Bayamo, but apparently he's not in. She won't leave a message with me, snooty cow.'

'His wife?' Celia felt her throat go dry.

'She wouldn't give her name. She says it's urgent.'

Celia handed the baby back to Mirella and picked up the receiver. 'This is León's sister-in-law. Can I help you?'

'Hello, Celia,' said a throaty, smoke-charred voice. 'He's told me a lot about you.'

'I'm afraid I didn't catch your name,' said Celia, rather thrown by this overture.

'Just tell him Sofía rang. I couldn't leave a message like this with a servant, or a hotel manager. He's got to get back to Havana right away. His wife has been arrested.'

She very nearly echoed, 'Arrested?' stopping herself just in time, aware that Emilia was listening. There was enough gossip flying around at the moment.

'What? But . . . why?'

'She's been charged with drug-dealing. The magistrate set bail at ten thousand pesos.'

Drug-dealing? What kind of woman had he married?

'What's happened to the child?'

'With her in prison, poor little wretch. Lily's a silly girl, she had it coming. But I feel sorry for the baby.'

'Yes,' said Celia, appalled. 'So do I. I'll give León the message.'

There was a short pause.

'Be kind to him, won't you? You broke his heart, you know. Spoiled things for all the rest of us.'

'I beg your pardon?'

'You're the reason he ended up with that little tramp. He went kind of soft in the head. I mean to say, it's not even his child. God alone knows who the father is, I'm sure she doesn't. Whatever it was he did to make you so mad, he's paid for his mistake, believe me. I just hope you don't live to regret your decision. Good men are hard to find.'

She hung up. Celia put down the receiver to find Emilia looking at her oddly.

'What's happened?'

'Send a car to the hotel. Get the driver to wait until León gets back and bring him here right away.'

'Bad news?'

'It's his wife,' said Celia shortly. 'She's been taken ill.'

His wife. A silly little tramp, whose baby wasn't even his. The heir to Buenaventura, despite all Enrique's efforts, didn't even have Soler blood in his veins, no more than Celia did herself. It wasn't fair, but it was a kind of justice.

León had had a long day. His father's office in Santiago, like the one at Buenaventura, had not so far yielded up the item he was looking for. Perhaps it was in his study, at the house. Or perhaps he had destroyed it, after Lidia's death. But León was determined to explore every possibility before he abandoned his quest.

He vividly remembered his father waving that envelope and shouting, 'I have all the evidence here, in black and white!' and now, at last, he had the chance to discover what that 'evidence' was. It wouldn't have mattered but for his growing conviction that Raúl was somehow involved.

It was with no great hopes that he began his search of the suite at the Casa Grande, but after working his way through stacks of documents, some of them dating back forty years, he was in meticulous mood, sufficiently so to go through the pockets of the suits hanging in the wardrobe, still redolent of rum and cigars. His patience was rewarded as his fingers closed around a folded sheet of foolscap, trapped between the lining and the fabric of a well-worn plaid jacket with a slit in its right-hand pocket. It was closely typed on both sides and headed,

> PRIVATE AND CONFIDENTIAL
>
> Report on subject for December 1956 in accordance with instructions previously received.

Every day of the month was logged from the moment Lidia emerged from her home till the moment she returned. It was a banal enough account of shopping trips, hair appointments and social engagements, timed to the minute, portraying accurately the barren indolence of her life, revealing nothing of interest until the entry for 15 December.

> Arrival of León Soler at family home, 15.55, in red Packard convertible reg. HV–2149, together with guest later identified as elder brother Raúl.
>
> *16 December*. 8.30. Raúl and Señorita Rodríguez accompanied Don Enrique to the mill. 10.00: León and subject left house together by above-mentioned vehicle, heading towards Manzanillo. After ten kilometres turned off main road onto dirt track. Surveillance operative waited five minutes before following, to find above car parked outside isolated shack later identified as disused property belonging to the estate. The couple emerged together at 11.30 a.m., returning to house at 11.50.
>
> *17 December*. León left house at 10.00 a.m., heading towards Bayamo. Subject left house alone with chauffeur at 10.45 a.m. Reached beauty parlour in Bayamo at 11.15. Dismissed chauffeur. Subject left beauty parlour at 11.20 and proceeded by cab to 4 Valdez Street. Red Packard convertible reg. HV–2149 parked outside this address. Subject emerged alone at 13.00, returning by cab to beauty parlour. Collected by chauffeur at 13.15. Arrived back home 13.50. Local estate agent confirms giving key of several vacant properties, including 4 Valdez Street, to León Soler, who claimed to be looking for an apartment in town and expressed wish to inspect properties alone in his own time . . .

León did not need to read any further. There was no reason why J. G. Fernández. private investigator, confidentiality guaranteed, should falsify information unless someone had paid him well to do so. And there could be no doubt as to who that someone might be. The only question was how Raúl had discovered their liaison – an indiscretion by Lidia herself being the most likely explanation. The other question, how Raúl knew that she was being watched, could have been an educated guess; it was likely, looking back, that his mother had been subject to the same surveillance, shared her suspicions with Raúl just as Lidia had shared hers with León – which was why their affair had been conducted strictly within the confines of the house. Acting on that assumption, it would have been easy enough for Raúl to identify the local firm on his father's payroll.

The clever part had been in exposing real guilt with fabricated evidence. The latter depended absolutely on the former, reducing their denials to a feeble 'yes, but', leading them to hang themselves. Literally, in Lidia's case.

Would it do any good to expose the report as a fraud, force the miserable snooper to tell the truth? It wouldn't absolve him of guilt, or Lidia either. After all, the half-dozen imaginary encounters described in the report were less damning, if anything, than an affair of ten years' duration. The only benefit would be in unmasking Raúl, in the hope of turning Celia against him, a grubby piece of tit for tat which would smack of desperation.

If Celia could be proud and stubborn, then so could he. Suddenly he saw himself through her eyes – or rather the self he had once been. Weak-willed, shallow, full of excuses, no match for a tough customer like Raúl. Well, not any more.

He arrived back at his hotel late that night to find one of his father's Cadillacs outside, with a chauffeur in attendance.

'Doña Celia asks that you return immediately to the house,' he said. 'She wishes to speak to you urgently.'

Suddenly there was hope again. 'I need help,' she would say, fighting back the tears. 'I have to get away, before he sends for me, somewhere he won't find me . . .'

No. That was wishful thinking. Just because Raúl had bullied his younger sibling didn't mean he was a wife-beater. And León preferred to shut his mind to the other, even more dangerous side to his character – the hypnotic charm, the sudden, disarming bouts of benevolence, the ability to wipe out all the hurt in an instant with a few gruff words and a fierce embrace. For every bad memory León had of him, there was a good one that was even more painful. Had he worked the same sinister spell on Celia?

She received him in the salon, alone.

'Someone called Sofía called from Havana,' she began frigidly. 'It's about your wife . . .'

León listened with growing alarm, tinged with hideous embarrassment at having to hear such news from Celia. Trust Lily to get herself into trouble the moment his back was turned; he should have known better than to leave her alone. Reinaldo was undoubtedly behind this; he must have called in his favour, been rebuffed, turned vicious.

Poor kid, she must be frightened out of her wits, locked up in some filthy cell with a bawling Leonardo. He would have to catch the first flight home, tomorrow morning. God, what a ball and chain she was! And now Celia would think he had married some low-life gaolbird . . .

'Thank you for taking the message,' he said stiffly. 'I'd better leave. I have an early start.'

'Before you go . . .' She struggled briefly with herself before blurting out, 'This Sofía says it's not your child. Is that true?'

Damn Sofía for opening her big trap.

'Is it true?' she repeated, no doubt expecting him to try to talk his way out of it, as the old León would have done.

'Legally, Leonardo is my son,' he said brutally. 'Just as Gabriel is legally Raúl's son. Fair's fair.'

'You've chosen to deprive your own child in favour of someone else's bastard?'

'My own child? I seem to recall you begging me not to claim paternity. Make up your mind.'

'You're despicable!'

'Whereas Raúl, of course, is noble and decent, for doing exactly what I did, for taking on another man's child. At least I didn't have any ulterior motives.'

'Raúl admitted that he knew about my father's will, there are no secrets between us. So don't try to poison my mind against him. This isn't some naïve, juvenile romance, like the one I had with you. What I have with Raúl is real.'

She thrust a piece of paper in his hand.

'By the sound of things, you have your hands full at the moment. So I'll make this brief. You need a steward here, someone who won't cheat you. I'm the only person you can trust. These are my terms. I'd like your answer before you go.'

León read through it quickly, irritated by its formal language, annoyed that she should put him on the spot at a time like this.

'This isn't necessary,' he said, dismissively. 'I'll make you an allowance. If you want to join Raúl, I'll finance the trip and accommodation. After what happened to my father, this is no place for a woman on her own . . .'

'Don't patronise me. Yes or no. I'm tougher than you think.'

It was a challenge, not a plea. If he refused her this, she would never ask him for anything again. León shrugged, affecting callous indifference.

'Do what you like,' he said. 'Why should I care what happens to you? I'm the bad guy, remember?'

She held his gaze for a moment. There was something in her eyes he hadn't seen before, something elusive, enticing.

'It suits you,' she said. 'Goodbye.'

Raúl was no run-of-the-mill recruit. Being half Yanqui, and an ex-officer of the US Army, he was treated with greater than usual suspicion and subjected to several days of ferocious preliminary grilling. No doubt they would check up on everything he said, but Harry's people had taken care of all that. They would find out all about his poverty-stricken adolescence, his distinguished combat record, and the affair with a Soviet agent which had cost him his career and left him with a deep grudge against his adopted country. All excellent qualifications for his present role. Meanwhile, his brief was to appear politically naïve and model all his future opinions on Fidel's own.

Eduardo took pains to avoid him, seeing himself, no doubt, as the reason for Raúl's enlistment, waiting daily for him to make a move. But Raúl kept his distance. One moment of folly could bring this mission to a sudden, inglorious end. And besides, he had sworn to himself that he would never weaken again.

He was impatient for his first taste of combat. Combat would stop him brooding about Celia, tormenting himself with images of her with León. He wanted to believe the unbelievable, that Celia truly loved him, wanted to put an end to the doubt and suspicion which made him feel like a wretched captive, not an honoured guest. But his jealousy was tempered by sympathy for her plight, a plight which he understood only too well. She had tried so hard, poor darling, to conquer her feelings for his brother, just as Raúl had tried to conquer his feelings for her. Perhaps, like him she loved two people at once, in very different ways. And if she did, who was he to blame her?

'I am distressed to find you in a place like this,' said Captain Reinaldo. The police station which served the harbour district catered for a low class of petty criminal – drunken sailors, streetwalkers, and smugglers who were unwise enough not to share their profits.

'But you realise,' he continued, 'that this is luxury compared to the Morro prison. Arrangements have already been made to transfer you tomorrow. You could be there a year, even two, awaiting trial. Unless you plead guilty, of course. In view of the statement you've already signed, quite frankly, you have no choice. That way you might get off with a lighter sentence. Think of your unfortunate child.'

The unfortunate child was asleep in the arms of one of Lily's cellmates, a big black woman in a tight pink dress.

'Bastard,' spat the third inmate, a skinny white girl even younger than Lily. She turned to her protégée. 'If you want to get out of here quick, love, you know what you have to do. These cops are all the same.'

Lily glared at Reinaldo mutinously. She wished now that she hadn't signed that piece of paper. She had only done so on the understanding that they would let her go immediately. But instead they had hauled her in front of a magistrate who put her on remand without bothering to hear any evidence, and then they had brought her back to this horrible place, only made bearable by the kindness of her two fellow criminals, who, moved by the sight of a wailing Leonardo, had taken her under their wing. They were rough and coarse and loud, but, like Lily's erstwhile neighbours in Tejadillo, they weren't so bad once you got to know them. 'Good for you!' they had crowed, when she told her story, slapping her on the back. 'Too bad you didn't bite it off!' They had made her feel quite brave.

'I demand to see an attorney,' said Lily, vaguely remembering from her visits to the movies that you were supposed to be allowed one phone call.

'A defence lawyer will be appointed by the court,' said Reinaldo. 'In view of the weight of evidence against you, his only function will be to plead for clemency. You will be able to help your case by giving evidence against Maguire. No doubt he led you astray, and in view of your extreme youth, we can only hope that the judge will decide to be lenient with you.'

'In other words,' said the black woman, making an obscene gesture, 'you gotta fuck him as well.'

'You skunk!' yelled Lily, playing to the gallery. 'You don't scare me!'

'You'll have plenty of time to consider your plea. In the meantime, prison will at least provide a roof over your head. I regret that your landlord has already changed the locks . . .'

Hearing a sudden commotion, Reinaldo turned round, just as a door flew open behind him.

'León!' screamed Lily theatrically. 'Oh, León, thank God!'

'Let her out of here,' said León. 'Now.'

Reinaldo smiled apologetically. 'I regret, that's not possible. In view of the gravity of the charge, bail was set this morning in the sum of ten thousand pesos.'

'I've just paid it,' said León, shoving a piece of paper at him. 'Now let her go.'

A cheer went up from Lily's cellmates, who began hugging and kissing her and showing two fingers to Reinaldo, sharing her moment of glory.

'So your father left you something after all,' hissed Reinaldo, reluctantly signalling to a warder to unlock the cell. 'How very timely.'

'Yes, isn't it.' León grabbed hold of Leonardo without ceremony. 'Come on, Lily.'

'Wait a minute,' said Lily. 'How much bail for them?' She indicated her two companions. 'Can you get them out as well?'

'For God's sake—'

'Please,' bleated Lily. 'They were kind to me.'

'We'll see,' rapped León, as the two women began blowing him kisses and hitching up their skirts. 'Just let's get out of this place.'

'It'll cost you plenty to buy your way out of this,' snarled Reinaldo. 'She's already signed a statement.'

Ignoring him, León led Lily away, stopping at the duty desk, where a sour-faced policeman returned Lily's jewellery.

'There was a gold charm bracelet as well,' said Lily.

'This is all you signed for.'

'I don't care what I signed. I want my charm bracelet. It was a present from my mother!'

'There's no record of any bracelet.'

'I'll buy you another one,' said León, impatiently. Such thievery was routine.

'I don't want another one! I want that one!'

'Move!' barked León.

She preceded him out into the street, weeping. 'You're mad at me,' she began.

'Too right I'm mad at you. We're going straight to a hotel, and you're going to tell me exactly what happened. I don't care how bad it is, as long as you tell me the truth. But if you try to lie to me, we're through. I mean it, Lily.'

He bundled her into a waiting cab.

'Has your father left you some money?' demanded Lily eagerly. 'Does that mean you can pay the judge to let me off?'

'That depends on whether or not you're guilty.'

'Of course I'm not guilty! Reinaldo framed me! He only did it because I . . . because I . . .'

'Because you did what?'

She did her best to edit what had happened, but León was a merciless cross-examiner. By the time he had finished with her, she had told him everything, from the day she had first run into Frank. She sat on the bed in the new Havana Hilton, clutching her baby in her arms, trying to look pathetic, but León's expression was hard, unrelenting, making her feel like the world's worst criminal. After making her tell her story for the third time, picking up on every tiny discrepancy, he fell to pacing the room, while Lily sat trembling, too upset to weep, waiting for him to tell her that he wanted a divorce. And with Frank in gaol, who would take care of her then? Who would take care of the baby?

For a long time he didn't speak, and for once Lily didn't either, dreading the moment when he would break the brittle silence. At last he said, 'To hell with bribing the judge.'

'You mean—'

'I mean you've just got yourself a lawyer.'

PART THREE

December 1957 – July 1958

ELEVEN

LÁZARO'S MOTHER had kept him abreast of the news at Buenaventura, using her neighbour as a scribe. At first the news had been all bad – Raúl Soler, far from languishing under the influence of the curse, seemed to be going from strength to strength. The *mayombero* had warned him that evil people were protected by evil spirits, but Lázaro had hoped to hear that his enemy had developed a mysterious rash or lost his appetite, or that his scar had started bleeding anew – sure signs that his body was being attacked from within.

But instead he had taken over as his father's second in command, married young Doña Celia and got her pregnant straight away. Obviously he was all set to take over the estate, once the old man was dead. Lázaro had begun to lose all faith in magic. To add to his woes, he had never got a second sight of that beautiful mulatta, despite several expeditions into town on market day. And to cap it all, he had still not had the chance to kill any rebels. Despite the attempted forced evacuation of peasants in the Sierra Maestre and random bombing of the area, the guerrillas continued to strike when and where they pleased, with apparent impunity. Lázaro was getting more and more depressed. Nothing seemed to be going his way.

When word reached him, following Don Enrique's murder, that Raúl had failed to inherit, it seemed, at last, like a step in the right direction, as did his departure for America; his absence would enable Lázaro to visit his mother without fear of running into him again. But as it happened, he did not have to wait for leave before he found himself once more at Buenaventura.

Alarmed by the number of successful raids on ill-defended positions, the military high command took urgent steps to reinforce vulnerable garrisons. The upshot of this was the sudden, unexpected transfer of Lázaro's unit to Bayamo, now deemed to be under-manned and liable to attack. His mother was overjoyed at the news, as was Emilia. As a full-time mechanic and chauffeur, Lázaro had ready access to the motor pool and would be able to call in whenever he had an excuse to leave the barracks.

This opportunity arose within two days of arrival in Bayamo, when he found himself driving three senior officers to a dinner appointment at the big house.

'So what's our position, now that Don Enrique is dead?' enquired Major Sánchez, who had transferred with Lázaro's unit. 'I gather that this León Soler is a bit of a Bohemian. Such types tend to favour the rebels.'

'So far we have seen little of him,' said the Colonel. 'He's appointed his sister-in-law to manage the business while he remains in Havana. I assume she's asked us to dine tonight because she wants to increase the size of the guard. Now that we have reinforcements, I can see my way to sparing another dozen men. But I expect she'll drive a hard bargain.'

'She runs that place with an iron hand,' agreed the third officer. 'Mind you, it needed it. The old boy was losing his grip, and Raúl Soler was all talk. But his wife is another story. The first thing she did was sack the chief accountant for cooking the books. Then she forced Don Enrique's old *mayoral* to resign. Poached a new one from the Rivero spread. Old man Rivero's hopping mad.'

'Sounds like she's making herself a few enemies.'

'And more than a few friends. The workers love her. As do their womenfolk. She plans to open a school, and a mother and baby clinic, and double the size of their allotments. Much to the disgust of the union leaders. They would rather she spent the money on upping their bribes.'

'She sounds like a liberal intellectual to me,' mused the Major. 'With a rebel for a brother . . .'

'The brother was a wet-behind-the-ears schoolboy who got in with a bad crowd,' snorted the Colonel. 'And the rebels killed her stepfather, remember. Doña Celia's neither liberal, nor intellectual. She's a shrewd businesswoman. She's figured out that discontented workers are easy meat for the rebels.'

'So what happens once she joins her husband in America?'

'He's been gone nearly three months now. Local gossip is that he's scarpered. It turned out to be a shotgun wedding.'

Lázaro hoped that there was some sinister reason for Raúl Soler's protracted absence; perhaps he had contracted some vile disease, or turned to drink, or found himself a fugitive from enemies or the law. Or perhaps his wife had discovered his secret vice and banished him. Or perhaps one of his victims had overpowered and killed him, perhaps even at this moment he was lying in a ditch somewhere, crawling with flies and maggots . . .

Having dropped his passengers at the front of the house, Lázaro parked the car and prepared to slip off to visit his mother's shack; there had been no time to alert her that he would be here this evening. But before he could make his getaway, Emilia spotted him from the kitchen window. She came pounding out of the back door, her huge bosom heaving with excitement, and crushed him in a voluminous embrace. It proved quite impossible not to return her open-mouthed, cavernous kiss.

'Don't you look smart in your uniform!' she cooed, taking him by the hand and ushering him inside. 'Come in and have something to eat.' She winked grotesquely. 'The Colonel always stays till late, we'll have plenty of time to ourselves.'

Lázaro was just about to say that he couldn't stay long, he must pay his respects to his mother, when he spotted a girl sitting at the kitchen table, eating a bowl of soup. He blinked, unable to believe his eyes. It was her. The beautiful peasant girl he had never thought to see again.

'Sit down, sit down,' fussed Emilia, not bothering to acknowledge or introduce her. She turned to a kitchen maid, who was filling a china tureen. 'Give some of that to Lázaro,' she barked, sawing off several slices of warm, fresh bread. She sighed as the bell jangled, summoning her to the dining room, and picked up a tray of canapés. 'I'll be back in a minute,' she said. 'Eat up, now.'

The girl looked up at that moment and met Lázaro's incredulous gaze, starting in confused recognition, as if she knew that she had seen him before but couldn't remember where.

'Hello,' said Lázaro awkwardly, fingering his cap. 'We met on the road out of Santiago, a few months back. I was one of the soldiers who searched you and your cousins, remember?'

Not for the first time, he found himself ashamed to admit he was a soldier. No doubt she thought he was crude and uncouth, like most of his comrades.

'I'm sorry if my mate frightened you,' he continued humbly. 'I wouldn't have let him hurt you.'

For a moment she looked panic-stricken, reliving, no doubt, the fear she had felt at that moment. Then she nodded her thanks shyly and managed an uncertain smile. She was even more beautiful when she smiled.

'What's your name?'

She didn't answer; he had forgotten that she was dumb.

'Mirella,' put in the kitchen maid, overhearing. 'She can't speak.'

Mirella. The name was beautiful, like her. Suddenly, to Lázaro's dismay, she jumped to her feet and quickly left the room.

'Baby's crying,' said the maid, by way of explanation. Lázaro picked up a faint wailing from above. 'She's Doña Celia's nanny.'

So she lived here! This was too good to be true.

He barely tasted the food piled before him, as Emilia moved back and forth between the kitchen and the dining room, summoning the maid to help her serve the soup, followed by sucking pig served with rice and beans. He kept one eye on the door, waiting for Mirella to return, but when she did so, briefly, Emilia was present, and Lázaro knew better than to show any interest. If Emilia realised that she had a rival, she would turn the girl against him for sure.

He watched covertly as Mirella placed the rest of her supper on a tray and took it upstairs, wondering how best to play it. He remembered her two cousins saying that she had been attacked by bandits; the poor girl was probably terrified of men. He had better curb his usual direct approach, for fear of scaring her off. Meanwhile he would have to keep Emilia sweet, to ensure an open invitation to the house . . .

It was with this in mind that Lázaro allowed the delighted housekeeper to bear him off to her quarters, after dinner, where he put up a creditable show of passion, fired by a vision of doing this, and this, and this to Mirella.

'I'll talk to the guards on the gate,' she told him, as he dressed. 'They'll wave you through any time. Just let yourself in by the kitchen door and if I'm not in, wait for me in my room. You know the times I go to market.'

Yes, thought Lázaro. If he timed his visits for when she was out, he would be able, with luck, to snatch some time alone with Mirella. For the first time in months he slept soundly and woke up full of hope. His luck was on the turn at last.

Reinaldo looked across his desk with naked, quivering hostility. León returned his scowl with a well-dressed smile. Every time he thought of what he had done to Lily, he had to contain a physical urge to beat him to a pulp. Which would have been to play straight into his hands.

'I refuse to give in to intimidation,' barked Reinaldo, rattled. 'This so-called evidence is nothing but a tissue of lies.'

'That's for the court to decide,' said León. 'Regrettably, I will have to call you as a hostile witness and ask you a lot of unpleasant questions. No doubt the court will treat your evidence as gospel. But the public . . . well, they're only too ready to believe the worst. A sign of the times, I fear. And foreign journalists, of course, are notorious for twisting the facts. In fact I was chatting to a reporter from the *New York Times* only the other day . . .'

Reinaldo opened the drawer of his desk; there was a gun in there for sure.

'Personally, I'm glad that you prefer to have everything out in the open,' went on León imperturbably, swallowing a sigh of relief as Reinaldo withdrew a lighter and helped himself to a cigar. 'Especially as I've managed to arrange an earlier hearing date.'

'To buy it, you mean. You young upstart! Just because you've come into a bit of money . . .'

Money alone would not have been enough. Money was for buying lies, and León had wanted the truth; it had taken him weeks of persistent, painstaking research to excavate and piece together all the facts. A surprising number of people had proved willing to speak to him, emboldened, perhaps, by the groundswell of popular dissent. Ex-employees of Addy's who had delivered bribes in cash. Families of boys who had been murdered by the police for failing to sell their quota of drugs. Beleaguered defence lawyers who had seen their clients go to gaol because they couldn't raise the judge's unofficial fee. Port officials who admitted that they acted under orders from the high-placed bureaucrats who ran the customs rackets and who paid them a commission on the proceeds in lieu of a living wage. It was like a huge interlocking jigsaw puzzle, linking Reinaldo with a vast network of corrupt officials and licensed criminals, whose lackeys were motivated less by greed than by poverty and fear.

'And whatever judge you dig up for the trial,' continued León blandly, 'I'm sure I can find something on him as well. Addy kept a photograph album that I managed to rescue from the bailiffs. A little insurance policy against a rainy day.'

Reinaldo's twitch became a full-scale tremor, and for a

moment León held his breath, still half-expecting to be shot; he had made careful contingency plans with that possibility in mind. But Reinaldo must have already worked that out, hence the look of feverish frustration.

'You think yourself so superior, don't you,' he snarled, 'on account of your inherited wealth and your fancy education. If you'd worked your way up from nothing, as I had to do . . .'

'If I'd been a gangster, in the thirties, as you were, perhaps I too would have been bought off by weak, spineless politicians and got myself a lucrative sinecure. In fact, there's a great deal about your past that doesn't bear close inspection.'

'Be careful what you say, Soler. I will not hesitate to sue you for slander.'

'And render yourself liable to cross-examination? I don't think so. And besides, there doesn't have to be any slander, or any scandal – as long as you drop the charges and as long as nothing untoward happens to me, or to my wife, or to Frank Maguire.'

It was bluff, of course. León knew that none of his unnamed witnesses would agree to take the stand. Nor could he blame them. 'I'll deny I ever told you this,' people had said, again and again. 'I've got a family to think of.' Frank had been the only exception.

'I'll testify against that sonofabitch any time you like,' he had said, heedless of the likely consequences. It was the second time he had demonstrated his what-the-hell self-deprecating courage. But León hoped that this particular bomb could be safely defused. Reinaldo, like all his kind, was beginning to lose his nerve. With every terrorist attack the threat of revolution became ever more real; deposits into Swiss bank accounts were increasing by the day.

'If you were to intercede with the public prosecutor,' continued León, 'it would serve to demonstrate your goodwill and sense of fair play. These days, it pays to keep on the right side of everyone. Who knows what the future may hold?'

Much as it irked him to let the bastard off the hook, this

was the surest way to play it. He didn't want to see his wife exposed as the daughter of a notorious madam, or watch the prosecution dissecting her morals in public. As for Frank, he was guilty, and this was his only hope of getting him off, bar bribery, a tactic which could well backfire, enabling Reinaldo to charge his opponent with obstructing the course of justice.

There was a long silence while Reinaldo considered his position, obscured by a pall of smoke. After an agonising delay he picked up the phone and issued curt instructions while León sat quietly listening, nothing in his face betraying the immeasurable relief within.

'It's been a pleasure doing business with you, Captain,' said León, retrieving his documents. He snapped his briefcase shut and picked up his hat, light-headed with the aftermath of adrenaline. 'And now, if you'll excuse me, I must go and collect my client.'

Frank was being held in a disused lunatic asylum in the old town, one of the many makeshift goals which had sprung up to house the growing prison population. He had been denied bail in view of the prosecution's claim that he might leave the country. But thanks to the generous gratuities paid by León to his warders, his time in custody had been relatively comfortable. Prison staff sold every kind of privilege to supplement their breadline wages – Frank had avoided the mouldy, bug-infested food fed to less fortunate inmates and was allowed regular exercise and reading material. If he wanted a woman, or drugs, or booze, those too would have been available at a price.

'Second time I've been in gaol,' he had shrugged stoically, without explaining what the previous charge had been. 'At least this time I managed to do something wrong.' It hadn't taken León long to establish that his love for Lily was genuine, reinforced by a massive guilt complex that cried out to be exploited. A pity he hadn't shown up in time to marry her, Still, better late than never.

Frank was waiting for him outside the prison gates, wearing clothes that were now too big for him.

'I never thought you'd pull it off,' he said, getting into the car. 'Thanks a lot. I owe you.'

'Call it quits. You saved my life, remember? But I'm going to ask you a favour anyway.'

'You don't need to say it. You want me to get the hell out of Havana and stay well away from Lily.'

'On the contrary. I want you to stick around until you can persuade Lily to leave Havana with you. For the States, preferably. Naturally I'll foot the bill.'

'What?'

'You got her into trouble, now I want you to get her out of it. You love her, don't you?'

'Don't you?'

'Not enough. I only married her for Addy's sake, because she was – is – incapable of looking after herself, let alone a child. It was a mistake. Good deeds aren't my style. I was never cut out to be a husband. I neglect her, she's unhappy, we fight like cat and dog. She needs someone who's willing to give her his undivided attention, make a fuss of her, put her first. If she stays with me, sooner or later she'll wind up getting into mischief again. If she's with you, I know she'll be safe.'

'Safe? With a bum, a dope dealer, a gun-runner, a gaolbird, a dried-out alcoholic, a—'

'A hopelessly old-fashioned and very shame-faced romantic who'd do anything for her. Safe.'

Frank looked embarrassed, but he didn't deny it.

'And how does she feel about you dumping her?'

'I'm not dumping her,' said León, rather defensively. 'I'm giving her a way out, a choice, a chance. I don't want her to know that I've talked to you, she'd only dig her toes in. I want her to think it's her decision.'

Frank shook his head in disbelief. For an intelligent man, Soler could be remarkably obtuse.

'You've misread the situation, pal. If she was your big mistake, I was hers. When she visits, all she ever wants to talk about is you. What a terrific guy you are, how kind you were to her when her mother died, how lucky she is to have such a wonderful husband . . .'

'She's rather more honest to my face, I'm glad to say. She threatens to walk out on me at least twice a week. And she would too, if she had anywhere else to go. Right now I'm the selfish, heartless ogre who won't let her sing.'

'So she told me. She's pretty sore at you about that and I can't say I blame her. The girl's got talent.'

'Keep telling her that and you'll have her eating out of your hand. It'll work like a charm, you'll see.'

'You're a cold-blooded bastard, Soler. Is that why you stuck your neck out for me? So that I'd take her off your hands?'

'Why else? I'll provide evidence of adultery, I'll give her all the alimony she wants. As long as she doesn't contest custody of Leonardo.'

'You'd deprive her of her child just so you can stay rich?'

'Leaving the child won't worry Lily. She's got no interest in him at all.'

'Well, I have. I'm his father.'

'Don't push your luck. I'm a lawyer.'

Frank fell silent, still trying to figure out what made Soler tick. He was a strange mixture of flamboyance and inhibition, candour and reticence. If he was really as ruthless as he made himself out to be he would simply walk out on Lily and pay her off, break the poor kid's heart . . .

León stopped the car outside a classy Spanish-colonial stone house, set well back from the road and shaded by banyan, oleander and eucalyptus.

'I expect you could do with a bath and a decent meal,' said León. 'It's all legit. I told Lily you had a right to see the baby. I won't be back till late, by the way.'

Frank gave him a long hard look.

'No wonder you got the better of Reinaldo.'

'If you need any cash . . .'

'Forget it. I'll sell the boat if I have to. Don't act like you've hired me, OK? I'm doing this for my own benefit, not yours.'

León wanted to say, 'Don't get me wrong. I respect you and I care about her. I'm not as selfish and insensitive as you think.' The habit of wanting people to like him was hellishly hard to break. But if Frank thought the worst of him so much the better. It would give him an added incentive

He had thought long and hard about this plan. Much as he wanted out of his hasty marriage, his motives were not purely selfish. If he hadn't made that speech, Frank would have done the decent thing and left Havana. Now that he knew how things really stood, at least Lily would have an option. Lacking that option, she would only find another, less acceptable one. Only last week she had gone off to an audition, without telling him, and been hired on the spot. León had lost no time in telling her prospective employer – a typical Havana sleazemonger – that the deal was off, resulting in a hysterical outburst and the old, childish threat to 'run away'. Short of tying her to a chair, as he had threatened to do in the old days, providing her with a guardian angel had seemed the next best thing. Frank would protect her against predators, flatter her ego, and provide a safe outlet for her need to rebel. The rest was up to him.

He waited till he saw the door open and Frank go inside. Then he put his foot down and roared off in the direction of his office, two unpretentious rooms above a warehouse in the old town, where the usual pathetic assortment of no-hopers were patiently waiting for free legal advice and representation, some the victims of bad landlords and bad employers, others seeking help for loved ones who had been rounded up, rightly or wrongly, on charges of terrorism.

His practice had been born out of his recent investigations. Promises had had to be made and kept, debts accrued and honoured. It wasn't so much philanthropy as a way of filling up his time, an excuse for avoiding Lily, with her insatiable demands, and Leonardo, whose chronic colic caused him to cry night and day. Between them they were driving him crazy. He felt sorry for them, but not sufficiently so to play the martyr. In any case, he was through pretending to be nice. Least of all with Celia, with whom he maintained a frigid, uneasy truce.

He had visited her once, back in October, on the flimsiest of excuses – an encounter he had relived endlessly ever since.

'I had to see my father's solicitor, in Bayamo,' he had said briskly, as he was shown into her office. 'There were a few loose ends to tie up about the will. I thought I would make a courtesy call while I'm here.'

Celia called her secretary, who was about to leave them alone.

'Stay here and take the minutes of our meeting,' she said, adding pointedly, 'That way there won't be any misunderstandings.'

She didn't trust him, thought León, with some satisfaction. Or could it be that she didn't trust herself?

'I found your last report lacking in several details,' he said, going on the attack. 'I'm well aware that you had manipulation of my father down to a fine art. But I find it unacceptable, not to say insulting, that you should employ the same tactics with me.'

She flushed, furious to be caught out.

'These plans for a schoolhouse,' he continued, enjoying her discomfiture. 'Your proposed budget is either wildly optimistic or deliberately misleading. Were you afraid I'd veto the project if I knew what it was really going to cost?'

He tossed the relevant papers on her desk. Celia underlined several words with a flourish and shoved them back at him.

'I stressed that the figures were "approximate" and "estimated". The actual expenditure would all have shown up in the monthly accounts. You know me better than to think I'd try to cheat you.'

'And you know me better than to think I'd penny-pinch.'

'Why on earth would I think that? Judging by the amounts you've drawn on the estate lately, money is no object these days.' She bit her lip, aware that she had risen to the bait. 'Your father's solicitor happened to mention it to me,' she muttered, by way of a disclaimer. 'He's very indiscreet. If I were you I'd sack him.'

'Perhaps you should sack him on my behalf,' said León, gratified by the slip in her icy control. Even her resentment was better than indifference. 'You're much better at breaking off relationships than I am. Talking of which, is there any news from my brother?'

'I had a letter yesterday,' said Celia, rattled. 'His step-father's been ill. He's hoping to visit soon.'

'Do give him my very best regards. And how's Gabriel?'

'He's in excellent health, thank you. While you're here, I may as well get your signature on some papers—'

He had found this confrontation incredibly erotic; it was like trying to touch her through glass, like holding his hands up to a sheet of ice and feeling them glow with reflected heat. She had written to him afterwards saying that such visits were quite unnecessary, undermined her authority, and broke the terms of their agreement. He had stayed away ever since, just to keep her guessing.

Two more months had passed since then, and there was still no sign of Raúl, fuelling León's hopes that he had gone for good, despite his parting shot. *I'll kill you. I'll kill you both.* It was just the kind of threat Raúl would make, for spite, whether he meant it or not, relying on León's old ingrained fear of him and his reluctance to put Celia in danger. But the longer he stayed away, the more likely it seemed that he had been bluffing. Perhaps he already had a wife and kids in the States, thought León. Nothing would have surprised him. God alone knew what hopes and heartache Celia hid behind that proud, capable front. More than once he had been tempted to telephone Emilia and recruit her as his eyes and ears, constrained only by the knowledge that the housekeeper was incapable of discretion. If she got so much as a whiff of León's real interest in her mistress, it would be all round the estate in a flash.

His last client despatched, he settled back to open his mail, starting with the big buff envelope from Buenaventura. Every week without fail Celia sent him a meticulously detailed report, listing the decisions she had taken, summarising expenditure, and keeping him abreast of developments. All very efficient and entirely impersonal, except for the signature at the end. Her handwriting had always given her away, its big bold black strokes belying the passive, secondary role his father had forced her into, a role which she had now abandoned with evident relish.

> ... On Monday I entertained Colonel Castillo to dinner, together with two other officers. They tried to put pressure on me to increase the size of the guard. I refused, on the grounds that an army presence is inflammatory and for the most part merely cosmetic. In fact the purpose of my invitation was to request removal of all military personnel, whom I propose to replace with volunteers from the estate. I trust that you will back me up ...

It gave him a thrill to think of little Celia thwarting his father's erstwhile cronies. She was through with pretending to be nice as well. As he turned the page his eye was drawn down towards the hand-written postscript.

> The enclosed has just arrived. As you can see it is addressed to you personally and marked 'private and confidential', otherwise I would obviously deal with it myself. I daresay it is something quite routine, in which case please return it for my attention.

It was anything but routine, and León thanked God she hadn't dealt with it herself. It contained a second, sealed envelope, inscribed with the words 'TO BE OPENED IN THE EVENT OF MY DEATH,' together with a short note from J. G. Fernández, Don Enrique's erstwhile private detective, written whilst in the throes of terminal cancer in hospital in Miami:

> I have left instructions for this to be posted once I am dead. In December 1956 your father engaged me to investigate his son Raúl's past. The facts I uncovered were so damaging that I foolishly gave your brother the opportunity to buy my silence. He said if I ever breathed a word of what I knew he

> would kill me. This threat dies with me, and therefore my original report is enclosed herewith, for you to use as you wish.

The report was dynamite waiting for a detonator. Firstly, there was no rich stepfather in Chicago. Secondly, Raúl was up to his ears in gambling debts. Thirdly, and most importantly, Fernández had uncovered a scandal involving a male prostitute in Berlin, which had led to Raúl's dishonourable discharge from the army. León might have dismissed this as malicious fabrication had its author had anything to gain by misleading him. As it was, the information was of no possible value to anyone but himself.

Kill me, Raúl had said, handing him a loaded gun. And now he could go one better than that. Now he could do to Raúl what Raúl had done to him. Or simply threaten to do it. That should be enough to keep him out of Cuba and away from Celia for good. Raúl, that most vociferous of queer-bashers, would undoubtedly rather die than be exposed as being bisexual. You could break every one of the ten commandments, commit every one of the seven deadly sins, and no full-blooded Oriente male would think any the worse of you. Except for the one which wasn't mentioned, the one for which even perverts like Reinaldo affected holier-than-thou horror.

To hell with it. Call it moral cowardice, call it the savagely inculcated habit of never telling tales on his brother, he simply couldn't bring himself to stoop that low. It seemed like weakness as he got out his lighter and burned the letter like the piece of putrid garbage it was. But afterwards he felt much stronger.

Expansion of the Buenaventura clinic and recruitment of an independent guard gave Celia a cast-iron excuse to purchase large quantities of ammunition and drugs. Even so, Raúl would not hear of her delivering supplies herself. A week after his departure, she received instructions to employ an extra chauffeur, one Luis Labrada, a member of a 26 July cell in Bayamo, who would make the trips in her stead. If caught, Luis would claim that he had been acting independently, without her knowledge or consent.

Meanwhile she got on with staging a quiet, bloodless revolution of her own. Already plans were in hand to convert a vast acreage of cane to mixed farming, in order to provide year-round employment. Long-disputed areas of land had been leased, at a nominal rent, to their dispossessed ex-owners, decriminalising former squatters and releasing the manpower formerly used to harass and exclude them. The bonus schemes for next year had met with an enthusiastic response, thwarting the venal union leaders whose power base depended on bad industrial relations. Now that every man had a stake in the harvest, profits for the next year should reach an all-time high. She would show León what she was made of. And Raúl too, come to that.

Her secretary tapped on the door and came in with the mail, collected each morning by Luis from the post office in Bayamo. Celia sifted through it quickly, searching for the letters the courier would have given him last night. As always, there were two for her and one for Mirella. She waited until she was alone before opening Raúl's, anticipating the usual sugared vinegar of love and doubt.

> Yes, my dearest, I am still alive. Survival is a natural instinct for a soldier, but doubly so for me, knowing that to die would be to lose you to my brother. Though perhaps this would be a kinder fate than losing you to him in life. Has it been hard for you, Celia, fending off his attempts to usurp me? Could it be that you keep him at arm's length out of love, to protect him from my wrath?

Celia sighed. How on earth would Raúl function if León didn't exist? His love seemed born of jealousy, rather than the other way round. Often she wondered how it would have been if Raúl, and not León, had been snatched back and returned to Buenaventura. Would he have taught her to ride and swim, as León had done, would he have chased her, shrieking, through the woods and put fat beetles down her back and allowed her to rain puny blows on his chest in a frenzy of furious glee? How would it have been if they had always been together, if she had never known his brother? She remembered the last time he had made love to her, how he had turned away from her afterwards and said, quite calmly, with infinite sadness, 'What a fool I am. It can never be the same.' He was right, it could never be the same, never as it had been with León. Not even with León. He had changed. He was harder, colder, tougher . . . more like Raúl.

> My continued absence makes you a subject of gossip, gossip which travels even to the top of this lonely mountain. To silence those who say I have deserted you, I shall visit you as soon as I get leave, which is likely to happen without warning. In the meantime, I continue to train new recruits in marksmanship and unarmed combat. The presence of bandits in the area, calling themselves rebels, has provided my only opportunity for active service so far. Your idealistic brother tends to their wounds before such scum are tried and executed. His foot is still badly swollen, and heavily strapped up. He is in constant pain. Later today I shall make one last attempt to persuade him to seek treatment.
>
> I trust Gabriel is thriving. I think constantly of you both.
>
> Till we meet again, my dearest darling,
>
> Your loving husband, Raúl.

As always, the letter brought tears to her eyes. This separation was proving an even greater strain than she had expected. Particularly after that visit from León, in October, when he had arrived at the office out of the blue, catching her completely unawares.

'You don't look well,' he had challenged her.

'I'm fine. Just missing Raúl, that's all.'

'How long has he been gone now? It must be getting on for two months.'

'It's six weeks, actually. But he hopes to visit soon.'

It had astonished Celia that her secretary could sit there, placidly listening, apparently deaf to the screaming subtext behind every word they uttered. Stripped of its veneer of courtesy, the conversation would have read:

'I hope you're good and miserable.'

'If I was, I wouldn't admit it to you, you swine.'

'He's run out on you, hasn't he? He never loved you. That'll teach you to give my son to another man.'

'So you've come to gloat, have you? For two pins I'd tell you where he really is . . .'

He had tried every trick in the book to make her lose her composure; when it came to sarcasm Raúl had nothing on León. And then, when their business was over, he had heard Gabriel crying in the room next door, and said blandly, 'I must say hello to my nephew before I go.'

Standing there, helplessly watching him as he held his son in his arms, she had had to struggle even harder not to lose control. And she could tell, by the look in his eyes, that it was even worse for him. She wanted to yell at him, 'You deserve this, damn you! What happened was all your fault!' but he must surely have realised, long ago, that she had contrived the pregnancy, and why. Just as Celia had realised, long ago, that her mother had not been blameless. Unable to withstand the tidal wave of emotion, she had made an excuse to leave the office, and by the time she had recovered herself sufficiently to return, he had already driven away.

'Don't ever do that to me again,' she had begged him, couching her request in formal, frigid language. And the worst of it was, he hadn't. She had never felt more alone.

There were two more letters from Eduardo, one for Celia and the other for Mirella. Those to his sister were invariably brief and contained no news, merely exhortations that she continue to 'serve the cause'. Presumably those to Mirella were more personal, but she no longer shared their contents with Celia, evidence of the growing distance between the two women. Gabriel, formerly the bond between them, was now a source of silent, unacknowledged strife.

It had begun when Celia fitted out the room next door to her office as a nursery, to enable her to look in on the baby during the day. Mirella, already used to having sole charge, clearly resented this covert supervision and had been making her dumb displeasure very clear ever since. Celia tried not to take it personally, knowing that her behaviour was rooted in the deep, dark trauma of losing her child, but such possessiveness boded ill for the future. Her body might have recovered well, but what about her mind? Mirella was subject to dreadful recurring nightmares in which some harm befell Gabriel; some nights, she would not sleep at all, keeping vigil over his cot for fear that he would stop breathing. Celia had even considered calling in a psychoanalyst, a tentative suggestion which provoked, in big black capital letters, the angry assertion: I'M NOT MAD. Celia wasn't so sure. But how could she get rid of her without feeling a perfect bitch?

She tore open her brother's letter, which was dated a day later than Raúl's. As usual, it was a bare half-page.

> Dear Celia
>
> By the time you read this I shall be on my way to a safe house in Havàna. In the end I decided to request a medical discharge, to get this damned foot seen to. A false ID is being arranged and a surgeon there who's a member of the movement will operate free of charge. So I won't be asking you for any of León's money.
>
> Take care of Mirella for me. I intend to marry her, once all this is over, if she'll have me. In the meantime, I know she's in safe hands with you.

Thank God Raúl had persuaded him to see sense at last! That much was a huge relief. As for his intention to marry Mirella . . . Celia quashed her misgivings about her mental instability, her limited intelligence, Eduardo's inexperience of women, selfishly hugging the solution to her problem. Mirella would marry Eduardo and have lots of babies of her own . . .

And besides, who was she to spoil their innocent romantic idyll? Perhaps Mirella's simple-minded devotion was a recipe for happiness, the kind of wholesome, naïve happiness Celia would never know again. And yet what she felt for Raúl was a powerful bond, less fragile than mere joy, more enduring. Illusions bloomed briefly and faded and died; hope was an evergreen.

Raúl knew that he was taking an insane risk. He had sworn to himself that he would stay well away from Eduardo, not just because of the risk of discovery, but because of this new, crippling loyalty to Celia, the feeling that if he betrayed her she would also betray him. And there was a third risk too – the risk that one more taste of the drug would renew his addiction.

Nevertheless, there was only one sure effective way to force Eduardo to leave the camp and seek the treatment he needed. This would be the last time.

Eduardo never strayed far from the hospital building, seeing it as a citadel that kept him safe. Raúl waited until he was alone in the dispensary, before going in and shutting the door behind him.

'What are you doing here?'

'What do you think?'

'I warned you. Touch me and I'll blow the whistle on you.'

'Go ahead,' said Raúl, advancing. He didn't want to sully the memories they shared by forcing himself on Eduardo, didn't want to invite a hysterical outburst of wounding abuse. But time was running out. He had just been told in confidence that he would soon be moved to a new base in the north of the province. He had to take decisive action, before it was too late.

'I'm fed up with your teasing,' snarled Raúl, steeling himself to play the role of rapist. 'You've been waiting for this since the day I arrived, and now you're bloody well going to get it.'

Eduardo took a step backwards, but he didn't call for help. Mud stuck, and in exposing Raúl he would expose himself, to suspicion if nothing else. Fidel's contempt for *maricóns* was well known; better to die than be pilloried as the lowest form of life.

'I enlisted because of you,' continued Raúl, keeping up the charade. 'And now you have the nerve to play games with me, to deny everything there was between us, to pretend that—'

'Let go of me!'

Raúl grabbed hold of his arm, whereupon Eduardo seized an open dispensary bottle with his free hand and hurled its contents over him. Raúl caught his breath against the sudden searing pain as the acid burned into his hands and began eating through the coarse fabric of his uniform. He could easily have stopped Eduardo as he limped past him and made his escape, but he let him go, relieved that it was over, watching the blisters rise on his flesh, ignoring the cold-water tap nearby, aware only of the dull ache in his heart. He hadn't realised that he loved him that much.

That very same evening, Eduardo duly applied to be invalided out, just as Raúl had known he would. By the time Raúl's transfer was announced, he would be safely installed in a hospital in Havana. Celia would be pleased.

Soon he would see her again, if only briefly. He was to be granted leave prior to his departure; this would give him the opportunity to report back to Harry's minion in Santiago. Raúl was increasingly convinced that Fidel was a closet Communist, one who was anxious not to alienate the middle classes until he had seized power. He found rebel plans for land reform particularly sinister, the tip, no doubt, of a gigantic iceberg. And yet, what poetic justice it would be if Buenaventura ended up as a collective farm! That would cook his brother's goose nicely. Raúl had always abhorred Soviet-style state control, but now he was beginning to appreciate the politics of envy.

As yet there was no official, clear-cut policy for the future. Advisedly so. The compulsory political lectures at the camp embraced a rag-bag philosophy designed to accommodate recruits of widely diverging views, from dyed-in-the-wool Marxist-Leninists to milk-and-water liberals. As for Castro himself, he believed merely in Castro, and encouraged others to do the same, thereby making himself the one uniting force in an otherwise disparate group. He would not show his true colours till he was home and dry, and Raúl resolved to follow his example, agreeing with everyone, upsetting no one, presenting himself as a guileless warrior who trusted his leaders to do his thinking for him, who would follow their orders to the death. In the past, he had revelled in antagonising his superiors, but now he took a sly delight in deferring to them, in winning their approval, earning their trust, a role which would have stuck in his gullet but for the saving grace of deceit.

Local 26 July groups were under strict orders not to attack Buenaventura, save for a few cosmetic acts of sabotage, designed to avert suspicion. This measure to protect the supply line would keep Celia safe, a source of great comfort to Raúl. Unfortunately, it also meant that his brother's property would survive the conflict virtually intact; it annoyed him to think of him getting richer and richer thanks to Celia's efficient stewardship and unofficial rebel protection. No doubt León thought that Raúl had abandoned her, that he was leading a soft life in Chicago, amusing himself with other women, licking his wounds at having been cheated of his birthright. No doubt he thought he had given in too easily. It was high time he did something to startle him out of his complacency . . .

Two weeks after Eduardo's departure he received his marching orders, to include a few days' leave. Raúl went home via Santiago, where he made an unscheduled visit to the Soler warehouse.

'I just flew in this morning,' he told the chief clerk, looking every inch the Yanqui businessman. 'I promised my wife that I would drop by on my way home. Bring me the books, I wish to satisfy myself that everything is in order. We don't want my brother finding fault, do we? What are your security arrangements these days?'

'Two armed men are on guard round the clock, in three eight-hour shifts. Civilians. Your lady wife believes that the rebels are more likely to attack when army or police are present.'

'Only two?'

'Only two are necessary, thanks to the alarm system. Would you like to inspect it? It's the latest American design, newly installed. Doña Celia asked the manufacturers to include several amendments. Doña Celia . . .'

Her name was mentioned every two minutes. They all seemed in genuine awe of his little wife, not that he should have been surprised. He knew to his cost how formidable she was underneath that innocuous façade. She was doing to Buenaventura what she had done to him – controlling it, moulding it, bending it to her will. After voicing gushing approval for all the measures she had taken, Raúl took his leave and telephoned the number Harry had given him. The rest of the afternoon was taken up by a briefing and debriefing session; by the time he was finished, the Soler warehouse would be deserted, but for the same two guards he had met that afternoon, whose shift did not end till ten p.m.

Raúl returned early that evening, still carrying his heavy suitcase. The two men, recognising him, swallowed his story without question.

'I seem to have lost my watch,' he told them, displaying his bare wrist. 'The strap must have snapped. It belonged to my late father. I'm most anxious to find it in time to catch the next train.' He gave them each five pesos. 'Can I ask you to help me search for it? I never went inside the warehouse, so it must be somewhere in the office building, probably upstairs.'

They scurried off to do his bidding, giving him time to switch off the alarm system, open his suitcase, and install several incendiary devices in the warehouse, timed to go off simultaneously later that night. This done, he switched the alarm on again.

He knew that to make a thorough job of it he ought to kill the guards then and there, to cover his tracks; that he didn't was another sure sign that he was getting soft. They would escape injury, as long as they didn't try to extinguish the flames, and would no doubt mention his second visit under questioning. No matter. Nobody would be able to fix the crime on him. They would be much more likely to suspect rebel sympathies among the workers than accuse the redoubtable Doña Celia's husband.

His work for the day complete, Raúl conveniently found his watch under a chair, distributed more largesse, and caught the next train home.

León heard the news on the radio early next morning, while he was shaving.

'. . . And in Santiago, the warehouse of the Soler Sugar Company was gutted by fire during the night. Guards alerted the fire services, but by the time they arrived the blaze was out of control. Police are mounting a full investigation into possible arson. At the police academy in Holguín, an explosive device injured two cadets when . . .'

He ran to the phone and put through a call to Buenaventura only to find that lines throughout Oriente had been cut again, part of the continuing rebel campaign to paralyse communications. Seizing on this excuse to visit, he dressed quickly and woke Lily to tell her he was leaving straight away.

'How long will you be away?' she grumbled sleepily. 'You promised to take me to the Tropicana tonight.'

'Frank can take you instead. Give him a call now to check if he's free.' Frank had sold the boat, moved into a cheap hotel and got himself a job as a barman. Officially, he was León's friend, rather than Lily's ex-lover, but she seemed more than happy to keep him on a string, hoping, perhaps, to make León jealous. At least Frank would keep an eye on her during her absence.

The loss of the warehouse did not concern León; there had been no casualties, thank God. What did concern him, more and more, was the possibility of a similar attack on Buenaventura itself. He should never have let Celia take over as manager, he thought anxiously. If anything happened to her or the child he would never forgive himself. But with her stubborn insistence on working for her living, any attempt to persuade her to leave would be treated with contempt, as would an offer to install her in some safe place, at his expense. What an impossible woman she was turning out to be!

By the time the flight touched down at Bayamo, he had convinced himself that he would arrive to find the entire estate in flames. But he reached Buenaventura half an hour later to a scene of perfect normality. The guards on the gate waved him through and rang the house to announce his arrival; the door was already open as the cab drew up outside.

'Hello, Emilia,' said León, as she ushered him inside. 'I heard the news on the radio. I tried to phone but the lines were down. How's Celia?'

'Very well,' boomed a voice from the top of the stairs. 'Celia, my love! Hurry up and put some clothes on! We have a visitor!'

León stared at his brother, unable to hide his surprise and disappointment, not to mention a sudden, savage stab of jealousy. He was tousled and bare-chested; the knowledge that he had just got out of bed, at two o'clock in the afternoon, did nothing to improve León's state of mind.

'What a pleasant surprise,' said Raúl, flinging on his shirt as he descended. 'Come in and sit down.'

'So you're back,' said León tightly, following him into the salon.

'Evidently. Sorry to disappoint you. Were you looking forward to a cosy tête-à-tête with my wife? Too bad about the warehouse. Obviously an inside job, the police suspect that terrorists have infiltrated the workforce.' He offered León a cigar. 'I was there myself only yesterday, as a matter of fact. As I said to Celia, I didn't like the look of those two guards. Shifty-looking fellows, both of them.'

He sat back in his chair and smiled, waiting for his words to sink in.

'You bastard,' hissed León. 'It was you, wasn't it?'

'That's a very serious allegation,' said Raúl smoothly. 'You'll have a dreadful job proving it. Strangely enough,

Celia made the same accusation herself and we had the most terrible row before I managed to convince her of my innocence. In fact, we've just spent a good three hours making it up. An exceptionally good three hours.'

León was tempted to tell him then and there about the letter from Fernández and wipe that smirk off his face once and for all. But at that moment Celia appeared, looking very pink, her long hair hastily tied back with a ribbon.

'León,' she said stiffly, extending a hand. 'I'm sorry about the warehouse. I tried to phone you but the lines were down. I'm already trying to make alternative storage arrangements.'

'Never mind about that. I was just saying to Raúl, I'm worried that the same thing could happen at Buenaventura. I'm sure he shares my concern for your welfare.' He turned to his brother. 'I assume you've come to take her back to the States with you? Oriente is no place for a woman on her own.'

He would rather she was safe with his brother than in danger here. Except that she could never be safe with a man like Raúl . . .

Raúl reached for Celia's hand, entwining each finger with hers, investing this simple gesture with a wealth of sexual meaning.

'Celia is most reluctant to leave her country in time of trouble. In fact, we've decided to build our future here, in Cuba. Not at Buenaventura, I might add. I have other plans, plans which she supports wholeheartedly. Plans which will keep us apart for a while longer. Make the most of your chances, brother, while you still can.'

Celia bowed her head, evidently embarrassed at the innuendo. To León's surprise and gratification she allowed herself one furtive, fleeting, agonised look in his direction, a look that seemed to say, 'I'm sorry.' A look that would stay with him, torture him, lend itself to any number of self-indulgent interpretations.

'Excuse me,' she muttered. 'I think I can hear Gabriel.'

'What plans are you talking about?' demanded León, as soon as she had gone. 'What the hell are you playing at, Raúl, leaving her here all alone? Where have you been all this time? Where are you going?'

Raúl didn't answer, staring him out with that infuriating crooked smile of his. León thought about the non-existent stepfather in Chicago, thought about the untimely end to Raúl's brilliant military career, thought of the burning warehouse in Santiago, and suddenly everything started to make sense. When a strong young man left home these days, in mysterious circumstances, there was only one place he could be . . .

'Does she know you're with the rebels?' he demanded, hoping to startle him into an admission.

Raúl raised an imperturbable eyebrow.

'What a vivid imagination you have. I do hope you won't repeat that question in anyone else's hearing, for Celia's sake, if not for mine. You can imagine how difficult life would be for her if a rumour like that took hold. I do hope you'll stay for lunch? You won't believe how much little Gabriel has grown, he looks more like me every day. Of course, it's hardly my place to offer you hospitality, given that I'm your guest, but . . .'

'No, thanks,' said León shortly, unable to bear this a moment longer. 'It was just a flying visit. I must be going.'

He couldn't stand to see Raúl with Celia, smiling at her, touching her, flaunting his rights over her, couldn't bear to see him play the doting father to his son. Under cover of false cordiality Raúl would take a delight in torturing him. He wouldn't let up until León lost his temper and provoked another undignified quarrel in which Celia would be duty bound to take her husband's side.

León had to bite his tongue to stop himself yelling, 'Does she know about your little boyfriend in Berlin? How many others have there been since then? Suppose I tell her that she's married to a part-time faggot?' He knew that he would only despise himself for it afterwards. More to the point, Raúl would despise him as well. Not to mention Celia herself.

'So sorry you couldn't stay longer,' said Raúl, showing

him out. 'I'll make your excuses to Celia. Remember what I said, won't you?'

I'll kill you. I'll kill you both. His eyes were steely, threatening, and oddly wary. For the first time it occurred to León that Raúl was in torment too, that behind that sadistic swagger his big brother was afraid of him. Perhaps he always had been.

Mirella was dizzy with elation. It had happened at last, just as she had hoped it would. Eduardo had asked her to be his wife. Her delight was dampened only by the prospect of delay; his letter had referred yet again to 'when the war is won' and 'once there is an amnesty'. That might not be for years. And Mirella was increasingly anxious to get married as soon as possible, to have a baby she wouldn't have to share with anyone, a baby who would caller her Mamá.

With every day that passed, Celia usurped her more and more, reduced her rightful share of little Gabriel's affections. He was a cheerful, contented child, who smiled and gurgled at everyone, who charmed everyone, who responded to everyone. Mirella felt diminished by this; she would have preferred him to be nervous and mistrustful of others, to keep his love exclusively for her.

Even Raúl had managed to find favour, for all that he was a stranger, for all that he had stayed only three days. 'How's my boy?' he would roar, sweeping a sleeping Gabriel out of his crib without so much as a by-your-leave. 'How's my little soldier-to-be?' You would think that the sight of a face like that would have reduced any infant to tearful terror. But Gabriel appeared fascinated by this new admirer, placidly accepting his robust embrace without the slightest sign of distress.

Mirella was heartily relieved that Raúl's leave had proved brief. And no doubt Celia felt the same way. She had overheard one of their frequent, noisy quarrels, through the nursery wall.

'What good can it possibly do,' Celia had raged, 'to

destroy premises that employed a dozen people, that earned export income for Cuba?'

'We have no control over terrorist groups in the cities. Your own brother, remember, was engaged on similar activities. I warned you that I could not guarantee immunity from attack.'

'But why did they pick on us? I'm a good employer. Whatever wrongs your father did, I'm trying to put them right. There weren't even any soldiers or police there!'

'Don't blame yourself. Who knows, it may not even have been the work of rebels. My father had many enemies, all kinds of old scores are being settled under the revolutionary banner. And remember, you yourself have made an enemy of the army. This could even be their doing.'

'You don't care! Just because it belongs to León, you don't care, you're glad it happened!'

'And why should you care? The days of the big landowners will soon be over.'

'Now that you can't be one, neither can anyone else, is that it? It wouldn't surprise me if you set fire to it yourself!'

'If you really think that, then by all means betray me to the authorities. Tell them where I've been these last months. Or ask my brother to do so. Call him now and I will wait, here, for them to arrest me and imprison me and execute me. Then you will be free of me at last.'

'God, how I hate you sometimes . . .'

With Eduardo it would not be like that. They would live together in tranquillity and harmony. The safety she had found in silence would no longer be marred by echoes of remembered fear, at last she would be quiet inside.

It was so peaceful today. Celia was in Santiago, negotiating temporary storage arrangements pending the rebuilding of the warehouse. Emilia was spending her half-day shopping in Bayamo. The maids had finished their work and left. For the next few hours she would have the baby all to herself, play at being mistress of the house. Gathering the child into her arms, she went down to the kitchen to prepare his afternoon feed, starting in surprise as she saw Lázaro, sitting at the table.

'Hello,' he said. 'I'm just waiting for Emilia to get back. Any chance of you offering me a cup of coffee? I'll hold the little fellow for you.'

After a moment's hesitation, Mirella handed over the baby and began spooning grounds into the pot. Lázaro was forever in and out of the house, she was getting quite used to seeing him. He was always polite and friendly and often brought something for Gabriel – a wooden rattle, a cuddly toy, and sweets which he was far too young to eat. Celia had spoken well of him, even though he had apparently deserted his former post without giving notice.

'Not all soldiers are thugs,' she had told Mirella, touched by his thoughtful little gifts. 'You can't blame him for joining the army after the rebels killed his brother. There's good and bad on both sides, whatever Eduardo says.'

'Thanks,' said Lázaro, exchanging the baby for a tiny cup of strong, sweet coffee. He downed it in one gulp, determined not to let this chance slip by. It was the first time he had been alone with her; she usually spent the daytimes in the nursery next to Doña Celia's office, thwarting his previous attempts to exploit Emilia's absences.

'You're so beautiful,' he blurted out. 'Ever since I saw you that day I've thought of nothing else.'

He cursed himself for his lack of subtlety. But she affected to ignore the compliment, her attention riveted on the baby.

'I would have asked you out by now,' he continued, recklessly, 'except that I was scared you'd turn me down. Emilia would have my guts if she knew the way I felt about you . . .'

Mirella was used to men making passes at her. Any number of workers at Buenaventura had tried it on, but she had ignored them all with haughty disdain. She looked up, intending to give Lázaro her standard, icy, keep-off look, when he said, 'I know what you're thinking. That I've got a cheek. A girl like you could land herself a white boy, easy.'

This touched a raw nerve. Mirella had been on the receiving end of too much racial prejudice herself to risk endorsing such an accusation. Her mixed blood was surely the reason why Raúl disapproved of her romance with Eduardo; her late *novio*'s parents had reacted the same way.

She shook her head in protest.

'Then can I take you dancing, next time I have a pass?' said Lázaro, encouraged by this denial.

Another negative, more vigorous this time.

'Would you prefer to go to the movies? We could do anything you like. I promise I wouldn't touch you, unless you wanted me to . . .'

Had it been any other man but Lázaro, she might have fled from the room, fearful that he might make a grab for her. But he made no move, respectfully keeping his distance, his eyes full of naked supplication. Mirella couldn't help feeling sorry for him. So that was why he was walking out with Emilia – so that he would have an excuse to visit the house. Mirella had always wondered what a good-looking chap like him saw in a fat, middle-aged woman like her. The housekeeper was forever bragging about Lázaro's skills as a lover, regaling Mirella with details which she had found undeniably titillating, reviving sensations she had never thought to feel again, sensations which Eduardo, ever the gentleman, had never even tried to arouse.

'Please, Mirella,' urged Lázaro. 'I'm not like all the other guys. You can trust me, I swear it.'

Mirella hesitated. She didn't want to lead him on, but neither did she want to hurt his feelings. Remembering that she had once seen Lázaro reading a newspaper, she rummaged in a drawer for pencil and paper and wrote, 'Sorry. I already have a sweetheart. We are engaged to be married.'

Lázaro stared at the words disbelievingly. His discreet

enquiries around the estate had confirmed that Mirella didn't have a boyfriend, reinforcing his belief that she was scared of men.

'A sweetheart? Then where is he? Why doesn't he ever come to see you?'

Mirella shrugged, belatedly regretting her revelation. Oriente was full of absent menfolk, it was an open secret where they had gone . . .

'Is he in the mountains?' She looked away; it seemed pointless to deny it. There was no harm done. She had not named Eduardo, after all. At least now he would leave her alone.

'Ah, well,' said Lázaro stoically, forcing a smile. 'Just my luck.' It was just his luck all right. It was bad enough that she had another man, but that his rival should be a stinking rebel was almost more than he could bear . . .

He longed for combat as never before. That way, perhaps, he would get the chance to kill him.

Eduardo received a warm welcome from his new comrades in Havana. His re-broken and re-set foot, strengthened by steel pins, was newly encased in fresh plaster, preventing active participation in sabotage. But his status as a veteran of the Sierra commanded instant, undeserved, but gratifying respect.

He was accommodated in the home of Carlos Díaz, a prominent radical lawyer, posing as his nephew, a bogus identity supported by immaculately forged papers. He had shaved off his beard – the badge of a Fidelista – leaving behind a moustache, which, embellished by a pair of hornrimmed spectacles, made him look quite different from the photograph on the wanted posters.

Carlos was a prime mover in the campaign to expose and publicise government corruption, a subject dear to Eduardo's heart. He was glad to act as his secretary, and felt honoured to be asked to take the minutes at a clandestine meeting to be held in the basement of a workers' café. Eduardo was introduced by his new *nom de guerre*, Eduardo Marquéz, and took up his place as scribe.

'We're just waiting on one more person,' said an elderly bespectacled man. 'He defended the two Rubio boys, managed to get them off on a technicality. A brilliant performer in court. I've referred several cases to him I couldn't handle myself. Turns out he's got a pile of stuff against Hector Reinaldo.'

'Reinaldo of anti-vice?'

'The title covers a multitude of sins. If we can get him arraigned, he might just decide to grass on some bigger fish in return for the chance to clear off to the States with his ill-gotten gains . . .'

'Here he is,' said the elderly man, standing up.

Eduardo turned his head to see the newcomer, a comradely greeting dying on his lips. His crutches prevented a haughty, dignified exit, and in any case, he did not want these people to know his private business. He could hardly stand up and say, 'I'm leaving. That's the bastard who screwed my mother and left my sister pregnant.' So he said nothing, acknowledging León with a stiff nod, and didn't deny it when he said coolly, 'Eduardo and I have already met, back in Oriente.' But the deadpan statement was negated by a powerful handshake and the *sotto voce* murmur, 'Good to see you. I was afraid that you were dead.'

Carlos gave the floor to León, inviting him to share the fruits of his recent researches. Eduardo listened, reluctantly spellbound. He was still the same old León, the virtuoso who worked all night for a month before his exams and shirked shamelessly for the rest of the year, who relied on a photographic memory rather than application, who was too talented for his own good. And yet, he wasn't quite the same old León. The engaging brand of cavalier modesty had gone; this León didn't give a damn about making friends or being the most popular guy in the class. He was impatient, arrogant and unashamed – for once – to show off his fearsome intellect, more agile and daring than Eduardo's own, capable of great intuitive leaps, fortified by a creative imagination. He displayed little respect for revolutionary dogma, made it clear that he found committee procedures tiresome, and when somebody asked how he had got sight of Reinaldo's private papers, he said casually, mockingly, tapping the ash off his cigarette, looking straight at Eduardo, 'I had a look through his bureau while his wife was asleep. She happened to let it slip – quite by accident of course – where he kept the key.'

'Would you admit to that in court?' someone demanded.

'Certainly not. I have the lady's reputation to think of. Not to mention my own.'

Eduardo knew very well he was trying to bait him, to make him feel like a prude. It was as if he was saying, 'Don't think I'm a reformed character. Don't think I'm after your good opinion. If you want us to stay enemies, that's fine by me.' Was this really the same good-humoured León who had played with him as a child, made life in that gloomy house bearable, filled it with the sound of defiant laughter? For the first time ever he saw a resemblance between León and Raúl, Raúl who never made excuses, who made and lived by his own rules.

Well, he wasn't going to live by Raúl's rules any longer, With Mirella, he would prove that he wasn't a freak. If anyone could save him, it was she. However great the temptation, he must never weaken again, never put his future career in jeopardy. His greatest fear was that Raúl would continue to pursue him, Raúl who was afraid of nothing and nobody, who would never give up, never allow him to forget . . .

When the meeting broke up, Carlos slapped León on the back and said, 'Come and eat with us. You and Eduardo here can talk about old times.'

'Thank you, I will. I have my own car outside. You go ahead in yours and Eduardo can ride with me and show me the way.'

It would look absurd to protest. Eduardo had no choice but to haul himself to his feet and accept a helping hand from León as he opened the passenger door for him and tossed his crutches on the back seat.

'What happened to your foot?' he demanded.

'I would have thought Celia would have told you.'

'Then you don't know your sister very well. We're barely on speaking terms, the only thing we discuss is the estate.'

'Trust you to get her to skivvy for you, just like your father did.'

'She volunteered for the job.' There was a short pause. 'I assume because Raúl thought it would be good cover for the wife of a rebel. Were you two together in the Sierra, by any chance?'

'I don't know what you're talking about. Raúl is in the States.'

'Cut the bullshit, Eduardo. He more or less admitted it to me himself.' He pulled up by the side of the road. 'We've got to talk. It's high time we cleared the air.'

'I've got nothing to say to you. Just because you've joined the movement doesn't alter what happened, and—'

'I haven't "joined the movement". As for what happened, I'm sure you've heard Raúl's side of it and I don't expect you to want to hear mine . . .'

Oh, but he did. He wanted to hear, and believe, ill of Raúl, anything that would reinforce his resolve never to see or speak to him again.

'. . . so I'll get straight to the point. Thanks to me, your sister married in haste, married a man she knew nothing about. A man whom I know to be ruthless, dangerous, and possibly even violent, who smells out weakness like some killer beast, who has no scruples at all. If she's happy with him – which I doubt – well and good, far be it from me to stir up trouble between them. If she isn't happy, you can bet your life she won't come crying to me. But she might just confide in you, you're the only family she has left.'

'Confide in me? She hasn't even told me it's your kid!'

'Then who did? Raúl, I suppose.'

'Well, why shouldn't he? I'm her brother.'

'Exactly. You're her brother. What I wanted to say to

you was this. If Celia was ever in trouble, or in need of help, I want you to let me know. Don't let your grudge against me, or your loyalty to Raúl, get in the way of your duty to your sister. If you ever suspect for one minute that anything's wrong, that she needs help . . .'

Eduardo felt himself blushing. Ruthless, dangerous and violent. Oh, yes, he was that all right. Did Celia feel this way about Raúl too? Torn between love and loathing, desire and distrust?

'What should be wrong?' he said, ashamed of his own duplicity. 'What gives you or me the right to interfere in her marriage?'

León hesitated for a moment. Then he said, 'It turns out my father hired some slimeball of a private dick to check out Raúl's past. Just the kind of thing the old sod would do. By the time he came up with the goods, the old man was dead, and he sent his report to me instead.'

'Well? What did it say?'

'Things that might catch up with him one day. Things I wouldn't want Celia to know. Or anyone else, come to that. But other people might try to use them against him. And Celia could get caught in the crossfire. Just let's leave it at that, shall we?'

Jesus Christ, thought Eduardo with a sudden stab of insight, he knows. He knows why Raúl got kicked out of the army and he's not going to use it . . .

'How very noble of you to keep it to yourself,' he said, struggling to stay on his high horse as it bucked and reared in protest at his hypocrisy.

'On the contrary. I'm hardly in a position to cast the first stone. Especially at my own brother.'

'Even though you hate his guts?'

'Because I hate his guts. Well? Do we have a truce? For Celia's sake? Or do we carry on this feud for ever more?'

His tone was take-it-or-leave-it, unapologetic, making it clear that he wouldn't ask him twice. He would rather be rebuffed than dish whatever dirt he had on Raúl, and Eduardo was bound to respect him for that. Like it or not, he had deceived Celia every bit as much as León had done, they were partners in crime. Like it or not, they had a common foe.

'Why not?' he said, extending a hand. He was hardly in a position to cast the first stone himself.

Lily twirled the umbrella in her cocktail moodily as the chanteuse in the Lido blew kisses to a barrage of applause.

'Fat cow,' she muttered to Frank. 'I could do better than that.'

'Sure you could,' muttered Frank, well used to this refrain. Lily had been working hard, increasing her repertoire to include popular Cuban numbers, but León had remained adamant: no auditions, let alone jobs. Though he was happy for Frank to whet her appetite for fame by taking her to see visiting cabaret idols like Lena Horne, Maurice Chevalier, Eartha Kitt and Nat King Cole. The tears would stream down her face as she applauded, and yet nothing would induce her to leave her husband in pursuit of her thwarted career. 'León loves me,' she would insist stubbornly. Perhaps she really believed it.

Frank found himself wishing, against his own best interests, that it was true. Certainly León was fonder of her than he cared to admit. Otherwise he would have laid it on the line to her long ago. 'I want it to be her decision,' he had repeated, when Frank had taxed him about it. 'Lily's had a lot of bad breaks. I don't want her to think I'm trying to kick her out.'

'I wish you would talk to León about me getting a job,' she went on. 'He might listen to you. I'm so glad you two are friends. I'd never do anything to spoil that friendship.'

This was her way of letting him know that he wasn't about to get lucky, not that he had expected to. Trying it on and being rejected had become a kind of ritual. Lily's fundamental indifference to sex, except as a bargaining ploy, was now cloaked in a new wifely virtue. Which suited him better than he cared to admit. The weeks of purely platonic encounters had revealed the real Lily, a

Lily he could love without feeling like a prize mug. If he had known the true story, right from the start, he would never have laid a finger on her. And if he ever got her away from León, he wouldn't so much be marrying her as adopting her.

'If we went to the States,' he ventured, 'perhaps we could open up a little piano bar. I'd run it, you'd sing in it. That way you wouldn't be working for some meat merchant.'

'But you haven't got any money.'

'I could raise some.'

She shook her head. 'If I took the baby out of the country, the inheritance would be forfeit. I couldn't do that to León.'

'We could leave Leonardo behind. You could always visit him. You could . . .'

'You think I'm a lousy mother, don't you?'

'I never said that.'

'Just because I don't slobber all over him doesn't mean I don't care!'

Perhaps it was a sign that she did care. Otherwise she would surely have played the doting mother the way she played all her other roles. Real emotion gave her stage fright. Real emotion hurt. And Lily wasn't in the business of being hurt. She was raw as an egg inside that tough, impenetrable shell of hers. But given time, and warmth, she would grow and hatch out of her own accord. It was just a question of waiting.

Raúl waited impatiently for the order to attack. It was a small garrison, on the northern coast of the province, the first target of his newly formed unit. Soldiers who surrendered would be re-educated and given an opportunity to change sides. The imminent rebel victory would be the signal for workers' committees to rise up all over the area and force the resignation of officials at gunpoint.

Castro had decreed that all Batista soldiers would be discharged as soon as the new revolutionary government came to power. By defecting now, they could protect their livelihood, retain their rank, and avoid possible future charges of war crimes. In similar vein, he had forbidden all citizens to pay their taxes; those who defied the order would have to pay them all over again to the new administration. Such edicts were issued largely for their propaganda value, to give the impression that the battle was all but won.

In actual fact the guerrilla forces still numbered hundreds rather than thousands; their real strength lay in the public imagination. And, more importantly, in the sudden decision by Washington to stop sending arms to Batista. Evidently they wanted him to fall sooner rather than later, before the Communists in the towns took charge of the revolution they had formerly condemned. Castro might be distinctly pink but he wasn't officially red, making him the lesser of two evils . . . or so they thought. Raúl disagreed, more than ever, but his warnings had evidently fallen on deaf ears.

But for the moment, he was a soldier, not a spy; combat was a blessed end in itself, whatever the issues at stake. When the order came, Raúl launched the first grenade, providing a dense cover of smoke for the advance. As the first wave of return fire spattered the ground either side of him, he ran towards death, as if to greet an old friend, knowing that was just a mirage, that it couldn't touch him. But that didn't damp the fear that fuelled him, propelling him through the barrier of self-preservation towards an elusive vision of peace.

He saw one man topple forward, and then another, felt the rain of bullets reduce to a drizzle and then an erratic shower of big fat isolated drops as rebel troops stormed the gates and drew off the enemy fire. He roared the command for his surviving men to join the main attack and then, while bullets continued to whistle past him, carried both his wounded comrades back to safety, before running back towards the fray.

They made a hero out of him, of course, they called it courage. The two men he had saved swore eternal friendship, he would be mentioned in despatches to the great god Castro himself. Courage. Was there nobody who recognised a death wish? Was there no one else who understood despair?

TWELVE

THE HARVEST was safely in, much to Celia's relief. Despite the immunity from attack afforded by the supply line, the firing of the Santiago warehouse had led her to redouble security arrangements. There were any number of rival anti-Batista groups, and each one was a law unto itself.

Wisely, Castro had changed tactics, abandoning agricultural sabotage in favour of a lucrative sugar levy, protection money by any other name, which most plantation owners had been only too happy to pay. This had served both to swell rebel funds and to moderate their public image. Despite this heavy unofficial tax, Buenaventura's annual profits had broken all previous records, despite, or perhaps because of, heavy expenditure on benefits and incentives, which would help ensure a similar success next year . . . not that Celia would still be around to see it.

By next year, according to Raúl, a new government would be in power, backed up by a revolutionary army in which he would hold a commission; he had already risen to the rank of captain following a string of daring exploits on the battlefield. Batista's big push, a major offensive designed to wipe out the rebels once and for all, had proved an embarrassing failure, resulting in heavy casualties and an ignominious retreat. The American press had taken Castro to their hearts, hailing him as a Caribbean Lawrence of Arabia; Batista, meanwhile, had ignored calls for his resignation and postponed elections from June until November, despite growing rumours of a revolt by junior officers. Few doubted that a rebel victory was in sight. As in any victory, there would be as many losers as winners. And she, Celia, would fall somewhere in between the two.

By next year, she would have a husband again. She would leave this place for ever, give up her short lease on power and authority. Buenaventura was not her baby, any more than Gabriel was Mirella's. She would learn to be an army wife; Mirella would marry Eduardo, have the child she longed for. It was best that the parting should happen, for both of them, before they became too attached.

Raúl's two brief, unannounced periods of leave had been the usual assault course of wild accusations, fulsome retractions, stormy quarrels and passionate love-making. León's visit, after the warehouse fire, was repeatedly thrown in her face as evidence of a thwarted assignation. He would interrogate her closely about her movements, just as Enrique had once done with Lidia. Celia would answer back with spirit; telling him that he was like his father was the cruellest and most effective way to bring him to heel. She had long since ceased to fear his violent temper; Raúl, like all bullies, backed off if you stood up to him.

Ironically, his remorse was more painful than his suspicion. Her own fidelity felt false, forced. León's own two visits had knocked her sideways, left her riddled with regrets, reminded her that she was nowhere near as innocent as she liked to believe. Useless to remind herself of his crimes against her; Raúl himself had lied to her, abused her trust, hurt her, taught her that you couldn't stop loving to order. Raúl needed her, she could never turn her back on him, however badly he behaved. She had given him everything she had to give, except the broken half of her heart that still belonged to León.

Part of her longed for a reconciliation, but she didn't dare suggest it, not only for fear of Raúl's reaction but for fear of what it might lead to. And besides, it seemed less dishonest to pretend to be enemies than to pretend to be friends. Erstwhile lovers could only be friends when the passion was dead, and hers still lived like a caged animal growing large in captivity. Not passion for the lovable, extrovert León of old, nor for the abject sweet-talking penitent, but for the proud, remote stranger who had taken their place. This new, unyielding, inaccessible León was an unknown quantity, a challenge, a man she liked a great deal less and admired a great deal more. If only they could meet for the first time, as unattached strangers, now that they were both older, stronger, wiser . . .

It didn't help that she owed her new strength and wisdom almost entirely to Raúl; perhaps they both did. Raúl had taught her, no, forced her, to fight, to discover and develop muscles she had surely never possessed until her marriage. Once, in a moment of weakness, he had admitted to bullying his brother as a child, 'to teach him to give as good as he gets'. Perhaps, belatedly, this painful lesson had stood León in good stead.

And yet Raúl's behaviour towards Gabriel was unfailingly good-humoured and affectionate. He had a knack for engrossing all his wandering, fickle attention, demonstrating the same hypnotic technique he used with dogs and horses; Mirella didn't get a look in when Raúl was around.

'He looks just like you, thank God,' he observed. 'Or perhaps I should say, like your brother. Yes, I think he will grow up to be the image of Eduardo. But in other ways Gabriel will take after me. I shall teach him to ride and shoot and defend himself. One day he too will be a soldier.'

Celia had expected him to ignore and resent Gabriel; this determination to love him as his own, to mould him in his own image, was in some ways more worrying than rejection would have been. She kept remembering León's William Tell story, found herself haunted by images of little Gabriel with an orange on his head, too afraid to admit his fear, overcome by dizzying elation when the ordeal was over. She knew exactly what it felt like. Metaphorically, Raúl had done the same thing to her, time and time again, infecting her with his own addiction to adrenaline. The prospect of his visits filled her with trepidation, but she felt bereft when he had gone.

Eduardo never asked after him, or vice versa, the result, no doubt, of Raúl's opposition to his marriage plans, made worse by the astonishing news of his truce with León – a move which Raúl regarded, inevitably, as a betrayal, for all that Eduardo ascribed it, rather defensively, to their joint involvement in some pressure group dedicated to legal reform.

Celia welcomed this rapprochement, in the hope that León would keep her brother out of trouble. His damaged foot had mended well, and although it would never be strong enough for active service – thank God – it was responding to exercise and massage. He seemed a lot happier these days and had become a model of brotherly concern, telephoning regularly, exchanging letters via the rebel communications network, and urging her repeatedly to contact him if she were ever 'in any kind of trouble'.

'A commercial traveller to see you, Doña Celia,' announced her secretary, just as she was preparing to leave the office one evening in July.

'It's too late. Give him an appointment for tomorrow.'

'I tried. But he insists that you are expecting him. A Señor Marquéz from Havana.'

'Señor Marquéz?' Celia cleared her throat to hide a gasp of surprise. 'Oh, yes, I remember now. Show him in.'

She would barely have recognised him. The moustache was new, as were the heavy tinted spectacles; he wore a hat with a brim that threw half of his face in shadow. Sheepishly he took it off, and bowed. He had filled out dramatically, the callow youth had become a man.

'Eduardo!' she hissed, embracing him. 'What are you thinking of, coming here like this! There's still a price on your head!'

'Never mind about that. Where's Mirella?'

Celia ushered him into the nursery next door, smiling as Mirella launched both herself and Gabriel into his arms. The baby had brought her out of her physical shell, taught her to touch again; Eduardo seemed quite taken aback at the warmth of her embrace. Gabriel, intrigued by the stranger, began investigating his glasses, producing a general outburst of mirth.

'What are you doing here?' repeated Celia. 'You're not in trouble, are you?' In the last few weeks there had been a savage purge of resistance groups, and many members of the 26 July movement had either been arrested or fled the country.

'No. I'm here on official business. Liaison work, for the legal action group. I've just been to collect some documents from a contact in Santiago, and I couldn't resist dropping in on the way back. I'm sure the police have given up looking for me by now.'

'You'd better come back to the house,' said Celia. He would be in less danger there than anywhere else. Hotels were subject to routine police checks and 'safe' houses were regularly betrayed. 'It's Emilia's half-day, she's gone into town. Lázaro's taking her dancing tonight and she won't be back till late. But you'll have to leave early, before she gets up.'

'Surely the old girl wouldn't give me away?'

'Not deliberately, no. But it's still best if she doesn't know, in case she lets something slip, especially to Lázaro. He's a soldier, after all.'

At the mention of Lázaro Mirella found herself blushing. Not that she had done anything wrong. In fact, she had taken care not to encourage him, but she could tell that he still wanted her.

'You should never have risked coming home . . .' Celia was saying.

'I was worried about you. And I wanted to see Mirella. Besides, even if they did catch me, León would soon get me off. You should see him in action in court. The prosecutors have had things all their own way for so long, they've forgotten any law they ever knew. Half of them bought their diplomas and their jobs. I'd like to see him get to work on the "evidence" they've got on me.'

'Well, I wouldn't. Put your hat back on and talk shop with me as we leave the office,' she added. 'People will think I've invited you to dinner to negotiate some deal.'

Eduardo amused himself on the way out by emitting a meaningless sales pitch in a nasal sing-song, keeping it up during the brief drive back to the house, reducing Celia to silent giggles; Mirella, who was not blessed with a sense of humour, didn't get the joke. Once they were safely inside, the two lovers retired to the privacy of Eduardo's room, while Celia fed and bathed the baby and put him down for the night. What a treat it was to be alone with him, she thought, free of Mirella's ever-critical gaze.

Once he was asleep, she assembled the cold meal Emilia had left in the fridge, adding a celebratory bottle of champagne, and took the tray upstairs. Having laid the table in her room, she sat nibbling at a piece of bread while she waited for Eduardo and Mirella to join her. They appeared rather sooner than she had expected, looking rather tense and upset, disheartened, no doubt, at the prospect of parting again so soon. The atmosphere was strained, and neither of them was hungry, although Eduardo, normally so abstemious, drank the lion's share of the champagne – Mirella was not allowed alcohol on doctor's orders. After the meal a subdued Mirella went off to bed early. Eduardo made no move to follow her.

'If you want to join her,' said Celia tactfully, 'go ahead. Don't mind me.'

'It's all right,' said Eduardo quickly. 'This is the way she wants it until we're married.'

This seemed a strange scruple in wartime; no wonder he seemed irritable.

'Perhaps I shouldn't have come,' he added morosely. 'It will only make things harder for her when I leave. But I couldn't go back to Havana without making sure you were all right.'

'Why shouldn't I be all right? Why all this sudden interest in my welfare?'

'As you've banned León from coming here, I thought I'd do him a favour. That attack on the warehouse put the wind up him. He worries about you being here alone.'

'I can take care of myself. There's no need for him to check up on me.' She knew she was fishing, but she couldn't help herself. She wanted to hear more. She wanted him to say—

'He's still in love with you, you know.' said Eduardo, making her feel transparent. 'Not that he would ever admit it.'

Celia hid a surge of elation behind a so-what shrug. She was glad he hadn't admitted it, it made it easier to believe.

'What about you?' said Eduardo.

'You don't honestly think I would admit it either, do you?'

'No, I guess not. You know, if we could choose whom to love, and whom not to love, life would be a lot easier. A hell of a lot easier.'

'What about Mirella?' said Celia, picking up the bitterness in his voice. 'Isn't she the person you would have chosen to love?'

'I did choose her,' said Eduardo. 'Not because she's beautiful, though she is. What matters is comradeship. Shared beliefs. A common cause. Respect.'

'Yes,' said Celia, rather uncertainly, wondering what would happen once Mirella fell off that pedestal of hers. This was her cue to share her doubts about his choice of bride. No doubt she would get little thanks for it, but she might not get another chance.

'Eduardo . . . are you sure she's right for you?'

'Right for me? I've just told you, we believe in all the same things. We've been through a lot together.'

'Yes, I know that. But you know how it is with wartime romances. It's easy to get carried away.'

'You're the one who gets carried away, not me,' said Eduardo, irritably. 'Sorry, I shouldn't have said that.'

'It's all right,' said Celia. 'It was fair comment. But if I can be perfectly frank in return—'

'This is a calm, rational decision. I suppose the class thing is bothering you, but that won't matter after the revolution . . .'

'Eduardo, you're highly educated. She's barely literate. You're an intellectual. She's a simple, very ordinary girl. I'm just afraid you're romanticising her, that once you get married you'll find that she—'

'That's enough,' said Eduardo. 'I've made up my mind. I've had enough of that from Raúl without you starting off as well.'

She could have continued. She could have said, 'I suspect that she's mentally unbalanced. She shows every sign of being an obsessive mother. She'll probably lose all interest in you once a baby comes along.' Instead she settled for a craven, 'Very well. Just don't rush into anything. Wait till you've qualified, at least . . .'

'I can't ask her to wait seven years,' said Eduardo touchily. 'I told her we'd marry as soon as there was an amnesty and I can't go back on my word. Look, it's getting late. I'd better turn in.'

Well, at least I tried, thought Celia. Having made such a spectacular mess of her own life, she was hardly in a position to advise others, as Eduardo would no doubt be quick to point out if she persisted on the subject.

'Goodnight, then,' she said, giving him a big hug. 'I'll set my alarm and wake you up bright and early.'

'Celia . . . you are all right, aren't you? With Raúl, I mean.'

Now it was her turn to be touchy.

'Of course I am. I told you, everything's fine.' How could she possibly begin to explain what it was like being married to Raúl? Even if she had wanted to confide in her brother, loyalty forbade it. And anyway, she thought, Eduardo was too immature to understand. 'Now go to bed.'

Before having her shower, she looked in on Gabriel, to find Mirella sitting up in a chair next to the cot, still fully dressed and wide awake. She looked upset.

'Don't be sad,' she said gently, putting an arm around her. 'Soon you'll be together for good.' Mirella turned away sulkily, refusing to be comforted. 'You haven't quarrelled, have you?' she ventured, sensing that all was not well. Perhaps Eduardo had tried to get her into bed and been rejected. That was another problem he would have to cope with; it would hardly be surprising if her dreadful ordeal had left her frigid. But Mirella just shook her head, taking refuge in her customary muteness, provoking an uncharitable surge of exasperation.

Celia went back to her room and got undressed. Just as she turned on the shower she heard the back door open and shut below. It was only eleven o'clock. She hadn't expected Emilia back till after midnight. Just as well Eduardo had already turned in.

He's still in love with you, you know . . . She shut her eyes, remembered what it felt like, succumbed to a sudden rush of remembrance. Her hand strayed soapily as she imagined what it would feel like now, now that she had lost all her girlish illusions. Better. That was the pity of it. Much, much better . . . She sat down in the shower stall and gave herself up to shameless fantasy, letting the tears roll down her face under the stinging spray, feeling like an adulteress. The more so when she finally emerged from the bathroom to find her husband sitting on the bed with a face like thunder.

'You don't look very pleased to see me,' he said, stubbing out his cigar on the polished wood of the bedside table.

'Raúl!' She sat down beside him and buried her hot, flushed face in his chest. 'Why don't you ever tell me when you're coming?'

'Because, my sweet, I keep hoping to catch you out.' He indicated the debris from the meal, the two champagne glasses and the empty bottle. 'I see you've been entertaining in your room. A pity your guest had to leave so early, we could have made up a threesome.'

Suddenly, savagely, he slapped her hard across the face. Incensed, Celia slapped him back, making her hand numb.

'Was it him?' he hissed savagely, eyes glittering. 'Was it my brother? If he's been here, I warn you, I'm going to kill him. But first I'm going to teach you a lesson you'll never forget—'

'You stupid bastard!' spat Celia, as he pushed her

roughly back onto the bed. 'It was Eduardo!'

He let go of her abruptly.

'Eduardo?'

'He called in to see Mirella on his way back from Santiago. He had business with the rebels there. He's asleep in his room.'

'The young fool! What if somebody recognises him?'

'He's leaving at first light. And now apologise! Get down on your knees, damn you!'

He did so, pulling her onto the floor beside him. 'I'm sorry.' He burrowed into her neck. 'Oh, God, Celia, I'm so sorry. You know what a jealous brute I am. Forgive me . . .'

She did so instantly, too relieved that he was still alive and in one piece to be angry. And besides, he was right to be jealous. In a moment she would have to make love for the second time that night . . .

But for once Raúl showed no inclination to seal their truce in the normal way. He seemed distracted, miles away, muttering his apologies over and over again, and when she reached out for him he said gently, patting her hand, 'Go to sleep, my love. We'll talk tomorrow. I'm sorry.'

Celia lay restless for a long time. Forgiving Raúl was easy; forgiving herself was not. Loving her husband was not an absolution. She had been unfaithful to him every day of her marriage, in the only way that mattered, in her heart.

Mirella eventually dozed off in her chair, waking with a jolt just before one a.m. She got up and began pacing the room, wondering if Eduardo would still want to marry her after what had happened. Looking back, she should have left it to him to make the first move. But her impatience had got the better of her. Anything could happen to him, he might be arrested, or shot, she might never see him again. She hadn't wanted to let this chance slip by.

He was used to well-bred girls, of course; he had

thought her shy and modest, instead of simply afraid. But she hadn't been afraid of Eduardo. She had wanted him to know that, wanted to make things easy for him. And instead she had disgusted him, killed his desire.

'It will be all right once we're married,' he had said, crimson with embarrassment at his failure. 'And besides, what if I were to leave you pregnant, and then die?'

And if she had had words to speak, she might have said, 'That's the whole point, don't you see? If anything happens to you, then at least I'll have your child!'

But instead she had turned away from him, ashamed and humiliated and angry. Angry with herself, not with him. Now he would think her coarse and low-class. And so she was. Perhaps she had been stupid to dream of being a doctor's wife, when she could have had her pick of working men. Lázaro, for example. He would jump at the chance to give her a baby. He might be black, and poor, and a soldier, but at least he *wanted* her.

Just as she wanted Eduardo. Having set her sights high, nothing less would do. She couldn't let him leave with this shadow hanging between them, couldn't risk losing him to some clever white girl in Havana. You didn't need a voice to say, 'I'm sorry. It was all my fault.' He would surely see it in her eyes.

Her mind made up, she crept quietly towards Eduardo's room, relieved to see the band of light leaking from beneath his door, indicating that he too was lying wakeful. She was just about to knock when she stopped short. He wasn't alone.

'Keep away from me! If you lay a finger on me, you'll be sorry!'

The other voice was low-pitched, quiet, too quiet for her to make out the words. It must be a bandit, she thought, who had broken into the house and was demanding money or valuables. Or perhaps it was someone on the estate, who had recognised Eduardo, and was threatening to expose him unless he bought his silence . . .

'I said, don't touch me! I'm warning you . . .' And then,

feebly, breathlessly, 'Oh, God. Oh, God. Oh, God . . .'

Mirella stood rooted to the spot, too horrified to move. Only the sound of Eduardo moaning, as if in pain, jolted her into action. He was in danger, she must do something. There was no time to run for help, no time to think, no time to do more than reach for the gun she wore strapped to her thigh. Trembling, she released the safety catch and threw open the door.

Eduardo was pinned down on the bed with his assailant astride him, his broad back providing a target impossible to miss. Without a moment's hesitation, she aimed and fired.

'What was that?' Lázaro sat up in bed. 'I thought I heard a shot.'

'It was just a clap of thunder,' murmured Emilia, annoyed to have their love-making disrupted. A second shot rang out.

'It's coming from upstairs,' said Lázaro, pulling on his clothes and seizing his rifle. 'You fetch the guard. I'm going to see what's happened.'

He ran through the kitchen and up the staircase; hearing the sound of a woman sobbing, he followed his ears and burst through the open bedroom door.

For a moment he stood motionless, transfixed by the tableau before him. Mirella was weeping hysterically in the arms of a pyjama-clad youth with a smoking gun in his hand. A man's body was lying face down on the bed with two spreading red stains seeping through the white bathrobe. Doña Celia was crouching over him and murmuring, 'Raúl? Raúl, can you hear me?' while the young man comforted Mirella, saying, 'It's all right, darling. Hush, now. It will be all right.' His voice startled Lázaro into belated recognition. It was Celia's rebel brother, Eduardo . . .

Emilia came thundering into the room at that moment and threw up her hands in horror. 'Oh, my God!' she shrieked, seeing the body. 'What happened?'

Celia jumped up, her face pale with shock. 'Emilia,

ring for an ambulance. Tell them it was an accident. An accident, do you hear me?' Hearing heavy footsteps in the corridor, she bundled Emilia outside and shut the door behind them.

'It's all right!' she called out, as the guards arrived on the scene. 'There's just been an accident, that's all. Everything's under control. Please return to your usual stations.'

It should have been a moment of triumph for Lázaro. At last the curse had taken effect, at last his enemy had been struck down, at last justice had been done. But all he could think about was Mirella with Eduardo. At last he was face to face with his rival, the man he had hated from afar for so long, never guessing his true identity . . .

But why would Eduardo shoot his brother-in-law? Had Raúl Soler tried to steal his woman? Had he laid his filthy hands on Mirella?

'Thank you for trying to help, Lázaro,' said Celia, shutting the door and returning to her husband's side. 'But there's really nothing you can do. The gun went off by accident, nobody's to blame.'

Lázaro went over to the body. There was blood dribbling out of the corner of Raúl's mouth, his breathing was shallow. It was a pity he was unconscious; he would have liked to see him writhing in agony. He suppressed a pang of pity for Celia, who was on her knees again, stroking his hair and murmuring, 'It's all right, darling. The doctor's coming. It's all right.'

He looked at Mirella, but she was too wrapped up in Eduardo to notice him. Another rebel victory, he thought bitterly. It was one rebel victory too many. The last six months had been one long succession of army defeats and retreats, and this seemed like the final, crushing humiliation . . . No. This was his chance to hit back.

'No one gets shot in the back by accident,' he said stonily, looking at Eduardo. 'I'm a soldier, Doña Celia. I have a duty to uphold the law. Your brother here is a known rebel who's already wanted for murder. I have no choice but to arrest him.' He pointed his rifle at Eduardo's chest. 'Hand over your weapon.'

Celia, still struggling to contain her tears, looked at him in horror.

'Lázaro, please! Don't do this to us. I'll handle everything, no one need ever know what happened.'

'You can't keep this quiet, Celia,' said Eduardo. 'All gunshot wounds are reported to the authorities, there's bound to be an investigation.' He handed over the gun, holding Mirella close while she continued to sob in his arms. 'My sister knew nothing about this,' he said to Lázaro. 'I came here in secret, to visit my girl. Raúl discovered us and threatened to turn me in. So I shot him.'

'In the back,' added Lázaro, sneering. 'That's the way you rebels do things, I know. You did the same thing to my brother. Start walking. I'm taking you in.'

Mirella flung him a pleading look, but Lázaro refused to meet her eyes, afraid that he would weaken. For once, he was glad that she could not speak. Eduardo seemed quite calm, unlike Mirella who clung to him, weeping hysterically and refusing to let go. 'It's all right, Mirella,' he said, disengaging himself from her tearful embrace. 'Celia will look after you . . .'

'Lázaro!' protested Celia. 'How can you treat us this way? I'll make it worth your while, I promise you . . .'

'Move!' barked Lázaro, in a hurry now. Doña Celia was a hard woman to say no to. If he didn't get out of here fast, she would talk him out of it.

Mirella began breathing very fast. She opened her mouth as if to say something, but of course no words came out, just a strangled cry of distress. Lázaro shut his ears against the sound, shut his ears against Celia's continuing pleas. He would get promotion for this, not to mention the reward. So what if Mirella hated him for it, he had lost her already . . .

'I rang for an ambulance,' said Emilia, returning. 'I said it was urgent . . .' She tailed off as Lázaro began pushing Eduardo out of the room and out of Mirella's life, overcome by a blinding, bitter sense of power, trying to find some solace in his triumph. Raúl Soler was dead, or as good as dead, and Mirella's rebel lover would soon be in gaol . . .

'No!'

The word struck him like a bullet. He turned slowly. There was no shutting his ears this time. For a moment there was a stunned silence, broken only by the thin, high voice none of them had ever heard till now.

'It was me that shot him,' said Mirella.

For once, it was everyone else who was struck dumb, staring speechlessly at Mirella and at each other, as if they were trapped in some collective dream.

'He was hurting Eduardo,' she said, quietly but clearly. Her words were slow and deliberate, like someone trying to speak a foreign language. 'He was hurting Eduardo, so I shot him.'

'She's just trying to protect me,' said Eduardo.

'It's my gun,' she said, lifting her skirt and displaying the empty holster on her thigh. 'It was me.'

Lázaro felt a shiver go down his spine. Mirella had been the servant of the spirits, the instrument of his revenge; it was surely a sign that their destinies were entwined . . . He had a sudden hideous vision of her in handcuffs, enduring interrogation and worse. Everyone knew what happened to women in prison. Especially young, beautiful women. The police would be queuing up outside her cell . . .

'Beat it,' he heard himself saying to Eduardo. 'The sooner you get her away from here the better.'

Relieved, Celia handed Eduardo his clothes. 'Hurry,' she said impatiently, taking charge. 'Do what Lázaro says, before the police show up. Take my car.'

Lázaro thought quickly. If he lost sight of Mirella now, he would never see her again. She owed him now. Owed him her life, and Eduardo's too. A debt he would not allow her to forget.

'A car's too risky,' he said. 'They could be stopped by a patrol. I've got the truck outside. They never bother to check army vehicles. You two can hide in the back. Once we're safely out of Oriente, you can make your own way from there.'

'Are you crazy?' protested Emilia. 'What if you get caught? The boy's a rebel, you'll end up getting shot!'

'Be quiet, woman!' Lázaro turned to Eduardo. 'We'd better go.'

There was no time for more than one brief, tearful embrace. Mirella wanted to say goodbye to the baby, but Celia wouldn't allow it, hurrying her down the stairs and out of the kitchen door, where the truck was waiting. Emilia looked on unhappily, muttering and wringing her hands, while the two fugitives stowed away in the back. Lázaro leaped behind the wheel and roared off down the driveway, through the front gates and towards the main road.

Eduardo huddled in the darkness, holding Mirella close. She had spoken for the first time in almost two years, out of love for him; she had tried to kill Raúl for the same reason. Proof that she had only heard the tail end of their quarrel. A quarrel that he had provoked. Raúl had come looking for a truce, a truce Eduardo had rejected, seeing it as a trick.

'I would never have forced myself on you, that day,' Raúl had said. 'I only did it to make you leave the camp, so that you would get the treatment you needed. I did it out of love, dammit!'

But Eduardo hadn't wanted to believe him. He had been so afraid of yielding to temptation that he had hurled all manner of insults at him, using abuse as a shield. And still Raúl had refused to lose his temper.

'Is that why you're marrying that half-witted peasant?' he had challenged him. 'To protect yourself against me? To prove to yourself that you're normal? It won't work, Eduardo.'

'Why shouldn't it work? You're married! You're married to my sister!'

'We're not the same, you and I. You've told me a million times that women leave you cold. My God, but I envy you that sometimes.'

'Well, Mirella's different! I love her!'

'Have you slept with her?'

'Of course not. She's not that kind of girl.'

'For God's sake, Eduardo! Are you crazy? I swear to

you this isn't jealousy. If I thought you could be happy with her, I'd give you my blessing. But—'

'Don't touch me! Don't touch me or I'll kill you!'

He couldn't remember clearly what had happened next. Or perhaps he didn't want to, didn't want to confront his own weakness. 'He was hurting Eduardo.' Let her believe that. Let everyone believe it. Raúl, if he survived, would not betray him.

Best if he died of his injuries. Not only for Mirella's sake, but for Celia's and León's, and ultimately Raúl's as well. It was the kind of violent, sudden end he would have chosen; of all things, he dreaded old age and illness and incapacity. He had courted death so many times in vain, perhaps he would see this as a blessing, one which relieved him of the awful pain of living . . .

The truck stopped at the first army checkpoint.

'Where are you off to at this time of night?' he heard a raucous voice demand. 'You going AWOL or what?' But the tone was joking, ribald.

'Give me a break,' said Lázaro. 'I've got a woman in Las Tunas, see, and I've only got a twenty-four-hour pass . . .'

After a few loud, lewd remarks, they waved him through.

'I'm scared,' said Mirella. Her voice was not as Eduardo had imagined it. It was rather squeaky, with the slack pronunciation that betrayed her class. It didn't suit the rest of her.

'There's no need,' he said. 'I'll take care of you. Once we get to Havana, we'll be safe. León will help us.'

'Can we still get married?' she said. 'Can we get married as soon as we get to Havana?'

'You still want to?' He felt himself colouring at the memory of his failure, Raúl's warnings echoing in his ears.

'Don't you?' she said, anxiously. 'Don't you love me any more? I only shot him to save you. I thought it was a bandit, trying to kill you. You're not angry with me, are you?'

How unnatural it felt, to have a two-way conversation. Suddenly she seemed like a stranger.

'Of course I still love you. It wasn't your fault.'

He couldn't back out of it now. Once they were married it would be OK. It was just that he hadn't been prepared, hadn't expected shy, sweet Mirella to take off her clothes and put his hand on her breast and reach for his flies. He had panicked, that was all. Love was what mattered, love would make everything come right. And he loved Mirella . . . didn't he?'

'León? It's Sofía. I'm just phoning to say goodbye. We're leaving for Miami tomorrow morning.' She sounded immoderately cheerful, having got what she wanted at last.

'I shall miss you,' said León gallantly. 'Thanks for everything. I couldn't have done it without you.'

'The pleasure was all mine. I've had enough of this godforsaken country. Fort Lauderdale, here I come. If you had any sense, you'd get out as well, before the Reds take over. If you do, look me up, won't you?'

'I'll do that.'

'Look after yourself, my darling. And good luck.' She blew him a stream of kisses and rang off.

Reinaldo was leaving behind him a fifty-page affidavit implicating a score of crooked associates in return for his own immunity. Tomorrow application would be made via the public prosecutor for the arraignment of three of his superiors. Until recently, such an action would have been doomed to failure, but now the regime was desperate for scapegoats, as a sop to public opinion.

Meanwhile, renegade sectors of the government, police and armed forces were making friendly overtures towards anti-Batista groups, well aware of the way the wind was blowing and anxious to win themselves favours for the future. León despised these time-servers even more than Reinaldo. At least Reinaldo was honest-to-goodness bad.

He got home from the office to find Lily and Frank waiting for him in deputation.

'Frank's found me a job,' she began meekly, perching

herself on León's lap. 'You did say it would be all right as long as he came with me. The thing is, they want me to start right away.'

'You mean tonight?'

'Please,' wheedled Lily. 'With Frank there as my bodyguard—'

'Business manager,' Frank corrected her. Nursemaid, more like. The discussion was purely for form's sake, he had already agreed the whole thing with León.

'You've seen this place?' growled León, turning to Frank. 'What's the deal?'

'It's a piano bar off the Malecon, near the Hotel Nacional. A high-class joint. A bit of soliciting, but no rooms upstairs or anything like that. Owned by an American, pays his protection money on the nail, no trouble with the Mafia or the police.'

'And he doesn't object to you hanging about?'

'He's getting a bouncer out of it for free. Lily would do three spots a night, I'd get her home by four. Mondays off.'

'And I get two hundred pesos a month,' put in Lily proudly.

'Correction. Frank gets two hundred pesos a month.'

'Does that mean yes?'

'It means I'm fed up saying no.'

Lily began smothering him with kisses.

'I'll make do with that old black thing this evening, but tomorrow I shall have to buy some new clothes, things that reflect the spotlights . . .'

León pulled some notes out of his wallet and flung them at her. God knew how many hours a worker toiled at Buenaventura to keep Lily in luxuries, but so what? Anything for a quiet life. Lily squealed her thanks.

'You're going to come with us, aren't you? I need you to be there!'

'Not tonight. I've got work to do.'

Lily's face fell. 'Tomorrow, then?' She was like a kid performing in a school play.

'Tomorrow, perhaps.'

Too delighted to quibble, Lily ran off to change. Frank was glad for her, though perhaps he shouldn't have been. Now she had got what she wanted, he would never persuade her to leave Havana. But he couldn't stand to see the poor kid miserable. And neither, in the end, could León.

'You treat her just like her mother did,' said Frank. 'It's not money she wants from you, except as a substitute for love. It's pathetic, how much she wants you to be proud of her. And so you should be. She's got guts, she's got talent, you underestimate her. Lily needs to know she's worth something. Just the same as you did. You shouldn't begrudge her the chance you gave yourself.'

'I got roped into this legal action shit. You make it sound like self-indulgence.'

'Isn't it? Since when have you been noble and selfless? You do it because you enjoy it. It brings out your sadistic streak, making those bastards sweat.'

'At least I don't kid myself it's any more than that. Lily's got stars in her eyes, she feeds on fantasy. I deal in hard facts. Talking of which' – he fished a piece of paper out of his pocket and handed it to Frank – 'I opened a savings account, in her name, in Miami, as a precaution. It made sense to get money out of the country before it was too late. Already there's no gold or jewellery in the shops and the banks are running out of dollars. If the peso collapses or assets get frozen, there's enough in there to set you both up, and I'm adding to it every month while the going's good.'

'While the going's good?' mocked Frank. 'Just as well your rebel friends can't hear you.'

'I don't care if they do. Sometimes their sanctimonious claptrap makes me want to puke. God knows, Batista's had it coming. But if the Communists take over . . .'

'You've been reading too much right-wing propaganda. Castro needs American aid, and he won't get it unless he sticks to his promise to run the place democratically. He can't risk American investors pulling out and he can't afford to lose the US market for sugar. If he goes to bed with the Commies, Cuba will end up bankrupt.'

'And if he doesn't go to bed with them, they could overthrow him. They control the unions, they've got a finger in every pie. They won't hesitate to discredit him as another Yanqui puppet, he's caught between the devil and the deep blue sea. One thing's for sure, he'll do whatever it takes to keep himself in power. Meanwhile, it's better to be safe than sorry . . .'

At that moment Lily reappeared, shimmering with jet black sequins, twittering with excitement, and anxious to be on time for her engagement. Once she and Frank were gone, León re-immersed himself in the preparation for the indictment of Reinaldo's henchmen. It was after one before he went to bed, only to be woken, half an hour later, by Leonardo's anguished cries, defying the attempts of his nanny to placate him. God, what strong lungs that child had! Wearily, he got up and looked in on the nursery.

'He's teething, Señor,' the girl said apologetically. 'I've given him some mixture, but it doesn't seem to help much.'

'What do I pay that doctor for? Call him in the morning and get him to prescribe something else.'

He put Leonardo over his shoulder, without much hope of shutting him up. First colic, now teething, what would be next? So far Leonardo had seen off half a dozen nursemaids, and this latest girl already had the harassed, sullen look that heralded yet another resignation. Lily, who expected twenty-four-hour service-with-a-smile, routinely 'forgot' to stay home on the nanny's half-day; if a girl objected, or 'played up' as Lily put it, she would phone the agency and demand an immediate replacement, panic-stricken at the thought of having to cope on her own.

'The Cuban girls are so lazy and unreliable,' she would complain. 'And the American ones expect so much time off! Perhaps if we had two girls, instead of one . . .'

Poor little bastard, thought León. No wonder he was

hopping mad. It was all very well having two fathers but what he really wanted was one mother, not a new one every few weeks.

'I took him to the doctor this morning, Señor,' protested the girl above the din. 'I told him I had not slept for a week. I have never looked after a baby who cried so much. All day, all night . . . and the señora acts as it if were my fault!'

'Of course it's not your fault, Elsa.'

'My name is Ana, Señor.'

'Ana. Of course. Well, you mustn't mind the señora, Ana. If I were to give you a raise, say another ten pesos a week . . .'

The sound of the telephone was almost drowned out by another deafening crescendo. Groaning, León looked at his watch. Two a.m. It would be some tearful woman whose husband, son or father had been rounded up and flung into gaol; the prospect was almost a relief. Yawning, he picked up the receiver.

'León? It's me, Celia. I'm in trouble. I need your help.'

'Donã Celia, I can well imagine how distressing these questions must be. But, you understand, all shootings have to be thoroughly investigated. When and if your husband regains consciousness, he will no doubt give his own account of events. But as you are aware, his injuries are extremely grave, and if he were unfortunate enough to die . . .'

'I'm sorry if I seem confused,' said Celia, struggling to stay calm. 'I already explained, I don't remember a great deal about the incident. It was all such a shock . . .'

'Let's go through your original story once more, shall we?'

The local police chief had every reason to dislike the new mistress of Buenaventura. Having been on Don Enrique's unofficial payroll for years, turning a blind eye to the old man's illegal evictions and land thefts, and arresting troublesome employees to order, he had resented the sudden and dramatic decrease in his monthly income. Doña Celia, despite her demure appearance, had turned out to be a regular virago, bullying her feckless stepbrother into letting her run the estate, and driving her reluctant husband away. Everyone knew it was a forced wedding, and few had doubted that Raúl Soler's continuing absence was the prelude to a divorce. Rumour was that the two of them quarrelled violently. Well, this quarrel had evidently been more violent than most.

'Now, when we first called at the house last night,' continued the policeman, 'following your husband's admission to hospital, we were told by your private guard that there had been an "accident" and that you had told them that "everything was under control". Is that correct?'

'That is what I assumed at the time.'

'Your housekeeper tells the same story. That she heard shots, that she found you in the spare bedroom with your husband lying on the bed, and that you told her to phone for an ambulance, because there had been an "accident".'

'That is what I told her, yes.'

'Did anyone witness this accident?'

'No.'

'You have a live-in nanny, I believe.'

'She heard the shots and became hysterical. The girl can't speak. She wouldn't be able to tell you anything.'

'Where is she now?'

'I imagine she has gone to stay with friends or family. I gave her leave of absence.'

'To stop her talking?'

'I told you, she can't talk.'

'But she can write, I understand. Why would you have been so keen to get rid of her? In case she gave evidence against you?'

'That's absurd.'

'To get back to your second story. No one shoots himself in the back by accident. And we can discount any theory of suicide. The shots were not fired at point-blank range, but from a distance of about three metres. And the weapon which fired them has yet to be found.'

'I can only suppose that my husband was shot by an intruder. But by the time I got to him, there was no sign of anyone. So naturally I assumed, incorrectly, that it was an accident.'

'Naturally. Even though you found no gun? Even though you heard two shots?'

'I didn't think about that. My only concern was to get him to a hospital, not to question how it had happened.'

'Doña Celia, why was your husband sleeping in the spare room? Had you had an argument?'

'No. He was simply restless and didn't want to disturb me.'

'According to the guard on the gate, your husband arrived at approximately eleven p.m., at which time the housekeeper was out at a dance. I understand that it was his first visit home in over two months.'

'That's right. My husband has been working in the United States since last year.'

'Why didn't he take you with him?'

'He wanted to have everything ready for us before we joined him. At the moment his business involves a lot of travelling, and he isn't sure where we will eventually settle. It seemed best not to buy a house until we were sure of our plans.'

'And then, after another long separation, you spend your first night together in separate rooms?'

'I object to these personal questions. Our sleeping arrangements are none of your business.'

'To get back to this intruder. Your premises are well guarded, or should I say simply guarded. You have chosen to eschew the help of the army or the police in protecting your property. But surely even amateurs would have apprehended the trespasser before he got as far as your living quarters?'

'Then perhaps it wasn't a trespasser, as such. Many workers live on our land. The dead season always gives rise to crime. I imagine the person concerned climbed over the railings, got in through an unlocked door or window and was bent purely on robbery. No doubt he panicked and shot my husband to avoid being identified.'

'And managed to disappear without trace in the time it took you to respond to the shots? Tell me, why didn't you raise the alarm immediately, why didn't you send for the police? Why did you dismiss your private guard with this talk of an "accident"?'

'I already explained, I was confused. Why do you keep asking me the same questions?'

'Would you agree that your marriage is on the rocks?'

'No, I wouldn't. My husband and I are very happy.'

'As happy as two people who live apart by choice can be. You have barely lived with your husband since the birth of your child, born, I understand, seven months after your wedding.'

Celia stood up.

'I find these remarks offensive. I refuse to allow you to address me in this insolent manner. Please leave.'

'If I leave, Doña Celia, I might be obliged to ask you to accompany me. It's so much more pleasant talking here, in this charming house, than it would be at the police station, isn't it?'

'Are you accusing me of shooting my husband?'

'Oh, I'd hate to do that. I keep hoping that you will say or do something to help us identify the true culprit.'

'If you want money, why don't you just say so?'

'Tut, tut, tut. Are you offering me a bribe? That could be construed as an admission of guilt.'

'If you want to charge me, go ahead and do it. I flatly refuse to say anything more until my lawyer arrives from Havana.'

'From Havana, eh? So you're calling in the big guns. Hardly necessary if you're as innocent as you say.'

'Either arrest me, or leave. Now.'

'One last thing. Our enquiries have revealed that your housekeeper returned to the house last night at approximately midnight, and that she was not alone, as she claimed. A witness reports that she brought Corporal

González, of the Bayamo garrison, one of your ex-employees, back to her quarters, and that he left, alone, by army vehicle, shortly after the so-called "accident".'

'Perhaps she was embarrassed to mention it. Her private life is hardly relevant to this investigation.'

'Perhaps it is. Perhaps it was this Corporal González who committed the crime. He could have slipped out of your housekeeper's bed while she was asleep, gone in search of valuables, been apprehended by your husband, shot him, and made his escape via the back door, no doubt with the housekeeper's connivance.'

'I find that theory preposterous.'

'Why are you trying to protect him? Have you paid him to keep quiet about what he knows? The same as you did the nanny? As for that housekeeper of yours she's obviously lying through her teeth.'

'I repeat, no one witnessed the attack. How can you harass me at a time like this? I should be at the hospital, with my husband, not wasting time here with you.'

'Naturally you wish to talk to him before we do. Perhaps even now it is not too late for a reconciliation. But I'm afraid we cannot permit a private interview until we have asked him a few questions. Perhaps, in the meantime, Corporal González can throw some light on the affair. Of course, the trouble with these blacks is that they'll say anything to save their own skins. I mean, if he thinks we're going to arrest him, he might decide that he saw you with the missing gun in your hand.'

'Please leave. I've been up all night and I'm very tired.'

'Of course. How insensitive of me. I'll be back when we've interviewed Corporal González. Meanwhile a police guard will remain outside the house . . . to protect you from further intruders.'

As soon as he had gone, Emilia came waddling into the room.

'Was he as rude to you as he was to me?'

'Probably. He thinks I did it. He thinks I shot Raúl.'

'What?'

'The police have found out that Lázaro was here,' she

added woodenly. 'They're going to question him.'

'Well, what did you expect? If he's wise, he'll tell them it was Mirella! And if he doesn't I will, rather than see my little girl go to gaol!'

Celia submitted to a tearful, all-enveloping embrace.

'Let's wait and see what León advises,' she said. Her brain felt numb from fatigue. 'His flight should be leaving Havana about now. I have to get back to the hospital. If he arrives before I get back, tell him to wait for me here. I don't know how long I'll be.'

The drive into Bayamo, followed by a police car, gave Celia time to reflect on her lack of foresight. If she had sent the guards chasing after an intruder, then she wouldn't be in this mess. But there had been no time to think. Her only thought was to keep prying eyes away, to get Eduardo away from Buenaventura before anyone saw and recognised him.

She would never forget the moment she had rushed into the room to find her brother with a gun in his hand and her husband lying on the bed with two bullets in his back.

'I'm sorry, Celia,' Eduardo had said. 'Raúl and I had a quarrel. The gun went off by accident.' She should have realised straight away that he was trying to protect Mirella. It was just the sort of quixotic thing Eduardo would do.

She remembered how strange her voice had sounded, it was as if a statue or a picture had suddenly come to life. 'He was hurting Eduardo. So I shot him.' Eduardo hadn't said what the quarrel was about. Perhaps Raúl, disapproving of Eduardo's marriage plans, had tried to talk him out of it, made some insulting remark about Mirella. Or perhaps the dispute had been over his new-found friendship with León. Either way, Mirella, hearing the commotion, must have pulled her gun, and rushed to Eduardo's defence.

She should never have let her keep a loaded weapon, even though she kept one herself in her bedside drawer, as did most of the population. Henceforth, she would never allow a gun in the house. And now Raúl was lying helpless in a hospital bed on the very brink of death . . .

Celia felt another cold wave of fury towards Mirella. She had been sorely tempted to name her as the culprit, constrained only by the need to give Eduardo as much time to get away as possible. If the police ever found Mirella, they would find Eduardo as well, and no doubt he would persist in trying to take the blame in her stead. Oh, if only he had never met the wretched girl!

Thanks to her, Celia had lied herself into a corner; she was simply too exhausted to think any more. León would have to do her thinking for her. Let that cold, sharp lawyer's mind of his dream up a solution, let that persuasive tongue of his do the rest. There was simply no one else she could turn to, no one else she could trust.

Raúl was white as the sheet, attached to a network of rubber tubing, still unconscious following major surgery that had lasted the best part of the night. Celia's wish to stay and wait for news had been overruled by the police, who had driven her back to the house, denying her rest or sleep in an attempt to break her down. That would teach her to make enemies in future. Even now, a policeman was keeping watch by Raúl's bed, waiting to question him. Celia sat down and took his hand, fighting back the tears. Raúl, who was so full of strength and energy, whose very presence sent tremors through a room, who had cheated death on the battlefield more times than he could count, had been struck down by a stupid, unbalanced, hysterical girl.

He opened his eyes.

'It's all right,' murmured Celia, kissing his hand. 'Don't try to speak. I'm here, darling. I'm here.'

He looked up at her and smiled in recognition, his eyes full of love.

'Eduardo,' he murmured, before drifting back into oblivion. 'Eduardo.'

She experienced a fleeting, foolish flutter of absurd unease, of insane, irrational doubt. But at that moment, a doctor appeared and asked to speak to her in private.

*

Lázaro kept driving westwards till daybreak. Only then did he stop the truck in a country lane and allow his passengers to stretch their legs. Mirella was hanging on to Eduardo's arm, as if afraid to let go. Lázaro averted his eyes.

'Just drop us off on the main road, where we can hitch a ride to Havana,' said Eduardo. 'You must already be absent without leave. If you don't get back soon, you'll be in trouble.'

'I'm not going back.'

'What?'

'Everyone knows you rebels are going to win the war. If I'm still in uniform when that happens, most likely I'll end up in gaol. I've had enough of the sodding army.'

'You mean it?' Eduardo beamed, misinterpreting his motives, and held out his hand in friendship. Reluctantly, Lázaro took it.

'You fought for what you believed in,' said Eduardo. 'I respect you for that. But you're wise to pull out now. This way you'll have nothing to fear once Fidel comes to power.'

That was beside the point, but it was true, none the less. No one would miss him. Morale was at rock bottom, with men disappearing every day, anxious not to find themselves on the losing side. Thanks to the shortage of manpower, deserters were rarely caught. To hell with the bloody stupid war. All that mattered now was keeping track of Mirella.

'I always knew Lázaro was a decent guy at heart,' said Eduardo, unsuspectingly, as they got back into the truck. 'It's good of him to drive us all the way to Havana.'

Mirella nodded, troubled. She knew very well that this was nothing to do with decency or goodness. She knew he would expect a reward.

'León.' It was odd to hear his name on her lips again. She looked dazed, exhausted. 'Have you been here long?'

'I arrived about an hour ago. How is he?'

'He came round for a few seconds, then drifted off again.' She took off her hat and handed it to Emilia. 'They sent me away. The police don't want me there when they question him.'

Emilia retired, shutting the door behind her. For a moment they both stood immobile, several feet apart, each waiting for the other to make the first move. Celia gave in first, rushing towards him with a strangled sob and throwing her arms around him. León held her tight, not trusting himself to speak, breathing in the achingly familiar smell of her. She drew back, regretting, or pretending to regret, this lapse.

'Thank you for coming,' she said sheepishly. 'I didn't dare confide in Papá's lawyer. I didn't know where else to turn.' And then, rallying, 'I thought if anyone could lie their way out of this, it was you.'

'I need to know the truth first,' said León. 'And before you say a word, I know where Raúl's really been all these months, Eduardo told me, so don't give me any more of that bullshit about him being in the States. Now, sit down and tell me in detail exactly what happened.'

She nodded, expanding on the garbled story she had given him on the phone, and the even more garbled version he had heard from Emilia.

'You're sure Mirella did it?' he said, when she had finished.

'Positive. Eduardo would never shoot anyone in the back. But I couldn't name her to the police without explaining why I let her go. You know how it is,' she added, with a hint of asperity. 'One lie leads to another.'

'Which is why you've got to tell the truth, if not the whole truth. If you don't, Emilia will, rather than see you or Lázaro arrested. The best story is that Raúl tried to force himself on the girl and she shot him. You attempted to cover it up because you wanted to avoid a scandal. That way we can keep Eduardo out of it.'

'But suppose Lázaro mentions him?'

'He can't. He'd be court-martialled for not turning him in.'

'But if they catch Mirella, they'll catch Eduardo too!'

'I doubt if they'll catch either of them,' said León.

'They'll be well on their way to Havana by now and once they're there they can go to ground. This way, at least, the police will have a culprit, so they won't need to pin the crime on anyone else. They'll circulate details, for the record, and with luck that will be the end of it.'

Celia sighed. León made everything seem so simple. He had always had a knack for that.

'So how's Raúl?' he asked, trying to keep his voice level. It was too much to hope that he would die, he reflected gloomily, feeling ashamed even as he thought it.

'They say he's out of danger now. They kept telling me how lucky he is to have such a strong constitution. They said anyone else would have died on the table.' She bowed her head and added vehemently, 'I wish to God he had done.'

'What?' He saw the anguished defiance in her eyes, rejoicing in it. She didn't love him. She had never loved him. She had wished him dead . . .

'The doctors just told me,' she said. 'One of the bullets severed his spinal cord. He'll live, but he'll be paralysed from the waist down. Can you imagine what that would mean to someone like Raúl? I'd rather he was dead than see him in a wheelchair!'

She burst into a fit of stormy weeping, mocking his flurry of wishful thinking. For a moment he let her cry uncomforted, battling with his own emotions. Then he put an arm around her and said gently, briefly, 'You love him, don't you?' She wouldn't look at him, sniffing into her handkerchief. 'I might have known he'd do it to you as well. Twenty years on, I can still recall every kind word, every pat on the head, every bear hug he ever gave me. I have to force myself to remember the other things, the clouts, the threats, the insults, the sheer god-awful terror. I know what hell it is, loving Raúl. Believe me, I've been there too.'

She shut her eyes and let out a great shuddering sigh, as if in the wake of some giant confession. He had never felt as close to her as he did at that moment. Unexpectedly, she reached for his hand and squeezed it. A squeeze that said 'if only', and 'please', and 'don't', a squeeze that told him that there was no hope, that she would never leave Raúl now.

He should have said, 'I understand. I respect your loyalty. He's lucky to have a wife like you. I don't want to make things any harder for you than they are already.' That was the only honourable position to take. He ought to settle for being her brother-in-law, bow to force of circumstance, be the world's worst hypocrite. He fought in vain to muzzle his despair, but his lawyer's tongue got the better of him, giving voice to a spate of wounding words, words he knew he would regret.

'Raúl couldn't have planned it better, could he?' he taunted. 'He's got you exactly where he wants you now. You know, Celia, you're like a firefly, you glow in the dark. The darker it is, the brighter you shine. And Raúl – especially a crippled Raúl – is the blackest night you'll ever find. You'll stay with him, no matter what, but it'll be out of vanity, not virtue.'

She looked up, shocked at the harshness in his voice.

'I can see now where I went wrong,' he went on relentlessly. 'I underestimated you. I blamed myself for treating you badly. But the truth is, I didn't treat you badly enough. Trust Raúl to figure out what makes you tick. You like things to be difficult, don't you?'

'Well, it's better than liking things to be easy!' she bit back. 'All right, I admit it, Raúl can be an absolute swine. He can be cold, and cruel, and sarcastic, and vicious, and heartless, and insanely jealous . . . same as you, in fact. But—'

'But you can forgive him for it. Why the hell can't you bring yourself to forgive me?'

She gave him the answer with her eyes, eloquently, explicitly, and suddenly all his anger melted away. It wasn't that she didn't love him enough. It was that she loved him too much.

He sat down beside her, took her face between his hands and kissed her, very gently, on the temple, where a small vein was throbbing, betraying the headache within.

'I'm sorry, Celia,' he said humbly. 'I was out of line, I didn't mean to hurt you.'

He caught just a glimmer of a smile.

'God,' she said wearily. 'You two are so alike.'

'I'll take that as a compliment,' he said.

Raúl was vaguely aware that he had been shot. It had happened on the battlefield, and the knowledge that his life was ebbing away had induced a blissful feeling of euphoria, to be quickly superseded by one of fear. One moment he had been floating, free of his body, on a cloud of perfect peace, the next he had found himself hurtled into a deep, hot, noisy pit of pain, where monstrous creatures attacked him with spikes, laughing and jeering, among them his father, wielding that familiar much-dreaded horsewhip and cackling in senile glee. He tried to fight back, only to find that his legs wouldn't move; however hard he struggled he was rooted to the spot. He tried to shout, 'I'm not afraid of you!' but there was not sufficient breath in him to do more than gasp. Above him, he could see Celia, and then Eduardo, and then Celia again, until they both merged into one. They were reaching down to him, dangling a length of rope, shouting at him to grab hold of it so that they could pull him to safety. And then he found, to his relief, that he could move his arms, and held on for dear life . . .

After that, he must have fallen asleep. When he awoke, there were three people staring down at him, people he did not recognise, a man and two women dressed in white.

'Where am I?'

'In hospital. Don't try to move.'

The pain in his chest was excruciating; it hurt to breathe.

'How long have I been here?'

'Since last night. Your wife is outside. So are the police. I'm afraid they insist on talking to you first.'

'The police?'

'Don't be alarmed. We won't let them stay long. They

just want to ask you a few questions about what happened.'

'What happened? I don't remember.'

'You were shot, in the back. Your spine and a lung were badly damaged.'

'My spine? Can I still walk?'

'Never mind about that just now. As soon as your visitors have left, we'll give you something to make you sleep.'

'I want to know now. Can I still walk? Tell me!' He was shouting at the top of his voice, but it came out as a dry, croaking whisper, they didn't seem to hear him. He thrust a hand under the bedclothes and felt his thigh, but his thigh couldn't feel his hand. He dug his nails into his flesh, drawing blood, but he felt no pain. Oh, God. Why had he let them haul him out of that pit, why hadn't he let the demons finish him off? He had thought he wasn't afraid of death, and yet he must have been, and now he had escaped it only to find that he had left his legs behind. He was nothing but a useless trunk . . .

The white-clad figures left the room, admitting a man who looked vaguely familiar.

'Five minutes,' someone said. 'He's still very weak.'

'I won't keep you long, Don Raúl,' said the stranger.

'Who are you?'

'Surely you remember me? Rojo, chief of police, we've dined together many times. Do you know who shot you?'

Raúl looked at him blankly. His face kept going in and out of focus. It seemed a stupid question. An enemy soldier had shot him, who else?

'Enemy,' he croaked. 'Soldier.' His head was swimming.

'A soldier? Are you sure?'

Raúl nodded irritably, wishing that he would leave him in peace.

'A black soldier?'

What difference did it make? Raúl shut his eyes and tried to sleep. If he slept, perhaps he would manage to die.

'A soldier who was in your house on the night of the shooting has deserted. Is there any reason why Lázaro González, your former chauffeur, should want to kill you?'

The name sucked him back to consciousness.

'Lázaro? The chauffeur?'

'Was he the one who shot you?'

And then Raúl remembered his fight with Lázaro. But Lázaro hadn't had a gun, he had had a knife . . .

'He tried to kill me,' he murmured, recalling the blade plunging deep into his arm. 'Then he ran away.'

'Who tried to kill you? Who ran away?'

'The chauffeur. Lázaro.' He must have had a gun after all. He must have shot him. How long had he been lying there, in the road, before they found him?

The effort of speaking was too much for him and he lapsed back into a doze. Eduardo was there, beside him, stitching up his arm, and then he heard Celia's voice saying, 'Sleep now. It's all right. Sleep now.' And he did so, anxious to get back to the pit and find his missing legs, but when he got there, they were gone. Even the demons had disappeared, leaving only their laughter.

'But Lázaro couldn't have done it!' wept Emilia. 'He was with me when we heard the shots!'

'Listen to me, Emilia,' said León. 'If they catch him, I give you my solemn oath that I'll defend him myself and call you as a witness. But at the moment, there's nothing to be gained by you coming forward. He appears to have deserted; for whatever reason, that's enough in itself to get him court-martialled and shot. Our best hope is that he's got well away, and that they won't find him. This way, at least, the police will stop hounding Celia.'

'That filthy liar. He's always blamed Lázaro for getting jumped by those bandits, and now he's trying to get even!'

But Raúl seemed genuinely convinced of Lázaro's guilt, and had signed a sworn statement to that effect; it seemed foolhardy to rock the boat by contradicting him. 'That bastard always had it in for me,' he had told Celia.

'The police reckon that he must have spotted me arrive, sneaked out of bed while Emilia was asleep, and then hung around upstairs, waiting for his chance . . .' Emilia dabbed a leaking eye.

'I still don't understand why Lázaro didn't come back,' she wailed, repeating her refrain. 'Why did he act like a guilty man, when he knew I could give him an alibi? Why did he run out on me like that?'

'Soldiers are deserting every day, Emilia. They're afraid they'll be rounded up and shot if – when – the rebels come to power.'

'But Lázaro hates the rebels!'

'He probably hates the army as well by now. Ordinary soldiers are just cannon fodder. How many lives have to be sacrificed before this wretched business is over? Look, all politicians are as bad as each other, I don't carry a brief for either side. I've fought injustice under this regime, and daresay I'll fight it under the next. And I'll fight for Lázaro, I promise you, if he ever shows up, which I doubt. Agreed?'

Emilia sniffed a reluctant assent.

'I'm relying on you to stand by Celia,' continued León. 'She's insisting on taking care of Raúl herself. But she'll need a lot of help. I'm going to hire two full-time nurses and employ a manager to run the business and report direct to me. I don't want her to have to worry about the estate . . .'

He broke off as Celia arrived back at the house, returning from her daily visit to the hospital. León never accompanied her, knowing that Raúl would think he had come to gloat. She was carrying Gabriel in her arms; she seemed tense, troubled.

'What's the matter?' said León, struggling as always not to stare at his son. He was the only person the child was shy of, perhaps because León was so shy of him.

'Raúl asked if you would go to see him before you leave,' she said uneasily. 'He wants . . . he says he wants to be friends.'

PART FOUR

December 1958 – September 1960

THIRTEEN

'WHAT ARE you doing here?' demanded Raúl, as his visitor was shown in.

'I came to congratulate you, Ralph,' said Harry Jordan, making himself at home.

'On what? Winding up in a wheelchair?'

'Come now. This is a new beginning for you. It's only a matter of time before rebel troops reach Havana. And word is, you're already lined up for a senior post in the new administration. You're not our only source of intelligence, you know. Not that it's any big secret.'

Raúl's military exploits were by now common knowledge, thanks to information judiciously leaked by himself. With the rebels in virtual control of the province, there was nothing to fear from the beleaguered rump of the army, or from a decimated police force. Both had suffered mass defections, and the most unlikely people now claimed to have seen the light, in a last-ditch attempt to avoid future persecution. Being shot in the back by an off-duty Batista soldier had effectively sealed Raúl's status as a war hero; due recompense was assured once the new government came to power, an event which was anticipated daily, as local uprisings throughout the country provoked more and more top level resignations. Rebel sabotage had left roads impassable and paralysed communications. The harvest was threatened by a severe shortage of fuel, making it impossible to run the narrow-gauge railway that carried the cane. To quote an anxious Celia, the whole country would soon be grinding to a halt when it should have been grinding sugar.

'So, I'm going to end up a fucking bureaucrat,' conceded Raúl sourly. 'Or rather, a non-fucking bureaucrat. What have you guys been playing at, letting this Castro jerk take over? I warned you—'

'It wasn't that we didn't heed your warnings,' soothed Harry. 'If Batista had agreed to stand down, months ago, the moderates could have taken over, restored the old democratic constitution, and pulled the rug from under the rebels' feet. But the sonofabitch wouldn't play ball. So now we're going to have to make the best of a bad job. Which is where you come in.'

'You can't blackmail me any more, you realise,' jeered Raúl. 'It hardly matters if you're a fag once you can't get it up any more.'

Harry smiled sympathetically. 'It would matter a great deal if your rebel friends found out you'd been working for us. You'd be tried and executed as a spy. Rather an ignominious end for you, and a very uncertain future for your charming wife. Believe me, post-revolution purges can be very ugly to watch. The innocent tend to get swept up along with the guilty.'

'You bastard. You swore to me that you'd get her and my boy out of the country if I was ever found out.'

'That promise still stands, Ralph. For as long as you're one of us. Rest assured, we'll take excellent care of them both.'

Raúl affected to give the matter some thought.

'What the hell,' he shrugged, by way of assent. 'But you people don't own me, OK? You think I've got no choice, but I'm still choosing. I'll do it to please myself. It was always to please myself.'

'Which is why you're so damn good at it.' Harry stood up to go. 'I have a feeling you're going straight to the top, Ralph. Fidel thinks the world of you, you know. Make the most of it, won't you?'

Don't worry, thought Raúl as he saw him out, I will. His show of reluctance had been just that, a show; he had been hoping for just such a chance as this. A pat on the back and a sinecure of a desk job would only be bearable if he found a way of biting the hand that fed him. Nobody seemed to realise what a dangerous animal Castro was, not even cynics like Harry, and least of all idealists like Eduardo, who had swallowed all that mealy-mouthed crap about freedom. In a couple of years, if things went the way he feared, Cuba would have lost any freedom it ever had . . .

Just as he had done, trapped in this damned chair. Why couldn't he have had the decency to die, instead of shackling Celia to a cripple? The survival instinct was treacherously strong. Far from turning his face to the wall he had made a remarkable recovery, confounding the doctors who had advised a slow and cautious convalescence. Every day he went through a punishing ritual of exercises, pushing the upper half of his body to its limits, strengthening his weakened lung and developing arm muscles that burst the seams of his shirts. He was beginning to feel like a man again. Celia, his scourge and strength, had seen to that.

He had expected her to kill him with kindness. But she was pitiless, impatient, supervising his painful progress with all the benevolence of a sergeant major. He had yelled abuse at her, cursed and reviled her, but she had never flinched. He would beg her to put him out of his misery, only to have his will to live exposed.

'Die then,' she would challenge him. 'I can't stop you blowing your brains out. Just don't expect me to do it for you.'

Not being afraid of death was one thing; finding the nerve to kill yourself was quite another. Too bad Lázaro was such a lousy shot. But at least Eduardo was safe from him now, and he from Eduardo. Raúl hoped for his sake that this ridiculous marriage wouldn't turn out to be the fiasco he had predicted. But he had no desire to find out. It was best if they never saw each other again.

He sat for a moment watching Celia through the french windows, playing with Gabriel on the lawn beyond the pool, holding him upright while he attempted to walk.

'Let go of him!' he shouted, wheeling himself down the ramp which led onto the terrace. 'Let him fall and pick himself up again. Don't mollycoddle him!'

Catching sight of his papá, the child wriggled free, took a few eager unsupported steps towards him and promptly fell over, unconsciously mimicking Raúl's own futile attempts to prove the doctors wrong. Several times Celia had found him lying like a beached whale on the floor, and had to summon help to lift him back into his chair, berating him all the while.

Sunny-natured as always, Gabriel didn't cry. He might look like a miniature Eduardo, but in every other way he reminded Raúl of his brother at the same age.

'Who was that man?' asked Celia.

'An American traveller for farm machinery. I sent him down to the office to talk to Gómez.'

Until recently she would have shown an interest; now she affected indifference to what happened on the estate, well aware that they would not be here much longer.

'You're bored, aren't you?' said Raúl. 'Bored and frustrated.'

'I don't like marking time, that's all. The sooner we leave here and get settled in a place of our own, the happier I'll be. And I'm not "frustrated". You're fishing for compliments again.'

Her voice softened. The one thing she was always kind about was sex. She might revile him, for his own good, in every other area, but the bedroom was sacrosanct. It had taken the crushing experience of impotence to teach him how to make love, to seduce, not subdue, to cherish, not conquer, to discover that elusive part of her that had defied brutal excavation, that only yielded to patience and humility. Ironically, he had never been so sure of her, or of himself.

'We won't be stuck in this backwater much longer,' said Raúl, pulling the child onto his lap. 'I expect to be summoned to Havana as soon as rebel forces reach the city.'

'To Havana?'

'If I'm to have a government post, that's where I will be based.'

'And that's what you want? A government post?'

'I wanted to be an officer in a new free army. A role for which I am no longer equipped. As it is, I shall volunteer for a job in agriculture. The sugar industry has to be completely reformed if Cuba is to prosper.'

'Nationalised, you mean?' He could hear the scepticism in her voice. Celia was no fool.

'The state has always interfered with farming. It might as well exercise complete control. Get rid of all these piddling *colonos* with their outdated methods and resistance to change. They're just parasites on the big *centrals*, like Buenaventura.'

'You're beginning to sound just like Papá! He never stopped complaining about the reforms of 1937, he was always saying how it gave small farmers too many rights, and how much better it would be if he could take over their land.'

'Which he did illegally, whenever he got the chance.'

'So what are you saying? I thought you supported reallocation of land to the peasants? I though you wanted to see Buenaventura broken down into small, privately owned farms?'

'You misunderstood me, my love.' Just as the peasants had misunderstood Fidel; they would never be allowed to own a thing. 'Small farms are not efficient. What we need is control of production by the state, with every worker guaranteed a year-round job, and with profits being ploughed back into the soil, not filling the coffers of the rich.'

'The rich meaning León, I suppose.' She no longer avoided any mention of his name, as if determined to blunt its edge. 'Would you feel the same way if you were in his shoes?'

Raúl smiled. He might disagree with state control in principle, but he might as well enjoy its perks. Poor old León. He would not be rich for very much longer.

'If I said yes, would you believe me?'

'Would you blame me if I didn't?'

'No. Luckily I don't have to make a choice between my beliefs and my self-interest. I thank God for that reason that I'm poor. Surely you don't begrudge me a career? Who knows, perhaps we can find one for you as well.

The revolution needs hardworking, committed, educated people, women as well as men.'

She looked at him dubiously.

'You really wouldn't object to me going out to work?'

'Why should I object?'

'You know very well why.'

'Ah. She thinks I'm going to interrogate her every time she steps outside the door. She thinks I'm going to accuse her of secret meetings with my brother.'

He smiled indulgently and ruffled her hair, mocking her. How she mourned the old, possessive Raúl already! The Raúl she could dominate by stealth, the Raúl she could blame for her own cowardice. The new Raúl even looked different. In the last six months he had re-grown the traditional guerrilla beard – shaved off each time he had visited Buenaventura – which hid part of his scar and softened his face, giving him an unfamiliar air of biblical benevolence.

'Haven't I told you that I'm through with jealousy and suspicion?' he said. 'Why do you find it so hard to believe? You expected the opposite, didn't you? You thought that once I was a cripple, once I was less than a man, I would fear my brother more than ever. Even now, you try to twist my political principles into a personal vendetta. Why? Is it because you prefer us to be enemies?'

'No. No, of course not,' said Celia, less than truthfully. This way was much more difficult to handle. And León surely felt the same way. But how could he spurn an offer of friendship, however unwelcome, when it came from a man lying helpless with a broken back?

'You thought I was a chip off the old block,' continued Raúl. 'And so I was, for my sins. But I've changed. I don't want you to stay with me unwillingly. You're free to leave any time, and I'll understand. All I ask is that you don't deprive me of Gabriel. You can have other children. I can't. He's the only son I will ever have.'

'Stop it! For the last time, I'm not leaving you and that's final!'

He believed her. Forcing this truce with León had been his most inspired move yet. Trust inhibited both of them more than threats could ever do.

'I've forgiven León for what he did to you, and to your mother,' he continued sagely. 'And now I want you to do the same. Neither you nor I is blameless, and it's time we stopped using him as a scapegoat. When we get to Havana, I shall invite him and his wife to visit us.'

'His wife?' Her face was a picture.

'Our sister-in-law. I want you to make them and their child, our nephew, welcome. Families should stick together. The war is nearly over, Celia, and what's past is past. Our watchword for the future must be peace.'

'Yes,' she said, not looking at him. 'I suppose you're right.'

She thought that suffering had mellowed him, led him to some deep inner knowledge. And so it had. He knew that Celia would never leave him; his brother surely knew it too. The most they could ever allow themselves would be some guilt-ridden, clandestine affair, which would give neither of them any joy. He had won.

And now he had to learn to lose, to repay all her undeserved loyalty and devotion. One day, if he truly loved her, he would have to find the strength to set her free. But not yet. Not yet.

Mirella was proving a real treasure. Lily, impressed by her sure touch with Leonardo, had lost no time in offering her a job before León got the chance to object. He had been less than happy about the arrangement, for no good reason that Lily could see, León having kept her in the dark about Mirella shooting Raúl, for fear that she might let something slip. But he soon came around to Lily's way of thinking, seduced by the blissful, forgotten sound of silence. And now that Eduardo had moved in, following their marriage, the live-in arrangement seemed permanent. At last Lily's childminding headaches were a thing of the past.

As Lily told Frank, she hardly knew that Leonardo was

there. The non-stop bawling had almost stopped, and on the rare occasions when he woke in the night, Mirella would get him back to sleep in no time flat. Better still, Lily didn't have to worry about giving her time off. Mirella had no interests outside the baby and her husband. In fact, to Lily's mind, she let Eduardo walk all over her – she was forever sewing on his buttons or shining his shoes and generally playing the dumb little Cuban wife, services which he took completely for granted, for all that he was always banging on about the emancipation of women and how both sexes would be equal under the dreary old revolution. His idea of showing Mirella a good time was to drag her along to some political meeting; small wonder, thought Lily, that she was glad to use Leonardo as an excuse to stay home.

Mirella was as taciturn as Lily was talkative, providing her with an on-tap captive audience, and wasn't above helping her with her hair, running the odd errand, and doing emergency repairs on her wardrobe. Lily showed her appreciation by giving her all Leonardo's cast-offs, for when she had a baby of her own, gifts which she seemed delighted to accept. But when Lily asked her one day, in front of Eduardo, when she was planning to start a family, Mirella blushed scarlet and Eduardo told her, politely but firmly, to mind her own business.

Which Lily was happy to do, her own business being much more interesting than anyone else's. Her latest engagement was a twice nightly cabaret turn at the Capri Hotel, which was suffering, like all similar establishments, from the fall-off in tourism, and could no longer afford to hire big names. It was a big step up, prestige wise, from the piano bar which had launched her career, or the two undistinguished nightspots which had followed; Frank was proving an efficient hustler, always on the look-out for a better deal, and in the last six months she had almost doubled her original fee. Part of the proceeds had been invested in a run of publicity posters, of which León would not have approved, depicting Lily in a very tight low-cut dress, one of which now adorned the foyer of the hotel.

Eduardo, whom Lily thought a dreadful prig, was not impressed by her success; he disapproved of entertainment, apart from boring cultural stuff which wasn't entertaining at all.

'People come to Havana to enjoy themselves,' Lily would challenge him. 'What's so wrong with that?'

'People come to Havana in search of vice. It's a Mecca for gamblers and adulterers. All that will stop after the revolution. It's time we stopped prostituting our womenfolk and educated them instead.'

'Who are you calling a prostitute?' demanded Lily, who was still ultra-sensitive on the subject.

'He didn't say that, Lily,' León would drawl wearily. 'For God's sake, Eduardo, stop preaching at her. She just wants to work for her living. I thought you approved of that.'

'I didn't mean to offend you, Lily,' Eduardo would say in that cool, condescending voice of his. Why couldn't he just be downright rude, like León? He was the most impossible man to argue with. 'It just seems such a waste, that's all. If you want to work, there are so many useful things you could do.'

Useful meaning boring. Lily wasn't much looking forward to the revolution. Everyone else seemed to welcome it, even the people who had formerly supported Batista (though according to León some of them were just putting it on). But as far as Lily could see, the rebels were a bunch of killjoys who wanted to stop people making money and having fun. She had ingested a horror of Communists with her mother's milk, and even though Eduardo kept saying that Fidel wasn't a Communist, León wasn't so sure. As for that other bee in Eduardo's bonnet – Yanqui imperialism – where would Cuba be without dollars?

None the less she found politics too tedious to discuss, and besides, her Spanish wasn't up to it. Whenever Eduardo started proselytising, she would drift off to her room and lie down with a face pack till he had gone out; fortunately their paths seldom crossed. Less fortunately, she saw even less of León than she did of Eduardo but, on the other hand, this gave her a certain amount of freedom. Between León and Frank, she enjoyed the best of both worlds. Frank satisfied her craving for praise and attention and affection, but he was hardly love's young dream; being married to a drop-dead gorgeous sonofabitch like León was fundamental to her ego. And, of course, it helped that he was rich. Especially as he wouldn't be rich if it wasn't for Leonardo. Lily was glad of that, it gave her a hold over him. If he ever tried to ditch her, she would take Leonardo with her, and he knew it; she had told him so, in no uncertain terms, every time they had a fight, which was pretty often. Lily felt closest to him when they were fighting. She could just about live with the knowledge that he didn't love her, as long as he didn't start loving anyone else.

Luckily her only rival, the girl who had thrown him over for his brother, was stuck in the wilds of Oriente, hundreds of miles away. Which helped assuage the anxiety of finding her photograph, tucked away at the back of León's bedside drawer. It was the same one he had used to paint that picture of her and wasn't at all flattering, not least because it had been torn in two (yippee) and pieced together with Scotch tape (not so good). Lily had replaced it without a word and done her best not to think about it. Thinking about it would hurt.

'Hi, sugar,' she cooed, surprised to see León home early for once, early being ten p.m. 'Frank will be here any minute, to take me to the hotel. Why don't you come along and see in the New Year with us?'

'You're not to go out tonight,' said León.

'Why not? Is it the dress?' Lily began fiddling with the bodice, vainly trying to hoist it up an inch. 'If you don't like it, I'll put on something else.'

'There's going to be trouble on the streets. I want you to stay home.'

'But I can't not go! It's New Year's Eve! I'm doing the midnight spot!' Hearing the doorbell, she ran to answer it, anxious to enlist Frank's support.

'León says I can't go tonight,' she hissed as she showed

him in. 'It's probably just this dress. You talk to him while I change.'

'Too right you're not going out tonight,' said Frank. He hailed León over her shoulder. 'Do we celebrate, or what?'

'What are you talking about?' demanded Lily.

'Where have you been all day?' said León wearily. 'Don't you ever listen to the news?'

Lily noticed Mirella smiling to herself. She had been glued all day, as usual, to Radio Rebelde, the illicit revolutionary station. The blaring voices had woken Lily up at some unearthly hour (twelve noon), whereupon she had yelled at Mirella to turn the volume down and gone back to sleep. At three o'clock the maid had brought her a tray, and then she had had her bath, and after that she had done her nails and had a little nap while they dried.

'I've been too busy,' she said. 'And anyway, the news is always the same.'

'Tell her what's been happening, Mirella,' sighed León, in Spanish.

'The rebels have taken Santa Clara,' said Mirella quietly, in her usual unemphatic way. 'They're on their way to Havana. They say Batista's about to flee.'

'So?' shrugged Lily. 'Why does that mean I can't go to work?'

'Because there's likely to be a free-for-all. Shooting, looting, and the rest. I expect Eduardo and his pals are already in the thick of it.'

Mirella's face registered a flicker of alarm, but she just said, 'I must go and check on Leonardo,' and disappeared into the baby's room next door.

'What about tomorrow?' said Lily, impervious to history in the making. 'Will things be back to normal by then?'

'Hyper-normal,' said León. 'Instead of just a few routine killings and bombings, there will probably be a full-scale bloodbath. By morning, Batista and co. will be safely out of Cuba in their private planes, leaving the small fish to take the fall. It's going to be pretty ugly. I think you and Frank should take a little holiday in Miami until it all blows over.'

León exchanged glances with Frank and knew what he was thinking. 'If you want out of this marriage,' Frank had told him, time and time again, 'you'll have to lay it on the line to her. Once Lily's got a hold of something, she doesn't let go. You, me, Leonardo . . .' León's plan to offload her had proved a crass miscalculation; he had underestimated her tenacity. But right now, all he wanted was to see Lily safe. God only knew what would happen here after tomorrow.

'No,' said Lily stubbornly, determined not to fall for it. León had made similar suggestions before, and she had been quick to read between the lines. 'I'm not leaving unless you come too.'

'That's not possible, Lily. I've got a lot of work on right now.'

'What about my work?'

'Frank can find you work in the States.'

'You're trying to get rid of me,' accused Lily. 'You're hoping that I won't come back.'

'I'm not stopping you coming back. Once things settle down again—'

'You're using the lousy revolution as an excuse to send me away. Well, if and when I ever leave, Leonardo goes with me. I could never bear to be parted from him. So there!'

'Don't be such a goddamned hypocrite,' said León, losing patience. 'You know perfectly well you wouldn't miss him in the least.'

'You're the hypocrite. You used my child to get rich, and now you want him to grow up without a mother, just like I grew up without a mother. She sent me away when I was six years old and now you're trying to send me away all over again!'

'Lily, I want what's best for you. Frank—'

'Stop throwing Frank in my face! Frank, tell him there's nothing between us. Tell him!'

'That's not the point, Lily,' said Frank.

'It is the point! He wants me to have an affair with you so that he can divorce me! Well, no such luck, buster!' She put her hands on her hips, B-movie style. 'And if you think *I'm* going to divorce *you*, you must be crazy. I'm not letting you kick me out, and I'm not giving up my son!' Right on cue, her eyes filled up and two strategic tears raced like rival raindrops down her powdered cheeks. Unlike most women, Lily looked even prettier when she cried, an art which could only have been perfected in front of a mirror.

Frank watched León expectantly, but as usual he was a lousy advocate when pleading this particular case; the killer instinct he displayed in the courtroom deserted him when it came to Lily.

'Don't cry, for God's sake,' said León irritably. 'Nobody's trying to kick you out.'

'Remember one thing,' went on Lily, unappeased. 'If Leonardo goes, you'll lose everything. I'll make damn sure your brother knows he's left the country. Don't think you can make a fool out of me!'

'Don't force me to fight you for custody, Lily. I'm a lawyer, remember?'

'You'll have to fight me in the American courts, under American law. And no American judge will give a child to a man who's not even his father! I'll call Frank as a witness, I'll—'

'Shut up, both of you,' said Frank. 'And leave the kid out of it. Christ, you two deserve each other. And neither of you deserve to have a child. Specially not my child.'

'My child!' roared León. 'Where the fuck were you when he was born?'

'Stop fighting, you two!' bellowed Lily. 'I can't bear it if you're not friends!'

She ran off to her room, from which emanated the sound of theatrical sobs. León raised his eyes to heaven.

'Don't blame me,' said Frank, lighting a cigarette. 'This cosy little threesome was all your doing, remember?'

'It was never meant to be a threesome.'

'Well, Lily had other ideas. I'd bow out, except that she

needs me. Not like she needs you, but I've come to terms with that. It's time you did the same.'

'She's got both of us just where she wants us, hasn't she? Me because I don't love her, you because you do.'

'That just about sums it up,' said Frank.

Mirella listened, heart thumping, ear pressed against the wall. Her lack of English was no obstacle to getting the gist of the dispute. Every time she heard the words 'Leonardo' and 'America' she knew what they were fighting about. It wasn't the first time Lily had threatened to leave the country and take the baby with her.

'It can't last,' Eduardo had predicted. 'León only married her because she was pregnant, he can't wait for her to run away with Frank. They've got nothing in common except sex. Not like you and me.'

Mirella knew all about Lily's sex life, a subject on which she spoke with her usual exhibitionist candour.

'León's the most wonderful lover,' she would sigh. 'I do hope we didn't wake you up last night . . .'

Lily's virtuoso performances, complete with grunts and squeals, often did just that, much to Eduardo's disgust.

'That girl's like a bitch in heat,' he would growl, burying his head under the pillow. 'I don't know how León can stand it. If only we could afford a decent place of our own!'

Mirella could vaguely remember making similar noises herself, long ago, with Silvio; she couldn't help finding them arousing, and kept hoping that Eduardo would too. But his attempts at love-making were infrequent, inexpert, and ended, more often than not, in dismal failure; Mirella's well-meaning attempts to help only made matters worse. He would seize on any excuse to avoid sex, trying to make it look as if he were being considerate and unselfish.

'Marriage is about loyalty and trust and respect,' he would say. 'Not self-gratification.'

But it was not frustrated libido that left Mirella dissatisfied. The whole point of getting married had been to have a baby, and how could she have a baby if they never made love? When she ventured to tell Eduardo how much she looked forward to having his child, he just said, 'There's plenty of time for that. We can't possibly afford to have a baby until I qualify. We're quite dependent enough on León as it is.'

If it hadn't been for Leonardo, she would have been thoroughly miserable. Lily, unlike Celia, was happy to give her a free hand and never interfered in any way. Frank was another matter. It seemed to be an open secret that he was the child's real father, and certainly he took an avid interest in him, much to Mirella's annoyance, not to say alarm. What if he decided to claim Leonardo as his own and abscond with him back to America? But when she confided this fear to Eduardo, he just said, 'The child could be anybody's, with a mother like that, and Frank probably knows it. León used the baby to do to Raúl what Raúl tried to do to him. And now he's paying the price. I told him the same thing to his face. It will end badly.'

But how badly? Mirella's nightmares returned with a vengeance. Over and over again she dreamed that Leonardo had disappeared; half a dozen times a night she crept out of bed to check that he was still there. She had already lost two babies, her own and Celia's. She couldn't bear to lose this one too. She couldn't bear it.

As León predicted, Eduardo was in the thick of it. The decisive rebel victory at Santa Clara, earlier that day, had paved the way for a rebel advance on Havana; pending the arrival of Che Guevara's forces, revolutionary groups had taken interim charge of the city.

The news of the government's imminent collapse had spread like wildfire. People were spilling out of their homes into the darkened streets, cheering, 'Long live Fidel!' and 'Viva Cuba Libre!' and 'Happy New Year!' while Havana's nightspots hurriedly closed their shutters and tourists fled back to their hotels, in fear of their lives. Eduardo thrust his way through the thickening crowds, yelling, 'No looting! No bloodshed! Everybody, please stay calm!' The fear was that people would go on the rampage, and discredit the revolution.

Ignoring these strictures, two youths were busy uprooting a parking meter – the latest and much-hated money-making racket for enriching corrupt officials. Eduardo was just about to intervene when he heard a loud crash behind him as a brick hit a plate-glass window. He collared the culprit, and got a sock in the jaw for his pains, reeling backwards as the lad ran away. But it didn't hurt. Truth to tell, he would have liked to smash the place up himself – it was only the office of a right-wing newspaper, after all, whose sole function had been to print propaganda. For once, there were no army or police in evidence – wisely, they were staying out of sight. Eduardo could hardly blame their erstwhile victims for seizing this chance to break the law with impunity.

'Are you all right?' said one of his *compañeros*, hauling him to his feet.

'I'm fine,' panted Eduardo. 'He was just letting off steam. But I'm afraid things are going to get out of control. How long before Guevara gets here?'

'Within twenty-four hours, assuming the call for a cease-fire is accepted. By that time Fidel should have taken Santiago. The word is that Batista's already scarpered.'

'Damn. We need to get the airport closed, before too many others do the same.'

Even as he spoke, there was the noise of a plane flying overhead, packed, no doubt, with the dictator's chief lackeys, fleeing the scene of the crime. At that moment a gang of raucous young women, gaudily dressed and heavily made up, advanced purposefully, arms linked, towards the two young revolutionaries. Prostitutes by the look of them, thought Eduardo. One of them grabbed him by the hand and planted a smacking kiss on his cheek.

'Come to the party with us!' she carolled. 'It won't cost you anything! Not any more!'

His protests were drowned out as her companions echoed her invitation, and propelled him, on a surge of bodies, towards the open doors of one of the dingier downtown gambling joints, still adorned with garish Christmas decorations, where people were having a field day overturning the tables, smashing bottles, attacking the fruit machines with hammers and crowbars, and ripping the upholstery.

'Isn't this fun?' the girl yelled in his ear, eyes sparkling. Eduardo jumped up on a table and fired his gun in the air, extinguishing one of the lights and producing sudden, sullen silence.

'I hate these places as much as you do!' he bellowed. 'They're temples to greed and corruption. Like you, I rejoice that the police have lost their authority. But Fidel has ordered that there be no private acts of vengeance, no theft or intimidation, no wanton destruction of property. The Yanquis would love us to behave like barbarians! They'd jump at any excuse to interfere, on the pretext of restoring law and order. Is that what you want? Act responsibly to protect our national pride! This isn't the end of law and order. It's the beginning!'

To his relief, it worked. Even those who weren't old enough to remember knew of the scenes of carnage that had followed the fall of the hated dictator Machado, in 1933, and the part the Americans had played, as always, in appointing his successor. Sheepishly, people began filing out into the street; two of the men secured the entrance and volunteered to help Eduardo prevent similar scenes elsewhere.

The rest of the night was spent breaking up fights, boarding up shattered windows, and repeating the appeal for calm. Next morning, Castro made a broadcast from Santiago outlawing further violence. By that time, self-appointed revolutionary police had occupied various government buildings and were patrolling the flag-bedecked streets, armed to the teeth, just like their counterparts of old. Guevara's troops arrived in Havana late on 1 January 1959, to a quiet, well-disciplined city, with people obeying the call to stay indoors until the official victory parade.

It was all over. Eduardo staggered home, after forty-eight hours without sleep, drunk with fatigue and euphoria. At long last, for the first time in five hundred years, Cuba was truly free.

Lázaro did not enjoy his work, driving a city bus, but he objected to the general strike. Not only because it would lose him a day's wages, but because it stuck in his throat to pretend to support the lousy revolution. Nevertheless, he joined the victory celebrations in the Parque Central, along with a gang of workmates who assumed he shared in the general jubilation.

It had all happened, literally, overnight. Guevara had arrived in Havana the previous day, forced the resignation of the military high command, and occupied the presidential palace, whence Batista had already fled. Within hours, Castro had taken similar control of Santiago. It had been inevitable, but it was still a shock; deserter though he might be, Lázaro's political sympathies were unchanged. In the last few months he had become more of a loner than ever.

Ecstatic Habañeros were out in force, thronging all the streets leading out from the central square, shouting, 'Viva!' and waving Cuban flags. Lázaro soon became detached from his mates and sloped off to the outer perimeter of the crowd, intending to make a quick getaway as soon as the speeches were over. What sheep people were, he thought, seeing the eager faces all around him. Still, at least the threat of a court-martial no longer hung over his head. As for his other crime, the one he hadn't committed, that was a burden he was happy to bear, for Mirella's sake.

He could have had a cushier job, and seen her every day, but pride forbade it. León Soler had offered him a job as a chauffeur, but to Lázaro's mind that smacked of being paid off. And it was more than he could stomach to have any dealings with Mirella's husband.

She had broken the news of her hasty marriage with obvious trepidation, well aware that Lázaro would be jealous, and terrified that he would betray Eduardo to the authorities, as he had so nearly done before. A fear which Lázaro had been quick to exploit.

'Will you let me see you now and again? There's no need for your husband to know. You owe me that much, Mirella. I saved your life, and his too.'

She hadn't dared refuse. And her debt towards him had deepened when the shooting was pinned on Lázaro. Not that she needed to feel guilty about that. He would have pulled the trigger happily, given half the chance, and in a way, he had done, through Changó, who had guided Mirella's hand.

Since then they had fallen into a regular, clandestine routine. Lázaro's shifts gave him three afternoons a week off, when he would meet her, well away from the house, and walk alongside her as she wheeled the infant in its pushchair. Gradually, her fear was dissolving into trust, and these days she seemed almost pleased to see him, grateful, no doubt, that he hadn't tried to force her into bed. Sex was easy to come by in Havana; love was worth waiting for.

He encouraged her to speak, just for the pleasure of hearing her high, sweet, bird-like voice. Her long silence had lost her the habit of speech, or being listened to. It was clearly a novelty for her to be asked questions and be made to answer them, because once she started talking she invariably said too much, a sure sign that she was used to being ignored. It hadn't taken him long to realise that she was less than happy with her husband. Eduardo might be 'good and clever and kind' but he was always 'terribly busy'. She might 'admire and respect him' but she didn't have the sensual glow of a woman in love . . .

Suddenly the loudspeakers blared into action. Speaker after speaker came to the microphone – ex-political prisoners, leaders of the various anti-Batista factions, union spokesmen, and guerrillas, fresh from their military triumphs – while tumultuous applause rose like incense from the crowd. There were stern appeals for public order; there was to be no looting, no lynching, no settling of private scores. Representatives of the people were already in control of the telephone exchange, government buildings, newspaper offices and television and radio stations. Lackeys of the old regime – policemen, soldiers, civil servants and politicians – would be formally arrested and kept in custody pending trial. No one was to take the law into his own hands.

Much of what was said was distorted or inaudible, but everyone cheered even so; no, not everyone. Lázaro noticed one man standing just in front of him, arms folded, conspicuous not just because of his lack of enthusiasm, but because of his unusual fair hair. It was León Soler. As he turned to speak to his companion – a tall, greying, middle-aged man – he spotted Lázaro out of the corner of his eye before he could take evasive action.

'Lázaro!' he mouthed above the din. 'Where have you been hiding all these months?' Lázaro shrugged, abashed. 'Let's find somewhere quieter, I want to talk to you. I've had enough of this, haven't you?'

He put an arm around his shoulder and shepherded him towards the far end of the street, away from the crush.

'This is Frank Maguire,' he said. 'Frank, this is Lázaro, the guy who saved Eduardo's life.'

The Yanqui extended a horny hand. Lázaro knew something of him, via Mirella. This was the man who had fathered Leonardo, who she feared would take the child away to America.

'Pleased to meet you, Lázaro. I've heard a lot about you.'

Lázaro gave an all-purpose grunt; he didn't want to get pally with these people. Between them, they kept Mirella prisoner. Thanks to León Soler, she had a comfortable home, better than any he could provide. Thanks to Frank Maguire, she had Leonardo, a far more formidable rival than her husband.

'So what kind of work are you doing these days?' said León, offering him a cigarette.

'Bus driving.'

'That can't pay too well.'

'I manage,' shrugged Lázaro.

'Look, I don't want to sound patronising, but I feel responsible for you. Especially now. Rumour is that my brother is going to be given a top job in the new administration. So you can bet your life the general amnesty won't apply to the person who shot him. You're in danger, and that's partly down to me, for letting you take the rap. At the time I thought it would be an easy matter to disprove the case against you, if they ever picked you up. But all that's changed. Now that Raúl's a hero of the revolution, his testimony will be sacrosanct. No one will believe him capable of lying, and in any case, he isn't. He's actually convinced himself that he saw you.'

Perhaps he had done, thought Lázaro to himself. Perhaps as he hovered between life and death, he had seen the man who had really struck him down . . .

'You don't want to be looking over your shoulder for the rest of your life,' continued León. 'Your best bet is to clear off to the States, start a new life. At my expense, of course.'

Lázaro shook his head. He would never leave Cuba, whatever happened, unless Mirella came with him.

'No, thanks. I'm not afraid of your brother, big shot or not.'

'Then you ought to be. Think it over. If you change your mind, or if you ever need money, or help, if you're ever in a jam, come and see me, either at home or at my office. Here's my card.'

Lázaro took it, just to be on the safe side. Raúl Soler wasn't dead yet.

Celia and Raúl spent the week after Christmas at the Casa Grande, in Santiago, in readiness for Castro's expected arrival in the city. After his triumphant entry, on New Year's Day, Raúl was able to congratulate his leader in person, an honoured guest at the private reception held in the wake of Fidel's victory address. Never mind that his injuries had not been received in battle; he was a living symbol of sacrifice, suffering, and survival, a member of the select inner circle who would soon be rewarded for services rendered.

Celia found herself in the company of other privileged wives, some simple working women, glad to have their menfolk home again, others activists in their own right, who had worked in resistance groups or followed their husbands to the mountains.

'Fidel will not forgot those who fought alongside him,' one woman assured her. 'They are the men he knows he can depend on.' Men whose numbers ran into a few hundred, not thousands; the vast influx of late recruits might have served to swell the parade, but they would not share the special status accorded to the tried and trusted few.

Like everyone else, Celia had applauded throughout Fidel's speech, moved by his spellbinding oratory, his powerful charisma, his promise of justice, freedom and equality for all. But unlike most of them, she harboured some misgivings. How often had similar scenes been re-enacted in Cuba's history, only to end in disillusionment and bloodshed? Twenty years ago, Batista had been hailed as the saviour of the nation, the standard-bearer of democracy, supported by Communists and capitalists alike . . .

Such doubts seemed cynical and mean-spirited in the prevailing mood of optimism and faith. Perhaps this time the dream would not turn sour. No doubt, as Raúl kept telling her, she was imbued with reactionary ideas, the result of her upbringing and education. Eduardo had told her the same thing, time and time again.

Eduardo. Soon she would see him again. He never asked after Raúl in his letters, although Celia reported on his progress, unasked; no doubt he felt guilty that his wife, unbeknown to Raúl, had fired the shot which crippled him. Neither man ever referred to their final quarrel. For all Raúl's talk of reconciliation and families sticking together, he showed no inclination to make peace with Eduardo. Perhaps it was just as well, thought Celia. She would never find it in her heart to forgive Mirella for the shooting; at least this way she would be spared the need to socialise with her.

Raúl's forced inactivity had driven him to raid Eduardo's library, and in the last few months he had made up for years of despising books and study, ploughing his way through thick tomes on Cuban history and political thought and reading the complete works of José Martí, father of the nation, who had led the second war of independence against Spain. His frustrated physical energy was now channelled into his mind, which he strove to make as tough and agile as his body had once been, combining Eduardo's painstaking pedantry with León's gift for bending facts to suit his case.

'Disagree with me!' he would urge. 'Give me something to pit my wits against!' And so she did, arguing from both the far right and the far left, playing devil's advocate, marvelling at the way in which he could contradict himself without any apparent inconsistency. Eduardo was a pure, unwavering idealist who believed in absolute truth, León a self-confessed sceptic who saw the value of lies, but Raúl, thought Celia, was a born politician, for whom truth and lies were as one.

The first week of 1959 was spent awaiting the call to Havana, where they would be allocated one of the many abandoned houses previously occupied by members of the old élite. Meanwhile, Castro's convoy of captured army tanks and lorries swept the length of the island towards the capital, attended by the world's press, and avidly watched by Emilia on television. Like most former opponents of the revolution, she had recently learned the error of her ways, if for purely personal reasons. Her passionate affair with Luis, Celia's new chauffeur – a good-looking, muscular mulatto who had proved a real tiger in bed – had survived the discovery that he had been working, in secret, for the rebels. Much to her delight Luis would be joining them in Havana, as Raúl's full-time driver and bodyguard, consigning the faithless Lázaro to a long line of forgotten former lovers.

On the day of their departure, as a farewell gesture, Raúl threw the house open to the workers on the estate and announced that its contents were now public property. Celia watched helplessly as people rolled up rugs, tore down curtains, fought each other for possession of an armchair or a food mixer, and pulled the bathroom fittings from the wall, causing a flood of water to bring down the ceilings below. A knife fight broke out over the television set, which resulted in it crashing to the floor, fracturing the screen, but still the two men continued to grapple, while a third made off with the damaged set. By the time the ravening horde departed, the house had been picked as clean as a bone.

'You did that for spite,' said Celia angrily.

'Rubbish. My brother would approve wholeheartedly. These people paid, in sweat and blood, for this house and everything in it.'

'Then we should have sold everything, with León's permission, and distributed the money. That way everyone would have got something. As it is, a few roughnecks got the lion's share and there will be feuding and fighting for months to come. It's mocking the poor, to treat them like that.'

'All your mother's fine furniture!' bleated Emilia. 'All those beautiful drapes! What's Consuela Fontanés going to do with a refrigerator? She's got no electricity in that pigsty of hers . . .'

'Stop whining,' snapped Raúl. 'You make more noise than the child.'

He gestured for her to put Gabriel on his lap. Gabriel adored riding in Raúl's wheelchair, especially when he drove it round and round in a manic circle, knocking over any obstacle that stood in his way, sending lamps and ornaments crashing to the ground. His favourite game was when Papá gave him some fragile object – a piece of crystal or china out of Lidia's glass-fronted cabinet – and urged him to throw it as far and as hard as he could. He would yelp with glee at the satisfying tinkle as the missile broke a window or hit the marble floor.

'Well done!' Raúl would roar in approval, clapping the child's hands together while Celia protested in vain. 'That's my boy!'

Luis, who had flown to Havana the previous day, met them at the airport and conveyed them by gleaming official car to their new home in Miramar – a specially selected one-storey house with five bedrooms and three bathrooms, the former home of an elderly politician who had fled to the US. It was expensively decorated and furnished, and thanks to the public response to appeals against looting – or more likely to the guard stationed outside – it had not been vandalised.

'Well?' demanded Celia, inspecting her new surroundings. 'Aren't you going to invite people in, to help themselves? Why should we live in luxury while others go without?'

But at that moment the telephone rang, summoning Raúl to a meeting, and a few minutes later the car bore him off again. He didn't return till the following morning, haggard from fatigue but still seething with energy. There were to be elections in eighteen months' time, he told Celia; meanwhile a provisional government would pave the way for long-term reforms. Raúl had been assigned to the Agrarian Reform Institute, which would supervise the expropriation and the redistribution of land. The initial proposals were less drastic than Celia had expected. Compromise was the order of the day, Raúl explained, to avoid damaging rifts between moderates and extremists.

'And which are you?' asked Celia.

Raúl smiled enigmatically.

'Which is Fidel?' he said.

'Don't you want to serve the revolution?' demanded Carlos Díaz, looking at León across his new gleaming mahogany desk in the Ministry of Justice. 'You realise what an honour it is, to be asked to serve in the new administration?'

'I appreciate you putting in a word for me, Carlos. But

I'm not sure if my idea of justice is the same as yours.'

'Look, I know your views about the recent trials—'

'Drumhead courts martial are hardly trials.'

'The accused are war criminals, man. If we don't execute them quickly, the people will take the law into their own hands. Murderers deserve to die.'

'They also deserve a proper defence. As it is, we're scapegoating corporals because the generals have got away, as a sop to the public bloodlust.'

'As a deterrent to a bloodbath, you mean. As for the big fish you're so worried about, they didn't all get away. We propose public trials, in the sports stadium, so that justice can be seen to be done.'

León let out a harsh, heretical laugh.

'How very reassuring. I don't want any part in your revolutionary circus, providing entertainment for the masses. Justice is one thing, revenge is quite another.'

Carlos sighed. 'Look, you're a good man, León, and I don't want to lose you. If you want to have any influence, let your voice be heard from within.'

'After you hold elections, perhaps. If you ever do. Eighteen months is far too long and you know it. Democracy means a vote for everyone, as soon as possible. And that includes people who oppose the revolution, rightly or wrongly.'

'Don't label yourself as a counter-revolutionary, my friend. That silver tongue of yours could be the death of you.'

'I'll take that as a literal warning. Goodbye.'

On television that night, he saw his brother's face flashed up on the screen as the names of new government appointees were announced. Agrarian reform, thought León, amused. I'll bet he volunteered for that one. It hardly mattered that he knew little about agricultural law or economics. A host of new posts had been created to accommodate heroes of the revolution, whether or not they had the necessary qualifications. With so many former bureaucrats discredited, expertise was thin on the ground, while untried theory was rampant.

No wonder Carlos had sent for him. Nearly all former judges had been dismissed, a purge which extended all the way through the system, leaving the judiciary perilously short of manpower. There was talk of a full-scale purge of teachers, which would leave the schools similarly understaffed. The university would remain closed until new uncorrupted professors could be found. Meanwhile commercial companies hastened to declare their allegiance to the new revolutionary government; prominent pro-Batista businessmen now wore 26 July armbands as a talisman against ruin. Uneasy allegiances were the order of the day, as uneasy as the peace pact between León and his brother.

'Let's be friends for Celia's sake,' Raúl had said, his face white with pain. 'Now's your chance to show how much you love her. Mine too, come to that.' And then, cracking a smile, 'That doesn't mean you have to treat me with kid gloves, I hasten to add. Or vice versa. I couldn't bear it, and neither, I hope, could you.'

León was bound to admire Raúl's courage and fortitude in surmounting his disability, but then Raúl had always been brave and strong. As a child León had wanted nothing more than to grow up as brave and strong as his brother; perhaps he would have done, if fate hadn't split them up. As it was, he still felt a long way behind.

This offer of friendship had the unmistakable flavour of a dare. It was as if Raúl was testing his nerve again, challenging him to show what he was really made of. Both of them knew that nothing had really changed, that however brilliantly they both played their parts, they would still be two men vying for the same woman, a woman who loved them both. And Celia surely knew it too.

'Your sister-in-law rang while I was out,' Lily informed him tartly, a few days later. 'Mirella took a message. She wants us to come to lunch next Sunday.'

'Well, then,' said León, picking up his newspaper, 'I suppose we'd better accept.'

'It was bad enough you rushing off every time she phoned from Buenaventura. Now she's in Havana, I expect she'll be pestering you every five minutes.'

'I've been to Buenaventura three times in the last two years. And only once at Celia's request, in an emergency. What's got into you?'

'Did you know she was coming to Havana? Is that the reason you've been trying to get rid of me?'

'For God's sake, Lily, she's married to my brother. She jilted me, remember?'

'And you've never got over it.'

'Don't be ridiculous. A lot has happened since then. I'm not the same person any more. And neither is she.'

'Meaning, you inherited all the loot, and she's stuck with a cripple. No wonder she's so keen to see you again.'

'I told you already,' said León tightly, 'I've patched things up with my brother. If he thought there was anything between Celia and me, he would hardly allow her to invite us, now would he?'

'Perhaps he doesn't know you still keep her photograph.' She produced it with a venomous flourish.

'What the hell do you think you're doing, going through my drawers?'

'I recognised her from that crappy painting you did of her. I expect you've got that hidden away somewhere too.'

'I don't want to hear any more of this nonsense. I'm going out.'

'Tell me you don't love her any more. Say it.'

'What's the point? You wouldn't believe me.'

'That's not an answer.'

'Don't cross-examine me, Lily. I'm warning you . . .'

'I'm the one who's warning you! If you've got any plans to start fooling around with her behind my back, you can forget them right now. And I shall say the same to her. If that's supposed to be beautiful' – she tore the photograph in two again and stamped on it – 'then thank God I'm not!'

'Bitch!' roared León, picking up the pieces.

'That's exactly what I am. And I'll fight dirty if I have to. If she so much as looks at you, I'll scratch her eyes out.'

'If you do or say anything to embarrass me, I'll pack your bags myself.'

'Go ahead. Once Leonardo's gone, Raúl will get all the dough and Celia won't be interested in you any more!'

'And you won't get any alimony.'

'I don't want alimony. I want you. And if I can't have you, then you can't have Leonardo!'

'Then good riddance to both of you!'

'Where are you going? I haven't finished yet. I—'

The door slammed, making the walls vibrate, whereupon Lily burst in on the nursery and got it all off her chest to Mirella with her usual lack of discretion.

'If he tries anything on with that gold-digger, I swear to God I'll leave him,' she ranted. 'And I'll take the baby with me. I don't need León to support me, Frank can get me any number of bookings. I'll show him . . .'

Next day, Mirella shared her fears with Lázaro.

'If she takes Leonardo to America, I'll never see him again. Even if she asked me to go with her I couldn't. Eduardo would never allow it. It wouldn't be so bad, if I had a baby of my own. But at this rate I never will!'

She was too upset to be coy. With a little prompting from Lázaro, it all came tumbling out.

'With Silvio, I got pregnant right away, I thought it would be the same this time. There's nothing wrong with me, the doctors said I would be able to have another baby. But how can I, if he won't – can't – make love to me? If Leonardo leaves, I'll have nothing!'

She burst into stormy sobs, attracting stares from passers-by. Anxious to get her away from prying eyes, Lázaro hailed a cab and took her to his lodgings, where he brewed coffee over a primus and dispensed cane brandy. The room was cramped, dingy and malodorous, but she didn't seem to notice, sitting on his bed, crying her heart out, while he held her close and comforted her, relishing his secret delight in her misery. Finally she dried her eyes and said,

'You told me once you'd do anything I asked . . .'

Lázaro didn't need asking twice.

Lily was no fool. Despite her outburst, she knew that the only way to play it was to pretend to like Celia. In any show-down, she would end up the loser. Taking Leonardo to the States to spite León would just make Celia and Raúl rich. And giving León an excuse to walk out on her would be to play into her rival's hands.

Celia, meanwhile, was bracing herself to be perfectly charming to León's wife. She didn't want him thinking she was jealous. Or Raúl, come to that.

León was ice-cool. This ordeal would be rather like going to court to defend a guilty man – it was always easier to be detached than when you knew he was innocent. Lily would be watching him like a hawk and, damn it all, he didn't want to hurt her.

Raúl, for his part, was looking forward to this little comedy: León avoiding Celia's eye, Celia avoiding León's, both of them far more crippled than he, by pride and scruples and guilt. Well, so much the better. Last time León had got her without even trying. This time he would have to wait, and struggle, and suffer.

'There they are,' said Celia calmly, as Emilia went to answer the door. Raúl wheeled himself into the hallway, with Gabriel on his lap, his face wreathed in hospitable smiles.

'Welcome, brother,' he boomed. 'Gabriel, say hello to your uncle León and your aunt Lily. I'm delighted to meet you, my dear. You're every bit as lovely as León described you . . .'

Raúl would soon have her eating out of his hand, thought Celia, following him, bracing herself for the encounter. Seeing the voluptuous redhead on León's arm, she smiled serenely. She might have known she would be pretty, she thought wryly, struggling hard not to hate her on sight.

Lily struggled not to do the complete opposite, disarmed by Celia's warm, spontaneous embrace, not realising that it was anything but. Celia had rehearsed this cordial welcome in her mind more times than she could count. Just as she had rehearsed the brief, sisterly hug she gave León, which he accepted but did not return.

Belatedly, Lily regretted the tight curve-hugging dress, the elaborate curled chignon, and the excess of costume jewellery and make-up. Celia was wearing a plain white blouse and a floral dirndl skirt; her long dark hair was tied back with a velvet ribbon. Despite this lack of adornment, or perhaps because of it, she looked striking, exotic, confident; she exuded a no-nonsense air of directness and goodwill. The hunched posture and downcast gaze of the photograph were gone; she might shy away from a camera, but met your eyes full on.

'What a beautiful dress!' said Celia. 'Where did you get it? I haven't had time to go shopping yet, or to find a decent hairdresser . . .'

Her husband displayed similarly impeccable manners, kissing her hand, his lip curling in amusement as Lily tried not to look at his scar and found herself staring at his legs instead. She was obliged to accept a wet sticky kiss from Gabriel – a much bigger, bonnier specimen than Leonardo – as was León, before Celia handed him over to the maid. Raúl led the way into a huge high-ceilinged reception room, resplendent with silk drapes, oriental carpets and polished antiques. Lily thought it rather ugly – she didn't much care for old-fashioned stuff – but you could tell it had cost a packet. Raúl must be quite important, to be given a place like this. And he was oddly attractive, in a spooky kind of way . . .

Lily prattled away to Celia, tongue wagging automatically to hide her nerves, while Raúl engaged León in some incomprehensible political discussion.

'I envy you, having a job,' said her hostess, handing her a dry Martini. 'I'm hoping to start teaching soon, part-time, they're desperately short since they sacked everybody. Raúl says it won't matter that I don't have a diploma. And it should leave me with plenty of time to spend with Gabriel.'

'He seems such a good baby,' cooed Lily, realising that a show of interest was *de rigueur*. 'Aren't you lucky? Leonardo is a dreadful handful, I don't know how I would manage without Mirella. You must have been very sorry to lose her.'

'Yes,' said Celia shortly. 'She was very conscientious. But since she left I've managed without a nanny, Emilia is always happy to babysit. Would you like to see the rest of the house? It's really much too big for us, but I suppose I shouldn't complain . . .'

'She's quite a looker, your wife,' said Raúl drily, as the two women left the room.

'Yes.'

'You should have brought Leonardo. The two boys could have played together. Or were you afraid that I'd try to poison him?'

'Terrified. You still adore playing the monster, don't you?'

'Relax. Owning land would be a great embarrassment to me at the moment. That should reassure you that I have no designs on your property.'

'Except in your official capacity,' said León.

'Quite so. But don't worry. You'll get to keep three thousand acres, perhaps even more.'

'And what happens to the other thirty thousand?'

'It will be made into a co-operative. You'll be allowed to retain the mill, for the time being. And you'll be paid compensation. In the form of bonds, of course.'

Raúl endorsed this speech with a crooked, satanic smile. León shook his head in a show of admiration.

'I have to hand it to you, Raúl. You never give up.'

'Come, now. You surely aren't taking it personally? Fidel's father owns large holdings in Oriente.'

'Never mind about me or Fidel's father. You can bet your life the American landowners will take it very personally. They'll recognise your bonds as worthless bits of paper. Foreign investments will dry up, trade agreements will be irrevocably damaged.'

'You're living in the past, brother. The days when we danced to the Yanqui tune are over.'

'Then whose tune are we going to dance to? Because we'll have to dance to somebody's. Cuba can't exist in a vacuum. Without a market for our sugar, we're dead.'

'There are other markets.'

'You mean the Soviet Union?'

'Really, León. Surely you haven't fallen victim to anti-Communist paranoia? It's all stirred up by the CIA, you realise. They have agents everywhere, trying to spark off a counter-revolution.'

'You don't say. Who's being paranoid now?'

'This is a time for extreme vigilance. Too many ex-Batistianos are now affecting support for the cause, some of them have even joined the new government. And the reverse is also true, it seems. I was sorry to hear you turned down that post in the Ministry of Justice.'

'I don't want any part in these show trials.'

'You prefer to waste your talents on common murderers? Nothing you can say can save them. The defence provided by the court is perfectly adequate.'

'Just like the defence provided for rebels was perfectly adequate?'

'I refuse to quarrel with you. We shall just have to beg to differ. You are my brother, after all.'

León caught the mocking gleam in his eye, reminding him that kid gloves were taboo, that it was still all right to hit back, that Raúl would be disappointed if he didn't. Well, he would give him more than he bargained for.

'Oh, yes. I'm your brother. That was my big crime against you, wasn't it? Is that why you bribed that creep Fernández? To get your own back on me for being born?'

Raúl didn't answer for a moment.

'So you know,' he said.

'I know everything. Including the reason they booted you out of the army. He sent me a letter, just before he died.'

Another eloquent silence.

'Well?' said Raúl at last, apparently unperturbed. 'What are you waiting for? Tell her. Tell everyone. Tell

Fidel. He's got a regular bee in his bonnet about *maricóns*. There won't be any room for queers in the new cleaned-up Cuba. Vice and depravity are the symptoms of a sick, corrupt, effete society, didn't you know?'

'What do you take me for? I've no intention of telling anyone anything. Not because you're a cripple or because we're supposed to be friends. Because it would hurt Celia more than it would hurt you.'

'That's not the reason,' said Raúl, fixing him with a knowing stare. 'You never once split on me as a kid, no matter what I did. And you haven't changed. Give me a child before it is seven and it is mine for life.' He reached for his hand and gripped it hard, making him wince. 'Listen to me, little brother. I make no excuses for myself, I am what I am. I married Celia for all the wrong reasons but now I love her more than life itself. No, that's not true. I love her . . . more than death.'

A split second of fellow feeling shimmered like a bubble in the air between them, defying either man to grasp it. They looked at one another in silent collusion, letting it pass unacknowledged, unchallenged, understood.

FOURTEEN

LILY'S SINGING career was in the doldrums. With gambling and prostitution outlawed, tourism had slumped, and many nightspots had closed down for lack of custom. Others were feeling the pinch, and her engagements at the hotel were down to two evenings a week. Thoroughly bored, she had astonished everyone (except Celia, who had suggested it) by volunteering as an 'alphabetiser', teaching adults to read and write as part of the new literacy campaign.

Celia knew what it felt like to be underestimated and made a point of taking Lily seriously – not in the paternalistic way Frank did, but as one equal to another. It had started off, admittedly, as part of a conscious effort to see the best in her; she had been determined to like Lily. Liking Lily had seemed like a good defence against loving León. But now liking her got to be a habit. Lily, with her mischievous sense of humour, never failed to cheer her up.

With both their husbands working long hours, they often dropped in on each other, uninvited. León's and Lily's house in Cristal Street was not far from Raúl's and Celia's; Celia drove past it every day on her way to and from the school where she taught part-time. One hot, sunny day in November 1959 she decided to call in on her way home, knowing that Mirella always went into town on a Wednesday afternoon. She preferred to avoid her sister-in-law if possible. Although she treated her civilly enough, for Eduardo's sake, she could not look at her without remembering what she had done to Raúl, and it irritated her to see the way she smothered little Leonardo, just as she had tried to smother Gabriel. Lily might make the nonchalant claim that she was 'the world's worst mother', but the flippancy masked a profound lack of confidence, which Mirella had done nothing to improve.

'The señora isn't back from her class yet,' the maid informed Celia. 'But she should be home shortly, if you'd like to wait.'

She showed her into Lily's frothy, feminine drawing room, a riot of different shades of pink, with fussy floral curtains and frilled cushion covers. Celia sat down on a rose-coloured settee and picked up one of the stuffed toys that littered the house. Lily spent a fortune on extravagant presents for Leonardo.

'Celia.'

She turned round, affecting to be startled. She had seen León's car parked outside, known that Lily wouldn't be home till three, and still she had pressed the doorbell, breaking her resolution never to risk seeing him alone. But depriving yourself of something made you want it all the more; perhaps that was why she did it.

'León,' acknowledged Celia with a bright social smile. 'I didn't expect you to be here.'

'I finished early in court today and decided to bring some work home. How are you?'

'I'm fine, thanks. And you?'

'For heaven's sake. Do we have to keep this up without an audience?' He sat down opposite her. 'I'm glad to have the chance to speak to you in private. It's about Gabriel.'

Celia felt herself squirming. She knew what he was going to say.

'I've already said this to Raúl and he laughed it off. He's spoiling him to death. Turning him into a little thug.'

'He's high-spirited that's all,' protested Celia, jumping to her son's defence. 'I happen to be very strict with him. Raúl tends to encourage him to show off when other people are there. But he's as good as gold when he's with me.'

'You call an unprovoked attack on Leonardo showing off?'

'Leonardo is a dreadful cry-baby. And he did provoke him. In fact, when it comes to being spoiled, Leonardo wins hands down. I've said it to Lily a hundred times, you've got to wean him away from Mirella . . .'

She knew as well as he did that this conversation was a blind, an excuse to communicate, to argue, to drop the posture of politeness they both used as a shield. But she ranted on, faltering only as León's unwavering gaze melted from pretend-hostility to barely concealed longing.

'Don't look at me like that,' she muttered crossly.

'You're one to talk. You never miss a chance to look at *me* like that, when you think nobody's watching. You've been leading me on for months.'

Celia flushed, but she didn't have the gall to deny it. He made it sound deliberate, but it wasn't. Quite the reverse.

'What am I supposed to do now?' continued León. 'Pounce on you so you can slap my face?'

'Stop baiting me. If you think I've been leading you on, I apologise. That wasn't my intention. You know perfectly well that I would never do anything to hurt Raúl, or Lily.'

'Of course not. Much safer to settle for hurting me instead. Not to mention yourself.'

'Please, León. Don't make this harder for both of us. Think how guilty we'd feel if . . .' She tailed off.

'Raúl's set us both up nicely, hasn't he? Talk about a poisoned chalice.'

'You're misjudging him,' said Celia. 'At the beginning, I thought, like you did, that he was just pretending to trust us, that he was waiting for a chance to catch us out. But he's changed. He's genuinely not jealous or suspicious any more. In fact, he's so busy these days, he barely notices I'm there.'

She bit her lip, regretting the admission. With every day that passed, Raúl became more independent of her, more wrapped up in his work. She ought to have been glad that his crushing, possessive need of her had abated. But Raúl's needs had become a welcome refuge from her own, which were now crowding in to fill the void.

So she was feeling neglected, thought León, with some satisfaction. Or perhaps Raúl's increasingly hard-line politics were driving a wedge between them; Celia might play the dutiful party wife in public, but León knew that she was bitterly opposed, as he was, to the indefinite postponements of elections, the growing numbers of political prisoners, and the muzzling of the press.

Either way, he ought to take advantage of the situation. Restless wives had always been his speciality, after all. Keeping up this charade was becoming intolerable, and what Lily and Raúl didn't know couldn't possibly hurt them. There were a dozen good reasons why he should revert to type and seduce his brother's wife. And one very good reason not to. The fear of losing her altogether.

Mercifully Lily came tripping into the room at that moment, all sunny smiles. Celia, cheeks still burning, got up to embrace her friend. Guilt. It had become a kind of vice in itself.

'Hi, Celia. Hi, honey. What are you doing home early?'

'Working. I was just keeping Celia company until you got home.' He kissed her absently. 'I'll leave you two to talk, then.' He left the room just as the maid arrived with a tray of coffee.

'How do I look?' demanded Lily. She pirouetted to show off her latest outfit – a battledress green shirt and a workmanlike pair of dungarees.

'Like a true heroine of the revolution,' smiled Celia.

'Even your brother was impressed,' said Lily. She adopted Eduardo's grave demeanour and precise, donnish diction. ' "I was wrong about you, Lily. I thought you were trivial and empty-headed. I beg your pardon." '

'Don't,' protested Celia, spluttering on her coffee. 'You'll make me choke.'

'León disagreed, of course,' continued Lily. ' "She'll get bored with it," ' she drawled, through a cloud of imaginary cigar smoke. ' "I give it six weeks at most." '

Both women erupted into schoolgirl giggles. No one was safe from Lily's powers of mimicry – her impersonation of Emilia was a *tour de force*, almost as inspired as the one she did of Fidel himself (good enough, in León's view, to get her ten years in the slammer).

'Seriously, though,' said Lily. 'You were right. I quite enjoyed myself. I'm fed up with everyone thinking I'm all boobs and no brains.'

It was not social conscience that motivated her but a frustrated desire to perform. The undivided attention of ten rapt women, all pathetically eager to learn, provided her flagging ego with a much-needed boost. Unlike a cabaret audience, they didn't chatter or fidget, and hung intently on her every word. It was a new and stimulating role in her repertoire, and one which she played, as always, to the hilt. Less admissibly, it fulfilled a secret need to copy Celia, now a fourth-grade teacher in one of the many newly established schools.

'Actually,' went on Lily, 'I think Eduardo's rather sweet. Does he realise how sinfully good-looking he is? I tried flirting with him once, just to annoy León, and it was a total dead loss. I envy Mirella, having such a faithful husband. I dread to think what León gets up to behind my back. At least you don't have to worry about that kind of thing with Raúl.'

'No,' agreed Celia. Whenever León's name came up, she affected a vague lack of interest; any minute now, thought Lily, she would steer the conversation on to some other topic. And for once she wasn't going to let her. She had noticed Celia's heightened colour, noticed the way León looked at her, the way she looked at León. All this pussy-footing around had gone on long enough; it was time to talk turkey.

'Mind you, I've never caught him out,' she went on. 'I guess I don't want to. And even if I did . . . I would never leave him.'

She knew now that it had been a mistake to put Celia out of bounds, to feed León's obsession. 'You don't have to worry,' he told Lily coolly. 'I've no intention of having a fling with Celia. I've got too much to lose.' Lily had assumed – quite incorrectly – that 'too much' meant

Buenaventura, a side-swipe at her ill-considered threat to decamp with Leonardo.

'Just like you'd never leave Raúl,' she added pointedly, 'what with him being in a wheelchair and all.'

'No,' agreed Celia, wondering uneasily what this was leading up to.

'You know, I started off all ready to hate you,' said Lily. 'I was jealous, you see. But then I figured if we got on, it would annoy the hell out of León.'

'And does it?'

'It drives him crazy. He thinks we spend all our time talking about him. Even though he's the one thing we never discuss. That's how I know. That you still care about him, I mean. Otherwise, you wouldn't change the subject every time I mention him.'

Celia steeled herself not to change the subject.

'Then why are you mentioning him now?' Oh, God. Did she think they had been up to something? Thank God they hadn't. Celia braced herself for an accusation.

'I just wish you two would have an affair and get it over with,' said Lily. 'It's the only way he's ever going to get you out of his system.'

Her candour quite took Celia's breath away. Clever girl, she thought. Lily might be lacking in intellect but her instincts were spot on. Reality was a great antidote to remembrance. It wasn't just guilt and loyalty that held them both back. It wasn't so much will power or moral fibre as a mixture of bloody-mindedness and cowardice and romanticism. Better to dream than be disappointed. And yet part of her wanted to be free of fantasy, with all the futile fervour of a drug addict.

'Don't be offended,' added Lily. 'I just thought it was best to get it all out in the open.'

'I'm not offended. I admire your honesty. I'd like to get him out of my system as well. That is—' Much to her annoyance, she found herself blushing again.

'It's OK. Whatever happens, I don't want to know. Like I said, I'm not going to leave him and you're not going to leave Raúl. Just as long as we're in agreement about that.'

Celia looked at her with new respect.

'You really love him, don't you?'

'You can count on it,' said Lily.

Frank was spending more and more time with Leonardo, much to Mirella's annoyance.

'I want you to teach him to laugh,' Lily had told him. 'I don't think Mirella knows how.' A job that Lily could have done better than anyone. But whenever Frank suggested that she get more involved, she would go all coy and moody and say infuriating, heart-rending things like, 'Leonardo doesn't like me, he never has. Smart kid, huh?'

Making him laugh was hard going. The boy was painfully withdrawn – a condition which Mirella encouraged – and prone to start grizzling at the slightest thing; he was exactly as Frank imagined Lily at that age, capricious, sullen, full of unspoken fears. That he didn't give affection readily, except in exchange for candy, reinforced the comparison. Every unsolicited smile was a major triumph.

With his role as Lily's business manager on hold – her singing engagements were now confined to weekends – Frank was working the remaining nights as a hospital porter, a job fixed up through a contact of Eduardo's which left his daytimes free. With Lily's connivance he would turn up on Mirella, uninvited, and gatecrash whatever activities she had planned. But on three afternoons a week, regular as clockwork, she went off to meet some girlfriend or other downtown, always taking Leonardo with her and making it very clear that Frank was not invited. It was on one of those afternoons, in late 1959, that he went to see his new doctor.

The old one, like so many of his profession, had recently left for the USA, along with most of his fee-paying patients. Lily, who was always fussing about Frank's ulcer, lost no time in fixing him up with a Dr Moreno.

'Celia recommended him,' she said. 'He looks after her husband. Apparently he was slung in gaol by Batista for treating rebels. If you mention Raúl's name you'll get VIP treatment.'

The surgery turned out to be in a run-down quarter of Old Havana, as befitted its revolutionary credentials. Several patients were waiting to be seen. One of them was Harry Jordan.

The only spare seat was the one next to him. Frank took it, neither man acknowledging the other. Harry fell to examination of the ceiling, Frank to that of the floor, his mind buzzing, the pain in his gut temporarily forgotten. He couldn't believe that Harry, who regarded all Cubans as a lower form of life, would visit a non-American doctor in anything other than the direst emergency – unless his business here was far from medical.

Frank cast his eye around the room, wondering who his contact might be. There were a couple of worn-out mothers with young children, a very pregnant black woman, and an elderly, wheezing mulatto, none of whom looked likely candidates for dropping a newspaper or leaving behind a briefcase or whatever else had been arranged. Perhaps he was waiting for someone else to arrive . . .

He looked up as the surgery door swung open; the nurse held it wide as a broad-shouldered man in a wheelchair propelled himself towards the exit. Frank had never met León's brother in the flesh, but he recognised him from the newspaper photographs; there was no mistaking the jagged scar that ran down one side of his face, half obscured by the obligatory veteran's beard. Harry, good citizen that he was, jumped to his feet to assist him, running ahead to open the two sets of double doors which led into the street.

Frank's curiosity got the better of him. He followed, just in time to see the second set of doors swing shut and Harry stuffing an envelope into his inside pocket as he walked back towards the surgery. Frank folded his arms and whistled.

'You've caught a big one there,' he said quietly.

'What are you doing here?' hissed Harry, unamused.

'Seeing the doctor. Same as you. Do you come here often?'

'Damn you, Frank. You've just gone and turned yourself into a security risk.'

'Me? You can't be serious.'

'I'm deadly serious. You're bosom pals with his brother. And even if you weren't . . . why the hell couldn't you just have sat there and played it dumb?'

'Old habits die hard, I guess. Relax, you can trust me. You even offered me a job a couple of years back, remember?'

'Too bad you didn't take it. I'm sorry, Frank, I can't ignore this. You haven't been vetted, and a leak is a leak.'

'Does that mean I'm going to get run over? Or fall out of the window? Or cop a stray bullet?'

It was supposed to be a joke. But Harry Jordan didn't laugh. Perhaps it wasn't that funny.

Three bombs had gone off in Havana in the last week. It was like old times, thought León. Only the perspective had changed. The new generation of saboteurs were no longer hailed as freedom-fighters but denounced as counter-revolutionaries – a new and proliferating breed of public enemy that lurked around every corner. Several likely culprits had been rounded up within hours of the latest blast, and were now awaiting trial, or what passed for a trial. León knew he hadn't a hope of getting them off.

Following the suspension of habeas corpus, police were now empowered to detain suspects indefinitely. Even high-ranking officials were not able to escape the purge. The former commander of the troops in Camagüey – a veteran of the Sierra – was currently rotting in gaol, branded a traitor for daring to oppose the Communist takeover of the army. President Urrutia himself had been forced to resign, falsely accused of plotting against the state, proving that no lesser mortal was safe from censure.

So what chance did these three youths have? Far from

being former Batista supporters, the wisest of whom were now ardent Fidel fans, they were long-standing members of the 26 July movement who felt, like Eduardo, that their cause had been betrayed. They had risked their lives for democracy, they said, only to find themselves ruled by a virtual dictator who had outlawed all opposition.

It was easier, and safer, to defect than dissent. Every plane to Miami took off packed with middle-class Cubans, including many former supporters of Castro, leaving behind it an ever-growing shortage of doctors, engineers, scientists, managers and technicians. Cuba was getting poorer every day.

But the poor adored Fidel, as well they might. Thanks to the revolution they enjoyed reduced rents and paid less for power and public transport. New labour laws protected jobs and incomes. Soon there would be free medical treatment and education. No wonder they turned out in their hundreds of thousands to applaud their hero's every speech. No wonder they were so keen to denounce anyone who sought to deprive them of the fruits of victory. Public vigilance – a witch hunt by any other name – was approaching fever pitch. One careless remark could cost a man his liberty or his life.

For this reason León dinned it into Lily night and day that she must button that big mouth of hers and never, ever say anything against the revolution to anybody, anywhere, at any time.

'You do,' pointed out Lily. 'So does Celia, she and Raúl argue all the time. So does Eduardo. Eduardo can't stand the Communists. He says that Fidel has sold out. He says—'

'Never mind what Eduardo says. That's his look-out. And Celia is Raúl's responsibility. As for me, I'm extremely careful what I say outside these four walls.'

Which he was. Even in court, he chose his words with care, avoiding any remark which could be quoted out of context against him. He had seen the inside of gaols too often to let his tongue run away with him. If he occasionally managed to get cases dismissed, or secure an acquittal, it was only because the courts couldn't convict everyone without losing all credibility, and he felt no self-congratulation at pissing a drop of sanity into an ocean of hysteria.

After another long, dispiriting day in court, he arrived at his evening surgery half an hour late to find the usual assortment of worried faces awaiting him. The most worried of them all was Celia's.

Alarmed, he ushered her into his office, wondering what crisis had brought her here.

'What is it? Is it Lily?'

'Indirectly. She's hysterical. Frank's been arrested. The police picked him up on the way home from the doctor's, this afternoon.'

'What's he supposed to have done?'

'Did you know he was with the CIA?'

'Frank? That's absurd.'

Or was it? he wondered. Frank had always been cagey about his past, perhaps with good reason.

'Absurd or not, someone has denounced him. He's being held in custody till tomorrow morning. Then they're putting him on the first plane out, as an undesirable alien. Lily wants you to apply to have the deportation order revoked.'

'Yes,' said León, automatically. 'Yes, of course. I'll get on to it right away.'

'No, you won't!' She caught hold of his arm. 'Why do you think I came here, instead of her? Do you want to put yourself in danger? With you being such a close friend of his, you're already under suspicion. And in any case, you won't be able to help him, whether or not he's guilty.'

Her fear for him was like a balm, one he couldn't resist rubbing in.

'As you say, he's a friend, and we don't have any proof that he's a spy. Innocent people are being accused every day. I can't just stand by and do nothing.'

'If he's your friend, then he wouldn't want you taking any risks on his behalf. Your first duty is to Lily. She loves you, in case you didn't realise. She'd be devastated if anything happened to you.'

Her eyes were bright, pleading, naked. León held on to her gaze, held on to the moment, savouring it, squeezing it dry.

'What about you? Would you be devastated too? Or would you be . . . relieved?'

'Don't do this to me, León. Every day Raúl keeps telling me how many enemies you're making. If he hadn't vouched for you, if you weren't his brother, God knows what would have happened to you already.'

'I don't want any favours from Raúl. I'm not in a position to return them.'

'Stop being so pig-headed! Whether or not Frank's an agent, everyone knows that the Americans are planning to invade us, that they have agents everywhere, observing and reporting back and trying to stir up trouble . . .'

'So do the KGB.'

'I didn't come here to argue politics with you. I have enough of that at home. Promise me you won't get involved. You've got to tell Lily that there's nothing you can do. Don't get yourself arrested and force me to plead with Raúl to save your life . . .'

'What would you do to convince me that it was worth saving?' He put his arms around her and held her close, luxuriating in the perfect alignment of two interlocking halves, reminding her of how things were, how they would always be, because they were apart, not together. If they had been together from the start, he would have lost her by now, through sheer carelessness and complacency. This way, Raúl or no Raúl, she would always belong to him. There was a perverse satisfaction in it.

'Please, León,' she murmured, with false diffidence, not even attempting to pull away. He took her face between his hands and kissed her, deliberately holding back, torturing himself as the price of torturing her. She didn't resist, which was a response in itself. She had been expecting this. She had been expecting more.

'Why did you really come here, Celia?'

Her silence was answer enough. Her eyes brimmed over and he caught two escaping tears with the tip of his tongue, savouring them, remembering the sweet, salty taste of her sweat mingled with the smell of her desire. He could almost smell it now, underlying her perfume, and for a moment he was tempted to seize his chance, here, now and on her terms. This way she could delude herself about her motives. This way she could have her cake and eat it too – for a while. And then afterwards she would blame him, blame herself, refuel the reservoirs of her resolve with self-indulgent guilt. No. This was her way of trying to end it.

'I'm not falling for it, Celia,' he said softly, releasing her. 'Don't ever try to tempt me again unless you've made up your mind to leave him.'

She went very red.

'That's not fair. I wouldn't ask you to leave Lily for me.'

'Which proves my point. I'm not interested in something secret and sordid, some hole-in-the-corner affair you can be ashamed of. It's got to be all or nothing. I'd rather do without than make do.'

She turned her back on him, rigid with rejection.

'I wish I'd never come here. Go to hell.'

'Failing hell, which prison is he in?'

'La Cabaña,' said Celia stiffly. 'But he's not allowed any visitors. Lily and I have already been refused.'

'They can't refuse me. I'm his lawyer. Will you stay with her, till I get home?'

'Of course.' She was formal, flustered, furious. 'Be careful. For Lily's sake, if not for mine.'

'For my own,' he said, showing her out. 'Raúl's the hero, not me. For my own.'

Frank knew he was being let off lightly, for old time's sake. It was his own stupid fault for not playing possum, not that Harry would have taken any chances, even if he had. Unlike Frank, he had always been careful to cover his own back.

Raúl Soler. One of Fidel's blue-eyed boys, due, it was rumoured, for a big promotion. Zealous exponent of land reform, passionate anti-Yanqui, a political chameleon who had timed his progression from moderate to extremist with perfect precision, survived the last few months of divide-and-rule with infinite cunning and skill. A valuable property, whose cover must be protected at all costs.

Frank knew that if he breathed a word of this to anyone, both he and that someone would be dead. And even if he didn't breathe a word, anyone he spoke to would be tainted with his knowledge. For this reason, he made it clear to his warders that he didn't want to see anyone, that any visitors, including his attorney, were to be sent away.

It broke his heart not to say goodbye to Lily. He would probably never see her again, or the kid either. He would never be allowed back in, and if Cuba went the way of other Communist countries, they might well not be allowed out.

He should have accepted Harry's offer of a job, back in 'fifty-seven. Then at least he would be guilty as charged. Seeing the stark terror on the faces of his cellmates, he began to wish he was.

Eduardo was late coming to bed again. As usual, he would be 'too tired' to make love. Mirella was getting desperate. She was already two months' pregnant, and if it didn't happen soon, he would know for sure that the baby wasn't his. The baby might be black, of course, like Lázaro, but that sometimes happened when a mulatta married a white man. The important thing was to stay married. If Eduardo divorced her she wouldn't be allowed to live here any more, she would have to leave Leonardo. And even with the solace of a child of her own, she couldn't bring herself to desert him now. What would become of him, without his Mimi to protect him?

Whereas Gabriel was bold, adventurous, fearless, Leonardo was timid, vulnerable, clinging, more lovable in every way. While Celia allowed Gabriel to fall over and hurt himself, Mirella anticipated Leonardo's every stumble, never allowed him to take the slightest risk. No wonder Celia was always meddling.

'He's much too dependent,' Mirella had overheard her telling Lily. 'Mirella means well, but she's holding him back. In another six months, you can send him to a nursery where he'll mix with other children. As it is, he bursts into tears if Gabriel so much as looks at him. It isn't healthy . . .'

At a nursery, he would be bullied to death by other rough, rowdy children like his cousin. They would make his little life a misery. What right did Lily or Celia have to plot behind her back? How could she leave Leonardo defenceless against two selfish, heartless women who cared nothing for him?

Two a.m. She could still hear Lily sobbing her heart out, while León and Eduardo tried in vain to comfort her. Mirella had never understood what Lily saw in Frank. He was old and sick and rather seedy. Not handsome and refined like Eduardo, not young and strong like Lázaro. Mirella had bitterly resented his habit of turning up, uninvited, and upsetting the child's routine. Thank God he was out of the way for good.

It was another half-hour before Eduardo finally came to bed.

'Poor Lily,' he said, yawning. 'She's in a hell of a state. Frank's obviously guilty, he refused even to speak to León, I suppose he was too embarrassed. I never would have believed it of him. God knows I loathe the bloody Communists, but not enough to sell out to the Yanquis. I don't understand how León can still think of him as a friend . . .'

Mirella sighed. At one time she had hung on Eduardo's every word, seen him as a bottomless well of wisdom. But now she wanted him to stop talking, talking, and start paying her some attention for a change.

Boldly, she put her hand inside his pyjamas, seeking the response she got instantly from Lázaro. Eduardo picked up her hand and kissed it.

'I'm very tired, sweetheart,' he said.

'You're always tired.'

'I'm trying to do two years' work in one. I want to qualify as soon as possible. I was up at five this morning, and now it's nearly three.'

'Please, Eduardo. I want you so much. Don't you want me?'

'Of course I do. But not right now. Lie down and we'll have a nice cuddle before we go to sleep.'

'I don't want a cuddle. I want to make love.'

'For God's sake, Mirella, keep your voice down.'

'It's been months now. You don't care for me at all.'

'Of course I care for you. I thought we agreed that love wasn't just about sex?'

Undeterred, Mirella burrowed under the bedclothes and took him in her mouth, doggedly working away at him, not caring if he was shocked or not, wanting only for him to do it once, just once, and then she would leave him alone. Just once, and he would never be sure that the child wasn't his . . .

'Stop it.' He rolled away from her.

'What's wrong?'

'Everything. Stop acting cheap, I don't like it.'

'What kind of man are you? What kind of man ignores his wife night after night and calls her cheap if she tries to show her love? A real man would want me every night. A real man would—'

'Shut up!'

'Are you sick? If you're sick, you should see a doctor.'

'I'm not sick. There's nothing wrong with me!'

'There's nothing wrong with me either! I never had any trouble like this with Silvio!'

'Be quiet! Do you want León and Lily to hear?'

Not for the first time, he wished that she was still mute; her voice sounded hideously shrill. Shrill enough to wake Leonardo, who began calling for his Mimi, not his mamá, not that he appreciated the difference. Mirella leapt out of bed and went next door to see to him.

Eduardo buried his head beneath the pillow, blessing

this intervention, weak with the aftermath of panic. Fear of failure was a vicious circle. The more often he failed, the worse it would get, couldn't she understand that? And now she had given voice to his deepest fear, the fear that he wasn't a real man. Because of what had happened with Raúl, what had happened on the battlefield, but most of all because of what was happening with his wife. He had looked to her to be his salvation, and instead she had become a threat, an infinitely worse threat than Raúl had ever been.

Physician, heal thyself. He had tried to. But the medicine had only made him worse. He had thought her modest, intelligent, sensitive but in fact she was rather a coarse, stupid girl, of limited understanding, whose commitment to the struggle had been personal, not political, whose nobility and dignity had been nothing more than the bovine stoicism of the poor and oppressed. He had fallen in love with a dream.

In more ways than one. Everything was turning to shit, everything. Where was the democracy Castro had promised, so eloquently, in the mountains? Even Raúl had sold his soul, knuckling under to the party line for the sake of power and privilege. And Frank, before whom he had spoken without reserve, had turned out to be a spy. Suddenly nothing was what it seemed. Least of all himself.

'So what do you want to do?' asked León gently.

Lily twisted a sodden handkerchief and re-read Frank's letter for the umpteenth time. It had arrived in a badly sealed envelope, evidence of a clumsy censor. Not that it contained anything of official interest. Just a simple invitation for Lily to join him. He had a job in a boatyard in Miami, and an old friend had given him a loan. He was already scouting round various night spots. He attached a list of songs, asking her to put them on tape and send them to him.

'You want me to go, don't you?'

'This is about what you want, Lily. You have to choose

between us now. They're never going to let Frank back into Cuba.'

More stormy sobs. Lily wept often, but the tears were seldom real. Real tears, like these, were trapped behind some internal dam, and on the rare occasions they burst through it, the resulting flood was awesome to behold. Real tears washed away all her artifice, stripping her emotions to the bone.

'I never wanted to choose between you. It was perfect the way it was. Even though you're a rotten lousy husband and I know very well that you don't care for me at all. But if I've got to choose, I'm choosing you. Whether you damn well like it or not.'

She flung her arms around him fiercely. He felt absurdly touched.

'You're the one who may not like it,' said León. 'I want you to know exactly what staying here involves.'

'Save your breath. I've made up my mind.'

'Let me finish. The receipts from the estate are less than a tenth of what they were. I can't raise any cash against the bonds, because everyone knows they're worthless, and I can't sell off any capital, under the terms of my father's will, not that anyone would be fool enough to buy it. By this time next year the mill itself may be nationalised. Life here is going to get tougher and tougher. We're going to end up poor . . .'

He broke off as Mirella came in from her afternoon walk, with Leonardo toddling alongside. Following her usual practice, she ignored both Lily and León and shepherded her charge into the nursery. León could hear him bleating querulously, 'Mimi! Mimi!'

'We also have to think of Leonardo,' he said heavily. 'The way things are going, I don't think it's fair to keep him here. Frank's devoted to him, you know that. He would jump at the chance to have him. I've already lodged enough money in a US bank to raise and educate him. Soon his inheritance won't be worth having, and besides, I don't want him to grow up parroting slogans . . .'

Lily listened with growing unease. She knew that León was right; Leonardo would be much better off in the States. But would he understand that she had given him up for his own good? No, of course he wouldn't, no more than she had done herself when Mom had dumped her onto Grandma. He would assume that she just wanted to get rid of him.

He had always made her feel helpless and stupid and inadequate. She had even made a botch of giving birth. No wonder he had been so angry the very first time she saw him. And he had stayed angry ever since. A mother was supposed to understand her baby's cries and Lily was no exception. Right from day one he had told her, in a language that required no translation, that she didn't make the grade. And now she never would. And once Leonardo was gone León would have no reason to stay with her, she would have nothing to bargain with any more . . .

'We have to think ahead,' continued León. 'As yet, there's no law against leaving the country. That could change.'

'Can't we go with him together?' ventured Lily, knowing what the answer would be. León would never leave Cuba all the while Celia was here.

'No. What I'm doing may not be worth much, but it's better than nothing. I've spent most of my life avoiding responsibility and taking the soft option. I've got to stay, for my own self-respect, even if it's a futile gesture. But it's not fair to force that decision on you, or on a child. Especially one that's not mine. You could fly out with him . . .'

'No! I won't go! Especially if you're in danger!'

'Of course I'm not in danger. If they were going to pick me up on account of Frank, they'd have done so by now.'

'You can bet your life they would have done, if it hadn't been for Raúl. Celia reckons he pulled some strings so they'd lay off you.'

He would do, thought León wryly, remembering the

time his father had threatened to beat him and an outraged Raúl had intervened and been thrashed black and blue in his stead. Afterwards he had dragged León off to the stables and administered the hiding himself, saying that he bloody well deserved it, spoilt little snot that he was. At the time it had seemed illogical.

'You could fly out with Leonardo,' repeated León patiently, 'and come back a few days later. Take Mirella with you, if you like. Perhaps she could stay out there till Frank finds another nanny. I'll talk to Eduardo, I'm sure he wouldn't object.'

Lily battled with herself, unsure if she would ever find the strength to come back again. Frank would be so persuasive. He would promise her bright lights and, unlike León, he really and truly loved her. But having failed so dismally as a mother, she couldn't bear to fail as a wife as well, couldn't bear for Celia to think she had run out on León the minute the going got tough, or for León to think she cared more for her career than for him, or for either of them to think she was scared of those bully-boy Commies. For once in her life she would do something difficult, prove that she wasn't as selfish and shallow as she seemed. Perhaps Leonardo would love her more, not seeing her, the way she had loved her absent father. He would keep her picture by his bed, admire her as someone mysterious and glamorous, forget what a useless mother she had been . . .

'Mirella can take him on her own,' she said firmly. 'We can put her on the plane, Frank can meet her at the airport. At least this way he'll have someone to care for,' she added, struggling against another wave of terrifying emotion. 'I can't bear to think of Frank all alone.'

It was the first time León had seen her decisive, rather than demanding. He was reminded of Frank saying, 'It's pathetic, how much she wants you to be proud of her,' and now, unexpectedly, he was. The little girl was finally growing up. Or perhaps, because they had grown up together, he hadn't noticed the difference until now.

'I'll arrange passports and visas, then,' he said. 'If we run into any bureaucratic problems, no doubt my brother will be delighted to use his influence.'

Worthless or not, Buenaventura – or what was left of it – would soon be his at last. León wished him all the joy of it.

A few days later, Lázaro turned up at León's office. It was the first time they had met since their chance encounter, almost a year before.

'What can I do for you?' said León, seeing his glum expression. 'Are you in trouble?'

'Some guy recognised me, from my army days,' said Lázaro, avoiding his eye. 'Claims I beat up his sister. I never laid a hand on a woman in my life. But you know how it is. No one's going to believe me. And once it comes out who I am, most likely I'll get nailed for shooting your brother. I know a guy with a boat who can take me to Miami. But he wants money. You promised you'd help me if ever I was in a jam.'

'How much do you need?'

León opened the safe and handed over double the amount he asked for, expecting to have to press him to take it. But he didn't protest, pocketing the cash without a word.

'Tell the US immigration people you're a wanted anti-Castro activist,' said León, repeating his standard advice to fugitives. 'Do you want to hide out here in the meantime?'

'No need. The boat leaves tonight. At least from tomorrow I won't have to pretend that I support the stinking revolution. Fidel this and Fidel that. It makes me want to vomit.'

'I'm sorry this had to happen, Lázaro. Good luck.'

'Same to you. They'll be gunning for you next, like as not.'

Lázaro left quickly, glad to have got that over with. He didn't like having to lie to someone's face, but there had been no other way to get hold of the money he needed.

Mirella was used to living in comfort and he wanted to give their child a good start in life. Otherwise he would never have stooped to asking for help.

At last his patience had paid off. Soon he wouldn't have to share her with her husband, wouldn't have to share her with Leonardo. Soon he would have her all to himself.

Raúl opened a bottle of champagne and filled Celia's glass.

'A toast. To the new mistress of Buenaventura.'

Celia ignored the libation.

'I thought wealth was an embarrassment to a man in your position?'

'Be assured, I won't be wealthy for long. Not if my latest proposals are accepted.'

Buenaventura would soon be state property. Raúl's last act, before taking up his new post, was to submit his recommendation for the seizure of all private companies, including those owned by the US. The suggestion was slightly premature, but he had little doubt that it would end up being accepted, as every day government policy shifted further to the left. There was no doubt about the way the wind was blowing, and Raúl took care to have the wind behind him.

His promotion to a senior security post had fallen into his lap. Every day, as more moderates fell by the wayside, vacancies opened up for loyal revolutionaries like himself. Fidel was careful not to empower old-guard party members who might seek to overthrow him; recent converts like Raúl, moulded by himself and his henchmen, stood the best chance of success.

His task was to hunt down and weed out any potential enemies of the regime and crush the underground resistance movement; a vast secret police force and an army of informers would be at his disposal. Raúl was looking forward to his new job, which would give him unprecedented access to confidential information. With a bit of discreet sabotage he should be able to save a few lives, an objective that was quite outside his brief – the Agency was only interested in pulling out people who were actually working for them. Or people who had worked for them in the past, like Frank Maguire.

Harry's request had been easy to meet. One telephone call was all it had taken to have his old crony deported. A whisper was enough these days to have a man condemned, and Raúl's whispers travelled further and faster than most.

Oh, yes, he had fooled Fidel, almost as well as Fidel had fooled the people. It sickened Raúl to see his predictions coming true, as Cuba slid inexorably towards full-blown Communism. A slide he was ever more determined to subvert, whatever the cost to himself. He wanted Gabriel to grow up free to choose his own beliefs, his own friends, his own enemies. One day, perhaps, he would find out that his father had been a hero.

In the meantime, it was often hard to keep up the pretence, especially in the face of Celia's unabashed opposition. She wasn't taken in by any of the propaganda, thank God; he couldn't have borne it if she had turned out to be just another human sheep, like the infinitely gullible masses. But confiding in her remained out of the question, not only because of the need for watertight security but because she would only worry herself sick on his behalf, whether or not she approved of what he was doing. León caused her quite enough anxiety already.

An anxiety which Raúl could not help but share. His brother's lethally efficient defence of 'enemies of the people' was likely to prove the death of him one day. Keeping him out of trouble was becoming a major headache.

'Is it true that you've been protecting me?' León had challenged him. 'Don't stick your neck out on my account. If you're afraid that I'll spill the beans on your murky past—'

'If I had thought for one minute that you would do that, I could have engineered an unfortunate accident long ago. You're useful to me, brother. If anything ever happens to me, I look to you to take care of Celia and Gabriel. A man in my position has many enemies. Why should he destroy his only friend?'

He had devalued the words with his usual sardonic smile, but he had meant them none the less. Jealousy had mellowed and ripened into something infinitely more complex and satisfying. He almost relished the knowledge that his wife was in love with his alter ego, the self he should have been, the rival he had felt compelled to beat, over and over again, the only man he could bear to lose her to . . . one day. A day that would arrive with savage suddenness if he was ever exposed. A day which he was preparing for, slowly and painfully, by loosening Celia's bonds, and his own.

'León and Lily are going to have trouble managing,' continued Celia. 'He doesn't charge his clients, and even if he did, they couldn't pay. I think we should split the remaining revenues down the middle.'

'What a good idea.'

'You agree?'

'Of course. Now will you raise your glass?'

Celia did so, rather taken aback by Raúl's bland acceptance of her proposal. She would almost have preferred him to argue.

'He won't accept it,' she commented. 'But he can't stop me giving the money to Lily.'

'Handle it however you think best,' said Raúl, looking at his watch. 'I must go. I'm already late for a meeting.'

'But you've only just got home!'

'I'm sorry, my love. Duty calls.' He gave her a brisk peck on the cheek, his mind already far away. 'Gabriel! Say goodnight to Papá.'

Gabriel was engrossed in his new toy rifle, bought by Raúl in defiance of Celia's wishes. He looked up and aimed it at Raúl expectantly.

'Bang, bang, you're dead!'

Raúl slumped forward obligingly, provoking a chortle of glee.

'That's my boy,' he said.

*

Frank watched the planeload of passengers arrive, elbowing his way forward as he caught sight of Mirella and Leonardo.

'Hi there, little fella,' he said, giving him a big hug. Mirella was unsmiling as always, but Leonardo favoured him with an uncertain grin, distracted by the bunch of brightly coloured balloons in Frank's hand. 'Did you have a good trip?' he asked, picking up Mirella's suitcases.

'I have never flown before,' said Mirella peevishly. 'I still feel sick. And Leonardo is very tired.'

'You can have a lie down, soon as we get home. I've got the car outside.'

Just as well Mirella was married, he thought. Otherwise he would have felt duty bound to offer her the job of nanny. Perish the thought. He had spent the last week in a frenzy of activity, moving from his cheap downtown hotel to a house in Coral Gables and interviewing prospective live-in child-minders. The woman he had in mind was a destitute Cuban widow who had fled in the wake of her soldier husband's arrest and execution, and whose own child would provide much-needed company for Leonardo.

'How's Lily?'

'All right.'

'She wasn't . . . upset?' León's cable had given nothing away.

'No. She cares nothing for Leonardo.'

That wasn't what Frank had meant, but never mind. He had kept hoping, right up to the last minute, that she might change her mind and come too. But at least he had his son.

He was not yet at ease in his neat new suburban milieu; it would take time to get used to having a proper home. In a determined attempt at respectability, he had bought himself a suit and jacked in the job at the boatyard. He didn't want Leonardo thinking his father was a bum. He had received an anonymous envelope (from Harry) containing a thousand dollars in cash, which, added to the money in Lily's bank account, would help keep the wolf from the door. But sooner or later he would have to find a proper job, which wouldn't be easy. Teaching apart, which he hadn't done in years, there was only one kind of job he was trained to do.

Mirella insisted on stopping off at the store to buy groceries, saying that she would cook their evening meal herself; Leonardo had never been in a restaurant and had a delicate stomach. Frank was happy to let her get on with it while he gave the child a piggy-back tour of the house and introduced him to a treasure-trove of welcome-home toys.

After giving Leonardo a simple supper of scrambled eggs and putting him to bed, Mirella served up a heavily spiced *picadillo* for Frank, a traditional Cuban dish of minced beef. Anxious not to offend her, he cleared his plate, even though his ulcer was playing up and hot peppers were the last thing he should have been eating. Afterwards he felt incredibly sleepy and dozed off in his chair.

The next thing he knew it was morning. He woke with a parched mouth and a splitting headache, which he took at first for a hangover, until he remembered that he was on the wagon. He stood up unsteadily and rubbed his eyes to clear his vision; it was already nine o'clock. He had been asleep for sixteen solid hours.

'Mirella?' he called, stumbling into the hall. 'Leonardo?' No answer. Both beds were made and the stroller was gone, she must have taken him for a walk . . .

His brain was still too fogged to think straight. He felt drunk, drugged. It took a cup of very strong coffee before the mists began to clear, before it occurred to him to take another look.

There was no sign of Mirella's luggage and all Leonardo's clothes had vanished from the closet. Frank went to the bathroom and vomited blood. Then he telephoned the police.

'Thank you for coming straight over,' said León, as Celia emerged from the bedroom and shut the door quietly behind her. 'How is she?' He had never seen Lily in such a state.

'The sedatives seem to have taken effect,' said Celia. 'With luck she'll sleep for a bit. Where's Eduardo?'

'He's moved all his stuff out, gone to stay with some student friend. Says he can't live here any longer. He seems to think that it's all his fault. Apparently Mirella wanted a child and he told her she would have to wait until he qualified. He reckons that's why she resorted to stealing one.'

'I knew it,' muttered Celia. 'She was always totally obsessed with babies. Oh, God. I should have seen this coming. I don't think Lily will ever get over it. She blames herself, of course.'

'I would never have expected her to take it so hard.'

'Then you don't know her very well. It was difficult enough for her, giving him up, thinking he was going to be with Frank. Just as well she doesn't realise that Mirella's got homicidal tendencies. I suppose we're lucky she made do with drugging Frank rather than shooting him in the back. But *you* knew she was unbalanced,' she added, accusingly. 'You should have known better than to take her on.'

'Unbalanced or not, she married your brother, remember? What was I supposed to do? Turn them both out into the street? I feel bad enough about what happened without you saying I told you so!'

'Ssh! You'll wake her!' And then, bleakly, 'I'm sorry I snapped.' Without thinking, she put her arms around him, sharing his pain. 'I didn't mean to blame you. It's just that I'm so angry. I keep thinking, it could have been Gabriel . . .'

Gabriel. Their son. León tightened his embrace, breathed in the lemony scent of her hair.

'It could have been Gabriel all right. If I had my way, he'd have gone to the States as well. And you with him.'

'Don't ever say that in front of Raúl.' Celia pulled away. 'I said it myself, only yesterday. And then I wished to God I hadn't.'

'You threatened to leave him?'

Celia hesitated. She hadn't meant to mention it, but the last few hours of raw emotion had worn down her reserve.

'It wasn't quite like that. I said that I thought you and Lily were doing the right thing by Leonardo. And of course Raúl disagreed. And then I lost my temper and said that I hated what was happening to Cuba, hated what was happening to him, and that if things got much worse Gabriel and I would catch the next plane to Miami.'

'And what was his reaction to that?'

'He just said, without even raising his voice, that it would be like history repeating itself and not to worry, he wouldn't send any gunmen to track me down. I felt like a perfect bitch.'

Abruptly, she began crying. She turned her back on him, ashamed, not wanting to be comforted.

'Celia . . .'

'It isn't me he'd miss. He doesn't need me any more. It's Gabriel. He adores him. Seeing Lily just now, I knew I could never put Raúl through that. I'd have to stay in Cuba, whatever happened.'

'In Cuba? Or with Raúl?'

She didn't answer for a moment.

'You remember what you said to me once? About not treating me badly enough? Well, Raúl treats me very well these days. He never shouts, he never gets angry, even when I try to provoke him by blaspheming against bloody Fidel. And you know what? I can't bear it!'

León pulled her round to face him and pressed her face into his chest while she wept her heart out. No matter that she was crying for the love, or loss, of Raúl; for the moment it was enough to hold, and hope, and try not to think about his wife, lying there drugged and desolate in the next room.

'Celia . . . I know I must have seemed cold-hearted towards you. But I had to make a choice. That time you came to the office . . .'

'I was the one who was cold-hearted,' she said, shamefacedly. 'You were right, I was trying to manipulate you, the way I did before. I wanted it to become something manageable, something I could control, and devalue, and destroy. Something easy. Or so I thought. You used to be so weak-willed, you see. And now you're . . . strong.' She wiped her eyes. 'And so am I,' she added defiantly. 'Whatever happens between Raúl and me, even if I divorced him, even if he died, I won't let you break Lily's heart. She's lost enough already. You and I are never going to be together, León. We have to accept that. We have to find a way of living with it. Without rancour, without resentment . . . with love.'

It should have been the end and yet it felt like a new beginning, one that was free, at last, of pretence.

'With love,' echoed León softly. 'We'll always be together, Celia. If you can settle for that much, so can I.'

It was like an exchange of vows, binding them closer than ever. The long game of hide and seek was over; they knew exactly where to find each other now. Celia looked at him for a long moment, silently sealing their bargain. Then she said, 'I'd better go. I'll come back to see Lily tomorrow. Call me straight away if she needs me. Be kind to her, won't you?'

He stood at the window and watched her drive away. Then he went into the bedroom, and looked down at Lily's tear-ravaged face, her vivid hair in disarray over the damp pillow. So she had loved Leonardo after all. It had suited him to think her incapable of love, but now it came home to him, forcibly, that Lily loved him too.

Lázaro had no trouble finding work and a place to stay. The Cuban exiles in Miami looked after their own, which was why it seemed safer to stay here, protected by a tight-knit community, than seek refuge further afield among possibly hostile strangers. He got a job driving a delivery truck for a bakery on the Calle Ocho, owned by an ex-Batistiano, and found a room above a *botánica* two blocks away, whose elderly proprietress was deaf and half blind – a great asset in a landlady, given Mirella's terror of being recognised.

The picture in the *Miami Herald* had been a very poor likeness, but even so she refused point blank to set foot outside the door, for fear of running into the police, or

Frank Maguire, who had posted a five-hundred-dollar reward for Leonardo's return. But the trail was getting colder every day. The cops had better things to do than search for a missing child who was probably already out of state.

The kidnap, supposedly a last-minute impulse on Mirella's part, had not been part of their agreed elopement plan. But nothing would induce her to part with the child, making Lázaro an unwilling accomplice to her crime. She had a ready answer to all his objections, leading him to suspect that she had planned this all along. Mulattas often had white children, she said, she would pass him off as the son of a previous marriage. In a year or so she would present herself to the authorities as a newly arrived refugee, giving a false name. Meanwhile she and Leonardo would simply lie low and avoid attracting attention.

Lázaro couldn't help resenting the cuckoo in his nest. But for him they would have nothing to fear, nothing to hide. Every night Mirella would wake up screaming, in the throes of yet another bad dream, and insist on taking Leonardo into their bed. During the day she would hide indoors with the blinds drawn, nursing the sick headaches which blighted her pregnancy.

Lázaro could not persuade her to see a doctor. A doctor might ask to see papers, she said. When the time came, Lázaro could fetch the local midwife. Meanwhile, she felt too ill to make love, or clean the room, or cook. She rarely bothered to get dressed, lying on the couch in her robe all day, too tired to do more than stare at the television with a restless Leonardo on her lap. Lázaro had to do all the shopping, and often the cooking as well, a great affront to his masculinity. A good argument might have cleared the air, but he couldn't bring himself to shout at her in her present feeble state. Once the baby was born, things were bound to improve.

Rather than go home straight from work, he took to visiting a café in Flagler Street which served excellent home-cooked Cuban food, almost as good as Emilia's. There was usually a game of dominoes in progress and the beer was cheap, as were the loose women he used to take the edge off his frustration. Eventually, inevitably, he ran into someone he knew.

'Lázaro González! Put it there, man! Put it there!'

It was his old Sergeant Costa from the garrison at Bayamo, a hard-drinking, thuggish white guy who had never been remotely friendly towards him in the past. But now he greeted him like a brother.

'I've a bone to pick with you,' went on his former comrade, shaking his hand energetically. 'You need to improve your aim. Why couldn't you have killed the bastard and saved Cuba a lot of grief? Still, it was a nice try. How did you find out that he was a stinking rebel?'

'I overheard him talking to his wife,' said Lázaro, thinking quickly. 'I was screwing the housekeeper, see. So I took my chance.'

'Good man. But you were wise to scarper when you did. I reckon the police knew all along what he was and were getting a rake-off to keep their mouths shut. They were always on Buenaventura's payroll.'

'That's what I figured.'

'I went AWOL a few weeks later. Caught a boat out of Santiago, before it was too late, got my wife and kids out of the country. I wanted to live to fight another day. Let me introduce you to a few of my mates . . .'

Lázaro found himself the hero of the hour. Anyone who had taken a shot at Raúl Soler, one of Fidel's most hated henchmen, had struck a blow for freedom.

'The sooner we get him in front of a firing squad the better,' said one man, calling for another pitcher of beer and refilling Lázaro's glass.

'How are we going to do that?' said Lázaro.

'Come to our strategy meeting at my apartment on Friday night, and you'll find out. We need good men like you . . .'

Their plans sounded pretty far-fetched to Lázaro. The idea was to form an exile army, with a view to returning to Cuba and overthrowing Fidel. Lázaro felt bound to put up a show of enthusiasm, even though he had no desire to go back to Cuba. He wanted to build a future here, in America, with Mirella.

But when Friday night came, he got home from work to find Mirella already asleep, with Leonardo occupying his place in the bed beside her. Yet again, there was no supper on the table, just the dirty crockery from breakfast that morning.

Thoroughly disgruntled, he turned on his heel and marched back down the stairs in search of food and beer and company. He might as well go to the meeting as not. At least it was something to do.

Day after day Frank trailed the streets of Miami, showing shopkeepers and passers-by a dog-eared photograph of Mirella and the child. But, as the police kept telling him, they could be anywhere by now; missing persons rarely turned up unless they wanted to be found, and he needn't expect any help from the Cuban expats, who always closed ranks against the Anglo establishment. But Frank remained convinced that Mirella hadn't gone far. She didn't speak a word of English, and would surely have relied on her compatriots to help her find work and shelter.

With this in mind, he got to know every inch of Miami's rapidly expanding Cuban ghetto. He soon learned that asking questions was counter-productive; it just made people wary of him. His best bet was to float around anonymously, posing as a burned-out soak, eavesdropping and watching for all he was worth.

What he learned in the process did nothing to improve his state of mind. Many recent arrivals expressed fears for the safety of the loved ones they had left behind, fuelling Frank's concern for León and Lily. It became clear, from the many heated discussions he overheard, that the talk of a proposed invasion was more than just idle rumour. The various exile factions, united only by their hatred for Fidel, were vociferously eager to overthrow their common enemy. A venture which appeared to have financial backing, albeit unofficial, from the US. Potential recruits had loose tongues, especially when lubricated; some boasted that they had already been vetted, and expected to start training shortly. If Frank had been younger, and able-bodied, he might have been tempted to volunteer himself.

As the weeks dragged by, he began to lose hope. If Mirella was in Miami, she must be living down a well. His funds were running low – he refused to touch Lily's money – and the temptation to blow what remained on a suicidal bender threatened to overwhelm him. But he had to stay alive, just in case. And he had to find something to do, to stay alive . . .

In a last-ditch attempt to stem the tidal wave of despair, he dialled the number on Harry Jordan's phoney business card. That bastard owed him more than a thousand lousy bucks.

Every word spoken in the bars of Miami found its way back to listening ears in Havana. Exile groups had been infiltrated by informers, hand-picked men who had been 'denounced' and hounded out of Cuba to give them credibility. According to these sources, the invasion was intended to trigger a nationwide revolt, inspiring the oppressed masses to rise up in unison against Fidel. This would empower a new dissident government to 'request assistance' from the US, who would send in troops to finish off the job.

As Raúl tried in vain to convey to Harry Jordan, the plan was laughable. The mere threat of invasion was proving to be a propagandist's dream, ideal material for whipping up nationalism and anti-Yanqui paranoia and giving Fidel the perfect excuse to step up his savage purge of so-called 'traitors'. But predictably, Harry ignored the good advice Raúl gave him. Like all his kind, thought Raúl, he showed a woeful lack of insight or imagination and preferred to tell his bosses what they wanted to hear. Just as Raúl himself told Fidel what he wanted to hear. Except the things he chose not to tell him at all.

The document on his desk was a case in point. It had come as no surprise to see Eduardo's name on a confidential report from an *agent provocateur,* who had successfully recruited over fifty students to an anti-Castro cell. The time was ripe, he had advised, to pull in the net.

Raúl's pride balked at warning Eduardo directly. He had kept his vow never to see him again, dreading pity even more than rejection. Using Celia as a go-between was out of the question; her hands must stay clean at all costs. Which left the only other person he could trust. His brother.

He telephoned him at his office saying he wanted to see him in private about a case that was awaiting trial, one of many in which Raúl's department was involved.

'I have appointments all day,' he told León. 'You'd better come to the house tonight. It's urgent.'

When the bell rang at the appointed time, Gabriel, in his pyjamas, beat his mother to the door. Now that he was tall enough to reach the handle, his favourite game was to let in visitors. Celia arrived in the hallway to find father and son looking at each other awkwardly, both of them uncharacteristically bashful.

'Do you want to see my machine-gun?' ventured Gabriel, tugging at León's jacket.

'Celia, it's time the boy was in bed,' said Raúl, emerging from his study to greet his visitor. 'Where's Emilia?'

'It's her evening off, she's gone to the cinema with Luis. Say goodnight to Papá, Gabriel.'

León watched stolidly while Gabriel climbed up onto Raúl's lap. 'He adores Gabriel,' Celia had said, and evidently Gabriel adored him too. León could well remember the seductive power of Raúl's smile, a smile which he had always rationed ruthlessly, a reward he had made him work hard for. But with Gabriel, it seemed to be freely given. León felt a sharp pang of regret. But it wasn't Raúl he envied; it was the happy little boy on his lap.

'Bed,' said Raúl, eliciting instant obedience. Gabriel clambered down and following some drill of good manners, mumbled an uncertain 'goodnight' at León before following his mother.

'He's a tough little nut,' said Raúl approvingly, wheeling himself into his study. 'Just like you were at that age.'

'I thought I was a cry-baby,' said León drily, remembering the oft-repeated taunt that had denied him the childish luxury of tears.

'If you had been, I wouldn't have been so hard on you. Don't worry, I've never raised a finger to him. Not because he's yours. Because he's mine. Shut the door behind you.'

He fished some papers out of a drawer, handed them to León, and watched while he read them. He took his time; Raúl guessed that he was trying to memorise as many of the names as possible.

'I take it you want me to warn Eduardo?'

'Evidently.'

'You're committing treason.'

'I know. Put him on a plane and get him out of Cuba, before it's too late.' He gave León an envelope full of money. León shook his head.

'He won't go. He despises *gusanos*.' It was the ultimate term of abuse used for those who fled the country, literally translated as 'worms'.

'Then talk him into it.'

'What about the other people on this list?'

'Naturally he – or you – will want to warn them too. In which case the leak will be traced, inevitably, back to me. And then my wife and child will be yours at last.'

It would be his final act of love, and love was meaningless without an element of danger. León would assume he was doing this for Celia's sake, rather than Eduardo's, and in a way he was. He loved her too, after all. Loving two people didn't dilute what one felt for either of them; rather it intensified it. Celia knew that better than anyone.

León handed back the document.

'I won't tell him his cell's been penetrated. I'll just say that someone in prison has given false evidence against him to save his own skin. That way he won't alert any of his comrades and there will be no come-back on you.'

Raúl raised an eyebrow.

'They'll all be rounded up, you realise. Some of them

will end up dead. You have it in your power to save them.'

'I'd rather save you. I don't know these people. You're Celia's husband, you're my child's father, whether I like it or not. You're my brother, damn you to hell.'

Raúl smiled and lit an outsize Montecristo cigar.

'I know exactly how you feel,' he said.

'I can't leave my woman right now,' said Lázaro. 'Not while she's pregnant.'

'You'll be paid a lot more at the training camp than you're getting at the bakery,' said Costa, 'so she won't go short of anything. And she can move in with my wife, if she's scared to be alone. We need army men like you. Unless we keep our end up, the ex-Fidelistas will have things all their own way.'

'I'll think about it,' said Lázaro evasively. If it hadn't been for Mirella, he might well have been fired by all this talk of liberating Cuba. He would have liked nothing better than to topple Fidel, not to mention Raúl Soler. But Mirella would get quite hysterical at the thought of being left alone, for all that she ignored him when he was there, except when she wanted something done.

'I have to get back home,' muttered Lázaro. 'The kid is sick. I only dropped by for a quick drink on my way to the drugstore.' To Lázaro's mind, Mirella was making a fuss about nothing, as usual. The only thing that seemed to rouse her from her torpor was the slightest cough or sneeze from Leonardo.

'Have another beer before you go,' persisted his comrade, refilling his glass from the pitcher on the table. Why not? thought Lázaro moodily, accepting it. He didn't want Costa to think he was henpecked. It was high time he showed Mirella who was boss. He seemed to spend half his life running errands. Do this, do that, it was enough to drive a man to drink.

By the time Lázaro had finished his beer, he knew the drugstore would have already shut. So he saw no harm in having another and another. A man had to have some pleasures in life. Costa droned on, introducing Lázaro to some new arrivals as the guy who had shot Raúl Soler, provoking more back-slapping and congratulations and yet another brimming pitcher.

It was late when Lázaro finally staggered home. He was just on his way up the dark, narrow staircase when his landlady called out to him.

'Your wife . . .' she began, and faltered. 'The police want to see you.'

'The police?' Oh, God, he thought. It had happened. They had tracked her down and taken her off for questioning . . .

'There was an accident. She was knocked down, by a truck, right in front of the shop. I saw it happen.'

Lázaro rubbed his eyes. He must be drunk. This wasn't real.

'Where is she? Is she hurt?'

'I'm sorry, *muchacho*. I called for an ambulance, but it was too late. They want you down at the morgue, to identify her.'

Lárazo sat down on the stairs.

'But why did she go out? She never goes out!'

'She asked me where the nearest drugstore was and then ran straight across the road without looking. She was in a hurry to get there before it shut. The little boy isn't well, he's in my apartment. I asked my daughter to come over. Come in, come in . . .'

Numbly, Lázaro followed her through to the back shop. A young woman was sitting in a decaying armchair with Leonardo on her lap. He was coughing and crying at the same time.

'The little one has a temperature,' she said, feeling his forehead. 'If you like, I will take him to the doctor for you, tomorrow morning. Which one do you go to?'

Lázaro didn't answer, his mind whirling round in a circle like a dog chasing its tail. He imagined the questions the police would ask, the lies he would have to tell. Suppose they recognised Mirella's dead body from the picture in the paper? He would be charged with kidnapping and wind up in the electric chair . . . But if he didn't go to the morgue they would come looking for him. He had to get out of here, quick.

'I'll take the boy to a mate of mine,' said Lázaro. 'His wife will look after him. Then I'll go to the police.'

The two women nodded sadly. Lázaro picked Leonardo up and mounted the stairs, two at a time. If he'd gone to the drugstore as promised, she would still be alive. He had lost her, lost his unborn child, both their deaths were on his head . . .

He packed a few essentials, leaving all Mirella's things behind, apart from photographs and anything else that might help them identify her. Then he hurried along the darkened street, heading for Costa's apartment on SW 24th Street.

'My woman's walked out on me,' he told him. 'Left me with her kid and a stack of unpaid bills. I had to do a moonlight. People all over town will be chasing me for money. Can I lie low at your place for a while?'

As Costa was quick to point out, there was nothing to stop him enlisting any more. His woman had no doubt found herself a fancy man, his first wife had done the same to him. But his second was a good-hearted soul, who would gladly take care of the child while Lázaro did his duty . . .

His duty. That was all he had left.

Eduardo filed off the plane along with the other *gusanos*, feeling like a deserter. Fleeing his country was the one thing he had sworn he would never do, but he had had no choice. If he stayed, he would put other people in danger.

'Think of others, if not yourself!' León had bellowed. 'The secret police will be watching your every move. Do you want to lead them to other members of your cell? You mustn't see or speak to any of your associates. Just go.'

According to León, the man who had borne false witness against him was a member of a rival anti-Castro group, who had sought to buy his life without betraying one of his own, a treachery which León had discovered through a fellow lawyer. And now his comrades would write him off as a traitor who had chosen a soft life abroad rather than carry on with the struggle. Following hard on Mirella's disappearance – a source of shameful relief – this seemed like the final humiliation. Not that anyone knew why she had really left him, thank God. He felt less of a man than ever.

The arrivals area at Miami airport was thronged with eager exiles awaiting families and friends. Amid the sea of waving hands and smiling, tearful faces, Eduardo spotted Frank Maguire, hands in pockets, looking old and tired. Damn. León must have let him know he was coming.

'Hi,' said Frank, approaching and grasping his hand.

'Hello,' said Eduardo stiffly.

'I thought you might need a place to stay. I'd be glad to put you up.'

'Thank you. But I can easily find an hotel.' Eduardo walked on, Frank's longer legs making it impossible to outstrip him without an absurd recourse to running. 'I spoke freely in front of you,' he said coldly. 'We all did. If I'd known you were an enemy agent . . .'

'You really see the US as your enemy? Then why are you here?'

'I don't intend to stay. I shall probably go to Brazil, or Argentina. I certainly don't need any help from you.'

Frank caught hold of his arm.

'Look. It wasn't like you think. I found out something I wasn't supposed to know, the deportation was set up to get me out of the country. But I wasn't a spy. I wish I had been. If the US had had better intelligence, they might have handled things better. Right now it's important to limit the damage. We need people like you, Eduardo.'

'We? Oh, I get it. You're a recruiting officer.'

'Come back to my place and hear me out. Don't condemn me out of hand. I'm on your side.'

Eduardo very much doubted it. If an exile army was being formed, he wanted no part in it; allying himself with ex-Batistianos and their Yanqui controllers offended his sense of national pride. But he was curious. There was no harm in listening, if only to expose Frank's ignorance.

Much to his surprise, however, Frank spoke not in right-wing clichés, but in the kind of precise, academic language Eduardo understood. The shambling, self-deprecating façade concealed a trained mind and an impressive grasp of Cuban history and politics.

'You don't talk like a typical American, I must say,' conceded Eduardo at length. 'You people have never understood how we Cubans feel. Now less than ever. Who put you straight?'

'My ideas are my own. Unfortunately. I wish I could find a few more people who shared them. Look, I'm not just some robot obeying orders. I got involved in this because I felt so useless sitting around doing nothing. After the kidnap, I got . . . depressed. When I get depressed, I drink. And if I drink, I'm going to wind up dead. So I'm doing this instead, to keep myself alive. In case the kid turns up one day. In case Lily decides she needs me after all.'

Abruptly he reverted to the old, familiar Frank, a washed-up ex-drunk with all the hard-edged pathos of a frustrated romantic.

'So what is your role, exactly?'

'Liaison work. Co-ordinating different rebel groups and trying to formulate recommendations that will keep all of them sweet. Right now the ex-Batistianos have got the loudest voices and they're pushing for an early invasion. According to them it will spark off a massive counter-revolution.'

'Rubbish,' snorted Eduardo. 'It would be a disaster.'

'My point of view exactly. The way I see things, we need to send people in small groups, train and equip underground outfits, like the one you belonged to, all over the island, do to Fidel what Fidel did to Batista. And that didn't happen overnight. It'll take a couple of years, perhaps more, by which time people will start to realise what Communism really means. There's no future in forcing this on Cuba from the outside, it's got to happen from within.'

'Isn't that obvious?'

'To you, perhaps, and to me, but we're in the minority. The whole thing is getting carried away by its own momentum. If Fidel repels an invasion – which he will – he'll be a national hero, which will make it even easier for him to set himself up as God Almighty. That's why I need more moderate voices like yours, to back my case. I'm looking to you to help persuade your fellow exiles to oppose a suicidal invasion and demand long-term help for resistance groups instead.'

'Because that's what you want?'

'No, because it's what you want.'

Eduardo looked at him, still mistrustful. He was CIA, after all. Frank's answering gaze didn't waver, but then he had no doubt been trained to appear sincere.

'You said you were kicked – or rather pulled – out of Cuba because you found out something you weren't supposed to know. What was it?'

'The identity of an agent. One of Fidel's right-hand men. At the time I only suspected it, but since then I've had confirmation.'

'Who is it?'

'I can't tell you that.'

'Because you don't trust me? And yet, you expect me to trust you?'

'It's classified information.'

'And I'm a blabber-mouthed spic, right?'

'Eduardo, we have enough security problems already. It's not that I don't trust you, it's just that—'

'If you think I would compromise you by betraying your confidence, then you're better off without me.'

He got up to leave. Frank sighed.

'Does it really matter who it was? It was someone who was with him in the mountains. Someone who was set up to infiltrate the rebels right from the word go.'

Eduardo continued to scowl, unmollified.

'You mean a traitor.'

'I think he'd call himself an anti-Communist. Same as you.'

'At the beginning Fidel wasn't a Communist. If this

man was with the rebels from the start, reporting back to the Americans, that makes him a traitor in my book. No wonder you're trying to protect him. And now you're trying to make me into a traitor as well.'

'You're quite wrong.'

'They own you, don't they? You just do whatever you're told, like all your kind.'

'That isn't true.'

'Then prove your good faith,' challenged Eduardo. 'Disobey your orders for once. Trust me with something I could use to destroy you. Then I might believe you're an honest man.'

Frank didn't answer for a moment. Then he sat back, arms folded in front of him and said, quite matter-of-factly, 'Very well then. It's your brother-in-law. Raúl Soler.'

The two words resounded in the air, leaving behind them an ominous silence. Eduardo could hear his watch ticking like a metronome, repeating the rhythm of the name.

'Does León know?'

'Are you kidding? If they thought I'd breathed a word to him he'd be dead by now. And so would I, most likely. Remember that. I've just wired my life up to a time bomb. Is that enough to convince you I'm on the level?'

'He used me,' said Eduardo quietly. 'All the while I thought he was my . . . my friend . . . he was just exploiting me.'

'I guess he thought it was his duty. It's not easy, leading a double life. Take it from me, I know.'

'He lied to me. Right from the start. All those hours we spent talking about the revolution . . . I believed what he said. I thought he was a patriot.'

'Well, so he is, by his lights. He's taking the most godawful risk. Can you imagine what they would do to him if they found out? The man has guts.'

'That's not the point!'

All those words of love had been fake, thought Eduardo bitterly; right from the start Raúl had identified him as someone who could help him infiltrate the rebels. The most intense, distressing, rewarding experience of his life had been a gross act of manipulation . . .

'So do you trust me now?' persisted Frank, wanting his pound of flesh.

'Yes. Yes, I trust you.' But it wasn't true. He would never trust anyone again. From now on, he would trust only himself.

FIFTEEN

WITHIN TWENTY-FOUR hours of Mirella's death Lázaro was installed in a training camp in Homestead, thirty miles from Miami. It seemed like the safest place to be. Given that the Cuban Brigade didn't officially exist, for security reasons, it followed that Lázaro didn't exist either. No one would come looking for him here.

He sent money to Costa's wife each week for Leonardo's food and board, resenting the child all the while. But for him, Mirella would not have died, but for him he would not be a fugitive. Self-pity and paranoia left no room for guilt. None of this was his fault, he told himself. All his misfortunes could be traced back to the rebels and the revolution, embodied in the devilish shape of Raúl Soler, who had survived the death-blow dealt by Changó, who continued to prosper while he languished. His only solace came in imagining the public execution which would send his enemy back to hell, where he belonged.

The time dragged slowly, each day much like another, with endless marching and drilling and no definite news as to when the invasion would start. Impatient exiles complained of the delay and demanded immediate action, while faceless Yanqui 'advisers' tried to keep the pot from boiling over. The lid finally blew off it one afternoon in August 1960, when a bunch of schoolkids hurled half a dozen fire-crackers over the camp wall.

The response was instantaneous and savage. Thinking that they were under attack from pro-Castro agents, the trainees responded with a volley of bullets, seriously wounding a young boy. This incident provoked a barrage of embarrassing questions from the press, with the result that the camp was hurriedly dismantled and transferred, in conditions of utmost secrecy, to a new, discreet location in Guatemala.

Neither Lázaro nor his fellow recruits had a clue where they were going until they arrived, only to find that the hastily erected barracks, built without foundations in the middle of nowhere, were in danger of being washed away by continuous torrential rain. They spent their first month digging ditches, under a permanent shower – which was no substitute for a lack of the plumbed-in variety, not to mention other luxuries like fresh drinking water. The surrounding hills were full of poisonous snakes, for which no antidotes were available, nor indeed any other medical supplies, let alone a doctor.

Several men succumbed to a virulent tropical fever, Lázaro among them. Medical orderlies dosed him with patent remedies, to no avail. He continued to vomit and dehydrate till his body felt hollow, desiccated. In his conscious moments he knew, with a terrible certainty, that he was going to die. In the fog of delirium, as his temperature soared, he thought he was dead already, being slowly consumed by eternal fire.

It was too late now to repent of his sins, too late to evade the retribution already visited on Mirella and her unborn child, the child who had been taken from them to atone for the one they had stolen. Too late to wish that he had returned Leonardo to his father, instead of compounding his original crime to avoid the fury of the law. He was trapped here for ever, among the damned, waiting for the evil day when Raúl Soler would meet him on home ground, surrounded by the evil spirits who protected him . . .

In the brief, fitful bouts of lucidity, he prayed. He vowed by all that was holy that he would make reparation, if only his life was spared. If he broke his promise, let Changó strike him down on the field of battle. If he kept it, he would happily accept his punishment in this life, rather than the next.

When at last the fever broke and the flames subsided, Lázaro crawled back thankfully from the gates of hell and set about keeping his side of the bargain.

*

'Be good while I am gone,' said Raúl, giving Celia a perfunctory kiss before he left for the airport. He was attending the United Nations General Assembly in New York, as one of Fidel's personal entourage. Preparations for the trip had kept him even busier than usual; Celia had hardly seen him all week.

'Is that remark meant for Gabriel as well as me?'

'Boys are not meant to be good,' smiled Raúl, giving the child his customary bear-hug.

Gabriel grinned. He positively enjoyed being in trouble. Whenever his mamá spanked him, Papá would slip him some sweets afterwards for being a brave boy and not crying.

'Gabriel, Emilia wants you in the kitchen,' said Celia sternly. As soon as he was out of earshot she turned on Raúl, eyes blazing. 'You want him to be bad, is that it? Does that explain why you gave him an army pistol full of blanks? That pot shot he took at Emilia nearly gave her a heart attack. You know how strongly I feel about guns in the house. What use is it me chastising him if he thinks you approve?'

'Boys will be soon learning military skills as young as eight years old. It's never too early to learn how to handle a weapon. You would be wise to do the same. Women have a duty to defend their country as well as men. The invasion could come at any time.'

'For heaven's sake! Three years old is much too young to learn about hating and killing people.'

'It's not too young to learn about patriotism.'

'The revolution, you mean. That's all you seem to care about these days. New ways to undermine and erode our liberties, new ways to bribe and manipulate the poor, new ways to suck up to Fidel.'

The same old taunt as always. Raúl knew that she either thought him a blinkered fanatic, who had suspended all his critical faculties, or a power-hungry opportunist. Proof, if proof were needed, of how brilliantly he had played his part to date. It was hard to sacrifice her hard-won love and respect, even harder to endure her mistrust and scorn. Yet again he had to suppress the insane urge to burden her with his deadly secret, to contaminate her with his crime, to condemn her to live in fear, to blurt out, 'I hate Communism as much as you do. I'm risking my life every day to see Fidel brought down.'

Not that she would necessarily applaud him. Despite all her anti-Castro heresies, Celia was Cuban to the core, like her brother, and would no doubt take a dim view of him spying for the US. He would have liked to explain, 'The Americans are just a means to an end. I'm doing this for my country, for you, for Gabriel!' And for himself, of course, He certainly wasn't doing it for Harry. It had always been Harry who served Raúl's purpose rather than the other way round.

But he looked at her expressionlessly, letting her think the worst of him, only too well aware that he was driving her further and further away from him. For her own safety, she must remain in ignorance . . .

And yet, ignorance was not a guarantee of safety. Despite all Harry's promises to get Celia and Gabriel out of Cuba if Raúl were ever caught, there was the ever-present, hideous possibility that something would go wrong, that Celia, as his wife, would also be arrested and charged with collusion. And yet, he was in this far too deep to pull out now, even if he had wanted to, even if Harry would have let him. To pull out now would be to leave a job unfinished, to retreat, to despise himself for ever more.

If he loved her he ought to end this marriage now, brutally, decisively. Then, at least, if the worst came to the worst, she would be less liable to accusation. And yet he was no more capable of doing so than of ending his own life. He could merely expose himself to risk and wait for Celia, like death, to choose her own moment. If only she and León weren't both as proud and stubborn as each other, it would surely have happened long ago . . .

'You certainly don't care about me,' she continued bitterly. 'These days I might as well not exist. You're not the man I married any more.'

'I should hope not. If I've changed, then you must take full credit for that. Would you prefer me to be as I was? Possessive, bad-tempered and cruel?'

'I understood you then. At least, I thought I did. But now I feel I don't know you any more. It's as if . . . as if you're hiding something from me.'

He always had done, of course. More than ever, he wished he could wipe out the past, start all over again from scratch. But there was no escaping the past. The past stretched back as far as he could remember, choking the very gutters of his soul with its foul debris, casting its long shadow all the way to the grave. All he could do was atone for it, die for something he believed in.

'That's inevitable, Celia,' he said. As always, he refused to quarrel with her, fearful that he might say too much in the heat of the moment. 'Much of my work is highly confidential.'

'What I know about it already is more than enough! And stop using your work as an excuse to shut me up!'

'I can't argue with you now,' said Raúl, looking at his watch, controlling another craven urge to win her back 'I'll miss my flight. By all means give Gabriel a good hiding for frightening Emilia. He has to learn to take his punishment like a man. Goodbye, my sweet. I'll phone you.'

After he had gone Celia broke down and wept, stifling the sound of it with her handkerchief for fear that Gabriel would hear. She had fought so hard to salvage something from the ruins of her marriage, but now, after months of struggle and heartache, she was ready to admit defeat. It was bad enough having to live with Raúl's job – confidential or not she knew that it entailed the systematic crushing of dissent, that it swelled the ever-growing numbers of political prisoners, that it contradicted everything she understood democracy to be. But it was even harder living with the man behind the job, a man blinded either by ambition or bigotry, she couldn't decide which was worse, a man she couldn't even argue with, a man who shut her out of his world, not that she wanted any part of it, for all that she was expected to share his views in public, to practise a religion she did not believe in, to sicken herself with her own hypocrisy.

If she had any self-respect, she would move out. Raúl probably wouldn't even care, just as long as he got to see Gabriel. Gabriel, whom he wanted to follow in his footsteps. She shuddered at the thought of Gabriel, some years hence, parading in some miniature military uniform, chanting pre-digested dogma, stripped of the right or the ability to think for himself. And yet to desert her homeland seemed like a betrayal. What would become of Cuba if everyone with a mind of their own simply ran away, leaving behind only the poor, the ignorant, the fanatics, and the new sinister élite who ruled over them?

Raúl would be gone two weeks. Two weeks in which to make up her mind, to pluck up courage, to get cold feet. She had sworn that she would never leave him, but perhaps León was right, perhaps there was more vanity in it than virtue. Virtue was its own reward but vanity demanded something in return, something which Raúl would not – or could not – give her any more. Something she would have to learn to give herself.

Ironically, if it hadn't been for León, she might have made the break long ago. They had stuck to their pact to make the best of a bad job, to accept the prospect of an indefinite separation, to spin a pearl around the grit of desire, storing up riches for a future that might never come. And now she was afraid of upsetting the status quo, of jeopardising the delicate balance they had achieved, of losing what little peace of mind she had left . . .

She wrenched her mind away from her dilemma and back to her errant son. Give him a good hiding indeed. It would have absolutely no effect, coming from her; the conspiracy between Gabriel and Raúl was absolute. She decided to try a different tactic.

'Gabriel,' she said grimly, marching purposefully into the kitchen. 'I want to talk to you.'

He looked up sheepishly, his mouth ringed with biscuit crumbs and a white moustache of milk.

'You've been very naughty. So naughty that I'm not

going to spank you. I've talked to your father and he suggests that I telephone your aunt Lily and tell her we won't be coming this afternoon.'

Gabriel's face fell. His giant-sized crush on Lily was his Achilles' heel.

'In fact, I shall stop your piano lessons for good if you disobey me again.'

'Don't be so hard on the boy,' said Emilia indulgently, ruffling his hair. 'He didn't mean any harm. Give him one more chance.'

'Only one. You are never, ever, to play with guns again . . .'

'But Papá—'

'Except with Papá. It's not manly to frighten women, the way you did Emilia. Do you understand?'

Gabriel looked at Emilia with heart-melting contrition. 'Sorry, 'Milia. Can I have another biscuit?'

'Not until you promise,' said Celia. 'No guns, except when Papá is there. Promise.'

'I promise.'

He wriggled down from his chair and held out his arms for forgiveness, certain that it would be granted. At moments like this he reminded her poignantly of León, the feckless, amiable, mischievous León of old. Surely Raúl could see it too? It was as if he had rewritten his relationship with his brother, learned from past mistakes, turned history on its head. He had turned his biggest rival into his staunchest ally, one who would always prefer him to his mother.

And yet Celia could not find it in her heart to resent it. She might be forced into the role of taskmaster and killjoy, but nothing could blunt the abject affection she felt for the little miscreant, or dent his supreme confidence in it. He would end up breaking some poor woman's heart. Just like both of his fathers.

Havana, 18 September 1960

Dear Frank

I enclose another tape of your favourite numbers, to keep you company. My old pianist at the Capri has left the country, and as you can hear the new one isn't half so good.

Thank you for the fifty dollars you sent, which I'm saving for an emergency. You'd be surprised how sensible I've become now that you're not here to keep an eye on me. The teaching job Raúl wangled for me is working out quite well, even though one of my colleagues threatened to report me for not using the lousy approved texts, which are full of anti-American slogans and such. But the kids seem to like me, which is the main thing. I wanted to work for León, anything to buck the system, but of course he wouldn't let me get involved, in case he's ever arrested. Last week a counter-revolutionary cell was blown wide open, so he's up to his ears in new cases.

I miss you a lot. If it wasn't for Celia I'd get really depressed, but she is on her own a lot as well and so we spend a lot of time together. Gabriel is turning out so cute and I often wonder if Leonardo has changed as much as he has. He says the funniest things. I'm giving him piano lessons and he's picking it up real fast. Celia says I have a knack with children, which is strange considering what a useless mother I was, but once they stop bawling and crapping all the time, kids can be a lot of fun. Celia says I just lacked confidence with Leonardo. I guess I was still a baby myself when I had him.

Lily paused, waiting for the sudden stab of pain to ease. Not a day went by when she didn't stop and seethe and wonder how her little boy was doing. Frank would never have let him forget her. But Mirella would make damn sure he did.

Celia says will you please get Eduardo to write, even if it's only a few lines. I hope that neither of you is getting mixed up in this invasion nonsense, not that you would tell us if you were. It's all people talk about in Havana these days, with even women and children joining the new people's militias. So unless the US send about a million people, it will just be a massacre. Most people who oppose Fidel have either left the country or are safely tucked up in gaol, and the rest think he can do no wrong. Even Emilia, who used to be dead against the revolution, thinks he's real sexy.

Keep looking, won't you?

Take care or else,

Lots and lots and lots of love

Your Lily.

She imagined Frank reading and re-reading the letter, listening to the tape over and over again. He had always needed her more than she needed him, she could see that now. But not having him around still hurt. She didn't miss being looked after: it pleased her to be able to come and go as she liked, to have León treat her as an adult, to hold down a regular job and pay her way and babysit for Gabriel. No, what she missed was looking after Frank – making sure he took his medication, keeping him off the booze, getting him to eat properly. Left to himself he was such a god-awful slob.

But more than that, with a terrible aching fury, she missed her child. The six months since the kidnap had put years on her, she would never be the same person again. And yet, somehow, she had survived, much to her own surprise, and not without a huge struggle. León had enough to cope with, after all, without her cracking up on him.

It sure as hell was tough, being a grown-up. Even tougher than being a child, and that was saying something.

Frank was drunk. So drunk that the barman had had to call a cab to take him home. Not that it would ever be a home. It was high time he moved on.

After handing in his resignation that morning, as a futile gesture of protest against this cock-eyed invasion, he had spent the rest of the day pouring Bourbon into his mangled guts, celebrating the latest failure in his life. It had been bound to be a failure, of course, he might have known that from the start. Never again. He should have stuck to his motto.

He crawled out of the cab and lurched towards the house, too drunk to walk in a straight line but not quite drunk enough to forget to check his mailbox, in case there was a letter from Lily. He groped around in the dark, withdrew a large packet and a thin envelope, and staggered inside.

Seeing Lily's writing on the former, he tore it open,

wound the enclosed tape clumsily onto the machine, poured himself another drink, lay back on the settee and let the sweet, soothing sounds wash all over him, cursing himself for a sentimental jerk as his eyes filled up with maudlin tears.

As usual, she rejected the hit parade in favour of torch-song classics: 'That Old Black Magic', 'Makin' Whoopee', 'I'm In The Mood For Love.' Her voice had grown stronger, richer, gained in both power and subtlety. And there was something else. A deeper appreciation of pain and disappointment and regret; a new, self-mocking wry humour; above all, an extra measure of confidence, a sense of indomitability that hadn't been there before. She had learned to live without him. He loved her enough to feel glad for her.

He wiped his eyes with his sleeve and began reading the letter. There was the inevitable message from Celia for her brother please to write to her. Frank rarely saw him these days – or more accurately, Eduardo did his best to avoid him. He was living in a rooming house downtown with a group of embittered ex-Fidelistas like himself, who spent all their time in secret meetings, plotting and planning God alone knew what.

Eduardo had worked hard to rally support for the anti-invasion lobby, initially with some success. Small specially trained groups had been sent into Cuba to swell the ranks of resistance fighters, including the new breed of anti-Castro guerrillas ensconced in the Escambray mountains. But such measures had proved insufficient to placate those exiles who were pressing for an early invasion. Frank's superiors could no longer resist this collective pressure without risking the embarrassing public wrath of the formidable human machine they had helped create. The whole thing was unstoppable now.

'This is what you people wanted all along,' Eduardo had said angrily. 'I wish I'd never got involved. And there are plenty of us who feel the same way. From now on we fight Fidel in our own way, on our own terms, without American help or hindrance.' Frank dreaded to think what that might mean. Certainly he showed little interest in his studies these days, for all that he was supposed to be starting medical school next month on a scholarship funded by wealthy Cuban expats. His sister was right to be worried about him.

He read the letter several times as always, savouring each word. 'Keep looking, won't you?' He hadn't looked for weeks, months. What was the point? Leonardo was gone for good, he would never see him again, nor Lily either. He refilled his glass, spilling some over the table, soaking the other item of mail – a thin blue airmail envelope addressed in an unknown hand.

He opened it without much interest. The writing was hard to read, smudged from the whisky he had spilt and fogged by the whisky he had swallowed. He stared stupidly as the words went in and out of focus, incomprehension giving way to disbelief and disbelief into wild, drunken hope. Frank rubbed his eyes, smoothed the page, and read the letter again very slowly. It must have made little sense to the censors at the camp, but it made perfect sense to Frank.

> Dear Señor Maguire
> I knew your address because I met Mirella outside your house, the night she disappeared. She agreed to run away with me, on account of being pregnant with my kid, but I never figured on her borrowing anything from you.
> You will find the item you lent her at 140, SW 22nd Street, in the care of a woman called Costa. I told her Mirella ran out on me, leaving me to take care of it. So she never knew where it came from. As for me, I won't blame you if you come after me for not sending it back to you before. Mirella got killed in an accident, and after that I couldn't think straight for a while. I never meant any harm.
> Yours truly
> Lázaro González

Frank doubled up in agony from sheer excitement. Sweating and shivering, he threw up a skinful of booze, cleaned his teeth, showered, shaved, and drank a couple of gallons of black coffee before putting on a clean shirt and his one and only suit, stuffing Lázaro's letter into one pocket and a good supply of cash into the other.

He rang for another cab, pacing up and down the room as he waited for it to arrive, wondering if he would recognise the child; they changed so quickly at that age. Leonardo wouldn't recognise him either. He would holler in protest at being taken away from the latest in a long line of mothers. He would look at him as if to say, 'Who the fuck needs a father like you? Beat it, asshole. I'm happy as I am.' Frank was as nervous as a gangling youth on his way to a blind date.

Señora Costa turned out to be a coarse, blowsy fishwife of a woman, voluminous in a grubby nightgown and ill pleased to be knocked up at this time of night. A truculent-looking man, clad only in underpants and a three-day stubble, surveyed Frank balefully from behind her shoulder.

'Lázaro sent me,' said Frank, in Spanish. 'I've brought some money, for the kid.'

Her manner changed abruptly. With a jerk of the head, she dismissed her consort and invited Frank inside. The place was a hovel, stinking of fermenting nappies and stale linen and recent copious copulation. She showed him into a windowless boxroom, where six children were crammed together on two single mattresses, on a bare, unswept floor. She gestured towards one of the sleeping heads, sandwiched between two pairs of dirty feet.

'I do my best,' she said, 'but with five of my own, I have my hands full. And everything is so expensive, here in America. With my husband away, doing his duty' – so much for security – 'life is hard.'

It was Leonardo, all right. The unformed features had begun to gel into a recognisable replica of Lily; the baby-blond hair was turning red. Frank would have known him anywhere. Even in sleep, he looked anxious.

'Can you read?' asked Frank, of the woman.

She shook her head. 'No, Señor. I grew up on a farm. What use are books to a working woman like me?'

'Then let me read you the letter Lázaro sent me.' He

fished for the sheet of paper and got out his reading glasses, in an attempt to look authoritative. ' "Dear Frank, I am very glad that you have accepted your responsibilities as Leonardo's father. Now Mirella has walked out on me as well, I can see what you had to put up with. I know that Señora Costa is having financial difficulties, so the sooner you take the boy off her hands the better." '

'You're the boy's father?' She looked from Leonardo to Frank and back again.

'I met his mother in Cuba. Then she ran off with Lázaro, took the boy with her. I'd got no idea where they were, till he wrote to me. I'm most grateful to you for caring for him, Señora. This is for your trouble.' He handed her a wad of money. Her face broke into a gracious smile.

'It was my pleasure. Poor little mite. What kind of mother deserts her own child? As I said to Lázaro, you're better off without her . . .'

'Leonardo?' Frank shook him gently awake. 'Do you remember me?'

Pre-empting a protest, he scooped the child up into his arms. Leonardo looked at him blankly, but he didn't cry. He had the stoical expression of a child who has long since learned the futility of tears. He was wearing nothing but a dirty singlet and by the smell of him, he hadn't had a bath in weeks. Frank noticed several dark bruises on his thighs.

'He is a clumsy child,' said the Costa woman hastily. 'Forever falling over and hurting himself. I'm afraid all his clothes are at the laundry . . .'

'Keep them. I'll buy him some new ones.'

'Well, that's handy, for when I have another. Let's hope that the next child will be born in Cuba.'

'Yes. Goodbye, Señora.'

'*Adios.*' She didn't bother to say the same to Leonardo; evidently there was no love lost on either side. Leonardo showed no distress at leaving her, just silent, wide-eyed alarm at whatever ordeal awaited him next. Frank laid him down on the back seat of the waiting cab and covered him up with his jacket.

'It's OK, kid,' he whispered. 'It's OK. We're going home.'

Raúl looked around his hotel room in disgust. Reservations had been made at the Shelbourne, one of the better New York hotels, but the management, faced with a gang of bearded Latin revolutionaries, had fallen instantly foul of Fidel by requesting payment in advance. As a result, the whole party had decamped in protest to the Hotel Theresa in Harlem, a budget establishment more in keeping with their proletarian image, not that this had prevented Raúl, or anyone else, from running up a small fortune in room service.

It had been a long day. Fidel's speech to the United Nations had lasted nearly five hours and had met with the expected cool reception. Henceforward, he had declared with a flourish, Cuba would cut itself off from all US aid and would request help from the Soviet Union in repelling any aggression. Comrade Khrushchev had given his new buddy a big embrace for the cameras. It had all been entirely predictable, not to say excruciatingly boring. Nothing worth knowing was ever made public, after all.

Raúl placed a tiny roll of film inside his paper napkin, screwed it into a tight ball, and left it on the room service tray. If Harry's people had failed to penetrate the kitchens of this place, rather than the scheduled one, then that was their look-out; they would have to search the garbage at their leisure. Raúl had photographed secret documents showing the truly formidable extent of anti-invasion measures, in a last-ditch attempt to persuade them to abandon the plan, rather than play straight into Castro's hands.

The information had been easy enough to come by. Simply because his wheelchair made him so conspicuous, he was deemed incapable of subterfuge; he could enter any office, ask for any file, and it would be given to him without question. The wide scope of his investigative powers, and his special brief to weed out unreliable personnel, made it reasonable for him to inspect the most confidential reports. As usual, he had courted danger with impunity. He had no fear for himself; only for Celia.

The telephone rang. Wearily, Raúl picked it up.

'Raúl? It's me, Eduardo.'

Suddenly he could feel his toes again.

'Where are you?'

'In the phone booth across the road. I've got something for you, and I don't want your people to search me.'

'What is it?'

'If you want to know, come down to the foyer and get me past them. I need to see you in private.'

His voice gave nothing away. Had he come, perhaps, to claim him as a comrade, alerted by Frank Maguire of his perilous undercover work, his commitment to the downfall of Fidel? No, that was wishful thinking. Maguire knew better than to breathe a word of what he knew. Most likely he had come to plead on behalf of some friend in prison back home, or give him some message for his sister.

'I'll be right there.'

He wheeled himself into the elevator and emerged in the lobby, which was swarming with armed bodyguards.

'It's all right,' he said, as they moved forward to frisk Eduardo, who was carrying a leather attaché case. The sight of him was as painful as ever. 'It's my brother-in-law. I'm expecting him. This way.'

'You should have refused to see me,' said Eduardo stiffly, as he followed Raúl back to his room. 'I'm a *gusano*. You'll bring suspicion on yourself.'

Raúl coolly summoned Luis, his bodyguard-cum-chauffeur, who was patrolling the corridor outside his door, and despatched him on some pointless errand, anxious to ensure that their interview would not be overheard.

'If there were anything sinister in our meeting, we would hardly rendezvous openly in the hotel.' He showed Eduardo in and closed the door. 'What brings you here? I assume it's not a social call. Though your sister will be greatly relieved to hear I saw you in one piece, she's always fretting about you. Can I offer you anything? Don't look at me like that, I can't jump you any more. You're quite safe.'

'You're not.' Raúl blinked, startled, as Eduardo withdrew a gun from his briefcase and pointed it at him, producing an orgasmic rush of adrenaline.

'We knew we'd never get near Fidel, so you were the next best thing,' said Eduardo. 'I reckoned you wouldn't refuse to see me, so I volunteered for the job.'

Raúl couldn't help smiling to himself at the superb irony of it. He imagined his huge state funeral, Celia revered as the widow of a hero, Fidel delivering some long-winded eulogy to the latest martyr of the revolution, a street in Havana renamed in his honour . . . But Eduardo's next words stopped him short.

'I knew you were working for the CIA, of course,' he hissed, his voice heavy with contempt. 'But I couldn't tell that to my *compañeros* without betraying Frank. And anyway, you deserve to die, you bastard.'

Eduardo gripped the gun more tightly, determined to go through with it. If he didn't, his comrades would think him a coward. 'You were working for them right from the beginning,' he continued, relying on his anger to give him the courage he needed. 'You never believed in the revolution. You were nothing but a lousy spy. You used me to infiltrate the rebels. You lied to me. You lied about everything.'

'You're wrong,' said Raúl calmly. 'I fell in love with you the minute I saw you, long before I was recruited as an agent.'

'Even if I believed that – which I don't – that's not why I'm killing you. I'm killing you because you're a traitor. It wouldn't be so bad if you were doing it out of conviction. But I've worked it all out. They blackmailed you, didn't they? They threatened to expose you unless you worked for them. Didn't they?'

'At first, yes, but—'

'You're despicable! What about Celia? What will become of her if you're found out?'

'That's all taken care of. Eduardo, please listen, please let me explain—'

'You lied to her too. You used her too. I should have

told her the truth. And now I'm going to do better than that, I'm going to set her free. This way at least she'll never know what kind of man she married.'

He cocked the gun with a trembling hand. Raúl braced himself.

'Kill me, then. I'm not afraid to die.'

'And neither am I. I'm not the coward you think I am. Otherwise I wouldn't be here. I know I haven't a hope of getting away, your bodyguards will shoot me in a minute. God, how I hate you. If it hadn't been for you . . .'

'Don't blame me for what you are. You're not here because you hate me. You're here because you still love me. That's why you're so angry. Because you know it can never be the same with anyone else. That's the trouble with loving someone like me. I'm an incurable disease.'

He held his gaze, daring him to shoot, hoping that he wouldn't, for Eduardo's sake, not his own. He didn't want to see him throw his life away.

'Give me the gun, Eduardo,' he said quietly, hypnotically, as if trying to soothe a frightened horse. He wheeled himself closer, Eduardo retreating, step by step, till his back was against the door. But still he didn't pull the trigger.

'Don't come any nearer.'

'Then let's talk. Hear me out. Let me—'

'No. I don't want to listen.' His hand was shaking so much that he couldn't hold the gun still; in a moment he would drop it. Raúl felt a pang of regret; it would have been the sweetest possible way to die. And as Eduardo said himself, it would set Celia free. But right now Eduardo's survival was more important than his own death.

'Then leave. Leave now and think the worst of me. Just don't destroy yourself for the sake of destroying me. Live your life, learn to be a good doctor . . .' He advanced till the barrel of the gun was pressing against his forehead.

'Damn you,' hissed Eduardo, retracting his hand. He was trembling from head to foot. 'I c-can't do it.'

'Of course you can't. Why should you kill the only person in this filthy world who loves you for what you are?'

'I'm not a coward!'

'I know you're not.' Slowly, Raúl reached for his gun. Eduardo jerked it away, beyond his grasp. Raúl wheeled himself another few inches closer. Eduardo sidestepped him clumsily, knocking over the coffee table, sending the tray with its plate and napkin crashing to the floor.

'No!' His eyes were wild. 'Don't touch me! I can't bear it!'

'Eduardo—'

'They'll think I'm a coward. They'll think . . . damn you!'

He fired once. And then the guards came running.

León arrived home that evening to find Lily in floods of tears. Eyes puffy from weeping, she handed him a cable.

HI MOM. I'M BACK. CAN'T LOOK AFTER DAD ALL BY MYSELF SO HURRY UP AND COME HOME. LOVE LEONARDO.

'Thank God,' said León, hugging her. 'Don't look so tragic. This is good news, isn't it?'

'I called Frank. He said it was a long story and he'll tell me all about it when I get there. But Leonardo's in bad shape. Terribly thin and covered in bruises. Mirella dumped him on some bitch who didn't look after him properly. . . If I go, I can't leave him again, the way my mother did me. You can see that, can't you?' She swallowed another sob. 'And I can't bring him back here, it wouldn't be fair on Frank, or on him. If I go it has to be for good.'

'It's all right,' murmured León, putting an arm around her, suddenly appalled at the thought of losing her.

'And then there's Frank,' continued Lily. 'His ulcer's playing up again. You can bet he's been hitting the booze on the quiet. It would be different if he was young and healthy, but—'

'Lily, you don't have to justify yourself to me.'

'Yes, I do. I want you to know this is for them, not for me. Otherwise I'd stick to you like glue, whether you wanted me or not. You might at least pretend you're sorry to see me go!'

'There's no need to pretend.' He took her face between his hands and made her look at what he was feeling; he would never have expected it to hurt this much. 'I'm going to miss you, Lily. You've driven me crazy but you've kept me sane.'

She couldn't hold his gaze; as always, real emotion embarrassed her. She blew her nose and said, 'You don't need me. They do. This way, perhaps Leonardo won't remember how things were at the start. I mean, if Gabriel likes me, perhaps he will too . . .' And then, with all her old childish insecurity, 'Do you think I'm up to it?'

'A year ago I would have said no. But now I think you're ready. I think you can do anything you want to do.'

'It's the wanting that's the hardest part,' she said. 'Knowing what I want, I mean. I guess you can't have everything you want, and that's all there is to it. You will be careful, won't you? You won't take too many risks?'

'Nothing's going to happen to me. Not without Raúl knowing in advance. So don't fret about me, OK?'

'Just as well you're the top toady's brother,' muttered Lily with her usual lack of reverence. 'But I shall worry all the same.' She dried her eyes and took a deep breath. 'I'd better ring Celia. I didn't want to tell her until I'd told you. Just in case you begged me to stay, ha ha.' She flung him a knowing, mocking look.

'What would you have done if I had?'

'You'll never know,' said Lily bravely, picking up the telephone. And neither, thank God, would she.

'Come in,' said Celia, flustered but not surprised. She had been expecting this visit, but that didn't mean she was prepared for it; Lily's phone call had made her turmoil worse, not better.

'I just dropped Lily off at the Capri,' said León, rather awkwardly, following her into the living room. 'They're throwing a little farewell party for her later on, she wants you to be there.'

'When is she leaving?'

'The day after tomorrow. All the flights till then are fully booked.'

'I'm going to miss her.'

'So am I.'

León sat down next to her, sensing her panic, well aware of why she wouldn't look at him. But this wouldn't wait. He didn't want to give her too much time to think.

'Celia, the rules we drew up don't apply any more. Not to me, anyway. Once Lily's gone . . .'

'Lily going makes it even more difficult, don't you see?' If she left Raúl now, thought Celia desperately, he would assume the two events were connected. Oh, why did this have to happen now? She covered her face with her hands, knowing that she was looking for excuses, ashamed of her own cowardice. 'Please,' she mumbled. 'I don't want to talk about it now.'

She had always dreaded this moment, for all that she had dreamed of it. No vision of bliss, however exciting, could quell the last-minute doubt and fear of the unknown. Happiness. She had almost forgotten what it felt like. Perhaps she had never felt it. Perhaps it was nothing but a figment of her imagination. She was afraid to reach out and touch it in case there was nothing there.

'Very well,' said León. 'Don't talk about it. Don't say another word. I didn't come here to beg or to try to force you into anything. I know you better than that.' He prised her hands away from her face, glad that she had forsworn speech, speech which would have clothed the nakedness in her eyes. 'Or rather, you know me better than that. What I said still stands, Celia, Lily or no Lily. No half measures. Don't ever try to tempt me again until you've made up your mind to leave him.'

She stared him out for a moment, knowing that this was nothing to do with her mind, that this was a decision for her heart, not her head, a heart that was beating away against her ribs like a prisoner trying to get out . . . Impulsively, recklessly, she reached up and pulled his head down to hers and tempted him for all she was worth.

Plucked too soon, the moment would have been green

and sour but now it was sweet, ripe, mellowed by four long years of waiting. Where there would have been guilt, there was an overwhelming sense of absolution, where there would have been deceit and delusion and disappointment there was truth and faith and hope. The way ahead might be strewn with pain and problems but it was paved with promise and possibility. There was no going back now.

Celia felt herself slip into familiar rhythms, began moving in time to that special, private music only they could hear. It was like one of those insistent tunes you could never get out of your head; she had hummed it so often, in secret, that she remembered every note, as if she had heard it only yesterday. She turned up the volume loud, to drown out her thoughts, inhaling the sound like a drug, wanting only to twirl and spin, to become breathless and dizzy, to lose herself in a deafening vortex of noise . . .

A noise that was prematurely silenced by the shrill, accusatory bleat of the telephone. They pulled apart just as Emilia put her head around the door and announced, 'There's an urgent call for you, from New York.'

León swore under his breath. Trust Raúl to ring up at a moment like this. He snatched the receiver from Celia's grasp, as if to protect her from it.

'Hello? Yes, this is his brother. What? When? Is he all right?' Alarmed, Celia began mouthing questions, but León gestured at her to be quiet, listening with growing horror. 'Yes. Yes, I'll tell her right away. Thank you for letting us know. Goodbye.'

'What is it?' burst out Celia. 'What's happened to him? Tell me!'

'That was one of Raúl's aides,' said León woodenly. 'There was an assassination attempt on him earlier this evening. It failed. He's not hurt.'

Celia sank back into a chair, limp with relief.

'He was too shaken to call you himself. Celia . . . it was Eduardo who tried to kill him.'

'Eduardo?' All the colour drained from her face.

'He couldn't go through with it.' He sat down and put

his arms around her. 'He turned the gun on himself. Raúl's flying home with the body tomorrow. Oh, God, Celia, I'm so sorry . . .'

He held her while she wept, grieving with her for Eduardo, giving thanks with her that Raúl had survived. Losing her to him in life had been quite hard enough without having to share her with his ghost.

Raúl pushed his untouched plate to one side and lit another cigarette.

'I keep seeing it happen, over and over again. I see him lying there with that bullet in his belly, and when I look at his face, it's yours. I've seen so many people die, I've seen men blown to pieces by grenades. But I've never seen a man kill himself. If he'd done it cleanly, painlessly, it wouldn't have been so bad. But his hand was shaking so much . . .'

'Don't torment yourself,' said Celia. The sight of his pain crowded out her own. He had arrived home that morning, pale and haggard, still in profound shock, unable either to offer comfort or to accept it. Celia had never seen him this way before.

'Fidel's own physician travelled with him in the ambulance,' continued Raúl. 'It took him nearly an hour to die.' He banged his fist viciously against the table, making Celia jump. 'I wish it had been me instead. I wish it had been me.'

'Eduardo would have died anyway. You mustn't blame yourself. You know the kind of people he was mixed up with. His death is on their heads, not yours . . .'

'You'll never stop loving me, will you?' It wasn't a question, but a statement of fact. 'No matter what happens.'

Celia bowed her head, unable to answer. Yes, she would always love him, or rather, the man he had once been, but she couldn't live with him any more. And tomorrow, or the next day, or the day after that she would have to find the strength to tell him.

'That's the trouble with someone like me. As I said to

Eduardo, I'm an incurable disease. I destroy everything I touch. I don't want to destroy you too. But then, of course, you're not an easy woman to destroy. Death and disaster have always brought us closer together, haven't they? Misfortune brings out the best in you.'

She could hear León saying, 'You're like a firefly. The darker it is, the brighter you shine.' Well, not any more. From now on she would draw her light from the sun.

'If I really loved you,' he said, 'I would have found the strength to do what Eduardo did. I tried, last night. But I didn't have the guts.'

The words sent a chill through her. She looked up and met his gaze and suddenly she was face to face with the old, vulnerable Raúl, the Raúl she couldn't resist . . . No, she prayed silently. Don't let him do this to me. Not now. Please . . .

Misreading the anguish in her face, Raúl steeled himself for something worse than death. She would never make the break of her own accord; he would have to force her hand. Otherwise Eduardo would have died in vain.

'There's something I must tell you, Celia.' And still he hesitated. He needed her now, more than ever. He loved her now, more than ever. Enough to let her go. 'Eduardo and I . . .' He swallowed hard. 'Eduardo and I loved one another.'

'I know. I know how close you used to be, before politics came between you.'

'We were more than close!' he rapped, impatient now. 'Eduardo and I were lovers. I was in love with him, and he with me.'

Celia shut her eyes. She didn't want to know this, she had never wanted to know it. She had studiously forgotten the expression on Raúl's face in that hospital bed, that time he had mistaken her for her brother. An expression she had never seen before or since. She had buried that moment at the bottom of her mind, so deep as to be inaccessible, and yet it had survived in the dark, in secret, dormant, but not dead.

'Well? Do you despise me?'

Celia shook her head. She was shaken, yes, shocked, yes, but how could she despise two people she loved for loving one another? All she could feel was their terrible shared pain, pain she must have compounded.

'I loved you too,' he said, weakening. 'I hated myself for deceiving you. It isn't easy, loving two people at once. But, then, you of all people should know that.'

He had expected her to shrink from him in horror, hoped that this would be enough. But he had misjudged her. There was nothing in her eyes but compassion. He could hear Eduardo's voice saying, 'What will happen to Celia if you're found out?' and forced himself to go further.

'Loyal as always,' he said. 'Very well, then. There's something else you must know. I was the one who exposed your mother and León. It was all part of my plan to take over Buenaventura. But for me, Lidia would still be alive.'

Still Celia didn't say anything. She should have been appalled by his confession. But yet again, it was as if she had always known, deep down, and refused to acknowledge it, as if she had conspired at her own ignorance.

'To all intents and purposes, I killed her,' he said, vexed by her lack of response. Was there nothing she would not forgive? 'The same as I killed my father, only that was quite deliberate.' This time, thank God, he got a reaction.

'That's enough!' she covered her ears with her hands. 'I don't want to hear any more!'

'I knew I might die in action, in the Sierra, and I didn't want the old man bringing up Gabriel in my place. I didn't want him doing to him what he did to me. I planted that bomb. I'm a murderer. Is that enough for you?'

'Enough for what? Why are you telling me all this now? Why are you doing this to me?'

'Eduardo said that he wanted to set you free. And now I'm doing it on his behalf. Now that you know me for a murderer and a *maricón*, you cannot in conscience live with me any longer. Your brother tried to kill me, no one will think it odd that we should part. I shall move to a hotel tonight, till the ministry finds me an apartment. You and the boy will be well provided for.'

His eyes were bright and strange. She was frightened for him. He had opened the door of the cage wide, invited her to flee, and yet she stood rooted to the spot, unable to desert him in his hour of darkest need.

'I won't let you go,' she said numbly. 'Not while you're in a state like this. No matter what you've done. I can't do it.'

'That's what he said. I can't. I can't do it. Poor Celia. I tried to deserve you, more than you will ever know. Remember one thing. I will love you till the day I die. And so will León. Let him, Celia. I can't bear to think of you with anyone else but him. It will be easier for me if you leave the country. I know that neither of you will speak ill of me to Gabriel.'

The long climb was over, but the rocks were slipping away beneath her feet. She was stranded; one false step and she would plunge into the void. She heard the door slam, heard the car engine start up as Luis drove him away. But she didn't dare look, for fear she would lose her balance before she began the long, steep, perilous descent. Without him.

'Be happy together, won't you?' said Lily, as her flight was called. 'Oh, Celia, don't cry. Don't cry or you'll start me off as well. I love both of you, you know that. This makes it easier for me, don't you see? This makes it easier for me.'

León knew that it wasn't easy at all, that this was the bravura performance of her life. He looked at her for the last time through a blur as she gave him one final embrace and hurried towards the waiting plane, turning every few seconds to wave and blow kisses, a real trouper as always. Though her heart might be breaking, the show must go on.

They stood watching until the aircraft was just a speck in the sky, arms linked, fingers intertwined, thinking of Lily, of Raúl, of Eduardo, neither of them trusting themselves to speak. Later, if not sooner, they would be together at last, but it was still too early to rejoice. León had learned the hard way not to tempt fate; he would never be complacent again. Raúl was a hard act to follow. Celia had been spoiled for simple happiness, lost her sweet tooth for ever. It was still a contest. Perhaps it always would be.

She had seemed such a safe bet, once. The ideal, compliant, trouble-free wife. And now Raúl had changed her, stretched her, left his indelible mark upon her, made her into a force to be reckoned with. She had always hidden a will of iron, but now it was made of steel. The soft option had become a formidable challenge. One he was ready for now. To fail it would be to let his brother down.

'Raúl arrived just as I was leaving,' said Celia, wiping her eyes. 'To collect some papers and see Gabriel. He wanted to explain things to him himself. He was afraid that he would think it was his fault he had gone, that he would feel rejected . . .'

'Shh,' murmured León, as she fought off another fit of weeping. Raúl had always felt rejected himself, of course. By his father, by his mother, by the army, by Eduardo, and ultimately, not without his connivance, by Celia herself. They would never know the depth of the self-hatred which had blighted his life, or the depth of the love which had led him to drive her away. But they could guess at it, obscurely, intuitively, and with infinite sadness . . .

'Excuse me, Señor.' León turned to see two men in blue overalls. 'May we speak with you one moment?'

'Who are you?'

'Friends of your brother. The lady is in danger. Señora, you should wait with us, until your husband arrives with your son. They will be here very soon.'

Celia's grip on León's arm tightened.

'In danger of what? What's happening?'

'It's imperative that you leave the country immediately. A private plane is standing by to take you to Miami.'

She turned to León, eyes wide with alarm. She had always dreaded something like this. No one was safe from sudden arbitrary arrest; it was a fear the most elevated lived with daily.

'Oh, God. Not Raúl. Surely they haven't cooked up

some charge against him too? What on earth can he have done to bring suspicion on himself?'

'Who told you my brother was in danger?' demanded León. 'Who arranged all this?'

'We can't tell you that,' said one of them smoothly. 'We have to protect our contacts. We just run our little plane out of Cuba, getting people out of trouble. A sort of Scarlet Pimpernel outfit, if you like. Your brother found out about us and decided to turn a blind eye, for humanitarian reasons. In return, we guaranteed to help him if they ever found out what he'd done. Looks like it finally happened. He saved a lot of lives, Señora. He's a very brave man. If you'll follow us, there's no time to lose.'

'Do what he says, Celia,' said León, seeing her hesitation. 'Think of Gabriel.'

'As long as you come too—'

'Señora, there is only room for yourself, your husband and your child. If your brother-in-law wishes to follow, he can take the regular flight tomorrow.'

'I'll be on it,' said León, knowing full well that it would be already overbooked. 'If I can't I'll get a boat. Don't worry.'

'But what if they stop you? You're his brother. If someone's pointed a finger at Raúl, they might want to question you too. You know how it is when someone's under suspicion. They interrogate the whole family. You've been skating on thin ice for months . . . I won't go without you!'

'And Raúl won't go without you. He won't leave you behind to face the music. If you refuse to leave, it could cost him his life. And what will become of Gabriel if they decide that you're implicated too?'

'The aircraft is this way. You may stay with the lady, Señor, until we take off.'

Celia clung to him, too horrified to weep. They had waited so long to find each other again, and now it was all being snatched away from them. León took her arm and led her firmly towards the waiting plane and safety, telling her over and over again that everything would be all right, knowing all the while that they would come for him next, that he would never see her again.

Raúl sat staring at the telephone, considering his options. The message from Harry had been short and sharp. 'Your cover's blown. We're taking you in.' Had Eduardo let something slip to Fidel's doctor, in his death throes? Or had they found out some other way? Too late, he remembered Eduardo overturning that table, upsetting the plate and the screwed-up napkin with the microfilm inside. By the time Raúl returned from hospital, the debris had been cleared away . . .

Not that it mattered now. Luis was waiting to take him to the airport. Luis who, unbeknown to Raúl, had been working for the Agency all along. God only knew how many people were on their payroll; clearly some other high-placed agent had alerted them to his imminent arrest. This rescue operation was for their benefit, of course, not his. They were desperate to get him out of the country before he was caught and tortured and put through a public show trial as a Yanqui spy.

Thank God Celia was already at the airport, with León. The poor darling would be terrified. This should have been the moment when he could have reached out to her through the barrier of deceit which had kept them apart, rejoiced that the long ordeal was over. But it was too late for that now. He hadn't given her her freedom just to snatch it back again. That would be to do to her what Castro had done to Cuba.

He looked up and smiled as Gabriel came running into his study, having changed into his outdoor shoes, glad now that he had not had time to explain that his papá wouldn't be living here any more.

'Can we go to the airport now, and see the planes?' said Gabriel, delighted at this unexpected treat. 'Can 'Milia come too?'

'Certainly she can,' said Raúl. 'Emilia!' He wheeled himself out into the hallway, shutting the door behind him. 'I have urgent business to attend to,' he said in a low voice. 'You'll have to take the boy in my place. Hurry up, Luis is waiting.'

'But you only decided to go a minute ago!'

'I've changed my mind.' He caught hold of her arm. 'Listen to me, Emilia. It's very important that Gabriel gets in that car and goes to the airport. I've arranged for his mother to take him to America.'

'What?'

'I've just got word that I'm about to be arrested. One of my enemies has denounced me falsely as a traitor to the revolution. It's imperative that Celia leave the country. Otherwise she too may be accused.'

'You mean . . . my little girl's in danger?'

'I daren't take any chances. They may be watching the house. If they see me leave, they might give chase. So it's safer if I stay behind. I want to say goodbye to Gabriel, and then I'll call for you. Take him away immediately. Do you understand?'

'Yes,' nodded Emilia, too taken aback to question him further, transfixed by the strange bright light in his eye. 'I understand.'

'Now leave us to make our farewells.'

Suicide was the coward's way out, so they said. Raúl knew better. He had never been afraid to die, but he had always counted on somebody else pulling the trigger. And now that blessed mercy had been denied him. Now he was finally on his own. As soon as they had left, he would do it, redeem twenty years of vacillation. He would die from a bullet, like a soldier, not a cyanide pill, like a spy. He wouldn't bungle it, as Eduardo had done, wouldn't talk under torture, wouldn't let them parade him in front of the braying masses, or brand him, unjustly, as a traitor.

He wheeled himself back into his study to find his desk drawer wide open and Gabriel playing happily with his loaded gun.

'Gabriel!' he shouted, propelling himself forward, fearful that he would hurt himself. 'Give it to me! Give me the gun!'

Gabriel pointed it at him, grinning, enjoying his favourite game. 'Bang, bang, you're dead!' he chortled, falling backwards with the recoil.

Raúl slumped forward obligingly, clasping a hand to the hole in his heart.

'That's my boy,' he said.

'Why couldn't Papá come too?' demanded Gabriel, still troubled. Normally Papá played possum for a minute or two, while Gabriel shook him to no avail, and then suddenly he would shout, 'Boo!' making him squeal in joyful terror. But Emilia, of course, had got all upset about the bang, and made him get into the car straight away. And then she had sneaked on him to Mamá, whisper, whisper, whisper, even though he hadn't really been naughty, because it was all right to play with guns as long as Papá was there. Just as well Uncle León was around. Otherwise Mamá would have walloped him and refused to let him go up in the aeroplane. He could tell by her face that she was upset.

'Your papá had work to do,' said León, forcing a smile, trying to sound normal. 'Look down there, Gabriel. See how small the cars are. We're going to have a little holiday in Florida. Won't that be fun?'

In a few days, Raúl would come to visit them, and his plane would crash into the sea. Gabriel was still young enough, thank God, to believe whatever lies they chose to tell him. And the most important lie of all would never be gainsaid. Raúl would always be his father.

Celia stared steadfastly out of the window, so that Gabriel wouldn't see her tears. *I will love you*, Raúl had said, *till the day I die*. And beyond. She could feel it, quite distinctly. It was as if he were trying to let her know that he had finally found peace.

GLOSSARY OF SPANISH WORDS AND TERMS USED IN THE TEXT

aguardiente cane brandy
arroz con pollo chicken with rice
bachillerato matriculation exam
batey group of buildings around sugar mill
bohio worker's shack
botánica shop selling herbs and charms
central sugar mill serving a large area
chica/chico diminutive (little one, kid)
colonia farm growing sugar cane
colono farmer growing sugar cane
compañero comrade
curandera healer
herradura horsehoe
maricón homosexual (pejorative)
mayombero witch doctor
mayoral overseer
medio 5 centavos
muchacho/a boy/girl
mulatto/mulatta person of mixed race
novio/a fiancé/e
Patria o Muerte (slogan) Motherland or Death
posada cheap hotel
precarista squatter
puta whore
santero Priest of *santería* cult